I'll Walk Alone

J. J. Smith

PublishAmerica

Baltimore

First printing

ISBN: 1-4137-0242-2
PUBLISHED BY PUBLISHAMERICA, LLLP
www.publishamerica.com
Baltimore

Printed in the United States of America

This book is dedicated to Carol, Deb, Margie and Karen who gave me encouragement and assistance and believed in me and to all those men who served in World War II and to the women who loved them.

PREFACE

At the Embassy dance was the first time I heard *I'll Walk Alone*, and at the time I didn't know that particular song was to play such a significant part in my life. Mark Purcell, who had dated my former roommate, had talked me into attending the dance at the Australian Embassy in Washington. The town was caught up in the frenzy of wartime and men in uniform were everywhere. Usually I wasn't one for attending these embassy affairs because the fever of wartime pervaded them and I much preferred to curl up in my apartment with a good book. Mark, however, had convinced me that I should attend with him and since he was a good friend I had finally capitulated.

I first saw David at the embassy dance. He was tall, at least six foot three with brown hair that tended to curl and brown eyes that lighted up with laughter. He exuded masculinity that I could feel even from across the room and he was so ruggedly handsome that my breath caught in my throat. He stood across the room from me at the dance and I watched him laughing quietly at something, which had just been said by a member of the group with which he was standing.

"Who is that?" I asked Mark.

"David Benton."

I watched David Benton as he crossed the room. His legs were so long that they gave him a natural grace of movement and when he smiled it lit up his entire face.

"Who is David Benton?" I asked.

"He's a broadcaster from Sydney, Australia."

"What's he doing in this country?"

"I understand he was on some sort of assignment here when Pearl Harbor happened, and now he's sort of stranded here because of the restrictions on travel," he said. "I hear tell he's trying to get a commission in our Army Air Corp since he has flight training," he said.

"Would you introduce us?" I asked.

"Sure, why not," said Mark.

We made our way across the room to where he was standing and as the people to whom he had been talking moved on into other groupings, Mark introduced him to me. "David this is Lauren Bennett from the Office of War Management here in Washington," said Mark. "Lauren, this is David Benton."

He smiled as we shook hands. "Nice to meet you Lauren."

As he shook my hand I noticed how long and slender his fingers were and my hand was lost in his.

"Nice to meet you, David. I understand from Mark here that you are trying to get a commission in the Air Corp?"

"Yes, I kind of got stranded here when the war in the Pacific broke out and since I would like to get into the fray and have a good deal of flight experience, I thought I'd see if they could use me," he said.

"Are you having any luck?"

"Not so far; I keep getting the word that I can't be a part of the U.S. Army Air Corp unless I'm a U.S. citizen, which I'm obviously not," he laughed softly.

"Why don't you stop by my office in War Management on Monday, I may be able to help you."

"That's very kind of you."

"Well, I figure we can use every pilot we can get and my specialty is solving problems, so at least it is worth a try."

"Would you like to dance, Lauren?"

"Yes, thank you."

He took my hand and put his hand on my back and we moved out onto the dance floor. They were playing *I'll Walk Alone* as we began to dance. He drew me close to him and my face rested on his chest so I could feel the beat of his heart and I felt his chin resting on my head. As the song ended I thought he would lead me off the dance floor, but as the next one started he still held me in his arms and we danced to that one too.

"You're a terrific dancer, Lauren."

"Not usually, but you have a way of making a girl seem better than she really is on the dance floor," I laughed up at him.

When the evening ended I realized that the two of us had danced every dance together. As the band played the last song of the evening he looked down at me smiling.

"Would you like to go somewhere and get a drink?"

"Yes, " I said smiling at him.

We went out for a drink at one of the local watering holes and we sat talking until the place closed. I learned that he had gotten into broadcasting on a fluke but that he found he enjoyed the broadcast business as it suited his lifestyle and so he had stayed in it.

"How did you end up in the Office of War Management, whatever that may be?" he asked.

"I was Bill McCoy's secretary before he got the job here in Washington and he brought me with him when he went to work for the government," I said.

"What is the Office of War Management, if it's ok to ask?"

"We take on all the problems of procurement and supply, that other agencies can't seem to cope with," I laughed. "We are kind of the problem solvers here."

"Do you really think you might be able to get me a commission?"

"Well, let's put it this way, I can introduce you to the right people and then it is up to them, but I'll do the best I can. Since we are working very closely with the Australian government these days, I think they just might see the benefit of offering you a commission on a lend-lease type of deal," I said.

"Much as I would like this evening to go on forever," he said, "I suppose I should get you home before dawn."

We left the bar and he hailed a cab. I gave him the address of my apartment and he took my hand holding it as the cab made its way up K Street. When we got to the apartment house he got out of the cab and gave me his hand to help me out, telling the cabbie to wait. He took me to the door and kissed my hand that he was still holding. "I had a wonderful time tonight Lauren and I'll see you bright and early Monday."

"I had a great time too, David," and standing on tiptoe I reached up and kissed him on the cheek.

Later as I lay in bed thinking about the evening I realized that I had forgotten to give him my phone number. *Dummy,* I said to myself. *Oh well, you can give it to him Monday if he asks for it,* I thought.

Sunday morning I was curled up on the couch thinking about David when my phone rang.

"Lauren, this is David Benton," he said when I picked up the phone.

"Hello David. However did you get my number?"

"I called Mark Purcell this morning and got him out of bed to find out what your number was, since like a jackass I forgot to ask you for it last night."

"I'm glad," I said.

7

"I was just wondering if you might like to go out to breakfast with me?"

"Why don't you come over here and I'll fix you breakfast?"

"That would be even better," he laughed.

"Come over now and by the time you get here I'll have breakfast underway. By the way, how do you like your eggs?"

"Over easy or scrambled."

"It's apartment 3B."

"I'm on my way."

As soon as he hung up I jumped into the shower then dressed in blue-gray slacks and sweater. I set the table in the kitchen and got out the fry pan. Fortunately I had plenty of eggs and even a couple of slices of bacon left out of my week's rations. Just as I was getting ready to put the bread into the toaster the intercom buzzer rang.

"Come on up, David," I said into the intercom.

I opened the door and waited for him as he came bounding up the stairs two at a time. When he got to my floor I saw him grin when he saw me standing in the doorway.

"How can anyone look as good as you do on less than four hours of sleep?" he asked. "I'd have waited till later to call you, but I thought you might go out somewhere and I wanted to thank you for the most enjoyable evening I've had since coming to this country."

"That doesn't speak very well for American women, that we've allowed you to invade our shores then not made sure you had the best time ever," I laughed. "Come on in and make yourself comfortable. Would you like a cup of coffee?"

He came into the apartment and sat down on the couch. "I'd love a cup of coffee," he said.

"How do you take it?" I asked.

"Black, thanks."

I went into the kitchen to get him a cup of coffee and brought back two mugs, one for him and one for myself. He took a long swallow of his.

"This hits the spot," he said.

"Mark said you were on some kind of assignment here. What kind of broadcast assignment are you on?" I asked.

"They sent me over here to get the real scoop on you Yanks because our people are not that familiar with Americans and now that we are allies, the powers that be thought we ought to get to know you Yanks better," he laughed.

"Well Washington isn't exactly the best place to get the low down on how real Americans live and work," I laughed. "In fact, we've got almost every nationality here but Americans."

"I'm finding that out," he said.

"Come on in the kitchen and talk to me while I'm making breakfast," I said. "Turn on the record player if you will, and pick out some records then we can have some music with breakfast."

"Lauren, you have enough records here to start your own *Juke Box Saturday Night*," he laughed.

"I love music and I've just collected them over the years."

"Do you sing or play the piano or anything?"

"I can't carry a tune in a bushel basket but I love to sing anyway, so when I'm alone I sing my heart out," I laughed. "Back in Ohio, on Sundays we would all gather around the piano and Mom would play and we'd all sing."

"How many of you were there?" he asked.

"There was just my two nieces one of whom was two years older than me and one who was nine months younger, Mom, Dad, and myself. I don't know how good we sounded but we sure were loud." I laughed.

"There were seven of us, all boys, except for one girl; my parents divorced when I was young so there was just my dad," he said.

"I always wished I came from a big family, but considering how much my nieces and I fought with each other, it may be just as well there were only the three of us. Of course, my sister and brother being so much older, they were just like an extra set of parents," I said.

"My oldest brother is twelve years older than me, and I always thought that was bad enough, but to have him old enough to have kids the same age as myself would have been the pits," he laughed.

"Sis, Mom, and I were never all that close, but I absolutely adored my brother and my dad. Could be I was just partial to men, since I was always a tomboy and I loved working on cars with them and going to baseball games and climbing trees. You name it, if it was a male activity I loved it," I said.

"I adored my sister but she had a feminine streak a mile long so I really never spent a lot of time with her," he said. "I think she tried to compensate for all the maleness in our family by being just crazy about dolls and babies," he laughed.

"She and I should have traded places, because Mom would have loved to have a girl she could dress in pretty dresses and fuss over, whereas, I was always in jeans and one of Dad's old shirts. If we had been able to trade, I would have been involved in everything you boys were, so maybe I would have been more pest than someone to adore," I laughed.

"I just can't imagine you as a tomboy, you seem so soft and feminine."

"Thank you, kind sir. I've learned to tame the tomboy in me to an extent, but I have the feeling it is always lurking just below the surface.

"Come on out to the kitchen and I'll finish up breakfast. David, please sit down, we don't stand on formality around this place," I said as I put the bacon on to cook and beat the eggs for scrambled eggs.

"You've got a lovely apartment," said David. "I'm billeted at the Y and this is pure luxury to me."

"Another girl and I found it when we first came to Washington, but she moved out about six months ago and I decided I liked living alone better than having a roommate. I suppose that sooner or later the powers that be are going to insist, because of the space shortage in this town, that I take on another roommate, but until they actually catch up with me, I'm going to enjoy the solitude."

"Are you seeing anyone, if you don't mind me asking?"

"No one other than Mark, and we are just good friends," I said.

"The men in this town must be deaf, dumb, and blind to let a beautiful woman like you get away from them," he chuckled.

"Oh men in this town are too busy trying to get a step ahead of the other guy to bother about some little secretary," I laughed.

I took juice from the icebox and poured it into large glasses, and then I put the rest of the food on the table. "Dig in," I said, "good manners make for cold eggs."

We talked as we ate. He told me something of his life and I told him something of mine.

"Do you plan on staying in broadcasting after the war is over?" I asked.

"I don't really know, right now I tend not to look too far into the future because it all looks a bit murky so I take each day as it comes. What about you, what do you plan on doing?" he asked.

"Probably just go on being Bill's secretary, but what I would really like is to find a small place maybe in Maryland or Ohio and raise some horses," I laughed, "although that is really asking for the moon, I think."

"Why is it asking for the moon?"

"Because I know of no way I would ever be able to raise the capital for such a project, but it appeals to me because I love horses; they are such beautiful, loving creatures."

"Have you ever thought of moving such a project to England or Australia?"

he asked.

"Can't say as I have for I've never been outside the U.S.," I laughed.

"Never?"

"Nope, never really had any desire, I guess. Geography was never my strong suit in school for it never made me dream of distant lands like it does some people."

"I'd love to show you Australia, I think you might like it there."

I felt the blush creep up my face and I mumbled something about how nice that would be.

Standing up he pulled me out of my seat. "Let's do the dishes then let's go for a walk?"

"No need to do the dishes, just let me put them in the sink to soak and I can do them later. We can go by the building in which my office is located so that you can find it easily on Monday."

As we walked he took my arm and placed it through his. I realized suddenly that I was almost running to keep up with his long strides. "Whoa," I said, "you are going to have to slow it down because there is no way in this world I'm going to be able to keep up with your long legs."

"Sorry, Lauren, I'll slow it down," he laughed. "I forgot I was walking with such a little bit of girl. How tall are you anyway?"

"Well with the shoes I have on today I'm exactly 5'2". Unfortunately, I also am short-legged, so keeping up with a long-legged fellow such as yourself is somewhat of a challenge for me."

He stopped then. "Catch your breath, then we'll try it again and I promise to not make you trot along beside me," he chuckled.

"Why don't we go over to Pershing Park and we can sit on the grass and talk?" I said.

"Sounds good to me."

With that he put his arm around my waist and cut his stride so that I no longer had to run to keep up with him. When we got to the park we found a grassy space under one of the trees and sat down.

"How long have you been flying, David?" I asked.

"Well I actually started flying when I was about 14 and got my private license at 16 and my commercial license and my instructor's rating by the time I was 18," he said.

"You beat me out by a couple of years," I laughed, "I didn't start flying until I was 16 and got my private license when I was 18."

"You fly?"

"Yup I do, I told you I was a tomboy," I said.

"How about if we charter a plane next weekend and go up and tool around for a while?"

"That sounds wonderful; since coming to Washington I haven't done any flying at all and it will be great to be airborne again."

"It's a date then, although I hope you will let me take you out before then because the weekend is so far away," he laughed.

"I'd be honored, sir," I said laughing up at him.

"You don't look very comfortable sitting there," said David, "but I think I can fix that."

He moved then so his back was against the tree and he pulled me so my back was against him and his arms were around me.

"Better?"

"Yes, much better," I said.

"Can I take you to lunch tomorrow?"

"That would be very nice, and I don't think I have anything scheduled, but check with me in the morning after I've had a chance to check my calendar," I said.

"Why don't I come by and walk you to work in the morning?" he asked.

"I'd like that," I said turning so that I could look up into his face. He had laughter in his brown eyes and I thought again how very masculine his face was and how very handsome.

We talked for a while longer then I said I had to be getting home because I had some work for the office I had to do before going to work in the morning. Getting to his feet he pulled me to mine so I was standing just inches from him.

"My God Lauren, I knew last night when we were dancing that you were small but I didn't realize how small," he laughed. "I was always told good things come in small packages, and you certainly are proof of that," he chuckled.

He walked me back to my apartment and when we got to my door he took my key and unlocked it for me. "Thank you for a wonderful day, Lauren," he said and bending he kissed me softly on the lips.

"Thank you. I don't remember when I've spent a better Sunday in a long time," I said returning his kiss.

"What time should I pick you up in the morning?" he asked.

"How about 8:45 since it is only a 15 minute walk?"

"See you at 8:45 then," he said kissing me one more time.

That night I had trouble getting to sleep because I wanted to stay awake and remember everything about this day. Finally I fell asleep and I dreamed of David though in the morning I couldn't quite remember what the dream was but I know I awoke with a warm cozy feeling.

THE DREAM BEGINS

David picked me up right on the dot of 8:45 and when I went to the door to greet him, he leaned down and kissed me good morning and then took my arm hugging it to him while we walked. This time he kept his pace slower and we laughed and talked all the way to the office.

"Why don't you come in and I'll give General McDowell a call and see if I can set up a meeting with him for you?" I said.

"First things first, check your calendar because I want to know for sure I'll get to see you again at lunch," he laughed.

I checked my appointment book.

"I'm free, no meetings, no nothing until after 2:30 today."

"Good, that makes my entire day," laughed David.

I went in then and called General McDowell. After explaining the circumstances to him I suggested that maybe considering our new allied status with Australia that it might be politic to extend David the courtesy of joining our air force and he said to send David over and he'd see what he could do for him.

"Turn right at our entrance and go to the second building, he's three floors up and last door on your right," I said.

"Wish me luck."

At noon David came back to the office.

"Ready for lunch?" he asked.

"Yes and starving," I laughed softly.

"Me too," he chuckled.

We found a small restaurant then by Pershing Park and after we were seated and our orders taken David reached across the table and took my hand.

"So aren't you going to tell me how you made out?" I asked smiling at him.

"I'm to take my physical tomorrow and if I pass it, then in about two weeks I report for flight training at Andrews," he said.

"David, that is wonderful if that is what you want," I said squeezing his hand.

"I couldn't have done it without you."

"Oh sooner or later you'd have gotten to the right person who could see the forest for the trees, but at least I was able to save you some time and aggravation," I said.

"I couldn't ask for a better assignment because that will keep me near you," he said returning my squeeze. "Lauren, I don't mean to rush you into anything, or make you think it is because of the wartime atmosphere, but I think I'm falling in love with you."

"Oh David, I think I fell in love with you when I saw you across the room that first night we met," I said.

"Come, let's get out of here for the only thing I'm hungry for right this minute is to hold you in my arms," he said dropping some bills on the table to cover our order.

We left the restaurant and he hailed a cab and said to the cabbie, "National Airport and step on it." When we got to the airport, he took me inside and we stood by one of the departure gates and he put his arms around me and hugged me close to him and his head came down his lips seeking mine.

"This is the only place I could think of where I could hold and kiss you and no one would think anything about it," he laughed softly.

"I'm just glad you thought of it because I wanted so much to be in your arms," I said.

"Finding a place to be alone is going to be difficult in this town," he laughed.

"No it's not, because we have my apartment," I said.

"Are you sure, sugar; won't your neighbors talk if they see me going in and out?" he asked.

"First of all so many people work so many different shifts and share so many of the apartments, that no one would notice just one more and for a second thing I don't care, I just know that I want to be near you as much as possible," I said.

"I love you, little one, and I want to be near to you as much as possible too," he said softly.

"David, why don't you just move out of the Y and move into my place?" I said.

"Are you saying what I think and hope you are saying, Lauren, darling?"

"All I'm saying is that I love you and want to be near you every minute that I can and I want you to hold me in your arms and love me; I've never felt like this before with any other man and I know I never will again, so if that makes me immoral I guess I can live with it," I whispered.

"You could never be immoral, you are the sweetest, most loving person I've ever met," he whispered back.

"Darling, much as I would love to stay here in your arms forever, I do have to get back to work," I laughed softly. "Here's the key to my apartment; why don't you go back and move your stuff in and I'll see you tonight when I get home from work," I said.

"What time do you get home?" he asked.

"I generally leave work around 4:30 or 5:00," I said.

He let go of me then and got a cab and deposited me back at work, kissing me goodbye and I went back to my job reluctantly for the only thing I wanted was to stay in his arms.

"Lauren, for God's sake what is the matter with you this afternoon?" said Bill. "I've never seen you so forgetful and absentminded."

"I don't know Bill, maybe I'm coming down with something," I said.

"Well, why don't you take off tomorrow and the next day too if you aren't feeling well," said Bill.

"I just may take you up on that, if you don't mind," I said feeling so guilty because I had never lied to Bill before.

"Well, leave now, you aren't much good to me the way you are acting, and I hope you feel better soon," he said.

I got my purse and left feeling terrible that I had lied to Bill and at the same time eager to get back to my apartment and see if David had arrived yet. When I opened the door, David came out of the kitchen and strode across the room and took me in his arms.

"I'm so glad you are home early, my love, for I thought five o'clock would never come," he said kissing me tenderly.

"Bill gave me the afternoon and the next two days off because I told him I thought I was coming down with something and that was why I was so absentminded," I said. "I didn't tell him what I was coming down with was love, and I do feel guilty for not telling him the truth," I said, "but I'm so glad to be here with you."

"For someone I want to always love and protect, I seem to be putting you in awkward situations," said David.

"You didn't put me into them, I chose them, because I love you so much," I said.

He kissed me then long and lingeringly.

"Come out to the kitchen, I stopped at a hotel restaurant and picked up supper for us," he said.

"You didn't have to do that. I could have cooked us supper, although to be truthful I'm not sure exactly what food I do actually have on hand," I said smiling at him.

We sat across from each other and both of us kept smiling at each other and every so often his hand would steal across the table and take mine. When we were finished and the food put away, we went back into the living room. I went to the record player and put on some records and he came and took me in his arms and we danced to the music.

"Did you find space for your clothes?" I asked.

"Yes plenty," he said.

"In the morning we'll get everything sorted out," I said, "but tonight I just want to stay in your arms."

"That is exactly where I want you, little one, in my arms," he said as he bent and kissed me and I felt his tongue part my lips as his arms pulled me more closely into his body. My arms tightened around his neck and my body of its own volition pressed closer to his.

"Are you sure, little one?" he asked.

"I think so David, but my emotions are all mixed up; you make the decisions for me because I can't think anymore," I whispered.

He picked me up then and carried me to the bedroom where he set me gently on my feet and proceeded to undress me and then pulled off his own clothes.

"You're trembling, little one," he said to me as he pulled me back into his arms.

"I've never been naked with a man before nor have I ever seen a naked man," I whispered.

"I will not hurt you, little one, and if you want to stop right now we will," he said.

"No I don't want to stop, I want to know what it is, all of it, but I feel awkward," I said.

He picked me up then and laid me gently on the bed. Then he slid in next to me and took me in his arms and held me so tenderly that after a few minutes my trembling ceased and I reached up to put my arms about his neck.

"I love you David, so much," I said.

"I love you too, little one," and he began to stroke me until I felt the fire within me flare up and I pulled him onto me and my legs went around his waist.

"The first thrust may hurt you a little, but I'll try to be as gentle as I can," he said as he came into me.

I let out a small cry at the first thrust, and he lay still within me not moving for a few seconds, then he began a long, slow, thrusting motion until my whole being was on fire and I felt the shudders throughout my entire body and I watched as his eyes became clouded with desire and he sought his own release.

"Oh I never knew how wonderful it could feel," I whispered.

"I hope I didn't hurt you too much," he said. "It will be better next time and you will enjoy it more, I promise you."

I nuzzled my face into his chest and the fine gold-brown hairs I found there kissed my cheeks and I breathed in the smell of him and my hands began to learn his body. He lifted my face up to his and I again felt his lips on mine and as his hands roamed down my own body, I knew that I wanted him once more.

"Oh God I never knew how marvelous it could be, I feel as if my entire body is on fire for the want of you," I said. "Please darling, please take me again."

"With pleasure little one," he said, "and this time it will be even better I promise you."

It was better because it brought me even closer to this dear sweet man, who I knew I loved more than life itself. We made love yet a third time. Each time it was better than the time before, until we were both exhausted then he pulled me back into his arms and I fell asleep cradled in his strong arms and I knew that for the rest of my days that is the only place I ever wanted to be.

When I woke the first stray light of the morning was just filtering in and I watched him sleeping for a while, then I could stand it no longer and I planted kisses across his chest and when I looked up I saw him smiling down at me. His lips came down and I felt him suck on my nipple and desire tore through me. I felt his hand between my legs massaging that which sent exquisite waves through my entire body. I pulled him to me and he entered me once again and I was content because he was within me. He looked down into my face and I could see his desire for me and his love for me in that look. He began to thrust once more, but this time it was more insistent and I felt the waves of pleasure go through him as he reached his climax and my own release came at the same time.

"I think you may have unleashed more than you bargained for," I laughed softly nibbling at his ear. "For my desire for you becomes stronger each time you take me," I said.

"You may be right, my darling, but much as I would love to accommodate you again, I need time to recover," he said laughing gently.

"Darling, I'll try to be good and let you rest because I know you have your physical this morning, so I'll just be content if you hold me in your arms," I said.

"I almost forgot about the physical, little one, I'm glad you reminded me because after all you did to get me the meeting with the general I'd hate to forget to show up," he laughed softly.

"What time do you have to be there?"

"My appointment is for 10:30 and it shouldn't take much more than an hour or so, then I'm all yours," he laughed.

"Would you like me to call the flight surgeon and tell him I've already given you your physical and you passed with flying colors?"

"Somehow, I don't think that would suffice, but I do appreciate the offer," he chuckled back at me. He pulled me closer in his arms and sleep returned to us.

We woke again about 8:30 and lay for a time in each other's arms until I gave him a small shove and said, "Go shower and shave and I'll get breakfast ready for you, my love."

He did as he was bid and I dressed in my robe and went to the kitchen to prepare breakfast. When he came out to where I was standing at the stove making him eggs, he was dressed in brown slacks and a soft brown sweater that made his eyes even browner and he came to where I was standing and bent down and kissed me.

"You look very domesticated fixing my breakfast in your robe," he said, "and I love to watch you."

"Sit and I'll bring you your coffee."

"Lauren, what would you like to do today when I get back?"

My face turned red as the flush crept up it.

"What I would like most is to spend the day with you here in the apartment snuggled in your arms and have you make love to me," I said.

He stood up then and came over to me taking me in his arms.

"Don't ever be embarrassed, love, for I'm beside myself with happiness that you want me to make love to you because I want that more than anything.

I love you so much," he said his head coming down to kiss me and I felt the whole long length of him as he held me and I loved the feel of him against my body.

"Oh David, I never knew that I could feel so wanton for I would love to stay naked in your arms forever and I love the feel of your body and I long to explore it. I want you to teach me everything that pleases you so that I can give back to you some of the pleasure you've given to me for I want to please you in every way possible for teaching me how wonderful sex between a man and woman can be and for loving me," I said.

"It will be my pleasure, for I would spend every minute of the day and night exploring and loving your body and I love that you want it as much as do I," he said as he hugged me closer to him and bent his head to kiss me. "I want you so badly right now that if I didn't have to report to the flight surgeon I would pick you up in my arms and we wouldn't move from our bed of love."

"You don't know how happy that makes me," I said my arms tightening about his neck, "but go now, sit down and eat your breakfast so that you will have strength to pass your physical and can hurry home to my waiting arms." I laughed softly.

We ate breakfast then and we talked of mundane matters until it was time for him to leave. "David, give me the key I gave you yesterday so I can have another made for you while I wait for your return. I'll get groceries and then for two days we need never leave this apartment," I said.

He pulled me to him and I felt his lips on the top of my head, "I'll be back as soon as I can. I love you."

"I love you too," I said as he left to go.

I cleared the breakfast dishes and then got dressed to go out and get a new key made. I stopped at a men's store and picked up a robe for him and I could not stop smiling because shopping for him made me so happy. As I was walking out I saw a beautiful gold ring with two intersecting braided ropes and on impulse I bought it. Then I went to the grocery store and stocked up on what food I thought we would need for at least the next two days. I went home to clean the apartment so it would look nice for him and to put the groceries and my purchases away. I finished cleaning about 11:30 and went in to take a shower and put on fresh slacks and a sweater. By the time I had finished I heard the front door opening and went running to throw myself in his arms as he came through the door.

I heard him laugh softly as I hurled myself into his arms and his arms came about me and I once again felt the thrill of his lips seeking mine.

"Darling, you don't know how much pleasure it gives me when you come running into my arms that way," he laughed softly.

"That's all I want is to please you in every way possible, my darling; it feels like an eternity since you left this morning," I said looking up at him so he could see the love I had for him shining in my eyes.

"Are you hungry, darling? I'll go and fix you some lunch," I said.

He pulled me back into his arms as I had stepped away preparatory to going to the kitchen to make him lunch.

"I'm hungry, but not for food," he chuckled as he lifted me up into his arms and headed for the bedroom. When we got there he set me on my feet and we both tore at our clothes. He pulled me to him and I felt his hands travel over my body and I reached up to pull his face down to mine and his tongue once again came into my mouth and I let out a little purr of satisfaction and lay down on the bed pulling him with me.

"Please hurry, darling, for I need to feel you within me once again because I'm only half alive without you," I said my voice husky with desire.

"Yes my sweet witch," I heard him growl as he came into me and I felt the first slow thrust and my back arched so that he was even deeper within me.

"Beg me for it, for I love to hear you beg for that which I so willing give to you," he whispered as he continued to thrust into me slowly.

"Please, please," I begged as my body began to writhe and I felt him increase the pace of his thrusts until I screamed softly as my release came, then I felt the shuddering of his body as his release came and felt the weight of him as he collapsed against me.

"Woman, you amaze me," he chuckled softly as he rolled to his back bringing me to lie on top of him. "For you so willingly comply with my every request and you seem to enjoy the act of love as much as I do."

"I never knew I could feel the things I do when you take me in your arms," I said, "and I want only to be as close to you as I can possibly get and to give you as much pleasure as you give me," I whispered, "so please my love, teach me how to care for and love your body for my heart already knows how to love you."

"My body loves the feel of your hands and your lips anywhere on it for it craves your touch," he said taking my hand and placing in around his penis and as I wrapped my hand around it he let out a low moan as it became erect and I felt his fingers checking to see if I were ready and finding that I was he came into me then as his hands cupped my buttocks squeezing them gently.

I was once again aflame with desire for him and I begged once again, "Please, please," and he brought me to climax twice before he sought his own release. We fell asleep then in each other's arms.

I woke to the feel of his hands caressing my body and mine reached for his hungry to touch and love that which had given me so much pleasure.

"Where are you going, woman?" he laughed softly as I crawled on my hands and knees to where I could run my hands up his long legs.

"Oh David, I've such a need to run my hands along your long legs and to explore every inch of your body," I said.

As my hands traveled from his feet up his legs my lips followed their course and he began to moan and reach for those places on my own body to which his touch gave such pleasure. He moaned gently.

"Please love, I need to be inside you," I heard him whisper and I moved so I lay on my back and my legs opened to accommodate him, but my hands would not stay still as they continued to roam over his body as he thrust into me and I felt his hand reach to that spot just above where we were connected and his finger teased and massaged until I too was screaming my desire for him and both of our releases came.

"You were right my love, I think I have unleashed more than I knew and I'm so happy and proud that you find the same enjoyment in our love making as do I," he said. "For your hunger and thirst for me gives me more feeling of my manhood than I have ever felt before in my life and I feel complete and whole in your arms."

"Come love, for while I would gladly stay in your arms and never move from them, I know that your body must be requiring food so let's go to the kitchen where I can re-nourish you so that we both have the strength to make love all night long," I said.

With that I stood up and went to the closet and pulled out the new robe I had bought for him. Coming back to the bed I pulled at his arm until he was standing and then wrapped the robe about him.

"What's this, kitten?" he asked.

"It's something I saw that cried out to me, 'take me home to David for it will look so good on the long length of his body'." I laughed.

"Thank you, love, it is handsome and because it came from you I will love the feel of it around me," he said.

He held my robe for me and wrapped his arms about me even as I wrapped the robe around my body. We went then to the kitchen and I made dinner for him. As we sat eating I could see the laughter and the love in his eyes.

"You look at me with such adoration that I feel very humble," he said softly.

"How could I keep from adoring you for you have become everything in the world to me and I am only happy when I can look at you and feel you close to me," I said. "When the day comes that you grow tired of me, I will live on the memories of you for the rest of my life, and I'll know that at least for a little while I got to give you all my love and a small part of me will still be happy because for this little time you loved me."

He stood up then and came around the table pulling me to my feet and his arms went about me as he tilted my head up so that I could see his face.

"I'll never grow tired of you, my little one," he said. "I don't think I could survive life without you close to me and loving me nor would I want to because for the first time in my life I understand all the poets and all the love songs because you give your love so freely to me," he said and I could read it in his eyes and knew that he spoke the truth.

My arms went around his neck and I stood on tiptoe so I could reach the small cleft in his neck with my lips letting him know that I was content and unafraid of whatever the future held for us because he loved me and had told me so.

"Please darling, tell me often that you love me so that my head as well as my heart will know it," I whispered, "for I love you so much that it is like an ache inside me that goes on and on."

"Coming back home to you today, I wanted to keep urging the cabbie to drive faster and faster because my need to see your sweet face on which your love for me is written every time you look at me, was so great that I don't think I even breathed until I walked back in and you came running to throw yourself in my arms," he said, "and I knew that I would always feel that way my whole life through."

"Come love, we'll leave the dishes for the time being for I want to put on all the love songs ever written and sit on your lap cuddled in your arms," I said as we moved into the living room.

We set the records on the turntable of all the love songs we could find that said the words we felt for each other. Then he sat down in the easy chair and pulled me to his lap wrapping his strong arms around me and my arms went about his neck and I let my lips nuzzle his neck and I felt his lips on my head. We sat there for a long while completely content and at peace for while we sat there we could lock out the world and all the terrors in it. Finally I heard his soft breathing and I moved from him then quietly so as not to wake him and went to the kitchen to put away the food and do the dishes. I heard his step and looked up to smile my love at him.

"Why didn't you wake me so I could help you?"

"You were tired and needed your rest and besides even when I'm doing such small tasks as doing the dishes after we have eaten I feel like I'm wrapped in your arms for they are tasks that give me joy because they are for you as well as me," I said.

We went back in the living room then and put more records on and he took me in his arms and danced with me and I heard his beautiful voice singing some of the words to me and I purred in his arms until he stopped and undid my robe so that my naked body was once again pressed against his; then he picked me up and carried me to our bed and we made love.

The next morning when I awoke, I saw that David was staring down at me.

"How long have you been awake?" I asked grinning up at him.

"I've been watching you sleep for the past half hour or so," he laughed softly. "You look like a little kitten curled up in my arms. Did you know that you tend to purr in your sleep?" he asked.

"Do I really?" I grinned. "It must be the contentment I feel being held in your arms."

"When I first woke up I pulled you closer to me and when I did you smiled in your sleep and just began purring, so I kind of assumed that you liked the feel of my arms around you," he laughed.

"I feel so safe and secure in yours arms, like nothing bad could ever happen as long as I was safe in them," I said.

"You make me feel so masculine because you put all your faith and trust in me and it makes me want to protect and love and cherish you always," he said.

"Though I may have been a tomboy once, the moment I first saw you it began to recede and now in your arms I feel more feminine than I ever felt in my life and I am very grateful that I am a woman and a woman loved by you," I said.

"While I was desperate to get home to you yesterday, I did make one stop along the way," he said and reaching behind my head so he could reach the hand that was around my neck he pulled something from his little finger. "I wanted to get this for you and I pray God you will accept it," he said. With that he placed a beautiful little diamond ring on my finger. "Will you marry me, my darling?"

"Oh David, you know I will for I love you with all my heart and soul," I said the tears coming to my eyes even as my arms went around his neck and my lips sought his.

"Baby, don't cry, for I love you too with everything that's in me," he whispered hugging me to him.

"I can't help it, I'm so happy," I whispered in his ear. "I just want to make sure that what I said about you getting tired of me, yesterday, didn't force you into anything you will regret later on."

"Actually darling, if you will think about it for a minute, you didn't say that to me until after I came home, so you can be sure that asking you to marry me was entirely my own doing," he laughed softly. "Besides, no man my age could be forced into marrying someone if he didn't want to, just by words."

"I love you, I love you, I love you," I said smiling up at him. He held me so that his face was against my cheek. "Ouch, you scratch, my love," I said to him.

"That does it woman of mine, come sit with me while I shave," he laughed.

Going to the bathroom I sat watching him shave and he would turn from time to time to smile at me.

"I love watching you shave," I said. "I feel so warm inside watching you."

He pulled me up into his arms then and his lips came down to mine.

"I can't think of a more uninteresting preoccupation than watching a man shave, but if you like it always sit with me when I do so," he laughed. "I've got an even better idea," he said going to the shower and turning it on then stepping in and pulling me with him.

As he did his arms tightened around me and I felt the long strong length of him against my own body and I smiled as I saw his manhood spring to life. He lifted me in his arms then and my legs wrapped around his waist as he backed me against the shower wall for support. His head came down and I felt him suck on my nipple and I reached to guide him into me.

"My love," I said as he began to thrust into me and then we were lost to the world.

Afterwards he turned me in his arms so that my back was to him and began lathering my body with soap until I began to moan with the desire for him to take me once more. Turning back in his arms I rubbed against him so that the fragrant lather from my body spread to his. We stood under the spray to the shower while the soap washed off of our bodies then he turned me in his arms once more and bent my body forward and I felt him enter me from behind and felt his hand reach between my legs and start to massage that place which hungered for his touch. His thrusts were strong and he came into me deeper than he had ever come before. I moaned like a wild thing as my body moved against his to match him thrust for thrust and I felt his hand reach for my breast and stroke the nipple till it stood up and still he thrust into me and I moaned my desire for him until my release came and then his. As he turned me toward him once more I collapsed against him and had he not had his arms about me I would have fallen because my knees had turned to water and I had not the strength to stand on my own.

Turning off the shower he grabbed for a towel and began to dry my body then he quickly dried his off as well. Picking me up he carried me to our bed and laid me down then slid in next to me. I felt his hand massaging my breast while his mouth came over the other sucking at it. His hand moved lower and he stroked my belly and the inside of my thighs until I began to moan once more. Spreading my legs so they were on his shoulders his mouth came down licking and sucking all those places where his body had so recently been. I felt his finger go inside my vagina and explore it and I moaned and writhed and still he did not let up as wave after wave of shudders went through my body and at last I was still. I looked at him in awe and wonder for I had never before felt such ecstasy.

I reached for him then gently encircling his penis and my hand moved back and forth over it until he began to moan and thrust within it and I guided him into me for though I was completely sated I wished only for him to have the release he wanted and needed and as he plunged back and forth within me I heard his moans of desire until at last his release came and he too was sated.

"Lay still my darling," I said as I got up from the bed going to the bureau drawer. When I returned I took his hand and placed on it the gold ring I had purchased the day before.

"Sweetheart," he said looking at the ring I had placed on his finger.

"This is my solemn pledge to you that I will love you every day for the rest of my life and beyond."

"I wish I had the words to say to tell you how much I love you, but Australian men are not taught words of love to say to their women because it is thought to be unmanly to do so," he whispered. "Just know that I love you with everything that is in me and that I always will."

"While a woman loves to hear the words from her man, the way you hold me whenever you are near to me, the way you look at me with love in your eyes, the way you see to my comfort and my well-being, tell me more than mere words how much you love me and my darling I am so honored that you do," I said. "I hope that you don't mind if I say the words to you for I've such a need to tell you how much I love you."

Then this man who was so tall and strong and loving put his arms around me and his lips came down to mine in such a tender, gentle kiss that tears once more came to my eyes for in that kiss were all the words he could not say.

The next morning I quietly slipped out of bed so as not to awaken David and went in to dress for work. Coming back into the bedroom I saw that he was awake and went over leaning down to kiss him.

"Good morning, love," I said.

"Where are you going woman?" he laughed.

"To work, you idiot, though I'd love to stay in your arms all day again today," I said.

"I'll pick you up at noon," he said yawning.

"Go back to sleep, you deserve it," I laughed quietly.

In the office I dreaded to face Bill. When he came in he looked at me. "Are you ok?" he asked.

"Yes Bill, but I need to talk to you."

"Grab a cup of coffee for both of us and come on in the office," he said.

"Bill, I've a confession to make; when I led you to believe Monday that I was sick, I was lying to you. I've met someone and the reason my concentration was broken and I was so absentminded, was that I've fallen in love," I said. "I apologize for not telling you the truth, but I couldn't very well tell you that I had met a man and fallen head over heels in love with him and that I needed time to know if he loved me as well."

"Who is this guy, Lauren?"

"His name is David Benton, he's a broadcaster from Australia that I met at a party a few nights ago. He got stranded in this country after Pearl Harbor when restrictions were put on travel and he was trying to get in the Air Corp and I told him I would try to help him."

"Were you able to help him?" he asked.

"Yes, I got him an appointment with General McDowell who pulled a few strings and he starts flight training at Andrews in about two weeks."

"Are you sure what you're feeling isn't just sexual attraction that because of it being war time you are making more of it and thinking it is love?"

"Very sure Bill, he's asked me to marry him and I've accepted," I said showing him my ring.

"When is the wedding?"

"I don't know, we've not discussed it yet since I only met him five days ago," I said laughing. "He has to go to Andrews for flight training and he may want to wait until he graduates from flight school."

"Lauren, do me a favor, bring him around so I can meet him, will you?"

"He's picking me up for lunch today and I'll introduce him to you then, I promise."

At noon David came to the office.

"Ready for lunch, kitten?" he asked.

"Yes darling, but I want you to meet Bill before we go," I said coming around the desk and taking him by the hand, I led him into Bill's office. "Bill McCoy, David Benton," I said introducing them. They shook hands and I could see each sizing up the other.

"I hope you know that you are getting one of the sweetest women in the world," said Bill.

"I know and I have to keep pinching myself to make sure I'm not just dreaming that she has promised to marry me," said David putting his arm around me.

"I love Lauren like a sister so you had better treat her right. I was prepared not to like you on sight because this all happened too fast for me to think it is anything more than a war time fling, but after looking at the two of you together I can tell that you love her and she loves you, so if Lauren loves you, I'm prepared to be your friend as long as you treat her with the respect and with the love she deserves."

"I'm not very good with words because we Aussies aren't given to expressing our feelings, but I love Lauren and it will be my entire aim in life to love and protect and cherish her forever," said David.

"In a case like that, just call me Bill," said Bill laughing and coming over to shake David's hand again and to hug me.

"Thanks, Bill, I appreciate your faith in me on just meeting me for the first time and under the circumstances," said David.

"Bill, thanks from me too, I just want you to love David as much as I do and to know how happy he makes me," I said returning his hug.

"Did Lauren tell me that you are to report to Andrews in two weeks?" asked Bill.

"Yes, I report for flight school on the 25th."

"In a case like that, Lauren, you've got vacation you've never taken saved up so why don't you spend the time between now and the 25th with your guy; I'll get one of the girls from the pool to fill in for you," said Bill.

"Thanks Bill, we appreciate it," I said hugging him.

"Now skidaddle you two lovebirds before I change my mind," said Bill shaking hands with David and giving me a kiss on the cheek. "And Lauren, I like your young man very much," he laughed.

Back in my office David pulled me into his arms and kissed me.

"Two weeks of having you all to myself before I have to report in," he laughed. "I feel like a miser trying to horde them, so what will we do first?"

"Oh David, let's go home and change clothes then let's go charter that plane like we were going to do this weekend. I have to be sure you are as good a pilot as you say and that my trust in your skills was not misplaced," I laughed.

"Oh, oh, me thinks I hear that tomboy in you coming out," he laughed. "You just want to see if you're a better pilot than I am, don't kid me."

"Foiled again," I laughed back at him.

We went home then so I could change clothes then went to a small field just over the Washington, DC line. David chartered a little two-seater Colt and after the paper work was completed and our licenses, medicals and logbooks had been checked, he lifted me onto the right seat then went around to climb in the left seat.

"Ready mate?" he asked smiling at me.

"Aye, Aye Captain," I laughed.

He taxied to the runway and after getting his clearances he pushed throttle and we began our take off roll down the runway, and I watched as he pulled back on the yoke lifting the little plane into the sky. After turning out of pattern we went to the local practice area and played around doing stalls and spins and climbs and banks.

"Your turn, mate," he laughed dropping the controls watching as I took over the flight duties. "You didn't exaggerate, kitten, you are a terrific pilot," he laughed reaching across the consol to kiss me on the cheek.

"You're pretty darn good yourself and the Air Corp is lucky to get you," I said.

"Let's hop over to Maryland for lunch, then we'll go back," he said.

"Yes let's," I laughed and he could feel my joy at flying once more.

He landed the plane at a small field in Maryland and taxied to a parking area. After telling the crew that we were going to be tied up for about an hour while we went across the street for lunch, we walked arm and arm across the field and up an embankment. The little restaurant was nothing more than a bar, but the food was excellent and we chattered back and forth about flying while we ate and laughed.

"My first lesson was almost my last," I said. "My instructor was one of those old timers who believed you flew right from the get go, and so he told me how to do the takeoff run and how to pull back on the stick. I did what he said but I was so excited that I forgot I had to look out for inbound aircraft and fortunately for me I flew right between two planes," I said laughing at the memory.

"My first introduction to a stall and spin was in an Air Coup and my instructor did it, but I darn near lost my lunch in the process," he laughed. "To this day I still hate doing them if someone else has the controls though when I'm in command I love doing them."

"I know what you mean. At the field where I learned I used to beg all the rides I could get and one day after they had done some work on the magnetos of one of the Apaches my instructor wanted to know if I wanted to go along on the check ride. Unfortunately, he didn't tell me it involved a power-on stall to check the magnetos and I nearly lost it too," I laughed.

"I think the biggest kick I got was my first solo take-off, and you are going to hate me for this, one of the radio stations had chartered a flight for one of their announcers to go to a football game. Well, he and the pilot were running up the engines at the end of the runway. I taxied up and started my take-off roll when Jeff saw me and keyed the mike so I could hear this joker of an announcer yelling, 'What the hell, is that a woman flying that plane?' and I was laughing so hard I nearly forgot to shutoff carb heat." I laughed remembering the look on the announcer's face. "Afterward Jeff told me that the guy kept saying women just didn't fly planes."

After lunch we sauntered back across the field and stood by the Colt for a little while watching the take-offs and landings of other aircraft. Then David lifted me into the left seat and ran around to the right.

"You take her off," he said to me.

I gave him a jaunty salute and set the little plane racing down the runway and into the air. When we got back to the home field he watched as I landed the little craft.

"Smooth as honey," he laughed. "Yes I'd say you are an excellent pilot, my love."

"That means more to me coming from you than when the inspector certified me," I said hugging him.

When we got back to the apartment David took me in his arms. "That was the most fun flying I've had in a long time," he laughed.

"For me too, I love watching you fly because you do it so well and I feel as safe in the air with you as I feel here in your arms," I said.

He moved over to the chair and sat down pulling me onto his lap.

"We've got to get our feet back on solid ground from Cloud Nine where we've been for the last five days," he laughed, "we need to discuss a few things like when are you going to let me make a honest woman of you?"

"That's entirely up to you, my love, for from now on I'm at your beck and call 24 hours a day," I said nuzzling my face into his neck.

"Behave yourself witch, I'm trying to be serious and you are totally distracting me from my train of thought," he chuckled hugging me.

"Ok, I'll behave, but I meant what I said, it is up to you for I really do mean that I'm at your beck and call and I leave all the decisions up to you because I'm too happy to think straight for myself," I smiled at him.

"Alright, how about if next week we get the license, then go over to Andrews and talk to the chaplain there about performing the ceremony right after I graduate from flight training?"

"Yes, my darling," I said looking him straight in the eye. "I mean it David, I want you to take the lead in all the decision-making in our family for everything in my life now revolves around you and what you want. I'm yours to command."

"I love you, kitten, and I love that you say that 'I'm yours to command,' but this is going to be a partnership and I want your input on every decision we make," he said hugging me closer to him. "Tomorrow we have to go to Andrews for my swearing-in then I have to pick up my uniforms, after that until the 25th we only have to be concerned with one another."

"Oh God when you get in uniform my worries really begin, because you are so handsome even in civvies that I see the female population eyeing you constantly, but in uniform you are going to cause them to drool."

"Come on kitten, I'm not handsome except maybe to you, but I promise I'll wear blinders where other females are concerned," he laughed.

"It isn't you I'm worried about, it's all those females with raging hormones, out there for they will be licking their lips to get at you and you definitely are the handsomest man I've ever seen and you just exude masculinity, a combination which no female can resist. I've known right from the minute you took me in your arms to dance with me that your arms were the only place I ever wanted to be."

"And my arms are the only place I ever want you to be, kitten," he said.

"I won't ever leave them again and I will always be reaching for you," I whispered as my arms went around his neck.

His head came down and his kiss was so full of love and his arms tightened around me and I was so full of emotion I could barely breathe because I loved him so.

"I will always be reaching for you too kitten," he whispered back.

The next day we went to Andrews and David was sworn in as a second lieutenant, he looked so handsome standing there and he towered over all the other candidates. Afterward we went to pick up his uniforms.

"I know I'll have to have these altered because the sleeves will be too short as well the trousers," he laughed.

"I can't imagine why, you're such a little guy," I laughed with him.

We saw General McDowell and he came over to shake hands with David and myself.

"Just thought I'd let you know you passed your physical 100 percent," said the general.

"Thank you, sir. I appreciate the information," said David. "Sir, I have a question. Do you think it will be alright if I have my dress uniform made to order?"

"That's rather unusual, but I don't think there is any military regulation which says you can't," said the general.

"It's just that my arms and legs are so long that I know I'm going to have trouble having even my everyday uniforms altered to fit me," laughed David.

"I can see where that might be a problem for you, young man," the general laughed. "Perhaps you may want to have all your uniforms tailor made."

"Thank you sir, we will go to the tailors when we leave here and I'll have them all tailor made for I want to look sharp since you Yanks have been kind enough to let me join your Air Corp."

"I want to thank you too, General, for all your help in getting David squared away, it was very kind of you," I said.

"It was my pleasure, Lauren, since you've always been so good about helping me with procurements when I needed them," said the general shaking my hand. He noticed my ring. "Lauren I see congratulations are in order, who's the lucky young man?"

"You're looking at him, sir," said David.

"Congratulations you two, and may you be as happy as my wife and I have been over the last 30 years," said the general.

We went to the tailor shop then and I couldn't help laughing when David came out in his uniform for the shirtsleeves were half way up to his elbows and the pants a quarter of the way up to his knees.

"You look like Huck Finn, all that is missing is the fishing pole over your shoulder," I laughed.

"Can you do anything with these?" David asked the clerk.

"Not much sir, perhaps you need to consider having us make your uniforms for you," said the clerk.

"Can you get them finished by the 15th?" asked David.

"That should be no problem, sir," said the clerk.

"Then go ahead and measure me up for I can't run around the base looking like this," laughed David.

After taking his measurements, the clerk inquired if he could come in within the next two days for a fitting.

"Yes I'll be here," said David.

"My God, I hope they have a flight suit that will fit you," I laughed as we were walking out.

"I hope so too," he laughed with me. "Let's go back to our place and sack out for a while, I'm beat—I hate standing around being measured," he said.

"Yes, let's and while you are snoozing I'll make chicken and biscuits for dinner tonight," I said, "providing you like chicken and biscuits?"

"That's one of my favorite meals," he said putting his arm around my shoulders and pulling me close to him. Bending his head down, he whispered in my ear, "But you're my favorite meal, kitten."

I laughed up at him. "Then you snooze and I'll get dinner ready, then I'll come wake you up and you can have your favorite meal first," I said.

"Oh you have the nicest suggestions," he laughed planting a kiss on the top of my head.

Later that night after the supper dishes were finished and we were sitting in our favorite chair I suggested to David that we might go horseback riding over in Virginia the next day.

"You've got to be kidding, it's been years since I was last on horseback," he said.

"Well it's like riding a bike, once you learn you never really forget."

"I wouldn't be too sure about that, sugar, because as I recall I was never any great shakes at it," he laughed.

"Oh, come on, we'll find you a nice gentle mount, and besides, I want you to meet Storm King," I said.

"Who in the hell is Storm King?"

"He's a black stallion I ride as often as I can, he stands about 19 hands high and has the nicest disposition of any stallion I've ever ridden," I laughed. "Tell you what, we can both ride Storm King, you can ride behind me and I'll do the driving, so to speak."

"Kitten, you've lost me completely—what do you mean 19 hands high?"

"It means in horse terms that he is about equal to your size in human parlance," I laughed. "Come on, David, I promise to keep him at a trot and no taking fences or anything."

"My God you were a tomboy weren't you? I think the only time I rode a horse we were on bridal trails and believe me there was no jumping of fences involved," said David.

"Tell you what, just come with me and meet him. If after meeting him you still aren't sure about riding, even with me, you can just stand and watch me ride him for a little while. I owe it to him for I've been neglecting him lately," I said.

"But kitten, I don't even have riding clothes," he laughed.

"You can just wear slacks and a sweater or we can stop and get you a pair of jeans and boots," I said. "Come on, at least say you'll come with me to meet him," I begged.

He looked dubious but finally agreed to come with me.

"Thank you, my darling, for Storm King is the only other male in my life that I love and I do so want you to meet him," I laughed.

Later when we were in bed and our passion had been assuage for a little while, I rolled David on to his back and mounted him.

"See you just let your horse know what you want by guiding him with your knees," I laughed as I pressed first one knee then the other into his sides.

"No wonder I've got bruises on my sides after you wrap your legs around me when we are making love," he laughed.

"You're kidding, aren't you?" I asked.

"Not entirely. The first time after we made love I wondered why my sides were so sore; I didn't realize then that you thought you were riding your stallion," he laughed.

"I promise to do better in future, but yes I was riding my other stallion in a manner of speaking." I grinned at him.

"You sweet little witch, you never cease to surprise me," he chuckled.

"To think just a few short days ago you'd never made love in your life, and now you are always as eager for it as I am and I love your insatiability," he said softly.

"Oh I love you so much and I can never have enough of you," I whispered back at him as I bent down and my lips found his.

He lifted me then and I felt him thrust inside of me and my body began to move in rhythm to his as his hands guided me teaching me yet another facet of lovemaking. I felt his finger find my clitoris and my movements became even more frenetic until I felt the shudders throughout my body and felt his release within me.

The next day I borrowed Mark's car and after stopping to pick up a pair of jeans and boots for David, we drove over to a farm in Virginia which I had found when I first came to Washington. I took him into the barn then to meet Storm King. As we approached his stall Storm heard us coming and put his head over the stall gate whinnying as he bid us welcome.

"Storm King, this is David," I said to the horse. "He's to be my husband and is to be obeyed just as you would obey me." Storm tossed his head and nickered at us and nuzzled David's shoulder. "He likes you," I said.

I took Storm King from his stall, placed his bridle on him, then grabbing a fist full of mane I swung up onto his back.

"Aren't you even going to saddle him?" asked David.

"No I always ride bareback," I laughed. "Go over and stand on that crate lying there, you should be able to mount him easily enough from there," I laughed.

David did as he was bid and after one false start he managed to swing onto Storm's back behind me.

"Now put your arms around me," I said. As his arms came around me I snuggled back into them and walked Storm out of the barn and down into the meadow, which lay just below. I gave Storm a gentle kick and he broke into a trot.

"I think I like this," said David nuzzling the back of my neck as we rode, "at least I like the part of you in my arms."

"I've only ridden this way once before in my life and I love it too because I love the feel of your body against mine," I laughed.

"Who were you riding with then?" he asked and I liked the little bit of jealousy I heard in his voice.

"I think I was about six and one of the neighborhood boys who was probably about 12 dared me to ride bareback with him and this was how we rode," I laughed.

"Whew, I'm relieved to hear that for I must say this is a very romantic way to ride," he chuckled.

After a little while I said, "Press your knees and calves into Storm's sides and hold on to me, and let's try a gallop."

"Are you sure about this, kitten?" he asked.

"Yes, hold on."

I set Storm to galloping across the meadow. After a few minutes I slowed him back down to a walk.

"Are you ok?" I asked David.

"I think so, as a matter of fact, I really enjoyed that," he laughed.

We rode for a while longer then I rode Storm back to his stall and gave him water and a rub down.

David came over and patted his neck.

"Thanks for a wonderful ride, Storm King," he said and Storm tossed his head as if he understood.

Driving back David said, "I'm glad you talked me into coming today because I did enjoy it and I really like Storm King. I must say that you were right, in horse circles I think Storm would be about my size," he laughed.

"He's very like you," I chuckled, "big and strong but gentle nonetheless."

He pulled me across the seat so that I was snuggled in his arm and my hand rested on his knee and his lips came down and he kissed my cheek.

"As good as you are with Storm King, I really think you ought not to dismiss your idea of a horse farm. Maybe if we put our heads together we can come up with some way of managing it," he said.

"I'd love to have a small farm with horses and dogs and lots and lots of kids," I said squeezing his knee.

"I'd kind of like that myself," he laughed. "I'd love to have a couple of sons to roughhouse with, but I'd also like to have a little girl who looks just like you," he said squeezing my shoulder.

"Even if she turns out to be a tomboy like her mother?" I laughed.

"Especially if she turns out to be a tomboy like her mom," he said smiling at me. "You know kitten, we've got to sit down and talk about what the future holds for us," he said.

"Yes, I know, but oh David I don't want to think of the time when you'll be on active duty," I said.

"Tonight, let's go out dancing somewhere then after I go for my final uniform fitting, let's sit down and talk seriously about where we go from here for I want to make sure that you are taken care of before I go overseas," he said and I knew he was thinking only of my welfare.

"Yes, darling, but tonight let's not think about anything for I just want to be in your arms and to have the whole world see the handsome man that has asked me to be his wife," I sighed.

"Where would you like to go tonight?" asked David, when we had returned to the apartment.

"Every place will be so crowded because everyone is frantically trying to forget this stupid war; let's just stay here and put on some records. I just want to feel your arms around me and I want you to be able to kiss me whenever you feel like it and if we go out, we can't do that," I said.

"What's the matter darling, you sound like you are on the verge of tears?" David asked coming to where I was standing.

"Oh David, I hate myself because I'm the one who got you in to see the general and as a result, I'm the one who will have ultimately put you in harm's way and if anything happens to you I don't think I could go on living because my heart would be torn completely out of my body," I cried leaning against him as the tears came. "I know I shouldn't say these things to you because you've enough to cope with, but I love you so much and sometimes I can't keep myself from thinking about it."

"Baby, you've got to stop thinking like that. You aren't the one putting me in harm's way, it is the Japanese and Germans who are doing that and even if you had not gotten me in to see General McDowell, I would have found some other way to enlist," he said holding me close to him. "You are the best thing that has ever happened to me and that is one thing I'll always be grateful to this war for and that was meeting you. Had I not met you and been loved by you, I wouldn't have the incentive I now have to make it through whatever is to come," he said.

"Oh David, hold me tight," I said my arms going about his neck as I buried my face in that cleft in his neck that I loved so much. His arms came around me and he pulled me into his body then his lips came down on mine in a long lingering kiss and the fear began to leave me.

"I'm sorry darling, I won't let it get to me again, I promise, it is just that you are so very dear to me. Make love to me, please, make me pregnant for I want to know a part of you will be with me when you are far from my arms," I whispered.

"No darling, that is what I won't do because I want to be with you when our child is born and that I won't be able to do that just now—love you, yes;

make love to you, yes—but now isn't the time to bring a new life into this world," he whispered back to me. He picked me up then and carried me to our bedroom. There he undressed me, and then himself, and lay down with me and cuddled me into his arms.

"I'm sorry my darling, I am only adding to your burdens, and I never want to do that, but just for now I need your strength, but I promise that never again will I put you through this," I said.

He tilted my face up then so I could see his face plainly.

"I hate this war as much as you do, kitten, maybe more because I know eventually it is going to pull us apart for a while and I just found you. But remember this is a partnership deal between us, and you use my strength when it is necessary because there may come a day I will need to lean on you and use your strength. Just know that I love you and if there is anyway humanly possible, I will come home to you when all of this is over, then we will start our family because I want to be there when our baby is born and I want to hear him or her give their first howl of life. I want to be there for everything, its first step, its first word, everything and right now I can't be and you know it and I know it. It isn't that I want to deny you having a child for I want that more than anything, it's just that I want to be here when it all happens," he said.

"Oh my love, I want you here for all of it as well and I'll be good and not worry you anymore because I love you so much and I want only to make you happy," I said.

"You do make me happy, little one, I never knew how happy one person could be before meeting you," he said.

I snuggled deeper into his arms and I was once more at peace and the dark thoughts left as his arms came around me holding me even more closely and we both fell asleep in each other's arms.

When I awoke I heard him in the bathroom and putting on my robe I went in and sat down watching him shave. He reached over and put a dot of the shaving lather on my nose and I grinned at him and he smiled back at me.

"Feeling better, little one?" he asked.

"Yes my darling, I'm at peace within myself and with the world once more thanks to you," I smiled. "How about if I heat up the chicken and biscuits from the other night for dinner? Then I can just sit on your lap in our chair and we can listen to records and pretend we've been married for a thousand years."

"Sounds perfect to me, little one," he said.

I got up then and went out to the kitchen to heat up the chicken and biscuits and I made an apple pie and popped it in the oven. When he had finished shaving he came out and stood in the doorway watching me.

"Sit down over there and talk to me while I finish up dinner," I said taking him by the hand and leading him to the kitchen table I pushed him down into one of the chairs. He pulled my body into him and his face came down and he laid his head against my body. We stood that way for a few minutes and I could tell he was relaxed and at ease and my heart swelled with pride in my man.

"How did one girl ever get so lucky," I said, "to be loved by such a handsome, adorable man?"

"No love, I'm the lucky one because you've allowed me the privilege of loving you," he said.

I put supper on the table then and as we ate I could tell he was thinking over something in his mind.

"Ok you big long drink of water," I laughed, "I can tell you are hatching up something so spill it."

"I've been thinking sugar, tomorrow let's go out and find a used car so that you can drive me back and forth to the base," he said.

"Wouldn't you rather keep the car on base so that if you get a last minute leave you can just drive into town?" I asked.

"Well I thought about that but on the other hand if you have it here and pick me up then we have just that much longer together," he laughed. "The only trouble is I don't like the idea of you driving back alone from the base because who knows how reliable a used car will be and what if you have mechanical problems," he said.

"Well then I fix whatever is the matter," I laughed.

"Oh, I forgot you were the tomboy who liked fixing cars," he laughed.

"When I first learned to drive, my brother and dad both said that if I was going to drive I was going to fix. I had an old Chevy and something was always breaking down on it, so they would supervise and I'd do the work on it," I said. "Before I finally got rid of that car I'd fixed brake cylinders, tires, master cylinders, batteries, and you name it on it."

"Maybe the Air Corp would take you on as a mechanic," he laughed.

"The mechanics at the airfield where I learned to fly always came and got me when they were working on a plane and needed to get in a tight place, because my hands were so small I could fit them into any part on the plane," I laughed. "So maybe the Air Corp ought to consider me for a mechanic's job."

"Oh God Lauren, when we do have a daughter, I hope she is exactly like you," he laughed.

"Well I figure I'll probably produce a daughter who is all soft and feminine from the get go and just doesn't like to get her hands dirty at all, then who will I teach to ride and fly?" I chuckled.

"Well maybe you can teach our sons, if our daughter is too hoity-toity to appreciate getting dirt on her," he laughed.

"I think I'll leave the flight training up to their father, but I intend to teach them to ride and you too, my handsome sky jockey."

"You know, kitten, I just can't imagine myself as a father although I can picture you as a mother," he said.

"You'll be a really great father, I think, for you can give your heart completely and that's what my own dad did with me; he made me feel that I could do anything I wanted to do and he always stood back and applauded all my efforts. You know what I hope, I hope we have at least one set of twins," I said.

"Yikes woman," he laughed.

"Well it's not impossible, for my second cousin had three sets of twins. She always said twins were easier because they entertained each other," I laughed, "and I'd like to find out if she was right."

"Just how many kids were you planning on?" he asked cocking his eyebrow at me.

"Well I'd like at least six or seven," I said.

"We better figure a way to get that farm if you want that many kids, because believe me coming from a family of seven I know how often they can get in each other's way in a small house," he laughed.

"I just hope the boys all look like you because all the little girls in the neighborhood will have such fun chasing after them," I giggled.

"And probably I'll have to swat off the little boys because if our daughters look anything like you I know I'm going to have my hands full," he laughed.

I got up then and cleared the table. I took the apple pie out of the oven and cut a generous slice for him and topped it with ice cream.

"Godfrey woman, but you sure are a good cook," he said licking his lips after tasting the apple pie. "This pie just melts in a man's mouth."

"Well there is a lot about being a homemaker that I've never been really good at, but cooking just isn't one of them. I love to cook, especially for people who like to eat," I laughed.

"Then you'll just love being married to me because if there is one thing I like to do, it is eat," he laughed.

"I'll just love being married to you period," I laughed back, "and I'll especially love cooking for you."

"You know, kitten, you may have been a tomboy and some of it may still be lurking in your soul, but you have a way of pleasing a man that just naturally makes him want to take care of you because you do so much for his ego and it isn't contrived, it just comes naturally to you," he said. "I think society is wrong in discouraging little girls from being tomboys, because I think they may just make the best wives because they understand men so much better than the average woman does."

"I always felt like I understood men better than I ever did my own sex," I laughed. "I was never really comfortable around other women, but I felt perfectly at home amongst the boys I grew up with. Of course, I was always the pal never the date, so maybe there is something in the way other more feminine acting girls acted that attracted the boys to them."

"Well possibly during the teen years a boy might be attracted to the clinging ultra-feminine type of girl, and that is because he doubts his own masculinity and is just trying to find his way into manhood, but I know for myself that a man is more attracted to the former tomboy type of woman who doesn't pretend."

"I keep telling you, darling, you are one man in a million and I'm so glad I found you and you found me because you make me feel so female," I said.

"Well, you very definitely make me feel all male," he grinned at me.

I got up then to clear the table and do the dishes.

"Sit and talk to me while I do the dishes," I said. "I love talking to you as well as loving you and I like to look up and see you sitting there watching me," I said.

"That's what I mean sweetheart, how many other women would tell their man that they love talking to him?" he said. "Most would just tell him that he was handsome or clever to flatter his ego, but you, you tell him something he can believe, that you like talking to him and it makes him know deep within himself that you do believe his thoughts are worth hearing. You tell him that you like to look up and see him watching you, whereas most women don't want a man watching them do things like doing the dishes, they only want us to look at them when they are trying to make a fashion statement or something. I don't say it very well, but I hope you know what I mean. And the way that you run into a man's arms like he was the total sum of your existence, you just don't play the games other women do. You never pretend to be something you aren't, and yet, you'll beg if I ask you to, but it isn't the begging of someone who feels inferior, it is the begging of an equal, but still it makes a man, at least this man, feel more masculine more of a man, than I've ever felt before with any woman."

"You are the total sum of my existence, you are everything to me, and I only feel half alive when you are not with me," I said. "David my darling, know one thing if you never understand anything else about me, that I'm a throwback to the pioneer women of this country, that I will follow you to the ends of the earth as they did their men and like them I'll stand at your side fighting off Indians or whatever, but also like them when the homestead is safe once again I want nothing more than to stay locked in your arms forever, seeing to your every need," I said softly. "All I want from life is to love you, to take care of you, to laugh and play with you, to fight along by your side against everyone and everything that might try to interfere with our life and our love."

He got up then and in two strides he was across the kitchen and his arms came around me and he pulled me in close to him so that I could feel every part of his body and his kiss left no doubt in my mind that he loved me as much as I loved him and I sighed my contentment in his love.

The next morning we went for David's first fitting on his uniforms. The expression on his face said that he hated standing there while the tailor did the fitting. I smiled at him.

"You look like a little boy whose mother is making him sit still while she cuts his hair."

"Well, if I were a 'little boy' I wouldn't have to go through this," he laughed. "I always liked that I was tall until it came to buying clothes, then it became a real liability."

Finally the tailor was satisfied. "I think sir, that you won't have to come in for any more fittings except the final one when you pick up your uniforms."

"Thank you for that and for your fast work, I really appreciate it," said David.

We went then to some used car lots and looked at cars. While David kicked at the tires I opened the hood and checked out the engine and had him get in and start it for me. We both doubled up in laughter at the salesman's expression when he saw a woman checking the engine not the man she was with.

"Can't help it, mister," said David, "I'm a mechanical failure but my wife is a whiz at it."

"I'm sure she is," he mumbled, but I noticed that he no longer offered up the information that a little old lady had owned the car.

We finally selected a maroon convertible and David wrote out a check for it.

"I think that guy will think twice before he tries to sell another car to a woman on looks," I laughed.

"You probably scarred him for life and he'll only deal with men from here on out," laughed David, "especially after the bargaining session you put him through. I was so proud of you, I could hardly keep from applauding you right in front of him."

"That's another thing I love about you, my darling, your security in your masculinity so that you don't ever feel I'm a threat to you when it comes to things usually reserved for men only," I laughed as we drove the car off the lot.

"Well now all we have to do is find a place to park this bucket of bolts," laughed David.

"There's a garage about a block from the apartment and I'm sure they have vacancies," I said.

So we headed over and the manager of the garage said they would be happy to stable the car for us and at a reasonable price. We left the car then and went back to the apartment.

"Let's go for a walk, I feel like I need to stretch my legs for a bit," said David.

"Wait till I get on my roller skates then you can stretch them as much as you like," I laughed.

"Now there's an idea," he chuckled.

I changed from the skirt and blouse I had been wearing into slacks and a sweater. We went out then and walked around and I pointed out the various government buildings to him including the White House. Then we crossed over to Pershing Park and found the same tree under which we had sat that first Sunday morning. David sat with his back against the tree and I sat with my back against him with his arms around me.

"I was so glad that first time when we came here that you suggested we sit like this so I'd be more comfortable, because I wanted very much to be in your arms even then," I said.

"I was hoping, but I really didn't have much faith that you'd fall for my line about making you more comfortable but it was the only excuse I could think of to get you in my arms," he laughed softly.

"If you had just put your arms around me, I would have snuggled into them, so you see you really didn't have to come up with any excuses," I smiled looking up at him.

"Well, I'll be damned," he laughed, "and here I wasted all that time trying to come up with an excuse when the direct approach would have worked."

"David, have you called your family or written them about us yet?"

"I was just thinking last night that I'd try and call them tonight and they can at least meet you over the phone, because my brothers are just going to go wild when they get to meet you in person and they are going to absolutely want to throttle me for getting to you first," he laughed. "My sister, on the other hand, may be a little standoffish at first until she gets to know you and realizes what good care you take of me."

"How about you, little one, have you called your family yet?"

"There really is no one to call, my folks are dead and I don't even know where my brother and sister are living these days. We've all gone our separate ways."

"Well my dad will absolutely love you and so will the rest of my family, so you aren't getting just me you're getting an entire family."

"Let's call your family when we get back home because I want to meet them all even if it is only by telephone," I said.

"I know you don't want to talk about me going on active duty, but sugar there are some things we need to talk about, so let's do it right now and get it out of the way," he said looking down at me and pulling me even closer into his arms.

"I won't fall apart on you again, I promised you that, so yes let's talk about them and then we can forget for the rest of the time we have together."

"I've signed all my insurance and allotment check papers over to you, so if anything should happen to me you'll be provided for, little one," he said. "I know you are independent as all hell, but I'll feel better knowing that you are taken care of no matter what happens. You know, I've been thinking about this whole farm business and I've some money set aside which I hope that you will use to find a little farm and to purchase Storm King, so when I get leave I'll have a real home to come home to," he said looking at me and his face was very serious.

"I'll do whatever you want, David darling," I said. "But won't you want to go home after the war is over?"

"I figure properties will appreciate after the war because all us servicemen will be coming home and we'll want to settle down and raise families, so even if we do decide to go back home the farm will still have been a good investment for us, because we can sell it and use the money we get from it for a down payment in Australia. Besides I'm kind of getting used to this country and by the time the war is over I'll probably have become a died-in-the-wool Yank."

"Can we go tomorrow and buy Storm King so he'll never again have to have strangers riding him, just you and me?"

"I think that's a great idea, and besides, I would kind of like to ride him again myself," said David. "Now that much is settled, what about our wedding, little one?"

"What about it?"

"I know we planned on being married in the base chapel, but do you want a big wedding or just us?"

"I'd like to invite Bill and Mark because they've been really good friends. I think I'll ask Bill to walk me down the aisle, because I think that would please him," I said.

"How about if I ask Mark to be my best man, since I don't know that many people here and I like Mark, at least I like him better since I found out you two weren't seriously involved," he laughed.

"I think he would like that," I laughed with him.

"It's settled then, Friday I'll pick up my uniforms, because I will have to be in uniform when we talk to the chaplain. Then we'll drive out to the base and get it settled with him about the wedding. I've also been thinking about the date for our wedding, I don't want to wait until I finish flight training, if the chaplain will perform the ceremony before I actually start my training, let's get married next week?"

"Are you sure, darling?"

"The only reason I originally said after training was in case I washed out, but I really don't think I will and I want you all tied up nice and legal while I'm in training, so no other guy can get his hands on you," he said.

"No other guy ever will because I'm definitely a one man woman and you are that man," I said pulling his head down so I could kiss him.

"Lauren, just one more thing," he said his face serious again. "If I'm ever declared missing in action, I want you to wait a reasonable amount of time, then I want you to look for another guy to love and who will love you, because you have so much love to give. Don't mourn me forever, go out and find your happiness, and know that it is what I want because you've given me so much happiness. I couldn't bear it if you spent the rest of your days alone."

"I can only promise that I will look, I can't promise that I will actually do, because I really am a one man woman and I don't ever expect to love again as I love you, but also know that I won't live my life in sadness because that would be blaspheming our love," I whispered.

"That's all I ask, kitten, for I want you to be happy because you've given me everything any man could ever want and more," he said kissing me tenderly. "Now let's go out to the farm and buy Storm King, then let's go back to our apartment and celebrate our love."

"Do you mean it, you want to go today to buy Storm King?"

"Yes, sugar, I mean it and maybe while we are at it we can check in with a couple of real estate agents in Virginia to see what kind of farm properties they might have available. We might get lucky and they will come up with something we can look at next week."

We went then and got our new little car and when we got in David put his arm around me and pulled me over next to him.

"I feel like it's Christmas," he laughed looking down at me, "I've a new wife, a new car, and now a new horse."

"We owe Mark a lot," I grinned.

"How so?"

"Well if it hadn't been for him I wouldn't have been at that dance at all because I had determined not to go and he talked me into it."

"Now I know I'm going to ask him to be my best man," he said squeezing my shoulder.

"Bill may have to walk me down the aisle and fill in as my maid of honor as well, because I don't have any close girlfriends to ask," I said.

"Kitten, I love you so much and need you so much," he said.

"Oh David, I love and need you too so much that there just aren't words to tell you how much and how glad I am that you came into my life."

As we drove to the farm, David serenaded me with all the popular ballads of the day and I curled up on the seat next to him and snuggled into the crook of his arm and every so often I'd reach for his hand and kiss it because the happiness within me was so great.

When we got to the farm, we went in search of the manager and we found him in the paddock looking at new horses.

"Bart James, this is my fiancé David Benton," I said introducing the two men. "Bart, we may be interested in purchasing Storm King if he is for sale," I said.

"Sure, all my horses are for sale for the right price," said Bart.

"What are you asking for Storm?"

"Well, I was thinking $500 but as a special wedding present for you two I'll come down to $300," said Bart.

I looked at David and he nodded his head. "Sold," I said. "We'll want to continue stabling him with you for the time being, so what is that going to run?"

"$50 per month vet bills extra," said Bart.

"Great, now that it is settled you get the papers drawn up and David and I want to go down and tell our new horse," I laughed. "Then we'll come back and sign them."

"Will you take my check, as it is on an Australian bank because I only keep what I actually need here in the States," said David.

"As long as Storm King is going to be stabled here, that won't be a problem because I'll know where he is until the check clears," said Bart.

"I have a Letter of Credit from my home bank which I'll send you so you can add it to the papers," said David.

"Great, glad we could work things out because I know how this girl of yours loves that horse," laughed Bart.

The men shook hands on the deal.

"By the way, Bart, do you know of any small farms around this area that are up for sale?" asked David.

"As a matter of fact I know that the Langley Farm just down the road about half a mile is going on the market within the next month," said Bart.

"You don't know what the asking price is do you by any chance?" asked David.

"I've heard that they are asking $10,000 for it and it is a nice little property of five acres with stables and a house. The house is an old farm house that probably needs work done on it, but it has two bedrooms, living room, dining room, kitchen, and a full basement," said Bart.

"Maybe we'll drive by this afternoon and take a look and if it looks like something we'd be interested in we can make an offer on it when it comes on the market," said David.

We left Bart's office and walked toward the barn. "Well my little tomboy, how are you at fixing up old houses?" chuckled David.

"Pretty darn good, smarty," I laughed. "Dad taught me a lot about plumbing and electrical, I've helped him put on a new roof and even helped with the addition to our house including laying linoleum and carpeting."

"God, woman, is there anything you can't do?" he chuckled.

"Lots of things, I'm not very good at housekeeping because I tend to be the type if I can wade through it's clean enough," I laughed.

"I'll bet! You look to me to be the type that would be so organized nothing would ever be out of place, and I'm going to drive you nuts because I tend to drop my towels on the floor and leave clothes laying around," laughed David.

"I've noticed," I said giggling, "actually David I'm not a great housekeeper but I love picking up after you although after we've been married 30 or 40 years I'll probably be yelling at you about not putting your clothes in the clothes hamper. Mostly I just try to not leave anything lying around so that I don't have to clean all that often because I really do hate housecleaning."

Storm King heard us talking as we came in the barn and his head came over the stall door and he whinnied calling to us.

"Storm King, you are our very own horse now and no one but David or I will ever ride you again, except maybe our kids when we have them," I said putting my arm around his neck and hugging him. He tossed his head and his nose came down and he nuzzled my neck. "I think he understands," I laughed.

"Well us men aren't as dumb as you women sometimes think we are, any excuse to nuzzle a beautiful woman's neck is ok with us," laughed David.

"Do we have time to take him out for short ride before we start back?" I asked.

"Why don't the two of you ride and I'll just watch this time, but next time I want to ride behind you with you in my arms," said David.

I put the bridle on Storm and swung up on his back. We walked out of the barn and down to the meadow with David walking beside us. David climbed up on the fence after shutting the meadow gate behind us and I gave Storm his head and we raced down the length of the meadow and back. As we got to the fence I leaned down to Storm, "Let's show him what you can really do," I said patting his neck. With that Storm leaped over the fence close to where David was sitting. I pulled him up once we had cleared the fence and turned to look at David.

"Darling, your mouth is hanging open," I laughed.

"My God, I thought you were only kidding about jumping fences," he said awe in his voice.

"Climb on and we'll take Storm back to the barn and I'll teach you how to rub him down," I laughed.

He climbed onto Storm's back behind me and put his arms around me.

"You know, just the time I think you are all feminine and soft the tomboy in you comes out again, but I think I like the tomboy part best," he said into my ear, "because you have such a look of joy on your face when you are jumping fences or flying a plane."

We slid from Storm's back and I put my arms around this man who gave me permission to be real, not some artificial doll, and I kissed him and my whole heart was in that kiss. He hugged me to him.

"Then just as I think you are all tomboy and that is the part I love best, you run into my arms and you're all female again, and I think no that is the part I love best. I see where life with you, little one, is never going to be dull," he laughed softly.

"I'm so grateful that the man I love is secure enough in his own masculinity that he allows me to be myself and not play games pretending to be something I'm not," I said hugging him.

I showed him then how to unbridle Storm and to rub him down. We made sure Storm had water and then we said our goodbyes to him and started back. On the way we drove by the Langley farm. The stables appeared to be in excellent condition but it was obvious that the farmhouse needed some work done on it.

"Apparently they took better care of their horses than they did of themselves," laughed David.

"Actually a coat of paint and new roof probably would make it look a whole lot better, but I'd be interested in taking a look at the plumbing and the wiring," I said, "not to mention the windows and the heating system."

"Well, sugar, I trust your judgment so if it does come on the market come take a look. If you think it is worth the price put an offer on it, I'll see that the funds are available in my account here. That reminds me, we've got to change the account to a joint account," he said.

Riding back, I said to David, "Once we talk to the chaplain and have a definite date, let's invite Bill and Mark over for dinner so we can ask them about being attendants at our wedding."

"Sounds like a plan to me, kitten," he said.

"Another thing I've been thinking about, since we both love music so much, let's pick out a song that can be our song so that when either of us hears it we will automatically think of each other," I said.

"I was thinking about that the other night, and was trying to remember what song they were playing that first time we danced together," he said.

"It was *I'll Walk Alone*," I said.

"Yes, that was it, how about we make that our song then, babe?"

"Yes David let's, because it says everything I feel about you and it was the first song we ever danced to together," I said.

As we drove David began to sing our song. *I'll always be near you, wherever you are, each night in every prayer. If you call, I'll hear you, no matter how far, just close your eyes, and I'll be there....*

"Oh my love you have such a beautiful voice," I said. "I get goosepimply just listening to you, chills actually run up and down my spine—Sinatra has nothing on you. I just wish I could sing along with you but believe me you don't want to hear me sing, for I wouldn't subject my worst enemy to my voice."

"I bet your voice isn't half as bad as you think it is," he laughed. "Come on sing with me."

He began to sing our song again and I joined in with him. He started laughing, "Well you told the truth, you definitely can't carry a tune, but you are the first person I ever heard who sings sharp not flat."

"I told you I couldn't sing," I laughed with him.

"Oh well, so what, you're perfect in every other way," he laughed hugging me.

I let out a hoot, "You've got to be kidding; I'm not perfect in any way, but I'm so glad you love me despite that fact."

"Well I think you're perfect," he said softly.

"The first night you're back after this stupid war is over, let's go for a moonlight ride on Storm and you can sing to me," I said.

"Yes let's do that, kitten," he said.

"We can take a blanket with us and find a quiet romantic spot and you can make love to me and get me pregnant right away," I whispered.

"Oh God, babe, I want that more than anything else in the world," he whispered back to me.

When we got home David placed a call to his dad.

"They say there is a six hour delay, but they'll call as soon as they can get through," he said.

"Why don't I get supper, then we can sit in our chair and I can cuddle in your arms while we wait," I said.

"Would it be terrible if I went in and stretched out for a while?" he said yawning and stretching.

"Come love, I'll even tuck you in," I said pulling him into the bedroom and shoving him down on the bed and pulling a blanket over him. I bent then and kissed him.

"Pleasant dreams, my darling."

Then I went out to the kitchen to begin preparations for dinner and as I left the room I heard him whisper just before he fell into sleep, "I love you, Lauren."

After I had finished putting supper on to cook I went back to the living room and called Bill McCoy.

"Bill, this is Lauren," I said.

"So how goes the honeymoon?" asked Bill.

"Fine, the reason I called is I'd like to ask a favor of you."

"What do you want, Lauren? I'll help if I can."

"David and I've decided to get married next week. What I called about is I was wondering if you would be my Maid of Honor, so to speak," I laughed.

I heard him chuckling. "Well that's a first, I must say," said Bill. "Lauren, I'd be honored and I'll also give you away if you like," he chuckled.

"I'd like very much Bill," I said.

"You sound happy, are you?" he asked.

"Oh Bill, I don't remember when I've been so happy. David is wonderful and I love him more with each hour that passes. He is the first man I've ever known other than Dad, you and Mark who let me be me and to whom I don't have to apologize for knowing about plumbing, wiring, cars, hoses, and such like," I laughed. "He's like the three of you, so secure in his masculinity that I pose no threat to him."

"That's wonderful, Lauren. I know I had my doubts at first because wartime can make people do things they wouldn't ordinarily do like rushing into marriage, but I liked David as soon as I met him. I think he is a very special young man and that he loves you very much so you two should be very happy together," said Bill.

"Thanks Bill, I love David more than life itself, and it's nice to know that someone else concurs in my feelings about the kind of man he is. Oh I almost forgot to tell you, David bought Storm King for me this afternoon and we are looking at buying a farm in Virginia near where Storm is stabled. We bought a car this morning and if we do place an offer on the farm I'll still be able to drive in so I can work for you while David is overseas," I said.

"You've had quite a day I think," laughed Bill.

"I'm having quite a life," I said. "As soon as we find out what day the wedding is going to be we want you and Mark to come over for supper with us, because David is going to ask Mark to be his best man, though don't mention it to Mark yet because I know David will want to do the asking."

"No I won't mention it to Mark and I know we'd love to have dinner with you two," said Bill.

"Bill, if you need anything just call me. I hope my being gone these two weeks hasn't caused you a lot of grief and I want you to know how much we both appreciate them."

"So far everything is going ok here but I'll call if I think of anything. Bye Lauren."

"Bye Bill and thanks again," I said hanging up the phone.

I looked up and saw David standing in the doorway to the bedroom. I got up and ran throwing myself into his arms.

"Did you have a good sleep, my darling?" I asked.

"I dreamed of you so it was a good sleep, kitten," he laughed wrapping me in his arms. "I didn't realize how tired I was, but then I think a lot of it was all the emotional ups and downs we've had today."

"Come," I said taking his hand and leading him to our chair and pushing him down then curling up on his lap.

"This is what I dreamed, you with your arms around me and mine around you sitting in front of a roaring fireplace and all our kids safely in bed upstairs," he laughed.

"Oh that sounds like a wonderful dream," I said hugging him to me. "I just talked to Bill and he will be my Maid of Honor and also walk me down the aisle. He really likes you, David, and he says he thinks we will be very happy together."

"I like Bill too, he seems like a nice guy. Of course, any guy you think is great will always get my vote," he laughed. "That is unless he tries to steal you from me, then he'd better watch out."

"No one is ever going to steal me from you because you are the only man in the world for me and I don't even realize there are other men around anymore for I can only see you," I said pulling his head down so I could kiss him.

"Kitten, you sure do know how to make a man feel like a million bucks," he said.

"Come on out to the kitchen and talk to me while I get supper on the table," I said taking his hand and pulling him up. We went to the kitchen then and he sat talking to me while I set the table and put the finishing touches on the meal. "Is there any of that apple pie left?" asked David.

"Yes at least half, why?"

"Tonight could I have a slice with cheese on it?" he said.

"You sure can my darling, just let me know anything you want fixed for you and you shall have it. Besides, I love apple pie with cheese as well," I laughed.

"What's for supper tonight? Whatever it is sure smells good," he chuckled.

"Roast leg of lamb, brown gravy, mashed potatoes, and new carrots," I said.

"I haven't had lamb since I left Australia, I didn't think they ever served it over here," he said.

"We used to have it every other Sunday in Ohio because it was one of the cheapest meats we could get. Then Monday or Tuesday night Mom would make hot lamb sandwiches with gravy."

I took the meat out of the oven and let it rest for a few minutes. "Would you slice the lamb, please?" I asked.

"You mean you can't slice meat?" he chuckled.

"No, Dad tried many times to show me how but I just never got the hang of it, it just comes out all mangled when I try it," I laughed.

He stood up then and came to the counter next to the stove. I handed him the knife and fork and he bent his head and kissed me.

"Some people wouldn't think this little scene of domesticity was romantic, but I do," he laughed.

"So do I," I grinned up at him. When he finished slicing the meat, I set it back in the oven to keep it warm. "Now if you will mash the potatoes, I'll make the gravy and dinner will be ready," I said.

"Oh God Lauren, put this food away before I kill myself, I can't seem to stop eating. Everything was just delicious," said David.

"What say we clear the table and I'll do dishes, then we'll go in the living room and listen to records for a while, then I'll bring you your dessert?"

I cleaned up the kitchen while David sat watching me, grinning at me like a satisfied elf.

"You do everything with such an economy of motion," he said to me.

"Is that good or bad?"

"Good! My sister for instance couldn't get an entire meal on the table warm to save her life yet you do it with no seeming effort at all."

"My sister couldn't either but Mom and I always had the knack for it," I laughed. "Mom worked and my grandmother took care of my sister's daughter and I when we were young. We were supposed to do the housework and Grandma would get so mad at me because I always waited until about an hour before Mom was due home and then start in with what I probably should have been doing all day."

"I bet you got it all done before your Mom got home though, didn't you?"

"Yup."

"That's what I mean, you have an economy of motion, you don't waste steps."

"Come on love, I'm finished, let's go in and put on some records and wait for your call to go through," I laughed.

Just as we got back in the living room the phone rang.

"You get it, it is probably your call," I said.

"Yes operator we're ready…hello Dad it's David. No nothing is wrong, in fact just the opposite. I called so I could introduce you to my wife to be," I heard him say. "Yes, you heard right, my wife." He motioned for me to come to the phone.

"Dad, this is Lauren, my bride to be," he said handing me the phone.

"Hello Mr. Benton," I said. "Ok then hello Dad," I laughed. "I'm so happy to meet the man who caused this wonderful tall drink of water to be born into this world. I'm very grateful to you because I love him so much."

I looked up and smiled at David. "He's calling your bothers Frank and Bob to the phone to meet me," I laughed. "Hello Frank, it's nice to meet David's brother. No I'll let him tell you all about how we met, but I did want the chance to at least meet you over the phone."

"I think Bob just shoved Frank out of the way," I laughed.

"Hello Bob, nice to meet you too. I'm going to turn you guys over to David now because he's straining at the leash to talk to you. I can't wait until I get to meet all of you in person and thank you for making me feel like a part of your family already. Here's David," I said handing him the phone.

"Dad? Oh Bob put Dad back on will you then I'll tell you and Frank all about it. Dad, you've still got a good ear, yes, she is just as beautiful as she sounds on the phone, and you guys are just going to love her. No I can't get home because of travel restrictions and I've just enlisted with the Yank's Air Corp and I start flight training on the 25th. As soon as this war is over I'll bring her home to meet all of you, I promise. I'll write you tonight and tell you everything. Dad let me give you our phone number here in case you need to get hold of me or Lauren. Put Frank and Bob on they can listen together because this call is going to cost a fortune."

"Hi guys, you guys are all going to want to beat the tar out of me when you see her because I found her first," he laughed. "When she meets all of you she's going to feel like she's living in a household of giants because believe it or not she's only 5'2" but I warn you she is a died-in-the-wool tomboy so I think she can hold her own with you. What? Well she may be a tomboy but she is the most beautiful, feminine tomboy you'll ever meet. Give Dad a hug for me, hope to see you soon, we both send our love."

I watched his face as he hung up the phone and I saw the emotion in it and went to him, putting my arms around him holding him to me, letting him know it was ok to feel homesick. The moment past and he straightened up and he kissed me soundly three times.

"That's for Dad, Frank and Bob," he said, "and this is for me," and with that he bent and kissed me with such emotion that I felt weak in the knees. "That is for always knowing what I need and when I need it and giving it to me with such love," he said.

"Thank you my darling, but you may have to hold on to me because I'm not sure I can walk after that kiss because my knees feel like water," I said.

Picking me up he swung me around then crossed to our chair and sat down pulling me on his lap.

"God woman, you are just amazing, every word that comes from your mouth makes me so happy I'm a man and loved by you."

"For a man who says he doesn't know the words, you do pretty darn well, my love," I laughed. "You make me very glad I'm a woman and especially a woman loved by you."

"You know sweetheart, even with the condition of the world these days, I'm so glad we found each other. Remember when I said I don't think about the future because it is too murky?"

"Yes I remember, it was when I asked you what you wanted to do after the war," I said.

"Now that's all I want to do is think about the present and the future because it isn't murky anymore, it's filled with possibilities and hope," he said.

Just then the phone rang. I got up and went over and picked it up.

"Hello."

"Hello, is this Lauren?"

"Yes it is, who is this?"

"I'm Carol, David's sister," said the voice at the other end.

I mouthed the words to David. *It's your sister.*

He came over then and took the phone. "Carol, is it really you?" he asked.

"Yes, I called because I just got home and Dad just told me the news and I wanted to meet your bride," she said.

"Just a minute and I'll put her back on."

"Carol, this is Lauren, I'm so happy to meet David's sister," I said.

"If you really love my little brother then I'm happy to meet you too, but if this is some sort of wartime fling, I could well be your worst enemy," she said.

"Carol, I love your brother more than life itself and I want only to continue to love him our whole life through and to take care of him and give him lots of sons and daughters," I said.

David came then and took the phone from my hand.

"Sis, listen to me, please," he said. "I love this woman more than I ever thought I could love anyone. She gives me everything and she is so sweet and loving that she makes me so glad I am a man and that I am the man she loves," he said.

"Let me talk to Lauren, again, please David," said Carol.

He put me back on the phone. "Yes Carol," I said.

"Lauren, forgive me it is obvious that you love David and he loves you very much. I've never heard him say those kinds of words about anyone to anyone ever, and so he must love you very much and you must be a very special kind of lady. It's just that he is my baby brother and I've always felt so protective of him, but if he loves you that much then I'm prepared to love you too," said Carol.

"Carol, I don't want to take him away from you, I want to help you take care of him because he is a very, very special man and I'm just glad he had you all these years to love and take care of him. I'm sure he is so special because you must have been a great influence on him. Just know that I would die to protect him and keep him safe."

I heard her soft sobs. "Lauren, thank you, thank you for loving him. Can I write to you because I'd love to know all the details of how you met and it would be so nice to have another woman to talk to about the man we both so obviously love."

"Carol, I would love that for I've no woman I can talk to about how wonderful David is and how lucky and privileged I feel that he chose me to love and I would love to talk to you about him. Please write often because I want to know everything about him from the day he was born, and you are the one person in your family who I know can tell me the things we women want to know about because it takes one female to understand another female," I said.

"Yes, Lauren, let's write often and I can't wait to meet you in person. You are everything that David told Dad you were and much more I think than any mere man will ever understand."

"You'd be surprised, Carol, because I'm teaching him to understand so that when we give you nieces he will know how to talk to them and none of this nonsense about men don't say those things in Australia," I laughed.

"Now I know I love you already; yes the two of us will have to work on him in that department, but I think between us we can make him see the light," she laughed.

"I love you too, Carol, and I can't wait to meet you either. Now I'll put your baby brother back on because he's about to tear the phone out of my hands if I don't let him speak," I laughed handing the phone to David.

"Don't scream at me, baby brother, we women have settled everything between us and I think you are one lucky man because Lauren is probably the best thing that is ever going to happen to you in your lifetime," she said.

"Sis, I want you to love Lauren as much as I do because you two are my two favorite women in all the world."

"I already do, bro and we both love you. Take care and send me a picture of you two so I can put a face with the lovely voice I heard here on the phone."

"Yes we will, goodnight big sis, I love you."

"Good night bro take care, I love you too and tell Lauren good night for me and that I love her too and tell her I said thank you she'll know what I mean."

"I will."

After he hung up the phone David came to where I was standing and his arms went about me.

"You are something else, because I've never seen anyone handle Carol that easily in my life. Normally any woman I've ever introduced her to has felt the rough side of her tongue in no uncertain terms, but in just seconds you had her eating out of your hand."

"It's because we both love you so much that we immediately understood each other. It is going to be so wonderful to have a sister who is really a sister not an additional parent," I said.

"What was all that about teaching me?" he asked.

"It is Carol's and my plan to teach you how to say the words you claim you don't know how to say because that isn't the way Australian men talk to women," I said. "But we both agreed that you had already come a long way and I think what you said to her about me and the words you used were what convinced her that you really loved me and I really loved you," I said. "I think growing up Carol had a really hard time because of some Neanderthal theory that real men don't tell a woman how much she is loved and valued. I was very lucky because Dad never felt that way and he told me often how much he loved me and valued me; Carol apparently wasn't so lucky. So we are making it our priority to teach you so that when we do have daughters they won't grow up the way she did, but the way I did."

"I'm really trying, Lauren, to be more forthcoming with you and to let you know how much I love you," he said.

"Yes you are, my darling, and you have made amazing strides in just a few short days and with the years ahead of us I know you will live up to your full potential and your daughters are simply going to be gaga over their dad because he won't be afraid to let them know that it isn't just sons who have value," I said. "You're not afraid anymore to tell me and don't be afraid to tell Carol, because she needs to hear it from the baby brother she loves so much. David, you are the most wonderful man in this entire universe, you have a great capacity to love and to make the women in your life feel not only loved, but safe, and secure and valued, for if you didn't I couldn't love you the way I do."

"Carol said to tell you she loves you and thank you. She said you would understand what she meant. What did she mean?"

"Come darling sit down and I will try to explain it to you," I said leading him back to the chair and sitting once again on his lap. "Have you ever in your entire life told Carol that she was one of the favorite women in your life? Think hard because this is important to your understanding."

"No, I guess the subject never came up," he said.

"Did you ever tell her that you loved her?"

"Not in so many words but she knows I love her," he said.

"That is why she thanked me, because you said those words to her just now on the phone and, darling, once in a while a woman just has to hear the actual words to really believe them. We can tell ourselves that we are loved through your actions toward us and mostly that is enough, but every so often we have to hear the actual words so we know that what we think we believe is real. Women are creatures of words, and to feel truly loved, we have to hear those words every so often coming from the men we love. I don't mean that you have to tell me every hour or every day that you love me because your actions tell me that you do, but once in a while I need to hear the actual words and so does Carol."

"I thought you said you never understood your sex," he said. "I think you understand both men and women better than anyone I have ever known," he said pulling me close to him. "I can understand your need for words, because I need to hear you say them to me so I guess it is only reasonable that you need to hear them said to you. I promise, kitten, I'll try to remember to tell you at least once a day how much I love and value you."

"David do you remember after I tucked you in today when you lay down to nap do you remember what you said just as you were falling asleep?"

"No I don't remember saying anything, I just remember thinking how much I loved you."

"Well, I heard what you said, you were half asleep already and you said, 'I love you Lauren' and it must have been when you were thinking about loving me. While I was getting supper ready I kept feeling so warm and so loved because you said I love you Lauren to me just as you were falling asleep. Words don't cost much darling, all they take are sincerity and that you have in abundance. Tomorrow, let's both sit down and write to Carol because we both love her and I think she needs to hear it from both of us that we do," I said.

"Ok, I'll write to her and I'll try to be more forthcoming with her than I've been in the past."

"That's my good boy," I said hugging him to me.

That night just before sleep claimed us as we lay in each other's arms, David whispered, "I love you, Lauren," and I answered him, "I love you too, David, with all my heart and soul."

After breakfast the next morning David said, "I'm going to run to the tailor shop and try on my uniforms, then I'll be home and we'll go to the base and talk to the chaplain, so get dressed while I'm gone."

"I will, darling. I'll be ready on time I promise."

I walked with him to the door and kissed him goodbye. "Love you," I said.

"Love you too, kitten," and he was out the door.

I went in then to pick out an outfit to wear. I finally chose a brown skirt and sweater and I went in and showered and put on my make up. I was just putting on my earrings when I heard David come back in the apartment.

"Be right there, darling," I called.

I ran out to throw myself in his arms, because I knew he liked it when I did, but halfway across the room I stopped. He was in uniform and he looked so handsome that I literally could not breathe.

I did run to him then and put my arms around him. "Oh David, you have got to be the handsomest man on this entire planet," I said reaching up to kiss him.

I kept my face against him until I could get my emotions under control because seeing him in uniform for the first time the reality hit me like a punch in the stomach that it was real and that I was eventually going to have to send my man into combat with a smile pasted on my face when I knew I really would want to cling to him and beg him not to go.

"Definitely an improvement from the ones the Army gave me, wouldn't you say?" he asked laughing.

Mustering my courage I laughed up at him, "Gee no more Huck Finn, I kind of miss him. It's going to be a toss up today whether I want to lord it over all those women who will be ogling you that you're mine not theirs or whether I just want to scratch their eyes out."

"There are so many guys in uniform now that I doubt they will even notice one more," he said.

"Oh believe me, one look at you and they'll notice, because none of the others are half as handsome as you, my darling," I said.

"You're just prejudiced," he laughed.

"I'm just truthful," I said smiling at him.

"Come on let's get going, I stopped and brought the car up and parked it in front of the apartment building," he said.

When we got to the base David asked where he would find the chaplain's office. "Building H-6 second floor," the sergeant told him.

We found a parking space right in front of the building and David made sure I was to his left in case he had to salute any officers. There was no one in the outer office when we went in so we knocked on the door marked 'Capt. Hollenbeck' and were told to come in.

"Captain, I'm 2nd Lt. David Benton and this is my fiancée, Miss Lauren Bennett," said David saluting him. "We'd like to talk to you about performing a marriage ceremony for us if we can."

"Sit down, Lieutenant, and you too Miss Bennett," said the captain. "I don't recall seeing you around base, Lieutenant."

"I don't actually report in for duty until the 25th, sir," said David. "Lauren and I would like to be married in the chapel on the base next week, sir, if that can be done before I'm actually on active duty."

"What day next week?"

"We were thinking about Wednesday, Thursday, or Friday, if that was possible, sir."

"Well first let me check the chapel schedule for those days and then we can go on from there," said the captain. He got up and moved over to a big appointment book and started to leaf through the pages. "Well it's available at 10:00 on Wednesday and 1:00 on Friday."

David looked at me so I answered for him, 10:00 on Wednesday would be great," I said.

"Let me just pencil you in for that time," said the captain writing our names in the book as I spelled them for him.

"Well Lt. Benton, as long as you don't actually report for active duty until the 25th then there will be no problem about getting Army permission. I can see no reason why I couldn't perform the ceremony for you on Wednesday. How many will be in the wedding party?"

"Just Lauren and I and my best man, Mark Purcell, and Lauren's boss, Bill McCoy, who will act as her Maid of Honor," said David smiling.

"I don't think I've ever had a male Maid of Honor before," laughed the captain.

"Bill is also going to give me away," I laughed.

"Bill McCoy, why does that name sound so familiar?" asked the captain.

"Bill is the Director of Office of War Management," I said.

"Oh yes, I've had some dealings with Bill and you must be the young lady I talked to when I've called his office," said the captain.

"Yes, I'm Bill's secretary," I smiled.

"Bill called me yesterday and said you two would be coming to see me sometime this week and that if I didn't get you two married he was going to make sure to sic General McDowell on me," laughed Captain Hollenbeck. "So I guess I better make sure you have a great wedding day."

"Thank you, sir, we appreciate your help because we decided not to wait until I graduate from flight school," said David extending his hand to the captain.

"Can't say as I blame you, son, you've a mighty pretty young lady here and I would imagine it will be easier to concentrate on flight school if you have her under lock and key, so to speak, before you start," laughed Captain Hollenbeck.

"Yes, sir, that was my thinking too," laughed David and we got up then to leave.

"See you Wednesday at 10 then, kids. Oh what denomination are you?" asked the captain.

"I'm Episcopalian," said David.

"I'm Methodist," I said.

"Why don't we just make it non-denominational," said the captain.

"That's fine with us, sir," said David extending his hand to the captain and then throwing him a smart salute.

When we got home I called Bill and Mark and invited them to dinner that night. Both accepted and I told them to be at the apartment about six.

"We'll have a week and a few days for a honeymoon, where would you like to go, Niagara Falls?" asked David.

"No, let's stay right here," I said.

"Are you sure, baby, because it is going to be a long time before we get a chance to have a real honeymoon," he asked watching me closely.

"I'm very sure, because anywhere you are and I'm with you will be a honeymoon to me for the rest of our lives," I said looking back at him.

"Is there a record store somewhere around here?"

"Yes a couple of blocks down. Why?"

"Let's walk over because I want to get two records, one for you and one for me of *I'll Walk Alone* so that when I'm not with you I can play it and think of you, not that I wouldn't think about you anyway, but you know what I mean," he laughed.

We went to the record store then and picked up the records. When we got back we put mine on the turntable and David took me in his arms and we danced to the record and he sang the words to me. When the song finished he pulled me even tighter into his arms and my arms went about his neck and we stood, just holding each other, for a long time.

"You will be in my prayers every night, my darling," I said. "Just know that no matter how bad it gets you can close your eyes and I'll be there with you holding out my arms to you and loving you."

His arms tightened around me until I could hardly breathe and mine were about him the same way.

"Lauren, I'll write every single day and please, darling, write to me every day because I will be leaving my heart here with you," he said.

"I'll write twice a day my dearest, and all of my heart will be with you until I can hold you in my arms again," I whispered. I leaned away from him then and took his dear, sweet face between my two hands. "Just know that I love you with all my heart and soul and being and that I consider myself the luckiest woman in the universe that you found me and that you love me. We've had this time and we'll have the next week and half and then the six weeks you are in training, and that is more than some people ever have and I'll live on the memories of it until you return to my arms."

He kissed me then and it was the most tender of kisses any woman had ever known and I kissed him back and we stood for a while longer murmuring our love to one another.

"I'm so proud of you, my darling, that I want to shout to the world, this man is the dearest man on all the earth and he loves me."

"I too want to shout to the world, see this woman here in my arms, I love her and I'm so honored that she is to be my wife and that she loves me," he whispered to me.

"Come darling, let's go write to Carol because I know she is so proud of her baby brother and she loves you as much as I do. Tomorrow let's go and get our pictures taken so you can have one, and I can have one, and we'll send one to Carol."

We went over and both of us sat at the kitchen table and each of us wrote a letter to Carol. David let me read his when he had finished.

Dear Sis,

Lauren and I are sitting at the kitchen table writing to you. You don't know how wonderful it is for me to be able to look up and see her beautiful face and she always seems to know when I'm looking at her and she looks up and smiles back at me, much as you used to do when we were kids working on our homework assignments.

Carol, I know I haven't told you often enough how much having you for a big sister has meant to me, especially after Mom left us. I don't think I could have gotten through those years if it hadn't been for you.

I'm a very lucky man for in my lifetime I've been loved by two very exceptional women, you and Lauren. I hope when I'm a father I will learn to let my daughters know how much their love means to me and how wonderful I think they are. Lauren is teaching me and your baby bro is learning so bear with me and I'll try to tell you more often how much I love and value you.

Take care, sis, and write to me often. I miss you more than I can tell you and I can't wait until I see you again and you get to meet Lauren because she is the other half of me and I love her very much.
David

"Oh David, I'm so proud of you. Carol is going to love this letter from you and I think she will take it out and read it often. Please read what I've written to her and tell me if it is ok," I said.

> *Dear Carol,*
>
> *You don't know how much your words meant to me on the phone and I can't wait to meet you and hug you.*
>
> *Your brother is sitting across from me and he looks like a little boy trying to write his first love letter. His face is all scrunched up and he is concerned with trying to get the words just right, I can tell. He is so dear and so sweet and he looks so handsome in his uniform.*
>
> *We are going tomorrow to have our pictures taken and we'll send one especially for you and one for his dad and brothers. Our wedding is set for Wednesday and I just wish you could be here for I'd love to have you as my Maid of Honor. As it is my boss (who has been like a second brother to me) is going to fill in for you and also walk me down the aisle.*
>
> *I haven't even told David this yet, but when our first daughter is born I want to call her Carol and I know she will love her Aunt Carol all over the place. We've talked about her and David says he hopes she is a tomboy just like me, but I said she'd probably be a little princess who wouldn't want to get her hands dirty.*
>
> *We are looking for a farmhouse to buy here in Virginia which is close to my work so I can be fixing it up while David is away. We think it will be a good investment so when this awful war is over we can sell it and come back to Sydney to live if that is what David wants to do. At any rate, wherever we live I'll keep a room made up for you, big sis, and you will always be welcome. Just hope you don't mind a houseful of kids because I want at least six or seven and I may even talk your brother into shooting for an even dozen...he just blanched as he read this.*
>
> *All my love,*
> *Lauren*

"Thank you, sweetheart. Carol is going to love this letter and you for writing it. I can almost see her smiling about the dozen kids because if we have that many I'm sure she will want to move in with us and help us raise them for she genuinely loves kids," said David.

"Ok my sky jockey, let's get this ready for the post and then I've got to get supper ready because it is almost three now and Bill and Mark will be here at six."

Mark arrived right on the dot of six as I knew he would because Mark had an overdeveloped sense of timing and I had never known him to arrive anywhere one second late. When the doorbell rang, I said, "David, get that it will be Mark."

"How can you possibly know that? It might be Bill," he laughed.

"Nope, it will be Mark. because I've never known him to arrive even a second late, so if you ever want Mark to arrive fashionably late to anything, just tell him to come at whatever time the fashionably late might be and he will be there right on the dot," I laughed.

David opened the door and Mark was standing on the other side.

"Hi Mark," I called, "come on in and make yourself at home." I had to laugh at the expression on David's face and at the fact he was trying not to laugh.

"Hi Lauren, Hi David," said Mark coming in and heading straight for the little bar to fix himself a drink. "What a hell of a day this has been. Lauren, do you still have any Teacher's Scotch left," he asked.

"Bottom shelf, Mark where it always is," I said laughing in spite of myself because I could tell David didn't know whether to be annoyed that this man knew exactly what kind of scotch I had or the way he made himself at home in my apartment.

"David, come help me in the kitchen, please," I said as I chuckled to myself.

"What do you need, kitten?" asked David coming into the kitchen where I was standing doubled up in laughter. "What's so damn funny?"

"You, my darling, the expression on your face is priceless and I love it that you are jealous," I said.

"How in the hell does Mark know what kind of scotch you have and where you keep it? He just waltzed in here like he owned the place," he said. "Stop it kitten, I don't think it's funny."

"Calm down, my love, and in a minute you will see the humor of it too," I laughed. "Mark dated the girl who used to room with me and since neither she nor I drank scotch, he brought his own bottle. I told you Mark was a good friend and he is, after Shelby moved out and they broke up, he used to come around and cry on my shoulder until he started dating Linda, so you see you have nothing to be jealous of," I said still laughing.

David calmed a little then, but I could still see he wasn't about to give it up that easily.

"You mean he just drops by whenever he feels like it and makes himself to home?" asked David.

"That's about the size of it, darling. Mark is like a brother to me and every time he gets dumped by one of his many, many girls, he comes here to cry on my shoulder and to get drunk as a skunk on his own scotch. I let him drink till he is blotto then I throw a blanket over him and he sleeps it off on the sofa. The next morning he always apologizes and says he'll never do it again and swears off all women till the next time. He's really quite harmless, I promise," I said.

"Well, if you say so, kitten, but I was just about to withdraw my offer I haven't made yet to him to be my best man and knock him senseless," he said and I could tell David still wasn't completely convinced he still shouldn't knock him senseless.

"I promise you, darling, Mark is absolutely harmless and there has never been anything even remotely romantic between us. Just think of him as another one of your brothers and you wouldn't want me to throw one of your brothers out under similar circumstances, would you?"

"Well, I guess when you put it that way," said David, his voice trailing off. "My God, I've never felt so jealous in my whole life, see what loving you does to me, kitten?" he said finally breaking into laughter.

"David my love, there has never been any man in my life before you, which you very well know, and there never will be another. You are more than enough man for me," I said smiling at him.

Just then the doorbell rang and I heard Mark go to let Bill in. "Hey Bill, how are things going," we heard Mark say.

"Fine Mark," said Bill eyeing the scotch in Mark's hand. "Don't tell me you and your current girlfriend have hit the skids already?" asked Bill.

"No Bill, it's just been one hell of a day and I needed a drink badly," we heard Mark chuckling.

"In a case like that I'll join you," said Bill going to fix himself a drink. "Where are the kids?"

"They're in the kitchen and I'm not sure what is going on but I heard Lauren laughing her head off a few minutes ago. I wonder if David knows how that woman can laugh in all the wrong places," mused Mark. "I love her like the sister I never had, but sometimes I would dearly love to throttle her."

David walked back into the living room and Mark looked at him, "Did you hear that?" asked Mark.

"Yup," grinned David.

"Well I mean that sometimes Lauren can start laughing when she really shouldn't be and I do get so mad at her I could throttle her, but I love her nonetheless," he said.

"Do I hear my three men discussing how they'd like to throttle poor little innocent me?" I said coming into the living room and I smiled at each of them.

"David, I think some explanations are in order before you get the wrong idea about things," said Bill. "Mark and Lauren have a love/hate relationship like most siblings have and neither of them can make up their minds whether to laugh or kill the other one most of the time."

"Oh God David, I hope you didn't get the impression that Lauren and I were ever romantically involved," said Mark. "When I first met her I did think about trying to add her to my stable but she just looked at me and told me I was an idiot so I gave that idea up in a hurry, because this gal is tomboy enough that I bet she could really land a haymaker on a guy if she felt the need," he laughed.

"You better believe I could, Mark, and you were damn lucky you saw the error or your ways because I could easily knock you flat sweetie because you're a lover not a fighter, whereas I grew up in a neighborhood of all boys and I've belted more than one male in my life," I laughed.

"God, maybe it's a good thing I didn't make a pass at you that first night, my love," laughed David.

"Well you being the long drink of water you are I probably couldn't have reached high enough to land a haymaker but I could have bitten your kneecap," I said giggling.

"Now I need a drink," laughed David.

"Make me one too," I laughed. "If you guys are going to get blotto I intend to get blotto right along with you."

"What do you want, kitten?" asked David

"Rum and Coke," I said. He went then and poured himself a double shot of bourbon and brought me back a rum and Coke.

"Hey, David, you look mighty spiffy in your uniform," said Bill. "How does it feel to be a Yank?"

"So far so good," laughed David, "but I have a feeling that it is going to get really interesting when my fellow cadets hear my accent the first time."

"Oh just tell them you're from south Brooklyn," laughed Bill. "Most of them probably won't know the difference."

While the men talked, I set up the card table and chairs and set the table on it. Then I went out to the kitchen to bring in the food. "Come on you wild men, come chow down before everything gets cold," I said.

We sat down to eat then and the conversation was lively and animated once the three of them got started on the 'can you top this' stories about me. David started it telling them about me jumping Storm over the fence. "I've never seen a woman jump a horse over a fence at least four feet high before and especially not bareback," he laughed remembering.

"The first day Lauren applied for a job with me while I was interviewing her all the lights in the place went out. Lauren asked me where the fuse box was and I told her I didn't know, so she pulls this flashlight out of her purse and goes in search of it. Fifteen minutes later the lights came on again and she comes back and sits herself down like the interview had never been interrupted. I decided then this was a gal I just had to have working for me and I wasn't wrong," laughed Bill.

"The first day I met her she came to our company picnic with some guy who worked for our Agency," said Mark. "There was a baseball game going on, mostly amongst the men, and Lauren goes right up to the pitcher and asks if she can play left field. The pitcher just looked at this little petite gal and started laughing. Lauren looks him straight in the eye and tells him that she'll make him a deal, that if she can strike out three batters in a row, then he would let her play left field, but if she couldn't she'd retire to the sidelines with the rest of the women. The first guy comes up to bat, a big 230-pound hulk, and you could tell he was thinking he'd make short work of this dame that thought she could pitch. One, two, three strikes and he's retired. I never saw anyone look so thunderstruck in my life. The next guy comes up, same scenario and then the third guy comes up and it's the same thing all over again. As I recall, by the time the game ended these guys were carrying her off the field on their shoulders," laughed Mark. "Every year since all the guys start asking me about three weeks before the picnic if Lauren is coming again this year."

"I love you three guys," I said, "because you always let me be me and it doesn't seem to bother any of you that I'm a tomboy," I laughed.

"But you're such an adorable little tomboy," said Mark.

"You look at her and you think oh this little thing needs a great big man to take care of her, then zingo, the tomboy pops out and you wonder why you ever thought she couldn't take care of herself just fine," laughed Bill.

"If you really wanted to see something funny you should have seen the expression on the used car salesman's face when she popped the hood on the first car he showed us and told him the thing would never run, because the distributor cap was missing," said David.

"David, I can guarantee being married to Lauren will never be dull and definitely will be full of laughs because she has the zaniest sense of humor I've ever run into," said Bill.

"I'm finding that out," laughed David. "It sure appears it's going to be a wild ride."

"It may be wild, but this little gal has loyalty to those she loves built right into her soul and she's a little wildcat when it comes to defending those she loves," said Mark.

"Before I forget to ask you, Mark, are you free at 10 A.M. this Wednesday?" asked David.

"I can be; what did you have in mind?" asked Mark.

"Lauren and I are getting married at the base chapel then and I'd very much like to have you be my best man."

"I'd be honored," said Mark.

"Bill is going to be my Maid of Honor and give me away as well," I said.

"Oh I can't wait to see Bill in a bridesmaid's dress," laughed Mark.

"Watch it, son, or I'll have Lauren make you eat those words," laughed Bill.

I cleared up the supper things as the men sat discussing the war and then I came back in and sat on David's lap while we laughed and talked.

"I hate to break this up, but I've got a 7 A.M. meeting in the morning with the Secretary of State," said Bill, "so I think I'd better call it a night. "Great dinner as usual, and the laughs were great as usual."

"I've got to be up early too," said Mark. "Thanks for the dinner, Lauren, and thank you for asking me to be your best man, David."

"Both of you are welcome," I said and David shook hands with both men and I kissed them on the cheek.

After they were gone, I turned to David going to him and hugging him, "Why don't you get ready for bed and I'll be right in, darling, because you look kind of beat," I said.

"Jealousy isn't what it's cracked up to be," he chuckled. "It's very draining. I think, sweetheart, you missed your calling, you should have been a diplomat for you sure know how to diffuse a difficult situation with humor," he laughed.

69

"David, I'll never give you any reason to be jealous, but the little you displayed tonight did a lot for this gal's ego," I said smiling at him.

"I've never been jealous before in my life, but then I never had such a gorgeous little bundle to be jealous over before either," he said.

"Thank you, darling," I said reaching up and kissing him on the cheek.

Later lying in David's arms, I said, "What do you want to do tomorrow, my soon-to-be-husband?"

"How about going out to see Storm? I'd kind of like to ride him with you again holding you in my arms, for I just love the way you snuggle into them."

"Sounds good to me but let's do it in the afternoon and sleep late in the morning."

"Good idea, kitten," he laughed softly pulling me close to him.

"Do you want to?" I asked looking up at him.

"I want to but I'm just too tired tonight, my love," he grinned down at me.

"Me too," I said.

"What a woman! You would have agreed if I'd said yes, wouldn't you?"

"Yes I would have, but I have a feeling you would have been making love to a corpse because I don't think I could have stayed awake," I laughed softly.

"Don't ever be afraid to tell me no, if you're too tired or just not interested," said David.

"I'm not afraid to tell you no, and I guarantee that the time will never come when I'm not interested...too tired maybe...but definitely not disinterested," I said.

"I love you, Lauren," he said and a minute later I heard his soft snore and I knew that no matter what we had to go through, our love was worth it.

I stretched as I woke up the next morning and looked at David to see if he was awake. "Are you awake, sleepyhead?" I asked as I saw him smile at me.

"No," he said laughing.

"Well go back to sleep if you want to," I said, as I put my arms around his neck and kissed him and moved deeper into his arms.

"What did you have in mind, kitten?" he asked chuckling.

"You know very well what I have in mind, don't kid me because you can read me like a book," I laughed. His arms came around me and he hugged me to him.

"I remember hearing a young lady I know, who said she would never be disinterested and I think she may be about to prove it to me," he laughed, as his head came down to kiss me.

"How'd you ever guess?" I laughed back at him as my hands and lips sought his body.

"Well sweetheart, you tend to telegraph your punches," he said rolling over so that I was pinned beneath him. "Oh God Lauren, I can't wait any longer," he said and with that he entered me.

"Oh that feels so good," I said and I began to meet him thrust for thrust.

We both climaxed almost immediately. "Sorry love, I just couldn't wait any longer," he said.

"Nor could I, so there is nothing to apologize for. Let's stay in bed all day and make love," I said.

"Sounds good to me but I think I'd better get up and shave first because I don't want to scratch you all up," he laughed.

"Oh goody, I get to watch you shave," I laughed.

"What is there about watching me shave that you enjoy so much?" he asked curiously.

"I'm not really sure, but I just get this warm, cozy feeling when I watch you. Maybe it is all those funny faces you make while you're doing it, then, of course, I just love watching you period," I laughed. "Also, there is always the chance that you'll drag me into the shower with you when you finish."

"That's no chance, that's a certainty," he chuckled.

I got up then and stood behind him and wrapped my arms about him. "I just love your body, it is so big and so beautiful," I said hugging him. "It is a toss-up as to whose body is more beautiful, yours or Storm's," I giggled. "I love watching both my stallions."

He wrapped his arms behind my back and pulled me into him.

"So you like stallions, do you?" he said. He pulled me from in back of him so that I was pinned between him and the sink. "I'm kind of partial to cute little mares myself," he laughed kissing me and getting shaving lather all over my face. Then he began to rub my body with his, until I began to moan and my hand went down to that part of him that could give me so much pleasure.

"Oh want to play, do you?" he asked.

"Yes, oh please yes," and the huskiness in my voice told him I was more than ready for him and he lifted me so that he could come into me and I began to beg. "Please, please darling," as my tongue licked at his nipples.

"Witch," he said as his thrusts grew deeper and I was a lost mad thing straining to get even closer to him as my breasts pressed against his chest and my hands roamed over his body, until I felt him explode within me and then my own shuddering explosion came and I slumped against him too weak to even stand on my own.

"My God, kitten, how I love you and I love hearing you beg for me to take you and the fact that you are incapable of waiting even to let me finish shaving," he said.

"Oh David, I want you all the time, it is like nothing I've ever felt before and I love the feel of you in me and I love that you want me as badly as I want you," I said still leaning against him. "I love the feel of your body under my hands and I love watching you become erect because I know that soon you will be inside me and when you are it is like exquisite torture. I love it when you watch me when I'm in the throes of passion for you and that little smile you get as you watch me."

"Kitten, I've never known another woman like you, who can so freely admit her need of me both physically and every other way. I ache for you just as you ache for me and I love watching you respond to my touch because you make me so grateful that I was born a man and that my body can provide you with so much pleasure which is written all over your beautiful face."

Later as we were sitting at the kitchen table having breakfast, David's hand came across the table and taking mine he brought it to his lips. "I love you so much," he said. "I love the way your eyes go all soft when I touch you, even to just hold your hand, like now. I love your desire for me and the way you reach for me whenever I'm near you. I love the way you curl up on my lap and you nuzzle my neck, and the way you snuggle into my arms at night or when we are riding Storm. I love it when I'm dancing with you and you caress the back of my neck. I love the way you tell me in a thousand different ways how much you love me."

My eyes filled with tears that this big, strong, wonderful man would say these things to me. I got up and went around the table and sat down on his lap my arms going around his neck.

"Oh David, I hope you know how much I love you and how grateful I am that you love me," I said. "For sometimes the love I feel for you just overwhelms me until I feel like I'm going to burst because my whole being is filled with so much love for you. I want nothing more in life than to love you and take care of you and to tell you what a very special man you are. I love the way you look down at me and laugh and the laughter is in your eyes and the love you have for me is there too. I want to just give and give to you because you make me so happy."

We held each other until the emotion had passed for both of us.

"Let's get dressed and go have our wedding picture taken and I want you to have your picture taken so I have something to carry next to my heart when I can't be with you," he said.

"Yes let's and I want one of you that I can keep on the night stand next to our bed so I can look up and see your face and know that this beautiful man loves me as much as I love him."

"After let's go ride Storm so I can feel you snuggle into my arms," he laughed.

"You know, darling, you've spoiled it for me for my ever wanting to ride just by myself because now I only want to ride snuggled in your arms for the rest of my life. Go on with you now and go finish shaving and I'll clear up the dishes and get dressed too."

"Aren't you going to come watch?" he chuckled.

"I think if we are going to get everything done today we want to do I'd better refrain because somehow you and I always get sidetracked when I watch you shave," I laughed.

"We do indeed, little one."

We went to the picture studio and had our picture taken together. David wore his uniform and I was dressed in the suit I planned to wear for our wedding. Then we each had individual pictures taken. Afterwards we went back to the apartment and changed into jeans and sweaters and we set out to go ride Storm King. When we got to the stables Bart was just coming out.

"Glad to see you both, because I was going to call you," he said.

"Is something the matter with Storm?" I asked anxiously.

"Not a thing is wrong with that horse of yours," he laughed. "I just found out that the Langley property is going on sale next week and that I could arrange for a special showing of it for you if you were still interested," he said.

"Yes, we're very interested," laughed David.

"I'll go in and call the real estate agent if you have time for a tour this afternoon," said Bart.

"Please do, Bart, and thank you so much for thinking of us," I said.

We took Storm out then and rode him for about an hour with me snuggled in David's arms.

"You know, kitten, I never thought I'd get so I really liked riding horses, but you've convinced me that it is almost as much fun as flying," he laughed.

"It really is a toss-up for me which I enjoy more, flying with you or riding with you," I laughed. "I kind of think riding might win out by a hair because I get to snuggle in your arms when we're riding which I can't very well do when we're flying."

"Remind me to buy a plane with an automatic pilot," chuckled David.

After we finished stabling Storm we went to the office to find Bart. "Were you able to get hold of the agent?" we asked.

"Yes and I told her you'd meet her at the farm at about two which gives you just fifteen minutes to get there," said Bart.

"Thank you again," we said.

When we got to the Langley farm the agent was just pulling into the drive.

"Hi, you must be the Bentons," she said getting out of her car and shaking hands with us.

"Well, actually we won't be the Benton's until Wednesday," I laughed.

"Congratulations then," she said. "My name is Wendy by the way."

She took us on a tour of the stables first.

"Wouldn't Storm King just love these stables?" I said to David.

"Yes, I think he might find them very comfortable, kitten," he laughed.

Wendy showed us the house then. It was a big old farmhouse but it had been well maintained and I could find nothing of any significance that needed doing on the interior. The kitchen was huge and the living room had a fireplace and there were plenty of closets and cupboards. The master bedroom contained a bath and had cross-ventilation. The second bedroom was small but comfortable as a guest room and also had its own bath. The dining room was big and could easily accommodate a table seating at least twelve people.

"I admit the exterior needs a little work done on it," said Wendy, "but a coat of paint is about it."

"How about the roof? It looks like it might need a little work as well," I said.

"Actually the roof is fairly new, but we had a really bad storm here a couple of weeks ago and some of the shingles came loose," said Wendy. "I can get someone to replace them, if you are interested."

"Give us a minute, will you Wendy?" asked David.

"Take your time, I'll just be out by the car," said Wendy.

"Well, what do you think, kitten, should we make an offer on it?" asked David hugging me.

"I love it and I think it is a good investment, but do you really want to take on house payments with everything else you've got on your mind?" I asked looking up at him.

"I want a real home to come home to when I get leave, but we could also rent it out if you'd rather stay in your apartment," he said.

"But David, suppose you get stationed somewhere across the country, I'd want to come there and be with you until you get sent overseas," I said.

"Well, you could still do that if that happens, but truthfully darling I have the feeling that as soon as flight training is finished, they will be deploying us right away," he said.

"It's up to you, my love; I love the farm and I want you to have the home to come home to that you want and maybe if our luck holds out you'll be stationed at Andrews for a while anyway," I said

"Let's put an offer on it, sugar, because I will love thinking of you here with Storm to watch over you and thinking about you furnishing our home," he said hugging me to him.

We went then in search of Wendy. "Wendy, we'd like to make a formal offer on the farm," said David. "What is the asking price?"

"Originally, they were thinking about $10,000 but I just got a call yesterday from the owners and they are dropping it to $9,000," said Wendy, "because they want it to go fast."

"Make them an offer of $8,000 but you have our permission to go to the $9,000 if they won't come down any lower," said David.

"Will do and I hope you both will be very happy here," said Wendy. "I'll be in touch with you as soon as I hear back from them," said Wendy. "Give me a phone number where I can reach you. What kind of a down payment are you planning on?" she asked.

"Well, I'd be willing to pay cash for the entire amount if you could get them down to $7,000, otherwise how about a 10% down payment," said David.

"I think with the offer of cash they might just see their way clear to letting it go for $7,000," said Wendy.

"My funds are in my Australian bank, but I'll contact them right away to transfer them to my bank here in Washington," said David.

We shook hands on the deal and David and I got back in our car and started back to Washington. "I can't believe it," I said. "We're going to be homeowners if we're lucky."

"Do you realize what a whirlwind it's been since we first met?" laughed David. "Both of our lives have changed completely."

"David, pull over, please," I said.

"What's the matter darling?" asked David as he pulled the car to the side of the road and turned to me, worry in his eyes.

"Darling, don't look so concerned, I just had to be in your arms for a few minutes," I smiled.

"Baby, you scared me there for a minute, I thought maybe you were getting cold feet."

"Never, but are you very sure this is what you want, my love?" I asked.

"Very, very sure," he said pulling me into his arms and his lips came down to mine and I knew then that we would be together forever and that this was what he definitely wanted.

"I love you," I said, "and I'll start fixing up the house as soon as we close and can move in so you'll have your own home to come home to and when you're away you'll be able to picture it and see me waiting to throw my arms around you and never let you go," I whispered.

"I love you too, kitten, and I never thought that I would ever be this happy and this content and it is you who has made me feel this way," he whispered back.

We started out again heading for home and David's arm pulled me in close to him and I stroked his knee as we drove. When we were back in the apartment we hugged each other and neither of us could wipe the smiles off our faces.

"I was just thinking, David," I said looking up into his face, "what would you say if when they lift travel restrictions and it is safe for her to do so, that I ask Carol to come stay with me while you are overseas?"

"I think it would be wonderful because then I could come home to my two best girls," he said hugging me to him. "Let's place a call to her right now and ask her."

"Yes let's, then you should telegraph your bank about transferring the funds just in case they accept the offer," I laughed.

"Tomorrow without fail, we have to go to the bank and get the account changed over into both of our names," he laughed and he sounded like a young boy just discovering how good life could be.

"I almost swooned today when Wendy called us the Bentons," I laughed. "Just think day after tomorrow I'll be Mrs. David Benton."

"What say after we go to the bank tomorrow, that we stay home so we can make illicit love while we still can?" he laughed.

"Lt. Benton, you proposition a girl so nicely," I laughed too.

We placed a call to Carol then and miraculously the circuits were clear so they put us right through.

"Carol," said David when he heard her pickup the phone.

"David, what's wrong?" she asked anxiously.

"Nothing's wrong, everything is right," said David. "Lauren and I just bought a farm here in Virginia and we have a proposition to put to you."

"You bought a farm, does that mean you don't intend to come back here to live after the war?" asked Carol.

"No, it just means that we will have a home here until after the war then we'll decide where we want to live, you little idiot," chuckled David.

"So what is the proposition?" asked Carol

"Lauren and I would like to have you come here and live with us until I get home for good."

"Let me talk to Lauren," said Carol.

"Carol, we mean it," I said as soon as David handed me the phone. "We want you to come and stay with me at the farm while David is overseas and that comes from me as well as David, especially from me," I said.

"Are you sure, Lauren, are you sure you want a sister intruding on your life, just when you are starting out?" asked Carol.

"Very sure, Carol, we will have so much fun together and it will help us get through missing this guy of ours until he's back with both of us for good," I said.

David took the phone from me then.

"Carol, as soon as it is safe for you to travel and you can book passage, we both definitely want you to come. You're such a good sister and I'll feel better knowing that you are here with Lauren in case anything should happen to me...which it won't, I promise you," he said. "You can help Lauren fix up the house, and you two can ride Storm King, and I bet if you ask she would even take you flying," laughed David.

"What is Storm King and what is this about flying?" asked Carol sounding completely confused.

"Sorry sis, I forgot you didn't know, we bought a big black stallion named Storm King and you and Lauren can take turns riding him. Also I guess I didn't tell you that Lauren is a pilot and a terrific one at that so you two could go flying sometimes.

"By the way, will you go and see Ted at the bank and tell him to transfer my account to my bank here? I'm going to send him a wire, but knowing Ted he'll feel better about it if he thinks you know about it too," laughed David.

"Yes, I'll go see Ted this afternoon. But about riding Storm King, you know I'm not much of a rider and I think I'd have to think twice about that," said Carol with a nervous laugh.

"You and Lauren can ride him together because she is a terrific rider, you should see her jump fences and she does it all bareback," laughed David.

"Oh my God, bro, I'm sure I could never ride bareback even with Lauren," she said.

"You'd be surprised, I thought I couldn't either, but I do it all the time now and I love it," he laughed. "Let Lauren know when you can book passage, can't wait until we both see you, at least if I'm still stateside when you finally get here," he said.

"Carol, it's Lauren again, please say you will come and you don't have to ride Storm if you don't want to, but he is a lovely horse and very gentle and I'll make sure you are safe," I said. "I can't wait for you to get here because I'm going to need lots of help furnishing the house and you know all the things David likes, which I don't know yet."

"I can't wait, either, to see you and believe you me if the Japanese think they are going to stop me they better have another think coming," laughed Carol.

"Bye sis, we'll write you again tonight and tell you all about the farm and Storm, I love you," said David.

"Bye Carol, I love you too and can't wait to see you," I said.

"Bye you guys, I love you too and can't wait to see both of you," said Carol hanging up.

"Thank you, kitten, Carol was right, you are a very special lady," said David.

"You're welcome but I'm nothing special, I just happen to love my guy and want to see him happy," I said, "and I really do love Carol as well, and look forward to her assistance in helping me make this a perfect home for you to come back to."

"I owe Carol a lot," said David. "When Mom left, being the youngest I think it affected me more than the rest of our family except maybe for Dad. Carol was always there for me and she kept the others from teasing me until I had a chance to find myself."

"Anyone who took such good care of my guy is my kind of woman," I said. "Actually, I should thank you for allowing me to ask Carol to come here to be with me, because it will be a lot easier for me to have someone around to whom I can talk to about you, someone who knows you and loves you as much as I do."

"Just do me one favor, convince Carol that I'm no longer her baby brother that needs her to run interference for him," he laughed.

"Forget it darling, once a baby brother always a baby brother, you'll always be that little kid even when you're 90 so just learn to live with it," I laughed.

"Baby, you are so good for me and to me, I actually feel special and it is all because of you," he said hugging me to him.

"How could I not be good to you?" I asked. "You are everything every woman dreams of finding in the man she loves. You are not only tall, dark and very handsome, but you're strong and with a gentle quality that is so often lacking in strong, self-confident men," I said hugging him back.

"Kitten, you are awfully good for a man's ego, especially this man," he laughed.

"You are the only man for whom I want to be good for his ego, my love," I laughed back.

Just then the phone rang. "Do you think Carol already has found a way to get here?" I laughed going to answer the phone.

"Hello. Oh Hello Wendy, yes he's here just a second."

"It's Wendy," I said as he took the phone from me.

"Hello Wendy, what's up?

"Definitely, I'll have Ted wire you the confirmation immediately. Talk to you tomorrow."

He took two strides across the living room and picked me up in his arms and swung me around and around.

"You idiot," I laughed. "Tell me immediately what is going on."

"We've just become owners of a farm in Virginia," he laughed finally setting me down and hugging me. "Wendy said they accepted the cash offer immediately and they are working toward getting the closing completed within the next ten days if possible and we can move in right after we close," he said.

I let out a squeal that I'm sure everyone in the apartment house heard and hugged him to me. "What was the confirmation all about?"

"I'm to have Ted wire them confirmation that I have the funds in the Sydney bank and they will take that in lieu of the funds actually being in the bank here until all the transfers can be completed out of consideration for world circumstances and the fact that I'm a G.I."

"Let's call Mark and Bill and go out and celebrate tonight?" I said.

"Yes, let's."

"Then tomorrow you and I are going to go window shopping for furniture so I can see the kind of things you like, so I'll know more about the way to furnish the house," I laughed.

"Ugh, I hate shopping," he laughed. "But I suspect doing it with you will be an experience not to be missed."

"You send your wire to Ted then I'll call Mark and Bill," I laughed. "As for window shopping, I'll try to make it as pleasant an experience for you as I can. If you're a good boy and go with me I'll make it very worth your while when we get home."

"How can a fellow resist an offer like that?" he laughed.

"Don't be silly, that's why I made it because I know from experience you can't resist," I laughed.

He went then and sent the wire. I called Mark and Bill and they said they would meet us at the Ritz-Carlton for dinner and that the dinner was on them as their wedding present to us. We agreed to meet them about seven at the Ritz.

"Could I have a sample of how you are going to make it worth my while if I go shopping with you tomorrow?" he chuckled.

"I was hoping you would ask," I laughed softly leading him toward the bedroom. "Let me undress you so I can hang up your uniform so it will be fit to wear tonight," I said.

"Tell you what, I'll take off the uniform and hang it up if you let me undress you," he said.

"Deal," I said hugging him.

He removed his uniform and hung it in the closet. When he was completely naked I stood back eyeing him.

"You know I just can't make up my mind whether you look better in uniform or stark naked," I said licking my lips, "but I'm almost of the opinion naked is better. Either way you certainly get my juices flowing."

"Come on stop stalling, you said I could undress you if I was a good boy and hung up my uniform," he laughed coming toward me his hands reaching for my sweater. I laughed as his hands pushed my sweater up to where he could pull it over my head and then he reached for my bra to unsnap it. "God you're beautiful, kitten," he said his voice soft.

He took me then and turned me in his arms so that my back was to him and I felt his hands trace down along my naked belly and unsnap my jeans and his hands went down to stroke my abdomen while at the same time he pushed my jeans off me. He knelt in front of me then kissing my body as he removed my panties.

"Please, darling, please," I whispered and I saw a mischievous smile come across his face as his hand went between my legs. He continued to stroke and kiss me until I was twisting and turning in my efforts to get closer to him. He stood then and pinned my arms behind my back with one of his as the other kept stroking me. He sat down on the edge of the bed and pulled me onto his lap and all the time his fingers kept up their steady stroking of my body and I kept pleading for him to take me, until I felt the first shudders course through my body and my body strained against the pressure of his hand which was giving me so much pleasure.

"Please darling, let go of my arms because I need to touch you to feel my hands on your body," I said.

He let go of my arms then and I reached for his penis and as I did so I saw his face contort with the same desire, which I knew was on my own. I got up then and lay on the side of the bed my legs going around him and my arms pulling him down to me until he could fight me no longer and he entered me. His thrusts were deep and intensely satisfying and I mewed my pleasure of the feel of him.

"Witch," he said pulling from me and I felt so empty that I cried out. He picked me up and moved me then to the center of the bed then climbed in after me and once more I felt him enter me and the thrusting began again and I heard him whispering his love for me.

"Please if you love me end this sweet torture for both of us," I said and his thrusts became more intense until I felt the shuddering rapture go through me once again as my release came, then he sought his own and finally we fell apart both of us gasping for air.

When we had both regained our breath we turned to look at each other and he smiled and I returned his smile,

"My stallion," I said laughing softly, as my arms went round his neck.

"What a filly you are, my darling," he said hugging me to him. "If that is a sample I can't wait for the real thing tomorrow," he laughed.

"I feel like you are playing 'can you top this' with me and I'm getting to the point I don't know whether either of us can top it," I laughed with him.

"But isn't it fun trying?"

"Oh David it is beyond fun, it is almost mind altering. I keep telling myself that it can't get any better and somehow each time you take me to another level and I'm afraid that one of these times I'm going to disappoint you and I don't think I could stand that," I said.

"Kitten, you could never disappoint me, for I love you beyond any dream of love I may ever have had and I want only to give you the same pleasure as you give to me."

"Oh God my darling you do give me such exquisite pleasure," I whispered as he pulled me back into his arms.

We fell asleep then and didn't awake until almost six.

"Oh God darling, wake up," I said shaking his shoulder gently.

"What is it, babe?" he asked groggily.

"We've got to get dressed it's almost six and we're suppose to meet Mark and Bill for dinner at seven. I'll lay out your uniform while you shave and shower, then I'll grab a quick shower and do my makeup," I said.

We rushed getting dressed and managed to leave the apartment by 6:45 and luckily for us we were able to grab a passing cab. We got to the Ritz a few minutes after seven and there was Mark waiting for us.

"I told you Mark is never late for anything," I whispered to David as we got out of the cab.

"David, Lauren, I thought for a minute I'd gotten the wrong date," he laughed.

"Sorry Mark, the cab ran into a bit of a traffic snarl," I said winking at David.

"Well Bill isn't here yet either," he said.

"Yes, I am Mark, I was in the bar," laughed Bill walking up to us.

"Lauren you look just radiant, you have a kind of special glow about you," said Mark.

"Godfrey, Mark," said Bill, "she simply has a well-loved look about her and if you really knew anything about women you would refrain from mentioning it."

"What do you mean, Bill?" said Mark looking at him with a questioning glance and then he noticed the blush creeping over my face. "Oh forget it, I get you now," he said his face turning almost as red as mine.

"Let's go get a table for I'm anxious to find out what this celebration is all about," said Bill.

When we were seated and our drink orders had been taken Bill turned to David, "So give what is this celebration all about."

"We just bought a farm in Virginia," said David.

"Well good for the both of you, I'm glad because I think this little girl of yours will make a terrific homemaker," said Bill.

"She's dragging me out tomorrow to window shop for furniture," sighed David.

"Oh, oh," said Mark grinning at David. "It's been my experience that when a woman starts picking out furniture, the honeymoon is over and you two haven't even gotten married yet."

"Your experience, indeed," I said to Mark. "You've never come close enough to marriage to know whether picking out furniture means anything at all or not, so don't pick on my husband to be," I laughed. "Besides which I don't intend our honeymoon should ever end even after we've been married 50 years."

"Well we bachelors talk you know and we do have a few married guys we associate with," laughed Mark.

"Mark, for your information, I'm looking forward to 50 or 60 years of wedded bliss with Lauren and believe me it's like she said, it is going to be one long honeymoon for us," said Mark.

"I can't wait till Mark falls for some gal and she reels him in hook, line and sinker," laughed Bill.

"That's just never going to happen, there are just too many fish in the sea for me to ever settle down with one…God think of waking up to the same woman day after day, it's absolutely frightening," said Mark.

"About two weeks ago I would have agreed with you, Mark, but then Lauren came into my life and I sure changed my mind in a hurry," laughed David, "and believe me you will too if you ever find a woman like Lauren."

"Next to David, I probably know Lauren better than you do, and if I could find a woman like her, I'd settle down so fast it wouldn't be funny," said Bill. "Being a bachelor isn't what it is cracked up to be because for the most part it is a lonely existence and it would be so nice to have one woman to come home to every night who would love you no matter what."

"Well if that's what you two want you can have it," laughed Mark. "For me, I'll take having a different woman every night."

"Mark, I told you when I first met you, that you were an idiot," I laughed, "and what you've just said confirms what I knew then. You've let your fellow bachelors convince you that marriage is a ball and chain, but I bet if you really talked to each other you'd find that Bill has it right, that bachelorhood is a very lonely existence."

"If you ever find the right girl, you're going to know what I found out, that it is pure heaven to come home at night and have her meet you at the door and throw herself in your arms, to look up across the breakfast table and see her smile at you and to see her love for you reflected in her face and eyes, to have her put her arms around you when things aren't going just right in your life and know that she understands and is lending you her strength, and the way she gives your ego such a boost because she will tell you every day in so many ways that you are perfect even when you know you are far from perfect," said David.

"David, I'd say you really have it bad," said Mark. "This tomboy here has got you wrapped right around her little finger."

"Maybe so Mark, but I wouldn't trade places with you for all the tea in China," laughed David.

The waiter came then and we placed our dinner orders.

"Not to change the subject," said Bill, "but I want to hear more about this farm you two have bought."

"Bill, it is wonderful, it is an old farmhouse but very well maintained with two bedrooms, living room with a big fireplace, dining room, kitchen and a full basement. It sits on five acres of pretty much wooded land and has a stable big enough to accommodate at least four horses," I said.

"Where is this dream house located?"

"You know the stables where I always went to ride Storm King?" I said. "Well it is about a half mile down the road from it. Storm King is just going to love the stables and it will be so wonderful to be able to ride him on our own property."

"I suppose you talked David into buying Storm King too?" asked Mark.

"Yes, we bought him and believe me Mark you haven't lived until you ride a horse like Storm with someone like Lauren nestled in your arms," laughed David.

"Well it does sound romantic, but considering I look like the original eastern bumpkin on a horse, I think I'll stick to transportation I can handle," laughed Mark.

"You won't get too lonely out there in the country when David is overseas will you, Lauren?" asked Bill.

"As a matter of fact, Bill, we've asked David's sister Carol to come over and stay with me while David is gone as soon as she can get transportation to the States," I said.

"Maybe I can help you with that one," said Bill, "I happen to know that we've got military planes going in and out of Sydney on a pretty regular basis these days and maybe I can pull a few strings and get Carol transport on one of them."

"Oh Bill, that would be wonderful if you could," I said.

"Yes Bill, we'd both appreciate it if you'd try because I don't want Lauren to be by herself while I'm in flight training and afterwards," said David.

"Give me her full name and phone number before we leave tonight and

I'll see what I can do," said Bill.

"Since you've purchased a farm here, does that mean that you'll be staying in this country after the war?" asked Mark.

"We might then again we might sell and go back to Sydney, we'll have to wait and see," said David.

"I hope you decide to stay here because I'd miss Lauren and you too, David," said Mark.

"We'd miss you guys too," I laughed. "But on the other hand, we are going to need a lot more room than what the farm has now because I want at least six of seven kids and it might just be a little crowded trying to fit them all into the one extra bedroom we have."

"Ye Gods woman, did you say six or seven kids?" yelped Mark.

"At least, but I would really like a dozen," I laughed.

"David, when are you going to have time to work?" laughed Mark.

"Oh I'll manage, but it will be difficult scheduling it in," chuckled David.

"All I've got to say, Lauren, is that you are going to be one great mother, especially if they are all boys, because you'll be able to do everything with them," laughed Bill.

"Even if they aren't all boys, I intend my daughters will be tomboys just like I was," I laughed back at him.

"David, you're a braver man than I am," chuckled Bill.

"Oh Bill, you haven't heard the best of it yet, she not only wants a dozen kids but she wants at least one set of twins," said David.

"Lauren, I think this guy has taken all the tomboy out of you," laughed Mark. "You sound much too feminine with the talk of all these kids."

"Well, Mark, since this guy of mine came into my life I find that I like being female more than I ever have before," I grinned at him.

"It must be love then," chuckled Mark.

"Where are you two planning on spending your honeymoon?" asked Bill.

"Right here, but I'm telling you right now, we don't intend to have company, so Mark be sure you don't breakup with whoever you're currently seeing until after David has to report for flight training, because you are going to get booted right out the door on your fanny if you try coming around for booze and sympathy," I laughed.

"Oh, Oh I guess there is still some of the tomboy left in you," laughed Mark.

"Enough to throw you out because I want only to spend my entire honeymoon in David's arms," I said.

"David, very definitely you have tamed this gal. More power to you," said Mark.

"Hey you guys, let's go into the bar and maybe we can talk David into letting us dance at least one dance with Lauren," said Bill.

"How much is it worth to you?" laughed David. "I could be talked into renting her out for one dance a piece after I've had six or seven."

"Do you mean I have to dance all but one dance with Bill?" laughed Mark.

"It's like I told you before, Mark, there's a lot to be said for having only one woman," replied David.

We went into the bar then and David and I danced the first dance, and then I danced with both Mark and Bill. The conversation was lively and the laughter flowed and all too soon it was closing time.

"Don't forget you two hooligans, the wedding is at 10 AM the day after tomorrow and Mark, I'll expect you to get Bill to the church on time," I said kissing each of them goodnight as David shook hands with them.

We hailed a passing cab and David and I got in and as we settled back into the seat, David took me in his arms and kissed me and I snuggled into his arms for the ride back to the apartment.

"What a pair," laughed David. "It is like being around Abbott and Costello when we are with them."

"I think Mark is like the son that Bill never had," I said, "and he enjoys the give and take between them."

The cab pulled up in front of the apartment and we got out and went upstairs. "I had a really good time tonight," laughed David closing the door behind us.

"Me too, but it is nice being back with just you," I said.

"For me too little one," said David. "You know I was thinking when Bill was talking about bachelorhood not being so great, if he and sis might not just hit it off."

"I was thinking the same thing, and Bill is such a terrific guy," I said.

"Do you suppose he really might be able to get Carol transportation to the States in the near future?" asked David.

"Well, if anyone can manage it, Bill can."

"It would sure take a load off my shoulders if I knew Carol was going to be with you before I have to report in," said David softly.

"Darling, I hope that she can, but you are not to worry about me, just worry about taking care of yourself," I said hugging him.

We got undressed then and crawled into bed and I snuggled into David's arms. "I do worry about you sweetheart, because I wouldn't want you to be alone especially once they send me overseas," said David.

"Darling, please, please don't worry about me. I'll be ok even if Carol doesn't make it over here before then. I'll miss you so much, but I'll also be busy fixing up our home so most of the time it won't be so bad. The worst times will be at night when I reach for you and you aren't there beside me."

"Kitten, when this mess is finally over with, I don't ever intend to let you out of my arms ever again," whispered David.

"And I don't ever intend to let you out of mine," I whispered back at him hugging him close to me.

"David darling, there is something I've been meaning to talk to you about," I said looking up at him.

"What is that, love?"

"I just want you to know, that if you need a woman for any reason, while you are gone, I want you to have one, but just don't tell me about it."

"You'd do that?" he asked and I could hear and see the amazement in his voice and his face.

"There may come a time with the horrors I know you will see, that you need the comfort of a woman's arms."

"Lauren, no matter the circumstances, I will never need the comfort of any woman's arms but yours, my dearest darling. I don't know of another woman who would ever give their husband permission, even under present circumstances, and that is another reason I will never take you up on your offer, simply because you made the offer."

"I love you David so much that I couldn't stand it if you were ever hurting, or wanting or needing," I said.

His lips came down to mine then and he pulled me into his body and he whispered, "Lauren, I swear before God that there will never ever be any woman but you, because it would be like betraying myself to ever betray you in any way."

"Please darling, make love to me," I whispered, "for I have the need to have you as close to me as possible."

We made love then and it was more beautiful than it had ever been before because there was only giving on both of our parts and the need to cling to each other in a world trying to tear us apart.

The ringing of the phone woke us the next morning and I jumped out of bed running to answer it.

"Hello."

"Hi Lauren, it's Bill."

"Oh hi Bill, is something wrong?"

"Nothing is wrong, I just wanted to let you know that Carol will be landing at Andrews on the 24th. She will be coming in via military transport which will also have a fighter escort."

"Bill, thank you, thank you, you don't know how much this will mean to David and how much it means to me," I said.

"Go tell David because I know you are dying to and I'll talk to you at the wedding tomorrow," he laughed.

"Bye Bill, and thank you again."

"Bye Lauren."

"David," I yelled as I went running back into the bedroom and jumped on the bed hugging him to me.

"Hey kitten, what's up? What are you so excited about?" he asked.

"That was Bill. David, he's done it, Carol will be landing at Andrews on the 24th," I said laughing as his mouth fell open in astonishment.

"You aren't kidding me are you, sweetheart?"

"No I'm not kidding you. Bill said he had arranged military transport for her with fighter escort and she will be landing on the 24th at Andrews," I said hugging him.

"Did he talk to Carol? Do you know what time they will be getting into Andrews?"

"I don't know. What I told you was all he said, but knowing Bill I'm sure that he has talked to Carol and as soon as he knows I'm sure he will let us know when they will be landing. He said he'd talk to both of us at the wedding tomorrow."

"My God I just can't believe everything that has happened to me, to us, since that first night we met," laughed David.

"I think God must have a very special place in his heart for us, my darling," I laughed with him.

"He must, but I don't see how he could with me, since I've never been particularly religious," he said. "It must be you he's rewarding for being the most wonderful person in the world and because you love me he is including me in it."

"I think it is because he sees what a wonderful man you are and how much you love me, and how good you are to me and for me, that he's decided even with all the evil going on in the world that we deserve happiness."

"Come on, let's get dressed and I'll fix you breakfast, then let's go window shopping for furniture, because I want to make everything perfect for you and I want you to be a part of it."

"Ok, little one, whatever you want just as long as I can be near you and see the look of happiness on your face," he laughed.

"It would be hard for you to miss it because I can't stop smiling," I laughed.

We dressed and ate breakfast then we started out.

"Let's stop at the bank first and get my account changed over into both our names and make sure that they've received word about the transfer of funds," said David.

We went to the bank then and changed the account. They told us that they had received word about the transfer of funds and we told them that as soon as they received the transfer that the money for the house would be withdrawn.

"We'll take care of it so not to worry," the manager said.

Then we went to several furniture stores and looked at furniture and my poor darling was tolerant enough not to let me see how bored he was with this feminine need to nest.

When we got back to the apartment, David took me in his arms. "You had fun today didn't you darling?" he laughed hugging me.

"Yes I did and thank you for being so patient with me and my need to feather our nest so to speak," I said hugging him back.

"You know I didn't expect to enjoy the window shopping, but I really did because I could just picture our home and how cozy it will be when you get finished with your feathering," he laughed.

"I love you, David, and I want only to make a good home for you and to love you for the rest of my life."

"You are such a contradiction in terms, kitten, the tomboy part of you is so practical comparing one type of furniture to another, and then the female side of you asserts itself and you are the most feminine woman in the world as you talk about making a home for me and loving me and I love both sides of you equally."

"Speaking of taking care of you and loving you, I think I'd better go get us some lunch because I don't want you to starve to death and I'll bet you are hungry…at least I know I am," I laughed.

I went to the kitchen then and began to heat up the lamb and the gravy for hot lamb sandwiches. As I was working, I heard the phone ring and David going to answer it.

"Hello."

"Carol, is that you?"

I ran in from the kitchen then so I could listen next to David on the phone with Carol.

"David, how did you manage to get me on a military flight and so quickly?" I heard Carol asking him.

"It wasn't me, sis, it was this bride of mine and her boss that did it all," laughed David.

"Is Lauren there?"

"Yes, hold on a minute and I'll put her on."

"Lauren, how can I ever thank you?"

"By being my sister too, Carol."

"I can't wait to meet you in person and do thank Bill for me for all he's done."

"You'll love Bill, he's the kindest man in the world, in fact he's a lot like your baby brother in that regard."

"I just wish I could have been there for your wedding tomorrow, but I'll be with you in thought if not in person. God I must sound so ungrateful wishing for more after I've just gotten so much."

"No you don't sound ungrateful at all, you sound like you're just wishing the same things I wish for."

"Did David tell you that we definitely have bought the farm? I can't wait to get you here to help me furnish it."

"Oh that will be such fun, I can't wait either."

David took the phone from me then. "Carol, we may not be able to meet you at the plane because they probably won't tell us exactly when it will be landing due to military regulations, but Bill will make sure that we get together with you as soon as humanly possible."

"That's ok bro I'm a big girl and can manage, but I can't wait to hug and kiss you both. See you on the 24th."

"We love you, Carol," we both said as we hung up.

He picked me up in his arms then and waltzed around the room with me in his arms. "How does one guy get so lucky?" he laughed.

"You nut, put me down," I laughed.

"I'm never going to put you down again," he said.

"You're going to have one heck of time saluting with me in your arms," I laughed, "not to mention flying."

"I'll manage it somehow," he laughed.

"Ok I give up; I'm marrying a nut case," I laughed hugging him around the neck.

"Kitten, I just can't wait until tomorrow, until you're really mine," he said grinning at me.

"I don't know how I could be any more yours than I already am, because I'm yours heart, body, and soul, but I too can hardly wait until I'm really Mrs. David Benton," I said grinning back at him.

"Oh baby that sounds so good—Mrs. Benton," he said.

"It sounds pretty darn good to me too," I said hugging him again.

He set me down then and his arms came about me and we were content to stand just holding each other. After a few minutes he went over and put our song on the phonograph, then he came back and took me in his arms again. We danced without saying anything until the song finished; then he bent his head and kissed me and all his love was in that kiss.

"Oh my gosh, I forgot all about the lamb sandwiches, come on let's eat while they are still hot," I said.

After we finished eating we went and sat in our favorite chair with me on David's lap and snuggled within his arms.

"What are your dad and brothers going to say with Carol leaving them to come here to be with us?" I asked.

"I'm not sure my brothers will even know she's gone until they try to find a clean shirt or come home starving and there's no supper on the table," he laughed. "Dad will probably miss her most because she is his baby girl, but I'm not sure it will bother him a lot because he doesn't spend that much time with her. I was always the one closest to her and who spent the most time with her and even I took her for granted," he said.

"Well my darling, I'm not going to let you get away with ever taking either me or Carol for granted, I guarantee you that," I said.

"I never will take you for granted, that I can promise, kitten, and I'm sure going to make an effort not to take Carol for granted either. I want my two women to know they are loved and cherished."

"You fulfill that part of the bargain and Carol and I will see to it that you know you are the only man in our lives and you'll be the best loved, best taken care of, of any man in the world," I laughed.

"I wish Carol would find someone to love and who would love her because she deserves to have a home of her own and to know that she is the center of some guy's world," David said.

"Well, I'll do my best to find someone for her who is everything you are, but that is going to be a tough order to fill, because I don't know any men who can match you, my darling. I hope maybe she and Bill will hit it off because he's a wonderful man, almost as wonderful as you, and I truly think that Bill needs someone to love him and who he can love," I said.

"You know, I've even been thinking about Mark for Carol," he laughed. "I have a feeling when he meets her that that young cock may get his wings clipped just a little," he laughed. "Carol is truly beautiful so I know that will appeal to him, and she has a way of making men look twice because she is so ultra-feminine that it just naturally brings out the chivalry in a man."

"David, I wouldn't wish Mark on any woman. It's not that he isn't a super nice guy because he is, but I'm not sure Mark is through sowing his wild oats yet," I said.

"Well, guess we will have to wait and see, but just don't count Mark out entirely," he laughed. "I have a feeling when he does fall, it is going to be the fall heard 'round the world," he laughed.

"Why would you say that?"

"Because Mark was me, up until 10 days ago," he laughed. "I was just as much of the happy bachelor as he is and as I told him last night I would have agreed with him wholeheartedly about there being lots of fish in the sea so who wants to settle for just one. But that was before a little tomboy smiled up at me and I fell head over heels in love, so I know when he does fall he's going to fall just as hard as I did," he laughed.

"I don't know why, I just can't imagine you the free wheeling bachelor that Mark is," I said.

"Believe it darling, because until you batted those baby blues at me I flitted around just like Mark. Maybe that was why I wanted to knock his block off that night he came to dinner because I couldn't stand the thought of any guy ever treating you like one of his harem put on this earth just for his pleasure," he laughed. "But believe me I know I've done the same thing to other women, though I'm not very proud of myself now."

"Maybe I can't imagine it because that first night you made love to me, you gave me the chance to back out and you were so gentle with me and somehow I can't imagine Mark not pressing his advantage under similar circumstances," I laughed.

"If it had been anyone but you I probably would have pressed my advantage as well, but I had fallen so in love with you that all I wanted to do was protect and love you," said David.

"Heavens, what a revelation," I laughed. "I always thought I understood men pretty darn well, but I'd never have guessed any of this and do you know how much fun it is to sit here snuggled in your warm, strong protective arms and discuss how men think about women?"

"Well, not being female…" laughed David.

"Thank God for that," I laughed with him.

"I may be betraying my sex letting you in on our little secrets," he chuckled, "but I find it kind of enjoyable too. And just for your information, I think you do understand men pretty darn well, except maybe for the way we think when it comes to our sex lives. What's it really like for a woman the first time?" he asked.

"I guess it would depend on the man involved, so I can only tell you what it was like for me with you. For me, most of my fear was coming from being afraid I wasn't pretty enough for you. Most women don't have a very high opinion of their own bodies and believe me my opinion of my body was that it was so, so at best and just plain ugly at worst, so I was definitely afraid that you would be disappointed because clothes can hide so many flaws."

"God, kitten you have the most beautiful body I've ever seen," said David.

"But how could I know you would think that, when I didn't?" I said. "I also was a little frightened of actually seeing a man's body naked because if it got that far, I had always been told there would be no backing out."

"Who in the hell ever told you that, sweetheart?"

"I don't remember but I know that it was common knowledge amongst the few girls I knew that once a man was ready for sex he couldn't stop and even though I thought your body was so beautiful that it took my breath away, I wasn't sure I could go through with it. Then you gave me the option of backing out and I knew for that alone I would love you all my life. When you didn't make any move and instead held me in your arms until I stopped shaking, I felt that you of all the men I'd ever known were the one who I wanted to teach me the rest of it because you weren't trying to force me into anything and you were so gentle and loving that my fear went away to be replaced by a love that filled my entire being and I wanted only to give to you. Then when you actually did make love to me, I was filled with such joy that I wanted to laugh and cry at the same time because you felt so good inside me and I knew that forever more I would want you to make love to me as often as you wanted to do so."

"Holy Gehossofat, it's no wonder women are afraid of sex with all the false knowledge they have about how men's bodies function," he said. "But it isn't really so different for a man his first time," he said. "Our bodies are demanding sex, but at the same time we feel awkward and a little scared too.

If I were making the rules, I'd make every man's first time be with an older woman who could teach him how to please a woman because when we do, it is much more satisfying not only for the woman involved but for the man as well."

"I wondered how you knew that it was going to hurt the first time you entered me," I said.

"Because a very wise woman who shall remain anonymous, told it to me when I was about fifteen," he said.

"I'm very grateful to that woman and to any others who instructed you along the way, because I'm the one who reaped the rewards of their teachings," I said. "Was I any good at all, that first time?"

"You were wonderful, kitten, because even though I knew you were scared, still your body pressed into mine and you answered every movement of my body with such love."

"I loved the way you held me in your arms afterward, I felt so loved and protected. I love sitting here in your arms and someday I will tell our daughters how wonderful it feels to be loved by a man like their father, how glad they will be to be women and how good it feels to be unafraid to respond to their man's touch," I said.

"Well, just don't make it too inviting to them so they want to sample for themselves before they actually fall in love," he said.

THE WEDDING

The next morning I woke before David and went in to shower and put on my makeup. Then I put on my wedding suit and went to wake up my soon to be husband.

"Wake up sleepyhead, it's your wedding day," I said leaning down to kiss his cheek.

"Lauren you're the most beautiful bride a man ever had," he said hugging me. Then he too got up and showered and shaved and when he came out to the living room dressed in his uniform I thought how handsome he was. We left for the base chapel and when we arrived there were Mark and Bill waiting for us.

"I was afraid you two were going to be late for your own wedding," laughed Mark. "Ready David, last chance to change your mind."

"Not a snowball's chance in hell of that, Mark," laughed David.

"Ready Lauren?" asked Bill extending his arm to me to walk me down the aisle. "By the way, I stopped and got you a wedding bouquet; a girl can't get married without one I'm told."

"Thank you Bill, thank you for everything," I said kissing his cheek. "I'm glad you're walking me down the aisle because my knees are shaking so badly I don't know whether or not I could make it on my own."

"You're not having second thoughts, are you Lauren?"

"No never that," I laughed. "It's just that I love him so much that if I had to maneuver the aisle on my own I'm afraid I would start running as soon as I saw David standing there."

We heard the bridal march coming from the chapel interior and we started down the aisle. When we got to the altar Bill took my hand and placed it in David's then stood beside me acting as my Maid of Honor.

"Dearly beloved, we are gathered here today to witness the taking and giving of vows between this man and this woman. Matrimony is an honorable estate not to be entered into lightly or unadvisedly.

"David, do you take Lauren Bennett to be your lawfully wedded wife, to love her, honor her, and keep her in sickness and in health forsaking all others keep her only onto you so long as you both shall live?"

"I do."

"Lauren, do you take David Benton to be your lawfully wedded husband, to love him, to honor him and obey him in sickness and in health forsaking all others keep him only onto you so long as you both shall live?"

"I do."

"Who gives this woman to be married?"

"I do," answered Bill.

Taking the rings from Mark and Bill the chaplain placed them on the bible then he handed David my ring. "Repeat after me, with this ring I thee wed and with all my worldly goods I do thee endow."

David repeated the vow and placed the ring on my finger.

Handing David's ring to me he said, "Repeat after me, with this ring I thee wed and with all my worldly goods I do thee endow."

I repeated the vow as I placed the ring on David's finger.

"In so far as these two have professed their love by the giving and receiving of rings before those assembled, then with the authority invested in me, I pronounce you man and wife from this day forward through all eternity. You may kiss your bride, Lieutenant."

David took me in his arms and kissed me and his kiss was like a seal to the vows we had both just said and my answering kiss was a seal to the vows I had given to him.

"Congratulations Lieutenant and Mrs. Benton," said Chaplain Hollenbeck. Bill handed me my bouquet and we left the chapel.

When we got outside I made Bill and Mark stand a little away from me and I turned my back and sent my wedding bouquet flying through the air.

Mark caught the bouquet. "What am I supposed to do with this?" he asked.

"Put it under your pillow and dream of the woman you are going to marry," I laughed.

"Forget it. Hell's going to freeze over before that happens," he laughed.

"Congratulations, you two," said Bill kissing me. "If I ever saw two people just meant for each other, you two are it." He kissed me on the cheek then shook hands with David.

"Congrats, Lauren and David," said Mark kissing me and shaking hands with David.

"Now let's go somewhere and have coffee so that I can tell you all the details about Carol's arrival, then go have your honeymoon and neither Mark nor I will disturb you till the 24th," said Bill.

We found a little diner a short ways from the base and after we had ordered coffee Bill said, "As I told Lauren yesterday, Carol will be coming in by military transport which will be escorted by fighter planes on the 24th to Andrews. I made sure that there was going to be an escort of fighters before I tried to get her a seat on the plane just to make sure she was as safe as I could make it for her. She'll be flying with the Assistant Secretary of State, so I think you can be assured she will be as safe as anyone can be in today's world."

"Thanks Bill, for that. I owe you a lot," said David.

"You don't owe me anything, it's my wedding present to you both. I'm not sure yet what time the plane will be arriving but State promised they would let me know as soon as the plane clears U.S. air space, so that should still give you time to get to Andrews in time to pick Carol up before they even get her luggage off the plane."

"Thanks Bill," I said. "That is the nicest wedding present we could have gotten."

"Your sister sounds like a real jewel and I'm looking forward to meeting her," said Bill.

"Aren't any of you going to tell me what in the hell you're talking about?" asked Mark.

"Sorry Mark, I forgot you haven't been in on any of this," laughed Bill. "David and Lauren had asked David's sister Carol to come be with them while David is in flight training and until he gets back from overseas and I managed to get her booked on a military transport so that she will get here before David has to report in for flight duty," said Bill.

"Well I'll be glad to show her around town, if you like," said Mark.

"Thanks Mark," laughed David, "I appreciate your thoughtfulness."

I could see that David was trying not to laugh because Mark was so transparent about a new face being on his horizon.

"Mark, I appreciate your offer too, but if you don't treat Carol well, I'll be taking it out of your hide," I laughed.

"Oh God, Lauren, you don't think I'd make a pass at David's sister do you?" he said.

"Well, as a matter of fact, yes I do think you would," I laughed.

"Do you think I'm nuts? David could flatten me without ever working up a sweat," he said.

"Well just keep that in mind," I laughed.

"Kids, we are going to head out and I know you two want to get started with your honeymoon so we'll leave you two alone. Congratulations again and as my Irish grandfather used to say 'May the road always rise up to meet you.' Whatever that may mean, but I'm assuming it means good luck," said Bill.

"Thanks again, Bill, for everything and especially for walking me down the aisle," I said.

Driving back to the apartment David put his arm around me and I snuggled into it, "I love you, Mrs. Benton," he said.

"I love you, Mr. Benton," I replied.

The days leading up to the 24th were wonderful. We made love, we laughed, we played and we began to learn so much about each other that every day was a revelation. Mostly we tried to keep at bay the thoughts that our days were numbered for being together and in trying to do this the time that we had together was so much sweeter.

Early on the 24th Bill called to tell us that Carol would be arriving at Andrews in about 45 minutes. We rushed getting dressed then got the car and drove at breakneck speed to Andrews. We arrived on the tarmac just as the plane was taxiing to a stop. The crew brought out the steps and we saw several men depart, then we saw Carol coming down the steps.

"Carol, Carol, over here," shouted David running to sweep her up in his arms and to kiss her. She hugged him back and I saw her look around so I waved to her.

I too went out to hug her. "Welcome to the U.S.," I said.

"My God David, she is a little bitty thing isn't she," laughed Carol who towered over me by at least five inches.

"She's little but she's mighty," he laughed throwing an arm around each of us. "She's proof of what you always told me about great things coming in small packages."

"What in the heck do they put in the air in Australia?" I laughed. "I feel like I've landed in the land of giants."

"Just wait till you meet the rest of the family," she laughed. "David is the runt of the litter."

"Oh my God, I'll be talking to everybody's bellybutton," I laughed.

"Lauren, I can't thank you enough for inviting me here. I didn't think I'd get to see David for a long time yet and look how you've managed it all so quickly," said Carol.

"Carol, I'm just so glad you could come and I can't wait to hear everything about this husband of mine from you," I smiled.

"Come ladies, let's get Carol's luggage and get back home," said David.

"Yes sir," I laughed. He went then to retrieve Carol's suitcase and Carol and I stood with our arms around each other watching this man we both loved so dearly. We started for the car then and almost immediately the two of them were about three feet ahead of me.

"Wait up, for baby," I laughed running to catch up with them. "I can't trot as fast in high heels as I can in flats," I laughed.

"Carol, that is something you're going to have to get used to, because this filly of mine has a very short gait on her so you're going to have to take baby steps when you walk with her," he laughed.

"Sorry Lauren, I didn't think. I'm so used to loping along with the men in our family," said Carol.

"No need to apologize, I'm thinking about keeping roller skates handy so I can keep up with you two," I said laughing.

When we got to the car David started to help me in but I pushed Carol ahead of me so she could sit next to her brother. "Darling, let Carol sit next to you this time," I said.

"No," said Carol, "you sit next to your husband where you belong and I'll sit next to you. I love watching you two together because you both just radiate love."

As we drove, we talked and laughed.

"How was the flight over?" asked David.

"Very uneventful, except the Assistant Secretary of State kept me in stitches all the way," said Carol. "You Yanks sure have a sense of humor," she laughed.

When we got to the apartment I told David to take Carol's case into the bedroom that had once been Shelby's. "I'll let you get settled while I go make us lunch, so come out to the kitchen when you're ready." I went then and changed into slacks and sweater then went to start lunch. I heard them laughing and talking while they were getting Carol settled in and I was so glad because there was a lightness to David's laugh that was good to hear.

Carol came into the kitchen. "Let me help, Lauren," she said.

"I've got everything just about ready to go on the table so you can help next time," I said. "Sit down, Carol, and talk to me while I'm finishing up; we are very informal around this house."

She sat watching me while I put on the finishing touches. "You don't look anything like what I imagined," said Carol. "I thought you'd be one of those long-legged blondes we always see in all your cinemas," she laughed.

"Hope I'm not a disappointment, but I think those kind of women are all in Hollywood," I said.

"No, you're definitely not a disappointment, in fact I'm kind of relieved to find out you look just like you sound on the phone."

"Well, I'm just me, nothing special, but it sure is going to be nice to have you around to reach things for me," I laughed. "I get so tired of having to go get a stepstool every time I want something from the top shelf of the cupboard."

"I always hated being tall when I was growing up because I towered over every girl in my class and just about every boy," she said.

"I hated being so short because all the boys would pat me on the head and none of them ever thought I would be good at sports or anything until they got to know me and found out I was a real tomboy."

"What are you two up to?" asked David coming into the kitchen and coming to put his arm around me.

"I was just telling Carol that I was so glad she raised you right and that I didn't have so much work ahead of me getting you presentable for the public," I laughed squeezing him and winking at Carol.

"And I was telling Lauren that it took a lot of work and that I had to pin your ears back a few times to get the massage across," laughed Carol.

"Oh bull, you two, I can see where I'm going to have to take you in hand and teach you how a man should be treated in this household," he said laughing at both of us and his love for us was in his face.

We laughed and talked while we ate lunch. When I got up to clear the table Carol got up with me, "I insist you let me help you with the dishes because I don't want to be treated like a guest here, I just want you to treat me like your big sister," she said.

"Thanks kiddo," I said. "Please don't consider yourself a guest, come and go as you please and I never turn down an offer to help with dishes," I laughed. As we were finishing the dishes I saw Carol yawn in spite of herself. "Why don't you go catch yourself a catnap, you must be exhausted with all those change of time zones," I said.

"If you don't mind I think I will, I'm at the point I'm not even sure what day it is anymore," she said.

"The bed is all made up, there's a comforter on the chest at the end of it to throw over you and I think maybe I'm going to catch a nap too, all this excitement has worn me out. Just make yourself at home when you wake up and I think maybe if you'd like, I'll call Bill and have him meet us for dinner tonight so you can meet the guy that arranged all of this for us," I said.

"Yes, I'd very much like to meet Bill. He was so sweet when he called me after making the arrangements and I want to properly thank him," she said.

"Why don't we invite Mark too," said David. "That way she'll get to meet the whole gang at once."

"Who's Mark?"

"He was the best man at our wedding," said David. "He's a nut and a free-wheeling bachelor type but you get him and Bill together and it's like talking to Abbott and Costello. He's like a big brother to Lauren and if you thought you and Bob had a love/hate relationship, wait till you listen to Mark and Lauren go at it," he laughed. "Remind me to tell you about the first time they came to dinner here, because I darn near punched him in the nose."

I went up to her and put my arms around her and gave her a hug. "Carol, go lay down, you look like you're about to fall asleep on your feet. We've got the rest of our lives to tell you all about everything that has happened since I first looked across the dance floor and saw this gorgeous brother of yours and fell head-over-heels in love with him," I said.

"Have a good rest, sis," said David going to her and hugging her.

After Carol had gone in to lie down, David came to me and put his arms around me. "How could one man get so lucky to have a wife like you and a sister like Carol?" he said.

"Well, I think Carol would agree that we are the lucky ones to have a husband like you and a brother like you," I laughed kissing him.

"She really likes you, kitty cat, she was telling me when I was helping her get settled. She said that you were everything she thought you'd be after talking to you that first time on the phone when she lambasted into you and you didn't go running for the hills, but backed her right down."

"I love her already," I said. "She's an awful lot like you, so how could I help it? Now husband mine, explain to me exactly why you decided to invite Mark to this shindig tonight?"

"Well, I figured that she might as well meet Bill and Mark at the same time and besides, if we go somewhere where there is dancing, she'll keep them both entertained while I get to dance every dance with you," he laughed.

"In a case like that, you better call Bill and Mark and tell them to meet us at the Ritz for dinner about seven," I laughed. "As for me, I'm going to go in and catch a quick nap for myself because I have a feeling I'm going to have to keep on my toes tonight once those two hooligans get a look at Carol."

"I'll give them a call and I may even join you in that nap," he said. "Who knows what might develop?" he said grinning at me.

"Nothing is going to develop; because you are going to keep your hands to yourself, because I really do need a nap," I laughed but I hugged him close to me to let him know that I wasn't really serious.

"Oh woman, you do like to wave a red flag in front of this bull, don't you," he chuckled.

I went in then and removed my clothes, and put on my robe, then I lay down and as soon as my head hit the pillow I was out like a light. A little later I felt David come in and lie down next to me taking me in his arms, but I was too sleepy except to rouse just enough to put my arms about him then I was out again.

When I woke, I looked at the clock, which read 5:00 P.M. I slid out of bed so as not to wake David and went in to take a shower. I heard Carol stirring in her room and went to see if she needed anything. "I'm glad you came in because I'm not quite sure what to wear this evening," she laughed.

"I'll show you what I'm wearing and maybe that will help you decide," I said going to get my dress from the bedroom.

When I got back in our room I saw that David was awake. "What's doing babe?" he asked holding out his arms to me.

"Well, not that love," I laughed as I went to him and kissed him on the cheek. "Carol is up and I'm just taking the dress I was planning on wearing tonight for her to look at so she can decide what she wants to wear."

"Oh guess I'd better get myself in gear then," he said. "I'll go shower and shave then you two women can have the bathroom all to yourselves."

"That's my good little boy," I laughed. "I'll see that you are properly rewarded tonight when we get home."

"God I love you, kitten, you always know exactly what to say to keep me interested," he laughed back.

"Carol, this is the dress I was planning on wearing tonight, do you have anything similar?" I asked.

"How about this one?" she said pulling a white sheath out of the closet.

"Zowie, one look at you in that and Mark and Bill are going to be reduced to basket cases," I laughed.

"Do you see any wrinkles in it?" she laughed.

"Nope, looks good to me."

"I just sent my little boy to shower and shave," I laughed, "then the bathroom is all yours."

"Does he really let you get away with calling him your little boy?" she asked.

"You'd be surprised what a woman can get away with when she promises her man a roll in the hay later," I laughed.

She let out a hoot of laughter, "Yes I can just imagine."

"Hope I didn't shock you, sis," I said.

"It would take more than that to shock me coming from a houseful of men," she laughed.

I went back then and David was just coming out of the bathroom with a towel around his waist heading for the bedroom. "What was the hoot of laughter I heard out of Carol?"

"I just told her I'd sent my little boy to shower and shave and she asked me if you let me get away with calling you 'my little boy' and I told her that she'd be surprised how much I can get away with if I promise you a roll in the hay later," I said.

"You mean to tell me that women talk like that to each other?" he laughed. "I thought it was only we men that did that."

"Well Carol wasn't shocked, she just said it would take more than that to shock her coming from a houseful of men," I said.

"My God, I can see where I'm really going to have my hands full with you two females," he laughed.

"Your uniform is all laid out, so go get dressed and as soon as Carol gets her shower, I'll grab mine and we should be ready to go by 6:30," I said.

I was just finishing putting on my earrings when I heard David give a long low whistle so I went out to the living room to see what was going on. Carol was standing there next to David and she looked absolutely spectacular in the white sheath with her tanned skin.

"Holy cow, Carol, I never knew you were so beautiful," said David.

"What a thing to say, husband," I said laughing. "You need to open up your eyes because believe me Carol is going to turn every male head in this town."

"The guys in this town are going to shoot me when I appear with both you beauties, one on each arm," laughed David.

"I can't wait to see Mark's face when he gets a load of Carol," I laughed picturing it. "This may just be that fall you said would be heard around the world."

"What are you two talking about?" asked Carol.

"Sorry, Carol, the other night when we were at dinner with Mark and Bill, David was saying that Mark was going to fall in love one of these days and the fall was going to be heard clear around the world. This just might be the night it happens when he sees you in that dress."

"I must say you two are very good for a girl's ego," she laughed.

"David darling, why don't you go get the car so we don't have to bother trying to find a cab tonight," I said.

"Sounds good to me, but you both better be down there because I don't want to get a ticket for parking while I come up to get you," said David.

"We'll be there."

When we got to the Ritz, Mark was there ahead of us as usual.

"Carol, one thing about Mark he has this sense of timing and I've never known him to be late for anything, not even by so much as a minute," I said.

We got out of the car and the carhop took it to park.

"Mark, this is Carol, David's sister," I said introducing them. I couldn't help laughing because I could almost see Mark panting as he got a really good look at Carol.

"Jesus, Lauren, just once in your life could you manage not to laugh in all the wrong places," said Mark taking Carol's hand, but I noticed he didn't let go of her hand either.

"Mark, you are to be on your best behavior tonight or I won't let you dance even one dance with Carol," I said.

"Carol, don't pay any attention to her, you can dance every dance with me if you want to," said Mark glaring at me.

"You two are like brother and sister," laughed Carol. "You act with Lauren just like my brothers do toward me."

"How could any brother fight with you?" he laughed.

"Probably because I tend to laugh in all the wrong places, too."

"David, why didn't you tell me you had such a beautiful sister? I'd have gone personally and escorted her to the U.S.," said Mark.

"Down Mark," laughed David.

"Hi Bill," I said as Bill came up to us. "Good timing, because Mark is threatening to throttle me again," I laughed.

"Bill, this is my sister Carol, Carol this is Bill McCoy who is the reason you are in this country," said David.

"Bill, thank you so much for all you did in getting me over here," said Carol and I watched as Bill too got the look like he'd died and gone to heaven just looking at her.

Bill took her left arm and Mark her right and started into the Ritz.

"Guess you and I are forgotten already," I laughed.

"I think they've both forgotten we even exist," laughed David.

After we were seated and the drink orders taken I said to David, "Maybe you and I should just go home because I don't think Bill or Mark even knows we are here."

"Yes, why don't you two go back to your honeymoon and leave Carol to us," said Mark.

"Just remember Mark, how easily David could flatten you and if he doesn't I could if you try to make a pass at Carol," I laughed.

"Oh Lauren, don't hurt him, he's so cute when he's trying to impress a lady," laughed Carol.

"Let's hurry and eat so we can get Carol on the dance floor," said Bill. "For once we won't have to rent Lauren from David at his exorbitant prices."

"Geeze, a girl just gets married and already she's off the market on the dance floor," I laughed.

"Not for me, kitten, I'll always pay top dollar for you," laughed David.

"Oh you're an old married lady now and considering David's size, I don't intend to see if he's the jealous type or not," laughed Mark.

"I can tell you that he is, so behave," I laughed.

"What time do you have to report in tomorrow, David?" asked Bill.

"At 0700," said David.

"Well we'd better not make this a really late one, I'd hate for you to fall asleep on the flight line," laughed Bill.

Bill and Mark spent the remainder of the meal trying their best to impress Carol. We adjourned then to the bar and Mark beat Bill out for the first dance with Carol. "Come on old married lady, let's you and I show them how it's done," said David escorting me to the dance floor.

Bill got in ahead of Mark for the second dance, then David danced once with Carol while Mark escorted me around the dance floor.

"If you want to cut out early, David, Bill and I can see Carol home," said Mark.

"Sorry boys," said Carol, "I'm the kind of gal who goes home with the man what brung me," said Carol. "Besides I'd kind of like to have some time with my baby brother before he has to report in for duty," she said.

"Sorry, guys, but I think we are going to call it a night, because 0530 comes awfully early when I'm not used to having to get up early," said David.

"Carol, could I take you out tomorrow night for dinner?" asked Bill and I could see Mark squirming because Bill had beaten him to the punch.

"Guys, I'm really flattered, but give me a few days to get used to the change of time zones and to get settled in. Give me a call at the end of the week," she said. "I'm assuming you know Lauren and David's number."

"We know it and we'll definitely be calling you," they both said at once. We left then and drove back to the apartment.

"I'll go stable the car then I'll be in sweetheart," said David.

"Now I know what David meant about them being like Abbott and Costello," laughed Carol as we were walking up to the apartment. "I haven't gotten such a rush since high school."

"They are both great guys, Carol, and I know you'd be safe with both of them. Oh you might have to swat Mark down a little, but basically he's harmless," I laughed.

"I'm going to get on my jammies, then I'll visit with you and David a little, but I think I better let him get to bed soon so he'll be fresh in the morning," she said.

"I'm going to do the same thing. Carol, I'm so glad you're here so I can't get maudlin tomorrow when he leaves. I know it is only for flight training right now, but it's going to be hard to let him leave even so."

"I imagine he'll get some leave before he gets assigned, then we two are really going to have to jack each other up so we don't get all weepy," said Carol.

We both went in to change and I heard David come in the door and I ran out to throw myself in his arms. "What's this, little one?" asked David looking down at me.

"Oh I just had to come hug you that's all," I laughed. "Why don't you go get ready for bed then the three of us can sit around and talk for a while?"

"Sounds good to me, kitten."

Carol came out then and she and I sat down to wait for David. When he came back he pulled me out of the chair and sat down again pulling me to his lap. Carol watched with an amused smile on her face.

"Well what did you think of the boys?" asked David.

"Quite a pair," laughed Carol. "Bill is a dear, but Mark peaks my interest more, he's just bad boy enough that he is irresistible to a woman," she laughed.

"Why is it you women always go for that type?" asked David.

"Because we long to reform them and just wonder if we can," said Carol.

"Are you putting yourself in the same category as Mark?" I asked. "Because I fell for you hook, line and sinker the first time I looked at you."

"Well, as I told you the other night, there was a lot of Mark in me before I met you," he laughed.

"You better believe it, Lauren, this brother of mine had a line a mile long," laughed Carol.

"He was the perfect gentleman with me and in fact it was me who had trouble keeping my hands off him," I said. "He didn't even kiss me goodnight the first night we met when he took me home."

"I was just trying to get you to let your guard down, my love. You'll notice I called you first thing the next morning and I didn't refrain from kissing you when I took you home then or the next morning when I walked you to work," he laughed.

"Well, I hate to tell you my darling, but if you hadn't kissed me then, I would have kissed you, because I couldn't have resisted any longer," I said.

"Why do you think I kissed you? I couldn't resist any longer either," said David.

"I must admit, though I may be a bit prejudice, this brother of mine is quite a catch," said Carol. "In fact all my brothers are tall, dark, and handsome which may be the reason I had trouble getting dates in high school, because I think they intimidated all the boys who were afraid they couldn't quite measure up," laughed Carol.

"I just bet they were, because if they look like David, they must be breathtaking."

"Come on you two, I'm getting embarrassed now," laughed David.

"Don't kid me bro, that ego of yours is enjoying all this adulation," laughed Carol.

"Well maybe, but it is still embarrassing," laughed David.

"So how did you two meet?" asked Carol.

"Mark had talked me into going to this dance with him and I looked up and there was this tall, dark, and oh so handsome guy standing across the floor from me, so I asked Mark to introduce us and he did," I said.

"I took one look at Lauren and I was a gone goose," laughed David.

"Me too, it's just like the words to that song. *I took one look at you, that's all I had to do.* Carol, when he shook hands with me it was all I could do to keep from throwing myself in his arms," I laughed.

"He does kind of have that effect on the female population," said Carol.

"He still has that effect on me," I laughed, "because no matter where I am as soon as I see him I still want to throw myself in his arms and I have the feeling that even after we've been married 50 or 60 years I will still feel the same way."

"Sis, this bride of mine always comes running when I come in the door and throws herself in my arms, and I hope she always will," he said.

"You know I always will," I said.

"Bro, to tell you the truth I've never seen you look so happy," said Carol.

"I don't think I've ever been this happy in my entire life and to think a little tomboy could make me feel this way," he chuckled. "Frank and Bob were concerned when I told them she was a tomboy, but I ask you, Carol, have you ever seen a more adorable, feminine tomboy in your entire life?" he said.

"You're just prejudice my love, so don't put Carol on the spot of having to answer that," I laughed.

"It is so good, Carol, having you here, but unfortunately 0530 is going to come awfully early tomorrow so I think I had better hit the sack. You two sit and talk if you want."

"Well, I for one am ready to hit the hay too, it's been quite a day for me," said Carol.

"Carol and I will have lots of time to talk and I think she'll understand if I want to spend every minute I can with my husband tonight," I said looking at Carol for confirmation.

"I understand perfectly and as I said I'm tired," said Carol. We stood up then and David went to Carol and hugged and kissed her.

"I'm so glad you are here, sis, not only because I've missed you, but I'm glad you will be with Lauren," he said.

"I'm glad I'm here too bro if it makes things any easier on either you or Lauren," said Carol returning his hug and kiss.

I went to Carol and hugged her, "Thanks for coming Carol, I'm so glad you are here. Now remember, make yourself at home because this is your home."

David put his arm around me and we went into the bedroom. "Kitten, I'm not going to wake you tomorrow when I leave, but I'll call you as soon as I know anything about when I'll get leave—in the meantime write to me please."

"Darling I'll be awake when you leave because I always know even when I'm asleep whether you are near me or not and I want to get up and make you breakfast and besides I'll have to drive you out to the base," I said holding him close to me.

"No you won't, kitten, I made a deal with Mark tonight to pick me up and take me to Andrews and as far as breakfast is concerned I don't think I'm going to be very hungry," he said. "I'd rather remember you curled up safe and sound in our bed."

"Darling, if you are afraid I'm going to cry or make a scene, I'm not; I promised you I never would again and I won't. I just want to be with you as long as possible and I especially want to hold you in my arms and feel your arms around me," I said.

"Kitten, it will be easier for both of us if Mark takes me to the base, but I promise you that I'll make sure you are awake so I can kiss you goodbye," he whispered.

"Whatever is easiest on you my love, but please don't worry about me, I'll be ok, and I'll write you at least twice a day or more; just know that I love you more than anything on earth," I whispered back, my arms going around his neck. His head came down then seeking my lips and his arms tightened about me. "Oh darling I love the feel of your body against mine," I said.

"I love you, kitten, more than life itself and someday when this stupid war is over I'm going to take you in my arms and I'm never going to let you go again," he whispered picking me up in his arms.

"Please my darling, if you're not too tired, please make love to me," I said.

"I'm not too tired to make love to you, kitten," he said laying me gently on the bed and sliding in with me and I pulled him to me my body straining to meet his. "I love you, Lauren," he said. "I never knew it was possible to love another person as I love you."

"David, my dearest darling, you are everything to me, you are my reason for being and every day I love you more than I did the day before and I always will. Please darling, please," I said straining my body upward and I felt him shudder as his release came.

"I'm sorry sweetheart, I couldn't wait any longer," he said.

"Don't be sorry, I'm happiest when you are climaxing in me, because my pleasure comes from you being in me as deep as possible," I whispered. "Just stay in me so I can feel you there all through the night."

Staying in me he turned so that I was lying along the length of his body and he fell asleep and I held him in my arms all through the night and as morning broke he woke and I felt his lips against my hair and I looked up and smiled at him, "Good morning, my darling."

"My God, little one, didn't you sleep at all?" he said.

"I snoozed but I was afraid if I slept you'd slip from me and I wanted you there as long as possible," I said.

He rolled then and began to thrust and I answered him and finally my release came and then his. "Go to sleep again, my dearest," I said. "I'll wake you in time to get showered and shaved before Mark gets here," I said.

"I don't want to sleep, I just want to hold you in my arms for as long as possible," he said. And we stayed in each other's arms until it was time for him to get dressed. I went with him then and watched him shave, and after he pulled me into the shower with him and we stood locked in each other's arms while the warm water washed over our bodies and it was enough for both of us.

"For once I wish Mark wouldn't be so punctual but I know he's waiting for me, so I have to go," he said as we walked to the door.

"I love you darling, hurry home to me," I said hugging him to me and his head came down and his kiss was so tender and said everything for which neither of us had any words.

"I love you, Lauren," he said and picking up his bag he almost ran from the doorway and I could no longer stand and sank to the floor and then the tears came that I had been holding back.

I heard Carol come out and she sank down with me and her arms came around me cradling me as I sobbed.

"I heard most of it and I didn't want to come out and spoil it for you both; you're braver than I would be, Lauren, because I don't know if I could have held out against the tears like you did. I'm proud of you, little sister."

"Oh Carol, I love him so much I feel like my heart has been torn out of me," I said. "But I promised him I wouldn't fall to pieces and cause him any worry, and I never will," I sobbed.

She put her arm around me and pulled me to my feet, then she guided me into her bedroom and laid me on the bed and crawled in still holding me in her arms, until my sobs ceased and I fell asleep from emotional exhaustion.

When I woke I heard Carol moving around the kitchen and I got up and went out to where she was making coffee. "Carol, I'm sorry to have put you through that and you didn't even get a chance to say goodbye to him and I know you love him as much as I do."

"Don't worry about it, Lauren. David and I said our goodbyes last night when he kissed me goodnight. David knows how I feel about him and I don't think he could have held up with two females to have to say goodbye to and it was more important that he had every minute with you."

I went to her then and hugged her. "Thank you for being so understanding, I know it's stupid for me to feel that way because I know he is safe for the time being, but it is the first time we've been apart since the second day after

I met him and my arms feel so empty without him."

She brought over a cup of coffee for me and for herself and sat down across from me at the kitchen table.

"Tell me everything about how you met, and how you fell in love, because I'm dying to hear and besides it will make you feel better," she said.

"It was like we told you last night, I had been invited to this dance and I had decided not to go, but Mark talked me into it and I'll be forever grateful to Mark that he did. Anyway, David was standing across the room talking to some people and as soon as I entered the room my eyes went directly to him and I think even in the first glance I knew I loved him. I got Mark to introduce me to him and I told him I'd try to get him a commission in the Air Corp if that was what he wanted.

"He shook hands with me when Mark introduced us and when he took my hand it was like there were no other men in the room, because I could only see him and I still feel that way," I said. "He asked me to dance and they played *I'll Walk Alone* and he pulled me close to him and I knew I never wanted to leave his arms again. We ended up dancing every dance together and then he asked me to go have a drink with him. We talked and talked until the bar closed and he hailed a cab and when we were seated in it, he took my hand and held it all the way back to the apartment. I wasn't kidding last night, he didn't even kiss me, he just kissed my hand that he was still holding and I kissed him on the cheek, and he left. I remember kicking myself that I hadn't given him my phone number because my number is unlisted.

"The next morning he called me after getting Mark out of bed to get my phone number and I invited him to breakfast. We went for a walk then and ended up in Pershing Park and he said I didn't look very comfortable so he sat with his back against the tree and pulled me into his arms so my back was resting against his body and his arms went around me and I never wanted to leave them. We talked about his flight training and I told him about mine and he asked me to go flying with him the next weekend. Then he asked me out to lunch the next day and he asked if he could come over and walk me to work. When he took me home he kissed me and I could barely walk in the door under my own steam because my knees were so weak.

"At any rate he walked me to work in the morning then came back to pick me up for lunch. We had just gotten seated and given our order when he told me that he was falling in love with me, and I told him that I loved him too, so we got up and left because he said the only thing he was hungry for was to hold me in his arms. He took me to one of the departure gates at National

Airport because he said it was the only place he could think of where he could hold me and kiss me without people staring at us.

"I'm going to sound like a tramp now, but I asked him to move into my apartment that same day and he did. The next day he asked me to marry him and of course I said yes and we've been together ever since."

"You don't sound like a tramp to me, you sound like a woman in love," said Carol. "I'm just sorry I gave you such a hard time when you called us to tell us you two were getting married. My only excuse was that I thought you might just be caught up in the madness of wartime and I didn't want my baby brother to get hurt. I always knew when he fell, he'd fall hard and it would be a lifetime commitment for him and if it was just a wartime fling, he'd be hurt so badly I don't think he'd ever get over it."

"Don't be sorry, Carol, because I realized that his big sister just had his best interests at heart and how could I be mad about that? It just made me love you right from the start," I said.

The phone rang then and I went into the living room to answer it.

"Lauren, this is Mark, just wanted to let you know that I dropped David off," he said. "That man of yours loves you so much it isn't funny and he asked me to tell you once more that he loves you and he'll write to you tonight."

"Thanks Mark, I appreciate your taking him this morning, because I know it made it easier on him making a clean break rather than having to say goodbye to me at the gate."

"You holding up ok, kiddo?" he asked.

"Yes, I'm ok now thanks to Carol."

"Speaking of Carol, how about if I pick both of you up and we go out to the stables so you can introduce her to Storm King and then we take a ride past your farm so she can see it?"

"Oh that would be great Mark, hold on a minute while I ask Carol."

"Carol," I called to her, "Mark wants to take us out to the stables so you can meet Storm King and then we'll take a ride so you can see the farm—is that ok with you?"

"Sounds like fun, if you're up to it," she said.

"Mark, Carol says yes. What time are you coming by for us?"

"How about if I pick you up about 11:00, then we can grab a bite to eat after you see that horse of yours and the farm?"

"We'll be waiting, and thanks again, Mark, you are the best."

I went back into the kitchen then, "Mark's picking us up at eleven and believe me with Mark if he says eleven he means eleven not one second before and not one second after—I told him we'd meet him downstairs, so I guess we better get ready since it is already ten."

"What should I wear, sis?" asked Carol.

"Jeans or slacks and a sweater, anything comfortable," I said.

We were downstairs waiting when Mark pulled up exactly at eleven. I let Carol sit next to Mark and I sat next to her. "You know where you're going, don't you Mark?" I asked.

"Yup, I remember the way and if I didn't my car would you've borrowed it so many times to go out to see that stallion of yours," he laughed.

"Do you ride, Mark?" asked Carol.

"Not me. I'm partial to gasoline driven cars, not horses," he laughed.

"Lauren wants me to ride this horse of hers with her, but I'm not exactly on speaking terms with horses and from David's description he sounds like a monstrous, big horse to me," she laughed.

"Well, he's no shrinking violet, that I can guarantee," laughed Mark. "I don't see how Lauren even mounts him so easily, but she just grabs a fistful of mane and swings up," said Mark.

"It's really easy, once you get the hang of it, but most people seem to have trouble getting the hang…I know David did, but he's getting better," I laughed. "The first time he tried, he almost went over Storm, but he's gotten so he can mount him in one try now."

"This is really beautiful country," said Carol. "After Australia, it looks so green and lush."

"Well it is fairly green and lush but if you want mountains you can have those too," laughed Mark.

"No wonder David is thinking about staying here instead of coming home," she laughed.

"Oh I think that has more to do with the tomboy here than scenery…well I guess you could call her scenery too in a manner of speaking," laughed Mark.

"Hit him for me, Carol, since I can't reach from here," I laughed.

Carol gave him a punch in the arm.

"Ouch, don't tell me you're another tomboy and you look so feminine?" said Mark.

"No I'm no tomboy, but when my little sister says punch you, I punch you," laughed Carol.

"Oh God, now I'm going to have two females on my case," laughed Mark.

113

"You lucky boy, two for the price of one," I said.

Just then we came to the entrance to the stables. "Just drive right up to the barn, Mark," I said.

He pulled up and parked and we all got out. As we crossed into the comparative darkness of the barn I heard Storm whinny.

"That's my baby calling for Momma," I laughed running ahead to hug Storm. I found his bridle and slipped it on him then led him from his stall.

"My God he is a monster; he's equal to my brothers in size," laughed Carol.

I grabbed a fistful of mane and swung up onto Storm's back. "Come on Carol, come ride with me," I said.

"No way little sister, he's all yours and you're welcome to him," she laughed back at me.

"We'll watch from a good safe vantage point," said Mark.

I held Storm to a walk until we had gotten almost to the meadow gate, then I gave him his head and we sailed over the gate.

"I don't believe you just did that," said Carol.

"I've seen her do it a dozen times and I still can't figure how one little itty bitty girl like Lauren manages to stay on that stallion while he takes that fence which looks as high as Mt. Everest to me," laughed Mark.

"I'm going to let him run to the end of the meadow then we'll be back," I laughed at the two of them. Storm took off like greased lightening and for the first time that day I felt like me, and for the few minutes we galloped I almost forgot about David and how I was already aching for his arms.

"Lauren, you're a braver woman than I am," said Carol when we returned. "How in the heck do you ever stay on him with no saddle, no nothing?"

"It's all in the legs, sis, you just clamp your legs into Storm's side and let him do all the work," I said patting Storm's neck. "I miss having David's arms to snuggle into, because riding double that way is so romantic and feels so wonderful," I laughed.

"If you promise to keep him to a very, very slow walk, I'll try riding with you," said Carol.

"Go climb up on that fence and I'll bring him alongside so you can mount him easily," I instructed.

When she was on board behind me I let him walk leisurely along until Carol could get used to the feel. "Want to trot a little?" I asked.

"Ok, I'm game," she said but I noticed she had her eyes closed. I set Storm to trotting and I looked back and saw that she finally had gotten the courage to open her eyes.

"Is this how you and bro ride him?" she asked.

"Yes, except he has his arms around me and I snuggle back into his arms," I said.

"I can see how that would be romantic, you suppose I could ever get Mark to do this with me?" she laughed.

"Tell you what, we'll come out and you can practice riding Storm and when you get so you can do it without fear, I'll trick Mark into coming with you, then you can cuddle in his arms. I bet before we're through with him he'll be chomping at the bit to get you to come riding with him," I laughed.

"You got a deal, sis," Carol laughed.

"What are you two giggling about?" asked Mark.

"Oh just sister talk," I laughed.

"Well come on and put Storm away and we'll take a ride out to the farm, then let's go eat because I'm starving," he laughed.

"Aye, Aye, sir," I said saluting him.

"Hey, I've got to tease David, I bet you never gave him an 'Aye, Aye' in your life," he laughed.

"I give David an 'Aye, Aye, Captain'," I'll have you know.

"What does he give you?"

"I'll never tell," I laughed.

"My heavens, you two sound just like me and my brothers," laughed Carol.

I unbridled Storm and gave him a hug, and then I went to find one of the grooms and asked if he'd rub him down and give him water. I made a call to Wendy from the stables to see if by any chance there were any keys to the house hidden on the farm. Then we set out for the farm.

"Oh Lauren, this is really a lovely farm," said Carol when she saw it.

"I see they have fixed the shingles on the roof, but I'm still going to have to give the house a coat of paint, at least on the outside," I said. Wendy had said there was a key hidden in the middle flower pot by the back door so I went to look for it and let us in.

"My God, Lauren, the kitchen alone is big enough to feed an army," said Mark.

"Well, I've got an awful lot of man to fill up," I laughed besides after the first two or three kids this place is going to get a little cramped, but of course we could always add on if we decide to stay here.

We toured the house and Carol said, "Lauren, this is going to fix up just beautifully. I can't wait to get started helping you."

"Oh, oh when women start talking about fixing up a house it's time for a man to get lost because I've always found that eventually they ask you to do one little thing for them and then it becomes an avalanche of one little things," laughed Mark.

"Come out and see the stables," I said.

"Lauren, you'll have plenty of room for at least three more horses," said Carol.

"I was thinking about that, maybe we can get a good deal on a nice little mare for you to ride, Carol."

"Carol, don't tell me you're going to turn into a horse lover too," laughed Mark.

"You just never can tell, Mark," laughed Carol.

We stopped at a little diner on our way back into town and had lunch and Mark kept us both in stitches.

"Thanks Mark, for the ride, we appreciate it," I said as Carol and I got out at the apartment.

"Aren't you going to invite me up?" asked Mark plaintively.

"Not today, but maybe we'll invite you and Bill to come over for dinner Friday night."

"I like Bill, but why can't you just invite me, who needs a chaperon?" asked Mark.

"Carol does," I laughed. "See you later."

When we got back in the apartment I said to Carol, "Why don't we make up some sandwiches for supper then we can eat in the living room where it's cozier."

"You look a little beat, Lauren. Don't you want to lie down for a snooze?" asked Carol.

"Oh, I'm ok, besides I don't think I could stand being in our bed and smelling David's scent right now. It's going to be tough enough tonight because I'm so used to having his arms around me when we sleep."

"Tell you what, let's go make those sandwiches, then we'll get on our jammies and get really comfortable and we'll talk until morning if you want to," said Carol.

"Oh I'd like that, because I want to hear all about David as a little boy and to find out all his likes and dislikes and you're just the person to tell me," I laughed.

"I can even tell you about changing him when he was a baby, if you'd like," she giggled. "He'd kill me if he knew I said that."

"Well while I don't keep secrets from my guy, I won't tell him this one, it's just between us girls and since we both love him I don't think he'd mind. In fact, I have the feeling he'd just as soon not know," I laughed.

"Why don't you go get comfortable because I want to set down and write him a letter so it gets picked up with the mail this afternoon," I said.

"Go ahead, I think I'll grab me a shower, because I smell kind of horsy," said Carol.

I sat down at the kitchen table and wrote a long newsy letter to David telling him what we had done today and asking him how his day went. At the end I couldn't keep myself from it any longer and I wrote:

My darling, I miss you so much already. I've no loving arms to cuddle into and I can't wait until I see you again, because darling I'm going to throw myself in your arms with such gusto that I'll probably knock you off your feet.

I love you so much, my darling husband, and I can hardly wait until you are with me again because taking showers is no fun alone.

Carol is wonderful and I love her more with every passing hour. It's like we've been sisters forever, but I'm glad we aren't actually sisters, because then I couldn't be married to you or else I'd have to commit incest which I'd gladly do as long as it was with you.

We're keeping the home fires burning and a lamp in the window. I love you, I love you, I love you. Just remember our song "close your eyes and I'll be there with you."

I sealed the envelope and went to the lobby to put it in the postbox so the mailman would pick it up when he delivered the mail, which he usually did late in the afternoon. When I got back, Carol was in her jammies as she had said she intended to be.

"Hold on for half a sec, Carol, and I'll get on my jammies, if I can find them," I laughed. "It's been a while since I've needed them."

I went in to change and while I was gone Carol made fresh coffee and when I got back there was a steaming mug next to each of our chairs. Coming back into the room I curled up in the chair that David and I always sat in and in some way it was a comfort because I could almost feel his arms around me.

"So what was my darling like as a little boy?" I asked Carol.

"David was just your normal average kid until Mom left when he was about eight years old," she said. "After that I think he always felt betrayed, and he didn't trust women."

"Carol, it must have been awful for him," I said.

"I think that is why he became a free-wheeling bachelor and his motto was love them then leave them before they could leave him. I don't think he ever dated any woman more than once or twice then he was on to the next. I always felt that if he found the right woman he'd fall and fall very hard because I think he was always looking for the love he didn't get from Mom."

"Did he ever reconcile with her?" I asked.

"Yes, I think he's seen and talked to her in late years, I tried to fill in as much as I could with him and I ran a lot of interference for him with his brothers. He loved Dad and his brothers dearly, but they did tease him a lot, especially during his teen years and they are the typical Aussie males who never give any sort of vent to the emotions, whereas I think David, had circumstances been normal, would have been more likely to have given his heart easily."

"Carol, I'm so glad he had you, but in some ways I may have that Aussie male mentality to thank that no woman ever got to him before I found him."

"That was why I was so hard on you when you called that night," she said, "because I knew how badly he could be hurt again and I was afraid of what it might do to him if it was just a wartime romance."

"I'm just glad that I was able to make you understand how much I loved him and would love him all the rest of my life," I said.

"The funny thing is, it wasn't so much what you said, although that even further convinced me; it was him telling me how much he loved you, because I don't remember of ever hearing David say he loved any woman, not even as a teenager when most boys fall in and out of love—I don't think he ever did."

"Carol, I wasn't kidding about falling in love with him the minute I saw him standing across that room," I said. "Until that minute men had always just been pals to me, which I guess goes back to the tomboy part of me, but when I saw him, for the first time in my life I felt all female and I wanted to love him and take care of him for the rest of my life. All my maternal instincts kicked in that night and every feminine part of me that I had denied for so long kicked in as well. When he danced with me that night I couldn't get enough of being in his arms and that was an emotion I'd never felt before in my life. That next day after he called me and came over for breakfast, I did a lot of hard thinking and I decided that if the time came when he told me he loved me, society could be damned because I was going to live with him and love him since I knew that sooner or later he would have to go into combat and if it ever came to something happening to him I could at least know that I'd given everything I had to give to him for whatever time we had together."

"What I can't understand about you Lauren is why you think you're a tomboy? All I see is a very feminine woman."

"Growing up I liked to do everything boys did and the men in my family did; I loved working on cars with my brother and dad; I loved doing all the unfeminine things like climbing trees, going to baseball games, and my mother and my sister told me often enough that I was a tomboy that I began to think of myself that way. Then as I got older the boys I grew up with let me know very definitely they didn't see me as a girl, but as one of them. I never got asked on dates or to dances, like the other girls. When I went to work for Bill he treated me differently; I was a girl who happened to know a lot of 'for men only stuff,' but he still let me know that he thought I was feminine. Mark too, let me be me and didn't look down on me for it, for which I'll be eternally grateful to both Bill and Mark."

"David must have sensed your femininity, your vulnerability, because I've never seen him treat another woman like he treats you," said Carol. "When he is around you the chivalry in him just comes out and his masculinity asserts itself with a vengeance."

"What's so funny, Carol, is up until I fell in love with David, I never wanted children, never wanted to pick up after any man, never wanted to be dependent on any man. Now I want to give him a houseful of kids, to wash his clothes, to cook and clean for him, and most of all to love him and be there for him no matter what happens."

"Lauren, I can identify with a lot of what you say. I too never got the attention of males, I suspect mainly because my brothers were such handsome, masculine men that other men really didn't think they could measure up. I just happen to go the complete opposite of you, I tried to be the clinging vine, the ultra-feminine woman which really isn't me either.

"Sometimes I wonder if the day will ever come when men and women don't play these stupid games with each other, where women can have careers in professions that are now exclusively male and where men don't have to be the so called big-silent types, but can admit that there are times they need to lean on someone else for support.

"Well I doubt we will ever see it in our lifetime, but hopefully, some day yes and it may just be this stupid war that is going to force the change. Our men are going to see terrible, monstrous things and when they get home I suspect they are going to need their women to hold them in their arms when the nightmares of what they have seen come calling and maybe that alone will begin the changes," said Carol.

"Carol, I love being able to talk to you like this, for I've never had a close girlfriend and I was never very close to my sister and mother," I said.

"I like it too because I've never had a really close girl friend to talk to, and as you know, I've not had a mother to talk to either."

"I've just got to tell you about the first time Mark and Bill came to dinner because David's jealousy almost got the better of him that night," I said laughing softly.

"I've never known David to be jealous in my life, this I've got to hear."

"Well, David had asked me to marry him and we invited Bill and Mark over for dinner so we could ask them to be my Maid of Honor and David's best man at the wedding. You've got to understand something about my relationship to Mark in order to see the humor in it. Mark used to date the girl I roomed with here and he was used to coming over to our place and in fact since neither she nor I drank scotch he brought his own bottle which we kept on the bottom shelf of the bar just for him. Well he broke up with Shelby and right after she moved out; since he and I had always been like brother and sister with each other, he'd still drop by and make himself at home. Every time he would break up with a girl he'd come over here to cry on my shoulder, drink himself blotto, then he'd pass out and I'd put him to bed on the couch. Well that night Mark got here first as usual, and when David opened the door for him he sails right over to the bar while asking me if I still had Teacher's scotch left and makes himself very much at home. I caught a look at David's face and though I was almost doubled over with laughter, I hauled David into the kitchen to explain the situation to him because I could see if I didn't he was going to sock Mark right in the kisser. I explained to him between laughs about Mark's habit of showing up on my doorstep between girls, and got David calmed down somewhat, but I think what really was the turning point and why Mark was still asked to be David's best man, was Mark telling him about making a pass at me the first time he met me and that I had told him he was an idiot. After that the two of them got along just fine."

"Oh God, Lauren, that is too funny for words, I wish I could have seen it all," laughed Carol.

"Well I can tell you, it got a little hairy for a few minutes, but thank God my darling is a reasonable man not given to hitting first and asking questions later."

"It kind of surprises me that he didn't because David, while he is easy going as all get out, does have a temper occasionally," laughed Carol.

"That is something I would never have guessed," I laughed. "He's always so sweet and kind and loving."

"That is one thing I'll say for Dad, he at least taught all his sons good manners and for the most part what he taught them seems to have stuck," laughed Carol. "It could be too that he loves you and has learned to trust you."

"I hope so, I try to tell him every day how much I love him and that there is never going to be any man but him in my life ever. Do you know what that sweet darling of a husband of mine did?"

"What?"

"We sat down and talked about what the future held for us and he told me that if anything happened to him that he wanted me to go out and find another guy to love and who would love me because he couldn't stand the thought of my going through life without love."

"What did you say to that?"

"I told him that I could only promise to look, not necessarily do, but that I wouldn't spend all my life mourning him because that would be like blaspheming our love, because we had been given so much more than a lot of people and that if we had to we could make a lifetime out of whatever time we had together."

"If anything happened to David, would you remarry?"

"No, because he is the only man I ever want. He's such a gentle giant of a man and I really am a one man woman; but if it makes him feel better to think I would at least try to find love again, then so be it," I said.

"Lauren, you've a wise head on your shoulders and I think you will do the right thing for both you and David," said Carol.

"Well I'm not very proud of myself for breaking down the way I did this morning, but at least I managed not to do it in front of him."

"I suspect you've kept those emotions bottled up inside for the last few weeks and the dam had to break or you wouldn't be able to send him off with a smile on your face."

"I did breakdown just once and I could see the pain it caused him and I promised David I'd never do it again and I won't," I said.

"Well I'm here now so if you need a shoulder to cry on I'm available," said Carol.

"Thanks for that, I may need one from time to time, but I promise that we'll have a lot of laughs as well."

"By the way, what did you mean about tricking Mark into riding with me, if I ever get so I can handle Storm King?" she asked.

"I've learned how to push all his buttons and I can pretty much get him to do anything I want and most of the time he thinks it is all his own idea," I laughed.

"I know I should probably go for Bill because I think he's a lot more stable than Mark, but there is just something about Mark that I can't resist," she laughed.

"Oh believe me, Mark is charming and he darn well knows it, and like you said this afternoon those types of men we women just love to try to reform," I laughed. "It's funny but before you came David and I were talking about it one evening and he said he'd bet on Mark over Bill if it ever came to you getting together. He maintains that he was just like Mark before he met me and that when Mark does fall it is going to be just as hard as David did when he fell for me."

"It wouldn't be hard for me to fall for Mark," she laughed. "How did he escape the draft by the way?"

"Primarily because he has a really important job here in Washington and I think the agency he works for was able to get him a deferment."

"I just wondered because I would think Mark would be the type who would love to be in uniform because all the ladies would fall for him," she laughed.

Just then the phone rang.

"Hello."

"Hello Lauren, it's Bill,"

"What's up?" I asked.

"I was just out at Andrews and happened to run into David."

"Is he ok?"

"He's fine and I've a bit of news for you that he doesn't even know yet."

"What's that, Bill? Don't keep me in suspense especially if it's good news because I miss that guy of mine so much."

"Well one of the recommendations that the Army is considering is if any of the enlisted men or officers live within driving distance of Andrews they are going to allow them to live at home just as the guys who live on base do so as to make room for more recruits."

"Oh Bill, do you really think that's going to happen?"

"I'd bet my bottom dollar on it, but you can't say anything to David yet because it is still top secret as far as the Army is concerned."

"If they do, do it, do you know how long before it gets implemented?"

"I'd say within the next week or so," said Bill.

"Bill, that is just about the best news I could hear, thank you so much for letting me know."

"Well I knew you'd want to know right away," he laughed. "Is Carol around?"

"Yes she's sitting right here."

"Could I talk to her, please?"

"Sure just a second and thanks again, Bill."

I motioned for Carol to come to the phone and whispered, "Bill wants to talk to you."

I went out in the kitchen then to heat up the coffee in order to give them some privacy on the phone. As I brought in the coffee Carol was just hanging up.

"I've got a date with Bill for Thursday night for dinner," said Carol.

"Good for you."

"Are you sure you will be ok?" she asked.

"Very sure, you just go and have a really great time as it will give you your first real chance to know Bill and he is just a super nice guy," I said.

"Do you mind if I ask what your conversation with Bill was about? I couldn't help but overhear."

"Bill was in a meeting and this is strictly confidential, but they are going to allow all their service personnel who live within driving distance of the base to live at home rather than on base and that it is due to be implemented probably within the next week or so," I laughed. "Isn't that just the best news ever? It means David will be home with us nights."

"Oh Lauren, that is good news," she laughed coming over to hug me. "Especially for you, although I look forward to it too."

"The only problem is that I wanted to go with you tomorrow to look at furnishings for the house, but now I'm afraid to leave the apartment in case David calls for me to pick him up," I said.

"If he couldn't get us do you think he'd call either Bill or Mark?" asked Carol.

"I would presume so, but I'd want to be the one to pick him up," I said.

"Tell you what, tomorrow I'll go to the stores you select and look at all the furnishings and then I'll make a list of what I think David would like, then once we hear from him and know when all of this is to start, you and I can both go and look at the selections I've made together. That way you won't miss his call and we can still accomplish something."

"Carol, you're a genius!" I laughed. "Remind me to give you my key tomorrow so that you can have another one cut for yourself," I said.

"Well I wouldn't say I was a genius, but if you want to I won't contradict you," laughed Carol.

"What do you think about the furnishings in this apartment?" I asked.

"It's very cozy, I like them."

"Well I hate to tell you but most of them Shelby and I picked up from thrift shops so it cost us next to nothing. Once I get an idea about what David likes, you and I will have to scour the thrift shops to see what we can find," I laughed.

"Your quite a gal, Lauren. That brother of mine really lucked out falling for you," she laughed.

The phone rang. "You might as well answer it Carol, because I have the distinct feeling that Mark is calling to ask you out," I laughed.

Carol got up and picked up the phone.

"Hello."

"Don't let on it's me, sis. I've just gotten some really great news and I want to surprise Lauren," said David.

"What's on your mind?" asked Carol.

"They've just told us that those of us living within driving distance of Andrews will be able to live at home, so I'll be home tonight if I can get a ride," laughed David.

"Hate to tell you, but she already knows, she just didn't know when you'd get the word and I think if I were you I'd tell her to pick you up right now," said Carol.

"How in the heck did she find out? Isn't she the limit? Guess you'd better put her on," said David.

"Lauren, I think you want to talk to this guy," Carol said.

"Who is it, Carol?"

"Just come here and take the phone," she said winking at me.

"Is it David?"

I grabbed the phone from her. "Darling, when are they going to let you come home to me?" I said.

"I can't wait to find out how you knew before me, but I can come home tonight so do you want to pick me up?"

"What time, my darling?"

"Pick me up at 1600 at the front gate," he laughed. "You do know what 1600 is don't you?"

"You better believe I do and I'll be there and if you think Mark is punctual wait until you see me," I laughed. "I'm on my way, just as soon as I can get some clothes on," I laughed.

"What in the heck are you and Carol doing, playing strip poker?" he laughed.

"No, for your information, we've been sitting in our jammies all afternoon and talking our heads off," I said. "Now shut up and hang up I'll be there by the time you get to the front gate," I said.

"No flying at low altitudes, kitten," he laughed.

"I'm on my way my darling and I can't wait to be in your arms again."

"Bye kitten, see you soon," he said. "I love you."

"I love you too."

"Carol, come on get your clothes on. We've got to get going," I said

"You go by yourself, Lauren, so you can have David all to yourself on the way back," said Carol.

"Normally I'd probably take you up on that offer, but I need you with me to keep me awake because I haven't had much sleep in the last 24 hours," I laughed.

"You'll be all right, Lauren, because you'll go on adrenalin until you hit the bed tonight then I've a feeling David is going to have to make love to a corpse, but at least you'll be in his arms," she laughed. "I think I'm going to call Mark and see if his invitation for dinner and dancing tonight is still open, that way you two will have the place to yourself."

"If that's what you want, but don't you want to see David too?" I asked.

"Now we know he'll be home every night I'll have plenty of time with him and after what you went through this morning, I want you to have him all to yourself tonight," said Carol. "You need to leave your key for me though or else I'll have to get you out of bed when we get home."

"You've got it, but remind Mark that I told him I'd beat the tar out of him if he tries treating you like the rest of his harem," I said.

"Believe me I can handle Mark, I've had a lot of practice on guys like him," she laughed. "Now go get your clothes on unless you are planning on meeting him in your pajamas."

"I'll be there on time if I have to meet him stark naked," I laughed.

"Oh I bet he'd love that," Carol said giggling as I went in to get my clothes on.

Forty-five minutes later I pulled up to the front gate of Andrews and jumped out of the car looking for David. I saw him then and as soon as he was through the gate I ran to him throwing myself in his arms.

"Baby," he said hugging me to him.

"Shut up and kiss me," I laughed. He did with gusto.

He got in the car then and I snuggled into his arm.

"You'd think I'd been gone a month instead of only one day the way you greeted me, kitten," he laughed.

"Oh David, it seemed like a month to me and to think that I'll have you in my arms every night for a while longer," I laughed softly.

"How did you know about this deal when we just only got the word about an hour ago?" he asked.

"Bill, who else?"

"I should have known. I was planning on hitching a ride and surprising you but Carol let me know you already knew and would have killed me if I didn't let you pick me up," he laughed.

"That sister of yours is wonderful, she insisted on calling Mark and taking him up on his offer of dinner and dancing tonight when you called so you and I could have time together alone," I said.

"She always was a thoughtful sister, but then I suspect it wasn't all just because she wanted to give us time alone," he laughed. "I've a feeling that if she can manage it Mark just may end up being our brother-in-law."

"That doesn't exactly come as startling news, darling. I think she already is falling for him; I just hope she doesn't get hurt."

"She knows how to take care of herself and Mark did an awful lot of talking about her on our way to the base this morning."

"He picked us up and took us out to see Storm and to see the farm at eleven today, and according to him all he did was listen to you talk about me," I laughed.

"I think it was pretty much 50-50," laughed David hugging me closer to him and my hand caressed his knee. "Oh that feels good and to think I thought it was going to be at least three weeks or more before I felt your hand on my knee again," he said huskily.

"You don't know what a heck of a time I'm having limiting my hand's access just to your knee," I said and I reached up to kiss his neck.

"All I can say is it is a good thing we're so close to home or I'd find a place to park and take you right here in the car," he said softly.

"Try to contain yourself about ten minutes more and then we'll be home in our own bed and we won't have to get out of it until tomorrow morning," I said softly.

We drove then in silence until we parked the car in the garage. When we got out his arm came around my waist and we both ran the block to the apartment. At last we opened the front door and I noticed my key was gone.

"Carol," hollered David.

"She's left already," I said. "She left the door unlocked so we could get in because she took my key with her so she could get back in when Mark dropped her off tonight," I said. "We didn't get a chance to get another made for her; we were going to do it tomorrow."

He shut the door then and pulled me into his arms.

"I love you, kitty cat," he said softly holding me tightly against his body.

"I love you, David," I said softly.

He walked over to our favorite chair, sat down, and pulled me into his arms.

"I was dreading tonight not having you in my arms, then came the wonderful reprieve," he chuckled.

"Oh darling, I've dreaded tonight all day knowing I wouldn't be in your arms tonight and even after Bill called and let me know about the reprieve, I wasn't sure when it would happen so I was still dreading tonight, until you called. Do you know yet what hours you will be on base?" I asked.

"For the time being they are saying 0700 to 1600 Monday through Friday until we get through ground school and basic flight training, which takes about six weeks."

"Then why don't you drive so you can leave whenever you get a chance; all I ask is that you make sure you wake me every morning before you leave so I can get your breakfast for you."

"You don't need to do that, I can grab something when I get on base," he said.

"Then wake me just so I can kiss you goodbye every morning, please darling."

"Ok little one, if that's what you want," he said bending his head to kiss me.

"So what have you and Carol been up to today?"

"As I told you we went out with Mark to see Storm King and the farm," I said. "Mark refused to ride as usual, but Carol finally screwed up her courage and rode with me. It was funny at first because she'd just barely let me walk him, but she finally decided maybe she wouldn't mind if I'd let him trot, but I noticed she had her eyes closed. After riding with me, she asked if I'd teach her how to really ride Storm, so she could maybe talk Mark into riding with her. Finally I told her when we were out of earshot of Mark, that once she got comfortable riding Storm alone, I'd get Mark to ride with her because I knew all the right buttons to push to get him to do almost anything."

"Poor Mark he isn't going to stand a chance against you two," laughed David.

"Oh I forgot to tell you Carol has a date with Bill for Thursday night for dinner."

"So Bill's beating Mark's time is he?"

"Well actually, Bill's invitation came before Mark's, it just so happened that tonight was the night she chose to go out with Mark and that was so you and I would have time alone," I laughed.

"Friday night let's get together with Bill and Mark and go to the Ritz again, it should be quite a show by then watching those two fight over who gets to dance with Carol," he laughed.

"What I can't wait to see is Mark riding on Storm, just remind me to take a camera so if they ever do get together we can show it to their kids so they can see what an eastern dude their dad was," I laughed.

"Did you and Carol go shopping today?" asked David.

"No, after little or no sleep last night I decided to wait until tomorrow so Carol and I just sat around in our jammies all afternoon and talked up a storm," I said.

"What do you think of Carol, now that you've had time to get to know her a little?"

"Oh David, she is wonderful. I love her just like we've always been sisters," I said. "Oh God, that reminds me, I mailed you a letter this afternoon, what do they do with your mail if you aren't on base when it comes?"

"You mean after the censors get through with it?"

"Oh my heavens, I didn't think about censors looking at it," I laughed.

"That must be quite a letter, sugar, can't wait to read it," he laughed softly hugging me close to him. "I really didn't think you'd write me today since I only left this morning."

"I told you I'd write you twice a day or more and I meant it," I said. "Are you hungry, darling? I think there is still some lamb in the icebox that I can heat up for you or there are cold sandwiches left that Carol and I were going to eat."

"I'll just grab a cold sandwich and a cup of coffee because I'm not really that hungry," he said.

"Sit still darling, I'll go get it for you and bring it in here," I said getting up and going to the kitchen. I came back with a thermos full of coffee and a plate of sandwiches and set them on the tray next to our chair. After I poured coffee for the two of us and gave David his sandwich I sat back down on his lap while he munched. "What was your day like," I asked, "or is that a military secret?"

"They put us through inspection and drill training for about two hours, teaching us how to salute, march, and all that jazz," he said. "Then we spent another couple of hours in ground school, and another couple of hours in basic flight training…I felt like I was back earning my private license all over again."

"I bet you could have taught ground school, not to mention flying," I laughed.

"The last captain that I flew with asked me why in the hell they had me in basic flight training, that I should be teaching the course," he laughed. "I had half a notion to tell him my wife could teach the course too."

"I bet some of the younger men especially would love that, having a woman show them how to fly," I laughed.

"It would do them a world of good, I think, because I was watching some of them today in-between check rides, and believe you me I think we both did a better job on our first flights than they did," he laughed.

"Oh darling, it's so good to be back in your arms again," I said snuggling in closer to him as my arms went around his neck."

"It's pretty darn good to be back in your arms too," he said hugging me even closer. "Lauren, you were such a good little soldier this morning and I appreciate it."

I didn't know whether to tell him about my breaking down and decided that what he didn't know would cause him less pain and worry. "I promised you, my love, that I would never put you through it again and I never will, for you've got the biggest burden and I will never cause you one minute of pain or worry, but I'm so glad I'll have you in my arms every night for a while yet," I said.

"Oh God Kitten, when they called us together and made the announcement, I wanted to shout I was so happy and I know a lot of the other men felt the same way," said David. "It wasn't even so much the not having sex with you, it was not being able to hold you in my arms and kiss you that really got to me, when I thought about it," he whispered.

"Does that mean you don't want to have sex with me tonight?" I asked grinning at him.

"Just try to stop me," he laughed softly.

"Do you think I'm nuts? No way would I try to stop you ever," I laughed.

"That does it, kitten, I've got to have you in my arms and feel your luscious naked body against mine right now," he said standing up with me still in his arms and heading for the bedroom.

"I thought you'd never ask, my love," I said.

"Darling, throw your clothes on the chair there and I'll wash and iron your uniform tomorrow, that way you'll always have one change here," I said.

"Luckily in my hurry to leave I did remember to bring a change of uniform," he said as his lips came down to my neck and then began to travel down my body. "I think you're overdressed, kitty cat," he chuckled.

"Not for long, love, not for long," I said as he stood me on my feet and I began to pull at my clothes.

When we were both naked he pulled me back into his arms and as he pulled me into his body, my own body was already responding to his touch. "Please darling, please," I begged and I pulled him to the bed and lay down as his body came down covering mine.

We made love then and it was slow and satisfying as both of us reached our climaxes together. "My insatiable little kitten," he said.

"My stallion," I said.

We lay there looking at each other for neither of us could tear our eyes from the sight of the other's body and the lust and the love that was between us overflowed and we came together coupling once again and reveling in our need of each other.

We got up then and went out in the living room. I put on some records and David took me in his arms and danced with me. "I wonder how Mark is making out with Carol," he laughed as he drew me in closer to him.

"Well I told him if he made a pass at Carol I'd beat the tar out of him," I laughed, "but I don't think he was very scared or at least he figured it would be worth it."

"While I think Bill is a great guy and I'll be eternally grateful to him for getting Carol over here, I kind of hope that Carol can bring Mark to heel like you did me, because I think he would make a great brother-in-law," he laughed.

"I suspect he would too, and what's more I have the feeling that he just may be falling for Carol and I'd kind of like to hear the crash," I giggled.

"What have you and Carol got planned for tomorrow?" he asked.

"We'll probably go window shopping like you and I did, then I may just ask Mark for the loan of his car so I can take her out and give her her first riding lesson."

"We may just have to go on another car buying trip so you won't be stranded if I take the car to the base every day," he said.

"Let's not, because for the most part I won't need a car around town and I can always borrow Mark's if I do need one or else I can take you to the base and pick you up. There's not much use of having two cars to have to pay garage fees for. I was thinking, however, that I might just talk to Bart about finding a cheap little mare for Carol to ride, because as soon as we move into the house, we won't have to pay stable fees anymore," I said.

"That's a great idea, sugar, while you are at the stables tomorrow ask Bart to look around for a mare for Carol to ride, then the three of us can ride together," he said.

"Well actually I was thinking that if I found a nice gentle mare that isn't quite as large and scary looking as Storm King, that maybe both Carol and Mark would ride with us," I laughed.

"Wait until Mark finds out how much fun it is to ride with Carol snuggled into his arms, I'll bet he'll want to do it 24 hours a day," laughed David. "Babe, much as I love dancing with you, I think I've got to hit the hay soon because 0530 is going to come awful fast; I'm just not used to these early hours yet," he said.

"Darling, that is fine with me because it is well over 24 hours since I've had any sleep," I said.

We went into the bedroom and crawled into bed. "Go to sleep little one, you look like you're half asleep already and as long as I can hold you in my arms, I know I'll sleep well too," he said softly.

My arms came up around his neck and I snuggled into his arms and I was asleep almost before I heard him whisper in my ear, "I love you."

I murmured, "I love you too darling," and I was out.

I woke the next morning when David got out of bed. "Go back to sleep, kitty cat," I promise I'll wake you to kiss you goodbye before I leave, he said pulling the covers around me and kissing my cheek. I slept again and David kept his word, just before he was ready to leave, he woke me and taking me in his arms he kissed me tenderly. "I'll see you tonight, my love," he said and my arms went about his neck and I kissed him goodbye, then he took his arms from around me and tucked the covers back in around me and I went to sleep again.

About ten I woke up and went to shower and dress. Carol was already up and in the kitchen drinking coffee. "Hi sis," she said when I came in to join her. "You and that brother of mine have a good time last night?" she laughed.

"You better believe it, Carol," I laughed.

"Did you manage to stay awake or did you fall asleep while he was making out with you?"

"Oh we took care of that before the adrenaline coursing through my system wore off," I laughed.

"Ok I'll stop asking embarrassing questions," she said.

"So how was your date with Mark?"

"Fantastic, Lauren. We went out to dinner and then we went to a little club he knows and danced until it closed," she said. "He's one of the best dancers I ever ran into next to David."

"Well tell me, did he make a pass? Did he kiss you goodnight?"

"Actually, he was pretty much a perfect gentlemen, not holding me too tight when we danced at first, until I asked him if he was scared I'd break if he held me closer," she laughed.

"What did he say?" I asked.

"Actually he didn't say anything he just pulled me closer in his arms and from then on it was perfect," she laughed.

"So did he kiss you goodnight?"

"Several times actually, and I loved every minute of it."

"Did you tell him you have a date with Bill Thursday?"

"I might have let it slip accidentally," she laughed.

"It will do him good to think he has a little competition," I said smiling.

"That's what I thought too, but God Lauren, I wish we could just cut out the games because I don't know how long I can wait for him to make love to me before I throw him down and rape him," she giggled.

"Well, I suspect that he might just have considered making love to you, but wasn't sure that David wouldn't kill him if he did," I said.

"I'm to the point of telling him to forget about David killing him if he does make love to me, because I'm going to kill him if he doesn't."

"You sound like a woman who intends to land her guy one way or the other," I said.

"Why does it always take men longer to know they are in love than it does us women, I wonder?"

"Oh, I think they are totally in denial right up till they finally get the massage that they can't live without us, and that giving up their precious freedom just might be worth it," I laughed.

"Well he at least admitted that he thought he might be falling in love with me, but he sounded a little scared when he said it," she laughed.

"Me thinks that your going out with Bill Thursday and then having Bill as competition Friday night when we all go out will send him crashing, " I laughed.

"I sure hope so. Ok, what's on the agenda for us today?"

"I thought maybe we'd go shopping and get you a key made, then after lunch I'd see if I can borrow Mark's car and we'll go out and ride Storm. Also David told me to look for a nice gentle little mare for you today while we are at the stables and to buy her if I found the right one," I said. "David is of the opinion that if you two ever ride together the way he and I do, that Mark just might be a gone goose," I laughed.

"Remind me to give that brother of mine an extra hug tonight. You think David is on my side in this then?" asked Carol.

"We talked about it last night and both of us decided that Mark just might make a very satisfactory brother-in-law."

We dressed then and went out to look in the stores and thrift shops until almost noon. Carol and I agreed on almost everything as far as furniture and furnishings were concerned and then I called Mark and he agreed to lend me his car so we stopped at his office to pick it up. He came down to the garage to give us the keys and before we left he took Carol in his arms and there wasn't a doubt in my mind that he was falling hard for her.

"From the looks of things I'd say your boy is about ready to topple," I laughed.

"Well, from the way he just kissed me I'd almost agree with you, but I don't want to count my chickens before they are hatched," she laughed.

When we got to the stables I went in search of Bart.

"Bart, this is Carol, David's sister," I introduced them. "We are in the market for a nice little mare to buy for Carol; do you have anything?"

"As a matter of fact I think I may have the perfect mare for you. Why don't we go down to the paddock and you can take a look at her," he said.

When we got to the paddock Bart pointed out a little sorrel mare. I went over and examined her, "I think she might be perfect, Bart, if we can come to terms on price," I said. "What do you think, Carol?"

"She is pretty and definitely not as scary as that big horse of yours, Lauren," she said.

"What are you asking for her, Bart?"

"Seventy-five dollars," said Bart.

"Sold, and we'll need a saddle and bridle for her," I said.

"That will be another fifty," he said.

"Let's go back to the office and I'll write you a check," I said.

We went to the office and I wrote him a check and he signed the papers over to me.

"We'll need to stable her here until after the closing on our farm, which I think should be any day now," I said. "No problem, Mrs. Benton," said Bart.

We went back to the stable then and I bridled Storm. "I don't know if I can ride him bareback like you do," said Carol looking a little scared.

"I'll be on him sitting behind you, but you will be doing the driving, so to speak."

"Just grab a handful of mane and give a little jump so your leg goes over his back," I said. It took several attempts but finally she was able to mount Storm in a reasonably proficient manner.

"Now hug him with your legs," I said, "and use your knees to let him know which way you want him to go, and pull gently on the bridle at the same time in the same direction as you are kneeing him when you want to turn him. To start him moving just give him a gentle nudge with your heels."

Carol did as I instructed and Storm moved out in a gentle walk. When we got in the meadow gate Carol practiced turning him. "This is fun," she laughed.

"There is nothing like the feel of a horse between your legs, except maybe the man you love," I laughed.

"You're terrible," laughed Carol.

"No, just truthful," I said.

"Now to get him moving a little faster just give him a gentle kick with your heels."

"He won't go too fast, will he?" asked Carol.

"Not if you don't kick him too hard," I said. "The harder the kick the faster the pace."

We practiced for almost an hour. "How about it, Carol, want to try him solo?"

"I guess so, but just stay close in case," she laughed.

I slid off and she gave Storm a gentle kick and she walked him about ten feet from where I stood watching, then turned him and walked him back bringing him to a halt in front of me.

"I think you've got it," I laughed. "Bring him over by the fence so I can get back on because there is one more thing I want to show you."

When I had remounted I said to Carol, "Now let's gallop just once to get you used to it."

"I don't think I'm good enough for that yet," said Carol looking scared.

"Just clamp your legs around him harder and grab a fistful of his mane," I said.

She did as I instructed and we galloped down the meadow. Pulling Storm to a halt I looked to see how Carol had made out with her first gallop and to see if her eyes were open. "How was that?" I asked.

"Great, I even enjoyed it," she laughed and patted Storm's neck.

"Well, let's get Storm re-stabled and then I'll show you how to rub him down," I said.

We went back then and I showed her how to unbridle him and how to rub him down. "Now let's go over and get acquainted with your new mare," I said.

"Do you know what her name is?" asked Carol.

"According to her papers it is Lady," I said.

When we got to Lady's stall she put her head over the gate and nickered at us. I put my arm around her neck and rubbed her nose. "Now you do the same, Carol." She did so and Lady nuzzled her neck. "She likes you already," I laughed. "How about if we take her for a short ride?"

"Yes, let's," said Carol.

I showed Carol how to bridle her and lead her from her stall. We mounted and rode out to the meadow and Lady picked her way along daintily. "She really is a lady compared to that monster horse of yours," laughed Carol and she even galloped her for a short distance.

"Just remember that she has a lot more sensitive mouth than does Storm so you'll need to be extra gentle in pulling on the reins with her compared to what you need to be with Storm."

We took her back then and I suggested we get going because we still needed to get a key made for Carol. We went to a little key shop and had a key made. When we got back to the apartment we went to the kitchen to get ourselves some lunch.

"I think you are going to make an excellent horsewoman," I said to Carol. "You just need to build up some confidence then I think we can coerce Mark into riding with you," I laughed.

"It amazes me how much I enjoy it because I would have bet you a million bucks I was never going to ride Storm solo," she laughed.

We heard the phone ring and I went to answer it.

"Hello."

"Hi Lauren," said Mark.

"Hi yourself and thanks for the loan of the car today," I said.

"Any time, Lauren."

"I'm betting that you didn't call to talk to me," I laughed softly.

"Well as a matter of fact yes and no," he said. "Are you alone or is Carol in the room with you?"

"At the moment alone."

"Did she say anything about our date last night?"

"She said she had a lot of fun with you and that you are one terrific dancer," I said.

"Lauren, I really think I'm falling in love with her and I was wondering if she'd said anything to you about how she feels about me."

"Why don't you just ask her, Mark?"

"Well I wanted to see what you thought before I say anything because if she definitely isn't interested I don't want to pursue it any further."

"Let me put it this way, if I were you Mark, I'd tell her how you feel about her," I laughed.

"God Lauren, I didn't think I'd ever feel about any woman the way I feel about Carol."

"I'm glad for you, Mark, because Carol is one terrific lady and I really think the two of you could be as happy together as David and I are."

"Let me talk to Carol, please Lauren," he said.

"Hold on while I get her," I said.

"Carol, there is a very moon struck young man on the phone for you," I laughed, giving her the ok sign.

She ran into the living room then to pickup the phone. I stayed in the kitchen to give her some privacy but I kept my fingers crossed until I heard her hang up the phone and return to where I was in the kitchen.

"Well?"

"Oh Lauren, he says he loves me," she whispered.

"Oh I'm so happy for you, Carol, " I said hugging her.

"He asked if I would break my date with Bill for tomorrow night because he had something he wanted to ask me," she said.

"What are you going to do?"

"I already called Bill and told him that I was very grateful for everything that he had done for me and that I thought he was one terrific guy, but that Mark and I had been seeing each other and that I thought I was falling in love with Mark."

"How did Bill take it?"

"He was disappointed but nothing that I think he won't get over quickly," she said.

"Maybe once we get you and Mark settled we can both look for a really nice girl for Bill," I said.

"So are you and Mark going out tonight?"

"Do you think David would be very upset if I invited him over here tonight? I want to be with Mark but I also would like to spend some time with you and my brother tonight. I thought maybe I could ask Mark to dinner and we could sit around and talk for a while, then Mark and I could go elsewhere."

"Sounds like a winner of an idea to me," I laughed.

"Why don't you go call Mark back and tell him to be here at six for supper and I'll see what we have in the way of food to serve our two big lugs."

When she came back to the kitchen she was laughing. "What's so funny?'

"Mark, he wanted to know if I thought David would mind if he put his arm around me tonight," she laughed. "Also he wanted to know if I thought we could cut out about eight or nine so we could go somewhere and dance because he had an important question to ask me."

"What did you tell him?"

"I told him that David wouldn't care, that I didn't need my baby brother's permission to have a man put his arm around me. Also I told him that it would be fine if we cut out early because David would be going to bed by ten anyway because of having to be up so early. I tried like heck to find out what the question was, but I couldn't get a thing out of him," she laughed.

"Does David like meatloaf?" I asked.

"He sure does, it was always one of his favorites."

"How about if we have meatloaf and mashed potatoes and gravy?"

"Do you have baby peas and pearl onions by any chance because that is one of David's favorite vegetables."

"I sure do and that's what I'll make. I've just got to sit down with you soon to find out what his favorite foods are, favorite colors, and favorite everything."

We got the food on cooking and went to shower and dress.

"What are you wearing tonight?" I asked.

"What about this dress?" she said, holding up a gold sheath dress.

"Wow, that ought to do the trick," I laughed, "but won't that be a bit dressy for dinner with us?"

"You know what, I think I'll put on my white pantsuit then I can always change before we go dancing," she said.

"I think that is a really good idea, that way you'll be comfortable around here and then you can knock his eyes out with the gold job, which ought to be the 1, 2, punch as far as Mr. Mark Purcell is concerned," I said laughing. "Should we eat in the kitchen or out here in the living room tonight?" I asked.

"Let's eat in the kitchen; it will be cozier," laughed Carol.

"Well it definitely will be a tight squeeze, but then I suspect that may be what you have in mind," I laughed.

"Actually the thought did cross my mind," she laughed back.

I heard the front door open and I ran out to throw myself into David's arms. "Welcome home darling," I said reaching up to kiss him. Carol had followed me into the living room and she stood smiling at us.

"Hi bro," she said coming up to give him a hug.

"Geeze what a deal I get hugged by two beauties," laughed David. "So what have you two been up to today?"

"Why don't you go get into civvies so you can be comfortable then we'll bring you up to date," I said. "By the way, Mark is coming to dinner tonight and then he and Carol are going out afterward."

"I'll just be a minute, then we can talk all we want before and after supper," said David.

When he came back I handed him a bottle of beer and Carol and I took our Cokes and sat down. As usual I sat on David's lap and Carol started to laugh. "What's so funny?" asked David.

"I never thought I'd see the day you'd sit holding a girl on your lap, drinking beer, and looking thoroughly domesticated," she said.

"Well to be truthful with you, I never thought you would either, but thank heavens this little kitty cat came into my life and changed all that," he said.

"So as I said before, what have you two been up to today?"

138

"Carol had her first riding lesson today and she is making really great progress," I said.

"Did you ask Bart about finding her a mare?"

"Better than that we bought a lovely sorrel mare named Lady for her to ride," I said.

"You're not going to believe this, David, but I actually soloed on Storm today and we even galloped him," said Carol. "However, I'm going to enjoy riding Lady over Storm because Lady is such a dainty little thing and I feel a lot better being closer to the ground," she laughed.

"I've got some news for you two as well," said David. "I was called into the colonel's office today and they are taking me out of Basic Flight School and giving me my wings at a ceremony on Monday."

"Then what will you be doing?" I said and it was hard to keep the fear out of my voice.

"For the next six weeks I'll be instructing then once my former class graduates, I'll be transferred to B-17 training for four to six weeks," said David.

"How did this all come about?" I asked.

"Well, you know that captain who wanted to know why the heck they had me in basic flight training?" he said.

"Yes, I remember."

"Apparently he went to the colonel and told him it was a waste of time me being in basic flight training when I could teach the course, so it was decided that they would make me an instructor for my old group of cadets. He gave me the choice between fighter planes and B-17s and I chose the B-17s," said David.

"Congratulations, bro," said Carol.

"Yes, darling, congratulations," I said. "Are wives allowed to attend the ceremony, and sisters?"

"Yup, I expect you both to be there Monday," he said. "Couldn't miss an opportunity like that to let the other guys see what a great life I live with two beauties like you two."

"Would you mind if I brought Mark too?" asked Carol.

"No, he's more than welcome," said David raising an eyebrow and looking quizzically at Carol.

"I'll confess all tomorrow night," said Carol, "because by then the situation should be a little more clear or Lauren can explain it to you tonight when you're alone after Mark and I leave."

"You better believe kitten will explain all to me tonight after you leave," laughed David.

"David, I've been meaning to ask you, where in the heck did you come up with the names kitty cat and kitten for Lauren? I don't think I've ever heard you call any woman by such cutesy names."

"Well, actually I started calling her kitten because when she's in my arms she tends to purr and I guess kitty cat just became a derivative of that. And no I've never given love names to any woman I ever dated, but that was before I met this baby doll of mine," he laughed.

"All right Lauren, fess up, what do you call David?" asked Carol.

"Well, I've been known to refer to him as my stallion," I laughed. "Otherwise, the only thing I've ever called him other than darling or my love or something like that is Captain."

"Well, I think it's cute," she said.

"Carol, you really ought to think about settling down because I can highly recommend it," said David.

"Believe me, I've thought about it more than once and a lot just lately," said Carol with a grin.

"Ok, spill it sis. I know you well enough to know when you are up to something," said David.

"Well bro, please don't let onto Mark tonight that I've told you anything, but today on the phone he told me he thought he was falling in love with me," she said.

"What about you, Carol?"

"I know I love him and he said he had something to ask me tonight."

"He better be serious, because I don't want him breaking your heart just for another notch on his belt," said David.

"Darling, I can tell you first hand that he's in love with Carol and I think you're going to hear the big crash for sure after tonight," I laughed.

"Lauren, how do you know that he's in love with me?" asked Carol. "I only told you today what he said to me."

"If you recall, when Mark called today he talked to me before he had me put you on the phone," I laughed. "He told me that he thought he was in love with you and wondered if I knew how you felt about him," I said.

"What did you tell him?"

"I told him he should ask you how you felt about him. He asked me if I thought you were interested in him and I told him 'let me put it this way, if I were you Mark, I'd tell her how you feel about her', then he said he never thought he'd feel about any woman the way he feels about you. And believe me after seeing the way he kissed you when we picked up the keys to the car today, I know he loves you because that wasn't the kiss of a guy on the make; that was the kiss of a guy who is head-over-heels in love," I laughed.

"I have to agree with Lauren," said David, "because a guy on the make kisses a girl one way and a guy who has fallen so hard he doesn't know what hit him kisses her entirely differently," he said. "Kitty cat here can tell you first hand that there is a difference, can't you darling?"

"Yes, I can from experience," I laughed. "The first time David kissed me goodnight it was definitely the kiss of a guy on the make, but when he dragged me out of the restaurant and took me to National Airport, it had changed, it was the kiss of a man who was entirely serious and entirely in love."

"But I still can't see how you could tell that it was love on his part, because you weren't on the receiving end like you were with bro here," said Carol.

"Because he kissed you exactly the same way David kissed me there in the airport, and when he held you in his arms, it was the way David held me like he never wanted to let me go, not like a man who has only sex on his mind and believe me Mark kissed and held you exactly the same way today."

"How in the hell do you women know the differences between the way we kiss and hold you when we aren't serious and when we are?" asked David.

"I don't exactly know how we know, but you can take it from me that we do…maybe it's because we feel the love and the protectiveness as opposed to 'this feels good let's hit the hay' of the other kiss."

"She's right bro, when Mark kissed me today it was different than last night and so was the way he held me in his arms," said Carol.

"Ok kitty cat, then answer me this, how come you went through that whole spiel about when I got tired of you, etc," asked David.

"I meant it," I said. "While we can usually tell the differences of serious versus let's have fun, we aren't infallible because we've got a lot of emotions going on inside us too. Sometimes we get tripped up just because we love you so much that we want to be right about the way you hold and kiss us, that we can misread the signs. Besides, I'd never asked a man to play house with me before and all I knew was that I loved you but I wasn't going to try to make you feel guilty if I'd misread your intentions," I said.

"Do you see why I love this woman so much, sis?" he asked as his lips came down to mine. "What other woman do you know of who would come to a man a virgin and then let him know she would never hold him to his promises of love?"

"Not taking anything away from Lauren," she said, "I think there are more of us than you know who are capable of loving a man so much that we would give up everything just to love and be loved for even a little while by that man," said Carol.

"The trouble is, David darling, that there are some women who play games, and give and withhold love to gain whatever advantage they can over a man and they are the ones who make it so hard on the rest of us who know we will only love one man in our lifetime," I said.

"Sis, is that the way you feel too?" asked David.

"Yes bro it is," she said. "I know that Mark is the only man I'm ever going to love, whether he feels the same or not, because I'm not Mom and neither is Lauren, we are one man women and that is just the way it is."

"How did you know I was thinking about Mom?" asked David.

"Because ever since she left when you were eight, you've always thought of all women in terms of Mom and her walking out on us, until you met Lauren and somehow she got through that shell of yours and made you believe in her," said Carol.

"You're right she did get through my shell and I don't know how she did it, maybe by being so honest and straight forward with me, no pretenses— even that first time I made love to her and she was scared and was shaking, she told me that I was the only man she was ever going to love and somehow the way she said it, I knew that I was always going to be the only man in her world. Even when I told her that if anything happened to me that I wanted her to find someone to love her because she had so much love to give, she would only say she would look but that if she didn't I wasn't to worry about her because she wouldn't mourn me for the rest of her life because that would be like blaspheming our love and I think I knew then that I had found me a woman worth loving worth giving my heart to, because she would never betray my love for her," he said.

"I know you and Mom have finally reconciled on some level, but I've often wondered why because I always thought you hated her for leaving us?" said Carol.

"Mom and I have talked and I understand something of her side of it now that I didn't know before, but I don't think I will ever completely trust her, but maybe with age I've learned that everyone is entitled to a second chance," said David.

My arms went around his neck and I held him to me. "I swear before Carol and God, my darling, that I will never leave you and never betray your love and your faith in me because it would be like cutting out my own heart if I ever did. I love you so much that every minute that you aren't with me is an agony to me and I only wish that it was like it was in the early days of this country and they'd let me fight right along side you when you have to go into combat, but even though I won't be there physically, my heart and my love will be there," I said.

"Lauren, I hope you won't hate me for this, but David has a right to know what you went through that first morning when you sent him off to report in," said Carol.

"No Carol, please my husband has enough to bear please don't add to his burdens," I said.

"Lauren, it won't add to his burdens that I promise you, it will set him free because he will understand once and for all that there are women in the world like you who will put themselves through hell not to add to their husband's burdens in a world gone nuts," said Carol.

"Please David stop her," I said, "because I don't think I could bear it if what she tells you makes you worry about me instead of concentrating everything in you on coming through this damned war," I said.

"No kitten, I want to hear what Carol has to say, because I have a feeling in some way it will give me peace of mind," said David holding me close to him.

"That morning after you ran out the door and down the stairs, I came out of my room and she was crumpled on the floor sobbing her heart out because she said she felt like her heart had been ripped out of her, but that she had promised you that she would never cause a scene and never break down in front of you and she never would. This woman loves you more than she loves her own life and that is why I love her so much because she does love you that much as do I, and that is just exactly the way I love Mark," said Carol.

I got up and ran into the bedroom so that David would not see the tears that were so close to the surface and Carol ran in after me. "Forgive me, Lauren, but David had a right to know how much you love him and how deeply you were affected by his leaving because he's spent so much time convincing himself that all women betray their men eventually and that would be an even bigger burden on him if he had to worry that you might not be here waiting for him when he returns," said Carol.

"I just hope you are right, Carol," I said as I slumped into her arms.

"Carol, give us a few minutes, please," said David taking me in his arms and holding me close to him.

"Lauren, Carol was right in telling me because while I knew in my heart you loved me that much, I still was trying to convince my brain that what my heart knew was right," said David pulling my body in close to his. "Please darling, don't think you have to shield me from your emotions, because knowing about this just makes me know both with my head and my heart that I am truly loved and it does set me free to love you the same way. I've spent a lot of my life despising women and using them for my own ends because of the betrayal I felt when Mom left us until you came along and I must have sensed right from the start that you would never betray me and that you loved me the way I always wanted to be loved. But at the same time I can't let you go through alone feeling the way you did that morning without knowing that you are my world, my life and leaving you was like tearing my heart out of me. Don't hate Carol for telling me and please don't ever hide from me the way you feel thinking that it will help me because we share everything."

"I don't hate Carol," I said, "I just didn't want her to tell you because it does put an extra burden on your shoulders and while I know they are broad, capable shoulders you should not have to carry all of the burden and if my sending you off with a smile helps you in any way, then it is a very small price for me to pay," I said hugging him to me. "I love you so much and you give me so much by loving me in return."

"Come on kitten, dry your eyes," he said handing me his handkerchief. "We'll talk more later when I can hold you in my arms, but we don't want Mark seeing you with red eyes because he just might think I've been beating you or something," he laughed softly.

When we went back in the living room Carol was watching me with such anxious eyes, so I looked at her and smiled and nodded my head to let her know that she was still my beloved sister and she returned my smile.

"Isn't it six yet, where is that man of mine?" Carol laughed.

"It can't be six because he would be knocking on the door if it was," I said.

Just then we heard Mark knocking and Carol went to the door and threw herself in his arms just as she had seen me do with her brother.

"You were right David, it does feel pretty damn good when your woman throws herself in your arms when you walk through the door," he laughed.

"There is nothing like it in the world and it just does wonders for a man's ego," laughed David.

"David, since you're Carol's brother, or at least one of them, I guess I need to ask you something," said Mark hugging Carol.

"What's that, Mark?"

"Do I have your permission to ask Carol to marry me?"

"You've got it Mark, but I think you had better ask Carol the question not me," said David.

"I was going to wait until later, Carol, but I can't wait any longer; will you marry me, please?" said Mark.

Carol threw her arms around his neck almost cutting off his ability to breathe, "Yes my darling, yes," she said softly. "I love you so much, Mark."

"I love you too, doll face, and I never in my life would have thought I'd ever be saying that to any woman," chuckled Mark.

"That's the truth, Carol," said David. "It was only a couple of weeks ago that Mark here was telling me how terrible it would be to wake up to the same woman every day of his life. Now I have the feeling that he knows exactly what I meant when I told him how great I thought it was," said David.

I went to Carol and hugged her. "I'm so happy for you, Carol. Mark is a great guy even if he does drive me to drink sometimes, but then you, of all people, know how aggravating brothers can be."

"Congratulations sis," said David hugging her. "I just hope you two will be as happy as kitty cat and I are," he said.

He went over and shook Mark's hand. "Welcome to the family Mark," he said.

"Thanks David, I really do love this sister of yours but I'm not quite sure how it all happened," laughed Mark.

"Welcome to the brotherhood," laughed David. "I know exactly what you mean, I'm still trying to figure out how it all happened."

"Welcome brother-in-law to be," I said kissing him on the cheek. "Don't ask how, just enjoy the ride."

"The only thing I feel bad about is Bill, because I know he liked Carol too and Bill is such a great guy," said Mark.

"Darling, I explained to him when I broke my date with him for tomorrow night, that I loved him like a brother and was so grateful for his bringing me over here, but that I couldn't help it, I just loved you," said Carol.

"Unfortunately, we don't have any champagne to celebrate with, but let's fix ourselves some drinks at least," said David.

"You guys go make yourself comfortable. Carol and I will get the drinks," I said.

"Yes, go sit down you two and let the women folk take over," laughed Carol.

We went then and fixed their drinks and ours. Bringing them back Carol handed Mark his drink and I handed David his then we both sat down on their laps and cuddled into their respective arms. "Here's to love," I said.

"To love," chimed in the other three.

"Carol, let's go get dinner on the table before these men of ours think we are trying to starve them into submission," I laughed. We went out to the kitchen then and I hugged Carol to me when we were out of eyesight. "I'm so happy for you, sis, and I'm glad you didn't have to wait through dinner and small talk to find out whether or not he was going to propose tonight."

"Yes, thank God for small favors, because I was already a nervous wreck wondering," laughed Carol.

We set the table and called the men into dinner while we put the food on the table. "Oh something smells like meatloaf," said David.

"That might be because it is," I laughed. "Carol said it was one of your favorites. Mark, I hope you like it too," I said.

"As a matter of fact it is also one of my favorites," laughed Mark. "Besides, I'm not sure whether I would notice if you fed me dog meat tonight, I'm so happy since Carol said yes."

"You know, I was just thinking, we've got all that land on our new farm, why don't you two think about building a house on part of it so we'd be living close by each other," I said.

"That's a great idea, sugar," said David.

"Give me a day to get used to even thinking about being married," laughed Mark, "before you start talking about houses."

"You and Carol talk it over and you can let us know anytime," said David.

"Yes, give my poor darling free-wheeling bachelor time to say goodbye to his bachelorhood," laughed Carol.

"Me married, it just blows my mind away," laughed Mark. "Not that I don't love the idea now but I just don't know how it happened. I feel kind of like I'd been hit by a bolt of lightning."

"No not lightning, Mark, by cupid's dart," I laughed.

"Believe me Mark, once you stop reeling you're going to find out that you wished it had happened years ago and that bachelorhood isn't all it's cracked up to be as Bill tried to tell you the other night," said David. "When Lauren said yes to me I felt like I was Atlas and could balance the world on my shoulders."

"That's exactly how I felt when Carol said yes to me just now," laughed Mark. "I've never felt so protective of a woman in my life."

"Believe me, it just gets better and better," said David. "I know from experience."

While Carol and I cleared the table putting the food away and putting the dishes to soak in the sink, the men sat watching us like two spaniel puppies with the silliest grins on their faces.

"You two look like tom cats who have just found the biggest bowls of cream in the universe," laughed Carol.

"We did," they laughed.

"Let's go in the living room and put on some romantic music and dance," I said.

"Yes, let's because I'm dying to get this woman back in my arms," said Mark.

"Do you two have a favorite song?" I asked.

"Well, the first dance I danced with Carol last night they were playing *Till the End of Time* and it pretty well says everything I'm feeling," said Mark.

I put on *Till the End of Time* and the one to come right after was *I'll Walk Alone* and Mark and Carol just held each other in their arms and kind of swayed to the music and kissed from time to time.

"Do you think we ought to excuse ourselves and adjourn to our bedroom to leave them alone?" whispered David in my ear.

"Right after our song, I think it would be a great idea," I whispered back.

"What are you two whispering about?" asked Mark.

"Oh David was just making lurid suggestions to me," I laughed.

"Ooh, that sounds like fun," laughed Carol.

"Well remember what I told you this afternoon about riding a horse," I laughed.

"Ok you two, what are you talking about?" said Mark.

"I'll tell you later, darling," said Carol winking at me.

"Come on kitty cat, let's leave these two love birds to their own devices, because I have something for you in the bedroom," laughed David.

"Oh goody and I know just what it is," I laughed back at him.

"David, why don't I drive you to the base in the morning then Carol and Lauren can have your car to do whatever they have planned for the day?" said Mark.

"Thanks Mark, I think maybe I'll take you up on that," said David. "I assume you plan on spending the night here so it won't be out of your way?" said David.

"David!" said Carol.

"Well, don't tell me you two weren't thinking about it?" laughed David.

"Oh shut up, bro, you're embarrassing us," said Carol.

"Maybe I'm embarrassing you, but I know damn well I'm not embarrassing Mark, because I know how much I wanted Lauren in my arms after I asked her to marry me," said David.

"As a matter of fact I was already in his arms when he asked me, and it's a little hard to say no to a man who's just given you a night of love like David did me," I laughed.

"Well I had to take advantage didn't I, while you were still under the spell of my lovemaking?" laughed David.

"Oh come on, Tarzan, let's give these two a break and I'll play Jane for you," I said taking him by the hand and heading for the bedroom. "Night you two, let your consciences be your guide," I laughed.

When we were getting undressed David said, "I told you Mark was going to fall like a ton of bricks, didn't I?"

"I knew he was a gone goose when I talked to him on the phone this afternoon. I'm just surprised that you suggested he might want to spend the night; I would have thought you'd want to protect Carol from the big bad wolf," I laughed.

"Well, I figured they were going to do it anyway, so it was kind of my way of letting Carol know that I approved of her choice in men and that I knew it was going to happen sooner or later and she had my blessing," he chuckled.

"I'm glad you did for Carol's sake because she would worry about sneaking behind your back and after all she is over 21," I said. "Besides, I want her to know how wonderful it can feel when the man you love makes love to you," I said.

"I just hope, if she is still a virgin, that he's gentle with her," said David.

"Well while she's never told me explicitly that she is a virgin, I can pretty well tell you that I think she is and Mark can be a very gentle person when he chooses and where Carol is concerned I'm sure he will be."

"I want to know what you told her about riding horses, today," said David picking me up and dropping me on the bed then crawling in beside me.

"All I said was that there is nothing like the feel of a horse between your legs except when you have the man you love between them," I said laughing softly.

"What did Carol say?"

"She just told me I was terrible, but I suspect she was hoping she would soon find out for herself so she could make her own comparisons," I laughed.

"You women aren't the shrinking violets we men give you credit for, are you?" he laughed.

"Not once we've been made love to by the man we love," I said. "Actually, women talk just like you guys do, only we aren't making comparisons we are wondering what it will really be like."

"Did it live up to your expectations?"

"Darling, you surpassed anything I ever thought it would be," I said.

"Come here, kitty cat, because I really do have a surprise for you," he chuckled.

"Like I told you earlier, it's no surprise, but I can't wait much longer or I'm going to ravage you," I whispered.

"Ravage away, my beautiful kitten," he whispered as his body covered mine.

In the morning as David started to get out of bed without waking me, I put my arms up and brought his head down to mine for his morning kiss. "How in the hell do you know when I'm leaving your bed?" he whispered. "I try so hard not to disturb you."

"Even in my sleep I can tell when you get up during the night," I said. "I told you and I meant it that every minute you're not near me I'm in agony."

"Kitten, whenever I'm away from you my arms ache to hold you," he whispered. "By the way, I meant to tell you that I finally got your letter," he said.

"And...."

"I damn near had to go take a cold shower after reading it," he chuckled.

"Then it's a good thing I didn't say everything I was thinking and feeling when I was writing it," I said.

"When I am called for active duty, darling, please keep on writing me the same kind of letters because it makes me feel like I'm in your arms," he said.

"If it affected you that way, I'm just wondering what it did for the censors," I laughed.

"I'm just hoping it was some old maid and she got as big a thrill reading it as I did," he laughed. "As long as you're awake why don't you come sit with me while I shave," he said.

"Only if you promise I get to shower with you too," I laughed softly.

"You can bet on it, my love," he said.

When we got to the kitchen, Mark and Carol were already there. "Well, I guess Mark spent the night," I laughed grinning at David.

"Mark, was I wrong, isn't it the greatest feeling to wake up with Carol in your arms?" asked David.

"You're not wrong and I look forward to a lifetime of waking up to my darling," said Mark.

"Aren't women just the most wonderful things in the world?" asked David.

"They are indeed," said Mark.

"We kind of think the same thing about you men," said Carol.

"So what is on the agenda for today for you guys while I'm slaving away trying to teach my students how to fly?" asked David.

"What's this, are you an instructor now?" asked Mark.

"Oh in all the excitement last night I forgot to tell you. Yes, I'm going to be a flight instructor for the next six weeks before going on to B-17 flight training. I get my wings Monday and I want you and Carol there as well as Lauren, for the ceremony."

"We'll be there, David," said Mark.

"How about us four going out to dinner with Bill Friday night?" asked David.

"Wouldn't that kind of be rubbing salt in the wound that Carol chose me over him?" asked Mark.

"I don't think so, Bill isn't that kind of guy and he'll be happy for you and Carol," I said. "I'll call him and ask him and tell him to bring a date if he wants to so he won't feel like a fifth wheel."

"Oh and last night, Carol and I talked and we'd like to accept your offer to build a house on your property," said Mark, "if you're still sure you want us living that close to you."

"We're sure," said David and I together.

"Come on Mark, it's time we get going if you want me to report in on time," said David.

"I'll go get the car," said Mark, "and meet you out in front."

"Be right down," said David.

Pulling me into his arms he said, "You're ok with my leaving now, aren't you little one?"

"Yes, because for a while longer I'll know that you're coming home to me every night," I said kissing him.

"I'll be home to you every night if only in my dreams," he said kissing me back.

"I love you, David, and you are always in my dreams and prayers."

"I love you too, Kitten."

I went into the living room and placed a call to Bill.

"Hi Bill, it's Lauren."

"How goes it kiddo, you holding up ok?"

"Yes, it's easier now that David gets to come home every night for the next six plus weeks."

"I bet it is."

"Bill, are you very upset about Carol and Mark?"

"No not really, I didn't think I had a chance because I could see right from the start the way Carol looked at him, but I thought it was worth a try."

"How about joining the four of us for dinner at the Ritz Friday night and do bring a date if you want to?"

"That would be fun and I'll have to think about the date, but I just may," he laughed.

"I'm so glad you aren't pining away for Carol because you are such a super guy that I wouldn't want you hurt for anything."

"Set your heart at ease, Lauren. I'm not carrying a torch."

"Bill, if it is ok with you I'd like to extend my vacation through Monday so I'll come into work next Tuesday because David gets his wings on Monday. By the way you are invited to the ceremony."

"That's fine kiddo, take more time if you need to; you've got it coming."

"Well, we'll see what happens, but I want to save some time for when David gets activated because I know I won't be much use to anyone the day after he leaves."

"Did Mark propose to Carol?"

"Yes, last night he asked David if it was ok if he asked Carol to marry him and then he asked Carol and she accepted."

"Mark is a nice guy and I was right, he did fall for someone hook, line, and sinker. He even called me to make sure I wasn't too upset," he laughed. "What I wonder is what he would have said if I had told him I was terribly upset and was thinking about committing hara-kiri or something."

"Well considering that big lug really did fall hard, I don't think he would have given her up to spare your feelings, but I'm sure he would have felt really bad about it," I laughed.

"It was only a matter of time till the law of averages caught up with Mark and he fell head-over-heels for someone. I'm just glad it was someone as great as Carol," he laughed.

"We offered and they accepted our offer of having them build a house on our farm property so we can live close together."

"I'm glad because at least Carol will be close to you while David is gone. Are you just as crazy about David as you were when you brought him in to meet me, now that you've been married a whole three weeks?"

"I'm even more nuts about him, Bill; he is the kindest, sweetest, most loving guy I've ever met and every hour I love him more than I did the hour before."

"You four sure sound like you have it bad, all of you."

"We do!"

"Actually I met a very nice woman and we've been seeing each other and I just have the feeling it might get serious between us."

"Oh Bill I'm so glad; you deserve someone to love who loves you the way I love David. What's her name?"

"Beth Knight; she works for the Secretary of State's Office and I think I'm going to ask her to go with us Friday so you guys can meet her."

"I can hardly wait to meet her because she must be a super person too or you wouldn't be thinking seriously about her," I said.

"What time do you want to meet Friday?"

"How about seven, because Mark is staying here with Carol and four people are a lot of people trying to get ready to go somewhere at the same time, especially with only one bathroom," I laughed. "How is my fill-in working out?"

"Actually pretty good, she's not you, but she does a very good job keeping my calendar and everything else straight."

"Would you consider her a replacement if the time comes that I have to follow David to another base?"

"Yes, I would. In fact I was thinking that I'd have her stay and work with you for a couple of weeks so you can teach her all the details just in case you do become a camp-follower."

"I've been thinking about talking to David about me quitting my job because I'm going to have a lot of work getting the house ready and I don't see how I can do that and work at the same time."

"If it comes to that, why don't you just take a leave of absence for a year, because once he's overseas you may want a job to keep you occupied and by then you'll have the house in shape."

"I hadn't thought about that and I appreciate you thinking of it for me. I'd really miss seeing you every day and once David is called up I know I'm going to want to go back to work, so that may be my way out."

"I miss seeing you every day too; this gal doesn't make me laugh the way you do, little one."

"I'll talk to David about it tonight and we'll see you Friday night at seven at the Ritz," I said. "Do me a favor, give Mark a little bit of a hard time Friday night just so he'll know another guy thinks Carol is wonderful too. It just might keep him on the straight and narrow, although I think he's so in love with her he's already forgotten how much he liked being the swinging bachelor," I laughed.

"Will do Lauren, see you Friday."

"Bye Bill."

I went into the kitchen then to see what Carol was doing. "What are you up to, sis?" I asked.

"I'm just sitting here thinking about everything that happened last night and pinching myself to see if I'm awake or only dreaming," she laughed.

"Well, if it was a dream, then I had to be dreaming the same dream and so did David so I think you can safely believe it. I just called Bill and he's going to meet us at the Ritz Friday night at seven," I said.

"How did he sound; was he upset?"

"No not really, he said he could tell the way you looked at Mark the first night he didn't stand a chance. Besides he's seeing a gal by the name of Beth Knight and it is getting serious…he's going to bring her Friday night."

"Wouldn't that be fantastic if Bill would get married and the six of us could pal around together?" she laughed.

"I told Bill that I would go back to work Tuesday, but that I wasn't sure just how long I would continue because when David gets activated if he's stationed in the U.S. at another base, I'll want to go with him and then there is the decorating of the house. He suggested I take a year's leave of absence then I could return to work for him once the house is finished and when David is sent overseas."

"That sounds like a winning situation to me," said Carol. "Who knows by that time you could even be pregnant."

"That's not going to happen till David gets home for good," I said.

"Why not, was that your idea or David's?"

"David's. He said he wanted to be here when the baby was born and while I'd love to start a family right now, I've got to respect his wishes," I said. "I don't want him worrying about me when he's overseas and I would really like him to be here when we have our first baby."

"Well, I can understand his thinking, but at the same time I hate to see you have to wait too long to start that family, especially if you really intend to have 12 kids," she laughed.

"Not to change the subject, but have you and Mark set a wedding date yet?"

"We talked about it and since we want you and David to stand up for us, we've been thinking about making it fairly soon, probably in about two or three weeks."

"What about your family, they won't be able to be here?"

"I know and I regret that, but the most important members to me are here and besides, I want to tie that man of mine up all legal and nice," she laughed.

"I told Bill to give Mark a bit of a hard time Friday to keep him on his toes thinking that another man could still be very interested in you," I laughed. "I know I'm a stinker, but I just couldn't resist.

"Oh Lauren, I'm just gaga over that man and last night was pure heaven," she laughed.

"You can tell me it's none of my business, Carol, but I was wondering if you were a virgin?"

"*Was* is the operative word, sis."

"God I hope Mark was as gentle with you as your brother was with me," I said.

"Believe me he was, I never would have thought Mark could be that gentle, because I was shaking pretty badly when he undressed me, but he gave me the chance to back out and after that I was a gone goose."

"That's exactly what David did with me," I laughed.

"Doesn't it feel wonderful? All the talking us gals do about it and none of what we thought it would be like compared to what it is actually like," she laughed. "Mark made love to me at least four times last night and every time it just got better and better. I can't get enough of him and I never would have thought I'd feel like that about any man. All he has to do is look at me and I'm ready for him," she laughed.

"Wait until he pulls you into the shower and makes love to you, it is just beyond belief," I laughed.

"What I couldn't believe is how beautiful I thought his naked body was," said Carol.

"Oh I know exactly what you mean, because I think if I had my way David would never put on a stitch of clothing, because I think he is absolutely the most beautiful sight in the world," I laughed.

The phone rang and I ran to answer it.

"Hi kitten, it's me. I only have a second but I wanted to let you know that Mark is picking me up tonight so we'll both see you around 4:30. Mark is going to stay to dinner, then he says he wants to take Carol out somewhere because he is going to give her her ring tonight."

"I'm kind of glad because I have a couple of things I want to talk to you about."

"Anything serious?"

"Not really; I love you darling."

"Love you too kitten, see you tonight."

"Who was that?" asked Carol.

"David. Mark is picking him up tonight and Mark plans on having dinner here then taking you out afterwards."

"Wonder what that is all about?"

"I'll tell you if you promise to act really surprised later tonight," I said. "I know I shouldn't but I'm so excited that I can't help myself."

"Spill already!"

"Mark is going to give you your ring tonight."

"Oh Lauren, I'm so glad you told me so I can dress extra special tonight."

"Why don't you wear that gold sheath you were going to wear the night Mark proposed?"

"I think I will."

The phone rang again then. "This is getting to be the most popular phone number in town," I laughed.

"Hello."

"Hello Lauren, this is Wendy."

"Hi Wendy, what's happening?"

"Can you and David be in my office by 4:30 Monday night?"

"Yes, I think so; David gets off at 4:00 and I don't think it will take us more than a half hour to drive to your office. Why what's going on?"

"Everything on the house went through and we are going to close Monday night on it, so you can move in anytime you feel like it."

"That's fantastic, how did you get everything done so quickly?"

"Well the sellers were anxious and fortunately the funds got transferred right on time, so there was no reason to delay since the owners weren't living in the house anyway."

"I can't wait to tell David, now I've really got to get busy to get it fixed up and furnished," I laughed.

"See you two Monday night," said Wendy.

"Thanks Wendy for everything you've done."

Going back to the kitchen I said to Carol, "You're not going to believe this but that was Wendy and we close on the house Monday night and we can move in anytime once the papers are signed."

"My gosh we'd better get busy and make a list of what needs to be done and get started right away on Tuesday," said Carol.

"Carol, we were planning on you moving into the spare bedroom anyway, and if it isn't too small for you and Mark, why don't you ask Mark tonight about moving in when we do so that you can be on site when you start building your house?"

"That's a great idea. Is it further away from the base than you are now?"

"No, as a matter of fact it is closer which means that David will be home every night by 4:15," I laughed. "Also, as soon as we get it furnished and move in we can bring the horses over from the stables and you and I can ride every day if we want to."

"I'll be a pro in no time then. I intend to get that husband of mine on Lady with me because more than ever I'll want to nestle in his arms," she laughed.

"Mark will have to sub-lease his apartment and I'll have to sub-lease this one as well. I think we better start that list, so maybe that's what we ought to do today."

"David suggested we get another car and I talked him out of it, but now I'm wondering if I did the right thing," I said.

"Mark told me last night he wanted to get me a car so you and I won't be dependent upon him and David giving up their cars when we need one, so maybe Friday he and I can go out and look for a car."

"Another great thing about our living so close together is that we can share a car because there is no use of us each having the expense, not to mention the gas rationing for a car of our own."

"Carol, thank God you are here because I don't think I could handle all of this on my own. I know I should get busy and start that list but I can't seem to settle down; my mind is going a mile a minute," I laughed.

"Why don't we go out and get the key for Mark made; maybe some fresh air will settle you down a little," suggested Carol.

"Yes let's do that," I said. "I've got to make a list too of everything I need to talk to David about tonight because I know I'm going to forget something."

"I need to make a list of what I need to do for Mark's and my wedding as well. My God we're going to have lists coming out our ears," she laughed.

We went out then to the locksmith and got a key made for Mark. We stopped and picked up lunch so we wouldn't have to bother fixing it and we also picked up groceries enough to last through Monday.

"What would you think about stew for supper tonight," I asked Carol.

"Well it sounds fine to me and I know David likes stew, but I don't know about Mark," said Carol.

"I've seen Mark eat stew so let's just assume he likes it. That way we won't have so many dishes to do tonight and you can get ready to go out with Mark and I can talk things over with David."

"When we get back home let's get the stew cooking and then we'll sit down and start making lists," she laughed. "Thank God you at least know something about what Mark likes in the way of food, because I haven't a clue."

"Yes and thank goodness you know what David likes; that's another list we need to make out," I laughed.

"One thing, you and I definitely are going to be too busy to get in any trouble in the next few weeks," she laughed.

"Oh damn," I said coming out to where Carol sat at the kitchen table paring potatoes for the stew.

"What's the matter, sis?"

"My stupid period had to pick today to start and by tonight I'm going to be getting cramps so bad I won't feel like doing much of anything. Besides it's the first time since David and I've been together which is kind of embarrassing."

"Well I'm sure the guys are aware that women do have periods, so why worry about it?" she said. "I could be mean and say I'm glad it's you not me, but I'm due next week so people in glass houses shouldn't throw stones. At least you and David are married, whereas Mark and I aren't, which makes it even more embarrassing."

"Guess it had to happen sooner or later, but I'd just as soon it was later. I don't know why the Creator didn't put in a switch so you could shut it off when it's inconvenient," I laughed.

"Probably because He wanted to populate the planet and figured we'd have it shut off most of the time," she giggled.

"Ok now that we have the stew on cooking, the bread ready to pop in the oven to warm and the cheese cake made, let's start making a list of what we need to fix up in the house before we start making lists of furnishings," I suggested.

"Good thinking."

"By any chance do you remember what color the paint was in the house?" I asked.

"I remember the kitchen was white and I think the dining room had wallpaper, but that's about my limit," said Carol. "Maybe we ought to go out to the house tomorrow and take a look and measure the rooms before we start this list."

"Why don't I make a list of things I have to talk to David about tonight and you make a list of things you need to ask Mark about," I suggested

"Then we'll make a list of preparations we need to do for my wedding," said Carol.

I glanced up at the clock. "How in the heck did it get to be 4:00 so fast? The guys will be home soon so I guess we better just stick to the lists of what we need to ask them about and start fresh in the morning."

"Yikes, I didn't realize it was that late either," laughed Carol.

We just got our lists finished when we heard the men at the door. Both of us ran out and threw ourselves in their arms.

"Hi guys, welcome home," we chorused together as we hugged our men to us.

"Hi kitten," laughed David hugging me back.

"Hi beautiful," said Mark hugging Carol to him. "David I just can't get used to being met at the door like this," laughed Mark.

"Well get used to it," said Carol.

"Come on you guys, go get washed up for supper; we're eating a little early tonight because we've got a lot to tell you," I said.

While the men went to wash up, Carol and I put the bread in the oven to warm and made the coffee. By the time they came into the kitchen everything was ready to put on the table.

"So what is all this excitement about and what have you two been up to?" asked David.

"Wendy called today and you and I close on our house Monday night at 4:30 at her office," I said.

"That was fast," laughed David picking me up and swinging me around. "Did she say when we can move in?"

"Yes we can move in on Tuesday, which means Carol and I have an awful lot to do starting right now," I said.

"Mark, you and I have got to go look for a car tomorrow because Lauren suggested we move into their spare bedroom until our house is built, and she and I are going to need a car to get back and forth," said Carol.

"Guess I'd better get on the ball and find an architect," laughed Mark picking her up and swinging her around as well.

"Yes and we've got to set a definite date for our wedding, and along that line I was thinking about asking Bill if he would give me away," laughed Carol.

"Well I feel a little creepy about that since I stole you right out from under Bill's nose," said Mark.

"Don't worry about that, I talked to Bill today and he's dating a gal by the name of Beth Knight and he's bringing her tomorrow night to meet us all. From what he said, I gather that it is getting rather serious between them," I said.

"Oh," said Carol, "before I forget here's your key to this apartment and I have mine so we won't have to wake up David and Lauren to let us in."

"Slow down you two; you're racing a mile a minute, give us time to absorb what you're telling us," laughed David.

"Sit down you two so we can eat," I laughed. "We've been making lists of everything we have to do today and if you think we're on the fast track now you should have seen us this afternoon trying to think of everything we needed to make a list for."

"What kind of lists are you making?" asked David.

"A list of what we need to talk to you two about tonight, a list of what we need to get before we can start making a list of house furnishings we need, a list of dates of when we can move what into the house," I said stopping for air.

"In addition to all of that, I need to make a list of what we want in our house when we build it, furnishings for it, but first a list of things to do for our wedding," said Carol also stopping to catch her breath.

"You two sound like list babbling idiots," laughed Mark.

"Don't be a smart ass, darling," said Carol. "You two just get to go off to work every day, while Lauren and I try to organize everything so that we have a proper home for you to come home to every night and at the same time plan our wedding, my love."

"When women get the nesting instinct and go into full throttle, I think it's time we men get out of the way before they throttle the two of us," laughed David.

"Oh darling, I want you in on all of this, but it just feels overwhelming to me when I think of everything we've got to do because I want to get it all done and us moved into our house in the next three weeks," I said hugging him.

"You little goose, I'll help on weekends, then you have Carol to help you, and by gosh Mark is going to help as well," laughed David hugging me.

"How did I get volunteered?" laughed Mark.

"I love you dearly, my soon to be husband, but we girls can't do everything and it's for you as well as for David and Lauren," she said.

"I didn't say I wouldn't help, baby, I will, but you two look so frazzled like you were planning a major campaign," laughed Mark.

"If you think the generals running this war are planning campaigns, trying to organize what we are organizing in the time we have to organize it in would send them all running to the peace table in short order," I laughed.

"That's an idea, Lauren, let's tell them to stop the war and get us settled; by the time they got through war would be the farthest thing from their minds," said Carol.

"Maybe we should get Bill to bring up your suggestion at the next Cabinet meeting," laughed Mark.

Carol and I got up and started clearing the table and doing the dishes. "I don't know about you, David, but I'm taking my babbling idiot out tonight," said Mark getting up from the table.

"You keep this up and I may be a widow before I'm a bride," threatened Carol, but I noticed she went over to him and put her arms around him even as she made the threat.

David got up then and came over to me taking me in his arms. "Come on babe, come watch me shave," he said.

"Oh that's another thing I've got to tell you tonight too," I said my face turning pink.

"What's another thing?" asked David.

"I'll tell you while you're shaving," I said.

"Mark, come help me zip up my dress and we'll get out of here and leave these two alone...at least it will be two less voices heard from," said Carol.

David and I went into the bathroom so he could shave. "David, I hate to tell you this but I got my period today so I'm going to be off limits for a few days," I said my face turning scarlet.

"What are you so embarrassed about, kitten? Contrary to popular belief, men do know about such things," he laughed.

"Well it's the first time since I've known you and it is embarrassing to me," I said.

"Since you want a dozen kids, you must know that I knew there were going to be times when you were going to be off limits as far as sex was concerned," he said.

"It isn't just that, but I get really bad cramps my first day and I figure by the time we go to bed I'll be in agony," I said.

"Then I'll just hold you in my arms and get you a hot water bottle if you need it," he said. "Stop worrying, little one; while this may be the first time we both know it won't be the last. In fact, why don't we make it an early night and we can talk about all the things you wanted to talk to me about."

The tears started to come down my face and when he saw them he pulled me up and cradled me in his arms. "Baby, take it easy, nothing is really wrong," he said.

"Oh David, I don't know how I'm going to get through five days of not having you make love to me and what are you going to do for those five days?"

He started to laugh. "I'm sorry kitten, I don't mean to laugh at you, but it really is funny because you're the one worrying about getting through five days with no sex, not me. So for the next five days I just hold you in my arms at night and that is just fine, because that is almost as pleasurable as having sex with you."

"Thank you, darling, for trying to make me feel better, but don't men have to have sex every so often or they get their systems all screwed up or something?"

"Where in the hell did you get your information about the male anatomy and its needs?" he asked.

"I don't remember exactly but that is what I always heard," I said.

"Well kitten, you've got it all wrong, so let me finish shaving and then let's call it a night and I'll try to explain it all to you while I'm holding you in my arms."

"I'll let you finish shaving while I go put the teakettle on because I really do think I'm going to need that hot water bottle," I said. I took the hot water bottle from the cabinet and went out to heat up the water. By the time I'd finished David was finished shaving.

I went into the bedroom then and rummaged through my drawers for a nightgown and put it on.

"Kitten, that's the first time I ever saw you in a nightgown and you look adorable," said David. "Come on, sweetheart, crawl into bed and I'll be there in a minute."

When he slid in beside me he turned me so that I was lying on my side with my back to him and he took me in his arms and cradled me like I was some breakable doll and he laid his face along side mine and I did feel very comfortable and very loved.

"First thing on our agenda to talk about is this nonsense you heard somewhere about men's needs," he chuckled. "You'd be surprised how long we can go without sex if we have to and going without definitely does not screw up our system. What I think you may have heard is that if we get an erection and we don't have sex it can cause physical problems. Even that is overblown, it is just if it happens too often and there are other ways to take care of that too," he laughed softly. "So put your mind at ease because holding you like this is very pleasurable. Now that that is out of the way, what else did you want to talk to me about tonight?"

"I talked to Bill this afternoon while I was inviting him for Friday," I said. "The subject of my coming back to work came up and I told him I didn't know how I was going to get a house furnished for you and work full-time. He suggested that maybe I should take a year's leave of absence and that once you were overseas and the house was done, then I could come back to work for him. What do you think about it?"

"I think it's a great idea, but darling you do know it's more likely to be less than six months before I get my orders, so will you want to be off a full year?"

"Well I thought of that too, but I think Bill would take me back on whenever I needed to come back," I said. "He's going to use the girl who has been filling in for me but she won't actually have a job change status, she still will only be a temp for however long I need to be off the job."

"Then by all means, talk to Bill again and tell him that you need to have some time off."

"I had planned on working the next two weeks or so to get her up to speed on everything in the office, but now with the closing being on Monday, I think I'll ask him to start my leave Tuesday and that if she needs help I'll be available for her to call me."

"Knowing Bill and how much he adores you, I'm sure he will be agreeable to whatever you need," said David kissing me on the cheek. "Now what else did you have on your mind, little one?" he asked.

"I invited Bill to your wing ceremony Monday," I said. "I thought he'd really be hurt if we left him out."

"I'm glad you did sweetheart, because I really like Bill," said David.

"Carol said that Mark told her he wanted her to have a car so we decided that we would share it, especially once we moved into the house, and that way we could save the added expense of two additional cars, not only the purchasing of them, but the upkeep and the ration points for gas. Then you and Mark could each have a car since you'll both be going in opposite directions once we move."

"You two are like a well-oiled team, what one doesn't think of the other does," he chuckled. "I didn't realize I was getting such a thrift-conscious wife."

"David what do you think about the furniture in this apartment?"

"In what way?"

"Do you think it looks ok?"

"I guess so, I've never paid much attention, too busy looking at my beautiful wife to really notice, but I don't see anything wrong with it, why?"

"Well all of it came from thrift shops and cost Shelby and I hardly any money at all and I was thinking that Carol and I could scour the shops again to furnish the house, then every year for Christmas we'd buy one new piece of furniture and retire the old and that would be our Christmas present to each other. That way we won't have a big outlay for new furniture all at once and if you do decide you want to go back to Australia after the war, we won't lose a lot of money if we sell the furniture," I said.

"You really are thrifty," he laughed. "I've been thinking about after the war, and since Mark and Carol will be building a house on our property, I've about made up my mind not to go back to Australia, because this will be our home."

"Well our house is going to be awfully small when the kids come along."

"We've plenty of land and can always put on additions as we need them; and you'll have the horse farm you always wanted, because we can always add on to the stables as well. I'm sure that I can get work here after the war, because they will probably need even more broadcasters and I've heard about something they are working on called television and that might be an area I can expand into if they ever get it working. In addition, I don't have to worry about becoming a citizen to get work, because by marrying you I am a citizen."

"Darling, do you really mean you'd stay in this country after the war?"

"I'm really becoming a true-blue Yank," he chuckled.

"I hope if we do stay here that we can go to Australia for a visit because I'd like to meet the rest of your family and I'd also like to see where my darling husband grew up," I said.

"Oh we'll go back for a visit, because I want you to meet the rest of the Benton household, and I also want to show you Australia because I think you'd really like it."

"I'd love any place as long as you were there with me," I said. While we had been talking I had begun to relax and as the hot water bottle had cooled off I dropped it on the other side of the bed, because suddenly the cramps were gone.

"Do you want me to reheat that for you?" asked David.

"No my love, my cramps are all gone. I never realized some of the other advantages of marriage; talking to you took all the tension out of me and what used to be a two-day siege of cramps became a few hours and the only explanation I have for it is that I'm totally relaxed here in your arms and talking with you."

"If you turn on your stomach, kitten, I'll rub your back for you and that should relax you even more," said David.

So I turned over and his strong hands began to massage my back and I began to purr because it felt so good.

"I have the feeling when I do get pregnant you are going to be very nice to have around," I laughed softly.

"I hope so babe, because I always want to take care of you," he said.

We heard the outside door open then and a soft knock on our door.

"Are you two decent? Can I come in?" said Carol.

"We're decent enough, sis, so come on in. What's up?"

"I just wanted to show you my ring," she said holding out her hand.

"It's beautiful, Carol," I said.

"You look like you're feeling better, sis," said Carol.

"I do feel loads better and this marvelous brother of yours has me so relaxed that even my cramps have disappeared."

"Well I won't disturb you any further. I just couldn't wait to show you my ring and besides Mark is waiting for me and I intend to show him my appreciation in full tonight," she laughed.

I heard David laughing and turned to see what was so funny. "I never thought I'd hear my older sister come up with such unladylike phrases," laughed David.

"She does seem to have become almost as forward as me; maybe we are a bad influence on each other," I laughed.

"It just tickles the hell out of me what you two come up with," said my husband, "especially when both of you look so demure and ladylike."

I turned then so I could put my arms around my husband and I yawned as I did so. "You've got me so relaxed I may conk out on you at any time, love," I said. "But before I do, do me a favor, please?"

"What do you want, sweetheart?"

"Tomorrow when you're driving into work with Mark, tell him to explain things to Carol the way you did me tonight, because I know she is due to get her period next week and she's as worried about it as I was and as embarrassed."

"Ok, I'll let Mark know that he needs to be prepared to let Carol know that we men can make it through five days without sex and that we know about female anatomy," he chuckled.

"I love you so much, my darling, every day I learn more about you and from you and maybe by the time we've been married 50 or 60 years I'll know enough not to be embarrassed by anything because I know you will understand and explain to me if I start getting embarrassed."

"I love you too, kitten, and I'm learning a lot from you as well and we've quite an adventure ahead of us I think. Now go to sleep because I'm tired too tonight and even if you'd been available I don't think I could have done much about it," he said kissing me tenderly.

In the morning I woke as David was getting out of bed. "How are you feeling, sweetheart?" he asked.

"I'm fine thanks to my adorable husband," I said pulling his head down and kissing him good morning.

"Why don't you go back to sleep for a while, you had quite an emotional night last night and probably a little extra sleep would do you a world of good," he said.

"I don't want to go back to sleep. I want to come watch you shave then get you breakfast," I said.

"Then come on and watch me shave, though I don't think I'll ever fully understand your fascination about my shaving," he laughed.

"I don't fully understand it myself," I laughed. "I used to watch my dad shave and it always gave me such a feeling of security and peace, but it's more than that when I watch you shave," I said. "It's hard to explain, I just feel so much love for you because it's such a masculine occupation it makes me feel so feminine to be sitting watching you. Besides I love to watch you all the time and especially when you're half naked or fully naked; you have such a beautiful body."

"It must be love," he laughed, "because I sure as hell can't see what is beautiful about a man's body, but if you say so, I'll take you at your word."

"Well, maybe you have to be a woman to fully appreciate the beauty of a man's body, just as I would have to be a man to understand what you see beautiful about my body. Carol says she loves to watch Mark shave too and she thinks his body is beautiful, so it must be strictly a feminine thing."

"Not to change the subject, kitten, but what do you think Bill's new girl will be like?"

"I haven't the faintest idea, but I just hope she is everything that Bill is looking for in a woman and that if it is truly serious that she loves him as much as I love you."

"I don't think Bill is the type of guy to get involved with anyone but someone as sweet and as nice as you, my love."

"I was telling Carol the other day that Bill has always been like a second father or maybe I should say brother, because he's not that much older than we are, and he was the first man who ever made me feel feminine and I'll always be grateful to him for that."

"How did he make you feel feminine?" asked David.

"He knew from the day he hired me that I knew a lot about things that women aren't supposed to know about and that are supposed to be the strict province of the male of the species, but he always opened doors for me and called me 'little one' and made me feel truly feminine and no one had ever done that for me not even my beloved dad, so it was the first time in my life I thought maybe I wasn't such a tomboy after all."

"All finished," said David wiping the soap from his face. "Did you say something about breakfast?"

"Yes sir," I said saluting him. "Coming right up."

As I was finishing up breakfast, Carol came out to the kitchen. "Enough left for Mark and me or should I get more breakfast going?" she asked.

"More than enough. Where is that man of yours anyway?"

"Oh he's coming, he got something of a late start this morning because I talked him into having sex just one more time this morning," she laughed.

"Carol, for God's sake, you are becoming as lustful as my bride here," laughed David, "and I bet Mark just hates that just like I do."

"Well bro, until I met Mark, I didn't know how wonderful sex is and how good it feels because most of us females don't get to practice like you men," she laughed.

"It must be Mark and I hit the jackpot and got the only two sex-starved women in creation."

"Unfortunately, I think there are more of us than the other kind," she laughed.

"What are you guys talking about?" asked Mark coming into the kitchen.

"Sex-starved females," said Carol.

"Oh the very best kind of female," laughed Mark.

"Carol was just telling us she can't keep her hands off you, and how much you hate it," I giggled.

"I could swoon from pure enjoyment, I hate it so much," said Mark.

"Carol and Lauren, make sure both of you are ready to go car shopping when I get back from taking David to the base," said Mark.

"Are you sure you want to take Lauren?" laughed David. "Because she is going to make you look very mechanically stupid."

"Oh I'm used to Lauren making me look mechanically stupid and besides she drives a harder bargain than I do," laughed Mark.

"Don't forget guys, you need to get home on time tonight if at all possible because we have to meet Bill and his new girl at the Ritz at seven and with four of us sharing the same bathroom we might get a log jam," I said.

"Can't you and Carol shower in the afternoon?" asked David.

"Probably not because when we get through buying a car, Carol and I have to go out to the farm and make some notes on paint and wallpaper and take some room measurements."

"If we happen to get home early from that we'll get our showers so that you two men can have time to shave and shower," said Carol.

"Why don't you leave the trip to the farm until Saturday, then Mark and I can go with you and help with measuring?" said David.

"I almost forgot you'll be home tomorrow and Sunday, I think that's a great idea because that is one of the tomboy things I'm not very good at and that's measuring," I laughed. "I'm just terrible at figuring fourths, and eights and whatnot."

"Saturday let's go to the farm and when we get done there, we can go over to the stables so I can see the new mare and maybe the four of us can go riding," said David.

"Yes Mark, I want you to meet Lady because she's such a beautiful mare and so much closer to the ground than Storm," laughed Carol.

"Well, I'm not guaranteeing I'll ride her with you, but I keep hearing all this propaganda that it's so romantic riding double, I just might work up my courage and try it," laughed Mark.

"Then Sunday we can laze around the house and you guys can help us with our lists," I said.

"Come on Mark, we've got to get going," said David. "This sister of mine is screwing up your timing mechanism."

We went to the door with them and kissed them goodbye.

"This is the life," said Mark.

"You better believe it," said David.

"You feeling better this morning, Lauren?" asked Carol.

"Much better, and just for your education I was informed by my husband last night that men have a working knowledge of the female anatomy so I got embarrassed for no reason at all," I laughed.

"What did he say about all that stuff we've always heard about men having to have sex or it screws up their system?" she asked.

"Apparently that was all wrong too," I laughed. "I asked David to talk to Mark so that when you get your period he can explain it all to you the way David did for me."

"Well we can always get together afterward and compare notes just to make sure they are telling us the truth. In some ways I'm not as worried about Mark not getting sex as I am about me not getting it," she laughed.

"I know exactly what you mean," I laughed.

"Guess we better get dressed because Mark will be back soon and you know how he gets if we're one minute late," said Carol.

"I was thinking about this afternoon; let's sit down and start our lists, then maybe after reading them the boys can come up with things we haven't thought of on Sunday. We can also get our showers in the afternoon so we don't get a log jam in the bathroom tonight with all of us trying to get ready at once. By the way, how did Mark like the gold sheath?"

"Well I got a very satisfying whistle when he saw me in it," laughed Carol.

We were waiting on the sidewalk when Mark came back from dropping David off at the base. As we got in the car, I asked Mark what kind of car he was thinking about.

"I thought maybe we could find a little convertible like yours, because they are so much fun to ride around in during the spring, summer and fall with the top down."

"They also can be cold in the winter," I said.

"I suppose, but humor me, I've never bought a car for a woman before," said Mark.

We hit several of the used car lots and finally found what we were looking for at the fourth one. After I gave my ok on it, much to the relief of the salesman, we went into the office to negotiate price. By the time I got through with the salesman and the owner of the place, we'd gotten the car down in price to reasonable terms and Mark wrote them a check for it.

"I just love putting those used car salesmen through the hoops," I laughed, "especially the ones that try to sell you a lemon based strictly on its looks."

"That guy probably will never wait on another woman as long as he lives," laughed Mark.

"Well at least he'll think twice about trying to convince another woman that a little old lady was the one owner of the car," I laughed.

"I'm going to drop you guys then head for work and I'll pick David up tonight on my way home so you won't have to bother and can clear out of the bathroom before we guys get home," said Mark.

As he pulled up to the curb and stopped, I got out and then realized that Carol was still kissing him goodbye. "Carol, if you don't stop he'll never get to work then you won't get to build your house," I laughed.

"Ok, ok, I'm coming," said Carol.

"Let's start on your wedding list first," I said as we sat down at the kitchen table with paper and pen. "Do you want a church wedding, or a town hall wedding, or I bet Bill could even arrange for a senator to marry you guys?"

"Well, since we've no one to invite to the wedding except the wedding party, how about finding a Justice of the Peace?"

"How about in the base chapel where David and I were married? I'll call Captain Hollenbeck if you are interested and see if due to your relationship to David you could be married there?

"Do you really think it's possible? Because I would love that."

"What about your wedding attire—gown or suit?"

"Suit I think, I've a cream one that should do nicely."

"Wedding rings—did Mark get the wedding ring when he got the engagement ring or do we need to remind him that he needs to get one?"

"No, he got the wedding band to go with the diamond."

"How about a ring for Mark, do you plan on having one for him?"

"I hadn't thought about that but I definitely want to make sure he's branded so I guess I'd better plan on buying one for him."

"Wedding bouquet?. . .Forget that one, I'll buy one for you as my wedding present to you."

"You don't have to do that, Lauren. I don't need a bouquet."

"I want to, sis, and besides it makes it feel more like a wedding—Bill bought me mine."

"Honeymoon?"

"We've decided to postpone having a honeymoon until after we get the house built and we move in...that way we'll stay on schedule and besides maybe by then this dumb war will be over and we can go somewhere really exotic."

"Take some advice from an old married lady, make every day a honeymoon because believe me a place does not a honeymoon make."

"Wedding date?"

"Next Saturday."

"Anything we've forgotten?"

"Not that I can think of, Lauren."

"Ok, first things first, let me call Captain Hollenbeck and see if we can get the chapel for your wedding."

I went in and phoned Captain Hollenbeck.

"Captain, this is Lieutenant Benton's wife Lauren, you married us in the chapel about a month ago."

"Yes Lauren, I remember you and the lieutenant very well? What can I do for you?"

"Lieutenant Benton's sister is getting married next Saturday and we were wondering if by any chance she could be married in the same chapel in which David and I were married. Her fiancé isn't military, but I thought maybe being David's sister, you might make an exception for her?"

"As long as she is related to an officer on active duty, that is no problem. I just checked the chapel calendar and there is an opening on Saturday at 1300 hrs."

"Please put us down for then, Captain, and you don't know how much we appreciate it. The bride's name is Carol Benton and the groom's is Mark Purcell."

"Do they also want a non-denominational wedding?"

"Yes please, and thank you again so much."

"My pleasure, Mrs. Benton," said Captain Hollenbeck.

"Carol," I yelled running into the kitchen and hugging her, "you are to be married in the base chapel at 1:00 P.M. a week from Saturday and I told them to make it a non-denominational ceremony like David and I had."

She jumped up then and hugged me back. "Thanks sis, it sure is nice to have influential in-laws," she laughed.

"I've got to call Bill about something anyway, do you want me to ask him to the wedding?"

"Definitely, in fact I'd like to ask him to give me away if you think that isn't too tacky a thing to do under the circumstances."

"I think Bill would love it if you did."

We went into the living room and I called Bill.

"Hi Bill, it's Lauren."

"Hi little one, what's up?"

"Carol and Mark are getting married at the base chapel a week from Saturday at 1:00 P.M.; you are invited and Carol is standing here and has something to ask you, so I'll put her on, but then I have something else to talk to you about when she's finished, so don't hang up."

"Ok Lauren, I won't. Put Carol on."

"Bill, if you don't want to do it under the circumstances, which I can understand, say so, but I'd like it very much if you gave me away at the wedding."

"I'd be honored, Carol. Thank you for asking me."

"Thanks for being one of the sweetest men in this whole blooming world," said Carol. "I'll put Lauren back on."

"Bill, David and I discussed the job situation last night and he agrees that I should take a leave of absence for whatever time we have before he gets sent overseas," I said. "But the kicker is I'd like to begin it now because we just found out that we will be closing on the farm on Monday and can move in anytime after that, so I've got just scads of things to do to get everything ready because I'd like to move into the house before David has to leave."

"That should be no problem, Lauren, as long as the temp can call you if she runs into any problems."

"Bill, you are such a dear, this takes a load off my mind."

"You do know Lauren, that you can come back to work for me anytime you want to, so the leave doesn't have to be for a full year if things work out that you don't need all that time."

"Remind me to give you an extra special hug tonight when I see you; you don't know how much I appreciate everything you've done and are doing for me and David," I said.

"Well, you're kind of a special person, Lauren, and I really haven't done all that much. See you tonight."

"Thanks again, Bill. See you tonight."

"Carol, how about if we go purchase Mark's ring and we can also stop at the florist and I can order your wedding bouquet?"

"Do you think we'd have time to run out to the farm and check the décor in each room this afternoon?" asked Carol.

"I think that would be cutting things a bit fine if you want us to be able to get our showers before the men get home," I said.

"Guess you're right there, well let's just run out to the jewelry store, then if there's time we can stop at the florist, otherwise, you can just call them. You know, we ought to start our own consulting business, you and I between us can out-organize any general living or dead," laughed Carol.

"Once we get everything done, let's think about that, because you just might have a gem of an idea there," I laughed back at her.

We went out then and Carol bought Mark his ring and then we stopped at the florist shop and I ordered a bouquet of lilies of the valley and white roses for Carol. The florist promised to deliver it to the apartment by no later than ten on a week from Saturday. We went home then and Carol took her shower then I took mine. We decided to just wait for the men to come home, in our robes, so that our dresses wouldn't get all wrinkled. I pressed David's uniform in case he would want to wear it instead of civvies and we sat down to wait.

At exactly 4:30 the door opened and the guys came in. As usual Carol and I threw ourselves in their arms.

"You two look like the cats who ate the canary," laughed David.

"Well you'll be proud of us," I laughed hugging him. "We've got everything planned for Mark's and Carol's wedding from the location to the bride's bouquet and we've even taken our showers so you guys will have the bathroom to yourselves tonight."

"You girls have been busy," laughed Mark. "And to think you've only had since ten this morning after we bought the car to organize all this."

"Have we got time to have a drink before we have to get ready?" asked David.

"More than enough time, let me get it for you."

After Carol and I made the drinks for the guys we sat them down in the chairs, sitting on their lap, to tell them everything we'd arranged about the wedding.

"I talked to Captain Hollenbeck and he said since Carol was related to an active duty member of our military, that he would be more than happy to marry her and Mark in the base chapel a week from Saturday, at 1300 hours," I said.

"I would never have thought about the base chapel," laughed David.

"We talked to Bill and he's going to give Carol away," I said.

"Are you sure Bill was ok with that, not just being nice?" asked Mark.

"Very ok," said Carol. "I also bought your wedding ring today, Mark,"

"And I bought Carol's wedding bouquet which will be delivered here a week from Saturday by no later than ten," I said.

"Geeze, you two have been busy little beavers today," laughed Mark.

"Well, Mark and I made a couple of plans too coming home tonight," said David.

"What plans?"

"We are taking you two ladies out for a celebration dinner after the closing Monday night," he said. "Also Bart arranged for the horses to be taken to the farm on Tuesday and he'll have one of his men water and feed them every day until we get organized enough to move into the house so we can take over."

Carol and I let out little squeals of delight and hugged our guys to us.

"Me thinks they like the plans," laughed David.

"I talked to Bill today too about starting my leave immediately and he said to go right ahead and that anytime I want to come back to work I can whether it is six months from now or a year," I said.

"You know, David, I'm really beginning to think these two women of ours could out-organize any general in the entire U.S. military and besides they are so much prettier than any general I've ever seen," laughed Mark.

"I agree with you, especially about them being prettier," laughed David.

"Ok you organizing demons, what's on the agenda for tomorrow?" asked Mark.

"We thought we'd go to the farm and take room measurements and check on décor, then we'd go to the stables and ride Storm and Lady," I said.

"Well I'm still not sure about the riding Lady part," laughed Mark.

"Carol has become quite the horsewoman and you'd be very safe, all we ask is that you keep an open mind about it," I laughed.

"What about Sunday?" asked David.

"Well Carol and I figured we'd work on our lists Saturday night then on Sunday you guys could go over them and see if we've forgotten anything, but otherwise we'd just play it lazy and lounge around the house for the day."

"Sunday sounds heavenly to me," laughed David.

"Ok you two, go shower and shave and when you are finished Carol and I will get on our dresses and we'll be ready to go," I said.

"David, why don't you go first," said Mark, "while I make out a little with my bride."

"Ok with me," laughed David, "but it better be a fast make-out if we're supposed to meet Bill at seven."

"Don't worry, David, it's going to be a very limited make-out session because I don't intend my hair should get all mussed up since I just got finished doing it," laughed Carol.

"Come on sweetheart, you can watch me shave and leave the field to these two," laughed David.

"Have we got time for me to hold and kiss you for a little bit before you start shaving?" I said putting my arms around him.

"There's always time for that, kitten," he said bending his head to kiss me and pulling me closer in his arms.

"Mmmmm, that feels so good," I whispered, hugging and kissing him back.

"I love the way you purr in my arms," he said.

"I love being in your arms. Ok enough; you need to get your shower and shave," I laughed. "Why not take your shower first and I'll lay out your clothes while you are doing that then I'll come back while you shave?" I said. "What do you plan on wearing, uniform or civvies?"

"Since I'll be out in public it will have to be uniform," he said.

"I pressed your uniform so put the one you're wearing in the hamper and I'll get it ready for Monday," I said giving him a peck on the cheek as I went into the bedroom to lay out his clothes for him.

I heard the shower shut off and went back to sit with him while he shaved. "You two really have done an amazing job of organization so far," he said smiling at me.

"Carol and I make a great team," I laughed. "In fact we were thinking this afternoon that if we manage to make all of this go off without too many hitches, she and I might want to think about starting our own consulting business, then we could pick and choose our hours of work and jobs."

"You might have a good idea there, because I think the two of you work so well together and that would allow you to work at home when I get back and we start having kids."

"I thought maybe I'd broach the subject to Carol seriously after she and Mark get married then she could talk it over with him."

"Why don't you do that, kitty cat?" said David.

"By the way, I forgot to properly thank you for thinking about bringing the horses to the farm next week," I said.

"Maybe by Sunday night or Monday night you can do just that," he laughed softly, wiping the remaining lather from his face.

I got up then and put my arms around his neck and kissed him lingeringly. "Well consider this a down payment till then."

"Oh kitten, I love you so much," he whispered.

"I love you too with all my heart," I whispered back. "Now go get dressed and I'll go see if Mark and Carol are anywhere near ready.

When I got out in the living room Carol was ready and waiting on Mark. "I thought it was we women who were always supposed to be the last ready to go and here you and I stand waiting on our men," she laughed.

"Probably it's like everything else we always heard, completely false," I laughed.

David came out of the bedroom then and I let out a long slow whistle. "Hey flyboy, want a date?" I asked.

He came up to me and put his arms around me. "Sure do little lady," he laughed.

Mark came in then and Carol whistled at him. "Hey big boy how about a date?" she laughed.

He too came and put his arms around her. "You better believe it, you scrumptious little tart," he laughed.

"Come on David, let's you and I go get the car before these two women corrupt us entirely," said Mark.

"We'll be down by the time you get here," we said.

"We've got to have found the handsomest men on this planet," I said.

"I agree; I just love the looks we get when we are on their arms," laughed Carol.

"The women just almost drool, then they look at us like they'd like to kill us; it's so good for a girl's ego," I laughed.

The fellows drove up just as we got to the sidewalk. "Can we give you two beauties a lift?" asked David jumping out to hold the door for us.

"I don't know if you can afford us," laughed Carol, "our prices are pretty steep."

"This is fun," I laughed. "I've never gotten to snuggle in the backseat before."

"Well we tossed a coin to see who drove and Mark lost and I couldn't be happier," laughed David.

When we got to the Ritz, Bill was on the sidewalk waiting for us with a beautiful redheaded girl on his arm.

"About time you guys showed up," laughed Bill.

"Well we almost didn't because David and I were having such a good time snuggling in the backseat, we had half a notion to make Mark keep driving while we made out," I laughed.

"David, Lauren, this is Beth Knight, Beth this is my secretary who has deserted me in favor of her husband for a while," said Bill. "And this is Mark and Carol who are soon to be married, Carol is David's sister and Mark is my best friend."

"Hi Beth, we're so glad to meet you," I said.

"Hi Beth, nice to meet you," said Carol, David, and Mark.

"Come on let's go because the place is rapidly filling up," said Bill.

We made small talk while we were being seated and our drink orders taken. "So Mark, hell froze over and you've finally decided to take the plunge," laughed Bill. "Carol, I would never have believed any woman could get this guy alter-bound."

"It was a struggle, Bill, but I finally managed," laughed Carol.

"When are you getting married?" asked Beth.

"A week from today at the base chapel," said Carol.

"I was Lauren's Maid of Honor and I also gave her away," laughed Bill, "but this time I only have to escort Carol down the aisle."

"Afraid your Maid of Honor dress will just have to be retired this time around," laughed Mark.

"And to think it was only a few weeks ago that you sat here telling me that you could never settle down to just one woman," laughed Bill. "My how times have changed."

"You know Bill, I'm still not sure how it all happened and so fast, but I'm just glad it did," said Mark.

"I keep telling him not to spend time wondering how it happened, just to relax and enjoy it," laughed David.

"Oh believe me, I'm enjoying," said Mark leering at Carol.

"I'm just glad you were waiting for us, Bill, because I hate running the gamut of those drooling females we have to put up with when these two handsome men take us out," I laughed.

"Well, I've got some news for you four for a change," said Bill.

"Oh did they make you Secretary of State?" laughed David.

"No even better, I asked Beth here to marry me and she has accepted me," said Bill taking Beth's hand.

"Oh Bill, I'm so happy for you both, when's the big day?" I said.

"We haven't actually set a date yet, I just asked her last night," said Bill and I could see the happiness in his face.

"Beth, you are getting the second most wonderful man in the world, next to David," I said.

"I think I'm getting the most wonderful guy in the entire universe," said Beth shyly smiling at Bill.

"We've got to be the three luckiest women in the world," said Carol, "finding three such great men who are also handsome."

"It must be something in the air this spring," laughed David. "Welcome to the lucky men's club, Bill."

"Beth, anything you want to know about Bill I can probably tell you since I've worked for this guy for over five years now," I said.

"Don't you dare tell her all my faults," laughed Bill, "let her find out for herself that I have feet of clay."

"Don't you believe it, Beth. Bill is just a super guy," I said.

"Well, Lauren, you just lost out being the girl all three of us men fight over to dance with tonight," laughed Mark.

"You mean the only girl you had to fight over," I laughed.

"So Beth, tell us all about how you and Bill met and how all this came about," I said.

"I work for the Secretary of State's Office," said Beth, "so I've known Bill ever since he came to Washington. About a month ago he ask me for a date and I went out with him and it just kind of progressed from there."

"I wanted to ask her for a date the first time I saw her, but you know me, I'm kind of backward where beautiful women are concerned," said Bill hugging Beth around the shoulders, "but I finally screwed up my courage and asked her out and it's taken me from then to now to muster the courage to ask her to marry me. I just couldn't believe it when she accepted, but I'm sure glad she did."

"You two make a darling couple," said Carol. "It's going to be so much fun for the six of us to pal around together."

"I'm glad Lauren has the four of you to look after her while I'm away," said David.

"Oh don't worry, David, we'll have her thoroughly corrupted by the time you get back," laughed Bill.

"Don't you change a hair on this tomboy's head," chuckled David, "or I'll sic her onto all of you when I get back."

"How can you call her a tomboy?" asked Beth. "Lauren looks like a very feminine lady to me."

"Oh she's a tomboy, but she's the most gorgeous feminine tomboy I ever ran into," laughed David.

"David and Lauren just bought a five acre farm in Virginia and Mark and Carol are building a house on their property," said Bill. "I've been meaning to ask you, David, does that mean you plan on staying in this country after the war?"

"Yes, I'm sure I'm going to stay here because everyone I love is here," said David.

"Would you consider maybe letting us build a house on your property too?" asked Bill.

"Definitely, if you're interested," said David.

"Oh Bill that would be so great having you and Beth close to us too," I said.

"What do you think Beth; is it worth exploring or did you have something else in mind?" asked Bill looking at her.

"Wherever you are, darling, is ok with me," said Beth.

"We're going out to the farm tomorrow to take measurements, why don't you guys join us then you can see the farm for yourselves," said David.

"Do you ride, Beth?" I asked.

"I've ridden once or twice but I'm no great shakes at it," said Beth.

"Oh thank God, someone else who isn't nuts over horses," laughed Mark.

"Well, we've a stable with two horses in it already and I'm teaching Carol and Mark how to ride, so I could teach you at the same time and then maybe the six of us could go riding," I said. "Because I know Bill likes to ride and it is so romantic with your man riding behind you and you snuggled into his arms."

"Maybe we could stop and see if Bart has a horse for sale that we'd like to consider buying," said Bill.

"I'm sure he does and you can meet Lady, the horse David bought for Carol," I said.

"It's a date then. What time tomorrow?"

"How about if we all meet at the farm at eleven tomorrow, that way none of us have to get up too early," said David.

"Where is this farm, David?" asked Bill.

"You just turn left out of the stables where Lauren keeps Storm, then go down the road about half a mile," said David.

"David and Mark arranged for the horses to be brought to the stables on Tuesday and to have one of Bart's grooms look after them at the farm until we get moved in," I said.

"These two nuts have organized everything right down to dotting the i's and crossing the t's," laughed David. "You should see the mountain of lists they've made, they make a general planning a military campaign look like a rank amateur."

"As a matter of fact, we've about decided to hire them out to the Army to do their organization for them," laughed Mark. "Beth, maybe the State Department would be interested in contracting for their services."

"I've often thought the State Department could do themselves a big favor if they just allowed us women to organize things for them," laughed Beth.

"I think we'd better order because that waiter is giving us the eye," said David.

We ordered dinner then and while we were waiting for it to be brought to us we told Bill and Beth everything we'd been organizing and all the news from the four of us.

"I'm just sorry Beth that we don't have another bedroom we could offer to you and Bill while you build your house," said David.

"Well since we both work in the city we might as well stay in my apartment until it is built and that way Beth can sub-lease her apartment," said Bill.

"Washington is going to be ecstatic with three apartments becoming available in such a short time," I laughed.

"If you could get everyone who has an apartment in this town to marry someone else who has one, the housing shortage would definitely be a thing of the past," Carol laughed. "That reminds me Beth, you are invited to our wedding too."

"There she goes leapfrogging again," laughed Mark. "These two jump from one subject to another so fast that sometimes David and I have trouble keeping up with them."

They brought our food then and as we ate we continued to discuss our plans.

"I have a feeling we may be overwhelming Beth with all the plans since she only got engaged last night," I said. "Don't be afraid to stop us if we start making too many plans involving you and Bill and you want more time to think about them," I said.

"Well things have been moving kind of fast for me to absorb, but so far I like everything I've heard," said Beth. "I have the feeling you, Carol and I have a lot in common and I want to be your sister too."

"I only wish you were on leave too so that we could get together and make our plans," I laughed.

"As a matter of fact, when Bill proposed to me last night he asked me to turn in my resignation because he didn't want me working after we were married, which I did this morning so in two weeks I'll be available," said Beth.

"That's great, another pair of hands and another brain to help organize, " laughed Carol and I together smiling at her.

"Do you get the feeling that we men might just be redundant in this project," laughed David.

"Never, love," I laughed. "Don't you know everything we are doing is aimed at keeping our men happy and satisfied?"

"Come on you guys, let's adjourn this knitting society to the bar and the dance floor because I'm longing to get Beth back in my arms," said Bill.

"Topper of an idea," laughed Mark.

"I'll vote for adjournment too," said David.

I noticed that on the way in Bill and Mark hung back a little from the rest of us.

"Oh I'd love to be the fly on the wall listening to that conversation," I said to David.

"I'm not worried, you'll worm it out of Mark on the way home," laughed David.

"You're darn right I will because my curiosity is killing me," I said.

After we were seated and our drinks were brought David turned to me, "Come on kitty cat, they're playing our song,"

All of us got up then and went out to the dance floor. "Oh darling, I'm so glad you asked me to dance the first night I met you and I love being in your arms even more now than I did then," I said.

"I'm just glad that Mark talked you into coming that night," said David, "and I like having you in my arms even more now than then and I wouldn't have thought that was possible then."

"You know, David, I've been thinking, with all three of us living on the farm, we're fast running out of room already and probably eventually all of us are going to need to expand our homes to accommodate the kids we'll have."

"I've kind of been thinking about that too and Mark and I discussed it. Mark wants to pay me for his plot of land and probably Bill will too, then

Mark also suggested that we might want to think about going in together and purchasing that five acres next to the farm. Do you think Bill would want to be included in that too?"

"Yes, I think he will. What do you think of Beth?"

"I think she and Bill make a nice couple and I think they suit each other's personalities," said David.

"I have a feeling that is what Mark and he were talking about because I think that Mark thinks his proposing to Beth was a little too fast after losing out to Mark for Carol's affections."

"You could be right, but then Bill said he'd been dating her, so maybe he wasn't as gaga for Carol as we thought, it was just a man's natural reaction to a beautiful woman who he had just met," said David.

"Keeping his options open, so to speak?" I said.

"Exactly."

When we got back to the table, I ask Bill and Beth if they had a song that meant a lot to them. "Well, the first night I took Beth out dancing they were playing *Stardust* and that has sort of become our song," said Bill.

I leaned over to David. "Darling why don't you go ask the bandleader to play *Till the End of Time* and *Stardust* next," I said.

"Ok babe, you've got it." He got up then and excused himself and I saw him go over and talk to the bandleader. "Done," he said coming back and sitting down next to me.

"Mark, let's dance again because they're playing our song," said Carol. All of us got up and returned to the dance floor. After that dance was finished the orchestra started to play *Stardust* and Bill who was dancing next to us with Beth leaned over. "Thanks David, for having them play our song," he said.

When *Stardust* ended I turned to walk toward our table, but David reached out his arm and pulled me back and then I heard them start to play *I'll Walk Alone* as I came back into his arms. "Thank you darling," I whispered into his ear.

The next song they played was a swing tune so we returned to the table. "Thanks David, for having them play our song," said Mark.

"You know if we were all as smart as we think we are, we'd build a dance floor in one end of the stables so we could go dancing every Friday night without having to spend a bunch of money," I said.

"I love that idea," said Carol.

"I do too," said Beth.

"Great idea," said the men. "Why don't you girls work on it and include it in your plans?"

"We will," we said together and then we laughed.

"It should be a lot of fun because every Friday night we can get together for a potluck and dancing," I said.

"I think I even know where we might be able to pick up a juke box cheap and we can fill it with all our favorite songs," said Mark.

"And when our kids get old enough we can teach them to dance, although by then they probably will think our music is old fashioned," laughed Beth.

"We ought to think up a name for the farm," said Carol. "You know like Oak Creek Farm or something like that."

"Oh God, not another list," laughed Mark.

"Do you ever get the feeling that these three will be making lists of when each kid is to be conceived and born and to which family?" laughed David.

"Next they'll be making a list of what nights we can have sex with them," said Bill.

"You got to be kidding," I laughed. "You know darn well it will be Monday through Saturday and twice on Sunday."

"That's one thing you've got to say for our women, they aren't shy about what they want," laughed Mark.

"Well if this one of mine still wants a dozen kids when I get back, I'll have to insist we be put down at least twice on Saturday as well as Sunday," laughed David.

"I can't wait until Carol and Mark have some sons so I can blackmail Mark not to tell them about his free-wheeling bachelor days, especially when he's trying to tell his son to take it easy," I laughed.

"She'd do it too," said Mark.

"We'll have to start a blackmail fund for college expenses and that alone ought to get at least one or two through college," laughed Carol.

"See David what you started by falling off the bachelor bandwagon," laughed Mark.

"Well I notice you followed my example pretty darn quick once you met this sister of mine," laughed David.

"Guilty as charged," said Mark.

"He didn't stand a chance once I threw my bridal bouquet at him and he like a dummy caught it," I laughed. "His bachelor days were numbered right then."

"Well all I've got to say is thank you, thank you, thank you, Lauren," laughed Carol.

"Yes kiddo, I guess I owe you one too," said Mark squeezing Carol's hand.

"Beth, I hope after meeting my nutty friends here you don't head for the hills," laughed Bill.

"Not a chance darling, you're hooked for life," laughed Beth.

"Thank God for small favors," said Bill and his love for her was written all over his face.

"Come on kitten, let's you and I dance again and leave these idiots to their own devices," said David.

"You know it's going to be so much nicer when we have our own dance floor because you can waltz me right to our door and up to our bedroom and we won't have that long drive in between," I laughed.

"We knew there was a reason we all thought it was such a good idea," laughed the others.

"You know kitten, I think Beth is going to make a great addition to our crazy group," said David once we were on the dance floor.

"I think so too and if Mark just looks at Bill he's going to see he has worried for no reason, because Bill just beams every time Beth looks in his direction," I said.

"It's like a whole world has been lifted off my shoulders knowing those four will be around to look after you and make sure you don't get too lonely while I'm gone."

"Oh darling I'll be lonely, never doubt that, because I could do without everyone in this whole cockeyed world, but you."

"Kitten, do you really know how much I love you?" he asked bending his head so no one could hear him but me.

"I know, my darling, and that is just exactly how much I love you," I said looking up at him.

When we got back to the table Carol said, "You two make a spectacular looking couple on the dance floor, but it's a wonder that Lauren doesn't have a stiff neck after dancing with you all evening."

"When I'm in David's arms I wouldn't even know if I have a neck," I said.

"It's just that you are such a little bitty thing next to this brother of mine I would think dancing with him would be uncomfortable," she said.

"Actually, Carol, I love dancing with this brother of yours. I have ever since the first night I met him, and he's just the right size for me in every way."

"Well God help you if David ever does take you back to Australia and you have to dance with my other brothers, because as I told you, he's the runt of the litter."

"My God darling, you mean you have even bigger brothers than David?" asked Mark.

"Yup, all of them are between six foot four and six foot six, while David here is only six foot three," she laughed.

"Thank the Lord they stayed in Australia because I don't think I'd have had the guts to ask you out, because I would have felt like a Lilliputian next to all of them," said Mark.

"Just remember what I can sic on you if you ever try to leave me, my darling," laughed Carol.

"Beth, do you have any brothers?" laughed Bill.

"No but if you try to back out of our wedding I'll borrow some from my new sister Carol," she laughed.

"Mark, I think you and I better watch our p's and q's," laughed Bill.

"Hey guys, it's nearly closing, why don't we break this up and head for home. It's been a long day and I suspect tomorrow these beauties of ours will have us doing all sorts of things around the farm," said David.

"I agree, this has been a roller coaster of an emotional ride for me this week and I'm afraid I can't stay awake much longer," I said.

"The men paid the check and we left. On the sidewalk waiting for our cars to be brought around, I hugged Beth. "Beth, I'm so glad you are going to be one of my sisters and I'm so happy for you and Bill. Do you mind if I hug your fiancé?"

"Go ahead, Lauren. I can't blame any woman for wanting to hug this man of mine," said Beth. "Thanks for including me as your and Carol's sister."

"Bill," I said, "I'm so happy for you and I wish nothing but happiness for you and Beth, as much happiness as my marriage to David has brought me."

When they brought the car up David relented and let Carol and Mark sit in the backseat and make out while we drove home. "I'll park the car then I'll be right up, darling," said David dropping us at the entrance to our apartment house.

"Come on you two," I said to Mark and Carol, "you can make out when we get inside."

"Point killer," said Mark.

When David came into the bedroom a few minutes later, he asked where

Mark and Carol were. "Guess," I said, laughing.

"I guess that was sort of a stupid question," he chuckled.

He came over then and took me in his arms and stood holding me close to him. "I meant what I said tonight, kitten, when we were dancing; I do sometimes wonder if you know how very much I love you."

"David, I know exactly because every day in so many ways you tell me how much you love me with or without words and I hope you know how much I love you; it's like I was only half a person until you came into my life and made me whole."

"You are everything in the world to me, little one; a million times a day I find myself not really concentrating on what I'm doing because my mind keeps coming back to you."

"Darling, promise me that when you are in combat, you'll keep your mind focused on what you are doing and coming home to me, but when you really need me, close your eyes and I'll be right there at your side and you'll feel all of my love surrounding you."

"Come kitten, let's get ready for bed because I want to hold you in my arms and feel your arms around me."

We got undressed then and when he slid in next to me in bed his arms going about me my arms reached for him and I felt him relax in my arms and all the tension drain out of him and I was content because while we held each other in our arms my world was complete and I knew that his was too.

When I woke the next morning I saw David smiling down at me. "Good morning my darling," I said reaching to draw his head down to mine so that I could kiss him.

"Good morning, kitty cat," he said kissing me.

"What luxury to be able to lie here in your arms and to know you don't have to leave me."

"When I get home for good, I'm not going to let you out of my sight even for a minute for at least a month and I'm never going to let you out of my arms."

"I don't ever want to be out of your arms again, my darling, nor out of your sight. I love you so much."

"You're like an ache inside me that never subsides, kitten, and I'm still counting my lucky stars that I found you and that you love me."

"It's such sweet agony loving you, David, but it's an agony I never want to be free of, I want it to go on and on even into eternity because you fulfill my every need and my every desire and you are the only man I am ever going to love."

His arms drew me in even closer to him and we lay there content in our love for each other.

"Are you hungry darling, do you want me to get you some breakfast?"

"No, let's just stay locked in each other's arms until it's time to go to the farm," he whispered.

"Oh yes, my love, yes," I whispered in return and his lips found mine once more.

"Kitten, Bill was right when he said bachelorhood isn't all it's cracked up to be and that it's lonely. Until you came into my life I played at happiness but I never knew what it was, and I realize now I've been lonely my entire life until you took it all away and for that I can't thank you enough."

"I can't wait to lay your first son in your arms, darling, then I'll have given you my ultimate thanks for your love," I said.

"I'm kind of hoping our first will be a girl who looks just like her mother and I hope she will love riding and flying and going to baseball games with me, just like her mom."

"Do you really darling, you mean you wouldn't be upset if our first was a girl? Because I'd hate to disappoint you in any way."

"You could never disappointment me and yes, I really do want our first to be a daughter and I want to name her Carol as you told sis we would in our first letter to her."

"I really liked Beth, I think she will be so good for Bill, actually even better than Carol would have been. Beth is more Bill's type than Carol would have been, I think, she's more, oh I don't know how to explain it."

"I like her too and I agree with you, where Carol has a playful streak to her Beth is more grounded and as you say suits Bill's temperament better than Carol ever would have," said David.

"Carol and Mark just suit each other's personalities as both of them have that playful way about them and their zany sense of humor."

"They'll have lots of fun with their kids; they will be able to get right down to the kids' level because neither Mark or Carol will ever quite reach adulthood," laughed David.

"Wonder how they see us?"

"That would be interesting to find out," he laughed.

"How do you see us?"

"Sometimes when we are around Carol and Mark I feel like we are the older not like Carol is my older sister."

"That's the way I see us too, and yet I think we have just as good a time with each other as they have with each other, so what makes it seem like we're the elders?"

"Maybe it is because our situation is different…they don't have separation hanging over their heads like we do. Mark's agency will always get him a deferment whereas we know the war isn't going to miraculous end before I'm called up."

"I think that has a lot to do with it, we've had to grow up, they haven't," I said.

"Speaking of being responsible adults, I hear the kids laughing in the next room so I imagine we'd better get up and get dressed if we want to meet Bill and Beth at the farm on time," he laughed.

"Ok; Mom and Dad will get up and see to the kids, but please give mom one more kiss before we do," I grinned at him.

"With pleasure, Mom," he chuckled.

When we came out in the living room Carol and Mark were sitting in the chair necking. "My God, don't you two ever get enough?" I laughed.

"Nope and never will," said Mark.

"Mark, what were you and Bill talking about last night when we were going from the restaurant into the bar?" I asked.

"Well, I was worried because it seemed awfully sudden that Bill asked Beth to marry him and I wanted to find out if he knew what he was doing," said Mark.

"What did he tell you?"

"Bill said I shouldn't worry because he loved Beth as much as I loved Carol," said Mark.

"Well Mark dear, if you'd open your eyes and look at something other than this adorable bride to be of yours, you would have seen what David and I saw, that Bill just beams every time Beth looks at him so you wouldn't have had to worry," I said.

"That's what I tried to tell him last night when we were dancing, but he still had a guilty conscience so he really didn't believe me," said Carol.

"Mark, watch Bill today and you'll see for yourself that you have nothing to feel guilty about, as David said he thinks Bill's play for Carol was more or less to keep his options open until he made up his mind that Beth was the one for him," I said.

"Lauren's right, Mark. I really don't believe that Bill was ever in any way serious about Carol and if he had been and Carol would have chosen him over you, I'd be worried because Carol and Bill don't have the personalities that would bode well for them being married," said David.

"How so, bro?"

"Carol, you have a playful streak in you that Bill has never had nor will he ever have it. Bill was a responsible adult even as a kid, I think, in fact I'd stake a bundle on it, whereas you wanted to play and laugh but was just repressed something Bill would never understand and eventually you would have made each other miserable," said David.

"Today at the farm, watch Beth and Bill together and you'll know that he loves her as much as you love Carol," I said.

"Not to change the subject, but Carol, I was thinking, we could use the furniture from my apartment and any Mark has in his apartment to furnish the house so we could move in right away then you and I can paint, paper, carpet and what not at our leisure since then we wouldn't be paying Bart for the services of his men to look after the horses. What do you think?"

"Lauren, you're a genius why didn't we think of that before and since Beth is going to sub-lease her apartment and move in with Bill maybe she has some furniture we could use too," said Carol.

"How about if I arrange for a moving truck on Wednesday, then they could load up our furniture and move it the same day to the farm and on Tuesday you and Carol could pack up what has to be packed," said Mark. "In fact, I could take the day off and help you girls pack."

"Whoa boy, let's think this thing through a little more. Monday is David's wing ceremony in the morning and the closing in the late afternoon and then you guys are taking us out to dinner afterward. Tuesday, Carol and I need to go out in the morning and make sure everything is scrubbed and cleaned at the farm before we actually move in anything. So if Carol and I packed up Tuesday afternoon and Wednesday morning and the moving truck picked up the stuff at noon, we could probably be moved in by Wednesday night and Mark that way you'd only have to take off a half day so that you could be at the farm to help us arrange the furniture and unpack," I said. "Of course, we wouldn't have any drapes or curtains up to the windows, but we're so far out in the country I don't think that would make a lot of difference."

"What about getting the electric and telephones turned on? That's going to take at least two or three days, I would imagine," said David.

"Why don't we talk to Bill today because he might be able to get the electric and phones changed over more quickly so they wouldn't be a hold up," I said.

"Good thinking, kitten," laughed David pulling me into his arms. "Wouldn't it be something if by Wednesday night we had our own home to come home to?"

"Then Thursday, we could talk to the landlord and see about sub-leasing the apartment, though with the shortage of apartments in this town I don't imagine that would be a problem," said Carol.

"Then the following week we could move in everything from my apartment and I could sub-lease it right away," said Mark. "And you girls could go shopping for drapes and curtains and things."

"Come on you guys, let's get going so we aren't late meeting Bill and Beth and we can talk everything over with them and then take room measurements and so forth," said David. "Wow, this will be our first real home."

We walked down to the garage and got the car. David drove and Mark sat in the front with him while Carol and I piled into the backseat. "Carol," I whispered to her, "have you ever seen David this excited?"

"I was just thinking that he looks like a kid who just woke up on Christmas morning and found out there really was a Santa Clause," she laughed.

"I think he was half afraid that he'd get called up before he actually got to live in his own home and now he'll be able to and can picture it in his mind when he's overseas," I said.

"Yes, that's part of it, but I think there's more to it than that. I think for the first time since Mom walked out on us he feels truly loved and secure and that the house is his way of putting down roots, of knowing he has a place all his own to come home to and knowing that you will never leave him," Carol whispered.

"What are you two females up to back there?" asked Mark turning to look at us.

"I was just telling Carol I feel like I'd died and gone to heaven, I have not only my darling husband, my equine stallion, now I have my own home to share with both of them and with you and Carol," I said.

"It is kind of miraculous, isn't it," said David. "Sweetheart, remind me when we get home that there is something I want to discuss with you."

"If it's important we can talk at the house," I said.

"Well, it's important in a way, but I want to have you in my arms when we talk," he said.

"Isn't that just like a man, to tell you just enough to peak your interest then leave you hanging," laughed Carol. "It's a good thing it's your husband

and not mine, Lauren, because if it was Mark, as soon as we got to the farm I'd take him out in the woods and ravage him until he told me what I wanted to know, you know, sort of torture him," she laughed.

"She only says that because she knows I'm weak willed and that I'd confess after only two or three ravages," laughed Mark.

"Bro, I never thought you had a mean bone in your body, but apparently somehow I raised you wrong, that you torture a woman by telling her a part of what you want to tell her then making her wait all day long for the other shoe to drop," said Carol.

"Carol, shut-up," I laughed. "If my husband says he wants me in his arms when he tells me, I for one can wait."

"I'll tell you how to get even sis, did you know this brother of mine is extremely ticklish?"

"No I didn't, but I'm glad you told me for future reference," I laughed.

"Oh God David, we should have known after these two roped and hogtied us so easily, that they wouldn't stop there and now they are in cahoots our lives are not going to be worth living," laughed Mark.

"Mark, you know darn well you've never had it so good," I said.

"Well with such a perfect life as I'm living now, a man just has to have something to complain about once in a while, Lauren," said Mark.

"MEN!" laughed Carol and I.

"WOMEN!" laughed Mark and David.

When we got to the farm Bill and Beth were waiting for us. Beth came up and threw her arms around me. "Lauren, this is a beautiful place, I bet you can't wait to move in."

"Well I think it is beautiful but it's nice to hear it confirmed," I laughed. "No, we can't wait to move in and this morning we came up with an idea that may allow us to move in next week."

"We nothing," laughed Carol, "it was Lauren, she is the genius who thought of it."

"Ok, give, what have you two been up to this morning?" laughed Bill.

"Well I thought if we took the furniture from our apartment and eventually from Mark's apartment, we could move in next week. There's two sets of bedroom furniture, and the living room furniture and even though the kitchen table is small, we could still set it up in the kitchen until we could get a larger table and chairs for the dining room, then we could move in next week," I said.

"Lauren and I could come Tuesday and clean and then do what packing we need to do Tuesday afternoon, then the moving truck could move the furniture and set it up on Wednesday so by Wednesday night we could be moved in," said Carol.

"By doing it this way, Carol and I could paint and wallpaper and what not at our leisure and Mark said we could move his furniture in the week after their wedding, so David, Carol, Mark and I will have our own home to come home to each evening," I said.

"Of course, we wouldn't have drapes and curtains right away but out here in the country it isn't such a necessity as it would be in the city, then Lauren and I could go shopping for them once we get the décor all figured out," laughed Carol.

"Tell you what, I'll ditch work both Tuesday and Wednesday and come help you," laughed Beth. "What are they going to do to me because I've already quit."

"Great!" said Carol and I.

"There is only one fly in the ointment that we can detect," said Mark, "and that's getting the electric and phones turned on in a reasonable amount of time."

"Well, I think I can help you there, I'm sure I can get them switched over into your name so the lights can be turned on and the phones installed on Tuesday," said Bill.

Carol, Beth and I ran and threw our arms about his neck. "I should have known you'd come through for us, Bill," I laughed.

"Yes, any man who can get me to the U.S. like you did, the electric company and Ma Bell should be no problem at all," said Carol.

"Darling, you're wonderful," laughed Beth.

"Hey don't we get hugs too? After all David bought the farm and I assisted him in getting the horses moved here next week," said Mark.

We all ran over and hugged both of them. "Aren't men wonderful?" laughed Carol.

"Ok now that that is all settled, how about a tour of the place?" said Bill.

I dug the key out of the flowerpot and David unlocked the door. "My God, I don't think I've ever before seen a kitchen the size of this one," laughed Bill.

"It is even bigger than I remembered and my little kitchen table is going to look like an ant sitting in it," I laughed.

"We could hold the next cabinet meeting in the dining room," said Bill.

"Let's take a look at the bedrooms because Mark and Carol, yours is rather on the small side," I said.

"Are you kidding, sis, this will do us nicely and it isn't forever anyway. As soon as our house gets built we'll be moving out and you can use it for a nursery or a guest room or whatever," said Carol. "Your living room furniture is kind of sparse for the size of the living room, but by the time we move in Mark's furniture, it should do until we can find some furniture to add to it."

"Well, I'm moving in with Bill next week so maybe between the three of us we will have enough furniture for the time being," said Beth.

"Does that mean you guys have set a wedding date then?" asked Carol.

"It does, Bill and I talked it over and we've set the date for a week from next Saturday," said Beth, "and you are all invited. Lauren, since you've known Bill the longest, would you consider being my Matron of Honor; and Carol would you consider being a bridesmaid?"

"Oh we'd love to, Beth," said Carol and I.

"Mark, I'd like you to be my best man. David, would you give Beth away?" said Bill.

"Where is all of this taking place?" asked Carol.

"We've decided to just have a small civil ceremony at a Justice of the Peace that Bill knows," said Beth. "We thought about a bigger wedding because of all the people in Washington that Bill knows, but we decided we'd rather just keep it simple and just have our nearest and dearest—meaning you guys, with us," said Beth.

"It is just mind blowing," I laughed. "Six weeks ago none of us were married nor even thinking about something so far fetched, now we're all married or about to be and soon we'll all be living right here on the farm," I said.

"If we time things right we could all be pregnant at the same time every time and then the kids would all have someone their own age to play with," laughed Carol.

"Come on you guys, let me show you the stables, then we'll go in and measure the rooms and measure for the draperies, and make notes on the décor," I said turning so that they wouldn't notice that I hadn't joined in on the discussion of children.

David came up and put his arm around me. "Don't look so sad kitten, because that's what I want to talk to you about tonight is kids," said David leaning down so none of the rest of them could hear.

I looked up to see if he was serious and he smiled down at me nodding his head to let me know that he was but he also put his finger across his lips to let me know not to say anything now in front of the others. I squeezed him around the waist to let him know that I wouldn't say anything to the others, but my smile told him how much I loved him.

"Down at this end is where I thought we might put in a dance floor and we could set up a couple of picnic tables for our potlucks on Friday nights," I said.

"There will be more than enough stalls for our horses," said Bill. "Beth and I stopped at Bart's on the way in and I bought a nice little Arabian stallion for Beth and I to ride."

"The only thing he still has to do is convince me I want to get on that giant horse he bought," laughed Beth.

"Just wait Beth, until Bill lifts you up the horse's back and swings up behind you and you snuggle back in his arms, you are just going to love it," I laughed.

"Besides Beth, your horse is going to look like a miniature once you see that monster of a horse of Lauren's," laughed Mark.

"David, have you thought about buying the land next to this place?" asked Bill.

"Mark and I have been discussing it and we think we can swing the deal for it which will give us more than enough room for everyone to have a plot of land big enough for our present houses and to expand on them when the need arises," said David.

"Well, I intend to pay you for our piece of it and I'll go in with you guys on the additional land too," said Bill.

"The farm will be in mine and Lauren's name as of Monday night and I'll sign a power of attorney so if I'm called up Lauren can sign any documents for your deeds to your parts of it," said David.

"You know I was thinking," said Bill, "if we bought not just the five additional acres but another five as well, we could put in a small landing strip on the back of it and maybe Mark and I could purchase a small plane then you and Lauren could fly it for us and we could all take trips together."

"I for one, never want you men telling Lauren and I that we leapfrog because after hearing you guys today, we've got nothing on you," laughed Carol.

"Come on you guys, we've stalled long enough, let's go measure the rooms then we can all go riding," said David.

The men measured the rooms and we women made notes on the décor and what needed to be repainted or re-wallpapered. When we finished David relocked the door and we put the key back in the flowerpot. Then we all rode over to Bart's to check out the newly purchased stallion and for the others to see Lady.

When we entered the barn, all three horses were stabled there. I went to Storm's stall and put his bridle on him then swung up onto his back. Just as I was about to tell David to mount, a small mouse skittered across the floor and Storm, at my instigation, reared up on his hind legs. It took me several seconds to get him calmed down again and when I had, David came up to me.

"My God Lauren, you could have been killed; I think we need to find you a smaller mount than Storm King."

"Darling, I was in no danger whatsoever," I laughed.

"I don't believe that, kitten. What if you'd not been able to hold on?" said David.

"David, take it easy," said Bill coming up and putting his hand on David's shoulder. "I've seen Lauren rear that horse on purpose dozens of times, believe me she can handle Storm King under any circumstances and that horse would no more hurt Lauren than pigs can fly."

"Bill, are you sure about that? Because it looked awfully dangerous to me," said David and I could still see the fear in his face.

"David darling, I promise you that I absolutely was in no danger. Haven't you ever seen a western movie? If you have you've certainly seen them put their horses through the same performance, and you can imagine no movie studio is going to allow superstars to take any chances," I said jumping down from Storm and going to put my arms around him.

"Actually David it looks more dangerous than it is, and Lauren could stay on that horse if he turned somersaults," said Bill.

"It's all a matter of just clamping my legs around Storm and grabbing a fistful of mane if need be, I'll show you by doing it again when we get outside, although I could do it in here, but there are too many bystanders and they could get hurt," I smiled at him.

"Don't try to get round me that way, Lauren, because I'm not amused," said David.

"But darling, you didn't object when I jumped Storm over the fence, which is infinitely more dangerous than him rearing up," I said. "David, you've got to trust me, I won't put myself in any unnecessary danger," I said.

David pulled away and walked out of the barn. I ran after him and pulled on his arm to make him slow down at least and stop at best.

"David, please stop and let me talk to you, darling," I said the tears coming to my eyes.

He stopped then and I threw myself into his arms. His arms came around me. "Promise me Lauren that you'll never do that again or jump fences either," said David. "If anything ever happened to you I couldn't stand it."

"David, I promise I won't rear Storm or jump fences with him, but please don't make me give up riding him," I pleaded with him. "Please let me bring him out and show you exactly what happens when he rears up that way, then you'll see that I was in no danger."

"No you won't do it again, you just promised me and I expect you to keep your promise," said David. "I still think he is too much horse for such a little girl as you, but I'll concede that you can ride him, but I want no more rearing and no more jumping fences."

"Darling I promised and I'll keep my promise to you, but you are taking away the only relief I get from being so scared that something will happen to you. I don't think you know what it is like for me every day wondering if this will be the last day I will ever see you, and jumping Storm gives me some feeling that I'm in control and so I can bear it another day and not burden you with my fear. When you got scared just now when Storm reared up, that is how I feel every single day because I love you so much and this damn war is tearing you from my arms and David I don't know if I could go on living if anything happens to you because it is hard to live when your heart has been torn out of your body," I shouted at him.

"Oh God Lauren, I didn't know that it was that bad for you, because when I saw that horse rear up and I was frightened for your safety, I thought I would go mad," he said pulling me close to his body his arms tightening around me. "I must be putting you through hell and I wanted only to love and protect you."

"Darling, our love is worth anything, any fear to be endured and I wouldn't go back and change it for anything in the world. Yes, I'm scared to death every day of my life because I love you so much, but I would rather live in fear than to know perfect peace and not have you in my life loving me."

"Ok kitten, show me how to jump fences with you in my arms, and how to let Storm rear up that way with both of us riding him because if I'm going to let you do it, I must understand the freedom from fear that it gives you. I trust your judgment that you can handle Storm and Bill says that you can. I don't think he would ever let you put yourself in physical danger, if he didn't think you could handle things, so I guess I've got to let you do it in order to let you know that I have implicit faith in your ability, but it is going to be hard because to me it looks so dangerous."

We stood then in each other's arms to let our emotions settle down a little and to recover from the words that had been said realizing that it was the first time we had not been in perfect agreement.

We walked back to the barn then and Mark, Carol and Beth looked at me in awe. "My God sis, you scared me to death. Would Storm or Lady ever do that when I was on them?" asked Carol.

"Actually Carol, Storm didn't do it, I told him to do it so he wouldn't trample that poor little mouse," I said. "Yes Storm was frightened and his instinct was to rear up in order to trample what he perceived as a threat, but he would never actually do it while I was on his back unless he knew by the way I was sitting him that I was safe."

"Lauren is telling it like it is everyone, Storm would no more put Lauren in jeopardy than he would run over a cliff of his own accord. I've seen her purposely rear him while patting his neck and holding onto him only by the strength of her legs. Storm loves Lauren as much as David loves her and they have an ability to speak to each other which even I don't understand and I've been riding horses all my life," said Bill.

"Look everyone, come outside, and I'll show you all exactly how it is done and if David is game I'll show him how to do it and we'll ride Storm together and you will see for yourselves that there was no danger involved," I said.

I took Storm's bridle and led him outside where I mounted him. "Watch my legs. See how my knees and calves are clamped to his sides? Now I'm going to tell him to rear just by moving my feet forward and nudging him and pulling back slightly on the reins." I did what I was instructing them and Storm reared up and when he was back on all fours he whinnied and tossed his head and I patted him on the neck telling him what a good boy he was.

"David, come try it with me," I said. Bill gave David a leg up and David put his arms around me. "Now clamp your legs around him just as you watched me do a minute ago," I said. "Are you set, darling?"

"I guess so," said David.

I reared Storm again and David had no trouble whatsoever staying on his back although I did feel the pressure of his arms tighten around me just a little. When I had Storm back on the ground I turned so I could look at David.

"Are you ok, darling?"

"Kitten, I just don't believe it, but I actually enjoyed that," said David.

"I'm sorry I made such a scene about you doing it and I'll never underestimate your abilities again, I promise," he said as his arms pulled me closer into his body.

"Darling, at worst you would have only landed on your backside on the ground, so you can see there wasn't any danger," I laughed.

"What did you mean that jumping fences was infinitely more dangerous?" asked David.

"Because if a person riding the horse didn't know about a horse's abilities the horse could actually get his feet tangled in the fence and fall taking the rider with him and maybe even falling on the rider or the rider could go head first over the horse's head. But I know Storm's abilities and he knows mine so we are in very little danger, much less than when I cross the street in Washington," I laughed.

"Now, let's go back in so you can meet Lady and Bill's new stallion," I said leading them all back inside.

"After that demonstration I don't know whether to be more or less fearful of riding," laughed Mark, "but I certainly like Lady since she is so much closer to the ground."

Bill took us then to see his new stallion Sheik who was small compared to Storm King but beautiful. "I looked at a couple of stallions who were more Storm's size," said Bill, "but I thought Beth would be happier on Sheik."

"Oh I definitely could never be talked into riding a horse the size of Storm King," said Beth.

"Let's go riding, folks," I laughed.

"I think we ought to call it a day," said Carol and everyone nodded their agreement.

"Would you mind if we rode Storm just down to the end of the meadow and back?" I asked.

"Go ahead we'll wait for you here," they said.

"We rode to the end of the meadow and back as I nestled into David's arms. "Please darling, promise we'll never fight again," I said turning my head so I could peer up into his face.

"No never," he whispered into my ear.

We drove back to the apartment and when we were inside David looked at Mark and Carol.

"Do you mind if Lauren and I spend some time alone in our room? Because I think we need to talk, because our world got pretty badly shaken up this afternoon."

"No we don't mind, because I think Carol and I want time alone too," said Mark.

When we got in the bedroom David pulled me into his arms and my arms went up around his neck.

"I learned several lessons today, kitten, and maybe that incident in the barn with Storm was meant to be so I could learn them," he said.

"Oh David, I was so scared that you would stop loving me when I told you how I feel every day about being so scared that it would be the last day I'd ever see you," I said. "I shouldn't have said it because it wasn't fair to you to make you bear the burden of my fear, but at the same time I didn't want you to take from me my solace when I ride Storm."

"Don't ever be scared, kitten; I will never stop loving you no matter what because I'll love you forever. You needed to say it kitten, and I needed to hear it, because up until you actually yelled it at me I guess I never realized how great your love for me is, not that you haven't told me over and over, but I guess I couldn't quite believe it. Part of my not believing it goes back to when Mom left us because she had always told me she loved me, but then she left me. All these years I've never been able to believe any woman who said she loved me, and I had taken a chance again when I believed you when you told me you loved me. But when you yelled it at me I saw the naked fear and torture in your eyes and face and I knew you loved me and always would and that you'd never leave me for any reason," he said. "As for burdening me with your fear, you haven't burdened me you've set me free of all my doubts and fears and for that I thank you little one."

"David I love you so much that if anything happened to you I don't know what I would do, because the pain would be so great. I know I told you that I'd look for someone else but I knew while I was telling you, that I never would because you are the only man in the world I'm ever going to love. I did mean it when I told you that I wouldn't mourn you all my life, because that would be blaspheming our love. I won't. I'll eventually be at peace again even with my heart torn out of my body, because I'll know that for whatever time we have together that you loved me and I loved you and that is more than a lot of people ever have."

His head came down then and he kissed me, and his whole heart and soul was in that kiss and it said that we had weathered a storm, but that our love had grown even stronger for having passed through the storm.

We lay down on the bed then and he held me in his arms and I held him in mine. "What were you going to tell me when we got home today?" I asked.

"I've been rethinking this for a long time but when I saw your face when Carol mentioned about all of us having kids at the same time; I knew how unfair I was being to you, because while I'm gone the others will undoubtedly have kids and you'd be left longing for them but not having your own," he said. "I realized today I no longer have to fear that if anything happens to me you'll be left alone to try and bring up a child, because you'll have Mark and Carol and Bill and Beth to help you and with the money they are paying for their piece of our land there would be a nest egg for you to use so you wouldn't have to work and could stay home with our son or daughter; and that Bill would see to it you had work when our baby was old enough to go to school if you wanted it. So I think we should try and get you pregnant before I leave."

"But David darling, I thought you wanted to be here when our first baby was born? I wouldn't want to deny you being in on all of it from the minute I could lay the baby in yours arms through its first words and first steps."

"I would like to be here, but if I'm not for the first one, I'll be for the others we have and I don't want to deny you the right you have to be a mother."

"David, I want a baby so badly, because if anything did happen to you I'd at least have a part of you with me the rest of my life and I'd be holding you in my arms whenever I held your son or daughter."

"I know that now and I hope you get pregnant before I have to leave because I love you so much that I want you to have whatever comfort our baby would provide for you."

"Thank you darling, thank you for understanding and in return I'll promise you that I won't jump fences and I won't rear up Storm King until you are back riding with me."

"No, kitty cat, you go right on riding Storm the way you always have and if it gives you peace then I'm glad."

"I love you so much David that I don't think if we had three lifetimes together it would be enough for me," I said my arms tightening around him. "I'll never leave you because I'd have to give up my heart to do it."

"I love you too, kitty cat, so much that there are no words to say how much, but it is with all my heart and soul and you're right three lifetimes won't be enough."

After a while we got up and wondered out to the living room. Carol and Mark were there, but the usual banter between them was missing.

"What's up you two?" I asked.

"Are you two ok now?" asked Carol.

"We're fine, Carol," said David.

"I don't mind telling you baby brother that you two scared the bejeebers out of us today," said Carol.

"You sure did," said Mark.

"I thought all of you were ok with the incident with Storm now that you know I was never in any danger," I laughed.

"It wasn't just that, although that was scary enough, it was the way you two fought, because we've never heard so much as a cross word between you before and it scared us to death," said Carol.

"Well adults, even those who love each other, do sometimes have disagreements, sis."

"Yes I know they do, but David I've only seen you really seething mad once or twice in our lifetime and today was one," said Carol.

"I wasn't seething mad, sis, I was terrified," said David. "I guess I always took it for granted that Lauren was relatively safe so I didn't worry about her, but when Storm reared up, for the first time I realized I could lose her and everything in me turned to ice because of my fear and that was why I spoke to her so sharply. I left the barn the way I did because I had to have time to get the fear I felt under control."

"But we heard you screaming at each other, bro, and that scared all of us even more than the incident with Storm."

"Lauren had to scream at me to get through the fear in me," said David.

"Carol, because of his fear David was demanding that I give up Storm and what I was screaming at him was not to take away the only way I had of coping with my fear that something would happen to him, because that is a fear I live with every single minute of every day and night," I said. "I never dared voice it to anyone because if I did I'd lose all control and then the fear would win. So I had to make David understand that the terror that gripped him when Storm reared up was exactly the same thing I feel every single day, but which I felt I had to keep locked away inside me because I didn't want to add to his burdens. Carol, you saw some of it last Monday when David left for camp, but that was only the tip of the ice berg."

"My God Lauren, how do you stand it?" asked Carol.

"You, Mark and Bill help, but when I'm riding Storm and jumping him over fences, some of it goes away or at least stays at bay for a while, and that is why I couldn't let David take away the only thing that saves me from insanity because of his own fear, especially since it was groundless."

"Are you two ok again then?" asked Mark.

"We've talked a lot of things out, things we'd both been hiding from each other because we didn't want the other one to have to deal with anything more than what we were already dealing with, but we've finally grown up enough to know that complete honesty is the only way to make a marriage work and because we've both found the courage to face our fears, we think our marriage has grown stronger as a result," said David.

"But why were all of you so scared; even if David and I had actually had a fight?" I asked.

"Don't you understand sis, if you two can't make a go of marriage none of the rest of us stands even a ghost of a chance and we might as well chuck it all now," said Carol.

"That's nonsense; what does our marriage have to do with yours and Mark's or Bill's and Beth's?" I asked.

"All of us have kind of looked to you and David to show us the way in this love game, because you two are so obviously in love and you both seem to have everything under control and neither of you ever had any of the doubts that we all felt," said Carol.

"Sis, don't look at us as role models, we're just feeling our way the same as you guys are; it's just that we maybe look at things differently than the rest of you, because I could be sent overseas at any time and there is the chance that I won't make it through," said David looking at his older sister.

"We look at things differently, but that is also what got us into difficulty, because David wanted to save me worry and I wanted to save him worry and while we didn't lie to each other we didn't tell each other our fears either, until we were forced into it today," I said. "We don't have the answers any more than you guys do, but I think David will agree we found out today that what we feel for each other is worth whatever we have to go through to have it because one of us without the other is only half a person," I said.

"Carol, come on it's time we got supper going because we still need to sit down and logically figure out every move if we are going to be moved in our home by Wednesday night," I said.

We went into the kitchen then and began to prepare supper. While we were working Carol asked, "Sis, what was it bro had to talk to you about when we got home tonight that he wouldn't tell you earlier in the day? I've been dying of curiosity."

"David rethought his position about me not getting pregnant until he was back home for good so we are going to work toward me getting pregnant before he has to leave," I said. "And personally since being abstinent for four days I am really looking forward to the trying," I laughed.

"I bet you are and I'm just afraid I'll be climbing the walls next week when it's my turn," she laughed. "People who think we get jumpy and edgy during our periods because of hormones don't know what they are talking about, because now I know I'm just plain horny."

"Me too," I laughed. "I think if I'd had to wait one more day to make love with David that shouting match we had today would have seemed like a love match. I'll tell you one thing sis it is going to be a really quick meal tonight and then you aren't going to see either David or me until well past noon tomorrow."

"Does David know yet that you are available?"

"No I'm saving that surprise until I get him locked safely in our bedroom, then I'm going to throw the key out the window so he can't get out. If you hear that six foot three brother of yours screaming for mercy, if you are truly my sister, you won't come rescue him," I laughed.

"I wouldn't think of it, us women have to stick together and I'll expect the same from you next week," laughed Carol.

"What are you two up to out here?" asked David and Mark coming into the kitchen.

"We were just thinking about demur little Beth getting initiated into sex by Bill," said Carol, "and wondering if Bill isn't opening a can of worms he never suspected."

"If you two are examples, maybe Mark and I ought to forewarn Bill," said David.

"Well Bill must know something otherwise how did he know about my so-called well-loved look that he chastised you for not knowing on the night we went to dinner, Mark?"

"Why that sly dog, I'd never have guessed it of old Bill; I bet he and Beth have been making it right along," laughed Mark. "Maybe the next time we see Beth we better have a close look at her and see if she has the same look as you had that night, Lauren."

"Go sit down so we can get supper over with because Carol and I have plans for you guys tonight," I said.

"Oh God, those damn lists," said Mark.

"Well darling, there are lists and then there are lists," laughed Carol.

"Don't you just hate it David, when the girls get mysterious on us? Although, I must say sometimes it turns out to be something really enjoyable,"

202

said Mark.

After super when the dishes had been done, Carol took Mark's hand leading him toward the bedroom. "I need your assistance, darling," she said laughing.

"A man's work is never done," complained Mark.

"Lucky you," laughed Carol.

When David and I were alone I put my arms around him. "I could use your assistance as well, darling," I said grinning at him.

"Ok sugar, what do you need?" he asked following me into our room.

"I need you naked and in my arms as soon as it is humanly possible," I whispered.

"You mean it, kitten?"

"I mean it, boy do I mean it, let's start trying to get me pregnant."

"Oh and trying is going to be all of the fun," laughed David.

"You said it, husband mine, if I'd had to wait one more day you would have seen me go around the bend," I laughed.

"Hurry up, don't talk, just strip," laughed David.

"Aye, Aye, Captain," I said.

"Oh God little one I've missed you," said David pushing me down on the bed.

"Not half as much as I've missed you, and don't talk; just hurry please, because I can't wait another minute," I laughed softly. His hand came between my legs and I pushed it away. "No, no foreplay, no nothing just you inside me as deep as you can get."

As he entered me I began to thrust against him urging him on wanting nothing but the feel of him thrusting deep inside me. "You are in a hurry, kitten," he said nuzzling my neck.

"Yes, oh yes, my darling, I want you and need you so badly that I feel like I'm on fire," I whispered.

"Then it's have me you shall," he said, and his thrusts increased in intensity and speed until I felt the familiar shudders go through my body and then felt him explode within me.

"Oh it's so good to have you home again," I whispered my hand going down to wrap around that which had just given me so much pleasure.

"You're going to have to wait a little while, witch, but I think I can make the waiting enjoyable for you," he laughed as his hand went between my legs and I felt his finger flick back and forth across my clitoris until I was moaning and writhing like someone possessed. "Feel good, darling?" he laughed softly.

"It feels wonderful, but I want you not just your hand," I moaned. "I need you, darling, I need to feel you giving me life," and my hand went down once more to encircle him and I could not repress my smile of satisfaction as I watched him spring to life in my hand.

"Oh God woman how I love you," he said as his body covered mine and I felt him once more come into me and I rose up to meet him until we both climaxed.

His hand came down to cover my breast and I felt him caressing it, and my hands roved over his body loving it and glorying in his need of me even when he could no longer maintain an erection. "I love the feel of your body and I love the feel of your hands on me," I said, my lips seeking his.

"Baby hold me, hold me for all those nights I won't be able to hold you so when that time comes I can close my eyes and the memory of the feel of your body will come back to me," he said softly as he drifted into sleep.

"My husband," I whispered and even as he slept my hands caressed him and I saw a smile cross his face and knew that he felt my hands on him and it gave him some sort of solace, until I eventually too drifted into sleep.

When I woke I saw him smiling at me. "It never fails to amaze me that when I pull you close to me when you're sleeping you always purr like a little kitten," he laughed softly.

"It's because I love having you reach for me and pull me closer to you because you make me feel so contented and so safe and loved. How can I do anything else but purr, my husband?" I grinned at him and my arms went around him. "Thank you darling, for an incredible night of love."

"Definitely, it was my pleasure," he grinned back at me holding me close to him.

I reached for him and tickled his ribs and he began to laugh. "I just wanted to be sure that Carol had given me the right information," I laughed with him. "Because a wife never knows when she might need such information."

"You have better ways of torturing me into submission, my little wild cat."

"From kitten to wildcat in one night, what an accolade," I grinned as my hands traced across his chest and down his belly seeking that which had given me so much pleasure the night before.

"Oh God Lauren, I love the feel of your hands on my body."

"As do I yours on mine, my love."

"You certainly know how to make your stallions rear up and take notice."

"Can I ride you, my stallion?"

"Please," he said lifting me so I was astride him and his hands came up to caress my breasts pulling me forward so that his mouth had access to my nipples and I began to moan my need for him as his hands came down across my belly.

"Please darling please," I begged as my hand reached in back of me to hold him.

He lifted me then and I guided him into me and for a few minutes I luxuriated in the feel of him, not moving, and then the need grew in me so strong that I could no longer stay still and began to ride him until we both moaned in ecstasy. He turned me so he was once more astride me and our love making went on and on until the pleasure was too much to be endured by either of us and our releases came, mine first, then his and he collapsed on top of me. He started to move off me and I pulled him back so that the full weight of him was on me. "Stay, my darling," I begged. "Let me feel you on top of me because even that is such pleasure," I said.

Finally he rolled so that I was on top of him and my body stretched out along his. "If we don't make a baby it won't be for lack of trying my darling," he said grinning at me.

"Well they do say practice makes perfect," I laughed back at him. "Viva la perfection."

We heard the phone ring and heard Carol answering it. "I suppose we really ought to get up and get going and I would imagine you must be starving, my darling," I laughed.

"Only for you babe, only for you," he laughed back at me.

"You make a girl feel really special, my knight in shining armor, but I definitely hear your stomach rumbling so let's go eat breakfast then we can take a shower," I laughed.

We put on our robes and went out to see where Carol and Mark were. We found Carol in the kitchen. "Is there anything left for us?" I asked.

"Plenty, go sit down and I'll even bring it to you," she laughed.

"Who was on the phone?"

"Oh that was Bill, he said to tell you that the electric would be changed over into your names on Monday and the telephone would be installed on Tuesday. I'll say one thing for Bill," laughed Carol, "he sure doesn't let any grass grow under his feet in getting things done."

"Where's Mark?" asked David.

"I let him go back to sleep for a while, bro, he had a rough night last night," she said grinning.

"This wildcat of mine left me a little winded too," laughed David.

"Congratulations Lauren, I see you've progressed from kitten, to wildcat," said Carol.

"Well Carol, I believe in do it again and again until you get it right," I laughed.

"Hey what are you guys up to?" asked a sleepy looking Mark as he came into the kitchen.

"Wildcats and practice makes perfect," laughed Carol.

"David, does that answer make any sense to you at all?" asked Mark.

"Fortunately, yes," laughed David.

"Oh you mean you and Lauren kissed and made up?" asked Mark.

"Something like that," I laughed.

"Come on, kitty cat, let's go get showered and dressed. We'll let Carol explain it to Mark," laughed David.

"When we get back, we expect you two to be wide-eyed and bushy-tailed so we can make out our list of what we have to do in the next couple of days, if you want us to be moved into the house by Wednesday night," I said.

"Godfrey, I'd never have believed my reserved big sister would ever have said some of the things I've heard since Mark came into her life," laughed David.

"Well, I definitely think she and I found an avocation at which we are perfectly well suited," I laughed up at him.

"Yes, I think you two have found an avocation to which you can devote yourself body and soul, or at least body," he chuckled.

"Are you complaining?"

"God no kitten, I'm exalting! In fact to prove it let's practice some more."

"Yes let's practice a couple of times because I want to keep improving until I master it," I laughed leading him into the shower.

His arms came around me and he pulled me in close to his body as his tongue parted my lips. "You feel so good, I love the way your body molds to mine like it was made just for me," he whispered.

"It was made just for you," I said as I let my hands run down his back pulling him even closer to me.

We made love then and it was unhurried as if each of us wanted it to last forever and as my release came I collapsed against him and then I felt him once again begin to thrust into me and I looked up to see him smiling down at me. "I love that dreamy look you get on your face, kitty cat, as if you had found paradise."

"Any time I'm in your arms I'm in paradise," I whispered my body beginning to answer his until he could continue no longer and he exploded in me.

He set me down then but continued to hold me close and began to sing our song to me. We stood with the warm spray cascading over us and swayed to the rhythm of the song and I loved the feel of him against my body. When the song had finished I pulled his head down and everything I felt for this giant of a man was in that kiss.

He turned me then in his arms pulling me in closer to his body and his hands came down so that they caressed my belly. "I hope our baby is already starting to grow within you," he whispered.

"I hope so too my darling," I said.

THREE FAMILIES

"Are you two about ready?" asked Mark.

"By the time you get the car we'll be down at the curb waiting for you," I said.

"What kind of a ceremony is this, Lauren?" asked Mark.

"I'm not really sure, I think it is the one where they present him his wings which would normally have taken place with his entire squad when they graduated from flight training; but since David was advanced to a flight instructor I guess they decided to give him his wings early," I laughed.

"I must say bro was very mysterious about the whole affair," laughed Carol. "I tried to worm it out of him last night but he just said it was no big deal, so I let it go at that."

"Well, I guess we'll all find out soon enough," laughed Mark.

When we got to the front gate we were directed to the building in which the ceremony was to take place. Inside we found Beth and Bill waiting and we all took seats together.

After the opening ceremonies, the men receiving their wings were marched to the front and presented with their wings indicating that they were equivalent to a private pilots rating. Then David was requested to come forward. "Second Lieutenant David Benton, you are hereby awarded your Instructor's Insignia and your First Lieutenant's Bars," said the colonel. "Congratulations, First Lieutenant Benton."

The new aviators were then dismissed so that they could join their families. "David darling, why didn't you tell me you were going to get your First Lieutenant's Bars?" I asked as I hugged him.

"Well kitten, I wanted to surprise you and we both know how hard that is to do," he laughed. "Bill, Beth, it was so good of you to come."

"We wouldn't have missed it for the world, David, congratulations," said Bill shaking his hand and Beth kissed him on the cheek.

"I guess I've got to stop calling you 'baby brother,'" laughed Carol. "By the time you make general it just wouldn't be appropriate anymore."

"Nice going, David," said Mark.

"Oh darling, I'm so proud of you," I said kissing him.

"I've got to go because I've got to give my kids a workout yet today," laughed David but I could see he was proud of himself. "See you tonight at 1600 hours. Wow to be made a first lieutenant and a new homeowner all in one day, it kind of blows my mind."

I reached up and whispered in his ear, "Tonight my darling you get your reward from me."

"Baby, I can't wait. It's going to be awfully hard to concentrate and believe me Carol and Mark are going to eat the fastest dinner they ever ate in their lives," he laughed softly.

After David left us Bill turned to me. "Did you guys get your priority list all straightened out for the move?"

"Actually no, we sort of got side-tracked Sunday," I laughed.

"Don't look at me. They started it," laughed Mark.

"I thought maybe the three of us or if you want to the five of us could go back to the apartment and work on the list until time for me to pick David up tonight," I said.

"Well, I've got to get back to work, but Beth can go with you if she wants," said Bill.

"Sorry, since I'm ditching work tomorrow and Wednesday I think I better go back today, but I promise tomorrow I'll be at the apartment by no later than 8:00 A.M.," said Beth.

"See you guys tomorrow then," I said.

As we drove back to the apartment we laughed and talked. Mark dropped us at the apartment and then went on to work.

"Carol, let's change and get comfortable and then we just have to get at those lists," I said.

"I'm with you kiddo," she said heading to her room to change, as did I.

"How long do you think it is going to take us to clean the house up?" asked Carol.

"I wouldn't think it would take much more than till noon then we can come back here and start packing," I said.

"Well we shouldn't have a whole lot to pack, just the dishes and the linens," she laughed.

"How about the table lamps and knickknacks?"

"Oh I forgot about those. Still we ought to be able to get everything packed up pretty much on Tuesday and the rest of it we can just throw in the car and take over to the house on Wednesday," said Carol.

"The moving truck is suppose to get here by noon then we vacate everything here and go to the house and Mark can help us arrange the furniture when we get to the house."

"Why don't I stay here and make sure everything gets loaded on the truck and you and Beth can go to the house to make sure everything gets unloaded at that end," said Carol.

"Good thinking, sis," I laughed.

"I know the guys are taking us out tonight but why don't we pick up some take-out food on Tuesday because I've got the feeling by the time we get through Tuesday neither of us is going to feel much like cooking," said Carol.

"Another winner, I'm sure glad you're here to think of all the things I miss," I laughed.

"Oh you're still on cloud nine from Sunday," said Carol.

"You bet I am. Did you ever explain to Mark what we were talking about when we told him wildcats and perfection?" I laughed.

"I went one better than that, I threw a complete demonstration for him," laughed Carol.

"I'm just glad that brother of yours is as insatiable as I am."

"Well, I don't know of too many men who aren't," she laughed, "but then usually it would my luck to find the one in a million who isn't. Thank God this time my luck held."

"Do you know what they do at a house closing?" I asked.

"Haven't a clue, but I imagine someone will lead you through it," laughed Carol.

"Just think, Wednesday we will be in our own home then we can chase the guys around a whole big house instead of just a tiny apartment."

"Remind me to wear my tennis shoes Wednesday night, sis," laughed Carol.

"What should we do about dinner on Wednesday? Because I've a feeling by the time we get everything moved in and put away none of us are going to feel much like cooking."

"Tell you what, as long as I'm going to stay here to see to the packing up why don't I fix dinner and put it in a hamper then we can just heat things up that night?

"The new champ," I laughed. "That's three great ideas in a row. Do you think that's enough for one day?"

"Yes, we don't want to wear out our brains," laughed Carol.

"In a case like that, I think I'll go get my shower and put on my makeup then I'll just slide into a dress when it's time to pick up David," I said.

"Mark and I will plan on meeting you two at the real estate agent's office around 5:30 then we can just follow you two to wherever we are going for dinner."

David came through the gate right on the dot of 4:00 and after kissing me hello he opened the car door for me then jumped in the other side pulling me next to him. We drove somewhat above the speed limit and managed to arrive at Wendy's office right at 4:30.

"Well, Bentons, are you ready to start signing your life away?" asked Wendy.

"I guess so," laughed David.

For the next hour we went over everything and signed papers until our hands were numb; when we came out there were Mark and Carol waiting for us.

"Where are you guys taking us?" asked Carol.

"There's a nice little roadhouse close to the farm with a big dance floor, what say we go there?" asked David.

"Sounds perfect to me, but let's not make it too late tonight because these two have to get up early to clean the new house," said Mark.

"Don't rub it in," laughed Carol.

We went then and had a really good seafood dinner, then we danced several dances and finally everyone agreed while the evening had been loads of fun, that we ought to call it a night, so Mark and Carol followed us home. The guys went to park the cars while Carol and I went upstairs to the apartment.

"Well, do you feel like a homeowner yet?" asked Carol.

"I don't think any of it has sunk in yet, but probably by the time we get everything moved it will," I laughed.

"Don't know about you sis, but I think I'll go get ready for bed just in case that man of mine still feels like playing games tonight," said Carol.

"I'm just hoping mine will want to play, but after Sunday I'm not sure he has any games left in him," I said laughing.

When the guys came in from parking the cars they hollered at us, "Where are you two wildcats hiding?"

"In here," said Carol.

"In our room," I said.

"Am I still going to get my reward?" asked David coming into the room and putting his arms around me.

"If you're not too tired," I said bringing his head down to my waiting lips.

"Well, I know I've got enough stamina left to practice at least once," laughed David pulling me closer to him.

"Oh I love you so," I whispered. "And I'm so proud of you."

"Kitten, I love you too and just think, Wednesday night we'll have an entire house to play in," he chuckled softly.

"Darling, get undressed for I've a need to give you your reward," I said.

"And I've a need to receive it, kitten," he said softly.

Later, lying in David's arms, I said, "I love Carol and Mark dearly, but I'll be glad when their house is built and it will just be you and me in our home. Is that terrible of me?"

"No kitten, for I've the same longing to be just us two again for a while. I love them both too, but I miss sitting in our chair with you curled up on my lap talking like we used to."

"Our room at the house is big enough, why don't I move our chair up there and we'll just have to get along for the time being with what furniture is left over in the living room?"

"Kitten, that sounds wonderful. They can have the living room and we'll sit in our bedroom…besides it's so much closer to the bed that way," he chuckled softly.

"You think the nicest thoughts, my love," I laughed.

"I've just got to tell you about one of my students today," he chuckled. "Remember how you told me on your first solo you almost forgot to shove off carb heat?"

"Yes, I remember."

"Well I was check riding this student today and since he'd done a thousand take-offs and landings, I wasn't paying too much attention to him and suddenly for some reason I looked up and noticed we were running out of runway and the plane still hadn't gained only a few feet of altitude; so naturally I started scanning the instrument panel, then it was like I heard you telling me that story and looked and by gosh he hadn't shoved off carb heat either," he laughed.

"You actually heard my voice in your head?"

"Yes, it was just like you were sitting next to me telling me the story again."

"Maybe I was sending my love to guide you just like our song says," I whispered.

"If you were, keep, on sending your love to guide me," he whispered back.

"My love is always with you, surrounding you, every minute of the day and sometimes during the day I'll be doing some inconsequential thing and all of a sudden I can actually feel your arms around me," I said.

"Kitten, my arms are always around you because whenever I shut my eyes I see you and I think about holding you in my arms," he said.

I snuggled deeper into his arms and my lips went to the little nitch in his neck and I began to purr my love for him. "I love you so much it's like I can't even breathe when I'm near you."

"You are everything to me, kitten, you are my world," he said hugging me even closer to him.

When the alarm went off the next morning I looked up to see David watching me. "How long have you been watching me sleep, my darling?"

"Just for the last fifteen or twenty minutes."

"Why didn't you wake me?"

"You looked so peaceful I didn't have the heart."

"Any time I'm in your arms I'm at peace," I said. "You make me feel so safe and so loved."

"What are you going to be doing today?"

"Beth, Carol and I are going out to the house to scrub it down this morning, then we'll come back here and pack up what has to be packed, the rest we will just throw in the car and take to the house tomorrow," I said.

"Remember to look for Bart because he'll be bringing over the horses this morning."

"I'm glad you reminded me, because I almost forgot about that."

"Should I drive to the farm after work today or come back here?"

"Come back here because we'll all be back by the time you leave the base."

"See you tonight, love," he said kissing me and getting up to dress.

Beth came at 8:00 and the three of us packed up all the cleaning materials we could think of that we might need and headed out to the farm. "I hope Bart brings over the horses before we leave, but if he doesn't he knows what to do with them," I said.

"Why don't we split the house up into sectors and each of us take a section of it then we'll meet in the middle?" said Carol.

"Carol you're so tall compared to Beth and I, why don't you take the kitchen because you'll be able to reach the higher shelving easier than we can, I'll take the bedrooms and baths upstairs and Beth you take the dining room and living room then we can all tackle the windows," I said.

"Did you bring shelf paper?" asked Carol.

"Yes, but it is just plain white so it will go with whatever room we need it in," I laughed.

"I brought some too, just in case we needed it," laughed Beth.

When we got to the farm we saw that Bart's truck was already there and he was unloading the horses.

"You girls go in and get started and I'll see to the horses," I said. "Bart, I don't even have hay to put in their stalls yet and those two non-horse-type men we married never thought of that I suppose?"

"Don't worry, Mrs. Benton, I anticipated that they wouldn't think about needing straw to bed the horses so I brought twelve bales and whatever we use I'll just add to your bill."

"Thank God, one of these days I've just got to teach all my non-riding friends what is needed to maintain a horse," I laughed.

"You go right ahead and do whatever you were going to do in the house and my men and I will see to the horses; although, we might just call on you when it comes to unloading that big baby of yours," he laughed.

"If you need me just come up to the house and get me, as we will be cleaning house all morning, and thanks Bart for all your help," I said.

We set to work cleaning and by ten Carol had the kitchen pretty well in shape and I had the two bedrooms and baths upstairs done so we went in search of Beth. "How you coming, Beth?" we asked.

"I've got the dining room done and most of the living room as well," said Beth.

"I washed the windows upstairs inside and out so we won't have to worry about them," I said.

"Do you have a step ladder so we can reach the outsides of the windows on the downstairs?" asked Carol.

"Godfrey, I forgot all about needing a step ladder, maybe we can run into the nearest hardware store and get one," I laughed.

"No problem girls, I brought one with me," laughed Beth.

"Oh Beth thank you," I said hugging her.

"When we leave here why don't we go to my apartment and you can see what if any of the furniture you might want to take immediately," said Beth. "Since I moved in with Bill I'm not using it anyway."

"I've got the keys to Mark's apartment and we can check it out too," said Carol.

"Mrs. Benton, could you come out and help me unload Storm?" hollered Bart from the back porch.

"Be right there, Bart," I said.

"We'll come watch then we'll get back to work," said Beth and Carol.

I went out then and led Storm from the truck and put him in his stall. "This is your new home Storm, I hope you like it," I said hugging him around the neck. He nickered and tossed his head. "I think he likes it, girls," I laughed. I helped him unload the rest of the horses and put them in their respective stalls.

"I'll feed and water them, Mrs. Benton, then one of my guys will be over later tonight and tomorrow morning to make sure they have everything they need," said Bart.

"Thanks Bart, I appreciate everything you've done," I said.

"Well ladies, back to the cleaning," I laughed.

"Slave driver," they laughed.

By noon we had everything done that we could do for the time being. We went then to Beth's apartment and I selected one or two chairs, which I thought might help fill up the living room. Then we went to Mark's apartment but we found nothing that we thought we needed immediately. "We can always get our husbands to help us bring some things out next weekend," said Carol.

"Carol, have you forgotten that Saturday is your wedding day?" I laughed.

"No believe me that I hadn't forgotten," laughed Carol. "But I figure we could put the men to work on Sunday if need be."

"Only if absolutely necessary because Mark deserves at least a two-day honeymoon," I laughed.

"Well he might just be a little tired on Sunday so maybe I'll let it go until the following week," laughed Carol. "Oh I forgot to tell you, Mark told me last night that he has booked a suite for us at the Ritz for Saturday and Sunday for our honeymoon."

"Have you two found an architect yet?" I asked.

"Yes, we have and we meet with him on Friday," said Carol. "I've got my wish list all drawn up."

"We're meeting with our architect on Wednesday and I've got my wish list all made out too," laughed Beth.

"We never did think up a name for the farm," said Carol.

"Why don't we call it Love Farms," laughed Beth.

"Actually that wouldn't be such a bad idea, but I suppose the men would just hate it," I said.

We drove back to the apartment after stopping at several of the local stores to pick up packing boxes. When we got inside we decided to take a break for lunch. After making sandwiches we sat down at the kitchen table to eat.

"I've just thought of a name for the farm," I said. "What would you think of the name Triad Farms, since all three of us will be living there?" I asked.

"I like it," said Carol.

"I do too," said Beth

"Ok, let's put it up for a vote with our men tonight and if it passes muster with them that is what we'll name it," I said.

By 3:30 we had everything packed that we could pack which left just the linens on our beds and the dishes we would need to use as well as a couple of table lamps.

"Well gals, I think I'll head for home," said Beth.

"Beth, thank you so much for all your help today, we couldn't have done it without you," I said hugging her.

"See you in the morning," said Beth.

Just then the phone rang and it was Mark saying that he would pick up something for supper on the way back to the apartment.

"I think I'll shower and change," I said.

"Let me know when you're through and I'll do the same," said Carol.

At 4:30 I heard the front door open and I ran out to throw myself in David's arms. "Hi darling," I said, my arms going around his neck and pulling his head down so I could kiss him.

"Hi kitten," he said putting his arms around me. "I'll never get enough of having you throw yourself in my arms when I come home from work," he laughed.

"That's good, husband, for I'll never get tired of throwing myself in your arms, either," I laughed.

"My God you girls have been busy today haven't you?" he said looking at all the boxes piled around the living room.

"We got the entire house cleaned and ready for the move tomorrow; we got the horses bedded down, and now we're all ready for movers tomorrow," I said.

"Where's Mark; isn't he home yet?" asked David.

"He's going to pick us up supper tonight."

"Good for Mark, I imagine you and Carol are beat after the day you've put in getting everything packed up and the house cleaned."

"Incidentally darling, the next time you move any of our horses you need to order straw for their bedding," I said. "Not that I'm complaining, mind you, but thank God Bart thought about it and brought plenty along. We're going to have to set up an account with the local store so they can deliver it to us."

"Well you will let us non-horsy types make the arrangements," laughed David. "Why don't we find out who Bart uses then they can just deliver to us when they deliver to him?"

"Good thinking, husband, by the time we've been on the farm for a few years you'll get the hang of it all," I laughed kissing him.

Just then Mark came in the door.

"Here Lauren, take this food will you while I go find my soon-to-be wife," he said handing me a bag of take-out food.

"Mark, Carol is in the kitchen so you might just as well take the food with you since you're going that way anyway," I laughed.

"No way Lauren, I want my hands free at least momentarily," said Mark.

"Ok Romeo," and just as he started across the room he stumbled over one of the boxes sitting on the floor.

"Serves you right, for being such an eager beaver," I laughed.

Just then Carol started on the run out of the kitchen. "Did I hear my man?" she asked as she too stumbled over a box and went headlong into Mark knocking them both to the floor.

"Are you two ok?" asked David laughing.

"Only my ego is bruised," laughed Carol.

"Well I think more than my ego got bruised," laughed Mark.

"As long as we're down here," laughed Carol hugging and kissing Mark, "might as well make the most of it."

"Come on kitten, I might as well go change to civvies because it may take those two idiots a while to sort themselves out," laughed David taking my hand and heading for our room.

"Just be careful, my love, because there just isn't room in here for you to fall."

"Why don't we give them a few minutes and us too?" said David pulling me into his arms.

"Mmmmm, I love that idea my darling," I laughed up at him.

"Thought you might, kitty cat."

"You know darn well I would."

"Yes, but I love to hear you say it," chuckled David.

My hands went up and undid his tie and pulled it from around his neck and I unbuttoned his shirt so that I could get at the nitch in his neck that I loved. Standing on tiptoe I let my lips seek the nitch and his arms tightened around me. "I love you so much, my husband, and I feel so safe and secure in your arms, that I could stand here forever and be perfectly content."

"I love you too kitten, more than I ever thought I could love anyone and I too could stand here forever and be content just holding you," he whispered back.

"Much as I'd love to stand here forever, you need to get changed so we can eat supper and we can tell you about the name we three girls came up with for the farm," I said.

"Tell me about it while I'm getting changed, kitty cat," he laughed as he stepped back from my arms and began to change his clothes.

"What do you think about the name Triad Farms, signifying the three families who will be living there?"

"I like it, it has a nice ring to it and especially considering what you three sex starved females could have come up with," he laughed.

"Oh you," I laughed. "Actually we first considered 'Love Farms' which in a way is far more appropriate, but considering we might make it a paying farm we decided we better go with something a little more mainstream."

"Did they get the phones installed today?"

"Yes. I had one put in our bedroom and one in the kitchen and one in the living room. It is a bit extravagant having three phones, but the house is so large I couldn't think of a central place to put just one phone where we could hear it from every place in the house," I said. "Eventually I'd like to put an extension in the stable as well, but that can wait for a while."

"Maybe us guys can get the dance floor started in the stable this weekend," said David.

"Not this weekend or next, darling, you forget your sister is getting married Saturday and Bill is getting married the following Saturday," I laughed.

"God I almost forgot about that—don't tell Carol I said that or she'd kill me for forgetting about her wedding," he laughed. "Come kitten, let's go see if Mark and Carol are ready to eat."

"Did you tell David the name we came up with for the farm?" asked Carol.

"Yup I did and he thought it was a good name. Mark, what do you think of it?"

"I think it is a good name especially if you are figuring on making it a real horse farm eventually, but I actually liked your first idea better except it wouldn't do very well for a business," laughed Mark.

"You know kitten, the more I think about it, why not name it 'Love Farms' because that is what it is, your love of the horses and all of our love for each other," said David.

"I agree Lauren, because that farm is going to be filled with love of all kinds both sacred and profane," said Carol.

"Let's ask Beth in the morning and if she agrees then let's name it Love Farms," said David.

"Doesn't Bill get a vote?" I ask.

"Yes, but that would be 5 to 1 so we'd still win," laughed Mark.

I yawned. "Sorry folks but I think I've about had it for the night," I said. "I didn't realize how much work there was to cleaning just one house."

"You and me too sis, I think I've found muscles I forgot I even had," laughed Carol.

"Why don't you take a hot shower, kitten, it will relax you and keep you from stiffening up," said David.

"I think I will; night all."

"When you finish with your shower I think I'll grab one too," said Carol.

I went then and got undressed and went into the bathroom.

"Want company?" asked David.

"Always my love, but I'm not sure I'm going to be a very functioning partner tonight," I said.

"You don't have to be darling, I just want to hold you in my arms," said David.

"Please darling, hold me in your arms for that is the only place I want to be."

David led me into the shower and turned on the water so it ran fairly hot and stood holding me in his arms. "Kitten, I love you so much and I've had to leave so much of all this work on your small shoulders," said David.

"Well they may be small, but they're strong, especially when it comes to making a home for you, my love," I smiled up at him.

"You are my home, kitten, if I'm with you holding you this way, then I'm home," he said softly.

His head came down then and he kissed me and all his love was in that kiss and I snuggled deeper into his arms.

"I wanted to make our home a refuge for us both so when we go in and shut the door the world is locked outside, but I'm just beginning to realize that it is only shelter it isn't a refuge, because our refuge is in each other's arms and each other's love," I whispered against his chest.

"I could stand this way forever, but I think we'd better give Carol a chance at a hot shower," he said.

"Yes, I suppose we must and to tell you the truth, I want to lie next to you and feel the long, hard muscled body of my love against me and feel your arms pulling me close and I want to lie there with my arms around you and feel your mouth on mine and tell you of the love I feel for you," I said.

He pulled a towel from the rack and dried my body then his, then he picked me up and took me to our room laying me on the bed and sliding in next to me and his arms were around me and I heard him softly singing the words; *"I'll always be near you wherever you are each night in every prayer, if you should call I'll hear you no matter how far just close your eyes and I'll be there…*darling, every night when I'm away, think of me and I'll be right here and you'll feel my arms around you," he whispered.

"David darling, I'll be thinking about you both day and night and if you need me I'll be there with you too, holding you close to me and loving you always for you are my whole world," I whispered.

"Go to sleep, little one. You are safe in my arms and dream of us watching our children and grandchildren riding their own Storm Kings," he said softly and I could only nod my head before I tumbled into sleep.

In the morning as the four of us were having breakfast Mark said, "By the way you guys, I wanted to tell you that I've booked a suite at the Ritz for Carol and I for Saturday and Sunday nights, for our mini-honeymoon, so don't expect us at the farm."

"It isn't that we don't love you guys, we do, but we thought maybe it would be nice for us to be entirely alone with each other and to give you guys the chance to be alone as well," said Carol.

I walked David to the door to kiss him goodbye. "Don't forget tonight you come home to Love Farms, not to this apartment," I said smiling at him.

"Don't worry, love, I won't forget," he said kissing me goodbye.

"I'll be back around noon time and I'll take a load of stuff to the house, then I'll stay there with Lauren so I can help unload and place furniture," said Mark.

"I always knew I loved you for some reason," I laughed, "even if I do want to strangle you like you'd like to strangle me a good bit of the time. It is going to be so nice having you as a real brother."

Beth came just as Mark was leaving. "Ready Lauren? I'm parked out in front so we'd better hurry before I get a ticket."

"Mark, grab a couple of those table lamps, will you please? Beth if you can get that floor lamp, I'll get the other one and we can take them out to the farm. See you later, Carol. You've got my phone number if you need to get in touch with us."

"Yup sis, I've got it. Go now and I'll wait for the movers then I'll be out."

On the drive out I asked Beth what she thought about naming the farm Love Farms after all. "I think it's great and in fact Bill and I talked about it last night and he said even if you did turn it into a business he thought that was a great name for a horse farm," she said.

"Then it's unanimous, Love Farms it is," I laughed.

"Well with a name like that if you don't make a success of the farm we can always turn it into a brothel," laughed Beth. "Bill and I went shopping last night and don't be mad at us, we bought some drapes for the front window in the living room…they aren't expensive ones so if you want to get rid of them once you get the decorating all finished just give them the pitch, but we wanted to get you guys a housewarming present. Also I cooked dinner for you guys and have it in a hamper in the backseat because I figured you'd be too tired to cook by the time everything got moved in and arranged today."

"You guys shouldn't have done that, but David and I do appreciate it so much, Beth," I smiled at her. "You're a gem to think of supper too."

"I just can't believe how much we accomplished yesterday and if we get half as much done today you guys should be in pretty good shape by the time for Carol and Mark's wedding," said Beth.

"Oh God, I just remembered that I told the florist to deliver Carol's bouquet to our old apartment which he was to do by 10 on Saturday and there'll be no one there to accept it," I said.

"Don't worry about it, I'll call them when I get home if you give me the particulars and have them deliver it to Bill's apartment then I'll bring it with us when we come out to the base," said Beth.

"I knew I wanted you as a sister," I laughed. "This is just another reason, because you keep pulling my chestnuts out of the fire for me."

We pulled up to the house and took in the things we had brought from the apartment as well as the supper Beth had cooked for us.

"Maybe while we're waiting we can find a grocery somewhere around here so that you can get the essentials for breakfast in the morning," said Beth.

"I hadn't even thought that far ahead," I laughed.

"Well you've had just a few things on your mind, so you're allowed," said Beth.

We found a small grocery store nearby and I purchased milk, eggs, bacon, and some of the staples like sugar and flower. These we took back and put away, then I called Carol at the apartment.

"How goes it there?" I asked as soon as she picked up the phone.

"Actually, not bad at all. Everything is just about loaded so we are ahead of schedule and I packed a hamper full of sandwiches and lemonade for lunch," she laughed.

"Beth, the doll, cooked supper for us which is sitting in the icebox just waiting for us to heat it up and I got some of the staple items like flower and sugar and enough food for breakfast in the morning, so we won't starve," I said. "Beth and Bill also bought us drapes for the front living room window as a housewarming gift."

"Tell Beth I love her to pieces for cooking us supper, not to mention for the drapes," laughed Carol.

"Will do. When do you think the truck will be leaving?"

"I think we'll be leaving in about a half hour and Mark will be along at any minute because he just left the office," said Carol.

"See you in a little while, then," I said.

"See you."

"Carol said the truck and she would be leaving in about a half hour and Mark is already on his way," I said. "I sure hope the unloading goes as well as the loading appears to have done."

"It will I'm sure," laughed Beth.

"While we're waiting let's take the horses a lump of sugar each," I said.

"Only if you promise to feed it to them," laughed Beth.

"There's nothing to feeding them sugar, you just lay it on the palm of your hand and they nibble it right off," I said.

"My hand or the sugar?" laughed Beth.

"The sugar, horses aren't meat eaters," I laughed.

"Tell you what, I'll feed mine to Lady because she looks the most gentle and you give the stallions their lumps," said Beth.

"Deal!"

We went into the stables then and I gave Sheik and Storm their lumps of sugar and hugged them. Beth fed Lady her lump but I noticed that she didn't offer to hug her, so I went to Lady and gave her a hug as well.

"I'm sorry Lauren, for I know how you and Bill love these horses but I'm petrified of them," said Beth.

"Well if you're not used to them Storm especially can be a bit daunting because of his size, but eventually I'll get you used to them so you'll no longer be petrified, because actually, Beth, they are such loveable creatures and so beautiful," I laughed.

"I hope you can because I want to ride with Bill like you do with David but I'm not sure I'll ever be able to do it except by gritting my teeth which doesn't make for a very romantic ride," she laughed. "How in the world did you get used to them?"

"I've been riding ever since I was five or six; some of our neighbors in Ohio owned horses and I fell in love with them at first sight," I laughed.

"Bill was telling me that you also fly; you must be the bravest person I know," said Carol.

"No, just a tomboy at heart and I love flying, it is so relaxing," I said.

"Relaxing! I'd be holding on for dear life," she laughed.

"You mean you've never ridden in a plane?"

"Nope and when Bill mentioned buying a plane so we could all go places together my heart was in my throat," said Beth. "I don't see how Carol ever had the guts to fly to the U.S. from Australia."

"Well I see I've got my work cut out for me, but I guarantee you that before I get through you'll love horseback riding and flying," I laughed. "Actually if the Army would ever get over its prejudice against women pilots I'd fly combat missions right along side of David," I said.

Just then we heard Mark's car horn and went out to greet him.

"What have you two been up to?" he asked.

"We got groceries for tomorrow's breakfast and Beth the dear cooked our dinner for tonight so all we have to do is warm it up," I said.

"Thanks Beth you're a doll," laughed Mark. "Have you heard from Carol?"

"Yes, I talked to her about fifteen minutes ago so they should be leaving in the next 15 minutes fully loaded," I said.

I had no sooner gotten this information out of my mouth than Carol pulled in along with the moving truck.

"We got away early," she said running to throw her arms around Mark.

"Bet my doll was right after them every minute or they wouldn't have," laughed Mark hugging her.

"You better believe it. I'd make a great sergeant," laughed Carol.

"Lauren, why don't you go in and direct the placement of the furniture so they'll know which floor and room to put it in," said Mark.

Within two hours the furniture was completely unloaded and placed in the area where it was to be used. The movers helped us set up the beds and to put the mattresses on them. When they left we four moved the furniture around and put up the drapes Beth and Bill had given us.

"Does anyone know where this dining room furniture came from?" I asked.

"Yes, I had them pick it up from a friend's apartment," laughed Mark. "I wanted to surprise you."

"You are a living doll," I laughed. "Now we'll have a kitchen and a dining room table."

"Come on everyone, let's start at the top and get the furniture arranged and the clothes hung up," said Mark.

We spent the remainder of the day getting everything placed and the clothes and the dishes put away as well as the beds made up. We'd just finished when I heard David's car in the drive. I ran out to greet him as usual. "Nice timing, my knight, for we've just finished," I laughed.

"My dad never raised any dumb boys," laughed David.

"I heard that bro and I quite agree, he taught you well to leave the work to the women and collect only the rewards," laughed Carol.

"Come in and see what we've done, my love," I said.

"My God you guys have done a fantastic job," said David. "I actually figured we'd be moving furniture around until late this evening. Kitten, come outside for a minute."

We went out on the porch and David picked me up in his arms and carried me across the threshold. Setting me down inside he pulled me into his arms.

"Welcome home, my husband," I said softly.

"Carol come on, I might as well carry you across the threshold too," laughed Mark.

"No way darling, that right is reserved for a husband and you won't be that until Saturday," laughed Carol.

"You sure are getting knit picky," laughed Mark.

"I'm going to get going and leave you four to your own devices and maybe I'll even carry Bill across the threshold tonight, husband or not," laughed Beth.

"Thanks Beth, for all your help and for the beautiful drapes, not to mention the supper awaiting us," I said hugging her.

"You're very welcome. Maybe you'll do the same for Bill and I when our house is built," said Beth hugging me back.

"You better believe it," I laughed.

"Come on darling, we need to get you changed into civvies then I'll give you a tour," I said.

"Babe, you've just done a fantastic job, it already feels like home," said David taking me in his arms when we got to our bedroom. "I see you did move our chair in here."

"We even managed to fit one into Carol and Mark's room too," I said reaching up to kiss him.

His lips came down on mine and his arms drew me in closer. "Want to initiate our room properly?" he laughed softly.

"Yes, later, but right now I'm starving so get changed and we'll eat," I said hugging him to me.

We ate the delicious meal which Beth had brought us and when the dishes were done we took a tour of the house.

"I don't know about you guys, but I think it is beautiful," I said.

"We think so too," said Carol, David and Mark.

"Mark, let's go initiate our shower," laughed Carol pulling him by the hand.

"She thinks she's getting sex, but I'm too tired to participate until I have a nap," laughed Mark.

"He just thinks he's too tired," laughed Carol.

"How about you, kitten? You too tired too?" said David.

"Never, my stallion," I laughed following Carol's example and pulling him toward the stairs.

When we got to our room David sat in the chair and pulled me to his lap and I curled up in his arms. "Darling, you are wonderful," he said pulling me tighter in his arms and kissing me with such love. "You've managed to make my dream of a real home come true for me."

"It was my dream too, my love, for I wanted to make you a home filled with love and joy and comfort before you had to leave me so you'd have something to remember when you are far from my arms," I said.

"Thank you, kitten. Thank you for all you've given me; the love, the caring, the needing, our home, our life because of you no matter what happens I've had everything any man could ever hope to have. I love you so much," he whispered pulling me in even closer to his body as his head came down and I felt his lips on my neck.

"Thank you too, my dearest, for you've given me more than I ever dreamed was possible by giving me your love, your faith and your trust and now a home and a dream to hang onto in the time ahead. I love you with everything that's in me and you've given me light and hope and the belief that somehow we will come through the darkness ahead of us to continue to share our love," I whispered in his ear.

"Come on, kitten, let's get ready for bed because you look like you are half asleep," he said standing me on my feet.

We undressed and climbed into bed and David pulled me into his arms. "Do you want to?" I asked.

"Kitten, I don't really think you could stay awake," he laughed softly.

"I'd manage somehow," I laughed back.

"Why don't we wait until tomorrow night when you are far less tired?"

"Give me a couple of hours and I'll be ready," I said.

"You're just amazing, kitty cat. I appreciate the offer but let's just get a good night's sleep and we can play tomorrow night and besides we'll have Saturday and Sunday to ourselves," he laughed.

"Well sweetheart if you change your mind you know where I am, right here in your arms, and all you have to do is wake me and you don't even have to wake me if you don't want to," I said. "Or if you wake up early I'll definitely be available."

"Go to sleep, kitty cat, it's enough just to hold you in my arms," he said bending his head and kissing me tenderly.

"Last chance," I yawned as my arms went about his neck. Much later I felt him leave the bed and go into the bathroom. When he returned my arms went about his neck. "Come love, let Momma love you," I laughed quietly.

"Are you sure?"

"Very sure."

His body covered mine and I felt him enter me as his lips sought mine. "Does Momma want Daddy to continue?" he laughed softly.

"Oh that feels so good, more, please Momma needs her Daddy," I laughed.

"What does Momma want her Daddy to do for her," he asked as his mouth covered my breast.

"Momma wants her Daddy deeper," I whispered and my body thrust up against his.

"Let Daddy help," he said as his hands went beneath my buttocks and he raised me so that he was deeper in me and he continued to thrust until I was softly screaming my need of him. "Does that feel better, Momma?"

"Yes, oh yes, Daddy knows exactly what Momma needs," I moaned pulling him even closer to me, and his thrusts became stronger and more frenetic until at last he exploded in me. As he moved from me his arms brought me close to him so that I could feel the whole long length of him and I purred my love for him.

"Go back to sleep, kitten," he whispered.

"Daddy, I love you so much," I whispered as once again I drifted into a deep sleep.

In the morning as he slid out of bed I opened one eye, "Isn't Daddy going to love Momma any more?" I asked laughing up at him.

"Momma, I think you've had all the loving I'm capable of for the time being," he laughed as he went into shave and shower. When he came back dressed and ready for work, he lifted me into his arms and kissed me goodbye and I snuggled in his arms.

"Have a good day, my darling daddy," I murmured already half asleep again.

"When I get home tonight let's take a ride on Storm," he said and his hand stroked my belly.

"I hope that's not all you want to do," I giggled through a yawn.

"Daddy has some ideas he thinks will please Momma," he laughed as he rose from the bed tucking me in. "I love you."

When I woke again it was well after ten and I got up putting on my robe and wandered downstairs in search of Carol. "Well was Mark as tired as he thought?" I asked giggling.

"Not last night, but he definitely was this morning. He was almost late getting started to work," she laughed.

"I think our men are wondering what they started when they initiated us into the sex act," I laughed.

"Well it serves them right, whatever they started we'll finish," she laughed. "I take it you weren't too tired either?"

"As a matter of fact I offered and David told me he could wait until tonight so I went to sleep, but about three this morning I got my second wind."

"Sis, I'm truly beginning to wonder if there is something wrong with me because I crave the feel of Mark's body I just can't leave him alone. I want his hands on me and I love stroking his body and watching him salute my efforts," she said.

"Carol, I know exactly what you mean because I feel only half alive unless David is making love to me and my hands seek every part of his body and I glory in his reaction to my touch," I said.

"Mark said last night that once we get to the Ritz we were not getting out of bed for the next two days until I beg him to stop," she laughed. "The only trouble is I think he's going to do the begging before I will, but it's going to be interesting to find out."

"Remember how the girls at school used to say that they heard sex was something we had to put up with in order to be mothers?"

"Like everything else they used to say that was about as false as it could get for I'd want it and procreation doesn't have a darn thing to do with it, it just feels so good," she laughed.

"Well I'm glad I'm not the only one who feels that way because I just keep coming and coming and I don't ever want it to stop," I laughed. "I don't know what I'm going to do when David is overseas, it actually scares me thinking about it and I thought it was always the man who had that problem."

"I bet the censors are just going to love your letters to David," she laughed.

"David told me he wanted me to write him those kind of letters, he may live to regret that request."

"Maybe we ought to start a letter writing campaign sending them to the Japanese soldiers and they'd get so horny they'd call off the war and go home to their wives and girlfriends," laughed Carol.

"Now there is a good campaign slogan 'Make Love Not War,'" I laughed.

"Well enough of this or I'm going to Mark's office," laughed Carol. "What's on the agenda for today?"

"We need to go looking for a washing machine and some window shades," I said.

"You know we actually did a pretty good job of furnishing this place, better than I would have thought when you first came up with the idea," said Carol.

"It may not be '*house beautiful*' but it is homey and comfy looking," I laughed.

"Why don't we go and pick up the stuff we need then I'll give you another riding lesson this afternoon."

"Come on, what are we waiting for? Go get dressed and we'll be off to the races in more ways than one," laughed Carol.

We found a washing machine and arranged to have it delivered on Friday and then we ordered window shades for all the bedroom windows, as well as curtains.

"At least we found some cheap ones until you decide exactly what décor you want to have," said Carol.

Riding back to the farm I told Carol about David thanking me for making his dream come true of a home of his own.

"I think David has actually wanted a home for a long, long time," she said, "but had made up his mind that it was never going to happen because he just couldn't trust another female after Mom left us."

"It's funny that he trusted me almost from the beginning," I said. "Maybe it was my asking him to move into the apartment, but you'd almost think that would be a reason not to trust a woman."

"I'd more think it was your little speech to him about when he got tired of you, because you didn't place any of the blame on him if he did ditch you eventually," said Carol.

"But I didn't say that to him until after he'd already purchased my engagement ring, so that doesn't make sense."

"Truthfully, I think he really fell for you hook, line, and sinker from the first night and he wanted to trust you so when you made that little speech to him it was the deciding factor for him that he would take the chance on you not betraying him."

"All I know, Carol, is that I love that man so much that it is like a constant ache inside me, not just the wanting of him in a sexual way, but wanting to make him happy and content with his life," I said.

"Lauren, he loves you just as much because he told me so that first night when I came over here when we were getting me settled in the bedroom," said Carol.

"What did he say?"

He said, "You know sis, I never thought I could love or trust any woman after Mom, but Lauren is different. When I'm not with her I feel lost and lonely and my arms actually ache to hold her. She completes me, for I'm only half a person without her and I love that she is a tomboy who obviously can take care of herself, yet I know that she needs me just as much as I need her. I love the way she laughs and I love the way she comes running when I come home and actually throws herself in my arms and I love the way I feel when I put my arms around her. For a tomboy everything about her is so feminine that I feel more masculine when I'm around her, I love the way she can even laugh when we are having sex and the fact that she wants it as much as I do."

"He's so big a strong and so male and I just want to give and give and give to that man," I said.

"I'd say you two were in love and likely to be for the next 100 years or so," laughed Carol.

"It's funny how both you and I fell for our men the way we did," I said.

"What's really funny was my dream man was always tall like my brothers, I guess because I was so tall myself," laughed Carol, "and who do I fall for, Mark, and I can't even wear high heels without being taller than he is. You'd have thought being small like you are that you'd have fallen for someone Mark's size and I'd have found me a man more my brother's size. But I think the reason I fell for this little pipsqueak is that he makes me laugh and he can say the most outrageous things to me; things I would never have let any other man get away with."

"Let's face it, we found our soul mates regardless of their size or anything else about them and fortunately for us we were smart enough to realize it," I said.

"I think you are right. All I know is I want to love Mark my whole life, I want to laugh with him, cry with him, bear his children and take care of him," said Carol.

"That's the way I feel about that brother of yours and I think that is the way that Beth feels about Bill as well."

"You know, bro was right when he said that if I'd fallen for Bill instead of Mark that we would have made each other miserable eventually," said Carol. "Bill is too straight laced for me. I need a man who will keep me guessing and who I can never take for granted."

When we got home we put up the window shades then we changed clothes and went down to the stable. "Do you want to ride Storm or Lady?" I asked.

"Lady. You can have your big brute," laughed Carol.

"Let me show you how to saddle her just in case you ever want to ride her that way, but if you're riding with Mark I'd suggest it be bareback because that allows you to snuggle into his body so much better."

I showed her then how to saddle and bridle Lady. "Why don't you ride her bareback because I suspect that is how you'll be riding her most of the time," I laughed.

"Yes definitely," laughed Carol.

"One thing I learned from the episode in the stable the other day, I think I need to know how to control her if she does rear up," said Carol.

"Go over to the fence so I can mount her with you until you get used to the feel of it when she rears up on her hind legs," I said.

After practicing several times, Carol asked to try it solo and she managed to stay on just fine.

"I just wish Mark would learn to ride her so that I could nestle in his arms better, but I suppose that is too much to hope for."

"Well, I don't think you are ever going to make a horse person out of Mark, so I guess you're just going to have to settle for the next best thing," I laughed.

"Hey, we better get going if we want to change before the men get home," I said looking at my watch. "Besides we've got to get supper on to cook. What do you guys have planned for tonight?"

"Mark mentioned something about going dancing, do you guys want to come?" asked Carol.

"I think you and Mark need some time alone and so do David and I," I laughed, "so I think we'll pass on the dancing."

"My God, do you realize that the day after tomorrow I'll be a wife?" laughed Carol.

"Well then you and Mark better enjoy your illicit love affair while you still can," I chuckled.

"Speaking of being a wife—I just thought of something," said Carol. "You told the florist to deliver my bouquet to the apartment and there won't be anyone there to receive it."

"All taken care of. Beth called the florist and they are delivering the bouquet to her and Bill's apartment and she'll bring it to the chapel with her," I said.

"Thank the Lord for sisters who keep their wits about them when us soon-to-be brides don't think at all," laughed Carol.

At 4:15 David came home and I ran to the door throwing myself in his arms. "Welcome home, husband," I said kissing him. "You better run up and change because supper will be ready in about an hour."

"Hi Momma," laughed David pulling me close in his arms and dropping a kiss on the top of my head. "Do you suppose I could catch forty winks after I change? I'm bushed after a certain young lady who shall remain nameless kept me up half the night."

"I think that can be arranged, besides I want you completely rested for later tonight," I laughed.

"Now I know I've got to catch a nap for Daddy wants to be especially good for Momma tonight," he whispered.

"Go then and I'll come up and wake you when supper is ready," I said giving him a shove in the direction of the stairs.

"What's with this momma—daddy stuff?" asked Carol when I came out in the kitchen where she was sitting at the table.

"Oh I'll tell you about it one of these days," I laughed.

231

Mark came in about 4:30 and Carol went flying into his arms. "Welcome home darling," she said. "How did your day go?"

"Fine except I discovered I still had sore muscles that I didn't even know I had in the first place," he laughed.

"Come on baby, go take a hot shower and Momma will scrub your back then I'll give you a good rub down, for I've already practiced on Lady," laughed Carol.

"Can we put this dinner on hold?" asked Carol. "Because Mark is out like a light and I peaked in at David and he is too."

"Yes, we'll just turn the fire down to low and give them an extra hour. Thank God we're women and have stronger constitutions," I laughed.

"So much for big strong men," laughed Carol.

About an hour later we heard Mark and David coming down stairs. "Well I guess our heroes are awake," laughed Carol.

"It appears so, so I guess we better turn up the burners and get supper on the table because I have a feeling they both will be starving," I laughed.

"Where is everybody?" hollered Mark.

"In the kitchen," said Carol

They came into the kitchen and Mark was dressed to go out. "I thought we were going out for dinner and dancing?" he said.

"Oh I thought we were just going out dancing," said Carol.

"Well run up and get dressed and I'll take you out to eat as well," laughed Mark. "Our going isn't going to cause a problem for you, Lauren, is it?" asked Mark

"No, I can store the leftovers and David and I can have them for supper on Saturday," I said.

"Don't you guys want to come with us?" he asked.

"Nope, we've got other plans for this evening," I laughed.

"Oh it's that way is it," laughed Mark.

"Well actually, Mark, it may turn out to be that way, but we'd planned to ride Storm tonight after I got home," laughed David.

"Oh, well every man to his own poison," said Mark.

Carol came into the kitchen then. "I'm ready, Mark," she said.

"I thought I was too, but after seeing you in that outfit I'm not sure whether to take you out or throw you over my shoulder and carry you back upstairs to our bed," Mark said leering at her.

Leering back, Carol said, "Well, big boy, why don't you take me out and then when we get home you can carry me upstairs and have your way with me."

After they left I brought the food to the table and sat down with David. "I'm kind of glad they decided to go out for dinner so you and I will have the whole house and evening to ourselves," I said.

"Daddy has been thinking about several things that Momma ought to enjoy," he laughed.

"Hurry Daddy and finish supper," I said my voice husky.

"Suddenly I'm not very hungry for food," he laughed.

"No eat, you are going to need your nourishment," I laughed.

When we had finished I put the food away and stacked the dishes in the sink. "Now what was Daddy saying about ideas for pleasing Momma?" I said.

"Come on, kitten," he said grabbing my hand.

"Where are we going?"

"You'll see," he laughed.

"Hey slow down remember Momma has short legs," I laughed.

With that he stooped down and swung me over his shoulder in a fireman's carry. I slapped him on the backside trying to get him to set me down again. "If Momma keeps doing that she's never going to get where Daddy intended to take her," he chuckled.

"Ok, I give up," I said as I stopped struggling.

"I think Momma has gotten some sense considering I'm 6'3" and she's only 5'2"," he chuckled.

I looked up then and discovered we were in the stable outside of Storm's stall. Storm put his head over the gate and whinnied at us. David set me down then and he went to get Storm's bridle. When he finished bridling him, he reached for me and set me up on Storm's back then swung up behind me and I automatically nestled back in his arms. As we rode out from the stable he grabbed one of the horse blankets hanging on one of the rails.

"What's that for?"

"You'll see," he laughed hugging me to him.

We rode out toward the back of the property threading our way amongst the trees until we came to a grassy area. David pulled Storm to a halt and slid down off his back.

"Stay where you are, Momma," he laughed.

"Exactly what is Daddy up to?"

"Pleasing Momma," came his curt reply. He spread the blanket out on the ground then came over to where I was still sitting on Storm. "Come to Daddy," he laughed holding up his arms for me to slide into. He set me down on the blanket then he moved off with Storm in tow and hitched him to a tree several feet from the blanket. Coming back he sat down beside me taking me in his arms and kissing me thoroughly then pulling me down so that we were both lying on the blanket locked in each other's arms. "Guess what Daddy has for Momma," he laughed softly.

"I don't have to guess, I know," I said my voice husky. We made love then on the horse blanket and it was as good as it had ever been. "Oh Momma loves Daddy's ideas," I whispered.

"I thought you might," he whispered back.

"When you mentioned riding Storm last night I didn't realize you meant I could ride both my stallions," I laughed softly.

"Well Storm doesn't get to have all the fun," he said smiling down at me. My arms went around his neck and I pulled his head down so that I could kiss him.

"I love you David, so much that I can't begin to tell you," I said.

"Lauren, when we were first married I thought I loved you then, but compared to now and the way I feel about you it was like I only liked you," he said.

"Darling, while I would like to stay here all night in your arms, it is almost sundown and I think we need to get back to the stables before it gets too dark and Storm stumbles in some gopher's hole and we both break our necks," I laughed.

"Well get dressed then and we'll ride back," he laughed.

"No let's not get dressed for I would love riding with you naked and to snuggle into your naked body," I whispered.

We gathered up our clothes and wrapped them in the horse blanket and he lifted me up to Storm's back and placed the blanket in front of me for safe keeping then he mounted behind me and pulled me back against his body. "Momma has some pretty good ideas herself," he laughed as he handed me the reins and as we rode he stroked my body until I was on fire for the need of him once more.

When we got to the stables he put Storm into his stall and I pleaded with him to hurry. When we closed the stable door he swung me over his shoulder once more and headed for the house. As he walked he stroked my buttocks and I reached down his back and did the same to him. He opened the door and took me in the house not stopping until we were in our bedroom, then he lifted me and carried me to our bed and once more we made love until at last we dozed.

We woke together and laughing he picked me up and carried me to the bathroom turning on the shower. "Momma smells like a horse and so does Daddy so I figured we needed a shower," he laughed, softly pulling me into the cascading water.

"Let Momma wash her Daddy," I said reaching for the soap and soaping him from head to toe.

"Daddy's turn," he chuckled doing the same to me.

"I think Daddy has more on his mind than showering," I laughed softly as my arms went around his neck and I gave a little jump and locked my legs around his waist and I guided him into my waiting body and immediately we fell into matching rhythms.

"Oh God, kitten, do you think we'll ever get enough of one another?" he whispered.

"I'll never get enough of you; not if we live to be a million years old," I whispered as he backed me against the shower wall for support.

"I love you," he moaned as we climaxed together. We stood then under the shower letting the soap which was still on our bodies wash off, then we stepped from the shower and I dried him off and he me and we returned to our bed of love and made love yet once again.

I woke the next morning when he leaned down to kiss me goodbye. "Daddy thanks you for a lovely evening," he whispered as my arms went about his neck.

"I'm very beholden to Daddy for such a wonderful night of love and just think, we'll have tonight and the weekend," I whispered as my tongue sought his warm wondrous mouth.

"If you don't stop that I'm going to be late for roll call and somehow I don't think the Army is going to understand," he laughed disengaging my arms from around his neck.

"They're all men; they if anyone ought to understand," I giggled. He laughed softly and I felt his hand come down between my legs.

"Just marking my spot," he laughed and ran from the room.

When I came down in the kitchen I found Carol sitting at the kitchen table drinking her morning coffee.

"Last day of freedom, sis. You still willing to give it all up for Mark?" I asked.

"Lauren, I just don't believe how much I love that man and I was just sitting here thinking I wish our wedding was today instead of tomorrow," she laughed.

"Did you two have fun last night? We never even heard you come in," I said.

"It was wonderful. If Mark had held me any closer while we were dancing we'd have been arrested," she laughed. "It's no wonder you didn't hear us because we didn't get in until after four this morning."

"I'm so happy for you, Carol, and I know exactly how you feel about Mark because that's just the way I feel about your brother."

"How about you two, did you have fun last night?"

"It was pure magic. We went for a ride on Storm and David actually took over the reins and it was so much better because I could snuggle into his arms and not have to worry about guiding Storm, just enjoy the feel of David's body against mine," I said.

"I was wondering what the clothes were wrapped in that horse blanket when I went out this morning to ride Lady," laughed Carol.

"After you guys left we finished supper and then David picked me up and threw me over his shoulder," I giggled, "and he took me out to the stable and we rode Storm out to the back of the property and he put the blanket on the ground and we made love. We didn't even bother to get dressed again, he just wrapped our clothes in the blanket and we rode home stark naked."

"Don't you just love it when our men act like cave men?" she giggled.

"It definitely is very satisfying," I giggled.

"Do you miss Australia at all, Carol?"

"I did at first but now home is where Mark is and where you and David are so I don't miss it at all," she said.

"I used to wonder that if after the war David decided he wanted to go back home whether or not I could stand being uprooted from the U.S., but now I too know that home is where David is, but I'm glad the four of us will be here together," I said.

"It amazes me that I ever thought I had to protect David from you," she laughed.

"Well, it was a shock to you when you heard that David was planning on marrying some girl you didn't even know and after all you'd spent the better part of your life protecting and caring for him," I said.

"I always felt closer to David than any of my other brothers and I guess to a certain extent I was jealous of you because I thought you were taking my brother away from me and I knew that you would be the one he'd turn to not me anymore," said Carol.

"Now I feel closer to you than I do even to David."

"I love you too, Carol, and you are truly my sister in every way. I really lucked out because I have the most wonderful husband in the entire world and a sister to match," I laughed.

"Come on, sis, I'll help you with dishes and then we can make the beds and tidy up the house," said Carol.

"What do you have planned for today?"

"I have to meet Mark at the architect's at one, but otherwise I don't have a darned thing planned. I'm too happy to think of anything constructive," laughed Carol.

The deliverymen came shortly after Carol left to meet Mark. They set up the washer next to the stationery tubs. When I got back upstairs the phone was ringing.

"Hello."

"Hi Lauren, it's Beth."

"Hi Beth. How goes things?"

"Pretty well considering I have absolutely no interest in my work and find my mind drifting off to much more interesting thoughts," she laughed.

"Carol was just saying the same thing before she went to meet Mark at the architect's."

"Is she all set for tomorrow? Anything I can do?"

"No, just bring the bouquet and you and Bill and that's about it," I laughed.

"How does David like his new home by now?"

"I don't think I've ever seen him happier and that was just what I was hoping for," I said.

"You sound happy too, or at least as happy as any woman could sound with what is before you two hanging over your heads," said Beth.

"I try not to think about it but sometimes I do, I just can't help it."

"You're a braver woman than I'd be if it was Bill," said Beth.

"No I'm not brave, I'm terrified," I laughed weakly.

"Well at least you'll have your home all to yourselves this weekend," laughed Beth.

"I love Carol and Mark dearly, but it will be nice to have our home all to ourselves for a little while," I said.

"I was thinking about coming out to see you and Carol on Monday if that is alright with the two of you."

"We'd love it. She and I were just talking about the three of us getting together so we could talk about our men," I laughed.

"I'll bring our house plans along and we three can check them out to see if there is anything I've missed," said Beth. "Besides which I need you two to distract me because I'm beginning to get a case of the jitters about our wedding."

"You're not having second thoughts are you?"

"Oh God no, I love that man so much, but I just wish the wedding was over with so we could begin our married life together," she said.

"Isn't it funny when we were young we thought about things up to and through the wedding and didn't consider anything after it; now all of us just want to get the wedding over with and get on with our married lives?" I laughed.

"That must mean something, but I'm darned if I know what it is," laughed Beth.

"Why don't you come out early Monday morning and we'll make a day of it, just us three," I said.

"Ok, see you Monday bright and early," said Beth. "Bye sister."

"Goodbye my sister," I said hanging up the phone.

Just as I hung up the phone rang again.

"Hi kitten," said David.

"Hi darling, I was just thinking about you and the weekend," I laughed.

"I just have a couple of minutes, but I was thinking about you and the weekend too," he chuckled.

"Momma wants to thank her Daddy for a lovely evening last night," I said softly.

"Are you still saving the place Daddy marked this morning?" he laughed.

"Too bad you aren't here right this minute Daddy, I'd gladly show you."

"I wish I were too kitten, but I'll see you in another couple of hours. Do you suppose Mark and Carol will make it an early evening what with the wedding tomorrow?"

"I have a feeling from the way Carol was talking this morning that Mark will be lucky if he has the strength to stand at the alter tomorrow," I laughed.

"Well I just hope you and Carol have the strength to walk down the aisle," he chuckled.

"I forgot to get our clothes from last night and Carol found them in the barn and asked me what in the heck we were doing," I said.

"Did you tell her?"

"Only part of it, she also wanted to know what the momma/daddy thing is going on between us."

"What did you tell her?"

"That I'd tell her one of these days," I laughed, "but I'm not sure I'm ever going to tell her, let her find out with her own man."

"Hon, I've got to run. See you tonight, my love."

"I love you, my husband," I said softly.

After I hung up I set about preparing supper so that we would only have to heat it up and Carol came back about a half hour later.

"How did it go at the architect's?"

"Well my wish list got a bit long so some of it had to be trimmed to meet our budget," she laughed.

"Beth called and she's coming out to spend the day with us on Monday and she said she would bring the drawings for their house."

"Mark was afraid I'd be upset by having to cut out some of my wish list, but I think he got the message that I'd live in a tent as long as it was with him," she chuckled.

"Just how did he get this message?"

"Well maybe my hand stroking his inner thigh under cover of the table we were sitting at might have given him some idea, at least I hope it did."

"I can't believe you were ever the reserved person David said you were," I laughed.

"Oh but I was, but after meeting Mark my shy, reserved self just sort of disappeared," she laughed.

"I'll say it did!"

"Do you guys have any plans for tonight?" asked Carol.

"I was just thinking about making it an early evening and I was also wondering if you'd mind if we had dinner later than usual tonight?"

"Considering what I was thinking about on the way home I think a later dinner and then an early evening is just what the doctor ordered," she laughed.

"Great minds…" I laughed.

"No great hungers," she laughed back at me.

David came home at 4:15 and came out in the kitchen where he heard Carol and I talking. "Hi babe," he said coming over and taking me in his arms. "Hi my love," I said snuggling into his arms.

"That man of mine better not be late tonight or I'll murder him," laughed Carol.

"Why what have you got planned, sis?" asked David.

"None of your business bro, but if he don't get here pretty soon I may start without him," she laughed. "Tell him I'm upstairs when you see him," she said turning and we heard her running up the stairs.

"I have a feeling just how she's going to murder Mark if he's late," laughed David.

"We've decided dinner can wait till later because all we have to do is heat it up," I laughed.

"That's the best news Daddy has heard all day," he chuckled rubbing his body against mine.

Just then Mark came in the door. "Where is that wildcat of mine?" he asked.

"I think she's waiting for you in her den," I laughed. "I understand she gave you quite a workout at the architect's today?"

"She and I are going to have a very frank discussion about what's appropriate and what's not, especially when I have to go back to work," he said turning and running up the stairs.

"What was that all about?" asked David.

"Come with Momma and she'll explain it all to you while she watches you strip," I laughed taking him by the hand and leading him upstairs.

When we were in our room he put his arms around me. "Hello Mommy," he said as his hands traveled down caressing my backside.

"Don't talk, just strip," I said already pulling off my own clothes and reaching to help him take off his.

"Is Momma in a hurry?" he chuckled.

"Don't talk, just find the place you marked this morning because it's been such a long day," I laughed softly.

"You mean here?"

"Oh darling hurry, I need you so much," I moaned as my hand sought his penis and I tugged slightly moving him toward the bed.

He pushed me down on the bed and came down on top of me and my legs went up to embrace his waist. He came into me then and I moaned my need of him rising to meet his thrusts and I heard his moans of desire, which matched my own. "Daddy needs Momma just as much as Momma needs him," he said jabbing into me again and again until he felt the shudders go through my body then he too climaxed.

"Does Momma feel better now?" he laughed softly.

"Ever so much better, thank you Daddy," I said smiling up at him. "Rub me darling, and I'll tell you what Carol did to Mark today."

His hand came down between my legs and he began to massage me, "So what did sis do to Mark?" he asked.

"When they were in the architect's office and David was apologizing to Carol because they couldn't afford everything on her wish list, right there under cover of the table Carol began to stroke the inside of his thigh as her way of letting him know she didn't care about not being able to afford everything," I laughed as I let my hand wonder to the inside of his thigh stroking it gently.

"Oh God poor Mark, I can see why he wants to murder her," laughed David and he increased the pressure of his hand as I continued to caress him.

"Daddy, please, please, I need you," I moaned and he came back into me and once again we were in the throes of passion until we both could stand it no longer and our releases came. We both dozed, exhausted from our lovemaking.

When we awoke we continued to lie there content now with just holding each other and murmuring our love for one another.

"Did sis really do that to Mark?" asked David.

"Yes she did and I think she has even more torture planned for him tonight," I giggled.

"What do you girls do all day, think up ways to torture your men?" he laughed.

"We just figured you guys started it teaching us about sex and we want you to know what apt pupils we've become," I laughed.

"No wonder we never stray. What would be the use? We could never find two wildcats to compare to you two," he chuckled.

"That's right, Daddy, you never will," I said.

"Babe, I don't even have the energy to look anymore," he said.

"Good. I'll just make sure you never do have enough energy," I giggled. "Mark told Carol that he was taking her for the two nights at the Ritz and he didn't plan on getting out of bed until she begged him for mercy," I laughed.

"I have a feeling that he's going to cry uncle before she does," said David.

"You can bet on it," I laughed.

"Kitten, I hate to say it but I'm hungry and this time not just for you," he said.

"Come on, darling, let's go eat supper so you'll have enough stamina to last the evening," I laughed.

When we got downstairs Carol and Mark were already eating supper.

"Well Mark, did you have your frank discussion with my sister?" asked David.

"Oh he had it, I just wasn't listening because I had other things on my mind," laughed Carol.

"Oh brother did she," laughed Mark.

I went to the oven to get our supper and I set it before David.

"Eat, husband, because you have connubial duties to perform yet tonight," I said laughing.

"Well at least I'm not alone, your Amazon is as bad as mine," said Mark.

"Men's work is just never done," laughed David.

"You men will start what you can't finish," said Carol.

"But what a way to go, my Amazon," said Mark.

"Carol, I do think these men of ours do protest too much, I've a feeling it is just to keep us trying harder," I laughed.

"You could be right, sis, but as my man said, 'what a way to go'," laughed Carol.

"Be honest now, you two. Would you have it any other way?" asked David laughing.

"NO!" said Carol and I together.

"Just wait till some of our G.I.'s get to Australia, the women are going to think they've died and gone to heaven," laughed Carol. "They are going to go around chanting 'they're oversexed and over here, Thank God.'"

"Well I'm an Aussie and I don't hear my wife complaining," said David.

"Nor will you ever, my love," I said.

"See, so we Australian men aren't taking a backseat to Americans," he laughed.

"Yes but, bro, what does Lauren have to compare it with?" she laughed.

"You got me there, sis," laughed David.

"Well, since I'm the subject here, I'll tell all three of you right now, though I may not have had any comparisons, I don't need them for this Australian stallion of mine is all the man this little filly ever wants," I said.

"Well actually, sis, I don't have any comparisons either but believe me if our women ever had a Mark they'd never want anything else either," laughed Carol.

"Since I have had comparisons, I definitely will tell you that my Amazon is all the woman I'll ever want or need and I'm just glad I found her and that she's mine," said David.

"Thank you, my beloved husband, that's all I really wanted to hear," I said squeezing his hand.

"As for me while I too have had comparison, I know I only want Carol for the rest of my life and I for one can't wait until tomorrow when she is truly mine," said Mark taking Carol's hand.

"Thank you, my soon-to-be-beloved husband, that's all I wanted to hear too," said Carol squeezing Mark's hand.

After the supper dishes were done, the four of us walked back into the living room.

"David darling, let's go down and say goodnight to the horses," I said.

"Let's, I need to stretch my legs a bit anyway," he said. "Do you two want to come with us?"

"No thanks, David. I think Carol and I are going to make it an early evening. We've a big day ahead of us tomorrow and besides I want to hold my bride in my arms," said Mark.

"And I want to very much be in his arms, bro," said Carol.

We walked down to the stables then with David's arm around my waist and mine around his.

"I think Carol and Mark are going to make a lovely couple," I said, my head nestling into David's shoulder as we walked.

"At first I thought maybe it was just sexual attraction and that they were playing at being in love, but now I know they love each other as much as do you and I," said David.

"Yes I know Carol loves Mark because she's told me often enough how much she loves him," I said. "As for Mark, I think he loves Carol maybe even more than she loves him."

"Do you remember that first evening when we went to dinner with Bill and Mark at the Ritz? I thought then when Mark was spewing all that nonsense about too many fish in the sea to settle for just one, that he was kidding himself," said David.

"Yes, I remember and I remember Bill saying that bachelorhood was a lonely existence and you agreeing with him and I wondered then if you really believed that or if you just wanted me to think you had been lonely," I said softly.

"No darling, I wasn't just saying it, I meant it, but I was only beginning to realize how lonely an existence it had been for me then," said David. "Now I know I'd been lonely until you came into my life and gave me love and contentment such as I'd never known before."

"I hope I have, my darling, for I love you so much and I want only to make you as happy as you've made me," I said hugging him to me.

"Hello Sheik," I said reaching to put my arm around Sheik's neck as David rubbed his nose. Sheik shook his head and nickered at us. "Don't worry boy, your master will be coming to see you soon and one day before long he will be around all the time."

"You even want to make the horses happy," said David.

"I want the entire world as happy as I am," I laughed softly.

"Lady, how is our beautiful lady tonight?" said David going to her and rubbing her velvety nose.

"Storm my love, I saved the best for last because you are so big and beautiful like my husband," I said hugging him around the neck.

David came to where I was standing next to Storm and put his arms around me and my arms went about his neck. "Kitten, I've never known a woman with such love in her as you have for everyone and everything."

"But I didn't have it until you came into my life and you've given me such love and happiness that now I want to share it with the whole world, but especially with you."

We walked back to the house then and turned off the lights and locked the door before going upstairs.

"Come here baby, I want to hold you in my arms," said David sitting down in his chair and pulling me to his lap. My arms went around his neck and I nestled my face in his neck.

"You know what I was thinking, when I get home for good, I'd like to enlarge this room and put in a fireplace so we could sit in front of it nights the way we are now and talk about our children and our grandchildren," he said.

"Yes darling, let's do that for it will be our own special hideaway from the world where no one but you and I will exist," I said.

"I'm glad we found this place, it's so peaceful and so beautiful and you've already made it more than a house, you've made it a home," he whispered.

"I think it is beautiful too and I'm so glad you've decided you don't want to leave it to go back to Australia after the war," I said.

"This is our home now kitten, and it's the only home I ever want to have although anyplace would be home where you were," he said softly.

"I've learned that too, the only home I need is you, the rest is just a shelter from the elements, but for me to be truly home it is wherever you are, my darling," I whispered back.

Saturday morning I awakened as David got out of bed at 5:30. "What's the matter, darling?" I asked.

"I've just gotten used to getting up at this time and now I automatically wake up and can't go back to sleep," he laughed.

"Come, crawl back in with me and turn over and I'll rub your back. Maybe that will relax you and you can go back to sleep," I said

He came back into bed then and turned over on his stomach and I began to rub his back and I felt some of the tension start to drain out of his body and he yawned. "Baby, that feels so good."

"Hush darling, go to sleep," I whispered as my hands went on stroking his back.

He turned so that he was on his side and pulled me into his arms and I put my arms around him and kept stroking his back until I heard his soft breathing as he tumbled once more into sleep. I continued to stroke his back until I too fell asleep. When I woke he was looking at me with a smile on his face and when he saw that I was also awake he said, "Mommy has certainly learned how to rub down a man as well a horse."

"You know darling, sometimes I wonder if everything I've done up to the time I met you wasn't in preparation in someway to take care of you and love you," I said. "Maybe I wasn't such a tomboy after all, maybe it was God's plan to teach me the things I needed to know to love and care for you."

"Like what, kitten?"

"Like learning to fly, learning to fix things around a house, learning to rub down a horse," I said.

"Maybe, now that you say it, it was God's plan for you and maybe it was His plan in some way to make me distrust all women so that I would wait until you came into my life so that you could show me what real love and trust were all about," he said.

"Oh David, I don't think God would do that to you because I don't believe in a vengeful God, but just maybe after those things had happened to you He decided that He would allow you to find me so that I could give you all that you had missed, because when He saw what a wonderful man you are He wanted you to be happy."

"Whatever the reason kitten, I'm just so glad it happened for I love you so and you make me so happy."

"What would you think about going for a ride on Storm this morning?" I asked.

"It sounds like a wonderful idea, sweetheart," he smiled.

"Go get dressed and I'll check and see if Carol is up and if she needs anything and if not you and I'll go for a ride."

I checked downstairs and didn't find Carol anywhere around so I went back to our room. "I can't find hide nor hair of either Carol or Mark, " I laughed. "I just hope they get out of bed in time to go to their own wedding."

"Maybe we should check out their room, they might have done each other in in their enthusiasm and we'll find them lying in each other's arms dead as doornails," laughed David.

When we got to the stables we noticed that Lady was not in her stall. "Oh they had the same idea," laughed David.

"What a relief, because I was actually beginning to think that maybe we'd better check their room," I laughed in return.

David took Storm out of his stall and bridled him. Coming to where I was standing he lifted me up on Storm's back so that I was actually riding side saddle then he mounted behind me and I put my arms around him snuggling into his body. "Did you happen to notice that there was a saddle blanket missing off the fence?" he asked.

"No can't say as I did as I was more interested in snuggling down into your arms. Was there actually one missing?"

"Yes, I saw it there last night when we came out to see the horses," he laughed.

"I just hope they didn't decide to take Lady out last night because it could be dangerous since neither of them are experienced riders," I said.

"I don't think that happened unless it was after you and I went to bed and I think I would have heard if they'd closed the back door."

"Knowing those two I'm sure the sun was up before they decided to wonder out so we don't have the pre-dawn hours to worry about," I said.

"Why don't we ride out a little way and if we don't see them we can start calling to them so we don't give them any really embarrassing moments," he laughed.

After we had ridden quite a ways back into the property we began calling, "Mark…Carol."

Finally we heard a faint answer, "We're here you guys but don't you dare come near us and in fact turn around and go home."

"Are you ok?" I called.

"We're fine, just go home," came Carol's reply.

"What in the hell do you think is going on with those two?" asked David.

"Well, the other day I was telling Carol about us making love out in the back forty then riding home naked and I've got a terrible feeling that those two are trying to emulate what we did," I laughed.

"Oh God save me from morons," laughed David. "Don't those two have any sense at all? At least we waited till sundown or nearly sundown and we knew no one else was in the house or about to be."

"If I had a camera I'd be awfully tempted to sneak up on them and get a picture just so when they start spouting off to their offspring about having some decorum we could show the kids the picture," I laughed.

"It would serve them right," he laughed. "I always thought Carol was sensible but since she met Mark, I'm beginning to wonder if she has a brain in her head," he laughed.

"Well I always knew that Mark didn't have a brain in his head especially when it comes to women which was why I was so surprised when he fell for Carol because she seemed to be so level headed," I giggled.

"I'm beginning to wonder if Bill and Beth know what they are letting themselves in for moving in so close to Carol and Mark," he chuckled.

"I sure hope those two don't contaminate Bill and Beth with their brainless lunacy," I laughed.

"You know what would really be a riot?" asked David.

"No what?"

"If they got into poison ivy back there in the woods, because I doubt if either of them would know it if they saw it," laughed David.

"What a way to spend their honeymoon, scratching," I laughed.

"Well I suppose we ought to give them some privacy, so let's go back to our room and at least let them get into the house and get their clothes on," he chuckled.

He turned Storm then and we started back to the house laughing all the way. We stabled Storm and then went back into the house and up to our room. We sat in our chair waiting to hear them come in. A short time later we heard the back door open and close and two pair of feet beating a hasty retreat toward Carol and Mark's room.

"Oh God, I wonder if they road out naked as well," laughed David.

"I'll bet that is exactly what they did," I laughed. "Carol probably thought you and I would keep each other busy and we'd never know that they left the house."

"If this wasn't their wedding day I'd really put them through the third degree, but I can't be that mean on their wedding day," laughed David.

"One thing you've got to say, my darling, is that it is never going to be dull living near them," I giggled.

"That's for darn sure."

We heard their bedroom door open and close and footsteps going down the stairs.

"Come on darling, let's go down because I can't wait to hear their tale," I laughed and we went down stairs and out to the kitchen where Carol and Mark were sitting.

"Hi bro, hi sis," said Carol when we entered the kitchen, but I noticed that her face was very red.

"Don't 'hi bro' me," said David trying to look severe. "Just what were you two up to out there?"

"We just went for an early morning ride," said Mark and his face was a bright shade of pink as well.

"Did you two ever stop to think it could have been Bill and Beth instead of Lauren and I who found you out there in the woods?" said David who could no longer control his laughter. "I'll bet if it was, Bill wouldn't have let you off so easy, he'd have come to investigate."

"Oh God, I never thought about that at all," said Carol.

"Carol, when I told you about David and I making love out in the woods, we at least had the good sense not to ride out stark naked," I laughed.

"We thought we'd be back before you two came downstairs," said Mark.

"In future, I'd like to make a suggestion," laughed David. "At least take some clothes with you, just in case."

"Well you guys rode back naked," said Carol.

"Yes but we had clothes with us if we'd needed them and we at least knew you two weren't coming back before we could get back to our bedroom," I laughed.

"We didn't think about that," said Mark.

"What you mean is when you two get horny you just don't think," laughed David.

"I guess you're right," said Mark, "but it sounded like such a great idea at the time."

"Believe me it is a great idea," I laughed. "But next time forewarn us and we'll stay out of your way."

"Sis, you're not really mad at us are you?" asked Carol plaintively.

"My God no, Carol, we love you we just couldn't help but tease you a little," I laughed.

"Sis, we love you both and we'd never be mad at you over something like this, but we just hope you two will think a little before Bill and Beth move in too," laughed David hugging her.

"Come on, let's get some breakfast because you'll soon have to get ready for your wedding," I laughed.

"I don't think I could eat if my life depended on it because I've got such butterflies," laughed Carol.

"As for me I think I've got big giant moths chasing each other around in my stomach," laughed Mark.

"You two aren't getting cold feet are you?" asked David.

"No, I love Mark so much I think I'd die if I didn't have him and he didn't love me," said Carol.

"That's the way I feel about Carol too," said Mark

"Then what are you so nervous about?" asked David.

"We're just afraid something will happen and someone will call off the wedding and we've just got to be married to each other," said Carol.

"Believe me, sis, no one is going to call off your wedding; we all love you both and we are all so happy that you found each other," I said.

"I think that it is just that everything happened so fast that it kind of scares us, but I love Carol and I want to take care of her and protect her all the rest of my life," said Mark looking at Carol with such love.

"We know what you mean, Mark, because we felt the same way, but you'll love Carol more with each day that passes and she'll love you more with each day that passes. You'll wonder how you could love each other more each day than you do right at this moment, but you will," said David.

"I think part of it is that we know we aren't facing separation like you and Lauren, bro, and we don't know how the two of you stand it," said Carol.

"Carol, we've learned, as will both of you, that it doesn't make any difference how long two people who truly love each other have together; it's making sure that every minute of it is spent loving the other person that really counts. I know that I've been given a wife who loves me now and always will, I've had a home of my own, and that if anything does happen to me I'll go right on loving Lauren until she joins me and then we will be together through eternity," said David quietly.

"Mark, Carol, it isn't how long you have together, its how you use that time. Yes, I still get scared but David and I have had it all and I know now that nothing can ever really separate us, not even death for I'll go right on loving him until I can be with him again," I said softly looking at David.

"How come when Carol and I are older than both of you, that you and Lauren seem to be the ones who are older and wiser, that you keep teaching us about this thing called love?" asked Mark.

"Maybe because from the very beginning Lauren and I have had to look at all the possibilities of what our loving each other could mean for the both of us and so we had to grow up really fast, and we had to learn the lessons right from the very beginning that you and Carol may have more time to learn. Mark, we don't have all the answers, we are still trying to find our way, it's just that in wartime everything is accelerated for those directly involved in the war," said David.

"We keep trying to tell you not to judge your feelings, your love, or anything else by our standards, because our standards have had to undergo a sea of change that I hope to God you will never know. It's funny in a way because all of you thought that it was a wartime fling for us and maybe by your standards it is, but by ours, it is just condensing a lifetime into whatever time we have together," I said.

"Enough of this, I want to be happy and it is getting maudlin," said Carol

"Just one more word, Carol, then we'll get on with the happiest day of your life," said David. "Don't ever think we are unhappy, Carol, because I'm happier than I've ever been in my entire life and I think Lauren will tell you the same thing, so don't feel sorry for us."

"Yes, my husband, I am happier than I've ever been in my life and if I had to do it all over again knowing what we now know, I'd do it again in a heartbeat," I said.

"Well enough is enough," laughed Carol. "Come my very soon-to-be husband, let's go get our showers and get dressed then let's get on with our lives."

"Yes my bride-to-be, let's get on with our lifetime together," said Mark.

They left then to go upstairs to get ready for their wedding. David looked at me and came over to put his arms around me. "I don't think I really want any breakfast either, my love, I'd rather spend the time holding you in my arms," he said.

"Yes, darling, let's go back and sit in our chair and you hold me in your arms and I'll hold you in my arms," I said and that is what we did until it was time for us too to get ready and then we drove to the base chapel to watch those we loved most dearly enter into what we already knew was the adventure of a lifetime of discovery of how much two people can love each other.

"Carol, you look just beautiful," said Beth handing Carol her wedding bouquet.

"Ready Carol?" I asked turning to hug her and when she nodded her head I set off down the aisle ahead of her.

"Ready Bill?" said Carol.

"Ready."

The ceremony was simple but beautiful just as ours had been. After the ceremony was over and we were once again outside the chapel Carol threw her bouquet and Beth caught it.

"Well Beth, that's proof, next Saturday it will be your turn to be the beautiful bride," said Bill.

"Thank you, darling," said Beth softly and all her love for him was in her eyes.

"Well Mr. and Mrs. Purcell, be off with you to your honeymoon suite and we'll see you on Monday," I said hugging and kissing them both.

"Admit it Mark, that wasn't half as bad as you originally thought it was going to be, was it?" laughed David and Bill shaking Mark's hand and kissing Carol.

"See you Monday," they laughed as they got in their car and drove off.

"They seemed somewhat subdued for them," said Bill.

"Bill, before we came over here today we had a somewhat frank discussion with them because they insisted on judging the standards of their love and marriage by David's and mine," I said, "and we tried to tell them that they can't judge it by us because our circumstances are so different from theirs and I think maybe the two of them grew up just a little bit."

"Beth and I were talking about you two last night and we just can't imagine how tough it must be for you two with the war and all, but I think you both have whatever it takes to weather the storm," said Bill.

"Lauren, I keep telling you that you're braver than me, and your circumstances are further proof of it because I don't think I could stay sane the way the two of you seem to," said Beth.

"Beth, it isn't a matter of being brave, I've no choice because it would be worse still if I didn't have David and he didn't have me and whatever happens we are just glad we got a chance to share our love with each other," I said.

"How is Sheik doing?" asked Bill.

"He's fine. David and I went out to tell all the horses goodnight last night and I promised him that you would soon be out to see him and that before long you'd be around all the time," I laughed.

"I'll bet you anything he understood every word you said to him too," laughed Bill

"Well the way he was whining and nickering and nuzzling Lauren, I think he did understand her," laughed David.

"Like I told you, David, I've ridden all my life and I've never seen anyone who can communicate with a horse the way this little gal does," said Bill.

"She's promised to teach me not to be afraid of horses or flying," said Beth. "I just hope she can."

"Well if anyone can darling, it's Lauren because she has some kind of metaphysical something with both horses and planes," laughed Bill.

"That she does and with husbands as well," laughed David.

"Take care, you two, and we'll see you next Saturday. Beth, I'll see you on Monday," I said hugging her.

"I bet you two are going to enjoy being alone together for a while," said Bill.

"Yes, it will be nice, not that we don't enjoy Mark and Carol being around because they keep us in stitches," said David.

"Remind us to tell you about their wedding day ride on Lady," I said. "Those two are like two kids in a candy store."

Driving home David sang different popular ballads of the day.

"Come on, sing along with me for I know you want to and I don't care if you sing off key," he laughed.

"You've such a beautiful voice that I hate to spoil what I'm listening to by joining in," I said.

"Oh come on, you'll enjoy it and so will I," he said.

"Yes I can just imagine how you'll enjoy it, especially if I try to follow you which is what I always do with someone with a strong voice and my voice really cracks," I laughed.

"Come on sugar, sing along with Daddy," he said, so I sang along with him and I noticed how hard it was for him not to laugh.

"See I told you," I said laughing in spite of myself, "you can barely keep from laughing right out loud at this voice of mine."

"Actually, you don't have a bad voice you are just tone deaf," he said.

"At one time I did have a good voice and could actually carry a tune until in choir in high school they put me between a real strong alto and a real strong soprano and since then I can't carry a tune in a bushel basket, and you've got to admit that while I may be rotten at singing at least I'm loud," I laughed.

"That's ok baby, I love you in spite of your tone deaf state," he laughed hugging me.

"Do you think we made any impression on Mark and Carol?" asked David.

"I think what we said to them upset Carol somewhat because she has a connection to this war because she knows you will be directly involved, but I'm not sure it really meant anything special to Mark," I said.

"Sometimes I think things mean more to Mark than we give him credit for because he seems to pass everything off as a joke or a game," said David.

"Wouldn't that be a good indication that nothing affects him very deeply?"

"Not necessarily, I'd hate to play poker with Mark because I think he keeps a lot hidden behind his wit and smiles," said David. "Maybe I identify more with him because I used similar tactics not to let anyone know if I was hurting or to let them see that I cared too deeply."

"Maybe you did, but why didn't you try to hide your feelings from me?" I asked.

"When you put your little tiny hand in mine that first night I felt something I had never felt before, the desire to protect you from the world and that you were the one person in this whole cockeyed world I could trust," he said softly.

"That is what I felt too when you took my hand I felt secure and unafraid for the very first time in my life," I said as I snuggled deeper into his arm and I felt his arm tighten around me.

We pulled into our drive and David got out of the car and came around to hold the door for me giving me his hand to help me out of the car. "Let's go in and change clothes and then take a ride on Storm," he said.

"Yes."

We went upstairs then and I pulled out a pair of jeans and a sweater for David to put on and I took off my skirt and blouse and hung them up. As I was hopping around on one foot trying to put on my jeans David came up behind me. "Let me steady you kitten," he said softly putting his arms around me. I stopped my struggle with the jeans and turned and put my arms around him.

"I love you," I whispered pulling his head down to mine until I felt his lips on mine and my body leaned into his.

"Kitten," he whispered, "I love you so much."

"Please make love to me," I said softly.

"Daddy would like nothing better," he said as his arms pulled me in even closer to him and as his hands unsnapped my bra then slid down to push my panties down until they fell to the floor.

"Oh Daddy, I love being in your arms knowing that you want me as badly as I want you," I whispered as my hands reached to remove his clothes.

He picked me up then and carried me to our chair where he sat down pulling me onto his lap. "Let Daddy love you," he whispered as his lips came down to mine and I felt his tongue enter and search my mouth as his hands caressed my body. "Daddy loves Momma and it's so good to have you all to myself," he said softly as he stood up carrying me to the bed. He laid me down then and I felt his body come down over mine as I pulled him down to me.

We made love and it was slow and unhurried because we knew we had the house to ourselves for the remainder of this day through Monday.

"Momma, Daddy's only going to ask this one more time, do you want to take a ride on Storm?" laughed David.

"Well, it's not entirely my fault, because you know how easily Momma can get distracted by Daddy's loving arms and sexy body," I laughed.

"So do you want to?"

"Do I want to what?" I giggled. "And the answer is yes to either question."

"If Momma doesn't start behaving herself Daddy's going to spank," he laughed.

"Oooh that sounds like fun too," I laughed hugging him.

"Do you or do you not want to go riding?"

"Yes let's, but let me get us some lunch first because I'm starving and I know you must be too," I said. "Now if you'll please hold on to me I'll get these dumb jeans on."

"I think that's what started this whole thing in the first place," he said chuckling.

We went downstairs then and I made us lunch. "I wonder who's wining, Carol or Mark?" I laughed.

"If you don't see them Monday morning you better call and have them check their room they might both be dead from excess," chuckled David. "But if I were betting I think I'd have to put my money on Carol, she has an awful lot of stamina."

"My money would be on Carol too because she has a really huge appetite," I laughed.

"When they are here I think how nice it would be to be alone in our home, but when they aren't I kind of miss them because those two can sure give you a lot of laughs," he said.

"You're right, they can and in a way I miss them too, but for just a little while I like being alone with my husband," I said. "Is that terrible of me?"

"No, or at least if it is I'm guilty too because I like being in our home alone, just the two of us," said David.

"You finished?"

"Yes, let's go riding."

We went out to the barn and David bridled Storm and brought him out of his stall. "Hello, my big beauty," I said hugging Storm's neck. Storm tossed his head and whinnied at me. "Yes I know we've been neglecting you lately, but we'll make up for it today."

I swung up to Storm's back and David mounted behind me, taking the reins and we walked out of the stable heading toward the back of the property.

"You know if we do buy that extra five acres, we ought to make a meadow for us to ride in as well as a runway for planes," said David

"Would we have enough room to have both?" I asked.

"Even if we built a north/south and east/west runway we should still have room enough for a small meadow something like what Bart has."

"I really can't believe that we would ever use a plane enough to make it worth while to own one, especially when there are airports all around us where we could charter a plane," I said.

"With the way Beth feels about flying and Carol isn't a whole lot better…she doesn't mind big planes but the small ones scare her to death, it does seem like kind of a useless expense because you and I are the only ones who would get any pleasure from it to amount to anything," said David.

"Once Beth and Bill are married I think we ought to sit down, the six of us, and lay out our plan for this place," I said.

"That's a good idea, then there will be no hurt feelings or recriminations later on," said David, "not that I think there really would be, but better to be safe than sorry."

As we rode I snuggled back into David's arms so I was leaning my back against his chest and his arms tightened around me from time to time and every so often he would bend his head and I would feel him kiss the top of my head. "Pull up for a minute, darling," I said.

"What's wrong, sweetheart?"

"Nothing is wrong, I just want to kiss you," I laughed softly as I tilted my head so that he could kiss me.

"Momma does think of the nicest things," he laughed and he allowed his hand to caress my breast.

"Daddy has some pretty wonderful ideas too," I said. "When we get back closer to the stable, Momma wants to try something."

"Let's head back," he said chuckling softly.

"Yes, let's."

When we got closer to the stable he pulled Storm to a halt.

"Just what did Momma have in mind?" he asked.

"Hold on to me so I don't fall off," I said as I turned so that first I was in a side-saddle position atop Storm then I threw my leg over to the other side and I was once again astride Storm but I was facing David and my arms went around him and I was able to kiss him at my leisure. "This wouldn't work except in the slowest of walks or when we were standing still, but it was worth a try."

"Kitten, you do get inventive, but I think there are safer ways," laughed David.

"I think you're right," I laughed.

We rode back to the barn and bedded down Storm King for the night. As we were passing the one empty stall I said, "Now if we had just had the foresight to spread some straw in here we could have really had a roll in the hay," I laughed.

"Remind me to spread some around tomorrow just in case we can't make it all the way back to the house, sometime," he laughed.

"I just hope that we don't give these two stallions any ideas if we use it," I said giggling. "Lady might never forgive us."

"God help us if Mark and Carol ever discover why we put down the straw," chuckled David.

"If we ever get the dance floor built, we may need to put up a sign which says 'occupied' on this particular stall," I laughed.

"Somehow I can't see Beth ever taking advantage of it, because if a mouse happened to skitter out of the straw just as things were heating up I have a feeling her screams would scare the horses," he chuckled. "But while Carol doesn't particularly like mice, I don't think she'd let a little thing like a mouse deter her," laughed David.

We went into the house then and into the living room. "Put on some records Daddy, Momma wants her daddy's arms around her again," I said.

He went then and put on several records on the turntable. "Why doesn't Momma take her clothes off so Daddy can really enjoy dancing with her," he chuckled softly.

"Daddy should take his off too," I said.

We took off all our clothes and David started the records playing then came back and took me in his arms pulling me in close to him as he hummed the song that was playing into my ear.

"This is a much better way to dance," he whispered, as his arms came down cupping my buttocks in his hands as we swayed to the music and I allowed my arms to do the same to him.

"Daddy has such good ideas that feel so wonderful," I said lifting my head so I could look into his eyes. As I did so, he bent his head and gave me a long, lingering kiss and I rubbed my body against his letting him know how much I loved the feel of him naked against me.

"Momma, if you keep doing that this dance is going to come to an abrupt end," he whispered.

"Daddy isn't telling me anything I can't already feel," I laughed softly.

With that he sank to the floor pulling me with him as his hand went between my legs, "Momma is all ready for Daddy, I see," he chuckled.

"Come to Momma, she has something for you which she knows you will enjoy," I giggled. As he rolled so that he was atop me, I moaned my need of him. "Please Daddy, Momma needs you so much."

He came into me then, "Does that feel better, darling?" he asked looking down into my eyes.

"Yes, please, more, deeper," was all I could get out for my desire for him was beyond words.

He plunged into me then until I was screaming because the ecstasy was so great and still he continued to thrust until the shudders ran through me and he backed off slightly then began the thrusting all over again and I came a second then a third time and finally he too exploded within me. "Daddy really needed that," he said.

I bent my head then so I could kiss him just below his bellybutton. "Spread your legs apart, darling," I said and my hand went down to cup his testicles and I stroked them gently for several minutes then I encircled his penis with my hand squeezing gently and I heard him moan. "Does that feel good to you, my husband, the way your hand between my legs feels good to me?"

"Oh God yes, it feels wonderful," he said as his penis became erect in my hand.

I rolled then so he was once more on top of me and as he came into me I said, "This time it's just for you, I want to give you as much as you give me, so don't try to please me, my husband, just do whatever makes you feel good."

He plunged back and forth within me and I rose to meet him with each thrust until at last he climaxed. "Kitten, you didn't come that time," he whispered. "Let me give you your release."

"No love, that was just for you and my pleasure came from you just being in me that deeply and that I was giving you pleasure," I said.

"But it's not fair to you, you deserve to reach a climax just as much as I do."

"Darling before, I climaxed three times before you did once, was that fair to you?" I asked. "Just because as a woman I'm capable of multiple orgasms, doesn't mean that I have to have them to feel contentment and pleasure, for my pleasure comes in loving you and giving you as much pleasure as I can."

"Kitten I love you so much, and you never fail to amaze me, and I'll never know how I got so lucky to find you," he whispered.

"Do you even begin to understand how much your telling me that gives me pleasure, it's not quite but almost as good as sex," I laughed softly.

"You've got to be kidding?"

"No I'm not, for every time you just hold me in your arms, or I hear your soft laughter when something I've done or said pleases you, or when you reach out and touch me whether it is for sex or just in love, I feel so warm and so complete and I get a sensual pleasure from it," I whispered. "I love you in every way possible both sacred and profane."

He pulled me closer into his arms then and I purred my love and my pleasure of being in his arms and my hands began to stroke him once more as his hands stroked my body.

"This is for the both of us," he whispered as he came into me yet once again and I moaned with pleasure as his lips came down and his tongue teased my nipple until it stood up strong and proud and then he went to the other one with the same result and I moaned as his hands slid down and he raised my buttocks higher so that he was still deeper within me. With every thrust my body pushed against his thrust to bring him even further into me and I could feel the muscles surrounding my vagina begin to spasm in my need to draw him in still farther.

"Please my love end this now for I don't want to hurt you and I'm afraid I will," I moaned, and his thrusts came quicker and quicker until at last I climaxed and then I felt his seed burst into me and he collapsed on top of me and we both tumbled into sleep our bodies exhausted.

When I woke I saw that David was still sleeping. I got up and dressed and threw an afghan over him. Then I went to the kitchen to prepare dinner for us and as I stood at the stove I wrapped my arms about me and I smiled to myself because I felt so loved and needed. As I stood there, I looked up and saw David standing in the doorway smiling at me.

"You look happy and content, kitten," he said.

"How could I feel anything else when you give me such love, my husband?"

"Now are we talking about sex or love?" he chuckled.

"Both. The sex was mind-blowing, but the love, oh that is just beyond my wildest dreams," I laughed.

He came over then and pulled me into his arms and kissed me.

"You are such a joy to me, kitten," he said.

"I have a feeling Daddy is feeling playful again, but this time Daddy is going to have to wait until after super because I'm hungry," I laughed.

"You mean to tell me that if I demanded my conjugal rights this very minute you wouldn't cooperate?" he chuckled.

"Well if I thought Daddy was really serious and needed me right this minute I'd cooperate but then I might take a chunk out of Daddy because my stomach is demanding food," I giggled.

"We can't have Momma starve to death so I guess Daddy is going to have to wait his turn in the scheme of things," he chuckled. "So what's for supper?"

"I'm heating up what was left the other night when Mark and Carol took off without eating, but I also made Daddy a banana cream pie," I said.

"In a case like that Daddy will definitely defer to the banana cream pie."

"Daddy does seem to have a problem as to whether he lusts more after Momma or her cream pie," I laughed.

"Well I could always cut me a slice and lay it on Momma's stomach and nibble my way down," he said.

"Just think what Momma could do with whip cream and Daddy's cooperation," I laughed.

"You paint such wonderfully vivid pictures in my mind, kitten," he laughed.

"Oh David I love you so," I said. "I love that we can both laugh at what, for some couples, is such a serious business."

"I think that is one of the things I love most about you, kitten, is that wacky sense of humor you have not to mention your inventive little mind."

"Well Daddy was the one who first inspired my so-called inventive little mind," I said hugging him. "You will admit that if it weren't for you it would never have been pointed in quite that direction. Now go sit down and let me get supper on the table," I laughed.

I set the table and put the hot food on and sat down myself. We laughed and talked as we ate and every so often David's hand would steel across the table and squeeze my hand.

"I know we said these next two days were entirely for us alone, but what would you think about inviting Bill and Beth out to go riding tomorrow for a couple of hours?" I asked. "We've not spent much time with them and they have been so good to us."

"Why don't you invite them for lunch, then we can go riding afterwards, kitten," said David. "I've an idea that Mark and Carol may want alone time too by next weekend and they might just want to spend it at Mark's apartment so we still will have time alone together."

"Thank you, darling, and I think you are right about Carol and Mark, that is if they survived this weekend," I laughed. "That brings up something else I've been thinking about."

"Now what?" he laughed.

"What would you think if we kept Mark's apartment sort of as a town house for when we need time alone, if we each paid half the rent it shouldn't cost us a great deal and if Mark is willing we can keep it until after you get your orders then we can always sub-lease it, that definitely wouldn't be a problem in Washington?"

"That sounds like it may be a great idea and maybe Mark or Bill would still want to keep it even after I'm gone as an alternative hotel room for overnight guests for their respective businesses, so let's get Bill's opinion on it."

"I know with Bill that at least once or twice a month he had people coming into town that we were always trying to find a hotel room for and this way he wouldn't have to hunt and it could be written off as a business expense," I said.

"Why don't you go call Bill while I'm clearing up the dishes then you shall have your banana cream pie," I laughed.

While I cleared the table and started the dishes David called Bill.

"Hi Bill, it's David."

"Hi how is the second honeymoon going?" said Bill

"It's hard to say since we seem to be on one continuous honeymoon," laughed David. "Lauren and I were wondering if you and Beth would like to come to lunch tomorrow and then the four of us could go riding afterward?"

"We'd love it but are you sure you two want company?" said Bill.

"Yes, we're sure Bill, and we've also got something else we would like to talk over with you."

"What time do you want us there?" asked Bill.

"Kitten, what time do you want Bill and Beth to come by?" David asked me.

"Tell them around one is fine," I said.

"Lauren says around one is fine, Bill," said David

"See you tomorrow at one then."

"See you."

"Come sit back down, darling," I said as I cut him a generous piece of pie.

After digging in David said, "Don't ever let your government say again that we are fighting for mom and apple pie, it should definitely be we're fighting for mom and banana cream pie."

"I take it that it is ok then?"

"It is more than ok; it is to die for," laughed David.

After the dishes were washed and stacked on the drain board to dry, we walked down to the stables and mucked them out and spread new straw for each of the horses. "What do you want to do about this empty stall?" I asked smiling at him.

"For the time being why don't we leave it as is, besides I think Carol and Mark will get the most use out of it, so why don't we make them do the spreading of the straw?" he laughed.

"That's a very wise thought," I said laughing at him.

We went then and took each horse for a short ride. "I can't get used to being this close to the ground," laughed David as he rode Sheik.

"Lady is so lady-like that I almost don't feel like I'm on a horse," I said.

Finally we came to Storm King. "Now this is my kind of horse," said David as I swung up on Storm and he swatted my backside as I mounted. "He has such obvious advantages."

"Get up here you, lecherous young man," I laughed as he mounted behind me.

I patted Storm's neck and leaned down by his ear saying, "Storm you are our favorite, just don't tell the other horses for we don't want them to feel bad."

Storm shook his head and whinnied. "Yes Storm, you are definitely our favorite," said David patting him on the rump. Storm pranced around as if he understood both of us and was telling us he wouldn't tell if we didn't.

"Do you think you'll ever get Mark to help with the mucking out of the stables?" asked David laughing.

"Probably not, but Carol has taken to it like a veteran," I said, "as have you."

"Maybe we could talk Bill and Beth into coming flying with us tomorrow afternoon, what do you think?"

"Well I know Bill would, but I'm not so sure about Beth because she's deathly afraid of flying."

"Maybe we could talk her into it if we promised not to do any aerobatics or anything like that," he laughed.

"Oh God, don't even mention that word to her or we'll never get her over her fear," I laughed.

"Well if they don't want to go, maybe after they leave we can drive over and charter a plane for an hour or so," he said.

"I know you love flying as much as I do, but wouldn't that sort of be like a busman's holiday for you?" I asked.

"Well yes and no," he laughed. "It is what I do all day every day but this time I could relax and enjoy it because my beautiful co-pilot is so much better than any of my students."

"Let's play it by ear and see what happens and if Bill and Beth don't want to go and you still want to after they leave, then it's fine with me," I said.

We walked back to the house and David put on some records. I sat on the couch and David stretched out with his head in my lap. He reached for my hand and brought it to his lips.

"This has been such a wonderful day, my wife. I feel totally relaxed...do you think this is how we'll always feel when I get back home for good?"

"Probably not, we'll probably be too exhausted from chasing the kids around all day," I laughed. "Then we'll have to get them all bathed and in bed and by the time that is done, we'll just fall into bed."

"Won't this be a great place for kids?" asked David.

"It will indeed, darling, they'll have five acres in which to roam and explore, the horses to ride, dogs to run with, and then they can always go visit Aunt Carol and Uncle Mark or Aunt Beth and Uncle Bill when Mom and Dad just don't understand them and the latest mischief they've gotten themselves into," I laughed.

"You know that sounds so strange when three months ago I'd never have dreamed such a thing were possible, but now it sounds like pure heaven to me," said David.

"It does to me too, sort of like it was a movie I'd seen, but we'll make it all come true," I said squeezing his hand.

"What would you think if on the back of the property I put in a small swimming hole which we could also use as an ice rink in the winter?" he asked.

"That would be pure heaven for the kids; the swimming hole sounds great to me, but unfortunately I can't skate," I laughed.

"My tomboy can't skate?" chuckled David.

"No, I've weak ankles and about a half hour of ice skating and my legs ache so badly that I'm in misery so I've just stayed away from it."

"Well Daddy will just pick Mommy up in his arms and skate with her then she won't have to worry about weak ankles," he said.

We were quiet for a while listening to the music and enjoying the warm comfort of our home. Finally I shook David gently. "Come on Daddy, it's time you were in bed because there is no way on God's green earth I could carry you upstairs," I laughed softly.

We turned off the lights and locked up and we walked arm and arm up the stairs. David yawned and stretch. "I didn't realize how sleepy I was," said David.

"Come on, Momma will help you undress," I said pulling his sweater over his head. When we were undressed I steered him toward the bed and pushed him gently down on his stomach and began to rub his back.

"Oh baby, that feels wonderful," he said

When I finished rubbing his back for him I crawled over him and lay down in his arms, kissing him on the cheek. "Go to sleep, my love, you are exhausted and so am I."

"Good night darling, I love you," he whispered as he drifted into sleep with me curled in his arms.

The next morning I heard David stirring around and I opened one eye. "What are you doing, my love? You don't have to get up early today," I said.

He came over and kissed me. "Go back to sleep, little one. I just can't sleep anymore and I thought I'd go down and feed the livestock," he said softly.

"I guess you can take the man out of the military but you can't take the military out of the man when it comes to early rising," I laughed softly. "Wake me around nine if you will, darling."

"Ok Mommy, now go back to sleep," he said as he left the room. I curled up with his pillow next to my face so I could still smell his scent and I went back to sleep. When I woke again the clock on the nightstand said 7:30 and I got up and went in to take a shower and get dressed.

When I got downstairs, I heard David in the kitchen and went out to see what he was up to. He sat at the kitchen table drinking coffee and when I came into the kitchen he looked up.

"What are you doing up? It isn't nine yet," he said.

"I couldn't sleep anymore without Daddy beside me," I laughed going to him and putting my arms around him and kissing him on the cheek. "Any more coffee left?"

"Yes, plenty, kitten."

"What would you like for breakfast?"

"How about scrambled eggs and toast?" he said smiling at me.

"You've got it darling," I said going to the icebox and getting out the eggs. "Would you like some bacon too?"

"No, just eggs and toast."

I got down the iron skillet and whipped the eggs, and then I put the toast in the toaster. I brought a plate full of eggs and toast to him and refilled his coffee cup.

"Aren't you eating breakfast, kitten?"

"I'm not hungry for some reason," I said. "I'll just have more coffee with you." I sat then sipping my coffee and watching him down his eggs.

"Why are you looking like that?" he asked.

"Like what?"

"Like a kitten that has just had her saucer of cream and is dreamily sitting in the sunshine," he laughed.

"That's the way I feel, you described it perfectly," I laughed softly. "I love sitting here looking at you and loving you."

"Come over here and sit on daddy's lap," he laughed.

I went over to him and he drew me down on his lap and he nuzzled my neck and I turned so that my arms were around his neck and my face was in his neck and my lips against it as his arms came around me.

"You make a man feel so contented and so loved," he said.

"That's what I feel contented and so loved," I said, as my arms tightened around his neck.

"You're purring again, little one," he laughed.

"I know. Anytime I'm in daddy's arms I can't help but purr."

"Well little one, I think I could purr myself," he laughed.

"Did you get the horses all fed and watered?"

"Yup, everything is ship shape and Bristol fashion in the stable," he laughed. "I'd never have believed you could make a horse person out of me, but you did it."

"You never believed I could make a husband out of you either, my love, but I did that too," I laughed.

"Yes you have, kitten. I love being a husband which is something I never thought I would hear myself saying."

"One day soon, you'll be saying you never thought I could make a father out of you, but I will," I said.

"Are you trying to tell me something, kitten?"

"Yes, I think I may be pregnant," I said hugging him tighter around the neck.

"What make's you think you are?"

"I've been feeling nauseated in the mornings, I get tired more easily, my breasts are more tender, just a lot of little things, but we'll know for sure in a week or so," I laughed.

"Oh baby, do you really think that's what it might be?" he said

"Bet you twenty cents," I laughed. "I think that is part of what caused me to get such a nesting instinct when we were moving, I wanted my nest all prepared for my baby's father and for our baby."

"Oh God my love, one part of me is praying that you are right because I want to have babies with you, but the other part of me is thinking about all you'll have to go through alone," he whispered.

"But I won't be alone, my love, part of you will be right inside me and your love will be all around me, and then I've got Beth and Bill and Carol and Mark who will take good care of me, so don't worry about me," I said looking at him. "I want this baby so badly, I want to give you a son or a daughter who will worship you just the way that I do. Besides women have been having babies since time began, and while I wish that you could be here with me through all of it, you did your part already, now I take over."

"Baby, I love you so much and I need you so much, just promise me that you will take good care of yourself," he whispered and I actually saw tears in his eyes.

"Mark has a movie camera and I'll make him keep a photographic record of everything so you'll be a part of it, and I'll tell our baby every day what a wonderful father she or he has and how you'll play with him or her and love him or her and how brave you are because you will be fighting for his or her right to grow up in a free country," I said.

"Do you care if we tell Bill and Beth today?" he asked. "I've just got to tell somebody or burst."

"Yes, let's tell them and Monday night we'll tell Carol and Mark."

He laid his hand on my stomach. "It is hard to believe that our baby is already growing inside you, and it's unbelievable how protective I feel of him or her already," he said and his mouth came down on mine in such a tender loving kiss.

"What would you like to name our baby, my love?" I asked.

"Carol if it's a girl and Mike if it's a boy," he said. "Is that ok with you?"

"That's more than ok with me, darling," I whispered.

"Baby, ought you to be riding?" he asked.

"I don't think riding will be a problem if I keep it to a sedate walk. See my dearest, all your worry about me jumping fences and so forth was for nothing, you've already seen to it and you'll know I'm not doing either of those things," I laughed. "So you see you got your own way after all. Now would you mind taking me upstairs and having sex with me because I want you so much."

"Is it safe for you and the baby?" he asked.

"It's safe and absolutely mandatory," I whispered.

He picked me up in his arms and carried me up the stairs and we made love then and it was better than it had ever been because I knew I was giving him his posterity and I reveled in the new love I felt not only for my baby's father but for my baby as well. Afterwards as I lay in his arms, I whispered, "Thank you my love, for loving me so much and for giving me our baby."

"Darling, it is I who thank you, you've given me everything and I owe you so much for you've always given it to me with such love," he whispered.

"Much as I would love to lie here forever in your arms, I think I'd better get up and get lunch ready because Bill and Beth will be here soon," I said.

I dressed and I went downstairs then. David decided to shower and shave before coming down. The phone rang as I was preparing lunch for us.

"Hi Lauren."

"Carol, how is the honeymoon going?"

"It's just absolutely great, but I've got something to tell you."

"What?"

"You're not going to believe this sis, but I'm pregnant," laughed Carol.

"You're what!"

"I'm pregnant, or at least I'm pretty sure I am because I've missed my period by better than two weeks now and I never do that."

"Oh my God," I laughed.

"What are you laughing at sis?"

"I'm pretty sure I'm pregnant too as I was just telling your brother."

"You're kidding?"

"No I'm not kidding and wait till I tell David he's not only going to be a father but an uncle and all at the same time."

"Now if Bill can just get Beth pregnant on their wedding night, then we'll all be right on schedule," laughed Carol.

"What did Mark say when you told him?"

"At first he thought I was joking, but now he's just plain dumbfounded to be a bridegroom and a father all in the same week."

"Well take care, Carol, and I'll see you Monday."

"Bye sis, and congratulations to you too," she laughed.

"David! David!" I shouted as I ran up the stairs. He came out of the bedroom to see what all the shouting was about. I ran into his arms and hugged him to me.

"You're not going to believe this my darling. I think you better sit down," I said leading him to our chair and pushing him down into it and curling up on his lap.

"What aren't I going to believe?" he laughed hugging me.

"That was Carol who just phoned and guess what?"

"I'll be darned if I can guess where that sister of mine is concerned anymore," he laughed.

"Well darling you are going to be an uncle as well as a father," I giggled.

"I'm what?"

"You heard me, that was Carol calling to tell me that she was pregnant," I laughed.

"Is she sure?" he asked dumbfounded.

"Very, very sure, my love, so you get to be a daddy and an uncle all at the same time. Maybe we can get a reduced rate in the hospital. You won't have to worry about me because Carol will probably be in labor at the same time I am," I giggled watching the confused expression on his face.

"You're not just kidding me kitten, are you?"

"No sweetheart it's for real," I said hugging him again. "What's more if Beth just happens to turn up pregnant as well, we'll be right on schedule of having all our kids at the same time so that they will always have playmates."

"Whoa slow down, kitten, I'm still reeling from the shock of you and Carol both being pregnant, let's not get Beth in on this too," he laughed kissing me. "Let's call Carol back so I can congratulate her and Mark," he said.

We placed a call to Carol and when she answered David said, "Congratulations sis, I'm in shock from finding out that Lauren is pregnant then I find out ten minutes later you are too."

"Oh bro, isn't it just the greatest news ever?" she laughed.

"How is Mark taking it?"

"Well he's in shock too and I haven't even had time to tell him the news about Lauren yet," said Carol.

"Put Mark on if he can still function," laughed David.

When Mark came on the phone David and I chorused together, "Congratulations Dad."

"My God David, how did all of this happen so fast?" he said sounding perplexed.

"Well if you don't know where babies come from I'm going to let my sister explain it to you," laughed David.

"I just can't get used to the fact that I'm a bridegroom and a father all at the same time," Mark laughed.

"Well, I'll tell you one better, old buddy, you're not only a groom and a father, but you are also going to be an uncle."

"Lauren's pregnant too?" asked Mark sounding more confused than ever.

"Yup, old buddy she is," said David.

"Oh my God, do you think those two women of ours planned it this way?" said Mark.

"I wouldn't bet against it," said David. "You know how they are when they get together."

I took the phone from David. "Mark, Bill and Beth are coming over for lunch, do you care if I tell them your news as well as ours?"

"No, what the hell, the more the merrier," laughed Mark.

"Now all we need is to find out Beth is pregnant and it will be perfect," I laughed.

"I wouldn't put it past any of the three of you," said Mark.

"Well Mark, if you guys want to play, sooner or later you've got to pay the piper."

"Oh well, it was worth it, Lauren," he chuckled.

"See you two Monday," I said.

"Ya, see you," said Mark still sounding bewildered.

"What an unbelievable day this has been so far," laughed David hugging me to him.

Just then we heard a knock on the door. "Come on in, Bill and Beth," I hollered as we raced down the stairs.

"Hi kids, how goes it?" said Bill.

"Great."

"David, what's the matter?" said Beth. "You look like somebody just gave you a punch in the stomach."

"Well two people have, in a manner of speaking," laughed David.

"Come on in the living room and we'll tell you all about it," I said laughing.

"You on the other hand, little one, look absolutely radiant," said Bill.

"Bill, Beth…you are not going to believe this one even when it comes from Lauren and Carol," said David.

"Ok give, what is going on?" asked Beth.

"Well, just a little while ago I was telling David that I'm pretty darn sure that he's going to be a father in about nine months," I said. "Then about two minutes ago Carol called to tell David he's definitely going to be an uncle."

"Oh my God," said Bill. "You're kidding?"

"Nope cross my heart, Bill," I said, laughing at his expression.

"Well kids, not to be outdone," laughed Beth, "but I just told Bill I was pretty darn sure I was pregnant."

"Oh Beth, that's wonderful," I said, running to her to hug her and then Bill.

"I'm still reeling from Beth's news, then we come here and find out you're pregnant as well Lauren, and that Carol is too," laughed Bill. "I can't seem to take it all in—my ears hear it but I don't think my brain has caught up with my ears yet."

"Let's call Carol and Mark back and tell them," I said. "You two can get on the extension in the kitchen and David and I will use the one in the living room."

We called Carol and Mark then.

"Carol, get Mark so he can hear this too," I laughed.

"Now what?" asked Mark.

"I'm pregnant too," laughed Beth.

"Oh my God, I just don't believe this," said Mark.

"Isn't it great, the three of us are right on schedule," laughed Carol.

"Why don't you two check out and come home right now and we'll have a celebration," I said.

"Is that ok with you Mark?" asked Carol.

"Yes, I think I need Bill and David to pinch me to make sure I'm not having a nightmare," laughed Mark.

"We'll hold lunch for you till you get here," I said.

"We're on our way, sis," laughed Carol.

About a half hour later Carol came running in the house followed by Mark. "Isn't this the greatest day?" she laughed. "All of us pregnant at the same time."

The three men in our lives stood back watching us.

"It's a great day for us girls, but our men look like we'd dropped a bomb on them," I laughed.

"They do look a little shell shocked," laughed Beth and Carol.

"Come on in the kitchen and we'll get the food on the table, maybe food will help," I laughed.

"A good stiff drink would help even more," said Mark.

"Come on, Bill and Mark, I'll pour," laughed David.

"What do you girls want?" he asked.

"Considering the condition we are all in, I think we'd better stick to soft drinks," said Carol.

"Good, we men can have one for ourselves and then one for you girls," laughed Bill, "because I think we need it."

"Just like men," laughed Carol. "We're the ones pregnant and they are the ones getting drunk."

"Oh they are just congratulating themselves," I laughed. "Their part is over, they don't get to have all the fun we three will have in the next nine months."

"How about you two?" asked Beth. "I've already got morning sickness."

"I do too," I laughed.

"Me three," said Carol.

"You three women are enough to drive any sane man to drink," laughed Mark.

"I just didn't think all of us men had it in us," laughed Bill.

"You two guys better get your houses built pretty darn fast," laughed David, "because I don't think there is room enough in this house for three babies, unless we turn the living room into a nursery."

"Yes you better," laughed Beth, "because Carol and I have a great urge to build our nests and get them feathered now."

"I just can't figure out how you three managed to all get pregnant at the same time," said Mark.

"Well darling, you guys taught us all about sex and we enjoyed it so we haven't exactly been denying you. What did you expect?" laughed Carol. "Besides this just proves that the three of us are really sisters."

"As I was telling David this morning, if Daddy wants to play then the piper he must pay," I laughed.

"Oh that's what you were talking about with the momma/daddy bit," laughed Carol.

"Well Lauren and I were the only ones actually *trying* to get Momma pregnant," laughed David, "you and Bill were just having fun," he laughed.

"Oh are you saying it wasn't fun for you?" I laughed

"Never darling," said David.

"So Carol, have you and Beth picked out names yet?" I asked.

"Bill and I were thinking if it's a girl we'll call her Kate and if it's a boy we'll call him Sean," said Beth.

"David and I've decided on Carol or Mike," I said.

"Mark and I haven't exactly gotten that far," laughed Carol. "But maybe Raggedy Ann or Andy would be good."

"We just didn't realize how appropriate our name for this farm is for 'Love Farms' it is certainly turning out to be," I laughed.

"Sit down, you guys, so we can get lunch on the table because I'm starving," said Carol.

"I am too," said Beth.

"Well after all the three of us are eating for two now," I laughed.

We three girls ate ravenously, but the men who usually could wolf down a meal in two minutes flat kind of pushed their food around their plates still looking like the three of them had run into a brick wall.

"I think we'd better put all this food in the icebox because I have a feeling that these guys of ours are eventually going to get over the shock and are going to be hungry," I laughed.

"Lauren, it isn't that we aren't happy, but I for one never thought I'd be a husband much less a father," said Bill, pulling Beth onto his lap.

"As for me, I'm still reeling from the fall I took when this baggage of mine looked at me because as you know only the week before I was proclaiming I'd never get married, and now I'm not only a husband but about to be a father as well," laughed Mark pulling Carol onto his lap.

"I'm probably the most shell shocked of any of you, because a little over two months ago I would have laughed in your face if you had told me I'd ever trust any woman enough to fall in love, let alone get married, and now I too am about to be a father," laughed David pulling me onto his lap.

"Just as long as all of you are happy about our news, and you still love us," I said.

"I can't speak for the rest of the men, but I'm so happy I can't believe it," said David hugging me to him.

"Mark darling, you are happy about the news aren't you?" asked Carol.

"Baby doll, I'm happy too. I never knew that life could be so wonderful," said Mark hugging Carol to him.

"Bill, I hope you are happy too," said Beth.

"Beth, I'm just as happy as the rest of the guys here and I thank you for giving me your love and now our baby," said Bill hugging Beth close to him.

"See what you started, Mark, by talking me into coming to that dance," I laughed.

"Oh my God, Lauren. I'd forgotten that I was the one who talked you into coming that night," he laughed. "It seems like a million years ago now not just two months."

"So what are all you guys hoping for, boys or girls?" asked Carol.

"A boy," said Mark and Bill.

"That's where we differ my brothers, for I've already told Lauren that I hope our first is a girl, just like her," he laughed.

"Why do you want a girl, David?" asked Bill.

"Because I want her to be a tomboy just like her mom and I want to fly with her and ride with her and eventually I want her to make some man as happy as her mother has made me," said David. "Besides I know from experience that if anything were to happen to me or Lauren that a girl will look after her brothers and give them unconditional love."

"Thanks bro," said Carol looking at him.

"Personally, I don't care what it is as long as it's healthy," said Beth.

"Amen," said Carol and I.

"Hey let's go riding," I laughed.

"Do you think we ought to?" asked Carol.

"Sure, as long as we limit it to a sedate walk," I said.

"Beth, are you ok with taking a ride if I hold you tight?" asked Bill.

"I guess so. I don't want to be left behind," said Beth.

"Beth, you'll have Bill right there with you and he's one of the best riders I've ever seen and David and I will be right next to you," I said.

"Ok what the heck, I guess riding a horse can't be any more scary than thinking about becoming a mother," laughed Beth.

We went out to the stable then and got the horses. The men lifted each of us onto the horse then swung up behind us cuddling us in their arms. Even Beth settled back into Bill's arms and seemed to enjoy the feel of the horse and Bill's arms around her. Mark even took the reins from Carol and guided Lady.

"Now you guys admit it, isn't this the most romantic way to ride a horse?" I laughed.

They all agreed it was and that I had been right all along. When we got back, we rubbed down the horses and gave them water.

"As long as we are all together, Lauren and I have some questions for you," said David.

"What's on your mind? That is if after today's revelations you still have one," laughed Bill.

"Bill, you mentioned buying that extra ten acres and putting a runway for a private field on the back end of it," said David. "Lauren and I talked about it and since none of you care that much about flying we were wondering if this wasn't just an additional expense for no reason since there are small fields where we can rent aircraft if we want to go flying. We figure the only ones who would get any use out of it are Lauren and I since we are the only ones with pilot licenses."

"What do you two have in mind for it?" asked Bill.

"We were thinking that we'd make a meadow out of it where we could ride and our kids could ride," said David.

"You may be right about the airfield, but I still think purchasing it now is a sound investment since after the war I'm sure the price for land around here is going to double and triple, and we could always sell it later if we don't use it for anything," said Bill. "As for the meadow idea, I also think that is a good idea."

"What do you think, Mark?"

"I agree with Bill about the price of land going sky-high after the war so it will be a really good investment for all of us even if we don't do anything with it. As for the meadow I'm inclined to agree that it makes sense, because when the kids are still small we won't want them riding amongst the trees that are on the back part of this property and besides we can always use it for a paddock to show horses, if we ever do make this a paying horse farm," said Mark.

"Another thing we were thinking about is we ought to sit down and make a drawing of the property so you guys can decide where you want to put your homes," I said.

"I've been thinking about that," said Mark. "Since we already have the drive, why don't we just extend it back further and Bill and I can put our houses along it, that would still give us plenty of room to extend the stable and you and David will have plenty of room on the other side to add on to your house."

"I hate to bring in a sobering note to this happy occasion, but I want you guys to promise me something, " said David. "As you know I most likely won't be around when Lauren gives birth and I want your promise that you'll look after her for me and that if anything should happen to me you'll take care of her for me."

"David, you know we will look after Lauren and take care of her," said Mark and Bill.

"Speaking for myself, I've decided that after the war I'll stay right here in Washington and start my own business here because this is our home now."

"That goes for us too," said Carol and Beth. "We're sisters after all, and besides at least for the birth process we probably are all going to end up in the delivery room at the same time."

"Yes, David, Bill and I will double time in the father's waiting room so you'll be included even if you aren't here physically," laughed Mark.

"Thanks you guys, that makes me feel a whole lot better," said David.

"Don't worry about Lauren, she'll be well looked after by all of us and so will your baby," said Bill.

"Mark, I know you have a movie camera, so will you document my entire pregnancy...in fact all our pregnancies so we can send them to David?" I said.

"Sure sis, we may even be able to sell it to the movies as a romantic comedy," laughed Mark.

"I almost forgot to tell you, when we talked to the architect, I asked him to include our dance floor," said Bill. "And our builder will also take care of installing it."

"Not to change the subject, but are you guys hungry now because none of you ate much lunch?" I asked.

"As a matter of fact I'm starving," said Mark.

"Come on girls, let's get lunch back on the table for all these fathers to be. We don't want our kids being born to emaciated fathers," I laughed.

We heated up everything again and all of us sat down at the table and this time the men ate with gusto. Afterwards we did the dishes and then adjourned back to the living room.

"This has certainly been quite a day," I laughed.

"That is the understatement of the century," laughed Mark.

"I was just thinking, as long as all of us are breeding, what would you think of breeding Lady to Sheik or Storm?" I asked.

"Oh God, you women won't be satisfied until every female both human and animal in the world is pregnant I suppose," laughed David.

"It would be kind of nice having my horse pregnant at the same time I am," laughed Carol.

"Do you really want to take on that responsibility just now, Lauren?" asked Bill.

"I suppose not, it just seemed like a good idea especially since I have all kinds of wonderful maternal instincts going on inside me right now," I laughed.

"Besides why should we be the only ones having the fun of getting someone pregnant? Storm, Lady and Sheik, ought to have some fun too," laughed Carol.

"Carol, I hate to tell you but to keep the blood lines straight, it would have to be either Storm or Sheik," laughed Bill.

"That settles it, we wait until we have another mare for one of them because I don't want one poor male left out of all the fun," laughed David.

"David and I had another thought last night," I said.

"I'm almost hesitant to ask what," laughed Carol

"Mark, since you are the only one who still has their apartment in town, would you consider keeping it if Lauren and I pay half the rent until your house is completed, that way if either of us want some alone time with our spouse, we have a place we can go for one or two days. It isn't that we don't want you here because we really do, but why waste money renting a hotel room when you have a perfectly good apartment? In between times we could lend it to you and Bill for visiting fireman rather than either company paying the outlandish rents they are getting for suits," said David.

"Hey wait a minute, David. Suppose my agency took over and paid the rent on the apartment then you guys could use it anytime you wanted to and the agency could take the tax write-off for the expense of it," said Bill. "All you'd have to do is call my secretary and book the apartment whenever you wanted it and you too Mark and Carol, and I doubt very much if there would be too many conflicts. Besides how many times a year would you want it for more than a day or two and probably those would be on weekends?"

"Bill, if you're serious I think that would be great, because though we love Lauren and David we do sometimes want to be alone together," said Mark.

"Just promise me you guys, that when Lauren gets near her time you won't leave her out here alone," said David.

"Oh that's a given," said Carol. "Besides Beth and I will be at about the same stage and we won't want to be alone either."

"You don't have to worry, David, because we will all look after Lauren and I may even check into the possibility of getting the same room in the hospital if they all go into labor at the same time, which knowing these three I wouldn't bet against," said Bill.

"Thanks you guys, you're the greatest and I wouldn't bet against it either," said David.

"Maybe we can ask Captain Hollenbeck to do the three christenings, since he's been in from the start on most of this?" I laughed. "You know, Bill and Beth, I was just thinking, while you probably can't be married in the base chapel, I'll bet Capt. Hollenbeck would preside at your wedding and we could hold it right here in the house or out in the yard."

"Lauren, that would really be great. I really liked him and then all three of us can tell our kids about being married by the same minister," said Beth.

"I'll go see him first thing Monday morning," said David.

"While I hate to break this up, Beth and I still have the drive home and I'm kind of worn out emotionally and every other way so I think Beth and I will head back for town," said Bill.

"I'll see you early Monday morning," said Beth.

"Yes come early and stay late," I said.

"Yes, Beth, we three have a lot to talk about," laughed Carol.

After they left, David turned to me, "What would you think about chartering a plane and flying for a little while? I think I need to be in the wild blue yonder while I digest everything that has happened."

"Mark, Carol, can we interest you?" I asked.

"I'm game as long as you two don't do any of that aerobatic stuff," said Carol.

"Believe me Carol, I'm in no condition for that aerobatic stuff either," I laughed. "I just like the perspective on everything that flying always gives me."

"I'm game too," said Mark.

"OK come on you guys, let's drive over to that little field that Lauren and I flew out of that first time since they have all our records," said David.

We drove then to the field and chartered a Cessna. After we got Carol and Mark settled in the back seat, David lifted me into the right and he climbed in the left seat. "Ready mate?" he asked just as he had that first time.

"Aye, Aye Captain," I saluted him as he pushed throttle and the Cessna raced down the runway and into the air.

"This isn't as scary as I remembered it," said Carol.

"Actually sis, you are safer in this small aircraft than you are in an airliner," I laughed.

"How so?" asked Carol.

"If we had to set this aircraft down for any reason there is a lot more space to pick out the perfect landing sight since it takes a lot less runway to land it," I laughed.

"Hey co-pilot, how about you taking over for a while?" asked David.

"Ok. I've got the controls," I said.

David turned then and looked over his shoulder at Carol and Mark, who both looked somewhat startled. "I knew Lauren flew but I've never flown with her before," said Mark.

"I just wish my students were half the pilot my little tomboy is," laughed David.

"Let's fly over the farm and get a view of it from the air," said Carol.

"Ok, you got it," I said putting the craft into a bank and turning toward the farm.

"It's even prettier from the air," said Carol when we got over the farm.

"It may not be a magazine picture perfect place, but it has already become home at least to me," I said.

"Just think by this time next year there will be kids running all over the place," laughed Mark.

"Darling, I don't think they'll be quite up to the running stage by then," laughed Carol.

"Let's go home., I want to have this wife of mine in my arms, and that's a little hard to do up here," laughed David.

I turned the plane and we started back for the airfield. As we were approaching the field Carol asked, "My God Lauren, how do you tell where the field is? It all looks alike to me."

"See that strip that looks like a concrete road down there?" I said pointing out the front window.

"Yes, you mean we land on that little bitty piece of concrete?" laughed Carol.

"That's it, sis," I said laughing.

I set the craft down on the runway. "You sure grease this thing right in, kitten, wish some of my students could get the hang of setting a plane down as gently as you do," laughed David.

"You mean you landed this thing, Lauren?" asked Carol.

"Sure," I said.

"Oh my gosh I knew that you flew but I didn't think you did landings and takeoffs too," laughed Carol.

"How in the heck do you think the plane gets in the air and back on the ground if I don't do it?" I asked.

"Well I thought bro probably did those for you," she said.

"Unfortunately I didn't know this brother of yours when I got my pilot's license so I had to learn to do it myself," I laughed.

"I sure wish I could have been her flight instructor," laughed David. "It would have been great having as an adept a student as Lauren is and besides she could have bribed me for extra flight time and signing her log book."

"If you had been, bro, you two would have had at least four or five of those kids by now," laughed Carol.

"That would have blown the inspector's mind if I'd ask to take my kids on the check ride for my license," I laughed.

"I've never tried to make it in an airplane," laughed Mark, "but I could see that it might be fun."

"I'll say one thing for you, Mark, you're single minded of purpose," I laughed.

I parked the aircraft and we drove home with Carol and Mark in the backseat and me curled up in David's arm in the front seat.

"I don't know about the rest of you, but I think I'm going up and stretch out for an hour or so because I'm bushed from all the excitement," I said.

"I'm for that, kitten. I feel a little bushed myself."

"This mother-to-be is definitely in need of a nap," said Carol.

"I just want to hold Carol in my arms for a while and think about all that's happened," laughed Mark.

We went in the house and went up to our rooms. When we got inside and shut the door David came to me and took me in his arms.

"This has been quite a day, kitten," he said pulling me in close to his body.

"That it has, Daddy," I said snuggling into him. "I just hope you are as happy about the baby as I am."

He picked me up and lay me down on the bed then he too lay down and took me in his arms. "Yes, darling. I'm very happy and especially now that I know you'll be looked after while I'm away."

"Oh David, I love you so much," I said as the tears streamed down my face.

"Baby, what's the matter?" said David.

"It's just that I'm so happy and I love you so much," I cried my arms going around his neck.

"I appreciate that darling, but I also think it's your hormones kicking into high gear," he chuckled.

"I guess you're right, David, for I can't seem to decide whether to laugh or cry," I said smiling up at him.

"Well you seem to be doing both at the moment, my love," he said hugging me to him. "I'm not laughing at you, really, because I kind of feel the same way myself and I sure as heck can't blame it on being pregnant," he laughed.

"Can you just imagine what that maternity ward is going to be like if the three of all go into labor at the same time?" I laughed.

"God help the doctors and nurses because you three will be giving them instructions right and left and coming up with new ideas on how to make the labor room more livable," he chuckled. "I really do think you three should start your own consulting business because you sure know how to get things done in a hurry and what one doesn't think of the other two do."

"Maybe one of us should get a real estate license then we could sell people the land and the house, then our consulting business could tell them how to furnish it especially for people on a limited budget."

"You could work in conjunction with Bart. You design stables for them and Bart could sell them the horses for those stables," said David

"Do you think we ought to reconsider the landing strip? That way when you get back you could take our customers for an air view look at their new homes," I asked.

"Now that wouldn't be a bad idea either and maybe I could even get a few charter trips and just quit the broadcast business altogether," he laughed.

"Just think, if you did that then you could be at home with me and your dozen kids all day every day," I chuckled.

"Do you really think I'd get any work done if that were the case?"

"Maybe not, but if we girls make a success of consulting we could keep all our men so that all of you would be at our beck and call," I laughed.

"Something that did occur to me when Bill was talking about starting his own business after the war, that if we bought the ten acres instead of just five, he could set up his business right here on the farm," said David.

"Daddy, I love you so much. You never stop me from dreaming the biggest dreams in the world and in fact you encourage me," I said hugging him close to me.

"I love you too, kitten. And I love to watch your eyes light up as you come up with new ideas," he said.

"David, what do you want for our child's middle name?" I asked.

"Kitten, I really hadn't thought about that, but how about Carol Lauren?"

"Then how about Mike David, if it's a boy?" I said.

"Guess that does as well as anything, or we could call him John after my father."

"Well you pick it out, whatever sounds good to you from a male perspective," I laughed.

"You know I'm still reeling first and foremost from your news, then also because somehow Carol and Beth got in on it as well," he laughed.

"Well, I'm not exactly surprised about Carol because since that week I had my period and she said she was due the next week, she's never mentioned it again," I said laughing softly.

"Maybe that is what all her nervousness about the wedding was all about because remember she said she 'just had to marry Mark,'" he laughed. "At the time I thought it was sort of weird comment to make, but I just took it for granted that it was because she loved him."

"So that must make her conception date about two weeks ago and Beth just moved in with Bill about two weeks ago so I think she must be fairly close to Carol's date and then I think it was maybe two weeks ago for me as well. That definitely should put us all in the delivery room at the same time."

"Well just call me a late bloomer, since I didn't get you pregnant quite as fast as Mark and Bill did their wives," he laughed.

"Actually you are right on their schedule too because it was about two weeks ago that we decided to try and before then I'd been taking precautions," I laughed. "So you see you are every bit as good as Mark and Bill at hitting your target.

"Hope I keep right on hitting the mark if you really want a dozen kids," he said laughing.

"I meant to tell you too, I really have been feeling nauseated in the morning so I'm afraid I may be in for a bout of morning sickness, so if you see me run for the bathroom in the mornings don't get scared, it's just natural," I said.

"How long does that last?"

"From what I've read usually about a month or a little bit less," I said.

"Oh God kitten, that's going to be really rough on you and I won't even be able to go in late for work like the other guys so I can hold your head or your hand or whatever," he said.

"Well, I once heard my sister and mother talking about it and they said if they kept soda crackers next to the bed and munched on one before they even tried to stand up in the morning that it seemed to help a lot, so guess it is worth a try."

"I'll try to remember to bring some up and put in the nightstand tonight so you'll have them if you need them," he said hugging me.

"Wouldn't it be wonderful if I had twins? That way I'd be one up on the other two and maybe by that time this war will be over and I can stay right on their schedule," I said. "Maybe if I talk to the military they'll let me know how long they expect the war to continue and if need be I could aim for triplets if necessary."

"Don't even kid about that, kitten. I think I'd go AWOL if I found out you were having triplets…I could maybe cope with not being here if it was twins, but I'd definitely defect if it were triplets," he laughed. "While we've been talking I've been thinking of the middle name if it's a boy, and I'd kind of like it to be John after my father."

"Then John it shall be, my love," I said.

"I just hope Carol and Mark's baby survives infancy with those two numbskulls doing the care taking," he laughed. "I figure by the time their baby is four or five he or she can probably take care of the parents."

"Somehow I can't see Mark changing diapers or walking the floor with the baby at night," I laughed.

"Neither can I. Now Bill I think could cope, but not Mark. Carol, of course, practiced on me and somehow I survived."

"Of all of us, Beth looks more like the eternal mother type. I'll bet she has everything under control right from the minute the baby makes his or her appearance."

"If she doesn't Bill will have," laughed David.

"Oh well, maybe Carol and I will just send our kids over to their house until they are old enough to fend for themselves," I laughed.

"I wonder if Carol has thought about calling your dad with her news?"

"Knowing Carol these days, probably not. What say we put in a call to them tonight and both you and Carol can break it to him? Maybe my other three brothers Ben and Brad and Jack will be home too since they've never officially met you over the phone," he said.

"Maybe you ought to check and see what kind of time delay there will be on the call so we can place it now if there is another six hour delay like the last time," I said.

"Good thinking, kitten. I knew I married you for some reason," he chuckled as I leaned down and bit his kneecap.

He picked up our bedside phone then and called the operator. "Yes operator, please place the call and thank you."

"How long a delay?"

"Five to six hours," he said.

"Come on Papa, let's go see what Carol and Mark are up to and maybe Momma can entice Daddy to dance with her," I laughed.

"Momma knows darn well she can get anything she wants out of Daddy for the next nine months," he chuckled.

When we got downstairs Mark and Carol were in the kitchen, Mark drinking coffee and Carol attempting to drink milk.

"Ugh, I just hate milk. And to think I've got to drink it for the next nine months," said Carol.

"Sit down, darling, and I'll get you a cup of coffee then I'll have a glass of milk along with Carol," I said going to the stove.

"I never could figure out why you hated milk so bad," laughed David.

"Dad used to make me finish my glass before I could leave the table and I didn't like the taste of it even then," she said.

"Well see, if you'd drunk more milk then you'd be closer to our size since all of us guys drank it by the gallon," laughed David.

"Thank God she didn't," laughed Mark.

"Well it's worth it, isn't it sis, to have a strong, healthy baby with good bones and teeth," I asked.

"I definitely want a good health baby with strong bones and teeth, I just wish there was some other way of doing it than by drinking milk," laughed Carol.

"Before we forget sis, we placed a call to Dad a few minutes ago which has a five to six hour delay," said David.

"Well bro, that should be something of a shock to him because he probably is just about now getting my letter telling him I'm getting married now I call him with the news that I'm about to become a mother."

"Yee Gods, Carol, those five big brothers of yours are likely to come over and kill me, because you know what they will be thinking," said Mark.

"Well if the shoe fits wear it," laughed David. "I was at least wedded to Lauren before getting her pregnant."

"How was I to know Carol wasn't taking any precautions?" said Mark.

"Don't blame this all on me, it takes two to tango," said Carol.

"Oh baby, I'm not and I just realized how terrible that sounded," said Mark pulling her over next to him so he could kiss her. "I love you so much and it is my fault for not checking it out, although I'm glad you're pregnant."

"Mark darling, I was only kidding you, we both are to blame for letting our hormones get the best of us," said Carol.

"I owe you two an apology too. I shouldn't have said what I did," laughed David. "I just couldn't help teasing you two, that's all."

"David and I were talking and I did some figuring and as nearly as I can figure it out we all got pregnant the same week so we very definitely will all be in labor at the same time," I laughed.

"My God, I pity those poor doctors and nurses in the maternity ward with you three all there at the same time," laughed Mark.

"That's what I said too," laughed David.

"Maybe we can get a group rate," laughed Carol.

"We decided that if we have a daughter her name is going to be Carol Lauren and if it's a boy his name is going to be Michael John," I said. "Have you two come up with any names yet?" I asked.

"I've been meaning to tell you, bro and sis, please don't saddle your daughter with the name of Carol for my sake because I've always hated that name," said Carol.

"Well then what's your middle name?" I asked.

"Laura," said Carol.

"David, what would you think if we called our daughter Laura Beth in honor of my two sisters?" I asked.

"I think it would be wonderful, Mommy," he said.

"Thank you, Lauren, and you too, David. I love you both so much," said Carol.

"Now what have you two decided on for names?" I asked.

"If it's a girl we'd like to call her Carol Lauren and if it's a boy we'd like to call him William David," said Carol.

"Thank you for that, Carol and Mark," I said.

"Yes thanks, sis and Mark," said David.

"I thought you just said you hated the name Carol?"

"Well Mark is kind of set on her being called Carol," laughed Carol.

"What do you say we all go into the living room and put on some records and dance?" I asked.

"Yes kitten, I definitely want to hold you in my arms," said David coming over to take my hand to lead me into the living room.

"Yes, I want to hold Carol in my arms too," said Mark.

We went into the living room and picked out a stack of records and put them on the turntable. The first song that came up was *Till the End of Time* and as we danced to it David sang the words in my ear and Carol sang them to Mark. Both Carol and David had beautiful voices and with the lights turned low the room took on such a beautiful, romantic atmosphere. As we danced I looked up into David's face and mouthed the words, "I love you," and he pulled me in closer to him. I looked over and Mark was holding Carol close to him and his love for her was written all over his face.

All the songs we had picked were love songs because of all the love that filled our home. *I'll Walk Alone* came up last and David pulled back a little so he could look into my eyes and sang it just to me and this time Carol didn't chime in because she knew that the words were very special to David and I. As the song finished I whispered back to him, *"I'll send my love and kisses to guide you until you're walking beside me."* He kissed me then and we stood holding each other.

Carol and Mark came over to us. "Bro, I'll take care of Lauren just as I took care of you all those years ago until you're back home and can take over from me," she said.

Mark put his arm around David's shoulders. "Yes bro, we'll take good care of her and your baby," he said.

We turned and hugged them both then because neither of us could speak because tears for us both were too close to the surface. Carol went over and put on our song again and she sang the words to us as David held me in his arms and we swayed to the song and the words were our pledge to each other.

"Thanks sis," said David when the song finished and there was so much love in his voice for both Carol and I.

Just then the phone rang and Carol wiped her eyes, which were full of tears and went to answer it.

"Hello," she said.

"Carol, is that you?" said her dad.

"Dad," said Carol.

"Carol is David there?"

"Yes he and Lauren are here," said Carol.

"We bought a new fangled gadget to put on the phone so we could all hear you," said her dad.

"Dad, did you get my letter?" asked Carol.

"Yes, I got it. Who's this fellow you're marrying?" he asked.

"Dad, I am married to him already and his name is Mark," she said pulling Mark over to the phone.

"Hello, Mr. Benton," said Mark. "I just want you to know how much I love your daughter and I promise to take care of her always," he said.

"Mark, please call me Dad," said Carol's father.

David and I had gone to the kitchen to get on the other extension. "Dad, this is Lauren," I said.

"Hi Lauren, how is my daughter-in-law?" he laughed. "All the boys are here with me," said Mr. Benton.

"Hi guys," said David and Carol together.

"Hi," they answered back.

"Well Dad, you might as well hear the whole thing right now, because there are going to be two babies around here in about nine months that will be calling you Grandpa, and you guys Uncle," said Carol.

"My God, you're pregnant already, Carol?" he asked.

"Yes Dad, I'm pregnant and so is Lauren," she laughed.

"Way to go Mark and David," yelled the guys in the background.

"Dad, if it's a boy we are naming him Michael John," I said. "And if it's a girl we are naming her Laura Beth after Carol."

"Thank you for that, David and Lauren," said John.

"Hey sis, what are you going to name yours?" yelled Bob.

"If it's a boy we are naming him William David and if it's a girl we are going to name her Carol Lauren," she said.

"I thought you always hated your name, sis?" said Bob.

"Well I do, but Mark insists so her name is going to be Carol and I hope she doesn't hate it as much as I always did," she laughed.

"Dad," said David taking the phone, "I guess I might as well spill the rest of the news to you. Lauren and I bought a five acre horse farm here in Virginia and Mark and Carol are building a house on our property so we'll all be living close to each other."

"Does that mean you won't be coming back after the war?" said John.

"That's about it, Dad, but we'll come visit you and you guys will have to come over here for a visit," said David.

"You bet we will. We want to see our nephews and nieces," yelled the guys.

"What did you say you bought, a horse farm?" asked John

"That's right, Dad. Lauren is one great horsewoman and it was always her dream to own a horse farm and Carol has gotten to be quite a horsewoman as well. Lauren and I own a big stallion named Storm King and Carol and Mark own a lovely little mare by the name of Lady," he said.

"What in the hell do you know about horses, son?" said John.

"You'd be amazed how much I've learned from Lauren about horses, Dad," he laughed. "Storm is about as big as Ben as horses go and you should see this little gal of mine mount him. She just takes a fistful of mane and swings up to his back and I'm finally getting the hang of how to mount him," laughed David.

"I've even taught him how to jump fences and to make Storm rear up on his hind legs," I laughed.

"Dad, I've gotten pretty darn good too. Mark and I ride Lady bareback just like David and Lauren ride Storm and while I haven't learned to jump fences I can make Lady rear just as Lauren does Storm," said Carol.

"You ride bareback?" asked John.

"Yup Dad, we do," said Carol. "You'll see when you come over because by then we'll be able to ride again because our kids will both be born," she laughed.

"Let's get back to the two of you being pregnant," said John. "When are you two due?"

"In about eight and half months," said Carol.

"Well Lauren, when are you due?" he asked.

"Actually Dad, both Carol and I should go into labor about the same time," I laughed.

Her brothers gave a cheer in the background. "You and Mark are our kind of men," they yelled, "keep them barefoot and pregnant," they laughed.

"Dad, my former boss and his new bride who is also pregnant are also building a house on our property so we three families will live here and Beth is due at the same time as Carol and I so three of us will probably be in labor at the same time," I laughed.

"My God what did you do, time it down to the minute?" laughed John.

"Well we didn't exactly plan it but since we all three feel like sisters, we thought if all of us could get pregnant at the same time every time then the kids would always have someone their age to play with," I said.

"Every time?"

"We plan on giving you lots of grandkids to spoil. I want at least six or seven and maybe if I can talk your son into it an even dozen," I laughed.

"Mark and I want at least four or five and maybe we'll settle for a half dozen," said Carol.

"My God, you two men are going to be busy," laughed John.

"As soon as I get back we're going to work on an even dozen," laughed

David.

"Do you expect to be called up soon, son?" asked John.

"All I know for sure, Dad, is that my kids have another three weeks of flight training then I'll be sent for B-17 flight training for another four to five weeks. After that, it is anybody's guess," said David.

"Lauren, are you going to be ok with David gone when the baby comes?" asked John.

"I'll be fine, Dad. I have Mark and Carol as well as Bill and Beth to look after me," I said.

"David, you take care and give those Japs what for, for us," yelled his brothers.

"I will and you guys take care and Lauren will write to you because I have a feeling I'm going to be kind of busy," said David.

"Carol, daughter, you better write to us too and let us know how all of you are doing," said John.

"I will Dad, I promise," said Carol.

"Congratulations on all your news my son, daughter, daughter-in-law, and son-in-law," said John.

"Thanks Dad, and you guys take care too," said Carol and David and Mark and I.

"Bye."

"Bye."

"Whew, at least your dad didn't seem to be upset and your brothers were absolutely ecstatic that I got you pregnant so quick," said Mark.

"I'm sure my brothers are delighted and they really meant it about keeping me barefoot and pregnant as retribution for all the hell I put them through over the years," laughed Carol.

Mark looked at David. "Is that true, bro?" he asked.

"Absolutely," laughed David.

"Are you included in that sentiment?" asked Mark.

"No. Carol and I always got along fine, but she did make life hell for the rest of the gang most of the time," laughed David.

"Well bro, they deserved it most of the time," laughed Carol.

"I agree with you there, sis, but you've got to admit with Bob and Ben you worked over time at it," said David.

"Considering what those two put me through at times, they deserved it," she laughed.

"Carol darling, did that phone call make you homesick at all?" asked

Mark.

"Not at all sweetheart, my home is with you now," she said quietly.

"I don't know about you guys, but I'm going to hit the hay because tomorrow is a work day," said David.

"Yes Daddy," I said. "I'm tired too."

"And we've still got Bill and Beth's wedding to get through next weekend then maybe we can call our lives our own for a while," laughed Mark.

"Goodnight you guys. Will you lock up for us please?" I said.

"We'll take care of it, sis," said Mark.

"Oh wait a minute, David. I want to get some soda crackers to take up with me," I said.

"What are they for, sis?" asked Carol.

"I remember my sister and mom saying that if they nibbled on soda crackers before getting out of bed in the mornings the morning sickness stayed at bay pretty well," I said.

"Guess I better get some and take up with me too then, sis," she said.

The next morning when David woke me to kiss me goodbye, he handed me a soda cracker.

"Here little mother, munch on this before you stir around very much. I'll sit with you while you nibble," he said taking my hand.

I took his hand and brought it up alongside my cheek. "Good morning, Daddy," I said. "You've a lot to tell your comrades in arms, today, I think," I laughed.

"Well sugar, no one but no one is ever going to believe my tale," he laughed. "How do you feel?" he asked anxiously.

"So far fine, I felt kind of nauseated when I first woke up but after getting the soda cracker down it's completely disappeared," I laughed. "Let me try standing up before you leave, just in case."

He helped me out of bed and even standing, my stomach decided to behave itself.

"How do you feel, kitten?"

"Chalk one up for old wives' tales," I laughed as I put my arms around him to kiss him goodbye.

"Now go back to bed and sleep some more and I'll see you tonight, kitten," he laughed kissing me goodbye.

I lay back down with a contented yawn and soon I fell asleep again. When I woke I didn't seem to have any nausea at all but decided to munch on another cracker just to be safe. When I stood on my feet, I felt perfectly fine so I went to the bathroom to take my shower and dress.

When I was ready to go downstairs, I heard Carol stirring around in her room, so I knocked on the door and she bid me enter. "How are you doing this morning?" I asked her.

"Fine, couldn't be better," she laughed. "The cracker seemed to help because when I first woke up I thought I was going to have a full-fledged case of morning sickness, but after nibbling on the cracker I felt fine. How about you?"

"It was the same for me, maybe we ought to call Beth and see how she's doing and if she isn't feeling so hot, tell her to go get a cracker."

"Good idea."

We called Beth from my bedroom phone and Bill answered.

"Bill, how is Beth doing this morning?"

"Not so hot, she's been sicker than a dog all morning ever since she woke up," he said.

"Go get her a couple of soda crackers and tell her to munch on those before she tries getting up again," I said. "It sure worked for Carol and I."

"I'll go get them for her right now and call you back in about a half an hour," he said.

About a half hour later while Carol and I were still lingering over our coffee, the phone rang.

"Lauren, it's Bill," he said.

"How's Beth doing now?" I asked.

"She got the crackers down and now she's up racing around here like she always has," he laughed.

"Bill, keep some in the night stand by your bed and make her eat one before she tries to do anything at all in the morning. It sure worked for Carol and I," I said.

"Hold on a second, Lauren," he said.

When he came back to the phone, he said, "Beth said to tell you that you are a miracle worker and that she'll see you in about a half an hour."

"Great, tell her we're waiting for her," I laughed.

"Thanks Lauren, we appreciate it because she was one sick kitten this morning," he said.

"So how are you holding up, Dad?"

"All I've got to say is it is a good thing it is you women who have the babies, because I don't think we men could take it," he laughed. "I just can't get used to the idea that I'm going to be a father."

"You'll make a good dad," I laughed.

"I hope so, Lauren, because I've never been so happy in my entire life, except for when you came to work for me, little one," he laughed.

"Go on you Irishman, you just liked the idea that I knew where to find the fuse box," I laughed.

"Well that helped too, but I've come to love you like a sister."

"I hope you know that David and I and Carol and Mark consider you our brother and Beth our sister," I laughed.

"Guess I better hang up because Beth just told me to get off the phone so she could kiss me goodbye because she has a very important date with her sisters," he chuckled.

"Bye bro," I laughed.

"Bye sis," he answered.

"Beth is on her way," I said. "Apparently she was sick as a dog ever since she woke up this morning, but after she ate the crackers she's fine."

"Thank God you remembered about them," she laughed. "I was thinking maybe I'd try eating some when I try to get a glass of milk down."

"Couldn't hurt, but I was thinking do you like buttermilk any better than sweet milk?"

"Yes, I can at least tolerate buttermilk," she said.

"Well milk is milk, let's go to the store today and stock up on buttermilk and soda crackers," I laughed.

"How was Mark doing this morning? Has the shock worn off?"

"I just wish you could have seen his face yesterday when I first told him that I was pretty sure I was pregnant," she laughed.

"Bet that was a sight to see, sorry I missed it."

"He really was sweet last night, he turned me so that I was on my side and my back was to him and he put his arms around me and his hands came down on my belly and it was like he was trying to protect the wee babe within me," she said, her eyes dreamy.

"That's exactly what David did. I think these men of ours are really enjoying being husbands and now fathers," I laughed. "Thank you for singing our song for us yesterday. I think it meant as much to David as it did to me."

"I hope you know that we meant it about taking care of you," she said.

"Yes, I know you did and both of us appreciate it, sis."

"What I hope is that when I'm out to here that Mark doesn't want to trade me on one of his old models," said Carol.

"Oh Carol, he'll think you are absolutely beautiful because you'll be the mother of his child," I said.

"I know I've got to start trusting him more to have higher ideals than I sometimes give him credit for," she laughed.

"Do you suppose by any chance that when you, Beth and I were born, that somehow the stork got mixed up and dropped us off to separate mothers when we were really meant to be triplets?" I asked.

"It wouldn't surprise me a bit; we were probably thinking up some project and forgot to give him explicit instructions and being male he couldn't remember it all by himself," she laughed.

Just then we heard a knock on the door. "Come on in, Beth," we hollered together.

"Hi my sisters," she said coming into the kitchen.

"Beth, you don't have to knock, just come in anytime you're here," I said getting up to give her a hug.

"How you feeling, sis?" laughed Carol, coming to hug her. "Aren't those crackers just the greatest invention ever?"

"They definitely are because prior to Lauren calling and telling Bill about them I was to the point I just wanted to drop dead I was so sick," she laughed. "Now I feel absolutely wonderful."

"Did I tell you that I've changed the name I want for my daughter if I have one?" I asked.

"No. How come?"

"Well Carol said she always hated the name Carol so we decided to go with her middle name and your first name and call her Laura Beth," I said.

"Oh Lauren, that is so sweet of you," she said.

"Carol and Mark decided if their baby is a boy he would be called William David," I said.

"Oh Carol, thank you so much. Bill will be so pleased," said Beth.

"You know sisters, I think we've got to get busy and do some research for getting all three of us the best doctor in town," laughed Carol.

"What I'm wondering is do we all three want to have the same one, if it turns out that I'm right about the conception dates and we all three go into labor at the same time," I laughed. "It might keep him just a little busy."

"Well since it was men that got us all in this condition in the first place, it would serve him right if we keep him hopping," laughed Carol.

"Why don't we make preliminary appointments with three different ones and all three of us visit at the same time, that way if we choose just one for the three of us he would know what he was letting himself in for?" I said.

"We probably should visit the nearest hospital to see what their facilities are like as well," said Beth.

"Oh I almost forgot to tell you, our architect said that we need to get our plans ok'd and return them to him within the next two weeks and if we did, our house could be ready to move into in about two months," said Beth.

"Ours gave us the same time schedule," said Carol.

"Well by all means let's go over the plans and give them our ok so that we can move in before we get big as barns," said Beth.

We spread the plans out on the table then and considered every aspect of both sets. "I can't see any changes. Do either of you?" asked Beth.

"They look great to me," I said.

"To me too," said Carol.

"Good. I'll call him tomorrow and tell him to get started," said Beth.

"I will too," said Carol.

"Maybe next week we can go into town and get the appliances and the furniture picked out and put a down payment on them so that they can be delivered in two months," said Beth.

"While we are at it let's look at baby clothes at the same time," I said. "I'd like to get a couple of small items so David will feel that he is a part of this too before he gets called up."

"Lauren, you must be absolutely petrified knowing that your husband won't be here when your baby is born," said Beth.

"Not petrified because I have you guys, but definitely as the time gets closer I get more and more anxious for David," I said. "I just hope at least he will get to feel the baby kicking within me before he has to leave."

We got out the phone book then and started looking for doctors' names. We found three names and called and made appointments on different days with all three of them. "Why don't we time the drive from the farm to the nearest hospital?" said Beth.

We went out and got in the car and drove to the nearest hospital and it turned out that it was a 10-minute drive. "Well that's not bad," said Beth.

"Can't you just imagine Bill and Mark trying to get all three of us into the cars to drive us with all of us yelling in labor pains?" I laughed.

"Oh I'm not worried about Bill, but with that husband of mine I'll probably have to do the driving," laughed Carol.

"Well if we timed it right they could both be at work and we three could drive ourselves to the hospital and just present them with the results when they get home from work," I laughed.

"No way sis, I want them both to have the satisfaction of walking the floor in the waiting room," laughed Carol. "I only wish they had to be in the labor room with us, but on the other hand by the time the birth process is through we'd probably be telling them in no uncertain terms to never come near us again."

We had Beth and Bill's wedding in the front room of our house and Capt. Hollenbeck was kind enough to officiate and also said that he would officiate at the christening of all three babies providing he was still stationed at Andrews. It was a simple ceremony but beautiful and David and Carol sang for the bride and groom. We kept our appointments and picked out the doctor we all liked who agreed to deliver all three of us even if we went into labor at the same time.

Then for the next three weeks we looked at furniture and appliances and made selections. The builders came out with their backhoes to lay the foundation and start the framework on the houses. I bought some booties and a couple of little shirts for my baby.

"Hey, Daddy's home," yelled David.

"I'm up in our room, darling. Come on up I've something to show you," I said

I heard him running up the stairs and when he came in I threw myself into his arms as usual.

"What you up to, kitten?" he asked.

I pulled him over to our chair and then went to the bed to get the boxes of baby clothes I had purchased. "I just wanted to show Daddy what I bought today," I laughed pulling out the booties and shirts.

"My God, they're so tiny, kitten," he said looking at them as I held them up.

"Well they are just right for a newborn," I laughed. "What did you think, the baby would come out the size of a two-year-old?"

"No, but they just look so small," he chuckled.

"They might even be a little big," I laughed. "These fit a seven pound baby, but the baby probably will weigh less than seven pounds."

"My God, I must have been born a giant because sis told me that I weighed nearly ten pounds when I was born, and my other brothers weighed over ten pounds each," he said.

"I almost hate to tell you what I weighed when I was born," I laughed.

"If you say you weighed more than ten pounds, I'll pass out from astonishment," he chuckled.

"No sweetie, I weighed two and a half pounds," I said laughing at the look on his face.

"My God, no wonder you're such a little itsy bitsy thing," he laughed. "In Australia we throw fish back that weigh more than you did," he said.

"Even then I was determined and the more they told Mom I probably wouldn't survive my first year, the more determined I was to prove them wrong," I laughed, "and I more than did that and buried two of the doctors who said it."

"That's my little wildcat for you," he chuckled. "How did your visit to the doctor go today?"

"I'm fine, the babies are fine, and as nearly as he can figure, all three of us ought to go into labor about the same time," I laughed.

"Whoa, there kitten, what was that about babies, plural?"

"Well that's the other thing; it is almost 99% certain that I'm having twins," I laughed as his mouth dropped open.

"What's the 1%?"

"Well they'll know definitely by my next appointment next month, but he definitely says he heard two heartbeats," I laughed hugging David in a bear hug.

"God kitten, it was bad enough thinking about having to leave you just when you need me with one baby, but with twins, it's worse," he said soberly.

"Daddy, don't worry about me, the others will take care of me, and maybe when you get home you'll have both a son and a daughter," I said. "Or identical girls or boys. It's no more trouble having two than it is one and I'm so happy about it and I hope you are too, my darling."

"Baby, isn't it more dangerous for you with twins than it is with a single birth?"

"The risk factor doesn't go up that much for twins, now if it were triplets or quads, then yes the risk factor goes up a lot higher," I said.

"Lauren, how do you take it all in stride this way when you know you'll have to go through most of your pregnancy without me around?" he asked looking me in the eyes.

"Darling, what choice do I have, but to take it in stride and personally darling I'm elated that it will be twins. Please David, be happy for us, because I couldn't stand it if I thought it would cause you worry and that you weren't happy about it too," I said.

His arms tightened around me and his lips came down to mine. "I'm happy kitten, and if I were just going to be around when you need me most

I'd be shouting for joy," he said.

"Please Daddy, I'll be ok, I promise you. When you get back I'll expect another set of twins so you can be here for it all," I whispered. "I promise you, and I've never broken a promise to you yet that I know of, that both me and our babies will be fine as long as Daddy takes care of himself."

"Do the others know yet?"

"No, I wanted my children's daddy to know first," I laughed, "and believe me it's been hard to keep the secret all afternoon when I wanted to shout it from the housetop."

"My little momma, I love you so much," he whispered hugging me to him and kissing me again and then he bent down and kissed my stomach. "I love you too you little imps and you better be nice to your mommy."

"Daddy, I love you too and I can feel already that your babies love you too," I whispered. "Now come on, let's go down and tell Carol and Mark then let's call Bill and Beth," I said.

"Come on let's go break the news and see if Mark can survive it. I can't wait to tell my brothers and dad that we're having twins."

"Considering how they congratulated you when they found you had made me pregnant already, they'll crown you king of the hill for twins," I laughed.

"You could just be right there," he chuckled.

When we came into the kitchen Carol and Mark were sitting at the table talking quietly.

"Hey Carol, do me a favor and get Bill and Beth both on the phone, for we've something to tell all of you and we want to do it all at the same time," I laughed.

"Oh I bet you're going to tell us you aren't really pregnant and it was just an April Fool's joke," laughed Mark.

"Wrong, wrong, wrong," I laughed.

"Beth, this is Carol, get Bill next to the phone because Lauren and David say they have something to tell us and they want to tell all four of us at once," said Carol.

"Now what are you two up to?" asked Bill as he came on the phone along with Beth.

"Go ahead Daddy, tell them what I just told you," I said to David.

"It seems my little kitten here is to be not only a mother but a mother of two," laughed David.

They all looked at him blankly as if he had told them in Russian or something. "Don't you get it you guys? I'm having twins," I laughed.

"Did you say twins?" asked Bill.

"That's what we said, Bill," laughed David.

"Jumping Gehossofat, leave it to Lauren to upstage us all," laughed Mark.

"I just don't believe it," laughed Carol.

"Me neither," said Beth.

"When did you find this out?" asked Carol.

"This afternoon at the doctor's," I laughed. "He said he's 99% sure that he detected two heartbeats but he'll be able to make it a 100% surety next month when I'm further along."

"You mean to tell me that you knew this afternoon when you came home and you didn't say a word to me?" laughed Carol.

"Well sis, I felt it was only right that I let your brother know before I did the rest of you," I said.

"David, old man, my hat is definitely off to you," laughed Mark shaking his hand.

"Mine too," said Bill.

"Don't take your hat off to me fellows, since there are no twins at all on our side of the family; I think you have to reserve that right for kitten here, because she told me once that her cousin had three sets of twins," laughed David.

"Well Lauren, you got your wish, first time out of the gate," laughed Bill. "You remember telling Mark and I when we first had dinner with you two after you'd announced your engagement, that you wanted at least one set of twins?"

"Yes, I remember because Mark almost collapsed right on the spot that time," I laughed.

"I may yet collapse as soon as this sinks in," laughed Mark.

"Wait until our brothers hear this one," laughed Carol. "Baby brother not only upstaged them all by getting married first, he also upstaged them by getting his wife pregnant first and now he's given them a real target to shoot for—twins."

"What did the doctor say when he found out not only was he going to have to deliver all of us at the same time but into the mix you've added twins?" laughed Beth.

"He said we definitely were his star mothers-to-be and it was a good thing that he was taking on a partner, because apparently he was going to need one," I laughed.

"If this keeps up we're going to need a moving van to bring home all the babies," laughed Bill.

"Well congratulations again, you two," said Bill and Beth.

"Thanks guys, talk to you later," I said.

"Bro, let's call Dad right away with your news. This I've just got to hear and I hope all of the boys are at home too," laughed Carol.

She placed the call and this time it went through right away. "Dad," said Carol, "it's me Carol, and David and Lauren are here too."

"Carol, is something the matter?" asked John.

"Are my other brothers there?" she asked.

"Hold on and I'll get them," said John.

When they all got on the speaker phone Carol and Mark went to our extension phone in the living room and David and I stayed on the kitchen phone. "Now tell me what's wrong," said John.

"Dad, nothing is wrong," said David, "but we've had a bit of news we thought you'd like to hear right away and I'm putting Lauren on so she can tell you."

"Dad, it's Lauren. We just called to tell you that I found out today that I'm having twins," I said.

"You're kidding," came a chorus of voices from Australia. "Way to go, David!"

"I don't want any of you ever teasing David again because he's outdone the whole blooming lot of you," said Carol.

"Carol, from the sound of things I don't think you have to protect your baby brother anymore," laughed John.

"I guess I don't, come to think of it," Carol said laughing.

"David, son, I just want to wish you and your family all the best; you're more man than any of us," said John.

"Dad, thanks for that, but everything I've become I owe to the two women in my life, Carol for being a wonderful big sister when I needed her most and Lauren for being the greatest wife any man ever had," he said.

I looked up into his eyes and brought his head down so I could kiss him and Carol looked at him with tears in her eyes.

"Son, I'd say you had it made," said John.

"I really do Dad, and it was all because I had two hellcats of women that give and give to this man and I only hope the rest of you guys are lucky enough someday to find women half as good and that if you get that lucky you cherish them because they are worth fighting and dying for," he said

"I'm glad you finally realized that there are some women in this world to whom we men should get down on our knees and thank the good Lord that he put them on this earth; unfortunately, I didn't until it was too late," said his father.

His brothers were unusually quiet. "Dad, thanks for telling me that," said David. "I can't wait for you to meet my little kitten because she is the most precious thing in my life and I love her more each day because she gives me so much."

"Then love her, son, and don't forget to tell her every day of your life what she means to you," his dad said quietly.

"Thank you Dad, for both Carol and me, because we love this man, this son of yours, who makes us feel so appreciated every single day of our lives," I said.

"Lauren, I don't know how you did it, but you've brought this family closer together than we've ever been and I can't wait to meet you because I think you are a very special lady, even if you are pint-sized by our standards," laughed John.

"Well Dad, years ago Carol tried to tell me that good things come in small packages and until I met Lauren I didn't have a clue as to what she meant, but now I do and Dad, if anything should happen to me, please take care of her for me and make sure she never wants for anything," said David.

"You've got it, son. Now let's get off this phone and your brothers and I are going to celebrate your good news. My God, I'll have three grandchildren to love and spoil all at the same time," he laughed.

"Bye Dad," said Carol.

"Bye Dad, and thank you," I said.

"Bye Dad," said David.

Carol came running in then and hugged David to her. "Thanks bro, that was worth waiting for all these years," she laughed up at him.

"I've got the best husband in all this world and our kids are going to have the best father ever born," I said kissing him.

"David, what I said before don't worry about Lauren or the kids, we'll make sure they are well looked after and loved always," said Mark.

"Thanks Mark you don't know how much I appreciate that," said David.

Later that night when we lay in bed talking over the happenings of the day, David said, "I've never known Dad to ever say that the breakup of his marriage might have ever been through any fault of his."

"Maybe listening to you talking about Carol and I tonight the way you did, finally woke him up to the fact that maybe there was blame on both sides," I said.

"It certainly blew my mind and I have a feeling it blew Carol's as well, and what's more, I think you, kitten, had an awful lot to do with his change of attitude."

"How so?"

"I'm not exactly sure I know, but like Dad said tonight, you've brought our family closer together than it has ever been and you do it with the love that just emanates from you toward everyone you meet," he said softly.

"Believe me, darling, I wasn't always that loving, as witness the estrangement between my own brother and sister and myself, but being loved by you has given me an entirely new prospective," I said.

THE CLOUDS GATHER

The following week after we discovered we were to be parents of twins, David's squad graduated from flight training and they and David were given three weeks furlough, then David was to report for B-17 training. In those three weeks we pretended that we had eternity together, not just the four or five weeks of training before David would be assigned. During that time Carol and Mark's house was finished and the six of us got together and helped them move in and get settled and a few days later we did the same for Beth and Bill.

"This house is so quiet now," said David holding me on his lap in our room.

"You know I thought it would be so great when we were finally alone in our own home for the first time, but I miss those two something fierce," I laughed.

"I love being alone with you, but I miss them too, especially their zany sense of humor," he laughed.

"Daddy, are you truly happy?" I asked.

"Kitten, I've never been so happy or so content, if it weren't for this damn war I'd be the happiest man on the face of the earth," he said.

"Remember it was this war that brought us together, so it hasn't been all bad, but I wish everyone would just quit and go home and forget conquest and all the rest of it," I said.

"Kitten, I got you something while I was in town today," said David. "It's over there on the bureau."

"Oh David, now we can listen to music up here just the two of us and Daddy can dance with me right here in our room," I laughed putting the records on the little portable record player he had setup on the bureau.

"Well, come on Momma, let's try it out," he laughed.

He took me in his arms then as the love ballads played one after the other and his arms held me close to him. "I've often wondered if Carol was right that night at the Ritz when she said you must get a stiff neck from dancing with me," he said.

"No, I never seem to or maybe it is as I told Carol that night, when I'm in your arms I don't even know I have a neck and that you are just the right size for me in every way," I laughed. Just then I let out a squeal.

"What's wrong, kitten?" asked David and I could see the concern on his face.

I took his hand and placed it on my belly. "Wait a minute and you'll see," I laughed.

Just then the babies both kicked again and he jumped a little when he felt them kicking his hand. "My God Lauren, does that hurt?" he asked amazement on his face.

"Yes and no," I laughed. "It isn't a hurt, hurt type of feeling but I imagine if they keep it up too long at a time it could get uncomfortable. It is a very strange sensation."

"Tell me what it feels like," he said.

I tapped on his stomach. "Kind of like that, but every time they do it, it lets me know they are alive and well inside me so it's not entirely an unpleasant sensation," I said.

"You know I knew you were pregnant with twins which meant that you had two lives growing inside you, but until this moment, I don't think it really registered that they were actually real," he said chuckling.

"Well Daddy, I can tell you very definitely these two are real," I laughed as the two of them gave another kick.

He leaned down and kissed my stomach. "Behave you two, don't keep kicking Mommy like that," he said. Just as he said it they kicked again. "It must be two tomboys just like their mom, because they don't let anyone stop them in their determination," he laughed.

"They're just anxious to get born and take on life on their terms," I laughed softly.

"Just like their mother," he said leading me to our chair and sitting down and drawing me to his lap.

I cuddled on his lap my arms going around his neck and his lips came down to mine. "Daddy, I love you so much," I said kissing him back.

"Kitten, I love you too with all my heart," he said and his hand came down to caress my breast.

"Ouch," I laughed. "Daddy, Mommy's sorry but my breasts are so tender that you're going to have to be really gentle with them."

"I'm sorry, Mommy. I'll be more careful," he said

I took his hand and laid it back on my breast. "Just don't rub too hard and I'll be fine, for I want Daddy's hand there, because when you touch them now I get so much more pleasure than I ever have before," I said taking his other hand from around my waist and moving it between my legs. "Please Daddy make love to me," I pleaded.

He picked me up then and laid me gently on the bed then he came down over me making sure that I was not bearing the full weight of his body. "Is Mommy ready for me?" he asked looking into my eyes and I could see the desire in his.

"Mommy's more than ready," I laughed, my legs locking around him as he guided himself into me. "Mmmmm, you feel so good."

"God kitten, you don't know how wonderful you feel to me too," he said.

"Promise me, Daddy, when you get home you'll spend at least the first month making love to me morning, noon and night," I whispered.

"Won't the babies get kind of hungry if I keep their mother constantly in bed with me?"

"We'll send them over to Mark and Carol's," I said.

"My insatiable little wildcat," he murmured as he thrust into me and I came in a matter of seconds and I felt his own explosion within me.

Later as I lay snuggled up in David's arms, I brought up the subject of the dance floor, which had just been completed in the barn. "How about if I get the gang together tomorrow around five and we have a potluck and dance the night away?" I asked.

"That would be great, kitten. I think we all need to celebrate all of you girls' achievements," he said. "I don't know of many people who could have done what you three did in just these few months."

"While I am proud of our achievements and I know I speak for the other girls too, we were inspired by the love of our men, not to mention the nesting instinct from being pregnant," I laughed.

"You three really ought to think about starting your own consulting business, because you are fabulous at organization," he chuckled.

"Maybe we'll think about it while we wait for our babies to arrive, but I don't think we'll have a lot of time after they do, at least not for a year or so, but it will really give us something to think about when we are all big as houses and moving around becomes a real chore."

"Why don't the three of you go together and hire someone to help you with the housework, because you'll have more than enough to do just taking care of the horses."

"I've been thinking about the horses too in that regard; because I don't think any of us are going to be able to do the heavy work with them after about our seventh month, would it be a terrible drain on the budget if we ask Bart to have one of his men come over and look after them?"

"No I don't, and I think Bill and Mark will agree. Let's face it, Mark is just never going to be a horse person and Bill can't do it all by himself," said David.

"Tomorrow let's call a council of war and get some of these issues straightened out, then we can also plan our potluck and dance. Also tomorrow, Daddy, let's see if we can't find a nice little puppy so that he'll be housebroken and trained before the babies get here?"

"Ok Mommy you got it, in fact, why don't we look for a couple of dogs so they can grow up with our kids," he laughed.

"You know Daddy, even though these two kick the bejeebers out of me from time to time, it still is hard to imagine being a mother," I laughed, "because until I met you I never wanted kids or for that matter I wasn't very interested in marriage either, if the truth be known."

"Maybe we should have waited until I did get back to give you time to get used to being a wife," he said.

"Hate to tell you Daddy, but I think we're a little too late to shift gears now," I chuckled. "Besides, since I met you I've wanted nothing but the whole nine yards, a home, kids everything."

"Well I've got to admit, kitten, that there definitely is no such thing as being a little bit pregnant, but I do know what you mean, because before meeting you this would have seemed like the dullest life possible to me, now I find it exciting and I want it all too," he laughed. "In fact, I always feel sorry for those men who are still bachelors, because they just don't know what they are missing."

"Thank you my love," I said yawning. "That's the nicest compliment I could get."

"Go to sleep, kitten and tomorrow we'll go find puppies for you to lavish your love on and whom I hope will help keep you company while I'm away."

"I love you, my darling," I whispered before falling into a deep and contented sleep.

In the morning I took a walk and stopped in at each household asking if they wanted to have a potluck and dinner dance that evening around five and that David and I had a couple of things to talk over with them. "If you are going to tell us that now the doctor thinks it's triplets, I quit," said Carol.

"No sis, nothing like that or even I would throw in the towel if he ever told me that," I laughed.

"Well in that case we'll be there. What would you like me to bring?"

"How about if you make the salad and the deviled eggs?" I said.

"Fine with me," said Carol.

At Beth's house I went through the same spiel and Beth said that they would be looking forward to this evening. She said that she would bring homemade bread and fried chicken.

Later in the morning after the chores had been done, David and I jumped into the car and went down to Bart's to see if he knew of any puppies available and also if he'd be willing to look after the horses for us when Carol and I would not be able to handle the chores. He agreed and told me just to call him when he was needed. As for the puppies, he took us out to the stables and there were eight of the cutest puppies you could ask for.

"What breed are they?" asked David.

"Mongrel, mostly," laughed Bart, "but I think primarily cocker and terrier."

"What do you want for two of them?" asked David.

"For you two, they are free," said Bart in honor of the twins.

"How did you know about the twins?" I asked surprised.

"You, Mrs. Benton, are the talk of the neighborhood," he laughed. "I think most of the ladies around here consider you more interesting than the radio soap opera *One Man's Family.*"

"How did they ever find out about the twins?" I asked.

"Well most of the ladies go to the same doctor you go to and he's been telling everyone that he had to take on the new doc because you were having twins and the other two ladies were due at the very same time as you."

"I'll be damned," laughed David. "Honey, you're a celebrity."

"I guess I am," I laughed. "Well Bart, put us down for two of your finest and let me know when they are weaned and I'll come over and pick them up."

"How's that other big baby of yours doing in his new home and Lady and Sheik as well?"

"All are just fine, but unfortunately I won't be able to ride him too much longer and I'm going to miss that," I said.

"I bet you will, but you'll probably spend just as much time with him because you never could stay away from that horse," he laughed.

"You're right there, Bart. I know my stallions and when I love them, I love them," I laughed.

"Bye Bart and thanks for the puppies," said David assisting me back into the car.

"I wonder if we dare tell the others we've just added two dogs to the family," I laughed snuggling into his arm and laying my hand on his knee.

"Well, they shouldn't be that surprised," laughed David. "You always told them right from the start that you wanted kids, horses, and dogs running all over the place," he laughed hugging me to him. "And they should know by now that my kitten always manages to get what she wants."

"That's what you get, sir, when you take on a tomboy," I laughed.

"If one of these babies is a girl, she better be every inch the tomboy her mother is or I'll disown her," he laughed, "because somewhere about twenty years from now there is going to be some man who will look at her and his life will be turned upside down when she looks back at him with pure love in her eyes, and he's going to be the luckiest young man in the world and every day of his life with her, he's going to thank God that he found a tomboy to love," he said.

"Pull over please," I said.

He pulled the car over and turned to see what was the matter. I put my arms around his neck and pulled his head down while the tears ran down my face. "Thank you my love," I whispered.

"Kitten, I meant every word of it because I've been there before that young man and I know I thank God every day of my life with you that I found you and that you are mine," he whispered back.

"I'll tell her that if she's lucky enough to find a man like her father, she better love him totally or I'll disown her because I've been there before her and she should thank God every day that such a man found her and loves her," I whispered.

He kissed me then and said, "Let's go home, my love, because I need very badly to hold you close in my arms."

"Yes, husband, let's go home for I've the same need to be in your arms."

When we got home we went in then and shut out the world and once again I found the world in his arms and he in mine.

When I woke David was still sleeping so I slipped out of bed and got dressed and went downstairs to put together the two cheesecakes ready for our potluck. He came down a little later and came over to where I stood by the kitchen sink doing the dishes and he put his arms around me and I cuddled back into his arms and we stood that way just letting the other know how much she and he were loved.

At five we went down to the stable and I took a carrot and a lump of sugar for each horse. When we got there the others had already arrived and the food was sitting on the table and we girls threw a tablecloth onto the picnic table we had placed next to the dance floor and set out the china and silverware. We set the portable record player on a corner of the dance floor and put records on so we could have music as we ate.

"Where did you guys go today? We saw you drive out," asked Carol.

"Well sis, we went to see about two additions to our family," laughed David.

"Oh God, what now?" asked Mark.

"Bart has some new puppies and he has promised us two of them as soon as they are weaned," I laughed.

"What breed?" asked Bill.

"Mongrels," I laughed.

"Does he have any more of them left?" asked Bill.

"There are six more cute as anything you ever saw," I laughed.

He turned and looked at Beth. "Yes daddy, we'll go see about getting at least one of them or maybe two," said Beth.

"Before you start begging we'll go over with Bill and Beth tomorrow and get two for us too, Carol," laughed Mark as he looked at her pleading face.

"I could handle one more if one of you guys can take one more, then all the littermates will be together in one home," I laughed.

"What the hell, the more the merrier," said Mark.

"We can bed them down out here in the empty stall so they'll have the comfort of the horses and each other to get used to their new surroundings," I said.

"When we first came up with this idea of a dance floor and potlucks for Friday nights, did you ever think for a minute it would become a reality?" laughed Mark.

"Oh I didn't have a doubt about it once these three women of ours got the idea in their heads," laughed Bill.

"Admit it you guys, isn't this better than paying out the big bucks to the Ritz and we don't have to elbow strangers out of our way," I laughed.

"The food is much better too," laughed David.

"Guys, we've got two more things we want to discuss with you before we get on with the festivities," I said. "David and I were talking this afternoon and we wondered if you would have any objections if we paid Bart to send his men over to take care of the horses in a few months' time until we all deliver? There's just too much heavy lifting for Carol and me to do and Bill can't handle it all by himself."

"Well if all three families chip in the cost shouldn't be that much and I agree you girls shouldn't be doing what has to be done to maintain three horses," said Bill.

"I for one will welcome it, because I hate mucking out stalls," said Mark.

"We've noticed," we all laughed.

"Ok, ok, rub it in," laughed Mark. "I told you long ago that you'd never make a horse person out of me."

"Yes you did, Mark, and you really meant it," I laughed.

"What's the other thing you wanted to discuss?" asked Bill.

"We were thinking that if we hired a girl to do the heavy work around all our houses, then the girls wouldn't have to do everything," said David.

"I think that is a capital idea," said Bill. "With all three of us chipping in it shouldn't cost any of us that much."

"What about a nanny for after the kids are born?" asked Carol.

"I'll go for that one because I think two are too many for one woman to handle," said David. "Then when you need her you can share her."

After we finished eating we set the dishes at one end of the table and what food was left over, to be taken back to our separate houses when we left for the night. "I'm going to go give the horses their carrots and sugar lumps, then I'm ready to dance all night," said Carol.

"Me too, sis," I laughed.

When we got back the men had moved the record player to the table and stacked the records next to it. We put on a stack at random and all of us went to the dance floor.

David pulled me into his arms as the song *Blue Moon* began to play. "I love dancing with you Daddy, as I told you years ago or at least now it seems like years ago, that you make a girl look better than she is on the dance floor," I whispered, nibbling on his ear.

I heard him chuckle as he leaned down and kissed me. We danced until about eleven and I yawned and said to David, "I don't know about you, Daddy, but I think this kitten needs her sleep."

"Hey guys, Lauren is tired so I think we'll cut out," he said.

"I think we'll call it an evening too, David," said Beth. "I'm tired too."

"Well Carol and I are going to stay for a while. We'll take the record player home with us and bring it over in the morning," said Mark.

"Why bother? Just leave it right here in the stable and we can get it in the morning," said David.

"By the way, Mark, whatever happened to the jukebox you promised us?" I asked.

"As a matter of fact, it should be installed by Friday in time for us to have another potluck and dance to initiate it and I found out I can get all our favorite music for it," he said.

"Nice going, Mark," said Bill and David.

"You're a good kid, I don't know what you're good for, but you're a good kid," I laughed hugging him.

"Thanks a lot, sis," he laughed.

"Oh I know exactly what he's very good for," laughed Carol hugging him.

"Good night all," I said as David put his arm around me to walk me back to our house.

"Yes goodnight everyone; it was wonderful fun," said Beth as she and Bill also left.

When we got back to the house we locked up and then went up to our room. "That was fun and much better than the Ritz," I said hugging David.

"Especially since I could kiss you whenever I felt like it," laughed David hugging me back. "Go get ready for bed, kitten. You look exhausted."

"I am tired for some reason tonight," I said.

"Are you ok, honey?" he asked.

"Yes, I'm fine but these kids of yours have been kicking me black and blue all evening," I said.

"Get undressed then come sit on my lap and I'll sing them a lullaby and maybe they'll give Mommy some peace," he said. I got ready for bed and went back to where David was sitting; pulling me down on his lap and putting his arms around me he laid his hands on my stomach and began to sing to his two unborn babies.

A few minutes later the twins settled down and I fell asleep in his arms. I roused slightly as he picked me up and carried me to bed, but as soon as he was in beside me and I was cuddled in his arms I went right back to sleep.

When I woke the next morning I looked up to see him watching me. "Feel better this morning, Mommy?" he asked.

"I can't believe how quickly these twins settled down when their daddy began to sing to them last night," I laughed. "Not to mention so did Mommy."

"Maybe I better cut a record so you can play it for them when I'm not around, just so they'll give you some peace," he laughed.

"Oh darling, that's a wonderful idea," I said. "That way after they're born I can play it for them every night when I put them down."

"Ok. I'll check into it," he laughed.

"Oh please do, darling, then not only will the twins be able to hear their daddy's beautiful voice, Mommy will too," I said hugging him.

"You've got it, darling, for I can't deny you anything if it's within my power to give you," he said hugging me to him.

Just as we got downstairs I heard Carol come up on the porch hollering to see if we were home.

"Yes Carol, we're home and in the kitchen," I laughed.

"I just had to come tell you we just got back from Bart's and those puppies are absolutely darling. I can't wait until we can bring them home," she laughed.

"Sis, you never could resist babies of any type," laughed David.

"Well it used to be mainly for show, bro, because I thought that is what they expected of a girl; was to love dolls and babies, but now it's for real and I can't wait until we have kids, dogs, and horses running all over the place," said Carol.

"Why don't we hunt for a couple of kittens as well, because they can keep the mouse population down in the stable," I said. "If we get them while the puppies are still little they'll learn to get along together."

"That sounds great to me but I sure hope they don't bring any gifts of dead mice to us," laughed Carol.

"I think while David's home I'm going to talk him into going shopping with me so I can get the kids' bedroom fixed up," I said.

"If you want to move the bedroom furniture into one of my empty bedrooms, you're more than welcome to, then you'll have more room for setting up beds for the twins," said Carol.

"Thanks sis, I think we'll just move the present furniture down in the basement then when the kids get old enough we'll have at least one big bed available for them," I said. "Unless, of course, you want to use the furniture in the meantime."

"No I don't really need it because I'm using the one bedroom as a storage room for right now," said Carol.

"You want some breakfast?" I asked. "I'm just starting ours."

"No thanks sis, I had breakfast earlier with Mark before he left for work," she said.

"Daddy, what would you like? How about some pancakes?"

"That sounds good, kitten," he said.

"I can't get used to you calling bro, Daddy," laughed Carol. "Guess it's just that I never expected him to settle into family life like he has."

"To be truthful, sis, I can't quite get used to it either, but I love hearing Mommy call me Daddy," he said.

"I tried calling Mark daddy, but somehow with Mark it just doesn't come off the same way. I tend to think more about Sugar Daddy, not just daddy," she laughed.

"What does Mark say?" asked her brother.

"To be truthful I think he prefers stud to daddy," she laughed.

"Not me. I love it when kitten here calls me daddy and I can't wait for my kids to call me daddy too."

"I always thought you were meant to be a husband and a father and now I know I was right," said Carol hugging David. "Well, I've got to get home because Mark said he thought he might take the afternoon off, so I suppose I need to get him some lunch."

"Why don't you two come over here for lunch? We miss you," I said.

"You're a glutton for punishment, sis," she laughed. "But count us in."

After Carol left, I said to David, "Why don't I call Beth and see if she'd like to come over for lunch as well, if you don't mind being surrounded by women?"

"Well if it was my bachelor days I would have been delighted being surrounded by three women, but now I hope Mark does come home," he laughed.

I put the pancakes on and got out the butter and syrup. "How would you like some sausages to go with those?" I asked.

"Mommy, that sounds good to me," he laughed getting up from where he'd been sitting at the table and came over to put his arms around me.

"You don't mind my asking Carol, Mark and Beth to lunch do you?"

"No, sweetheart. I was only kidding," he laughed.

"Tonight, my darling, I'll devote myself to you body and soul," I said turning in his arms to hug him.

"Oooh, I like the sound of that," he said returning my hug, "especially the body part."

"Somehow Daddy, I thought you might, and that will be my down payment for going shopping with me this afternoon because we really do need to get the babies room ready for them," I said.

"Mommy knows just exactly how to bribe Daddy, doesn't she?" he chuckled.

"Yes but Momma loves bribing Daddy," I laughed. "Now go sit down and I'll bring your breakfast to you."

"Yes Mommy," he said

As we ate breakfast, I said, "Will you still be able to come home nights while you're in B-17 training?"

"As far as I know now, they said I would get my orders through the mail so then I'll know for sure. I expect that sooner or later I'll have to be gone on long distance flights while I'm in training, but until that time, I am assuming that I'll still be home nights with you, sweetheart," he said.

"Maybe Carol had the right idea," I said. "When she and Mark first fell in love I was telling her about you wanting me to write love letters to you and she said maybe we ought to write them to the Japanese soldiers so they'd get so horny they'd quit fighting and go home to their wives and sweethearts."

"I must say you and that sister of mine do come up with some inventive ideas," he laughed.

"Oh David, I love you so much I'd do anything in the world to keep you safe and near me," I said.

"I know you would sweetheart and I'd do anything in the world to stay near you always," he said. "But I also need to keep not only you, but our babies and their babies safe and right now the only way I can do it is by making sure these bastards don't continue to take over the world," he said softly.

"I know darling, and I love you for it, it is just so hard to think about being parted from you even for a minute."

"Come here, baby," he said sitting down and pulling me onto his lap. "Just know that I love you with all my heart and that I'm going to do my damnedest to come home to you hopefully all in one piece, but if it isn't in the cards, I want you to know that you've given me everything any man could ever want in life and that I'll always be watching over you and our babies," he said quietly.

"Just promise me, my darling, that if you ever get to a point you think you can't go on close your eyes and I'll be near you holding you in my arms and loving you, but if it gets so bad you can't stand the pain anymore don't try to hold on because I'll survive and so will our babies and then someday you'll come to me and we will have all eternity together," I whispered through my tears.

"Don't cry, kitten. I can't stand it when you cry, because it makes me feel like I've let you down somehow and I don't know how to make it right," he said holding me close to him.

"I'm sorry, sweetheart, I'm being unfair to you, but it's all these hormones bouncing around inside me that make me so emotional, and know always and forever that you've never let me down, you are simply incapable of doing so," I said hugging him around the neck.

"Kitten, I hope I never ever let you down because you are everything to me and I want to go on record right now, even knowing what we've yet to face; I wouldn't change a minute of our time together."

"Thank you, my love, for everything you've given me; your love, your faith and trust in me, our twins, our home, thank you because you've given me everything any woman could ever want."

We sat for a while longer holding each other close and we found a comfort in each other's arms as we always had and would continue to do so for as long as we had together. We both knew our love for each other would keep growing stronger through all the years to come no matter what happened.

"Let's go for a ride on Storm," I said, "then I'll get busy and get lunch ready for all of us."

When we got to the barn I heard Storm whinny when he heard us approaching his stall. "Storm, I think you love this little girl of ours almost as much as I do," laughed David.

"I think I first fell in love with you because you reminded me so much of Storm; you are both big, strong stallions, but you're also both gentle and loving," I said.

He bridled Storm then led him from his stall. He reached down and lifted me onto Storm's back so that I was sitting sidesaddle not astride him, then he swung up behind me taking the reins and I snuggled into his arms. "You definitely have a way with horses and men," laughed David.

"Only with this horse and this man," I said. "You both give me so much love, how could I help but love both of you in return?" My arms went around David's neck and I nestled my face in his throat as we road out to the back of our property with Storm picking his way carefully so as not to jar me unnecessarily, as if he understood that for the time being I was the little mother to be protected and loved.

"I suppose you can't wait to teach the twins how to ride and jump fences," laughed my husband.

"I want them to be throw backs to our pioneering ways, not sissified city people," I laughed.

"To tell you the truth I can't wait to teach them how to fly and then sit back and watch them watch their mom in awe that she's every bit as good a pilot as I am," he chuckled.

"You amaze me so much, David, because you are one of the few men I've ever known in my life that really doesn't care that I'm as good as you at flying, or that I know mechanics as well as you do or better," I laughed softly.

"You know love, I don't think you ever were really a tomboy, I just think the male population used that as an excuse when you wanted to do the same things they did and you proved to them that you were every bit as good as them in doing those things."

"It's strange because since knowing you and having you love me, I sometimes think I was never a tomboy either. I feel even more feminine than I ever thought I could feel and yet I can still do all the tomboy things I so enjoy," I laughed. "It's just that I never liked the frills and laces and all the other stuff that went along with feeling feminine but with you I don't have to go along with them and you still love me anyway."

"I just think you were born out of your time element, you should have been born when the west was getting settled because you would have made a great pioneer woman," he chuckled. "I can almost picture you and I walking next to our covered wagon hand-in-hand and you reloading my rifle and I yours to ward off the Indians and us making love in that covered wagon at night with you snuggling into my arms ready to face whatever adventures or adversities came our way," said David.

"Maybe in some past life we were those two people," I said. "And maybe in the next one we will be space pioneers, flying out to investigate the stars. All I know is that I'm sure we will be together in all our lifetimes to come, until at last eternity is here and we will spend that together locked in each other's arms sitting on Storm King."

He reined in Storm, then and bent his head and kissed me. "All I know, my love, is you're the only woman I ever want no matter how many lifetimes we have together," he said softly.

"Let's go home, Daddy, and get on with our lives for I think we have a whole lifetime of adventures to face together," I said softly.

We turned Storm then and went back to the stable. After putting Storm back in his stall we went up to the house and I started to prepare lunch for the five of us.

"Beth," I said as she answered the phone.

"Hi Lauren, what's cooking?"

"Just wanted to invite you for lunch, Carol and Mark are coming over and I thought maybe you'd like to come too."

"What time do you want me? I never turn down a lunch with you guys."

"How about noon?"

"Sounds good to me. Can I bring anything?"

"Nothing but your own sweet self."

"See you at noon then."

At noon everyone showed up at once.

"At least we don't have far to come anymore," laughed Beth.

"Are you guys getting settled into your new homes?" I asked.

"Pretty much, we've still got a couple of rooms to be furnished and I want to make some changes in another room, but otherwise so far so good," said Beth.

"Oh you know us, we're always a day late and a dollar short in getting things done, but actually we aren't in too bad a shape," laughed Carol.

"We're going out this afternoon to look for baby furniture," I said.

"Yes, I've got to do that too," said both Carol and Beth.

"Mark, what have you heard about the jukebox? Is it going to be ready for us to use Friday night?" ask David.

"Yup, that's one reason I decided to take this afternoon off, it's supposed to be delivered today along with 500 records and I wanted to make sure they had it set up and working," he said.

"Did you say 500 records?" laughed David. "That's almost as many as Lauren has."

"I beg your pardon," I laughed. "I only have a little over 100 records."

He laughed, "I could have sworn it was more like a 1000."

"You know I was thinking, why don't I build a bookcase in the stable so we can put the extra records in it then we could make up a list of all the records by title and by artist?" said Mark.

"How many actually fit into the jukebox?"

"I think about 100-200," he said.

"Then I think that's a wonderful idea. Three cheers for Mark," I laughed.

"If each of us takes a stack of 166 or 167 records a piece it wouldn't take too long to catalog them then the three of us could intersperse the three lists into one," said Beth.

"Leave it to a secretary to have that all figured out," laughed David.

"I was just telling Lauren the other night that you three girls really ought to consider starting your own consulting business because you're so good at organization," said David.

"That's for sure for what other three women could all turn up pregnant and likely to go into labor at the same time?" laughed Mark. "Now that's organization."

"Well when we all get too big to move around comfortably we can hold meetings and see what we can come up with," laughed Carol.

"Has anyone heard from Bart yet as to when we can pick up our puppies?" asked Beth.

"No but I would imagine sometime next week," I said.

"God can't you see it, all of us chasing eight puppies around the place trying to get them corralled into that extra stall?" laughed Mark.

"I'm just wondering how the horses are going to take to them," laughed David.

"You'll see everyone will get along just fine," I said.

"That reminds me, sis, I talked to a lady in town who has kittens that she wants to give away next week also," laughed Carol.

"Now if our kids were just old enough to play with all of them, we could keep the cats, the dogs, and the kids all entertained while we adults sit back and enjoy the show," laughed David.

"I hate to tell you, but Bill is already talking about buying a pony for our baby," laughed Beth, "and he or she hasn't even made an appearance yet."

"I wouldn't mind buying mine a hotrod or a motorcycle," laughed Mark.

"Well if you really want to be practical about the whole thing, maybe we ought to consider buying a couple of milk cows, considering the amount of milk that will get drunk around this place," I said.

"Oh God sis, I want to barf just thinking about milk and you want to buy milk cows yet," laughed Carol.

"Carol, I think it would be great fun watching Mark trying to milk them," I laughed.

"You know that might make it almost worth it," said Carol.

"And to think I thought I was getting a nice demure city girl and what do I end up with, a latent farmer," laughed Mark.

"For myself, I don't care what she is as long as she's mine," said David smiling at me. "However, I think that when this war is over I'm going to start my own airline and put Momma to work."

"God David, don't give her any more ideas than she already has," said Beth.

"I kind of like the idea myself as long as Daddy here is willing to ride the right seat while Momma takes over in the left," I laughed.

"Oh, oh there is my little tomboy coming out again," laughed David.

After lunch was finished and the dishes done and everyone had left, I pulled David to his feet. "Come on, Daddy, let's go look at baby cribs."

We spent the afternoon going to thrift shops, furniture shops, secondhand shops, and we found two matching cribs and a little chest of drawers which matched the cribs. When we got home David carried everything inside and stored it in the living room for the time being. "I'll get Mark and Bill to help me set these up and take the other furniture to the basement this weekend," said David. "In the meantime, I'm bushed and I think I'll go up and stretch out for a little. I don't know how you do it, kitten, you just seem to be able to go, go, go and I'm not that much older than you. How in the heck do you do it?"

"Well for one thing you don't have all these hormones racing around your system telling you to hurry and get everything ready like I do," I laughed.

"Come on Momma, let's both go up and take a snooze," he laughed.

"Daddy knows darn well it isn't a snooze he's thinking about when he invites Momma to lay down with him," I giggled.

"Now why would Momma ever say a thing like that?" he said pulling me into his arms and letting his hands travel down my back to massage my buttocks.

"Stop twisting my arm, I'm coming, I'm coming," I laughed. "On the other hand please keep twisting because it feels so good and I can definitely tell that Daddy has some interesting ideas on his mind, none of which have to do with sleep."

He picked me up then and headed up the stairs to our room. "Daddy wants some loving," he said huskily.

"So does Momma," I said and he could tell from the huskiness in my voice just how much I wanted him to make love to me.

After our passion had been assuaged somewhat, he held me in his arms while he allowed one hand to stroke me from my breasts down to my thighs as I murmured my appreciation of his efforts.

"Daddy's still hungry," he said.

"Yes and so is Momma," I moaned. "Come to Momma," I whispered as I reached to hold his penis in my hand and let my finger gently stroke its head.

"I've got to have you now, this minute," he moaned as he rolled over me being careful not to put all his weight on my stomach and entered me. As he did so I reached behind him so that I could massage his buttocks as he had mine earlier.

"Baby, that feels so good," he whispered as he continued to thrust into me.

"I'm glad for I love holding you like this," I whispered then I began to moan as I reached my climax and shortly afterwards felt him explode into me.

Later as we lay in each other's arms he laid his head on my chest. I stroked the back of his neck and his hair until he fell asleep and I continued to hold him as he slept. *Dear God*, I prayed as I held him, *this is the best man in all the world, take care of him, please, bring him home safely so that he can see his children grow up and I swear that I will never again ask you for anything. I love him more than life itself and he deserves only the very best of life.*

I felt him stir and he turned his head so that he could look up into my face and he smiled at me and my arms went around him holding him to me as if my arms could protect him and I whispered, "I love you, my darling," as he once again drifted off to sleep.

When he woke again I bent my head to kiss him and his arms reached for me. "I love you, kitten," he whispered and once again I beseeched God to spare him. We lay quietly letting our love surround us.

"Why don't we run over to the hardware store and I'll get some paint and paint the babies' cribs and chest of drawers?" he asked. "That way they'll be ready to move into their room this weekend."

"Let's stop and see Bart while we're out and take another look at our puppies," I said. "And while we're at the hardware let's pick up a big old fashioned alarm clock and a hot water bottle."

"What is that for?" he asked.

"So the puppies will hear the ticking of the clock and think it is their mother's heartbeat and the hot water bottle will be something for them to snuggle against so they will think they are next to their mother."

"Little mother, you just can't resist mothering everyone, can you? Me, our babies, the horses and the puppies," he laughed softly.

"I just want all of you to be happy and content," I said softly.

We got up then and got dressed and went to the hardware store. Then we stopped at Bart's on our way back.

"I was just going to call you, Mrs. Benton," said Bart. "The puppies have been weaned and you can take them home with you now. If you'd tell the others that they can pick their puppies up too, I'd appreciate it. I'll find a box to put them in so you can carry them home."

I went over to the mother of the puppies and reached down and stroked her head and she looked up at me as if to say "take good care of my children" and I whispered to her, "I'll take the best care of them I know how and they are going to be in a good home for all of them will be raised together and you can come over and see them whenever you like." She licked my hand then and it was one mother to another.

When we got in the car Bart handed me the box of puppies. "Here you go, Mrs. Benton. I hope your kids learn to love them," he said.

"Thanks Bart, they will." I laughed as all three puppies began to lick my face.

David reached across and scratched behind each puppy's ear and they began to give little yips of delight. "I never had a dog when I was growing up and now I have three of them," he laughed as he put the car in gear and we drove home.

Carol was out in the yard when we drove in our driveway. "Hey guys, they are installing our jukebox right now then as soon as she saw what I had in the box she came running over, then Beth saw them too and she came running over.

"Aren't they darling?" said Beth picking up one of the puppies and holding it close to her face and the puppy yipped and licked her face.

"Oh my gosh," laughed Carol. "They are the cutest little devils I ever saw." She picked up one and held it laughing as he licked her face and yipped at her.

I picked up the third one and cuddled it to me as the puppy sucked on my little finger. "Don't you just love them to pieces?" I laughed.

Bill drove in just then and Beth went racing over to show him the puppy and Mark came out to see what all the commotion was about.

"I suppose you want to go pick up our brood right away," laughed Mark.

"You got that right," said Carol dragging him toward the car as she handed me the puppy she had been holding.

"Here, David," said Bill handing him the puppy Beth had been holding, "I suppose this wife of mine wants to go right away too."

"Yes, Bill, please let's go right away," begged Beth.

A little later all eight puppies were happily playing in the stall in the barn as the six of us watched and laughed at their antics. I went in Storm's stall and led him out so that he could see what was going on. He sniffed at the puppies, but I noticed that he was careful where he stepped so as not to step on any of them. Bill led Sheik out of his stall and the stallion sniffed them once then lost interest. Lady sniffed at the puppies and she allowed them to run around her hooves and even try to climb up her legs. "Storm definitely shows tendencies to fatherhood, but Lady is just meant to be a mother," laughed Bill.

"Yes, we should breed her before too much longer, because she will make a very good mother I think," I said laughing.

David went in and got a big bowl in which he put their puppy food and brought it out to them. All six attacked the food as if they had not had a meal in weeks. One even tried to climb in the bowl. When they had finished we took them outside the barn so they could do their business and I took a shovel and cleaned up after them putting it in the compost pile I was building. We let the dogs romp for a while then put them in the stall where they would sleep for the night. I put the alarm clock in with them as well as the hot water bottle. All eight cuddled up to the hot water bottle and were immediately asleep.

"We've got to figure out names for all these puppies," said Mark.

"Well I for one don't want to think about it tonight. I'll think about it in the morning," I laughed.

While I got supper, David painted the cribs and chests. Coming in from the back porch where he had been working, he came up behind and put his arms around me as I stood at the sink and nuzzled my neck.

"How's my little mother?" he asked.

I turned and put my arms around his neck. "I'm fine, Daddy, now that we've got the kids bedded down for the night," I said.

"You know, kitten, I never particularly liked babies—not even puppy babies—but now I've such a longing to hold our babies in my arms," he said.

"You were just meant to be a daddy," I said. "And I'm just grateful that you chose me to be the mother of your children. These twins will have such fun with their father, and they will adore you almost as much as their mother does."

"Will they know me or will they be scared of me the first time I meet them because they may be three or four years old before I have that privilege," he said.

"No, they won't be afraid of you at all and they will love you right from the moment they first see you, because I'm going to make very sure that they look at your picture every day and play the record of your lullaby so they'll know your voice and I'll tell them every day of their life about the wonderful man who is their father and how much he loves them even if he can't be with them right now," I said.

"Oh God how I wish I could be here when they are born," he whispered.

"I wish for your sake that you could be here too, as well as for mine, but I'll tell you everything they do each day when I write to you and honestly the first year isn't a lot of fun for fathers, at least I don't think it is, because babies do very little but cry, eat, and sleep but by the time you get home they'll be little individuals in their own right and they will love playing with their daddy and having him tuck them into bed at night.

"Go, darling, and wash up. I'll get supper on the table then after supper we'll put records on and you lie on the couch with your head in my lap and we'll talk about all the things the four of us are going to do when you get home."

"Thanks sweetheart, you always know just what to say to make me feel better," he said kissing me and going upstairs to wash up.

After dinner we wandered into the living room and put on some records and I sat on the couch and David lay on the couch with his head in my lap holding my hand. "What are you hoping for kitten? Two girls, two boys, or a girl and a boy?" he asked.

"I don't know, I guess I'm hoping for a girl and a boy so that you will have both a son and a daughter. You know when you told me I could never disappoint you when I was worried that I might give you a daughter as your first born and you told me I never could disappoint you; well if we have both a girl and a boy, then I know I can't disappoint you unless you were hoping for a horse or something," I laughed.

"How about you? What would you like?"

"I really don't care, I'd love two little girls or two little boys, or one of each."

"When you get back I promise I'll get pregnant again just as fast I can so you will have the experience of what you'll be missing now," I said bringing his hand to my lips and kissing it.

"I'm going to hold you to that, sweetheart, because I don't intend to let you out of bed for at least a month," he laughed.

"You do know our twins are going to try to play both of us against each other to get their way, don't you?

"What do you mean?"

"Well your daughter will work on Dad and your son will work on Mom to get whatever they want, because that's just the way it works."

"I wonder why girls are more partial to their fathers?"

"Well even though mothers and daughters can be close, every little girl just naturally gravitates to the man in her life, kind of like a precursor to giving up everything familiar to her to go with the man she will eventually marry and love."

"How do you women do it? You give up your name, your home, everything familiar to you to follow the man you love to the ends of the earth if necessary?"

"Because we know that a man worth loving is worth giving up everything for."

"Come on sugar," he said getting up. "Come to Daddy's arms and let's dance."

"I love dancing with you, you have such a natural grace and then I get to be in your arms," I laughed.

"I'm sure glad I was born a man, because I'd never be able to follow someone instead of leading," he laughed.

"Learning to dance, I was always told, is the first way a woman learns to know what a man is going to do before he does," I laughed.

He laughed softly and pulled me even closer into his arms and he bent his head slightly so that his chin rested on my head as he always had. "Do you know how much my arms ache to hold you when you're not in them?"

"Yes Daddy, I do, because when I'm not in your arms it is as if my entire body were in agony. Let's go out and check on the puppies just to be sure they are ok," I said.

"Sure, just so we don't end up with eight puppies in our bed because Momma feels sorry for them," he chuckled.

We went out to the barn then and the puppies were all asleep curled up against the hot water bottle which by now must have turned cold, except for one who had somehow gotten out and into Lady's stall and he was curled up around her hoof and she being the patient female stood very still so she would not trod on him. "I think you're right, we need to breed her soon because she, like you, was born to be a mother," whispered David.

When we got back to the back porch David stopped to admire his handiwork with the baby furniture. "Oh Daddy, it's beautiful. Thank you."

The next day when the mail came there was a letter for David from the Air Corp. I took it and handed it to him. He extracted his orders and read them. "Well, I'm to live at home for the next five weeks of training and the sixth week I will be expected to make several long distance flights which may keep me away from home for a day or two at a time," he said.

"Do they say what comes after training?" I said with a lump in my throat.

"No, except I'll receive further orders during my training," he said.

"Well at least we know we'll have another five or six weeks together," I said going to put my arms around him. "Do they say what hours you'll be on base?"

"Just that I'm to report at 0700 each day, but it doesn't say whether we'll have weekends off, so I have a feeling that they are not planning on letting us have them off," he said.

I went to him then and put my arms around him, for I knew his disappointment was as acute as mine. "Darling, at least we have another five weeks, so that is something to look forward to and whatever time we have together during those five weeks is more than we first expected," I said tightening my arms around him and holding him.

"It was that I was just hoping they would give me something more definitive so we could at least plan our life a little more easily," he said his arms tightening around me. "I hate this living in limbo, why can't they just tell us and at least we'd know where we stand?"

"Well we will just play it by ear. We'll do the same as we have been doing, then if you don't get here for supper on time, I'll just figure they've kept you flying later and I'll keep your dinner on until you do get here. As for the weekends we'll also play them by ear and whatever time I have with you I'll just thank my lucky stars," I said.

"Kitten, how do you take everything so philosophically?" he asked.

"What else can I do? I can't hold a gun to their head and demand answers," I laughed. "If I could I'd definitely worm it out of them."

"Maybe I ought to sic you, Carol and Beth on them, gun or no gun. You three would get the answers somehow," he chuckled.

"Well we can't bribe the whole military the way we do you guys, so it would make it a little harder," I said.

"It's just not fair to you."

"Darling, I learned long ago there is nothing fair under the sun, so I don't expect it and therefore can't be disappointed when I don't get fair play," I laughed.

"Come on babe, let's go feed the livestock and see what our second family of puppies is up to," he laughed.

We took the puppies some breakfast, then watched as they chased each other around the barn yipping and climbing all over each other. Then we mucked out the stable and walked the horses. By the time we'd finished it was time to go in and get lunch ready for us.

Just as we were finishing lunch Carol came bouncing in the door. "Look what I have," she laughed holding up two small kittens.

She handed one to David and one to me.

"They purr just like you do, kitty cat," he laughed.

"Let's go take them down to the barn and introduce them to the family," I laughed.

We took them to the barn and held them up for each of the horses to inspect and sniff, and then we set them in amongst the puppies. Immediately the puppies began to yip and chase the kittens until one of the kittens hissed at them, then they backed off a little.

"I hate to say this, bro, but I think we need a bigger barn," laughed Carol.

"It does appear that this one is getting full rather fast," he laughed. "I think I better get a builder in here and plan an addition, if he starts now he should be finished by mid next week."

Beth came in. "New additions?" she laughed.

"Yes, two prime mousers eventually," laughed Carol.

"Oh they're darling," said Beth.

"No coddling of the kittens. They've got to learn to hunt for their food, or they'll never become mousers," I laughed.

"If you want to enforce that rule, I think you're going to have to feed the puppies in the tack room because the kittens will probably dig right in with them," laughed David.

"Hey guys I was just thinking, why don't we build a chicken coop and get some hens and a rooster then we can have fresh eggs whenever we want them?" I said.

"That's a great idea. But do you know anything about chickens? Because I sure don't," laughed Carol.

"We raised chickens for eggs and meat at home in Ohio," I said.

"You don't mean to tell me that we have to slaughter our own chickens do you?" said Beth alarmed.

"Well, I'm not even up to that," I laughed, "so the answer is no, we'll keep them just for eggs and then when they get too old to lay we'll sell them to the butcher shop."

"And you guys thought my tomboy here was just another pretty face," laughed David.

"Well if we let them brood once or twice a year, we'll always have new hens and if we get too many roosters, we can sell those to the butcher as well," I said.

"I for one, have no idea about eggs or chickens," laughed Beth, "I just assumed they came from somewhere but I never made too deep an inquiry in how the grocery stores came by them."

"We also need to dig up a small plot in which to raise vegetables," I said.

"Can we plant some roses and other flowers too?" asked Carol.

"Sure, why not? We've plenty of land," I said. "You know, David, if you do add on to the barn, I really would like to get at least one milk cow, then we could make our own butter as well as having fresh cream and milk and even buttermilk," I said.

"I think I did marry me a pioneer woman," he laughed. "But the answer is yes, why not have at least one cow and maybe two."

"I thought this was suppose to be a horse farm, not an actual farm," laughed Carol.

"Well, just think of all the ration points we'll save if we grow most of our own food," I said.

"At the rate this kitty cat of mine is going, I think we need to have another war council Friday night before the dance," laughed David throwing his arm around my shoulders and giving me a hug.

Later as we sat in the living room talking over things that had happened throughout the day, I asked David, "Am I getting too ambitious with this place?"

"No kitten, I don't think so, but the others might not see it as you and I do," he laughed.

"It's just that I want to accomplish as much as I can while you are still here to advise me and to see it taking shape so that you can picture it later when you are far away," I said.

"I know you do, kitty cat, and for that I'm very grateful to you, but I think you've got to decide if you want a fully functioning farm, a horse farm, or what other goals you really have for our place."

"First and foremost my husband, I want to make it a real home for you and our kids where all of you will feel safe and secure and happy," I said softly. "After that, I would like to make it into a real functioning, not to mention, paying, horse farm. But as I see it, the more of our own needs we supply like eggs, vegetables, milk, and so forth, the less it will cost us for everything else we want, plus if we raise the food ourselves then we'll know where it came from."

"In a case like that, I think you do have clear and definite goals for Love

Farms and I'll back you all the way on whatever you want to do, kitten," he said.

"One of the things we are going to have to do is fence in some portion of it where the horses and cows have a pasture, but I don't think we have enough land to sustain all our livestock so I'd limit it to just one cow and the horses we currently have. Once the war is over maybe we can purchase more land to use as part of the horse farm, but for the time being I don't want to add any debt if I can help it, because I'm not really going to have the time to devote to a real horse farm, but once you are home and can help then, yes, let's shoot for the moon," I laughed.

"You are just determined, kitten, aren't you to make a country boy out of this city boy you found and brought home like all your other strays?" he laughed. "Your only problem is that except possibly for Bill, the rest of the brood you've assembled are very definitely city folk and I don't think you'll ever change them."

"Well I know Mark and Beth are definitely lost causes, Carol has a lot of potential though and as for you, my beloved stray, I think you've already crossed the line from city boy to country boy," I laughed.

The rest of the week until Friday we tried to live as normal a life as we could under the circumstances. We did make love more often but it was because we both knew that very soon David would have to leave and we wouldn't get the chance for however many years it was before he could return to his family and also because we loved each other and making love was the greatest expression of that love.

On Friday, I awoke almost as early as David and went to the kitchen to make his breakfast and start the preparation on the food I was taking to our potluck. "How come you're up so early, kitten?" asked David when I entered the kitchen.

"I just couldn't sleep so I decided to come down and start the dinner preparations while I talked to my favorite man," I laughed softly going to where he was sitting at the kitchen table and kissing him.

He put his arms around me and pulled me into his body laying his face against my breasts. My hand went up then to stroke his hair and my lips came down to kiss his head.

"I love you, Mommy," he whispered. "I love you more than I can ever tell you."

"I love you too, Daddy," I whispered. "I love you so much." We stood that way for several minutes until he turned his face up to look into my eyes and I leaned down seeking his lips.

"What would my darling like for breakfast? Anything special?"

"In the way of actual food, no," he laughed. "But after we do the chores, Daddy definitely has something special in mind."

"And Daddy knows how much I like his specials," I laughed. "Go start the chores and as soon as I get the food on for tonight, I'll come out and help you."

"Will you bring out the dogs' food when you come?" he asked.

"Yes, Daddy," I said giving him a little shove toward the door. "Hurry Daddy, because I'm eager to find out just what your special might be this time."

"If Mommy keeps on, Daddy is going to say to hell with the chores," he laughed.

"Go you sex fiend, and I'll be out in just a few minutes."

By the time I got the food on cooking and the dogs' food ready, when I got to the barn, he had finished mucking out all the stalls and had laid fresh straw down. He was bent over cutting the wire on the last bale of hay so I went up behind him and put my arms around his waist rubbing my body against his. He turned then and threw me over his shoulder.

"To hell with the horses getting exercise, Daddy needs his own," he chuckled carrying me back toward the house.

When we got inside he continued up the stairs pulling off my jeans as he climbed the stairs. I reached down, "Unbuckle your belt, darling," I said laughing, "so I can get my hand inside your jeans."

I felt him tug at his belt and heard him unsnap several of the buttons on his jeans. I slid my hand beneath his clothing and I began to stroke him.

Once in our room he set me on my feet.

"Hurry darling, don't talk just take your clothes off," he said.

I pulled my jeans the rest of the way off as he did his jeans.

"I can't wait one more minute," he said pushing me down on the bed the upper half of our bodies still clothed and my legs went around his waist and my arms pulled him down to me.

"Hurry Daddy, Momma needs you," I whispered as I began nibbling on his ear. Then he was thrusting deep inside me and I sighed a sigh of utter contentment at the feeling of him within me.

"Momma likes that, does she?"

"Daddy darn well knows Momma loves that."

"Momma sure knows how to please her daddy," he said thrusting even harder and deeper as his hands went down to lift my buttocks higher so that he could come even further into me.

"Daddy," I moaned as my climax sent spasm after spasm throughout my body, and then I felt his release burst into me.

"Kitten, you have the most inventive little mind, and you don't know how appreciative Daddy is that you do," he laughed.

"Isn't sex wonderful with the person you love most in all this world?"

"Yes kitten, it is," he laughed hugging me to him.

Later David came into the kitchen,

"When is this shindig supposed to get underway?" he asked.

"Around 5:30," I said taking a banana cream pie from the oven.

"Kitty cat, can Daddy get a piece of that pie to tide him over?"

"As a matter of fact, Daddy, I made one just for you. It's over there on the counter," I said handing him a plate and a fork.

He cut himself a wedge and came over to where I was standing.

"Thanks Mom, I appreciate it," he said dropping a kiss on the top of my head. "This is so good, guess I'll keep you."

"Thanks Dad, but I hope you give me better payment than just a kiss on the head," I laughed.

With that he set the pie down and came over and gave me a very thorough kiss. "Does that pass muster as payment?" he chuckled.

"Yes indeedy, it does," I laughed back at him.

"I was just out in the stable and the dogs are trying to gang up on the cats, but so far the two of them have kept the eight pups at bay," he chuckled.

"We've got to name those dogs and cats pretty soon," I laughed, "or they are never going to get to know their names."

"How about Tarzan, Jane, and Boy?" he laughed.

"Well I don't think Jane is going to appreciate the name because he's a male too," I giggled.

"What do you expect from a man who never owned a dog?" he laughed.

"Come on Daddy, get your thinking cap on. I need name suggestions," I giggled.

"How about Rusty, Spike, and, and, and…I can't think of another name," he laughed.

"King. How's that for the third name?" I asked.

"Sounds good to me, I hate to think what Mark will call his three probably stud and stud muffin or something equally as ridiculous," he laughed.

"Hopefully Carol will keep his suggestions within reason," I laughed.

"I'm not sure that Carol won't come up with even more lurid suggestions than Mark," he chuckled.

"What I'm wondering is did Mark and Carol even think about having their female spayed because if they don't plan on doing it, we could end up with litter after litter," I said.

"Oh God, you better mention it to them tonight because knowing those two idiots they probably think they won't breed because they are brother and sister," he laughed. "Are you about ready to go, kitty cat?"

"Yes, can you get that tray of food and I'll bring the dishes," I said.

"You got it kitten, if you can just hold the back door open for me," he said.

When we got to the stable, the others had already arrived. "Well it's official now, the Benton, Purcell, McCoy dance and potluck is underway," laughed Mark.

We spread the tablecloth and set the food out as well as our table service. "Come on everyone, chow down before the food gets cold," said Carol.

"What would you guys think about putting in a vegetable garden out behind the stables and raising our own vegetables?" I asked. "Also what about getting some chickens so we have our own eggs and maybe a milk cow for milk and butter?"

"Lauren, I think the vegetable garden is a great idea, but none of us know anything about chickens and cows," laughed Bill.

"There's nothing much to raising chickens, as for the milk cow I've never raised one but if 4-H'ers can do it, why can't we?" I laughed.

"Why don't we start out small with a garden and chickens and then after you girls have your babies we'll think about the milk cow," said Bill.

"One other thing we need to do and that is fence in some pasture area for the horses," I said. "Then if we get a milk cow she will need to be put out to pasture as well."

"I'll vote for the fencing and I'll get someone on it this very week," said Bill. "Also I'll get someone to build a chicken coop. I'm assuming you intend to give them free range of the barnyard?"

"Yes, no reason not to and when they get too old to lay we'll either sell them to the butcher or take them to the butcher and have them slaughtered and dressed for our own consumption."

"Oh my heavens," said Beth, "I could never eat one of our own chickens that I actually got to know."

"Honey, where do you think the chicken in the grocery stores come from?"

laughed Bill.

"I don't know, but I think I'm going to become a vegetarian," said Beth meekly.

"What do you think about enlarging the stable?" asked David.

"For right now why don't we leave it just as it is because winter will be here all too soon and I think we are going to have our hands full with what we already have, not to mention the babies that will be making an appearance," said Mark.

"Mark, do you care if Lauren and I park our car in your garage since we don't have one until we do add on to the stable, at which time I'll have a garage built as well?" said David.

"Why don't you park it in our garage since Carol and David have two cars and we only have one?" said Bill.

"I'm glad you brought that up because I'd forgotten they have two cars," laughed David.

"Oh for anyone who has elected to take home a female pup, you may want to think about getting her spayed in the not-too-distant future unless you want an awful lot of puppies running around this place," I laughed.

"Well, I think our husbands ought to take care of that problem, since as a pregnant female, I just couldn't condone spaying another female right now," laughed Carol.

"Hear, hear," said Beth and I.

"OK, you guys, let's dance," laughed Mark.

"Come on kitten, let's go cut a rug," laughed David leading me to the dance floor as the others too went to the floor.

"Well, I guess my ideas weren't terribly popular," I laughed.

"Well two for two isn't all that bad," said David. "You've got to remember these guys have never been around farm animals all that much and besides, I tend to agree that everyone is going to have their hands full for the next nine months, especially since I won't be around to help."

"Oh, I'm not that disappointed, I kind of figured what would win and what wouldn't, but I just wanted to begin getting this farm on somewhat of a paying basis or even a break-even basis," I sighed.

"Kitty cat, can I make one suggestion for future reference?" asked David.

"Sure, darling. What's your suggestion?"

"Next time only present them with one thing at a time, then it won't seem like overload to them," he said chuckling.

"I guess you're right, but I'm just so eager to get everything underway before you have to leave so it will all be accomplished when you return, that I do tend to come off as an eager beaver," I laughed.

"But you're the cutest eager beaver in the world," he chuckled bending his head to kiss me.

"You're just prejudice, Daddy," I laughed returning his kiss.

"No just truthful, as you always tell me, Mommy," he said.

"Have you got anything planned for tomorrow?" asked David.

"No, I just thought we'd do whatever we felt like doing," I laughed. "Of course, I realize what we usually end up doing when I say that."

"Mommy, you do bring up such wonderful thoughts," he laughed. "I was thinking the other day when we were flying over here and I spotted a drive-in movie theater about a mile from the farm that Momma might like to go with me tomorrow night to see a movie."

"Oh goody, then we can sit in the car and neck like teenagers," I laughed.

"I take it that you would like to go then," he laughed.

"Yes, as long as Daddy doesn't get me pregnant at the drive-in," I said laughing softly.

"I think it's a little too late for that to be an issue," he laughed pulling me closer to him as we danced.

"It's a good thing this is our own dance floor because the way your holding me if it was a public one we'd probably be arrested," I whispered.

"Let's go neck behind the barn," he said taking my hand and leading me off the dance floor.

"Where are you guys going?" asked Carol.

"None of your business, sis," laughed David.

"And you call Mark and I sex crazed," laughed Carol.

We went out the back door of the barn, and there I saw our car in a very secluded and dark place.

"Get in, kitten," said David opening the door for me.

"Sir, just what are your intentions?" I giggled as I slid into the front seat and watched him go around to the driver's side and get in.

"It's been years since I've made out in a car and I just want to make sure I still know how," he laughed taking me in his arms as his lips came down to mine.

Giggling I looked up at him, "But sir, I'm not that kind of girl."

"I've got evidence to the contrary," he laughed softly.

"David my darling, I love you so much; I love the way you laugh and how your eyes crinkle up when you do; I love your hands which are so big and strong and beautiful but which can hold me so tenderly; I love the strength of your arms but also their gentleness when you pick me up in them; I love the way you hold me when we are dancing or making love or just sitting in our chair; I love everything about you, but most of all I love you, the man who gives me so much love," I whispered.

"Baby, I love you too in a million different ways, but most of all for always knowing what I need and giving it to me without ever once asking anything for yourself except that I love you."

His arms tightened around me and his mouth came down to mine as my arms, which were around his neck tightened. For more than a half hour we sat there holding each other and kissing one another not in passion but in love knowing that very soon now we would no longer have the comfort of each other's arms.

"Let's go back in and play our record one more time and dance to it," he said.

"Yes my love," I whispered and we walked back into the stable and once more he took me in his arms and my head rested on his chest and my hand caressed the back of his neck.

Carol saw us and was about to make a wise crack then she saw her brother's face and mine and it died on her lips. Instead she walked over to the jukebox and punched the buttons for *I'll Walk Alone* and when it started to play she sang the words in a hushed voice and Mark came up behind her and put his arms around her and Bill and Beth came over to stand beside them allowing David and I to be the only ones dancing. As the song faded David bent his head and kissed me pulling me into his body as though somehow we could become one.

"Darling, I'll always be with you, you'll never be alone ever again, I promise you that," I whispered. "Just close your eyes and I'll be there; just come home to me that's all I'll ever ask for in my lifetime." I took my arms from around his neck and we walked from the stable, and as we did so I looked over at Carol and mouthed our thanks.

We walked across the yard then and to the house then up to our room, our hide-a-way from the world, and I undressed him then myself and as we slid into bed I felt the racking of his shoulders as grief had its way with him; grief that he had to give up all that he loved best; fear that I would need him and he couldn't be with me; fear of what was to come when he went into combat. I held him in my arms and whispered my love for him until he quieted in my arms and when he would have spoken, I put my hand across his lips.

"Darling don't apologize, if that is what you were about to say, for none is needed; I'm here for you to lean on when you need me, just as I've leaned on you when I've needed to, for that is what marriage is all about and I don't consider you any less a man because you had the need of my strength tonight. You are the most wonderful man in this entire universe and I love you so much and always will my darling, my love."

His arms came around me once more and we clung to each other and at last, exhaustion claimed us and we fell asleep wrapped in each other's arms. In the morning when I awoke David was already awake and I pulled his head down to mine to kiss him.

"Thank you, Lauren, for loving me so much," he whispered and we made love then, a slow unhurried almost passionless lovemaking of two people who needed to be as close to each other as it was possible to get. Afterwards he slid down so he could lay his cheek on my stomach while he looked up at me and he could feel our babies kick and he kissed my stomach.

"Hush, Mike and Laura," he whispered as his hand stroked my stomach and mine caressed his hair so that it was almost as if the four of us were one. Later we dressed then with his arm around me we went down stairs.

"What would Daddy like for his breakfast?" I asked my hand going up to stroke his face.

"I don't care, kitten, I'm not really hungry," he said and I could see that he was still troubled about last night and the fact that he had broken down in front of me.

I turned then and put my arms around this gentle giant.

"David, stop brooding about last night. You've carried so much on your capable shoulders since we met, it had to come sooner or later. You've been on an emotional roller coaster ever since we met; it had to take a toll on you. Think about all the things that have happened just in these few short months. You fell in love, something you never expected to do; you got married, another thing you never expected to do; you became an owner of a horse farm; and last but not least you found out you're to be a father, not of just one child but two. And on top of all that you've had to worry whether I would hold up when you had to leave," I said.

"But, kitten, men just don't breakdown like I did last night," he said quietly and I could hear the embarrassment he felt in his voice.

"Don't you ever believe that men don't breakdown, they do and there are going to be a lot more of them who do after this bloody war is over; because they are going to wake up at night from nightmares of what they've seen, heard and experienced, because it will be the only way they can stay sane. And you know something, I for one hope to God they do, because maybe this stupid male pride thing will become a thing of the past and the world will finally realize that men can't always be strong and silent that sometimes they have to break and become little, hurt boys again just to stay sane in this insane world. I'm tired to death of the world believing the myths of what is proper male or female behavior. I've had to pay all my life because I didn't fit the mold of what it is to be female. I've had to apologize over and over again for liking and being interested in what is considered male things and you, you silly gander, have had to pretend you weren't hurt when you were, that you didn't really need women because one let you down badly. Why do we do it? I don't understand. Why is a man less of a man because he has emotions since all humans have them? Why does the world demand that a man should never cry when he's hurt and scared or lonely? And why is it considered feminine when a woman cries, but if she tells some jerk that is annoying her to bug off, she's aggressive and unfeminine? I won't have you think less of yourself because of last night, because to me it made you more masculine in my eyes; because part of what caused you to break is fear that you won't be here when I need you, but don't you understand my love, you are always here with me whether you are physically or not. All I have to do is close my eyes and I feel your love surrounding me. I can almost feel your arms around me. At the apartment that first day you were suppose to go on active duty, when Carol and I were sitting there talking, I sat in our chair and I could feel your arms around me then because we had sat there so many times with you holding me in your arms. When I tell you that I feel safe and secure in your big strong arms, it is because I do, but I don't feel any less secure or safe because you have need of my arms to hold you when the world gets too tough to bare. I love you. Do you understand me? I'll love you all of my life and no matter what happens I'll go right on loving you. I didn't fall in love with you because you were handsome or strong, or any of those things, I fell in love with you because of your gentleness and tenderness. So stop this nonsense—I love you and even you are not going to make me change my mind."

He held me even closer in his arms.

"Kitten, thank you for that and for holding me when I needed you so badly last night. I think you are right that this war is going to demand changes in how masculinity and femininity are perceived. I think too, you are going to make me understand that you love me no matter what my perceived shortcomings are even if you have to pin my ears back to do it," he laughed softly. "Another myth that has been perpetrated on the human population is that women are the weaker sex and that they are scatterbrained little imbeciles; neither of which are true. Women look life squarely in the eye and they don't flinch from the truth where as sometimes men try to evade the truth and definitely women are the practical, pragmatists of the species." He bent his head down to mine and kissed me tenderly. "Now I know little Momma is hungry so fix whatever appeals to her because Daddy's hungry too," he laughed.

I set about getting our breakfasts then and afterwards we went to the stables to do the chores.

All too fast David's furlough came to an end and during his B-17 training his hours varied so we could depend on nothing. We chose to spend what time we had together alone and the others respected our need to be alone with each other. In the last weeks of his training he was often gone over night and would appear at any hour exhausted from the long distance trips he made. Finally his training period was over and his new orders said that he would have temporary duty in England and that he was to report for active duty on the 5th at 0700. With his orders he received a week's leave.

The first night of his leave we got together with the others for our normal dance and potluck so that they could bid him goodbye with the understanding that the rest of his leave he would spend with me. We tried our best to make it a party atmosphere but it failed miserably and it took its toll on him although he did not let the others see it, but his smile now was an artificial smile and his laughter was hollow.

That night he made arrangements with Mark to drive him to the base on the morning of the 5th and he asked that Bill and Carol stay with me on that day, although he didn't tell me about these arrangements until the night before he was to leave.

We didn't even bother with supper on his last night of leave we, chose to spend it together in our room where we sat in our chair holding each other or dancing quietly.

"Baby," he said pulling me down to his lap where I cuddled in his arms, "I wish I didn't have to put you through this, you deserve better, you deserve a husband who is going to be here with you when you give birth."

"Darling, it's not you putting me through it and there are millions of other wives going through the same thing. Don't worry about me, just take care of yourself, my dearest love."

"I love you so, kitten," he said wrapping his arms around me. "And I love the twins, so please, the three of you, take care of each other."

"Please darling, don't worry about us, we'll be fine and the three of us will be waiting for you when you return, ready to give you all our love for the rest of your life."

"Kitten, Mark is going to drive me to the base in the morning because I want to say goodbye to you here in our room not at the base because I want to remember you here safe and secure."

"Please darling, can't I ride along with you and Mark because I want to spend every second I can with you?"

"Kitten, I want to be with you every second too, but it will be easier on me if you don't come. I don't think I could stand looking back and seeing you standing there alone."

"Then I'll stay here for I don't want to make it any harder on you than it already is. Just know my heart and my love will be with you, as well as all my prayers until you're back in my arms."

"Baby, I left something for you on the dresser. Don't open it until after I'm gone."

I tightened my arms around his neck and his lips came down seeking my waiting mouth and I purred as he kissed me.

"You know I'll write to you every day and twice a day most days," I whispered. "Please write as often as you can. Don't you dare fall for any of those English beauties, my Australian stallion."

"Not a chance of that, love, because you are all the woman I ever want or need."

"Damn the Army, why don't they let women fly combat, because if they did I could be flying right along side you in the right seat."

"That right seat might be a little tight for both you and the twins," he chuckled.

"Well you know me, I'd squeeze them in somehow," I laughed softly.

"Give Dad a call and let him know where I am and my address, will you?"

"You know I will, darling."

"And let me know which of you three go into labor first, I may start a pool amongst the guys."

"Bet on me then because since I've got two to go against their one. I intend to get first dibs on the doctor's time."

"Hon, I'd never bet against you on anything."

"You better not. What are you hoping for two girls, two boys, or one of each?"

"That's another pool I could start, maybe I'll come home rich if you just cooperate."

"I'll do my best, love, just let me know which way you're betting."

"I'm kind of hoping for a boy and a girl, but whatever they are is fine with me as long as you're ok."

"Sweetheart, I'll be fine and so will the twins, that I absolutely promise you."

"Come on kitten, let's dance," he said going to the recorder and putting on our song which he sang softly in my ear as we danced.

"Hold me, darling, because I love you so much," I said fighting back the tears that were threatening to get the better of me.

His arms pulled me in even closer to him. "Baby, I love you so much."

"Have I finally convinced you, my darling, that I love you more than life itself?" I asked.

"Lauren, I think you've finally convinced both my head and my heart of your love for me and I'll never doubt it again."

"Kitten, let me make love to you all through the night for all the time I won't be able to," he whispered.

"Please Daddy, please make love to me for all the time you won't be able to because I will be needing you as much you will be needing me."

We made love then, neither of us in a hurry wanting it to last forever, because as long as we were in each other's arms we were both content. Toward dawn we were finally too exhausted to continue our love making so instead we held each other close and crooned our love to each other. At 0530 David pulled from my arms to go in to shower and shave and I went with him watching him as I almost always did while he shaved. When he had finished he pulled me into the shower with him and we held each other under the warm spray of the shower. "Let me dry you off, my husband," I said taking the towel from him and drying his body trying to memorize everything about it for the months and years we would be apart. He did the same to me and finally we could put off the inevitable no longer and he dressed, then he came to me and kissed me holding me in his arms then he grabbed his flight bag and ran from the room.

I waited until I heard the front door shut, then I raced to the window to catch the last fleeting glance of him as he and Mark drove out of the driveway.

This time I did not dissolve in tears for there were no tears left in me to shed. I went to the dresser to see what he had left for me. Sitting there were three recordings and a little box holding a heart-shaped necklace, which I opened to find his picture. I put the necklace on and I knew that it would never leave my neck again until he was safely home with me. Then I put the first of the three recordings on the record player. It was David singing our song with the instrumental recording that we had always played playing in the background.

The second recording was a lullaby that he had recorded for the twins. As I listened I patted my stomach. "That's your daddy singing to you," I said softly to the twins.

The third recording was David talking to me, and this was the one that brought the tears that I thought had all been used up.

Lauren, my love, my dearest wife,

I'm recording this so that you can listen to it when the time comes that you will no longer be able to hear my voice. Kitten, I want you to know that I love you so much and how grateful I am that you have chosen to give me your love, your faith, and your trust. You are everything to me and I think I'm the luckiest man in the world that you love me.

Since the first night we met, I've never been so happy in my life and it is all due to you, little one. It was you who took away all my loneliness and all my distrust of love. Since that first day you asked me to share your life with you by moving into your apartment, you've given me unconditional love and you've never asked for anything in return except that I love you. Through your generosity you even gave me the option of backing out without recrimination saying only that you'd be happy because for a little while you had been loved by me and had the chance to give me your love. I can't think of another woman who would say those words to the man she loves the way you love me. Even after our marriage you wanted me to be free to look for comfort in another woman's arms if I needed to while we were separated because of this war because you did not want me to ever be hurting or lonely or needing. Kitty cat you are a very amazing woman and how I got so lucky to find you I'll never know, I am just eternally grateful that I was.

Just know that I have loved loving you and being loved by you. That I am so grateful that you share not only your love with me, but your adorable body as well.

Every time you run into my arms when I come in the door makes me know how much you love me. Your sexual generosity in never denying me, the way you will beg me to take you, the way you laugh during our most intimate moments that makes me feel even closer to you, all these things you have given me and I will be forever grateful to you.

The times you've held me when you knew I was hurting, the way you tell me not to be ashamed when I've needed your strength, has all meant more than you will ever know to me.

Sharing our flight times together have been more extraordinary than anything I've ever known before. The way you snuggle in my arms when we ride Storm or are just sitting in our chair, make me feel more masculine than I've ever felt before in my entire life. And now, in addition to all of that, you are in the process of giving me children and your doing it all when I can't be with you makes me love you even more.

Mommy, somehow I'm going to come through this mess and I'm going to run home and throw myself in your arms and I'm never going to leave them again. But if for some reason I don't make it I want you to know that I'll love you forever even through eternity and to know that I will be waiting for you. Live your life as happy as you can and tell our twins how much I love you and them. I know now that you will never look for another man if something happens to me, but you've also taught me that you won't be unhappy because we shared everything for a time.

I love you my darling, with all my heart and soul and I want you to know that I think you are the greatest woman who ever lived and what a privilege it has been to know you and to love you and to be loved by you.

Dear Twins,

This is your daddy, who you've never seen, but who loves you beyond anything in this world. I'm sorry I can't be with you, but I know I leave you in good hands for you have the most wonderful mother any babies have ever had.

If for some reason I can't make it back to you, know that I will be watching over you and loving you always. Make sure, my little ones, that you love your mother without question, because she will do more for you than I could ever do and she will give you her unconditional love through all of your lifetime, just as she gave me her unconditional love.

When I do come home, if I'm lucky enough to do so, I want to play with you, teach you how to fly a plane, ride horses with you, go to baseball games with you, and watch you grow up to be the wonderful adults I know you will become.

I love you both.

The recording finished and I took it off the record player and held it to me as the silent tears cascaded down my face. I heard the door open softly and Bill came into the room followed by Carol. Bill came to where I was sitting and pulled me up and into his arms until the tears stopped.

"Lauren, don't cry, he'll come back to you, I just know that he will," he said.

"Oh Bill, I hope so, I pray so, but even if he doesn't he's given me everything in the world and I'll be forever grateful that he loved me."

"Sis, I've known that brother of mine a long, long time and I can tell you that if there is anyway possible he'll return to you for he loves you so much," said Carol.

"What's the record you're holding, sis?"

"David recorded it for me and for the twins. I want you both to hear it, not the others, but you two because Bill you've been in on our love almost from the beginning and I want you to know what kind of a man I married and you Carol, because you've known and loved David all your life. I want you to hear it too so you'll know even more what a wonderful man he is. Even if the worst should happen I want you both to know that I don't regret one minute of the time and the love David and I have shared, because I've known the ultimate in happiness through loving him and his loving me."

"Lauren, you must pull yourself together because you've got two other lives to think of, not just your own," said Bill.

"Yes, sis, you've got to think about your babies now."

"You don't have to worry, either of you, I'm not crying out of grief I'm crying because I'm so happy that I've known love like exists between David and me. Please, both of you listen to recording while I go take a shower and get dressed, because I don't want to share it with anyone except his children when I listen to it. I think you both will understand when you hear it."

When I came back in the room after taking my shower and dressing, Bill and Carol sat there looking at each other in awe at what they had both heard.

"Now do you both see why I love David so much?"

"You know Lauren that I was concerned when you and David first came to me to tell me that you were getting married because neither of you had known the other more than five days and I thought you were running headlong into something that couldn't possibly last; but after hearing that recording whether or not he makes it through, I think the love you two have for each other will last through all eternity," said Bill.

"Sis, after hearing David's recording, I am just beginning to realize, like Bill, how much love you two share and like Bill I think no matter what happens it will go on forever and that you two share something that none of the rest of us will ever know in our own marriages, much as I love Mark and Bill loves Beth, it somehow doesn't compare to what you and David share."

"That's why I wanted you both to hear it, so that you would know that no matter what happens I don't regret one second of the time David and I had together and that neither of you have to worry about me, because I know now that nothing can destroy what we feel for each other not even death."

THE WAITING BEGINS

The months passed and our lives became routine. I wrote at least once a day to David and most days I wrote twice. We still had our Friday night potluck and dance. The men tried their best to make sure that I was included in the dancing, but it wasn't the same for they weren't my husband's arms holding me and so often as not I declined their invitations to dance. I know the women grew concerned because they thought I was withdrawing into my own world of misery and they would urge me to dance. I tried to explain to them that mine wasn't a world of misery, it was more like a waiting time, that I preferred to wait until David returned then I would always dance only with him because no other arms felt right and I didn't enjoy the dancing as I had when David held me in his arms. Finally to save everyone being uncomfortable I told them that I would come to dinner with them, but that afterwards I preferred to return home to write to my husband.

During those months I spent a lot of time with Storm, not riding him, of course, but he was a comfort to me because he always nickered and whinnied when I came to the stable to see him and he would nuzzle my neck as if he knew the loneliness I was feeling and tried to be David's stand in for me.

The puppies were now full grown and I played with them and eventually began to school them, which filled up the hours of the day because I no longer cooked meals, but just prepared food and ate it only because of the babies growing within me.

> *My Darling,*
> *Thank you again so much for your recordings and for the beautiful necklace which I will never take off not even in the shower, because as long as I wear it I feel you are here with me just like you used to be and I stand there and I can almost feel your arms around me, loving me. It's a good thing you have such long arms because I'm getting bigger every day and you need your long arms to get them around me these days.*

The twins must have been playing football in my stomach all day and quite frankly I think they were practicing drop kicking until Momma could stand it no longer and I went up and lay down and put your lullaby recording on patting my stomach telling them to hush and listen to their daddy singing to them. Believe it or not darling as soon as they heard your voice they settled down and there was no more kicking. So you see, my dearest love, even when you are not near to them they love hearing your voice and know that Daddy is thinking about them and loving them and they send their love to you too.

I've spent most of the day schooling the dogs or at least trying to school them. Spike definitely has a mind of his own and he's determined that no one shall be master over him, but I think he is finally getting the message that this tomboy is not to be messed around with. Rusty and King are definitely more docile and their training is going much faster. I've been spending a lot of time with Storm even though I cannot ride him now. He always nuzzles my neck as if he's trying to let me know that until you come home again he'll do his best to love me and take care of me just as Daddy would if he were here. I'm glad I at least have one of my stallions with me, of course, his nuzzling isn't nearly as satisfying as yours but if I close my eyes, I can almost believe it is you.

At least once a day I play your recording to me and I feel so honored every time I do that you love me so much. My arms ache for you too, and night and early morning are the worst times for me because I miss the comfort of your arms and the warmth of your body lying next to me in bed. Out of habit I usually wake at 0530 and I reach for you which you would think after all these months I would no longer do, but I've begun to understand that I always will until you are safely home in my arms again.

On Friday nights I go to the potluck but I don't stay for the dances anymore. Bill and Mark were so sweet asking me to dance, but it wasn't like being in my daddy's arms and rather than make everyone uncomfortable including myself, I just excuse myself and leave before the dancing begins. Instead I come to our room and put on the recording you left me with you singing our song. The other night I fell asleep in our chair while it was playing and I dreamed that you were here holding me and you were asking me to beg you to make love to me. When I woke, I was running my hands over my body the way you used to do and I went over and lay down on the bed and held out my arms to you.

You are going to think your little tomboy has become quite unhinged because I saved the pillow case after you left that morning and I've not washed it so that if I bury my face in it I can still smell the scent of you and I'll not wash it until you are back home with me. I keep it instead in a silk bag and I only take it out when the need for you becomes too great to be endured then I take it out and put it on your pillow and hug it to me and at least some physical part of you is still with me.

Yesterday morning I was wishing you were here (which I do every minute of the day and night) because I've gotten so big I can't see my own feet anymore and about half the time Carol and I laugh at each other because we both have on two different shoes and I was thinking my darling would be laughing at me and telling me I just wanted to play Cinderella and make him try the glass slipper on me.

The other day Carol and I decided we'd go charter a plane and fly around for a little bit. Unfortunately, both of us are too big and we couldn't fit into the cockpit because if I put the seat back where I could comfortably fit in then my arms aren't long enough to reach the control column nor can I reach the rudder pedals and very definitely not the brakes. We've decided that I will teach Carol how to handle the rudder pedals and brakes and I would handle the stick. We've been practicing at home with a makeshift cockpit, but I have a feeling by the time we get in sync enough to actually do it, the babies will be born and we won't need to do it anymore. I told her that once we deliver then I'm going to teach her how to fly a plane enough so that if we ever find ourselves in similar circumstances it won't prevent our flying. But then we got to laughing because Carol said in order for me to be in that condition, you'd be home so I wouldn't need her.

You'd get a kick out of Beth, she is definitely the most motherly amongst us, for she already has an entire wardrobe for her baby completed and in fact has made garments for both Carol and I for our offspring.

The closer our time gets the more nervous Mark and Bill are becoming. We may have to drive them to the hospital instead of they us. I have a feeling that trip is going to be just like a movie comedy where the husband forgets everything and starts to the hospital without the mothers-to-be. Even Bill isn't his usual calm controlled self; it is a riot to watch.

Darling, I'm going to close this letter out so I can get it in the post before the postman arrives. I love you, my dearest, and I miss you like everything. The twins send their love to you too. Remember dearest, if ever you need me just close your eyes and I'll be there with you. Even with this darn separation I wouldn't change anything; in a heartbeat I would love you and want to be your wife.

All my love and kisses.

I waited every day with such impatience for the postman hoping for a letter from David. Most days there was at least one letter waiting for me and I'd take it to our room and sit in our chair to read it.

My Darling Kitten,

My letter to you will be on the short side tonight, because I don't think I can keep my eyes open, for there has been a push on here and we've been flying almost around the clock, but I didn't want to let even one night go by without writing to my love.

The fellows have named our plane KITTEN in your honor, so in a way you are flying with me and your picture hangs right above the left seat so I can look up and see your beautiful face and I know my tomboy is guiding me.

The fellows look at your picture and none of them can understand why I refer to you as my tomboy. I tried to tell them that if you were here and one of them made a pass at you they would certainly know why I call you tomboy, not to mention that you can fly as good or better than most of the pilots. They said to tell you they wish you were here too because they'd rather fly right seat next to you than me, since you are so much prettier.

I'm glad my lullaby works so well on the twins when they are pestering you by kicking so much. When I recorded it, I was hoping that it would do just that, like when I was at home with you.

You mentioned your dream in your last letter and I know what you mean because sometimes when I dream about you I wake up and have to go take a cold shower just to keep from going nuts for the wanting of you. I wish I had a pillowcase like yours only with your scent on it; I'd probably take it right into the cockpit and sniff it instead of using oxygen. God how I love you, and miss you and I miss so much the way you snuggle in my arms. Do you feel my arms around you right this minute? I don't care how big you get I'd find a way to get my arms around you.

Goodnight my dearest darling, all my love and kisses to you.

The day finally arrived when I awoke to a terrible ache in my back and I felt the first contraction just as my water broke. I called Bill.

"Bill, this is Lauren. I hate to bother you so early, but I just wanted to warn you that I've gone into labor so sometime today I'll need a ride to the hospital."

"Beth and I will be right over, Lauren."

"No don't bother. Take your time and go back to sleep and I'll call you again when the contractions get a lot closer together than they are now."

"Beth has been restless all night so I figure she's next to go into labor."

"I wonder when Carol will make it a threesome?"

"Well knowing Carol she won't be far behind you and Beth," laughed Bill.

"Go back to sleep, Bill, because this could turn out to be a long day for all of us," I laughed as I hung up the phone.

I sat in our chair looking at David's photograph. *Well Daddy, it's not going to be long now before we find out what these twins are.* I could almost hear his voice telling me that he was with me and that he loved me. Shortly before nine Carol called to say that she was in labor.

"What took you so long? Beth and I've been in labor since early this morning, or at least I think Beth is because when I called Bill at dawn he thought she was going into labor."

"I wish you could see this, sis, every time I have a contraction Mark gets one too out of sympathy."

"Tell him to buck up and be a little man or else I'll come over there and clobber him," I laughed.

"Maybe I should just call Bill and have him drive Mark to the hospital then I'll drive you, Beth and myself," she laughed.

By noon all three of us were definitely in labor and Bill and Mark decided they were driving us to the hospital right then and there. Somehow they got all three of us in the back seat of the car and Bill drove while Mark groaned in sympathy pains every time one of us girls had a contraction. When we arrived Bill went to get a nurse and intern to help him get us out of the back seat of the car. The admitting nurse took one look at the three of us and called the doctor and told him to bring his new partner along because all three of us were having contractions about 10 minutes apart.

Somehow they got all three of us into the labor room and when they did the examinations all three of us were completely dilated and they rushed us into the delivery room. Somehow the doctor and his partner managed to get there just as I delivered my first baby who was a girl and ten minutes later I had the second, which was a boy.

Well, I won that bet for David, I laughed, *because in the pool the guys all bet it wouldn't be both a girl and a boy except David who said he knew he could count on Momma to do right by him.*

Carol was the next to deliver and she had a beautiful little girl, then Beth had a boy that was almost as big as she was.

When the guys were allowed up to see us they looked like they had been through a battle all their own.

"Lauren, your twins are beautiful and so is my son and Mark's daughter," Bill laughed.

"I guess we needn't have worried, because as usual you three had everything under control," laughed Mark kissing Carol.

"Did you expect anything else from us?" laughed Beth as Bill kissed her.

Both Mark and Bill came over and kissed me on the cheek.

"By the time David gets home and we go through this again, you guys will be experienced and you can take care of my husband," I laughed.

"Little one, I have a surprise for you," said Bill.

"What?"

"Pick up the phone. I've had them install next to your bed and you'll see," he chuckled.

"Hello," I said picking up the phone.

"One minute please," came the operator's voice. "Go ahead sir."

"Kitten," I heard David's voice and the tears came down my face.

"Oh my darling," I whispered.

"Darling, you've got to talk a little louder because this isn't the best connection in the world," he said.

"Daddy," I said, "Laura Beth and Michael John send their love to their daddy."

"Baby, are you all right?"

"I'm fine and so are the twins," I laughed. "So how much did Mommy win for Daddy in the pool?"

"Mommy won $500 for Daddy and the three of you won me another $300 for all of you delivering at the same time," he laughed.

"Oh David, I love you so much and you're going to love the twins, they are just beautiful."

"Daddy loves you too, kitten, and the twins. Kiss them for me and tell Bill or Mark they have my permission to kiss you for me," he said.

"I don't think they have either the time or inclination darling, they are too busy kissing their own wives and I'd rather wait until you get home and deliver the kiss to me because nobody can kiss me like you do."

"Believe me, darling, I intend to do more than kiss you when I see you."

"Oh goody, then Daddy can be here for the next set of twins in nine months after he gets home," I laughed.

"Kitty cat, you are just the most amazing woman in all this world and I love you my darling. Thank you for our twins."

"You're welcome and thank you too, because I definitely couldn't have done it without you."

"Baby, I've got to hang up because they only gave me five minutes, but know that I love you and I can't wait to have you back in my arms and our babies too."

"Goodbye for now, my love. I love you too," I said.

"Thanks Bill for that," I said hugging him.

"Well what's the use of being on a first-name basis with the Secretary of State if you can't ask for a favor under these happy circumstances?" laughed Bill.

We all came home from the hospital after only a week instead of the normal two weeks because it was so crowded with all the war babies being born. The ride back from the hospital was almost as hectic as the ride to it had been by the time the three of us crowded into the back seat all holding babies. Mark drove this time and Bill held my son in his arms while I held my daughter.

As soon as I got the twins settled, I sat down and wrote to David telling him everything about the trip home with all the babies. Then I lay down for a while as the babies slept.

The years passed slowly for me and it was 1945 and the twins were now four years old. During the intervening years I had made sure that the twins realized that the picture on my night side table was their daddy and the voice on the recording was his and that he loved them so much. Laura was a double of me including being an out-and-out tomboy. Mike looked most like his daddy and even he noticed it telling me that he looked like his daddy. We had been down at the stable playing with the dogs and talking to the horses and when we got back there was a delivery boy from the telegraph office. My heart stopped when I saw him and my hands were shaking as I took the telegram from him.

> **We regret to inform you that your husband, Captain David Benton, is reported missing in action STOP His plane was last reported over the Channel and it is believed that he may have parachuted along with his crew; a search is now in progress to see if any of the crew survived STOP You will be hearing from the War Department if there is any further news STOP**

I called Carol immediately and ask if she could come over right away and to bring Mark if he was home. Two minutes later both Carol and Beth were running up the steps of our back porch and when they saw my face they knew that the news was not good. I gave the telegram to Carol to read first because David was her brother then Beth read it.

"I'll take the twins to my house to give you time to decide what to tell them," said Beth hugging me to her.

"Thanks Beth. That would be a big help."

Carol came to me then and we held each other each giving the other the support to face what had to be faced.

"I just don't believe it," said Carol.

"I don't either," I whispered, "and I'm not giving up hope because I truly think I would know if David were dead."

"I think I would too and maybe I'm just not facing this head on, but I don't think he's dead either," she said. "I'm going to call Mark and Bill to see if they can get any more information."

"I've got to get the twins' dinner ready and I've got to decide what I'm going to tell them when Beth brings them home," I said.

"Lauren, I don't know how you are taking this so calmly because if it were Mark and not David, I'd be a basket case," said Carol.

"Maybe it's that it hasn't sunk in yet, Carol, or the fact that I think I would know if he were dead and I don't feel that he is, that I can stay calm,"

I whispered.

"Let me get the twins' dinner going. Why don't you go up to your room where you can be alone until Mark and Bill let us know if they can find out anything?" said Carol.

"No, I'll get dinner then I'll go up until the twins come home, right now I have to be busy so my brain can shutdown or I might just start screaming and besides I know you are just as upset as I am," I said.

We got dinner on cooking, and then Carol and I went upstairs. Carol lay down on one of the bunk beds in the twins' room and I went to sit in our chair and look at David's picture as if by looking at it I was keeping him alive somehow, somewhere.

"David, am I being stupid about this?" I asked his photograph. "Should I accept the fact that you are never coming home to me?"

I swear I heard David's voice then saying, "Don't give up hope yet, my love, for I'm trying to come home to you."

"Then I won't, my darling, and please try very hard to come home to me because I need you so badly."

"I'm trying, my love," I heard his voice say again to me and this time I was sure it was David himself speaking across the miles.

When Bill and Mark came Mark went in first to be with Carol while Bill came in and put his arms around me. "Lauren, what can I do for you?"

"Nothing Bill, unless you've heard something then I want it straight. Don't try to shield me from whatever you've heard."

"They apparently bailed out over the Channel and another crew that was next to them saw all their chutes open and sent out their coordinates so a search could be started."

"Bill, I know you want me to be practical but where my husband is concerned I can't be, I know I'd know if he were dead and I just don't think he is. While I was sitting here I heard David's voice not once but twice telling me not give up hope that he was trying to get home to me."

"It wasn't just that you wanted to hear it so much was it, little one?"

"No, I tell you I actually heard his voice and no one is ever going to convince me differently."

"Well, if you say so, Lauren, I believe you, but we aren't going to know anything until it's daylight over there so they can mount a search."

"You'll let me know just as soon as you hear anything won't you, Bill?"

"Yes. I told the War Department that I would be at this number and that I wouldn't leave until I heard something from them."

"Thank you, Bill, I appreciate it, you've always been David's and my guardian angel."

"What are you going to tell Laura and Mike?"

"I don't know, I want them to understand that there is still hope but at the same time I don't want them to get their hopes up either."

"Why don't you let me talk to them first then I'll bring them up, after that I'll tell Beth to take them to our house for the night."

Mark came in then and he and Bill had a whispered conversation while I sat motionless staring at David's photograph and mentally sending my thoughts to him telling him that I believed him that he was trying to get home and to please try as hard as he could that my love was there with him and for him to reach for my arms.

Bill went down then to go to his house and talk to the twins and Mark came to me and took me into his arms. "Kiddo, if there is anyway humanly possible for him to do so David will come home to you," he said quietly.

"I know he will, Mark. Don't worry about me because either way I've got to carry on because I've his two children who need me...I don't know how I'm going to do it if he can't come home to me, but I told him so long ago that I wouldn't be unhappy because that would be denigrating the love we have for each other and we have crammed a lifetime into the few short months we had together. Go home now and take Carol home for she is going to need your love tonight because she may have lost a baby brother that she loved and took care of ever since they were kids."

"Do you want me to call David's dad?"

"No, not yet, when we're sure one way or another is time enough."

He left then to collect Carol and take her home. Bill returned with the twins who came up to my room.

"Mommy, does this mean that Daddy is never coming home?" asked Laura.

"I don't know, my sweet, it may, but then they might also find your daddy, I just don't know right now. Mommy feels that Daddy is still alive and trying to get home to us, but I could be wrong, I just don't know," I said hugging both she and Mike to me.

"Mommy, I'm sure Daddy is ok, he's so big and strong. I'm just sure he is ok," said Mike.

"Pray for him, my darlings, because I know he's struggling so hard right now to get home, pray that God sends him a special angel to help him."

"We will, Mommy," they said in unison.

"Now go with Uncle Bill, and Aunt Beth will give you your supper, then they are going to take you to their house so you can play with Sean and I'll let you know just as soon as I hear anything about Daddy," I said kissing them hugging them once more.

For the next three days while we waited for news, I alternately paced or sat in our chair staring at my darling's picture. As I paced or stared I still heard David saying, *I'm trying kitten, don't give up on me yet.* So I clung to hope even though I knew the rest of them had given up hope and had already begun to mourn for David.

On the fourth day I heard Bill come running up the stairs to David's and my room. "You've heard something?" I asked fear knotting in my stomach.

"Lauren, it's good news, they've located the entire crew and they are all alive," he said as he caught me when I began to collapse.

"While he's alive he's also been injured and he may lose a leg, so I want you to be prepared for that."

"Oh Bill, I don't care. I won't ask for miracles, as long as he comes back to me, that's all I ask," I said the wracking sobs that I'd held off for four days finally over taking me and Bill held me in his arms while I sobbed.

"You may need to convince him if they do have to amputate his leg, that it doesn't make any difference to you as long as you have him, that you won't be repulsed by his having only a stump instead of an entire leg," said Bill.

"Will they ship him home before doing the surgery, Bill?"

"I talked to his doctor and they think that they will be flying him home as soon as they get his leg stabilized, and I've requested that he be returned to Andrews so that he will be at Bethesda Hospital so you can be near him."

"What did the doctor say?"

"That he would be coming back through Andrews and would be at Bethesda, until he's able to be discharged both from the hospital and from the Air Corp."

"Thank you Bill, thank you so much for helping. I can't wait to hold him in my arms and know that he will never have to leave them again."

"Depending on what happens about his leg you may have a long, hard haul ahead of you convincing him that he is still all the man you'll ever want, because he's likely going to feel less of a man and you're going to have to convince him a leg doesn't a man make."

"I wouldn't care if he'd lost both legs and both arms, all I want is David, body parts don't mean a darn thing to me."

"I know it and you know it, little one, but it's David that has to know it, because he'll feel that he let you down and the kids down because he won't be able to play with them like he'd planned on doing."

"Yes he can, and I'll prove it to him, just as once I had to prove to him how much I loved him and always would, just get him home to me and I'll take it from there," I said.

"As soon as I hear when he'll be flying back to Andrews I'll make sure that you are there to welcome him home. You've been such a brave girl so far and I've every faith in you that no matter what, you'll convince David once more that he is the most important thing in your life."

"Did you tell the twins yet?"

"No, I came here first and I think you need to be the one that tells them that their daddy is safe and about his leg."

"Will the twins be able to go with me to meet him when he comes in?"

"Do you really think that's a good idea, Lauren?"

"Yes, I do because they love him so much and it will be further proof to him that his family only wants him home with them."

"Maybe you're right, I'll see what I can do, but I can't promise that the military will go quite that far for me."

"Thanks Bill, thank you for everything and if it works out the twins can't go with me, if I have to fight everyone at the hospital I'll make sure they get to see their daddy and their daddy gets to see them just as soon as humanly possible because I think that will do David more good than anything and the twins as well."

"Well at least I can help you there, if not at Andrews," he laughed.

"I'll go let Carol know the news now and Beth, then I'll round up the twins and bring them home."

I kissed him on the cheek then, "Thank you, Bill. I'll be forever grateful to you for all you've done for me and mine."

When the twins came home I sat them down with me and told them that their daddy was coming home and they started to jump around and yell with glee.

"Laura, Mike, Daddy has been wounded in his leg and they may have to take a part of daddy's leg off in order to make him well. If they do, Daddy is going to need to know from both of you that it doesn't make any difference to you as long as you have your daddy with you."

"Mommy, will Daddy be able to walk?" asked Laura.

"Eventually, yes, but at first he'll only be able to walk with crutches but eventually they will give him an artificial leg then he'll be able to walk just fine."

"Will he be able to play with us like you told us he would when he came home?" asked Mike.

"Until Daddy gets his artificial leg he won't be able to lift you up in his big strong arms because he will need to walk with crutches, but eventually, while he'll never be able to run with you, he'll be able to do lots of other things with you, but you will have to be patient, my darlings, and just show him that you love him with all your hearts."

"Do you think Daddy will love us?" asked Laura

"Daddy already loves you with all his heart, but he might not show it right away until he gets used to you so you'll just have to show him in every way how much you love him, then eventually he'll know that you do and he'll be able to better show his love for you."

"When will Daddy come home?"

"They are going to have to fly him home, probably within the next week or so, but they'll take him right to the hospital. Uncle Bill is trying to get permission for you both to come with me to meet him when his plane lands, but the Army may not allow you to go to the base. If you are allowed to go, you need to know that they will probably bring Daddy out of the plane on a stretcher so I don't want you to be frightened."

"We won't be frightened, Mommy, we just are so glad that Daddy is coming home and at last we'll get to see him in person," said Laura.

I hugged them both to me. "Your daddy is going to take one look at you and fall in love with you all over again, so you must not feel shy about meeting him the first time when you do."

"Can we give him a hug and kiss like we do you, Mommy?" asked Mike.

"I think Daddy would like that very, very much, my darlings."

The next day Bill called to say that David would be landing at Andrews the following day and that he would drive the three of us to meet his plane. "Will Carol be coming too?"

"Yes, she said she wanted to be there to greet David and also to help you with the children."

"Knowing Carol she might just box his ears for being so dumb as to get lost in the first place and wounded in the second place," I laughed.

"I wouldn't put it past her," laughed Bill. "I know you won't get any sleep tonight anyway so I'll call you just as soon as I hear what time they will be landing tomorrow, so get dressed and get the kids dressed so we can go as soon as I hear for it will be like Carol's arrival, probably we'll only get an hour's notice."

"We'll all be dressed and ready, the twins are so excited I doubt if they sleep tonight either. We'll probably all three of us look like tired hags, but at least we'll be there to kiss and hug him."

"I don't think it will matter what you look like, Lauren. David won't notice he'll just be so glad to get home to his family. I talked to his doctor again today and there has been some improvement to his leg."

"Oh God Bill, that's too much to hope for."

"Well don't get too excited because he'll still require surgery to get the fragments out, and he probably will always need to use a cane, and, of course, they still may have to amputate, but we'll all hope for the best."

When the kids came back from whatever they had been up to around the yard, I called them to me. "Daddy is coming home tomorrow and we three and Aunt Carol are going to go meet his plane, so I want you to both eat your dinner tonight then go to bed because we'll have to be up early and you'll both have to get yourselves dressed early in the morning, because we won't know exactly when the plane will land so we have to be prepared to leave for Andrews at a moment's notice," I said.

"We promise, Mommy, but I don't know how we'll be able to sleep because it is so exciting to know that we are finally going to meet Daddy," said Mike.

"Well when you finish supper and get your baths I'll put Daddy's record on for you and usually when you hear your Daddy's voice singing to you, you both fall right asleep."

"Somehow we'll go to sleep," promised Laura.

I got their supper on the table and when they had finished I sent them up to get their baths. "I've hung the clothes I want you to wear tomorrow on your door so you can find them in the morning. Give me a holler when you're ready for bed and I'll come up and tuck you both in," I said.

After I had tucked them in and kissed them goodnight, I walked down to the stables to tell Storm. He nickered at me when I came in and I went up to him and hugged him. "Storm, Daddy is coming home tomorrow," I said and he whinnied as if he understood and also knew that at last I was truly happy once again. "He won't be able to ride you just at first because he's been wounded, but as soon as he's better we will both ride you again just like we used to do." I kissed his velvety nose then went back to the house to our room.

I lay down on the bed and turned David's picture toward the bed so I could look at him. *Thank you God, thank you for bringing him back to me.*

I'll take it from here, I prayed. *David, I'll be in your arms tomorrow and you'll be in mine. Just wait until you meet your son and daughter, for Laura looks like me and Mike looks just like you, so neither of us would ever be able to deny them. Don't be scared, my love, for we all love you so much and we can face anything as a family now that you are back with us, just know that we love you so much and only want you home with us.*

All night long I lay looking at his picture and when the dawn came I got up and showered and put on my makeup. I debated wearing a dress or slacks and decided on the blue gray slacks I'd worn the first morning when I had fixed him breakfast in my apartment, because I felt he'd feel more comfortable with his tomboy than with his woman. The clothes I had put out for the twins were matching slacks and sweaters so they would feel more comfortable and less formal when they first met their father. Bill called at nine and said that he was picking us up in about five minutes. We all got in the car, the twins sitting in back with Aunt Carol and me next to Bill in the front seat. We drove slightly over the speed limit to Andrews and arrived on the tarmac just as the plane was just coming to a stop. The big rear doors opened and they began to unload the wounded. At last I saw David on a stretcher accompanied by a nurse. I ran then to him and being careful not to jar the stretcher I put my arms around his neck and kissed him. "Welcome home my darling," I whispered in his ear. "I love you."

His arms came around me and he hugged me to him so tight that he almost upset the stretcher.

"Please be careful, Captain, we don't want an accident," said the nurse.

"I don't care if I end up flat on my face, nurse, I've got to hold my wife in my arms because it's been four years since I've been able to," he laughed.

"I'll be careful nurse, just let me hold my husband in my arms for a minute or two," I said.

"Baby, I love you so much and I'm so glad to see you," he said.

"I love you too my darling husband and I'm never going to allow you out of my sight again for the next 100 years," I said my lips seeking his. "Darling, there are four other people who are waiting to welcome you home," I said pointing to where Carol, Bill and the twins stood. I motioned for the twins to come over to meet their father. They came running over to him and both of them would have thrown themselves in his arms had I not caught them in time and admonished them to be careful not to jar Daddy.

"Daddy," they said in unison going up and putting their arms around his neck and kissing him. I saw tears come to David's eyes as he hugged them both to him and kissed them.

"Daddy is so glad to get to meet you at last and to hold and kiss you," he said and each of them took one of his hands as we walked along toward the terminal where they were taking the wounded prior to loading them on ambulances to go to the hospital.

They bubbled over telling their daddy all about their dogs and the farm and their day-to-day life. Finally I said to the twins, "Give Aunt Carol a chance to greet Daddy because she's his sister just like Laura is your sister and Mike is your brother." They moved a little away but stayed as close as they could and still allow Aunt Carol to hug and kiss their daddy and for Uncle Bill to shake his hand.

"I'm sorry folks, but we've got to get these men to Bethesda," said the nurse.

I leaned over David kissing him and hugging him to me once more. "Go darling, and I'll meet you at the hospital."

"Can we come too, Mommy? Because we want to be with Daddy," asked the twins.

"No darlings, not this time, they have to get Daddy settled and we don't want to tire him out too much, but I promise as soon as they will let me you'll go with me to see Daddy."

"Bye Daddy, we love you," said Laura squeezing his hand once more and Mike squeezed his other hand and bid him goodbye.

"I'll see you at the hospital too, bro, but I think I'd better wait until tomorrow for you'll want only Lauren with you today which is only right," she said leaning down to kiss him.

"Beth and I will be up to see you after you get settled, David," said Bill shaking his hand. "It's good to have you home. We've all missed you."

We all watched as they carried him inside, then we went back to the car and got in.

"He looks amazingly well for what he's been through," said Bill.

"He does look well," said Carol. "Almost like the brother I remember."

"Daddy liked us," squealed the twins in unison as usual. "He looks just like his picture."

"Daddy not only liked you he loved you and I'll bet he's already counting the hours until he can see you again," I laughed.

"Will Daddy be as tall as you showed us on the wall?" asked Mike.

"Of course he will be, my darling, you two will come about up to his kneecap," I laughed.

"Are you ok, Lauren?" asked Bill.

"How could I be anything else? My darling is back home with me again and I'm never going to let him leave me," I said.

"I'll drop Carol and the twins off, then I'll drive you over to the hospital and wait for you in the lobby until they kick you out," said Bill.

"Thanks Bill, it seems like I'm always thanking you for something where David and I are concerned, but I hope you know how much I love you for what you've done over the years for our family."

"No thanks necessary, Lauren. I'm just glad everything turned out so well," said Bill taking my hand and squeezing it.

We went home and dropped Carol and the twins off, then Bill stopped in to tell Beth that he was driving me to the hospital and he wasn't sure what time he'd be home. He also took a minute to hug and kiss Sean, and then we were on our way. When we arrived I went to the front desk to ask when I could see my husband.

"They're just getting the captain settled in so I would imagine you will be able to see him in about fifteen minutes or so, Mrs. Benton. He'll be in room 203, just take the elevator to the second floor and turn right and his room will be the third room on the right," said the receptionist.

"Let me buy you a cup of coffee, Lauren, while we wait," said Bill.

"No Bill, you go get coffee if you want it, I just want to wait outside David's room until they let me go in."

"Tell him I'll see him in a few days and show him pictures of all our kids," he laughed.

"Will do. I'll look for you in the lobby when I come down," I said.

"I'll be waiting, Lauren, so stay as long as they will let you," he laughed.

I stood then in the hallway outside of David's room until the nurse told me that I could go in. As soon as I walked into the room, David said, "Come here, baby, let me hold you in my arms."

I ran to his side then and put my arms around him as his lips sought mine. "Kitten, it's so good to hold you in my arms again," he whispered.

"My love, it so good to be in your arms again and to have my arms around you as well," I purred as he held me.

"I see you haven't forgotten how to purr, kitty cat," he laughed.

"You'll never hear anything but purring from me now that I've got you back with me for good, my love."

"I wish you could crawl in bed with me and I could make love to you," he said.

"Well, while I'm sure the nurses and doctors have seen everything here, still it might just be a little shocking for them if they discovered me in bed with you, though I want to be there as much as you want me there," I laughed.

"Sit in the chair there, kitten, but pull it up so I can at least hold your hand if nothing else," he chuckled.

"Well, Daddy, what did you think of your twins?" I asked.

"They're wonderful and they weren't afraid of me at all, which I was afraid they might be not having seen me before," he said.

"They are already planning what they want to show you when you come home from the hospital. I don't think I've quite gotten it across to them that we lived at Love Farms before they were born," I laughed.

"Do they know that I'll probably be on crutches when I first come home?"

"Yes, I've told them that you will be and that they are not to rush to your arms until you are seated and that you would hold and kiss each one of them in turn," I said.

"I should know my little organizer would have thought of everything," he laughed taking my hand and bringing it to his lips so he could kiss it. "Laura looks just like a miniature version of you," he said.

"Mike looks just like you and he's just exactly like you," I said. "So I guess, husband mine, neither of us will ever be able to deny their paternity."

"Is Laura a tomboy just like you?"

"Exactly like me. She already rides on Storm and loves jumping fences on his back; she has absolutely no fear at all," I laughed. "Mike, on the other hand, is more reserved, like his daddy," I said getting up and going to kiss and hold him once again.

"Oh baby, it's so good to have you back in my arms, I'm almost afraid to fall asleep tonight for fear this will all turn out to be a dream," he whispered.

"Please my darling, don't ever let me out of your arms again for as long as we live," I whispered.

"Believe me, darling, I'm never going to, I've dreamed of you in them for four years," he said.

"At last I can throw away that damn pillowcase because now I have the real thing and I can't wait to get you home so that I can show you just exactly how much I love you."

"Please love," he said softly as his hand came up under my sweater seeking my breast, "I've dreamed of this so long that I have to touch you to reclaim my territory."

"I would love to reclaim my territory too, but I don't want to make things difficult for you when we can't do anything about it right now," I said.

"I don't care, I'll take care of it later, just hold me there," he said taking my hand and moving it down so that I could hold his penis in my hand. "That feels so good, kitty cat."

"It feels wonderful to me, my love, for you know how I love holding you like this," I whispered.

There was a knock on the door and the doctor came in as I pulled back sitting down in the chair and taking David's hand once again.

"How you doing, Captain?" asked the doctor. "Any pain?"

"Only the pain of wanting desperately to make love to my wife," said David.

"Most of our returning men have the same problem," laughed the doctor.

"Well when are you going to let me do something about it?" asked David.

"For tonight we'll just make sure you get a sleeping pill, so you'll be fit tomorrow when Mrs. Benton comes to visit," said the doctor.

"When do you think I'll be able to get out of the hospital? I've got twins at home that I've never seen until today and a wife I want to spend the rest of my life holding in my arms," asked David.

"Twins, you must have kept your doctor busy, Mrs. Benton."

"Actually doctor, David's sister, and our best friend's wife, and I all had the same doctor and all went into labor at the same time, so yes, I think you could say he was a very busy man for a while," I laughed.

"My God, all three of you in labor at the same time and you delivering twins, now that's one for the record book," he laughed.

"Once you get to know the three women in my life, everything they do is one for the record books, now that I'm home all three of them are planning on getting pregnant at the same time again, so all our kids have kids their ages to play with them."

"How many children are you planning on, Mrs. Benton?"

"Well I've always said I wanted at least six or seven, but I've just kind of rounded it off to an even dozen," I laughed.

"Captain, we definitely have to get you fit, because you are certainly going to be one busy man," laughed the doctor. "I'll see you tomorrow morning, Captain, because we'll be taking you down to X-ray early, then we'll have a better idea of where we go from there, but you should be ready for visitors by visiting hours which start at 09:00."

"Is there any chance that David will be able to come home on weekends, if nothing else?" I asked.

"Once we determine the course of treatment, and get the infection under control, we usually furlough our patients who are able for weekend leave at home," said the doctor.

"Well I'll say goodbye to you now. It was nice meeting you, Mrs. Benton, and I look forward to meeting the other two women who all managed to deliver at the same time as well as their husbands. I may even write you up for the medical journal," he laughed.

"Thank you, Doctor. We appreciate everything you are doing for us," I said.

When the doctor left, I put my arms around David once again. "Darling, I think I'd better let you get some rest. I'm going to go home and get the twins settled for the night," I said kissing him.

"I hate to admit it, but I am tired. It's been quite a day so far and I'll be able to dream of tomorrow and really holding you," he said kissing me with such love that I knew that my man was really back with me.

"See you in the morning, my love," I said blowing him a kiss.

When I got back to the lobby I searched for Bill. "You'd better get me home because I think my emotions are about to erupt all over the place, but this time they will be tears of joy so bear with me, Bill."

THE CLOUDS ROLL BY

The next day the twins were disappointed when I left for the hospital without them.

"Daddy will soon be home at least on weekends and then you can spend the day with him and he'll be able to kiss you goodnight and tuck you into bed at night," I promised them. "In the meantime I'll take him the cards you both made for him," I said.

"Tell Daddy we love him and can't wait for him to come home to us," said Laura.

"Tell Daddy when he gets home we'll take very good care of him," said Mike.

"Yes, my darlings, I'll tell Daddy and take him your cards."

When I got to David's room there were now two other men in it with him. I went to him and bent and kissed him. "Captain, you're one lucky man," said one of his roommates.

"You don't know the half of it, Joe. This is my wife Lauren and at home I've got twins waiting for me," he laughed. "Jack, this is Lauren. Lauren, this is Jack and Joe."

"Hi guys," I said. "Are your wives or sweethearts coming to see you today?"

"My wife lives in Ohio and she won't be able to get here until tomorrow or the next day," said Joe.

"My girl lives in Spokane so our reunion is going to have to wait till I get discharged," said Jack.

I went over first to Joe then to Jack and gave them a hug and a kiss on the cheek. "That's for your wife and sweetheart, until they can deliver a much better version in person," I laughed.

"Captain, you've sure got one sweet little lady here," said the guys. "Thanks, Mrs. Benton."

"Please call me Lauren," I said.

"She's no lady, she's my tomboy," said David hugging me to him.

"How can you call this doll a tomboy?" laughed the men.

"Oh I'm definitely a tomboy and maybe when you get weekend leave you can come to our horse farm and I'll let you ride Storm King, my stallion, with me," I kidded them.

"I don't think so, because I've never ridden a horse in my life," laughed Jack.

"I'm not exactly partial to horses or they to me either," laughed Joe.

"You guys have got to see this tomboy of mine ride our horse. Storm is about as big as I am in horse size and this little gal just swings up on his back like it was nothing and you should see her jump Storm over fences and rear him up just like the cowboys do in the movies," said David.

"My God, she is a tomboy," laughed the two men.

"Baby, why don't you go get the nurse to bring a wheelchair and then we can go out to the solarium for a while," said David.

"Are you sure you feel up to it?"

"You better believe I am," he laughed.

I went and got the nurse and one of the orderlies got him settled in a wheelchair and I pushed him out in the hallway. "See you guys later," I said.

"See you, Lauren, we'll be looking forward to it," they said.

"Where to, my captain?" I asked.

"Take the elevator to the fifth floor, then to room 517," said David turning to look up at me and smile.

Room 517 apparently had once been a regular hospital room, but had been furnished to accommodate the families of the servicemen. The hospital bed had been pushed into the corner and comfortable couches and chairs had replaced the straight-back chairs of a normal hospital room. On the door a schedule was hung listing visitor hours so that the men could schedule the room to have some privacy with their families.

"I heard about this room from Joe and Jack," said David. "It was meant as a place that the families visiting returning servicemen could have some privacy. But according to Jack and Joe, the men let their conscience be their guide as to what uses the room is actually put to."

"Don't the hospital personnel ever check on the patients that actually use this room?" I asked.

"From what I've been told, they tend to accidentally forget this room exists. Kitten, wheel me over to that couch and hand me my crutches, then if you move that chair so I can put my leg up, I can hold you in my arms for the next hour," he said. "Go lock the door, so we won't be disturbed.

I got him settled on the couch with his leg on the chair then I sat down beside him and as soon as I was seated he pulled me into his arms. "Oh God baby, it feels so good to have my arms around you again," he whispered.

"My darling, I never want to leave your arms again. I've missed you so much and I love you so much," I said raising my head so that I could kiss him and all my love for him was in my kiss and his love for me was in his kiss.

"I want to make love to you so much," he whispered.

"And I want you to, but I'm not sure how we are going to manage it without my hurting your leg," I said.

"We may have to improvise a little and settle for less than our usual way, but hold me and let me hold you," he said. "Baby, please take off your clothes so I can look at your body and touch it."

I stood up and removed my clothing. "Now come over here," said David, pulling me so I was astride him a knee resting on either side of his hips. His hand went between my legs seeking that part of me, and his fingers flicked back and forth over it. My hand reached down to caress his penis and I saw him spring to life and we both moaned with pleasure of being able to touch each other again. I moved then so that he could insert himself into me and I moaned as he did,

"It's so good to have you back inside me again, my love," I said and I began to move up and down on him and he tried to thrust back.

"No love, let me do it so you don't hurt your leg," I whispered and he brought me down to where he could suck at my nipple.

"Kitten hurry," he said and I increased my thrusts until I felt him explode into me and my own release came too.

"Oh my love it feels so good to be back inside you again," he said.

"Daddy, I love you so much and it feels so good to have you inside me and to feel your hands on my body again."

Reluctantly I got up and dressed once more and I stretched out on the couch so that I could lie in his arms and feel his lips on mine. All too soon our hour was up. I helped him back into the wheelchair and pushed him back to his room. A nurse and orderly came to help him get into bed. Joe and Jack were not in the room when we came back and I pulled a chair up next to his bed so that I could look at him and hold his hand.

"God, kitten, that was so wonderful."

"It was for me too, my stallion."

"I'm really surprised the Army ever came up with that room for us men, but all of us no matter how sick have such a longing to make love to our wives again, just so we know that we are still men and are really home and our wives still love us so it definitely has to be therapeutic," he chuckled.

"It is very therapeutic for the wives as well," I laughed. "Before I forget my love, the twins sent you cards and their love."

He took the cards and looked at them chuckling at their childish attempts at drawing. Laura's card showed a stick man which we assumed was her daddy and there was two other stick people in his arms which we figured out was she and Mike and standing right beside them was another figure which we assumed was me. Mike's was a really tall stick man and beside him was a stick woman representing me and two little stick figures hugging their daddy's legs.

"Lauren, thank you so much for making me real to them, because I know it was your doing that allowed them not to be shy around me."

"Believe me, darling, those two are not shy about anything and especially their daddy because they've been talking about you ever since they were old enough to talk. Talking about how much their daddy loved them and how much they loved their daddy and all the things they were going to do with you when you came home."

"I can't wait to be home with them and also get to meet Mark's daughter and Bill and Beth's son," he said.

"Carol Lauren stole Mark's heart the first time Carol put her in her daddy's arms and she wrapped her little fingers around his finger and that child already knows all the buttons to push to get her daddy to do anything in the world for her," I laughed. "Sean looks just like Bill but with Beth's red hair and he adores him."

"What is so amazing is that neither of them got pregnant again while I was away," laughed David.

"We made a pact, the three of us, right after the children were born that they wouldn't get pregnant until you came home so that I could be pregnant right along with them just as we had always planned."

"Tell Mark and Bill that I plan on getting you pregnant just as soon as they release me from this place so they can be prepared," he chuckled.

"You tell them, love, when they visit you, one man to another."

There was a knock on the door and the doctor who had talked to us the day before came in. "Hi you two. Everybody ok this morning?"

"We're more than ok," laughed David winking at me.

"Mrs. Benton, I was telling some of my colleagues about you three women going into labor at the same time and they all want to meet the three of you," he laughed.

"Please, Doctor, call me Lauren and we'll be more than happy to meet with all of them, because as soon as this husband of mine is released we are planning to do the same thing all over again."

"Have they had any additional children while your husband has been gone?"

"Nope, we three made a pact that it's all for one and one for all."

"I've just got to meet them because I think you must be the most amazing women I'll ever meet," he laughed.

"You'll have to bring your colleagues out to Love Farms so you can see for yourself because those three got us all moved in in only three days and the other two have built houses right on our property," said David. "We even have a dance floor where we have potlucks and dances every Friday night which is located in the stable."

"I'd like very much to see it," said the doctor. "I'm also looking forward to an explanation of the name Love Farms."

"The first chance you get after I get home, come out and we'll tell you the whole story," said David.

"I've had a chance to look at your X-rays and I think I have some good news for you. It appears that the infection is clearing up so we should be able to do surgery to put in the pins in your leg probably by next week and the big one, you definitely are not going to lose your leg, but you probably always will have to walk with a cane."

I got up and hugged the doctor then. "Cane be darned, that's the best news I've heard since they called me and told me David was alive."

"You've got to forgive my wife, she goes on impulses and when she's happy anyone within her vicinity gets hugged," laughed David and I could see the relief in his eyes.

"You don't see me objecting, Captain," laughed the doctor. "After we do the surgery you'll be in a cast and on crutches for probably six weeks or better, but as soon as we determine the infection is not going to be returning I'll release you to your wife here who I think will do more for you than any nurse in this hospital can do, then we'll take off the cast after about six weeks and you'll be permanently discharged. Your leg will always be stiff to a degree, and it probably will ache like all get out when the weather changes, but otherwise I think you'll be able to live a perfectly normal life including dancing on your dance floor."

"When do you think you'll do the surgery?" asked David.

"Probably, if the infection continues as it is doing now, we'll do the surgery on Tuesday, then if it doesn't recur, I should be able to release you by that Friday just in time for your Friday night get togethers. The cast will be fairly heavy but I don't think you'll have any trouble getting up and down short flights of steps and we'll have the therapy department teach you how to get around on your crutches before you leave."

"Will I be able to ride a horse while I have the cast on?" asked David.

"I don't see why not if you're careful."

"He'll be careful, Doctor, because he'll ride with me and I'll make sure he's careful and Storm, our horse, will see to it as well," I laughed.

"That's right, your farm is a horse farm," laughed the doctor.

"You've got to see this little tomboy of mine ride, Doctor. Storm is about my size in horse terms and she just grabs his mane and swings up on his back and I always ride behind her since we ride bareback."

"Well I was about to warn you not to put your foot in a stirrup, but I see now that warning won't be necessary, but I do want to caution you to ride slowly; we don't want to take any chances on a spill."

"Please Doctor, we both mean it, we want you to come out to the farm and see our setup and do bring your wife and family because your kids will love playing with our four kids and riding and playing with our eight dogs and two cats," I said.

"I'd like that very much, Lauren, and I'm sure my kids will be pestering me to buy them a farm after they see yours and when I release David next Friday we'll talk about a time for me to bring them out. I've told my wife about you three women and she wants to meet you three remarkable women and by the way please call me Chris and my wife's name is Betty and our four kids are Brenda, Kelly, Ben, and James," he said.

"Oh we can't wait to meet them all," I said.

"I am going to ask that you limit your visits to your husband to two hours because he needs his rest in order to fight the infection, but I don't think that will be such a hardship on either of you since he'll be back home with you shortly."

"No we won't complain, Chris, and we appreciate all you are doing for us," said David, "and your kids are welcome to come out to the farm whenever they like. With the menagerie we have four more won't matter at all."

"Did you tell me that you had eight dogs?"

"We have four kids, eight dogs, two cats, and three horses, so far," I laughed. "And this with a husband who was a city boy born and bred."

Just then Jack and Joe came back from therapy. "Hi Doc, Lauren, David," they both said. "What's the good word?"

"Well you two may lose your roommate in the next week," said Chris.

"Way to go, Captain," they laughed. "Just make sure you let Lauren come back and visit because we've both got a crush on her."

"While I'm flattered I think you've both kissed the blarney stone trying to tell me you have a crush on an old married lady like me with two kids," I said going to each and giving them a hug.

"Lauren, I think we should hire you as a cheerer-upper person around here because you definitely provide the men with a pleasant distraction," laughed Chris.

"Tell you what Chris, I'll bring Carol and Beth with me tomorrow and we can go to all the rooms and talk to the men, and believe me those two are even better at cheering people up than I am, especially David's sister Carol."

"What do they look like?" asked the fellows.

"Carol is a 5'7", a long-legged brunette who is absolutely gorgeous and Beth is a petite little redhead," I said.

"Oh by all means bring them along," the fellows laughed.

"Just be careful because I've got five other brothers at home who are all bigger than me by a good two to three inches, so behave yourself with the girls," laughed David.

"Yee Gods, we didn't think anyone was taller than you," the guys laughed. "But we'll take your warning to heart."

"Well I've got to get back to my rounds. I'll see you Tuesday, Lauren, if not before and I'll keep you informed of our progress in surgery so you won't have to worry and wonder because the surgery will probably take at least four to five hours," he said.

"See you Tuesday, Chris, and thank you so much," I said.

The nurse came in then to let us know that visiting hours were over for the morning.

"We need to get these two cowboys back in bed," she said.

"Goodbye, my darling," I said kissing David. "See you tonight. See you two tonight too and I just might bring at least one of the girls along with me to keep both of you entertained," I laughed going to each and giving them a hug.

"Bye Lauren, can't wait for tonight," laughed the guys.

When I got home the twins came running to the car to meet me. "How did Daddy like our cards?" they asked.

"Daddy loved your cards and he's got them taped right to his wall so he can look at them all day long and think of you two," I laughed.

"Will we get to go and see him?" they asked.

"Tell you what, I've got even better news for you than that. Next week Daddy's going to have surgery and then he's coming home for good at the end of the week, so I think we should let Daddy rest while he's in the hospital because he'll soon be home for good with us."

They jumped up and down and squealed with delight. "Oh Mommy, that's the best news in all the world, now we'll be a real family just like Sean's and Carol's," they said.

"Yes we will be and won't it be good to have Daddy home with us and know that he'll never leave us again?"

"Yes, Mommy, yes that is great," they shouted hugging each other and me.

Carol and Beth heard the shouting and came out to see what was going on. I went first to Carol and hugged her.

"David will have surgery next Tuesday and then the doctor says he most likely will release him for good on Friday, so Friday night he'll be back home with us."

"Oh Lauren, that is such good news," said Beth coming up to hug me. Then all of us broke down and started crying tears of joy and relief.

"Mommy, why are you and Aunt Carol and Aunt Beth crying?" asked Laura, fear coming on to her face.

"We're crying because we are so happy," I laughed hugging her to me.

"Girls are so crazy," said Mike coming up for me to hug him once more too.

"Come on in the house and let's have a cup of coffee to celebrate," I said to Carol and Beth.

"Tell me exactly what the doctor said," said Carol.

"He said that the infection was definitely receding and as soon as it was completely gone, he would do surgery on David and put pins in his leg to allow the bones to knit and that David would be in a cast and that if there was no sign of the infection recurring by next Friday that he would release him from the hospital for good on Friday."

"How long will he be in a cast?" asked Beth.

"He'll have to wear a fairly heavy cast for about six weeks."

"What effects will his wound have on him in the long range?" asked Carol.

"Chris, his doctor, said that he'll probably always have some stiffness and that he'll probably always have to use a cane. He also said that it would ache like crazy when the weather changed like when it rains or snows, but that he should be able to walk alright and he'd still be able to dance with me on Friday nights."

"That's the best news in the world," said both Beth and Carol.

"Do you realize that a week from Friday I'll have my husband back in my arms?" I laughed.

"You've been so brave through all of this, Lauren. I don't know how you kept your sanity," said Beth.

"I definitely feel ashamed of myself that I let myself believe that he was dead when you got the telegram," said Carol.

"Sometimes it was even hard for me to believe that he was still alive," I said, "but I kept hearing his voice telling me he was trying to come back to me and I just had to listen to that voice and send my thoughts to him to keep on trying and to take my arms because I'd be there helping him," I said the tears sliding down my face.

"You never told me about hearing his voice," said Carol.

"I would sit and stare at his picture on the night stand and I'd hear him say that he was trying to come home to me just as if he was right in the room with me. It happened not just once but several times, so I had to put my faith in his love and that he was telling me to believe that he was struggling to come home," I said.

"During those three days while we waited for news, Bill often commented that you never shed a tear, that you just seemed to pull inside yourself as if you knew that it wasn't the end of your life with David," said Beth.

"I had to believe it and if I had ever started crying I would never have been able to stop," I said. "But let's not rehash those bad times, I want to look forward now to having him back with me and being able to love and take care of him for years and years to come," I said.

"Yes we all must try to forget and look forward now," said Beth.

"Speaking of which, David has two roommates at the hospital and I've told them all about you two. They want me to bring you guys with me so they can meet you. Would you come with me tonight to the hospital to meet them?" I asked. "They are wonderful men who have been through so much. Joe's wife will be joining him here in a few days, but Jack's girl is in Spokane and can't be with him, and both of them need some cheering up."

"I'll come," said Carol.

"I will too," said Beth.

"Good, will Bill or Mark mind taking care of the twins for a little while tonight so we can go?"

"Mark will look after them or both he and Bill can take care of them, because I have a feeling that four kids are just a little much for one man to handle on his own," laughed Carol. "And Lauren, I'm going to be with you at the hospital on Tuesday providing Beth will look after Carol for me."

"I'll be glad to look after her because someone needs to be with Lauren, she shouldn't have to do the waiting by herself," said Beth.

"It will be a long surgery four or five hours or so, Dr. Chris told me," I said. "But Chris said he'd make sure we got hourly reports from the operating room."

"I take it that Chris is David's doctor?" asked Carol.

"Yes, and he's a wonderful man, he says he's going to write the three of us up in the medical journal for our having gone into labor together," I laughed. "He's going to come out and bring his wife and four kids, because he wants to hear our story and see our farm."

We heard a car door shut and heard the kids hollering their hellos to Mark as he came home from work. Carol jumped up and went to the door to shout at Mark to come over to our house. Just then Bill drove in and Beth hollered at him to come over as well.

"Now what are you three up to?" laughed Mark as he came in the door and gave Carol a hug.

"That's what I want to know too," said Bill coming to hug Beth.

"While I was at the hospital today, the doctor told David that he'll be doing surgery on him next Tuesday and that if there is no signs of recurring infection, he'll release him from the hospital for good on Friday, then he'll be home to stay," I said.

"Wow, Lauren, that is good news," said Bill coming over to hug me.

"Sis, that is just the best news I've heard in a month of Sundays," laughed Mark also giving me a hug.

"Did the doctor tell you what the prognosis is for his complete recovery?" asked Bill.

"He said Tuesday would be a four- to five-hour surgery and that he would be in a fairly heavy cast for six weeks, but that although he will probably always have to use a cane because his leg will always be stiff, that other than it aching like crazy when the weather changes, he should be alright and should be able to walk normally and even dance with me," I said.

"While I'm happy as all get out for David, I'm even happier for you, Lauren, because you've been such a trooper through this whole four years," said Bill. "I don't know how you've managed to stay so normal, especially since the day you received the telegram that he was missing in action and somehow you kept the faith that David was still alive when the rest of us lost hope."

"Bill, I tried to tell you I heard David's voice telling me that he was trying to come home to me, but you never quite believed me, but I knew it was for real because it was like he was standing right in the room with me," I said.

"It will be interesting to hear David's version of that," said Bill.

"All I can tell you is it happened just the way I told you then and am telling you now and no one will ever make me believe that it wasn't David's voice I heard," I said.

"Do you think David will feel like coming to our Friday get together the day he's released?" asked Mark.

"I imagine walking on his crutches will be hard work, but if we got together for dinner here in our house where he could sit in a comfortable chair and keep his leg up, I don't think it would be too much for him and if he gets tired I'll just kick all of you out and take care of him," I laughed.

"You ask him how he feels about it after he recovers from the surgery and if he thinks he's up to it, we'll bring all the supper over here and have dinner with you then he won't have to walk clear down to the stable," said Mark.

"Are you going to let us dance with you again then?" asked Bill.

"No my darling brothers, I'll wait a little while longer because I never want to dance with anyone but my beloved husband ever again," I said.

"Lauren has asked me and Beth to go to the hospital tonight to meet David's roommates because she and David have talked so much about us, so we told her we would go, so you guys are going to have to baby-sit the four kids until we get home tonight," said Carol.

That night when we got to the hospital I went into the room ahead of Carol and Beth and right away the guys asked where my friends were.

"We're right here," said Carol and Beth coming in behind me.

"Wow, Lauren, you weren't kidding, these two are beautiful," laughed Jack and Joe.

"You guys, this one is Carol and the other is Beth," I laughed.

David hollered, "Carol, get over here and give you brother a kiss, and you too Beth."

They went to him then and hugged and kissed him.

"Now do you guys see why I'm so anxious to kick over the traces of this place and get home?" he laughed.

"Well if we were you with this setup I'd crawl out if I couldn't get there any other way, now I know what we were fighting for," laughed Jack.

"I tell you American women are the most beautiful women in this whole world," laughed Joe.

"I'm beginning to wonder if this was such a good idea," I laughed. "You guys' temperatures will be spiking and the nurses will blame it all on us."

"It's worth it," laughed the guys.

I went over then to kiss my husband and I sat down so that I could hold his hand and kiss it from time to time and Carol and Beth each took a chair next to one of the other men's beds.

Throughout the visit Carol and Beth kept the other men royally entertained regaling them with stories of how we had all gotten together and even telling them about the move into our house. While they kept the others entertained I sat holding David's hand next to my cheek and smiling at him.

"Did kitten here tell you about my good news?" asked David.

"She sure did, little bro," said Carol.

"Little bro," laughed Jack, "if he's a little bro I'll eat my hat."

"Well Jack, remind me to get your hat out of the closet because this is my little brother," laughed Carol. "He's not only the youngest of my brothers but the smallest."

"I don't believe it," laughed Jack.

"I've five other brothers who are all 6'4" to 6'6" tall," she laughed.

"Do you mean to tell me that any man had the guts to date you much less marry you with an arsenal like that at your beck and call?" laughed Joe.

"Well my husband may be smaller than my brothers, but he's determined," laughed Carol.

"I hate to tell you guys, but when I first met Lauren, I almost punched out Carol's husband because I thought he was entirely too familiar with her apartment, but I'm glad I didn't because my big sister here took him off the market so I never had to worry again," laughed David.

"I think I better clarify that a little, Mark, Carol's husband, used to date the girl I roomed with that was why he was so familiar with my apartment, but of course David didn't know that at the time," I laughed.

"Honey, did you tell the twins that I would be home with them a week from Friday?" asked David.

"Yes and they are both so excited that I think they may just hop right out of their skins in their joy. I think they are going to drive me nuts for the next week asking me every two minutes how long it is before their beloved daddy comes home," I laughed.

"I can't wait until they are old enough that you and I can teach them to fly," laughed David.

"Don't tell me Lauren flies, too?" asked Joe.

"Yup guys you've met one of the best pilots I ever had the privilege of flying with and if she'd had her way, she would have flown combat right along with the rest of us," said David.

"Can you imagine having a co-pilot that looks like Lauren? It would almost make this war worth it," laughed Jack.

"I tried to tell you this gal of mine was a tomboy, but you just wouldn't believe me."

"If you really want to see something, you guys," said Carol, "you should see her jump her big stallion over fences."

"Jesus, she's a triple threat," laughed Jack and Joe.

"Yes and the best part is she's all mine," laughed David.

"Some guys get all the breaks," they laughed.

We talked and laughed and I think Carol and Beth enjoyed the give and take as much as did the men. When it was time to leave, I hugged and kissed my husband. "Goodnight, my dearest, sleep well," I said.

"I'll try, but I don't promise to sleep well until I'm back home with you," he whispered in my ear.

"Knowing you, you probably won't sleep well then either for at least the first month, then we'll both have to play catch-up on our sleep," I laughed softly.

"You know it, kitty cat," he said pulling me down for one more kiss.

"See you guys," said Carol and Beth going to each man and giving him a hug and a kiss on the cheek.

"Thanks for coming, ladies. It has been a privilege," said Jack and Joe.

When we got back to the car, Carol said, "That was fun, but I just can't understand how men on the one hand can be telling you all about their wife or their girl and in the next instant, they are whistling at us," she laughed.

"It's all a big front, sis. Just let their wife or sweetheart walk in and we three would be forgotten in an instant," I laughed.

"Lauren's right," laughed Beth. "I think it is just a big front so the world won't see how lonely they are."

"I told Dr. Chris that we three would drop by the hospital from time to time after David is discharged and try to cheer up the men, so I hope you two are both game," I laughed.

"They've all been through so much and yet they all try to make us laugh and feel good, how can we refuse?" said Beth and Carol. "Besides it is so good for one's ego."

On Tuesday Carol and I went to the hospital to be with David during his surgery. Before they rolled him into the operating room, I got a chance to kiss him. "I'll be right here waiting for you, darling, just be careful what you say when you come out from under the anesthetic," I smiled at him.

"I love you, darling," he said groggily from the pre-operative meds he had been given.

"I love you too, my handsome husband," I said kissing him just before they rolled him into the operating room.

Six hours later, Dr. Chris came out to the waiting room. "Everything went very well, Lauren, and you'll be able to see him in the morning, for tonight we'll keep him under sedation."

"Dr. Chris, this is Carol, David's sister," I said.

"So you're part of the remarkable trio I've heard so much about," he said shaking her hand. "You three have been the talk of the hospital what with all of you going into labor at the same time."

"Well as soon as David gets strong enough we plan on trying for the same outcome again, and we'll let you know so you can be on hand to observe," laughed Carol.

"I'll just bet you three will manage it somehow," he laughed. "Thank God my wife didn't know you three when we were having our kids, because I'm not sure I'd be up to it."

"Well bring her and your kids out to the farm, because the three of us have been together right from the moment we first met our husbands, just about, and we've truly become sisters," laughed Carol.

"I understand you have quite a menagerie, I don't know how you do it, but my four kids are certainly looking forward to meeting your four and the dogs and the horses," he said.

"We'll let you go and get off your feet, you must be exhausted, but I just want to let you know that the three of us intend to come to the hospital to visit the men, even after David is discharged, and thank you for everything," I said.

"The guys will love that," he said. "Now go home and get some sleep yourself because it has been a long day for you too and I promise your guy will be bright eyed and bushy tailed tomorrow when you get here, in the meantime I'll keep him as comfortable as I can."

The next morning I tiptoed into the room to find my husband sitting up in bed and the other two guys not in the room. "Hello my darling," I said going to him and kissing him. "How are you feeling?"

"Well I'm fairly uncomfortable, but I didn't want to take my pain medication until after I saw you, but I think I'll survive," he smiled holding me to him.

"Call the nurse and take it now, because I don't want you in pain, my darling, and I'll sit with you until it takes affect, then I'll come tonight to be with you," I said kissing him.

"You're the best pain medication in the world," he said.

"Where are the rest of the crew?" I asked.

"They said they were going to vacate the room and give us some time alone together," he said. "So come up here beside me," he said patting the bed next to him.

"Are you sure, darling? I don't want to cause you more pain."

"You could never cause me pain, kitten. I can't do much of anything but hold you and have you hold me, but that will do for the time being," he said.

I climbed on the bed and lay next to him laying my head on his chest with my arms going around his neck. "This is from Laura and from Mike," I said kissing him on the cheek. "They send all their love to their daddy. And this is from Mommy," I said kissing him long and lingeringly.

"The gang is wondering if you think you'll feel up to having them come to our house for supper Friday night, that way you won't have to struggle walking to the barn and I told them if you got tired I'd kick them all out and administer only to you," I said.

"I think I will be up to it and I look forward to seeing everyone again, but most of all kitten I'm looking forward to being in my own bed again with my kitty cat curled up in my arms," he said softly.

"Believe me, Daddy, Mommy is looking forward to that too, because it will be the first time in four long years that I will feel contentment again," I said hugging him closer to me.

"I'll be glad when this cast comes off so I can really hold you and make love to you," he said.

"We've waited this long my darling, six weeks will be a walk in the park," I laughed. "Besides we'll figure something out even if it won't be quite as good as normal, because Mommy wants her daddy inside her again."

"Once this cast comes off, Daddy is definitely looking forward to showering with Momma again," he chuckled.

"Believe me Momma is looking forward to that too and to sitting watching you shave again," I said softly. "Just remember we've got two problems on our hands, because if I know your son and daughter they are going to wake us every morning by jumping into bed with us."

"I hadn't thought about that. What time do they get up?"

"Usually around seven or so," I said.

"Well then we have between 0530 and 0700 if you don't mind getting up that early."

"I wake up almost every morning around 0530 and at least this time when I reach for you, you will really be there," I said.

"Do you think we'll ever get used to waking up at a normal hour?"

"Probably, but it may take a while and besides think about all the lovely things we can accomplish by still waking up early," I giggled.

"Yes, baby, I've been thinking about nothing else," he chuckled.

"Now Momma is going to go get the nurse to give you your pain medication and I'll stay until you fall asleep, my love."

"I think maybe you'll have to because my leg is beginning to feel like they are putting the pins in it all over again," he said.

I called the nurse and she brought him his medication, which I could see he badly needed. After she left I sat in the chair holding his hand in mine and kissing it from time to time. After about fifteen minutes I could feel him relax and knew that the pain was subsiding for him. "Baby, I'm afraid I'm going to conk out on you at any moment," he said groggily.

"Go to sleep my love, and I'll be back tonight to see you," I said kissing him and by the time I started out of the room I could hear his gentle snore and knew that he was no longer in pain.

When I got back to the hospital that night there was a very lovely woman sitting next to Joe's bed holding his hand and I knew that his wife had finally arrived. "Lauren, I want you to meet my wife, Sherry," said Joe introducing us. "Sherry, this is David's wife Lauren and she's just top drawer in all our books around this place," he said.

"It's nice to meet you, Sherry. I know how much having you here means to Joe," I said shaking hands with her.

"It's nice to finally meet you, Lauren. I've heard so much about you from all the guys," she said smiling at me.

"Kitten, aren't you going to come kiss me?" asked David.

"You better believe it you tall drink of water," I laughed going to him and kissing him soundly.

"I've heard nothing from any of these three since I got here except about the three women who all gave birth at the same time," laughed Sherry.

"I don't think we three are ever going to live that down, and what's more we are going to try repeating history once David gets strong enough," I laughed.

"Believe me, Sherry, if it's possible the three of them will do it too," laughed David.

"He laughs now, but wait until he hears I want another set of twins, it won't be such a laughing matter anymore," I said squeezing David's hand.

"You have twins?"

"Yes a girl named Laura and a boy named Mike," I laughed.

"I don't think I could handle twins," laughed Sherry.

"Well my cousin had three sets of twins and she always said it was easier because they entertained themselves, and by golly she was right," I said.

"What do you think, Joe, want to try for twins?" asked Sherry.

"Oh God this woman of mine is going to infect the whole female population in the belief that having twins is great," laughed David.

"Well husband mine, if we intend to have a dozen kids this way I'll only have to be pregnant five more times so look at all the time we'll save," I laughed.

"I was telling Sherry that David has five more brothers at home bigger than he is, not to mention a beautiful sister who is no slouch either when it comes to height," said Joe.

"I keep telling David if he ever does take me back to Australia to meet all of them I'll be talking to everybody's belly button," I laughed.

"Well I'll tell you one thing when the seven of us walk down the street in Sydney everyone gives us a wide birth," laughed David.

"I'll just bet they do," laughed Joe.

"Come on, Sherry, help me into that wheelchair and let's give David and Lauren some time together," said Joe.

"Where's Jack tonight?" I asked.

"He's down in physical therapy then he said he was going to call his girl," said Joe, "so you've plenty of time."

"I feel like I'm driving you two out," I said.

"No, we want some time together alone too and there's a certain room here that I want to show Sherry," he laughed.

"She's going to love room 517," I laughed and winked at Joe.

"I hope so," said her husband.

After they left the room I slid on the bed next to David and put my arms around him and his arms came around me.

"I wonder if he's told her what 517 is all about yet," laughed David.

"Well if he hasn't she's in for a wonderful surprise," I giggled.

"Maybe by Thursday I'll feel up to paying a return visit," said David pulling me over so he could hold me.

"Much as I want what it represents, let's just wait until Friday when I can really administer to my stallion," I laughed kissing him. "In the meantime get your rest so you'll be up to it."

"Is that a promise, Mommy?" he chuckled.

"It's more than a promise, my love, it's a sure thing," I laughed.

"The nurses were telling me how I could wrap my cast in canvas so that I could take a shower, the only thing they didn't realize is how active I can get in a shower with my kitten," he chuckled.

"You do realize, my darling, that not only will the twins come bursting into our room when they wake up in the mornings, they are probably going to want to watch their daddy shave just as much as Mommy does?" I said.

"Maybe I ought to sell tickets," he laughed.

"I get the first dozen or so," I laughed.

"David, I want to ask you something but if it's too painful, you don't have to answer," I said.

"What's that, kitten?"

"When you parachuted into the Channel, did you call to me?"

"I remember when I was thrashing around in that ice cold water and I wasn't sure if I could keep up the struggle, I remember telling you in my mind that I was trying to come home to you and I swear I heard you answer me to keep trying and that I should take your arms because you were there with me," he said and I could tell the memories were painful. "Why did you ask that, kitten?"

"Because I'd gotten the telegram telling me that you were missing in action and I was sitting there staring at your picture loving you so much and it was like you were right there in the room with me telling my that you were trying to come home to me."

"Oh my God, kitten, did you really hear my voice?"

"Yes, just as if you were standing right next to me and in my head I called out to you to tell you to keep trying and to take my arms because my love was all around you," I said with awe in my voice. "Bill tried to tell me that I was just imagining things because I wanted you to be alive so desperately, but David, I knew in my heart that you weren't dead when I got the telegram and I knew just as certainly that I heard your voice calling to me, reassuring me, that you were trying to come home to me."

His arms tightened around me until I could barely breathe.

"I heard you telling me to hold on and to keep trying, then you said to take your arms and that your love was all around me, I could hear your voice as if you were right there with me and I remember trying to lift my arms up and I could almost feel your arms around me and for a few minutes I could feel you right there in the water with me and the chills going through my body stopped and I felt warm like I do when you are in my arms," he whispered. "Later in the hospital I told the doctor about what I had experienced but he just put it off as delusions caused by hypothermia."

"Oh my love, neither of us were delusional, we did hear each other, our love transcended distance and time to give each other the strength we needed for our love to survive."

"If Mark and Carol had told this story about them to me I wouldn't have believed them," he said. "But it did happen to us, Lauren. I know that it did happen just as I know you are lying here in my arms."

"I once told you, my dearest, that I would love you even into eternity and you made the same promise to me on your recording and I think somehow God heard us and knew that neither could survive without the other one and he gave us the power to speak to each other…something like when your student forgot to shutoff carb heat and you heard my voice telling you again the story of how it happened to me on my first solo flight, we were meant to be together and love like ours was meant to survive so that our children will know that if you love someone as much as we love each other, then miracles are possible because that love can transcend anything of this earth," I said looking up into his eyes.

Bending his head his lips came down to mine and we knew that forever our love would go on and it would last though all eternity just as we had promised each other.

On the next day which was Thursday I went again to the hospital and when I went to him my kiss was tender and full of love for this man and his returning kiss was just as tender and full of love for me. Jack was in the room and he lay watching us as we greeted each other then he turned his face to the wall and I heard him softly crying.

"Jack, what's the matter?" I said going to him and putting my hand on his shoulder. He turned then and put his arms around me while he cried.

"Lauren, the doctor told me today they were going to have to amputate my leg and I can't go home to my girl with only one leg," he said.

"Why ever not, Jack?"

"What woman wants half a man?" he said.

"Jack, she doesn't love just your leg or your arm or anything else, she loves you the man, because most women don't see men the way you men see us," I said. "We see what's inside you and that's what we fall in love with, not your looks. We fall in love with your gentleness and your tenderness, we fall in love with the way you hold us in your arms. Jack, call her, tell her and I'm sure she will tell you she doesn't care just as long as you come home to her."

"But Lauren she's so beautiful and she can have any man she wants," he said.

"Then there is your answer, Jack; if she can have any man she wants why did she pick you to love…aren't there men more handsome, wealthier, taller, stronger?"

"Yes, because I'm not handsome, wealthy, tall or particular strong," said Jack.

"Don't you see, she fell in love with something within you not the exterior trappings, so do you really think she will not love you just because you have one little itty bitty leg missing?"

He quieted then. "Go Jack, go call her right now and I'll bet you anything she'll tell you the same thing I just have and I'll bet you anything she'll go through fire and flood to get here to be with you," I said.

"Listen to her, Jack," said David, "because if it had been me, Lauren would have told me the same thing and she'd have told me that she'd pin my ears back if I didn't listen to her and believe her, and I think your girl will tell you the same thing."

"Jack, we women are a lot more practical than you men give us credit for being, because your girl is looking for someone who will love her even when she's big as a barn because she's pregnant, who will look at her when you are both old and gray and see only the girl you married so long ago not the impractical thing we call looks, because eventually all of us are going to get old and that beauty is going to fade, but love and gentleness and tenderness never fade," I said smoothing back his hair and I leaned down and kissed him tenderly, not as a lover but as a woman who understood how much he was hurting and was kissing away the pain. "Now you ring for the nurse right this minute and go call that girl of yours and if she doesn't have enough money to get the next plane here, I'll personally go and wire it to her and it will never have to be repaid."

He rang for the nurse then and she got him into a wheelchair and as he was going out the door he turned back to look at David and I. "Captain, you've got one hell of woman here and I sure hope you appreciate her," he said.

I sat on the edge of David's bed and he took me in his arms. "Babe, you are one hell of a woman," he whispered. "I just hope his girl is exactly like you."

"I think she will be for like you I don't think Jack would love someone not worthy of his love."

We sat there holding each other and a little later Jack came back into the room. "She said she didn't care; she didn't love my leg; she loved me, just like you said Lauren," he said smiling at me. "Thank you so much Lauren for being here when I needed your strength," said Jack.

"Is she coming to be with you?"

"She said she was going to catch the red-eye and she'd be here tomorrow and she was going to fall into my arms and she was never going to leave them again," he smiled.

"Well, she will teach you the same things Lauren has taught me, that women like them are just absolutely amazing people and that they love us, even our imperfections," said David.

"Well you two, visiting hours are almost over so I've got to get going, but David will give you our home phone number and you tell your girl to call me day or night if she needs me to be with her and tell her to let me know when your surgery will be because I'll come and sit with her."

"Thank you, Lauren, thank you so much. You are one special lady," said Jack taking my hand and kissing it.

"Blatherskite, I'm nothing special, you're just in love and every woman appears to be something special to you, and if you don't believe me just ask my husband," I said waving to the two of them.

Driving home I pulled over to the side of the road and the tears came for all the men who had given so much to keep us safe and free and were wondering if we would still love them or what was left of them and I prayed that all their sweethearts would tell them and make them believe what I had told Jack.

When I got home the twins came running. "How's Daddy? Is he still coming home tomorrow?"

"Daddy is just fine and yes I'm picking him up at the hospital tomorrow morning and I want you both to remember that you can't go running to Daddy when he gets here that you are going to have to wait until he's inside the house and sitting down then you can hug and kiss him as I know you will want to."

"Momma, if we promise not to get in his way can we come out and walk with him into the house?" asked Laura.

"Certainly love, but we have to be careful so we don't accidentally knock him down in our joy of his coming home to us," I laughed. "We'll have to be careful until his cast comes off but once they take it off and Daddy gets used to walking without it and his crutches and only needs a cane to help him walk, then you can run to him as much as you like and I'm sure he'll pick you up and throw you up in the air and catch you and he'll love having his darlings run to meet him."

Bill called to say that he would go with me to the hospital to pick David up just in case I needed any help getting him in the car. "Thanks Bill. I'll be glad of your company because that tall drink of water may be more than I can handle as far as getting him in and out of the car," I laughed.

The next day driving to the hospital I told Bill about what had happened with Jack the day before. "As usual, little one, you handled it just right I think," he said.

When I got in the hospital room there was a beautiful young girl sitting next to Jack's bed and holding his hand like she never wanted to let go again. "Lauren, this is Cindy, my soon-to-be-wife," said Jack and the happiness he was feeling was written all over his face, happiness that not even the prospect of losing his leg could dim.

"Cindy darling, this is David's wife Lauren who convinced me that I should call you and told me just exactly the words you did say to me."

"Cindy, I'm so glad you're here with Jack and so glad to hear that you two are getting married soon," I said to her going up and hugging her. "In case Jack forgot to tell you, I intend to be with you while Jack is in surgery because we wives have to stick together."

"Lauren, thank you for making Jack see that I didn't love him for his leg, that if he'd come back with no legs and no arms I would still love him just as much as I did before he left," said Cindy.

"See Jack, I told you, we women are far more practical then you men, we don't just fall in love with every pretty face we see," I laughed.

I went over then to David and kissed him.

"Ready, Daddy, to go home? Because if I don't get you there pretty soon your twins are going to have fits; they've been up since seven this morning asking me every fifteen minutes was it time for me to go get their daddy yet," I laughed.

"Ready Mommy," he laughed. "I'm almost as bad as the twins because I think I've asked Jack every fifteen minutes if he was sure that clock was right."

"You have twins?" asked Cindy.

"Yes, twins I'd never seen until they unloaded us at Andrews," said David.

"You mean, Lauren, that you gave birth to twins while your husband was overseas?" asked Cindy.

"Well, I wasn't exactly alone, David's sister and our best friend's wife all gave birth at the same time in the same delivery room and with the same doctor," I laughed. "They are four years old now and so full of life they wear me out."

"What are they, girls or boys?"

"One of each," I laughed, "although Laura is just as much a tomboy as I was so it is kind of like having two boys at times."

Just then Bill came in the door. "Bill," shouted David. "It's so good to see you."

"Hi David, it's good seeing you up and around. I just came along to help get you in and out of the car."

"Jack, Cindy, this guy was Lauren's boss when I first met her and in fact he was her maid of honor at our wedding. Now he and his wife have a house on our farm and we are like brothers," said David.

"I'll bet you made a beautiful maid of honor," laughed Jack.

"Jack, that's not nice," said Cindy.

"Well if David and he are like brothers, then I know he won't take offense," laughed Jack.

"Absolutely none taken and I did look stunning if I do say so myself," laughed Bill.

"Ready darling?" I asked David.

"Ready kitten," he laughed.

"Now remember, Cindy, I'll be here with you while Jack is in surgery and you are to call me if you need anything at all, or just another woman to talk to," I said. "Jack, when you get ambulatory and they give you weekend leave from this place, you and Cindy are to come out and stay at the farm with us; Bill and Beth or Carol and Mark will put you up in their house because unfortunately ours only has one extra bedroom right now which is currently the twins' room, but you'll love all four of them although as David will tell you being around Mark and Bill is like talking to Abbott and Costello."

"Thank you so much for everything," said Cindy coming to hug me.

"Come over here so I can thank you too," laughed Jack and when I went over to his bed he reached up and hugged me. "Thanks for being here when I needed you," he whispered in my ear.

"Hey by the way, what's happened to Joe?" I asked.

"He was discharged yesterday," said Jack. "He said to tell you goodbye and what a pleasure it was meeting you."

"We all look forward to seeing you both at Love Farms," said Bill. He left then to go bring the car up to the front entrance.

The orderly came in then and helped David into the wheelchair then he pushed him out to the elevator and rode down with us and he helped get David settled in the back seat of the car so he could keep his leg elevated, while I got in the front seat and turned so I could hold his hand and Bill drove.

When we arrived home the twins were waiting in the yard and I heard their shouts of "hi daddy" when we drove up. I got out of the car then and went to where the twins stood jumping up and down.

"Remember now, you two, you're not to rush at Daddy until we get him seated in a chair in the living room."

"Yes Mommy, we remember," they said.

Bill and I got David out of the car and made sure he had his crutches.

"Hi my darlings," David waved at the twins. They started toward him, but one look from me and they slowed their pace and just walked beside him as he walked into the house giving him a wide birth so they wouldn't knock his crutches out from under him.

Once in the door, Bill got David seated in a chair in the living room and then shook hands with him.

"We'll all see you later tonight for dinner, David, but now I have the feeling you want to spend time with just your family," he laughed.

"Thanks once again for all your help, Bill, and I'm looking forward to this evening to seeing all of you again and I hope I get a chance to meet your kids too, but yes I would kind of like time to get to know my family again."

"Well you two, aren't you going to come give your daddy a hug and a kiss?" asked David holding out his arms.

"One at a time, because until Daddy gets his cast off he can't hold both of you on his lap at the same time," I admonished them.

Laura went to him first and David reached down and swung her up on his lap and her small arms came around his neck and she kissed him on the cheek and he kissed and hugged her.

"Oh Daddy it's so good to have you home, now we're a real family just like Aunt Beth's and Aunt Carol's," she said.

"That we are, my little one, and it feels very good to be home with my family and especially with my children," he laughed hugging her. She crawled down off his lap being very careful of his other leg and went to stand next to his chair so she could remain close to him and so as to let Mike have a chance at sitting on their father's lap.

"Mike, aren't you going to come give your daddy a hug and kiss too?" asked David and Mike went over to him then and David swung him up on his lap and hugged and kissed him. Though Mike was somewhat more sedate than his sister, he put his small arms around David and hugged him back.

"I'm so glad you're home, Daddy. We've waited such a long time to meet you."

"You don't know how much I wished I could come home and be with you from the moment you were born, son," said David hugging him to him once again. Mike got down then and went to stand next to his sister.

"See Laura, I told you I look just like Daddy," said Mike to Laura.

"Well I never said you didn't, but in person you do look more like him than you do to his picture," she said.

"Daddy, will I be tall just like you? Because you are a giant," asked Mike.

"I imagine you will be or you might even be taller," laughed David.

"Daddy, is it ok with you if I only grow to be Mommy's height?" asked Laura.

"It's ok with me whatever height you finally grow to be, my darling love," laughed David.

"Daddy, do you care if we go out and play for a while? Because we want to tell Carol Lauren and Sean all about how wonderful you are," asked Laura.

"Sure my darlings, we'll have the rest of our lives to get acquainted because I'm never leaving either of you again," he laughed.

They went bounding out then, letting the door slam and I heard them yelling to Carol Lauren and Sean.

"They are quite a pair, my darling," said David taking my hand and pulling me so that I could sit on his lap.

"Darling, are you sure you want me sitting on your lap until you get your cast off?"

"I want you nowhere else, my love," he said softly.

I sat down on his lap then and his arm came around me and my face nestled into his neck and I sighed a sigh of utter contentment because I was back home at last in my husband's arms.

"Happy, my love?" he whispered kissing the top of my head.

"Happy doesn't begin to say what I'm feeling, Daddy. It is so good to be back in your arms and sitting on your lap again," I whispered.

"I'm never ever leaving you again baby; I want to be right by your side every minute of our life from here on," he said.

"Oh my love, I love you so much and it's so good to have you home again with me and believe me nobody is ever going to take you away from me ever again," I said lifting my head to kiss him.

"Those kids of ours are something else," he laughed. "I half expected my cast and crutches to intimidate them just a little, but it didn't seem to bother either of them at all."

"Nothing intimidates them as long as they are together, for they are very definitely twins and have a way of communicating with each other which even I don't quite understand, but separately Mike is the shy one, Laura is too much like me to have any fear in her," I laughed.

"Kitten, do me a favor, run up and get my civvies. I want to get out of this damn uniform and I never want to wear it again."

"Right away, my darling," I said jumping up and running up the stairs. I came down with his brown slacks and sweater.

"Let me help you get out of that uniform and into your civvies for I never want to see you in it again either," I said.

"Well as I recall, when Momma helped Daddy get undressed it always led to other things," he chuckled softly.

"For the time being and since we don't know when the twins will come bounding back in again, I think it will have to be just me helping my husband get into more comfortable clothing," I laughed.

I took his tie off then unbuttoned his shirt and helped him get out of it. Then I unbuckled his trousers and pulled them off of him. Next I helped him into his brown slacks and after something of a struggle getting them over his cast, I finally got them on him then I pulled the sweater over his head. "Why don't you lie down on the couch, sweetheart, where you'll be more comfortable and maybe take a snooze before lunch?"

"I think I will, if Mommy will come over and let me put my head in her lap like she used to do," he laughed softly.

I helped him get to his feet then and went over and sat down on the couch. He half fell half lay down on the couch with his head on my lap and he took my hand kissing it.

"Mommy may have to help Daddy shave in the morning not just watch because I'm not sure I can handle the crutches and the shaving gear all at the same time," he said.

"I can bring a bowl of water into the bedroom so you can sit down to shave if you'd like?"

"I'd rather feel your body against mine holding me up," he laughed.

"Do I get to give Daddy a sponge bath in the morning?" I giggled.

"Definitely, but unlike the nurses you get to bathe everything," he chuckled.

"Oooh, Daddy says the nicest things to me."

Just then the twins came bounding back into the living room.

"Daddy, are you alright?" asked Laura concerned because her beloved father was lying on the couch instead of being in his chair.

"I'm just fine. I always used to lay like this, with my head on your momma's lap, before you were born, but I would like another kiss and hug from you two," he smiled at her.

She came over to where he was lying and put her arms around his neck again and laid her head on his chest and he kissed the top of her head.

"Daddy, I love you so much," said Laura.

"I love you too, peanut," said David, which caused her to start giggling because her daddy had called her peanut.

"Mike, aren't you going to come over here too?" asked David seeing that his son hung back.

Mike came over then and put his arms around David's waist and David reached down and ruffled his hair.

"I love you too, Daddy. And I'm so glad you are home."

"I love both of you and I'm so happy to be home with you," said David and I heard the emotion in his voice.

"What have you two been up to?" I asked.

"We talked to Sean and Carol Lauren and told them that Daddy was as big as Storm King and they didn't believe us, but they'll see tonight for themselves," laughed Mike.

"Then we went for a ride on Storm and then we played with the dogs for a while," said Laura.

"Do you two ride Storm?" asked their father.

"Sure Daddy, we've been riding him ever since I can remember," laughed Laura looking up into his face.

"Well when I get this darn cast off I want to ride with both of you and Mommy on Storm too," laughed David.

"You'll have to reach down and pull Mike up because he still can't get the hang of mounting him, but I can do it so you won't have to worry about me," she said giggling at the punch Mike gave her.

"Hey Mike, son, men don't punch girls," said their father.

"Well Daddy, she punches me all the time so why not when I get the chance?" asked Mike.

"I guess you've got me there, son," chuckled his dad.

"Why don't you two run up and play in your room for a while so Daddy can catch a catnap, then as soon as he wakes up the four of us will have lunch," I said.

"Don't go away, Daddy," said the twins.

"I'm not going anywhere ever again," said their father ruffling the hair on both of their heads.

They ran up the stairs then talking and giggling.

"Laura is definitely a tomboy like her mother," he laughed.

"Mike was telling the truth, every time they get into any sort of argument, which thank God isn't often, she punches him out, and most times he doesn't retaliate," I laughed.

I moved to get up then, "Hey where are you going, sweetheart?"

"I'm just going in to start lunch so why don't you have yourself a snooze," I said leaning down and kissing him.

"Maybe I will, I am kind of tired," he said yawning.

"That's my good little boy," I laughed, but he didn't hear me because he was already asleep.

About a half hour later the twins came running down the steps asking when lunch was going to be ready because they were starving. I put my finger to my lips telling them to shush because they'd wake their father.

"I'm already awake, so come here, you two," he laughed as they ran over to him where he still lay on the couch.

"Daddy, come on get up because we're starving to death," they said as they ran to him and threw themselves on his chest.

"How can I get up with both of you laying on top of me?" he laughed hugging them.

"We'll help you, Daddy," they said each taking a hand.

"Laura, Mike, be careful. Remember Daddy has a cast on his leg, why don't you get his crutches for him then stand back while he gets on his feet," I suggested.

"Thanks you two," said David when the kids handed him his crutches.

I went over then, allowing him to attempt to stand on his own, but to be available in case he needed help. He managed to get on his feet by himself.

"Didn't think I could do it did you, Mom?" he laughed.

"Guilty as charged," I laughed.

"What's for lunch, Mommy?" asked the twins.

"Hot lamb sandwiches," I said.

"Oh goody," said the twins and my husband.

"I thought that might appeal to my Aussie and the twins are just like their daddy, I think they'd eat them every day of the week if I made them," I laughed.

"What's an Aussie?" asked the twins.

"It's a person who was born in Australia," chuckled their dad.

"Were you born in Australia, Daddy?" they asked looking up at their father.

"I was, I didn't meet your Mom till I came to America," he said.

"Daddy, where is Australia?"

"It's a country almost as big as this one in the South Pacific ocean."

"Can we go there sometime, Daddy?"

"We most certainly will, because you have five uncles and a grandfather living there who haven't met you yet, but it will have to wait until the war is over," he laughed.

"We've talked to them on the phone, so they have met us," said the twins.

"Did Mommy tell you that your uncles are even taller than I am?"

"Yes, but we can't believe anyone in the whole world could be taller than you, Daddy," they laughed.

"Well my little ones, my brothers are taller than me. I was the runt of the litter."

"What does 'runt' mean?"

"It means the smallest one," he laughed

"Come on you chatterboxes, go wash your hands and let Daddy get set down at the table," I said shooing them out to the kitchen sink.

"Doesn't Daddy have to wash his hands too?"

"Yes, he does," said David going over to the sink to wash up.

"Ok, you two, go sit down while daddy finishes so you'll be out of his way," I laughed in pure happiness seeing my entire family assembled at last.

When David finished washing his hands, he came over and kissed me.

"Look, Daddy's kissing Mommy," laughed Laura and Mike clapping their hands.

"Daddy loves kissing your mother," laughed David, "and as soon as I don't have to be on crutches anymore you're going to see daddy not only kissing Mommy but putting my arms around her and hugging her."

"Like Uncle Mark does to Aunt Carol and Uncle Bill does to Aunt Beth?"

"Exactly, only more often because I've had to be away from Mommy for so long," he said smiling up at me.

I put the food on the table and the twins looked at me. "Do we have to say grace and ask God to bless and take care of Daddy, now that he's home?"

"I think it would be nice if just this once more you said it and thanked God for bringing Daddy home safely to us," I said softly and I felt David squeeze my hand under the table.

"Dear God, thank you for the food we are about to receive, and thank you so much for bringing Daddy home to us safe. Amen," said the twins and I whispered my own heartfelt amen with them.

"Daddy, are hot lamb sandwiches your favorite food too?" asked Mike.

"Yes they are, Mike," laughed David.

"Then can you talk Mommy into making them more often for us?"

"I'll do my best."

"Ok you two eat, and give Daddy a chance to eat his food too, instead of answering questions," I laughed.

They dove in then like they'd not had a meal in their entire life, as they usually did.

"Well, I must say, they definitely have my love of food," laughed David.

"Very definitely, trying to keep these two filled up is a full time job," I laughed.

"What do you two like to do for fun?" asked David.

"I love ridding Storm and mucking out his stall," said Laura, "but I also like to play with the dogs, gather the eggs from the chickens, and play baseball with Uncle Mark and Uncle Bill," she said very seriously.

"I like making model airplanes and playing with Sean and I like to help gather the eggs too," said Mike. "But I like to play with the dogs and ride Storm too."

"Who helps you with mucking out the stables?"

"Mostly it's Mommy, Uncle Bill and Aunt Carol," said Mike. "Sometimes Uncle Mark helps, but he doesn't like to do it and Aunt Beth said she didn't want any part of it. I can't understand why Aunt Beth said that because while getting the old straw out is kind of stinky, I love spreading the new straw down and sometimes Laura and I get into wrestling matches in the straw."

"Do you have any chores you have to do around the farm?" asked David laughing at Mike's description of mucking out the stable.

"We are responsible for gathering the eggs twice a day, then we have to feed and water the dogs and the chickens, and Mommy asked us to help with the mucking out," said Laura. "I don't see why they call them chores, because all of it is such fun."

"Well I don't like gathering the eggs," said Mike, "because the hens peck at my hands and it hurts sometimes."

"I keep trying to tell you, Mike, that if you just push the hens over you can get the eggs without getting pecked," said Laura.

"What are you laughing at, Daddy?" asked Laura noticing that their father had begun to chuckle.

"It is just so nice to be home and hear my two babies chattering a mile a minute, because Daddy waited four long years to sit here with you two and Mommy," he said.

"Daddy, we aren't babies and four years ago you wouldn't have heard us talking because we didn't learn to talk until we were two or three," said Mike, always the practical one.

"You've got me there, Mike, and I didn't mean to call you babies, but to me you will always be my babies no matter how old you get, even when you are grown because you two were my first born."

"Mommy said when you got back to help her we were going to have brothers and sisters," said Laura. "Will they be twins like us?"

"Mommy and I will definitely work on giving you brothers and sisters, but I can't promise they will all be twins," laughed their father.

"Mommy, you said they would be twins if you had your way, so please talk Daddy into twins too," said Laura.

"Mommy and Daddy will discuss it and we'll see what we can do for you. Have you two finished eating? If so, why don't you run out and play, then I want you to come in for a nap so you'll be wide awake when the gang comes over for supper tonight," I said.

They got up, going to their dad and hugging him then coming to hug me as they ran out the door shouting to the dogs.

"My God, Lauren, those two are so much like you, it's unbelievable," he laughed. "Baby, it's so good to be home with all of you."

"They have a lot of you in them too, especially Mike, but wait till you've been home for a while you'll wonder how to shut them up from their incessant questions," I laughed getting up and going to kiss David.

"Come here, kitten," said David pulling on my arm and indicating he wanted me to sit on his lap.

"Thank you, my love, for doing such a great job of raising them while I've been away. They are just as I imagined them and I know it is your doing," he said kissing me.

"You're very welcome, love, but I do want to warn you, anything you say within their hearing is going to be picked up and repeated, so be careful what you say when they are around," I laughed.

"They certainly are little chatterboxes and I notice that nothing gets by them," he chuckled.

"It will be interesting to see what happens when we go to bed tonight, because I don't think I've quite gotten it across to them that Daddy will be sleeping in Momma's bed, so you may get even more questions," I said hugging him.

"I can't wait to tuck them in for the first time," he laughed, "and thanks for the warning about my sleeping in your bed."

I got up then and went to the sink to start dishes.

"Do you feel like sitting here with me while I do the dishes or would you rather go sit in a more comfortable chair?"

"I'm fine here, kitty cat. I've dreamed of this for so long; sitting watching you clear up like I used to do."

"Oh my love, it's so good to have you back watching me, and especially knowing that you'll not be leaving ever again," I said turning to smile at him.

"When I finish, if you feel up to it, I'll call the twins in for their naps and you can tuck them in, then we can lie on our bed and you can hold me until they come bouncing into our room," I said.

"I wouldn't miss it if I have to sit down and take one step at a time to do it," he said.

"The twins can carry up your crutches, and you can hang on to the railing with one hand and put your arm around me for support, so I don't think that will be necessary. Besides, it's such fun walking beside you when I don't have to run to keep up," I laughed.

"While I love the thought of being alone with you, Mommy, it will be nice to see the whole gang again, especially now that I'm not an object of their pity, that our time together is limited," he said softly.

"Darling, I don't think you or I either one were ever an object of pity with them, but they did feel bad to think they would be together when we were being torn apart. David, they've all been such a help while you've been gone. I don't think I could have gotten through it had they not been here, especially when I got that damn telegram," I said softly.

"Well, baby, I'll definitely let all of them know how much I appreciate them looking out for you and the kids and for everything else, but from what little Bill said about the telegram, you held up better than they did," he said.

"Darling, I didn't have much choice because I had to stay strong for your children, but also I think I would have known had you really been taken from me. I think I would have felt it somehow, then when you called to me, I knew I was right and that I had to make you know that I was giving you my strength to come home to me."

"I'll never get over the fact that you heard me and I you," he said softly.

"It was a miracle in a way, but I think the real miracle is the love we share," I said.

He stood up then and came over to where I was standing by the sink, setting his crutches on the sink, he took me in his arms and though he had to lean on me somewhat to keep his balance, he held me in his arms and kissed me with such love.

"Come on Daddy, let's get the twins in and bedded down so we can lie in each other's arms without you having to do a balancing act," I said.

I went then and called the twins in.

"Do we have to take a nap, Mommy? We aren't tired at all," they begged.

"You want to be wide awake for tonight, don't you?" I asked.

"We will be even if we don't take a nap," they cajoled.

"Come on you two, because I'm going up and take a nap too and so is Mommy," said David.

"Where are you going to sleep, Daddy, because we only have the two bedrooms?"

"Daddy will be sleeping in Mommy's bed with her from now on," he laughed.

"That's what Mommy said but we didn't believe her," they said.

"Why didn't you believe Mommy?" asked David.

"We just didn't think there was room enough for you to sleep in Mommy's bed because Mommy showed us how tall you were," they said.

"Well, there is definitely room enough for me and that reminds me, now that Daddy's home, Mommy and I would appreciate it if you didn't come running into our room, because it is only polite to knock and be asked to enter a bedroom of people who are married like Mommy and me."

"Why, Daddy?"

I couldn't help giggling quietly at that question because I could tell that David didn't expect it.

"Because it is, so would you please do Mommy and I the favor of knocking before you come into our room? Now run upstairs you two and please take up my crutches and Mommy is going to help me get up the stairs," he laughed.

They ran up ahead of us and watched as David jumped up each stair step on one foot holding onto the railing and me.

"Oh Daddy, that looks like fun. Can we try it?" they chorused.

"No you can't try it, you could easily fall and get hurt, and believe me I don't think Daddy is enjoying it at all," I said as David paused at the head of the stairs to catch his breath. "Now go in and get undressed and get into bed and Daddy and I will be in to tuck you in as soon as Daddy catches his breath."

"Are you ok, darling?"

"I think so, it's just that I haven't played hopscotch in quite a number of years," he chuckled.

We went in then and tucked in the twins kissing them and wishing them pleasant dreams. When we came out of their room, I saw tears in David's eyes and I hugged him to me.

"Daddy, you'll enjoy it even more when we put them to bed for the night because then they will smell of soap and water and they'll be half asleep and they love to cuddle for a few minutes in your arms. I usually put on your record for them to fall asleep to, but now you'll be able to sing it to them as you are tucking them in."

"Do you think I got it across to them about knocking on our door?" he asked. "And you, you just had to laugh didn't you?"

"Daddy, I couldn't help it because I knew that was going to be their next question because it always is when you tell them to do something. We'll find out later this afternoon how much your instructions were understood."

We went in then and I got David onto the bed then crawled over him to lie in my usual place. His arms came around me and my arms went around him and it was as if we had never been separated.

"Kitten, it's so wonderful to be back in your arms and holding you in mine," he said softly, bending his head to kiss me.

"Yes and so much nicer than being in room 517," I giggled.

"I can't wait for tonight after the twins are bedded down," he whispered. "Daddy's waited a long time to make love to Mommy here in our own room."

"Darling, some nights I'd get so desperate to feel your arms around me, that I'd take out that darn pillowcase and I'd hug your pillow until the stuffing was almost squeezed out of it," I said.

"I took an awful lot of cold showers," he chuckled.

"Do you know how much I love you and how happy I am that you're back beside me?"

"I love you too baby, and I'm just as happy as you are," he said kissing me again.

We lay then in each other's arms savoring our love and our closeness until we heard the twins getting up. We heard a knock on our door.

"Come in here you two, because we've missed you," hollered David.

They came in then and when they saw their dad lying next to me on the bed, they started to giggle.

"What are you two giggling about?" I asked.

"It looks so funny to see you and Daddy lying on the bed together, we've never seen that before," they laughed.

"Oh it does, does it?" laughed David. "Then you better come crawl in with us because I want my whole family with me."

They climbed up on the bed with us then, both of them taking care not to land on Daddy's bad leg. David put one arm around them and one arm around me and hugged all three of us as we hugged him back.

"It's so good to be home with my family," he said squeezing all of us.

"Daddy, are you going to dance with Mommy the way Uncle Bill and Uncle Mark do with Aunt Beth and Aunt Carol?" asked Laura.

"Much as I'd like to, peanut, I'm not going to be able to dance with Momma until I get this cast off, but then I will because I've missed dancing with her."

"Will you dance with me too when you get your cast off?"

"I certainly will, peanut," he laughed.

"I wish I could dance with you too, Daddy, but men don't dance with men," said Mike.

"Tell you what, when I get this cast off, I'll pick both of you up in my arms and dance with both of you at the same time," he laughed.

"Do you and Mommy have a favorite song like Aunt Beth and Aunt Carol?"

asked Mike.

"We sure do, hasn't Mommy ever played the recording of our song I left with her?"

"Oh, *I'll Walk Alone*, is that your favorite song?"

"Yes it is but I think now Mommy and I are going to have to pick another song, because we need to find a happier song now that I'm home for good."

"But Daddy, that's such a beautiful song. Why don't you think it is happy?" asked Laura.

"Because to Daddy it was a promise to Momma that no matter how far I was away from her I loved her and would try to come home to her," he said. "Now I'm home and I'm never going to leave her again for any reason."

"I know a good song, Daddy, for you and Momma," said Laura.

"What's that, peanut?"

"I'm *Glad There is You*, because that is just as beautiful and it doesn't say a word about you being gone," said Laura.

"I think that is a great idea because it tells Mommy how much I love her," he said.

"Mommy, are you going to throw out Daddy's recording of *I'll Walk Alone* now that Daddy is back home with us?"

"No, my darling, I'm not because that was the first song I ever danced to with Daddy and even though it has some sad memories for us it also has a lot of good memories from all the times we danced to it," I said. "Besides I'd never throw out a recording that your daddy made just for me."

"Do you and Daddy love each other very much?" asked Laura.

"Yes peanut, your mother and I love each other so much you just can't imagine it, but we also love the two of you just as much," said David.

"Ok you guys, go get dressed and I want you to help me set the table because the gang will be here shortly," I said.

They climbed down and started for the door, then looking back at us still lying on the bed they asked, "Aren't you and Daddy coming too?"

"We'll be right there. Now scoot," I said laughing.

"What a pair," laughed David. "So Mommy promised them twins did she?"

"With Daddy's cooperation," I laughed.

"Oh Daddy definitely intends to cooperate, starting tonight," he laughed hugging me to him, "and I hope the next pair turn out to be just like these two."

"Well I was kind of thinking about a set of girls then a set of boys, that will make six and they'll be evenly divided between girls and boys," I laughed.

"I can see where Daddy is definitely going to be busy."

"Well, maybe I could have four all at once, that way Daddy will have more free time," I giggled.

"Oh God woman, and it would be just like you to do just that."

"Ok then will Daddy consider giving Mommy more time and I have two sets of twins, then?"

"Whatever happened to twelve?"

"Well I'm not opposed if Daddy isn't," I giggled.

"Neither am I, kitten," he laughed.

We went downstairs then and it was easier on him hopping down the stairs than it had been going up. I got him settled in his chair, and then went to see what the twins were up to.

"Hey, you two, don't bother setting the table except for you two, Sean and Carol out here in the kitchen because I've decided to use trays for the adults so Daddy won't have to get up and move around too much."

Just then I heard Mark, Carol and their daughter Carol Lauren come up on the porch. "Is that baby brother of mine here?" hollered Carol.

"In here, sis," he said as she came running in to throw her arms around him and kiss him.

Mark came over and shook hands with him. "It's sure good to be a six pack again," laughed Mark. "On the other hand we've added four extra to the pack so I guess I can't call us a six pack anymore."

"Who is this beautiful young lady?" asked David holding out his arms to Carol Lauren. She approached him slowly but then decided he was ok if her momma had hugged and kissed him so she went running into his arms. He swung her up on his lap.

"Hi kiddo, I'm your Uncle David," he said hugging her.

She returned his hug. "Are you really Mommy's baby brother?" she asked.

"Yes, I am. Your mommy took care of me when I was a little boy," he laughed.

"Well you and Mommy do look a lot alike," she giggled.

Just then Bill, Beth and Sean came in. Beth went to David and hugged and kissed him.

"Welcome home, David. It's so good to have you back."

"It's pretty darn good to be back, too," he laughed hugging and kissing her.

"I bet you're Sean," said David holding out his arms. "You look just like your daddy."

Sean was a little more hesitant than the others had been about going to David. "Go on, Sean. This is your Uncle David, go welcome him home," said Bill.

"Maybe Sean would rather just shake hands, until he gets to know me better," said David smiling at the boy.

"Go on Sean, Daddy doesn't bite," said Laura.

Sean came up to David and stuck out his hand, which David solemnly took and shook, man to man.

"It's nice to meet you, Sean. I bet we are going to have lots of fun together," said David.

Sean smiled at him, then ran back to where his father stood and Bill reached down and picked him up in his arms.

"It takes Sean a little while to warm up to people, but once he gets to know you, David, he'll talk your head off," laughed Bill.

"Come on you guys, put the food on the table in the dining room and then let's chow down," I said. "I've set up trays in the living room for the adults and the kids will eat in the kitchen."

"But Mommy, we want to eat in here with Daddy," said the twins.

"You four are too sloppy to eat in the living room, besides we adults need some time with your daddy," said Aunt Carol.

"Ok, but when we're finished can we come back in here?" asked Mike.

"You bet you can, sweetie," said Aunt Carol.

"You guys help yourselves, and David I'll bring you a plate, then we women will fix the kids plates, then we'll all meet back in here," I said.

Carol, Beth and I went and got plates ready for the kids and took them into them in the kitchen, then I went back and filled up a plate for David. Mark and Bill fixed their plates and came back in to talk man talk to David until the women could get their own plates fixed.

Once everyone had their plates and were seated, the chatter like in the old days bubbled up as if none of us had ever been apart.

"Mark, Bill, are you two ready for more kids? Because Lauren promised the kids another set of twins," laughed David.

"Yes, and thank God you'll be here this time to help us get them all in the car, because believe me it was a show not to be missed the last time," laughed Mark.

"Bro, this guy of mine had sympathy pains right along with us on the way to the hospital; every time one of us had a contraction he had one too," she laughed.

"Oh God, I'd have given anything to see that," laughed David.

"Well, if we hadn't been so busy at the time, Lauren and I would have shot home movies for you, because believe you me it was the funniest thing I ever saw," laughed Beth.

"It's hell having sympathy pains not for just one woman but three," said Mark.

"David, Mark and I double timed around the waiting room, so you were included too, because we couldn't see you not being in on the wear and tear like us," laughed Bill.

"Thanks guys, I appreciate it, and while I'm at it, I want to thank all of you for taking care of my family while I was away," said David. "I really mean it because knowing you guys were looking out for them was a real load off me."

"You know your welcome bro, we wouldn't have had it any other way, now we can all look out for each other," laughed Carol.

"You know, it's awfully quiet in the kitchen for our kids," I said.

"I think we better go see what they are up to because little pitchers really do have big ears," laughed Beth.

"What are you kids up to out here?" I asked.

"We were just listening to you guys talk and laugh," said Mike. "It's so nice now that we have a daddy here too, we're just like you guys."

"Yes you are and you will be from now on, my loves," I said.

"We're almost through, so can we come into the living room?" asked Laura.

"What, no second helpings and no dessert?" asked Aunt Beth.

"We're too excited to be hungry, Aunt Beth."

"Ok you rascals, come on in the living room, but be sure you wash your hands and faces first, because I can see from here that half of the food is on the outside of you," I laughed.

The kids came trooping in then: Carol Lauren going to sit on Mark's lap, Sean going to Bill, and Laura and Mike going to David's chair, Laura sitting on her father's lap and Mike sitting on the arm of his chair so he could be near him too.

"Would you believe that all of us would be sitting around with our kids on our laps when you and David first met?" laughed Mark. "We've sure become a domesticated group."

"I would believe it because from the first minute I saw this guy of mine,

I knew I wanted to be in a scene just like this one with him," I said throwing David a smile.

"Well, I didn't quite go that far that night, I just knew I wanted you to be in my arms," said David smiling back at me.

"What you mean, bro, is that you were h-o-r-n-y," laughed Carol spelling out the word.

"What does 'h-o-r-n-y' mean, Aunt Carol?" asked Sean.

"It means that when you get as old as your daddy that you'll know exactly what it means," laughed Carol.

"Don't you get it, Sean? They don't want us to know what it means now, that's why they are spelling," said Laura.

"I think it's about time you four were in bed. Go up and get your baths and then you can come down to say goodnight, then I want all four of you asleep, no giggling, no rough-housing, no nothing, just sleep," I said.

"Oh Mommy not yet," they begged. "Daddy, do we have to go to bed now?" they turned pleading eyes on David.

"Ok, five more minutes then off you go like your mother told you," said their father.

"See, I told you Daddy would let us stay up longer," said Laura to Mike.

"Yes and Daddy and I are definitely going to have a talk about backing each other up where you two are concerned," I laughed.

"Oh Mommy, you know you are too happy to scold Daddy," said Laura.

"Ok smarty pants, you got me there, you're right. I'm too happy to scold Daddy, but it is only for this one time. Do you understand?"

She laughed then and I saw her wink at her brother.

"I saw that, peanut," said her father, "and believe me you're not going to talk me into something when your mother says no, from here on out."

"Yes, Daddy," she said but I knew she wouldn't stop at just one try.

"Now you four your five minutes are up, so run up and get your baths and put on your pajamas and then you can come down to kiss everybody goodnight," I said.

"Ok, ok we're going," they said as they went running up the stairs.

"Well Dad, you learned your first lesson, never give in when Momma says no because they'll play one of you against the other every chance they get," laughed Bill.

"You guys are going to have to catch me up on all their little tricks," chuckled David.

"Lesson one David, where four-year-olds are concerned, they know more psychology than any Ph.D. I know of and they don't mind using their knowledge of reverse psychology on either parent," laughed Mark.

"I think I'd better go up and see how they are coming with their baths because those four can get in more mischief in five minutes than any four individuals I've ever known," laughed Beth.

When she came down she was laughing so hard she could hardly walk down the stairs.

"What are they up to?" I asked.

"Mike was trying to get Sean to dive into the water from the back of the tub," she laughed. "I have the feeling that Mike had already tried it, but you know Sean, he's a little less brave than your two."

"Oh God, what your two don't think of, David, isn't worth thinking of," laughed Carol.

"I'm finding that out, sis. What a pair, neither of them seem to know any fear at all, just like their Mom," said David, beckoning me over to sit on his lap.

"Now I know you're really home, bro," laughed Mark, "now that I see Lauren seated on your lap again."

"I just hope I don't wake up and find out I'm dreaming again," said David.

"Has Laura told you that she and Mike ride Storm just the way you and Lauren always ride him?" asked Beth. "It absolutely terrifies me but they seem perfectly able to control him."

"Beth, that horse would no more hurt those children than he would me or David and both of them are very competent riders," I said.

"I know you've told me often enough," laughed Beth, "but Storm is so big, although I must say Laura mounts him just like you do, although she has to stand on a box to do it right now, but by the time she's six she'll be doing it just like her mom without a box."

"Give it up Beth, my two girls will just always be tomboys, and believe me I'm finding out that Laura is every inch a tomboy like her mother," laughed David.

"Bro, you should have seen Lauren when the twins were born. Beth and I were screaming our heads off and threatening to kill our husbands, while she just grunted with every contraction and patted her stomach and smiled as if giving birth were no more difficult than menstrual cramps," laughed Carol. "In fact she got out of bed the next day and went down to see them in the nursery while Beth and I were content to sit and contemplate our flat stomachs."

"Well I wanted to see our babies and tell them all about their handsome father," I said. "I'm just glad this time I'll have David here so he can feed one while I feed the other, because boy did the twins yell when they got hungry."

"Not to mention changing them," laughed Carol.

The kids came running downstairs then dressed in their pajamas. Carol and even Sean came up to David to kiss him goodnight then went to their parents. The twins made a beeline for David and discovered Mommy was sitting on his lap and they both stopped and stared.

"Mommy, that's our place, not yours," they said.

"Who says so?" I laughed. "This was my place long before you were a gleam in your daddy's eye."

"Well Mommy, get up so we can kiss Daddy goodnight, then when we go to bed you can sit back on his lap again," said Mike, the practical one.

"Come on you two, I think Mommy will relinquish her place just this once, and when I have two good legs again I can hold all three of you on my lap," laughed David, swinging them both up on his lap after I'd gotten up.

"Good night, my darlings," said David kissing and hugging them both. "Tomorrow night Daddy will come up and tuck you in and maybe even sing you your lullaby, but I don't think I could make it twice more tonight."

"That's ok Daddy, we put your recording on and all of us listen to it, so it will be like you're in our room with us tucking us in," said Mike.

"I love you both so much and it's so nice to be home with you," he said hugging and kissing them again.

After all of them had returned to the twins' room Carol said, "Well Lauren, you were right again, this brother of mine is a good father, which at the time you told me he would be, I just didn't believe it."

"Don't ever try to second guess Lauren where I'm concerned, because she knows more about me than I do myself," chuckled David taking my hand and pulling me back to his lap.

"Darling, if I don't get off your lap, your good leg won't be much good either," I laughed. "Why don't I just sit here at your feet and adore you?"

"I want to tell you all a story," said David.

"Dirty or clean?" asked Mark.

"No, a story of a miracle," said David.

"What kind of a miracle?" asked Beth.

"The miracle of love," said David. "I know you guys doubted Lauren when she told you that she heard my voice calling to her after my plane went down, but I want you to know that she did hear my voice, for she repeated to me the very words I cried out to her while I was splashing around in the Channel trying not to freeze to death. At the same time when I thought I couldn't keep from falling asleep and drowning one more minute, I heard Lauren's voice calling to me to keep on trying and to take her arms because her love was all around me. I remember trying to lift my arms up to reach her and then suddenly I wasn't freezing anymore and I felt warm, and I know now it was her love surrounding me lifting me up."

The room grew deathly silent as he spoke and I saw tears in Carol and Beth's eyes and even the men's eyes were moist. "My God," whispered Beth.

"Amen to that, Beth," said the rest of them.

"That's almost unbelievable," said Bill. "I don't think I would believe it even now if I hadn't heard it separately from both you and Lauren. I'd say you two have a very special kind of love between you."

"Bro, I know I didn't believe Lauren when she told me about hearing your voice, because I'd lost faith that you were still alive; now I have to agree with Bill, you two definitely have a very special love between you."

"So that's why you never shed a tear, sis," said Mark. "During those three days when David was missing, you really did know he wasn't lost and that he was coming back to you."

"I tried to tell you then, but everybody thought I'd gone off my rocker with grief and I even got so I only half believed me. I kept thinking that maybe I just wanted it so badly I'd really convinced myself. That is until I asked David what he had experienced and he told me about calling out to me that he was trying to come home to me and that I told him to take my arms because my love was all around him."

"I don't mean to put a damper on the festivities, but I just had to tell all of you to never doubt Lauren if she ever tells you a similar story," he said quietly.

"We're glad you told us, because we definitely would have kept on doubting that she actually heard you calling to her, but with both of you confirming the story, it has to be true and it is a miracle of love," said Bill.

"I think we better collect our kids and let these two get some sleep. It's been a really big day for both of them, in fact all four of them," said Carol.

"Mark, Bill, can I ask you a favor? Just this once, could you help me up the steps because I'm not sure I've got enough energy in me tonight to hop up them again," asked David.

"Sure old man, no problem at all. What else are brothers for?" said Bill

"You betcha," said Mark.

David stood up then gathering his crutches and hopped over to Beth and Carol and gave them both a kiss and a hug. "It's so good to be back with all of you again and I promise no weird stories next Friday," he said.

"It wasn't a weird story, it was a beautiful story," said Beth.

"Yes bro, it was beautiful. Get a good night's sleep, that is if you can keep your hands off Lauren long enough," she laughed.

"I make no promises, sis," laughed her brother.

"Lauren, bring up David's crutches if you will please," said Bill.

"Right behind you," I said.

They each got on one side of David and he put his arms around their shoulders although he had to hunch over a little bit to do it and they half carried him up the stairs. Once there they took the crutches from me and gave them to David.

"You ok, buddy?" asked Bill.

"Yup just fine. Thanks for the help, guys."

"Darling, go on in and sit down and I'll help you get undressed when I come back up," I said.

"Lauren, don't bother coming down, we'll put the leftovers in the icebox and stack the dishes in the sink, then we'll lock up when we leave," said Carol.

"Thanks sisters, you're just the best," I said.

"Thanks Bill and Mark," I said going to kiss and hug each of them.

"No thanks necessary," they said.

Bill and Mark went into the twins' room and picked up their sleeping children in their arms and descended to where their wives were waiting for them.

"I'll come over and see you and David in the morning, after I get my crew going," called Carol.

"If you two need anything during the night just call us," said Beth.

"Thanks again, you guys, but I'm sure the only thing we'll need tonight is to hold each other in our arms," I said.

I went in then and David was sitting in our chair and I could tell he was exhausted from all the emotions and newnesses of the day, but he also looked relaxed and happy, something that I had not seen for a very long time.

"Let me help you get undressed, my love," I said. "You look absolutely exhausted."

"I am a bit tired, but for the first time in over four years, I'm content," he said.

I helped him get undressed and got him into bed. "Be right there my dearest, I just want to check on the children," I said throwing him a kiss.

When I came back I saw him smile at me.

"The kids ok?"

"Yes, I just check on them before I go to bed at night because Laura always has the bedclothes half off her," I laughed.

"Now it's Daddy's turn," he chuckled softly. "Daddy wants to watch Mommy undress because I've dreamed of this moment for so long."

"Why don't I come sit with Daddy and he can help?" I said

I went over then and pushed the pillows up behind him so he was half sitting and I sat down on the bed. "Has Daddy forgotten how?" I whispered.

"Never, my love," he whispered back pulling my sweater over my head and reaching behind my back to unsnap my bra. "Oh God, you're just as beautiful as I remember," he said as his hands came down to caress my breasts and he leaned down to suck at my nipple while his other hand kept up the caresses on the other breast.

"Daddy, it feels so good to have your hands and lips on my breasts again. I've missed your touch so much."

I stood up then and wiggled out of my slacks and panties, and pulled the pillows out from behind his head that were propping him up and he slid down so he was lying flat, then I climbed across him.

"No you don't, Momma. I want you right here, he said and his arms lifted me to straddle him as his hands caressed my belly than went between my legs and I began to moan my need and love for him.

He lifted me then so I could guide him into me and as I settled down on his shaft he sighed, "It feels so wonderful to be back in you again, Mommy."

"Daddy, I have a feeling this is going to be a quickie for both of us, because I don't think I can contain myself much longer," I said leaning down to kiss him and then I began to move up and down along his shaft until the shudders began to pulse through my body and I heard him cry out softly as he exploded within me.

I stayed connected with him for a few minutes then I let him slide from me and lay at his side laying so my head was on his chest and my arms were around his neck and his arms came around me and I began to purr.

"Guess Daddy hasn't lost his touch," he laughed quietly, "and Mommy definitely hasn't lost hers."

"I love you so much my dearest and it's so good to be in your arms again, but I'll be glad when Daddy's cast comes off, because I miss feeling the weight of you on my body," I said.

"I miss being astride you too, my little filly," he laughed, "and also I can't wait until I can pick you up in my arms again."

"Momma's going to spend the rest of her life making up to you for all the time we lost, so Daddy better hurry and heal because I think he's going to be exhausted some nights," I chuckled.

"Is that a promise, Mommy?"

"It's a pledge, my dearest," I said hugging him to me.

"I meant it tonight, I keep having to pinch myself to make sure I'm not dreaming all of this because I've longed for it for so long," he said.

"Yes my darling, but you can be very sure that in the morning when you wake up I'll be right here in your arms, so sleep peacefully, my darling, because you must absolutely be exhausted."

"I am tired, but for the first time in four long years I'm at peace and content, because I'm back with my love once more," he said yawning.

"Sleep then, my love," I said holding him even closer to me and so we fell asleep in each other's arms our world restored once more.

In the middle of the night I felt David sit up in bed and I felt him shaking.

"What's the matter, darling?"

"It's just the stupid nightmare I have about ditching all over again and I keep trying to struggle to stay above water because I know I have to get home to you," he said and I could hear the residual fear in his voice.

"Lie down darling and let me hold you, so you'll know you are safe in my arms once more," I said and he lay back down but I could still feel the quivering of his body as he worked to throw off the nightmare. "You're safe, my darling," I crooned to him. "You're safe in my arms and you always will be from now on."

"Lauren, do you think this nightmare will ever leave me?" he asked.

"Yes, I do my darling, once you get used to being home, and being safe, it will just fade away," I said.

"God, I hope so, because it is so terrifying. I'm in the cold water again and I'm so tired," he whispered.

"Sleep again my love, I'll stand guard over you the rest of the night," I whispered to him and I felt his arms go around me and his body begin to relax as the tremors left him.

At dawn I looked up to find David awake and I smiled up at him and I felt his arm tighten around me. "Kitten, have you been awake all night?"

"I told you I'd stand guard over you and I meant it, darling."

"Baby, why are you so good to me, when all I've done is make you worry through our entire married life so far?" he whispered.

"Listen my dearest love, I'm not good to you, don't you understand even yet that I love you and have since the first minute I looked into those eyes of yours and saw the man I wanted to spend the rest of my life with and while I've worried about you it wasn't your doing that caused the worry and if I had to do it for the rest of my life I'd be willing to give up peace of mind just to have you in my life and be able to love you and have you love me. You've given me so much love as well as my children that whatever worry and fear I had to endure was worth every minute just to have you in my life loving me."

"I promise baby, if it's within my power I'll never make you worry again because I love you so much and I'm so grateful that you love me."

I reached up and pulled his head down to kiss him and in my kiss was all the love I felt for him and all the joy I'd known and would continue to know because I loved him and he loved me. "Sleep kitten, you need your rest too and as long as you are in my arms I'll be content," he said.

I fell asleep then knowing that he would be alright the rest of the night. When I woke again around six he was sleeping peacefully so I too went back to sleep until I felt him trying to get out of bed around seven. "What's the matter, darling?"

"Nothing kitten, I just have to go to the bathroom. I didn't mean to wake you but I've never been able to get out of bed without you knowing I was going," he laughed softly. "Especially now when I'm so awkward with this darn cast."

"Do you want some help?"

"No I think I can make it."

I lay there while he struggled to his feet, but I knew that he had to feel that he wasn't entirely dependent upon me, but it was hard not to help him when I knew he was struggling. He finally made it and went out of the room. A couple of minutes later I heard him going into the kids' room and then I heard him coming back. "Everything ok, Daddy?"

"Yes, the kids are still sleeping, and I could just stand and watch them forever," he laughed.

"Well come back to bed with Mommy, because it is lonesome here without you next to me."

He got back into bed then and put his arms around me.

"While I was laying here with you in my arms I was thinking about what

I wanted to do with my life from here on out. If I do go back into broadcasting it's definitely not going to be a job where I have to travel at all unless you can come with me and they guarantee that you can come with me, because I never want to be away from you again."

"You don't have to worry about that now. Wait until your entirely well."

"I know I don't have to, but what I was thinking was that I want to find some way that we can make this a paying horse farm so I can be with you all day every day of our lives."

"Yes, my dearest, that is what I want too, to know that you'll be right here every minute of the day and night. But do you really think we can do it?"

"I'll get my mustering out pay and we can use it to enlarge the stable, then I imagine if necessary Mark and Bill would float me a loan and we could use that to buy some horses then all we'd have to do is get the word out, or else we could just stable horses here for the time being because I'd hate to be in competition with Bart in the selling of horses."

"I could give riding lessons and school horses and you could run the business end of it, because I'm not that great at marketing and so forth. We might even be able to work out a deal with Bart that when he sells a horse he recommends us for instruction and schooling. Then you once had the idea that when Bill starts his own business after the war, that he might want to house it right here on the farm so we might want to investigate that possibility with Bill."

"That's what I mean sweetheart, you have such really good ideas and by the two of us working together I think we could make this a paying proposition, because neither of us care if we get rich, just have a large enough income to make sure our kids can go to college and we have a little bit left for our old age."

Just then we heard the twins running toward our bedroom. They burst in on us and hopped on the bed narrowly missing David's bad leg. "Hey you two, what did we tell you about knocking before you enter our room? You almost landed on Daddy's bad leg so you've just got to be a little more careful."

"We're sorry Mommy, we forgot about knocking and we should have been more careful of Daddy's leg," said Laura.

"Come here you two, and all is forgiven, just try to remember next time," laughed David, hugging both of them to him and kissing them.

"Daddy, will you help me with my model airplane today?" asked Mike.

"What model are you working on, Mike?" asked his father.

"It's a B-17," said Mike hugging his father around the neck.

"Sure, I'll help you and that was the kind of plane I flew so we should make it pretty authentic, in fact if you want son, we can name it 'Kitten,' because that was what my plane was called."

"That's a funny name for a plane," laughed Laura.

"My crew named her after your momma."

"Mommy, did you hear that they named a plane after you?" squealed Laura looking at me in awe.

"Yes sweetheart I know, because Daddy wrote and told me."

"Momma, have you ever flown with Daddy?" asked Mike.

"Mommy has flown with me any number of times and I've flown with her as well."

"Do you mean that Momma flew the plane?"

"That's exactly what I mean, peanut. Your mother is a very good pilot."

"Oh Mommy, can you teach me to fly when I get older?"

"Daddy and I will teach both of you how to fly when you are a little older so that by the time you're 16 you'll have your own pilot licenses."

"Can we go flying sometime?" asked Mike.

"Once I get my cast off the four of us will go flying and we'll even fly over this farm so you can see what it looks like from the air."

"Ok you two monkeys, go get dressed and then go do your chores while Daddy and I get dressed, then we'll all have our first breakfast together," I said. "And please be careful getting down off the bed."

"We will, Momma."

We heard them chattering away at each other as they went back to their room and in five minutes we heard them running down the steps.

"Are you sure you want another set of twins, sweetheart?" asked David grinning at me,

"There are days with those two I'm not sure I even want any more," I laughed hugging him to me.

"Maybe we'd be better off just trying to get you pregnant without ever quite achieving it," he laughed softly. "That way we'd have the fun without having to pay the piper."

"I seem to remember a very handsome sky jockey who wanted me to get pregnant as soon as he got home so that he could experience it all right from the start," I giggled. "Is Daddy getting cold feet?"

"Maybe just a little, I think I need time to get used to these two before we go branching out, because I have a feeling that they are going to be a handful."

"You're right they are a handful, but a very loveable handful, don't you think?"

"Yes baby, I already love them so much and believe me I don't think life will ever be dull with them around," he chuckled.

"Come on, Daddy. Do you want me to help get you bathed and shaved?"

"I especially want the bath, just like you promised," he laughed.

"When I made that promise we were talking about getting up a lot earlier, so if you want to run the chance of two little imps invading our privacy, I'll go along with you."

"Guess we better wait, I keep forgetting that it isn't just the two of us anymore. I've got to start picking my hours better."

"Mommy will take care of her daddy tonight if he'll just be patient."

"Ok I'll be patient, but it's just so hard to be good where Mommy is concerned," he laughed pulling me to him where he sat on the edge of the bed and kissing me.

"If you're a good little boy, maybe Mommy can talk Aunt Beth into taking care of the twins this afternoon for an hour or two so Daddy and Mommy can play," I laughed.

"Ooh Mommy, that sounds wonderful," he said hugging me.

"Come on, let's get you bathed and dressed and maybe you'll feel up to walking to the stable to say hello to Storm and watch your son and daughter ride him."

I brought in a bowl of hot water and his shaving kit and watched him as he shaved sitting on the bed next to him with my arm around his waist. I went out and poured out the water and put in fresh so he could give himself a sponge bath, then I helped him dress. By the time we were finished I could tell he was tiring again. "Darling, lie down for a little until you get your strength back and I'll stay with you."

"I hate being this dependent on you, my love," he said.

"I love having you this dependent on me because it makes me feel needed by my handsome husband," I said.

"I'll always need you in every way, kitty cat."

"I'll always need you too so we are even," I said snuggling into his arms once again.

"Let's try getting down stairs then after I rest for a little while, I think I can manage to get to the stables, because I'd really like to see Storm and besides I want to see that tomboy of ours mount him."

"Why don't you conserve your strength and just slide down the stairs on your backside?"

"Maybe I will though I must say that isn't the most elegant way to get down them."

"Elegant be damned, I'll take practicality over elegance every time," I laughed. "I learned that when I was pregnant with the twins because I was so big I couldn't see my feet and more times than not I'd get down stairs to find out I had on two different pair of shoes. Finally, I just gave up and put them on the shoe rack then I fashioned a stick I could use to get them off the rack, and that way I at least knew I had on the same two shoes."

"Kitten, you've been through so much that you should never have had to go through by yourself."

"Maybe so, but neither of us had any choice in the matter and in some ways it is a blessing, because I really did get huge and I preferred that you remember me as my slim self."

"I'd love you, Mommy, if you were out to there," he said holding out his arms to indicate my girth.

"Add about four inches to that and you'd be a lot closer to my size," I laughed. "I looked like one of the twins' drawings two little stick legs and arms and a gigantic middle."

"I bet you were adorable even so," he laughed.

We got him downstairs then and into his chair.

The twins came running back into the house and handed me the eggs they had gathered. "When's breakfast, Mommy?"

"Just as soon as you two get washed up," I laughed. They ran into the kitchen then to wash their hands and faces and David and I followed them into the kitchen.

"Hey, don't I get a hug?" asked David.

They came running over to him, but managed to stop short of throwing themselves in his arms. By leaning on the counter, he was able to balance enough that he could pick each one up in turn in his free arm.

"Daddy, it's such fun having you pick me up this way, it's like I can see forever when I'm clear up here in your arms," laughed Laura.

"Well peanut, soon I'll be able to pick you both up in my arms at once," he said.

Mike, who had been patiently waiting his turn, pulled at his daddy's pant leg. "My turn now, Daddy," he said.

David set Laura down and picked up Mike in his arm. "You're right Laura. You can see forever from up here," he said hugging David and kissing him on the cheek.

"If you two are good and don't dawdle over breakfast, Daddy said he thought he might be up to going to the stable to watch you ride Storm," I said.

"Yippee!" they hollered.

After breakfast David went down to the stable with the twins and I. Laura went into Storm's stall and bridled him leading him back to where her father stood. Storm neighed and nuzzled David as if bidding him welcome home.

"Storm knows you, Daddy. How does he know you?" she asked.

"Your mommy and I used to ride Storm even before we were married," he laughed.

"Watch, Daddy," she said going over to stand on her box and grabbing Storm's mane mounted him, then she leaned down to give her arm to Mike so he could get on behind her.

"If that isn't you my little tomboy all over again," laughed David. "I don't see how you both mount him so easily," said David.

"It's easy, Daddy. I'll show you how if you don't know," said Laura.

"Your mommy has tried to show me, but I've just never gotten the knack," he laughed.

"I'll take a couple of the chairs from the dance floor out so you can sit down and put your leg up, while you watch these two hooligans ride," I said.

I brought out the chairs and David sat down and put his leg up and I stood behind him with my arms around his neck.

"Watch, Daddy, what I taught Storm how to do," said Laura as she reared the horse on his hind legs much as I had done the day when David had gotten so upset with me.

Both youngsters stayed on with absolutely no trouble and David looked up at me. "Like mother like daughter," he laughed, "and to think I worried about you when you were 20 some years older than peanut here."

"Mommy, when are you going to make the fence so we can start jumping him?" asked Mike.

"One of these days soon," I said.

She gave Storm a kick in the side and they were off galloping threading their way between the trees.

"Lauren, are you sure that's safe for them with all the trees?"

"Darling, they've been riding him like that since they were three so I think they are safe enough."

"Maybe it's a good thing I wasn't here to see that," he laughed.

"Well Daddy, I'm sure your heart would have been in your throat a few times, I know mine was in my throat, but those two are absolutely fearless and I've learned that if they say they can do something, they usually can."

"Do they do everything together?" he asked.

"Just about, most of the time they are inseparable."

"Hey you guys, where are you?" called Carol coming into the stable.

"Out here, sis, watching the kids on Storm."

"I'll be right out as soon as I get Lady bridled," she called.

"Darling, I'm afraid I spent your money unwisely when I bought that saddle for Carol, because she has never once used it," I laughed.

Carol rode Lady out then and stopped beside her brother. "Hi bro, how goes it today? You still pinching yourself?"

"Sis, I'm black and blue from pinching myself especially after watching that daughter of mine mount Storm, it was like seeing kitten here in miniature," he laughed.

"She does have a familiar look to her when you watch her mount him," laughed Carol.

"Sis, even you've joined the horsy set," he chuckled. "I never would have thought I'd see you sitting on Lady with your leg draped across her neck and not even holding on."

"These days I do everything the kids do only on Lady. I'm still a little leery of Storm," she laughed.

"Did you ever get Mark to ride with you?"

"Reluctantly he will some of the time, but I always have to promise no galloping, no jumping, and no rearing before he'll get on Lady's back."

"Been riding out to the back of the property in your birthday suits lately?"

"God that was embarrassing, bro! No, these days we only go fully clothed."

"Is that because you learned your lesson or because there are so many kids around?"

"Both!"

The twins came riding back to where we were. "Aunt Carol race you," they shouted.

"You're on," said Carol and the three of them were off at a gallop.

"I just don't believe it, kitten. I'd never in a million years believe I'd ever see that sister of mine racing a horse in and out of trees that way," laughed David.

"You'd be surprised, darling. She jumps her, rears her, she's gotten as bad as I am," I laughed remembering the time he had taken me to task.

I could tell he was remembering too. "God even in combat, I was never as scared as I was that day," he said.

"Well as I told you then, love, there is nothing much to it and if four-year-olds can do it, then you know now I was perfectly safe," I laughed.

"They don't even hold on while they are doing it," he chuckled. "Are they always that fearless?"

"Most of the time, at least together they are. I don't think either of them is quite as fearless when they are apart," I laughed. "Although I must say that Laura comes closest to being fearless."

"Sweetheart, you've done an amazing job with them," he said.

"I had to because I couldn't let their father come home to find two scaredy-cats," I laughed. "They had to be perfect for you, although I'm not sure they are quite perfect."

"They are perfect, darling, and every minute I'm with them I love them more."

"Well I can tell you they think their daddy is just the best daddy in all the world," I said bending down to kiss his upturned face.

"Oh look, Mommy's kissing Daddy," laughed the twins as they pulled Storm to a halt near us.

"Who won?" I asked.

"We did, you know lady can't keep up with Storm," they giggled.

Carol came up then pulling Lady to a halt in front of us and draping her leg over her once again.

"You'd think at my age I could beat a couple of four-year-olds," she laughed.

"Probably you could, any four-year-olds but these two," laughed her brother. "You've got to remember they've been raised by a tomboy."

"What's a tomboy?" asked the twins.

"A tomboy is a girl who likes to do everything a boy does," said their father.

"Who's the tomboy?"

"Your mother."

"Oh, is that why you married Mommy?"

"Yes, in part," he chuckled.

"Mike, do you understand adults when they give us half answers?" asked Laura of Mike.

"Laura, I think Daddy means that he fell in love with Mommy because she was a tomboy, but also he loved her because she is nice and soft," said Mike.

"Mike, my son, you've said a mouthful. That is exactly why I fell in love with your mother, because she was the most feminine, softest, sweetest tomboy I ever knew in my life," chuckled David.

"Ok you two, go cool down Storm and rub him down, then come up to the house for lunch," I said.

"Carol, could you look after the twins for a couple of hours this afternoon?"

"Sure Sis, what are you two going to do?"

"None of your darn business, sister mine, we've got plans to get to know each other again in every carnal way I can possibly think of," I laughed.

"How about if I take all four kids to the zoo this afternoon and we stop in at Mack's for supper? That should give you enough time to wear this wounded brother of mine out," laughed Carol.

"As soon as I get this cast off, sis, maybe we can talk you into taking care of them for a full day and night," laughed David.

"Ok bro, I'm game, but I expect you to take on Carol Lauren in return so Mark and I can get reacquainted one of these days soon, but I'll give you a couple of weeks after your cast comes off."

"You have a deal, sis."

"Hey kids, please cool Lady and rub her down too while you are at it will you, and I'll help your mom get your dad up to the house again."

"Ok Aunt Carol," they hollered back to her.

We managed to get David back to the house; awkward though it was because he was so much taller than Carol and I and Carol was so much taller than me. When we got there David was definitely happy to see his comfortable chair.

"Well bro, we made it, but I'm afraid it was worse for you than either Lauren or I," she laughed.

"I'll be so darn glad when this thing comes off my leg and I can get around on my own again without having to depend on everyone else," he said.

"Stop it, David. If I had to carry you piggy back it would be all right with me because if it means not having you back and having you back I don't care what it takes," I said.

"Yes, bro, stop feeling sorry for yourself because in six weeks you know you'll have two legs on which to stand and there are so many men who will only have one or none at all," said Carol.

"I'm sorry girls, I guess I did sound like I was feeling sorry for myself, it's just that I've never had to depend on anyone for such a long time, that it's hard to take sometimes, but believe me I know how lucky I am not only to have two legs, but to have a sister and wife like you to help me," he said quietly.

"That's better bro, and don't you ever forget, because both Lauren and I would walk through fire if it was necessary just to have you back with us again," said Carol. "Gee that felt just like old times when we were kids and I bawled you out about something," said Carol laughing.

"You definitely haven't lost your touch," laughed David.

"Well, I'll leave him to you, Lauren, and send the kids over after lunch and I'll make sure all little pitchers with big ears are out of your way for the afternoon and you two have fun," she laughed going out the door.

"You're very quiet, kitty cat. What's the matter?"

"Carol shouldn't have spoken to you that way and I shouldn't have either, it's only your second day home and you've been through so much, of which I am sure, we've no idea."

"Come here, baby."

I went then to him and sat on his lap and put my arms around his neck. "Daddy, I don't ever want to be a scold like I was just now, it's just that I love you so much and it is as I told Jack. I wouldn't care if you had no legs or no arms I would love you and want you with me."

He hugged me to him and his head came down to kiss me gently. "Baby, you and Carol had every right to scold because I was feeling sorry for myself and I promise I'll try not to ever do it again."

"I promise too, I'll never scold my beloved darling again for the rest of our life together because I love you so much and I'm so grateful that you are back with me."

"Kitten, I love you too and I'm so happy to be back and I did sound very ungrateful when heaven has smiled on me so much sending you to find me and to love me and the fact that I came through this damned war relatively unscathed. I should never complain about anything."

"Enough sack cloth and ashes for us both, just kiss me and hold me, my love," I said softly.

"With pleasure, kitten," he said hugging me to him and kissing me.

"Sit here and rest or lie on the couch while I get lunch for my two men and my daughter," I said.

"I think I'll just sit here and gather my strength for this afternoon," he chuckled.

"Do that, love, for you are going to need it, I promise you that," I laughed as I went into the kitchen to get lunch going.

"Mommy, Daddy, we've finished cooling and rubbing down the horses," yelled Laura as she and Mike bounded in the door. "When is lunch going to be ready, I'm starving."

"Yes Mommy, I am too," said Mike.

"Hey you two, how can you possibly be hungry after that enormous breakfast you ate?" chuckled David.

"That was hours ago, Daddy," laughed the twins.

"Well come over here and talk to me while your mom finishes up lunch," he said holding out his arms to them.

They ran over to him then, Laura crawling up onto his lap and Mike perching on his chair arm.

"Do you beat Aunt Carol every time you race with her?"

"Most of the time, because Storm is so much faster than Lady," said Mike.

"Daddy, how did you like the trick I taught Storm?" asked Laura

"You two scared me half to death with that trick, because once, before you were born, I scolded Mommy for doing the same thing," he laughed.

"Daddy, did you really scold Mommy?"

"Yes, I did until she showed me that it wasn't all that dangerous. How long did it take you to learn to do it?"

"Well the first time I tried I slid off Storm onto my bottom, but the next time I tried it I just held onto him better with my legs, then after that it was easy," laughed Laura.

"I noticed that neither of you hold on to Storm with your hands when you do it, do you just stay on him using your legs?"

"Yes Daddy, that's how we do it," laughed Mike.

"Ok you two get out here and get washed up, because after lunch Aunt Carol is taking all four of you to the zoo and then out to Mack's," I called to them.

They came bounding out to the kitchen.

"You really mean it that Aunt Carol is taking us all to the zoo?"

"Well she's taking you two, Carol and Sean," I laughed.

"Can't you and Daddy come with us?"

"Not today, but once Daddy is getting around better we'll take just the two of you with us. How is that?"

"Oh Mommy, that will be fun, maybe we can ride the elephant when you take us, because Aunt Carol won't let us ride her," said Mike.

"Well, we'll see when the time comes. I'm making no promises," I laughed.

"What's this about riding an elephant?" asked David coming into the kitchen.

"Daddy, Mommy said you and she would take Mike and me to the zoo when you are getting around better. Make her promise that she will let us ride the elephant, will you Daddy?"

"Mommy and I will discuss it and we'll let you know later," he laughed.

"What are Mommy and you going to do while we're at the zoo?"

"Probably talk about you two," he chuckled.

"Oh Daddy, you're so funny."

"Well what do you think we'll be doing?"

"I think you two will be hugging and kissing."

"We might just do that too," laughed David.

"We like to watch you and Mommy hugging and kissing," said Laura

"Why?"

"I don't know, it just makes us feel all warm and cozy," she said. "Because for so long Mommy looked sad some of the time, but since you've come home Daddy, she just smiles all the time."

"Ok you two clean up your plates and then run up and change into your flight suits," I said pretending to glare at them.

"Oh Mommy you're so funny sometimes, especially when you pretend you're mad at us."

They finished their meal then ran upstairs talking about all they wanted to see at the zoo.

"Those two are the living end," laughed their father.

"Well they're your children, darling."

"I kind of think Mommy had a hand in it too, as I recall," he laughed.

"Oh Mommy had much more than a hand in it," I said laughing and going to him to kiss him.

"Yes, I do remember Mommy saying something to the effect that practice makes perfect," he chuckled hugging me to him.

"Well Mommy and Daddy had to get really perfect to produce a pair like that and besides practicing was always so much fun."

"It was indeed, kitty cat, and I can't wait to practice some more this afternoon."

"Nor can I, my love."

"If you don't mind, kitten, I think I'm going to go upstairs so that I can rest before you come up," he said.

"I'll help you, and why don't you snooze a little while I finish cleaning up the kitchen and get the kids off."

Just then the two of them came clattering down the stairs. "Come in the kitchen and show Daddy the flight suits I made you," I said.

"See Daddy, we have flight suits just like you wore," they laughed.

"Yes you do, you two ragamuffins," he laughed hugging them both.

"Go over to Aunt Carol's and try not to get dirty on the way," I laughed.

"Bye Mommy," they said coming to kiss me. "Bye Daddy," they said as they went to hug and kiss their father. "Daddy, promise you won't leave while we're at the zoo?"

"I'll be right here when you get back because I'm never leaving either of you again. Bye you two, have fun," laughed David.

"Bye darlings, have fun and mind Aunt Carol," I said.

"We will, Mommy."

"Come darling, I'll help you upstairs so you can nap and I promise as soon as I get the kitchen cleared up and I see Carol drive out with the kids, I'll be up and join my darling," I said.

"Kitten, I'd rather wait for you and just sit here and watch you," he said softly.

I turned to look at him. "What's the matter, my love?"

"It's just that for four long years, I'd go to sleep and I'd dream of you and it would be so real, then I'd wake up and you were thousands of miles from me," he said.

"Then sit and watch me dearest if that makes you more comfortable, for truth be told I don't want you more than an arm's length from me because I can't quite believe that this is real, because I've dreamed it for so long too that I'm half afraid I too will suddenly wake up and discover this is all a dream," I said softly going to him and putting my arms around him and feeling his arms come around me. "Oh to heck with the dishes, I want to lie in my husband's arms so I'll know I'm not just dreaming anymore."

He stood up then and we went up to our room and I helped him get undressed and I too undressed and we crawled back into the still unmade bed. He pulled me into his arms and my head rested on his chest and there was no passion in us for the moment only the need to hold each other close and know that we were no longer dreaming.

"Baby, I know I keep telling you how much I love you and how glad I am to be back, but it is true and I still can't believe I'm not going to wake up and discover that it is all a dream like it has been so many times before," he whispered his lips coming down to kiss the top my head.

"David, my love, I just want to be in your arms and hold you in my arms every minute of the day and night so I too can begin to believe it is real and eventually both of us will know it isn't just a dream anymore," I whispered as I looked up at him and pulled his lips down to my eager waiting ones.

"Do you think, kitten, that we'll ever get so we really believe it isn't just a dream?"

"Yes, the time will come when we both know it is real, but I don't think either of us will ever take it for granted being able to hold and love each other."

"The night before we ditched, we had a really big push on and I'd just returned from a flight so tired I couldn't even think anymore. I lay down on my cot and turned on Armed Forces radio and Jane Froman was singing *I'll Walk Alone*. I fell asleep thinking about you, about holding you in my arms and dancing with you, and I dreamed we were here on the farm and you were in my arms and our song was playing on the juke box—there was no one around it was just you and me; I could almost smell your perfume it was so real, then just as I went to kiss you, I woke up and I almost cried because my arms ached so for you."

My arms tightened around him and my lips that were nestled in his neck kissed him, my heart aching for all that he had had to endure.

"You are here now, my beloved, and every time you wake I'll be near to you so you'll never again have to endure empty arms because I'll always stay very close to you and all you'll have to do is call me and I'll come running to your arms."

"God I hope our twins will never have to go through what we've been through."

"I pray too that they'll never know war and separation, that the world has finally learned its lesson."

"Baby, slide over so I can feel the weight of your body on mine, so that I know I'm not dreaming again," he whispered.

I moved then so I lay full length on his body and both of us took comfort from the feel of our bodies pressed together and he dozed, as did I, our arms wrapped around each other.

We both woke at the same time and I saw him smile at me when I raised my head to look into his face.

"Daddy, make love to me, please," I whispered and he lifted me in his arms so that I could guide him into me and for a while we lay just enjoying the closeness and the joy of being connected totally once more; finally the passion flared up and we each of us gave everything to the other.

The next day, I told him that I was going to leave him in the twins charge while I went to sit with Cindy during Jack's surgery. "I want to go with you kitten, because I think when Jack wakes up he's going to need another man to be with him while he gets used to the idea that a part of him is missing."

"Then you shall come, my love. I wouldn't go if I hadn't promised that I would be there, but I think that Jack is going to need the support of all of us."

I got him into the car and he sat as close to me as he was able and we rode together to the hospital. When we got there, Cindy was sitting on the bed holding Jack in her arms while the premeds took affect on him. When David and I walked into the room she started to get up. "No Cindy, stay in Jack's arms and we'll sit in chairs here by the bed," I said to her.

She lay back in his arms again and I moved a chair up so David could sit down and drew another up so he could put his foot up, then I got one for myself. Jack kept one arm around Cindy but he also reached out his arm to take my hand. "Thanks for coming, you guys," he said.

"We'd be nowhere else today and we'll stay as long as Cindy and you need us," I said.

"I'm so scared," said Jack. "This is worse than flying a bombing run through flack."

"All three of us will be right there in the operating room even if physically we are sitting in the waiting room and you'll know that our love is surrounding you, Jack," I said.

They came then to wheel him up to surgery. Cindy went with him and we told her we'd meet her in the waiting room, so that she would have the few minutes with him to tell him again of her love for him.

Dr. Chris came to us three hours later. "The surgery went off without a hitch and Jack is in recovery. We'll be taking him down to his room in about an hour," he said.

David stood up then and leaning on one crutch he pulled Cindy into his arms while she cried her relief. When she had finally recovered David said to her, "Why don't you come with us and we'll get a cup of coffee?"

"No I want to wait for Jack so I'll be there when he's returned to his room," she said. "Thank you so much for sitting with me."

"We'll go get coffee and bring some back to you then we'll stay with you until they kick us out and we're taking you back to the farm with us tonight so you don't have to be alone, then Lauren will drive you back to the hospital in the morning to be with Jack," said David.

"That's too much to ask of you both," said Cindy. "I'll be all right at the hotel."

"Cindy, you're coming home with us tonight, no arguments," I said.

"Thank you both so much, especially you, Lauren. Jack told me how you held him and convinced him to call me when they first told him about his leg, and for that I'll be eternally grateful to you."

"This war has made us all sisters and brothers, so don't thank me," I said.

"Lauren, David, if you don't mind I'll go get a cup of coffee with you," said Dr. Chris.

"We'd love your company," we both said.

When we were seated in another lounge and I had brought coffee back for both the men and myself, Dr. Chris said, "I'd like to hear the story of what you said to Jack when he heard about our having to amputate his leg. He's had far less depression than some of the men who are in his circumstances, and maybe I can learn what to say to them by hearing what you said to Jack. David, as long as you're here, I'll save you another trip in and take X-rays of your leg while you're here today."

"I was lying on the bed next to David when Jack came back after talking to the doctors and he watched us for a while then he turned his face to the wall and I heard him crying. I went to him and asked what was the matter. He turned over then and put his arms around me and I held him in my arms while he told me what the doctors had said. I don't even think the news that he was going to lose his leg was what bothered him most, it was the fact that he felt he could not go home to Cindy 'being only half a man,' as he put it."

"Lauren told him then that Cindy wouldn't care about his leg, that she loved him not just his leg and that he should go call her immediately so she could tell him that herself," said David. "When she told him that he said he couldn't because Cindy was so beautiful she could have any man she wanted. Lauren said then that there was his answer, that if she could have any man she wanted, then why did she choose him because there must be lots of men who were handsomer, more intelligent, stronger, than he was. He had to admit that that was true. She said, 'Then that is your proof' she fell in love with him not for his looks but for the man he was. She told him that women were far more practical than men because women don't just fall in love with a pretty face, they fall in love with what is inside a man like gentleness and tenderness. She told him that looks fade, that a woman wants a man she knows will love her when she is pregnant and big as a barn and who, whenever he looks at her, will always see her as the girl he fell in love with because even the most handsome man or beautiful woman will one day grow old and what passes for looks fades, but that Cindy would never see him that way or even notice that his leg was gone, because she would always see him as he looked when she first fell in love with him, just as he would always see her as the beautiful young girl he fell in love with."

"I told him then to go call his girl and if she didn't have the money for the air fare to be with him, that I would give it to her and it would never have to be repaid," I said.

"When he came back from that call, he was all smiles and I don't think it mattered to him that he was going to lose his leg, because Cindy had told him the same thing exactly as had Lauren and that she was catching the red-eye and she'd see him the next day," said David.

"Lauren, I wish to God I had about a 100 women like you to talk to these guys who are facing deforming surgery, because it would make my life a 100% easier because you'd take the depression out of the picture and that is the toughest part of the surgeries," said Chris.

"But Dr. Chris, I didn't tell Jack anything that wasn't true or that had David had to face similar surgery that I wouldn't have told him because it's true that women don't look at men like men do us, we don't just fall in love with a pretty face no matter how handsome the man might be—that is just a bonus."

"But that's what makes them know it in both their hearts and minds, they can feel your sincerity and so they believe you," said Chris.

"Dr. Chris, would it help you any if I got the women in our area together so they could visit men who are facing what Jack was facing to come visit them and tell them the same thing that I told Jack?"

"You bet it would, Lauren," said Chris

"Then I promise you that I'll do my best to organize a group of women and tell them what I said to Jack and I'll bet you every one of them will volunteer and believe me they will all be just as sincere in what they are telling the men as I was."

"Chris, if you need anyone to organize anything for you, just let Lauren and Carol and Beth know because I've never met three women who could organize anything like they can. If the generals had had them organizing this war it would have been settled way back in 1941," laughed David.

"David, I'm going to make arrangements for you to visit X-ray while you're here right now then while you are busy with that, I'm going to take Lauren back to my office and give her a list of men who could use the services of these women right now. We'll meet you outside of X-ray and I'll take a look at the films and let you know what I find," laughed Chris.

He made the arrangements and put David in a wheelchair and took him personally to X-ray then he grabbed my hand and we headed for his office. He gave me a list then of six men who would be going through amputation within the next week, their room numbers, and a brief history of their wounds.

"I realize this is short notice, Lauren, and that you haven't even gotten anything organized yet, but if you could find six women, preferably beautiful women, who could visit these men, it would go a long way toward their acceptance and eventual recovery."

"Chris, I will go and visit two of them, I know Carol will visit two, and I know also that Beth will visit two, so that will take care of the most immediate cases, then the three of us will work on recruiting more women for whenever you need them."

He came over to me then and hugged me, kissing me on the cheek. "I just hope that David realizes what a woman he has," he laughed.

"Oh I think he does, or at least he's told me often enough so I believe him, but I got me quite a fellow too," I laughed.

"I agree with you there, I can't think of too many men who would be willing to let their wives hold other men in their arms and comfort them."

When we got back down to X-ray, David was finished and Chris asked that we wait while he looked at the X-rays. When he came out, he was grinning all over the place.

"Lauren, I don't know what you do for this man at home, but whatever it is keep right on doing it. If you bring him in next week, I'll remove his cast, because his leg has knit perfectly. I couldn't have asked for better results. I've never known anyone to be out of his cast in this type of surgery in under six to eight weeks, and after only five weeks is unheard of," he laughed.

I hugged David and then Chris. "Chris, this is the nicest present you could have ever given to us."

"Chris, thank you so much, it will feel so good to be able to make love to my wife without this thing getting in the way and to be able to walk with my kids and let them both sit on my lap at once," said David.

Chris noticed the blush creep up my face with David's outburst.

"Lauren, don't get embarrassed. Every man would say the same thing," laughed Chris. "I know I would if it were me. As for you, David, at first it's going to seem like you can't even stand on that leg, but use your crutches for the first couple of days until you get used to it, then you can trade them in on a cane. I know I told you you'd probably always have to walk with a cane, but I wouldn't bet against your being able to throw it away eventually too."

"Thanks Chris," said David shaking his hand and I hugged and kissed him on the cheek too saying my thanks.

"Go you two, go back and sit with Jack and Cindy, because you've made this entire day for me," he laughed.

"We're going to stay with Cindy till visiting hours are over then we're taking her back to the farm with us tonight, then I'll drive her in here tomorrow," I said.

"That will do even more for Jack's recovery because he'll know his bride won't be left alone tonight and that you two will be taking care of her," said Chris.

When we got back to Jack's room as we came in we saw Cindy sitting by his bed holding his hand and Jack looked not at all like a man who had just lost his leg, but more like a man who had found the whole world.

"Hi Jack," I said going to the bed to hug him. "You sure don't look like a man who has just undergone major surgery."

"Hi Lauren, David, I don't feel like a man who has either. I was so worried when they were wheeling me back to my room that Cindy would be repulsed when she saw them getting me in bed and saw my stump. But she came over and laid her hand on it and asked if I was in pain, then she said she thought my stump was really quite sexy because it made me look just like a pirate," he said.

"I definitely think Cindy is right, you do look very sexy and if your bride and my husband weren't here I might be very tempted," I laughed.

David went to him then and hugged him. "I've learned from this wife of mine that hugging another man is quite permissible especially when that man is just like a brother to me," he laughed.

"David, I think you and I must have done something right in our lives to have such amazing women as these love us," laughed Jack softly.

"You are right there, Jack."

"Now you two, we'll tell you what we've planned," I said. "We'll stay here at the hospital until visiting hours are over then we're taking Cindy home with us for the night, then I'll bring her back in the morning. I'm sure a good night's rest and a home cooked meal will make her feel like a new woman and I bet you 50 cents that by this time next week you'll be introducing her to room 517."

"What's room 517?" asked Cindy.

"Jack will explain it to you, but believe me, Cindy, you're just going to love it," I said. "Now David and I will leave you two alone and when visiting hours are over, Cindy, just come down to the lobby because we'll be waiting for you."

"Thank you both so much for everything you've done for us," said Jack.

"No thanks necessary. Have a good night's sleep and I'll bring your bride back to you first thing tomorrow morning so she can hold you in her arms again."

"David, I didn't even ask, why are you in a wheelchair, your leg isn't acting up is it?" asked Jack.

"No buddy in fact I get my cast off next week, Chris just had me down in X-ray and besides it's easier on both Lauren and me if I use a wheelchair around here."

"Way to go, buddy. I can't wait until I'm on crutches and they give me a weekend pass so that I can see your farm too," said Jack.

"Well Cindy can tell you all about it in the morning and if she doesn't run in here screaming about our crazy menagerie then you'll know it's safe to come see for yourself," I laughed.

We went then and sat next to each other holding hands in the Lobby. "Baby, I want to kiss you so much, but I guess I'd better refrain while we're here," said David squeezing my hand.

"Don't let a little thing like a lobby full of people stop you darling because I don't mind and I don't care if they do," I laughed and he leaned over then and kissed me rather thoroughly.

About seven Cindy came down and when we saw her we waved at her across the lobby. "Are you sure you want to leave now, Cindy, before visiting hours are over because David and I don't mind?" I asked.

"Jack has had his dinner and they've given him his pain medication, so I stayed until it took affect, so he won't even know I've gone."

"Believe me, Cindy he'll know, but with the joy juice they give you here he just won't care," said David. "Besides you look like we need to get you home and get some food into you before you collapse."

"I don't feel hungry, I just feel like I've been through every emotion imaginable and I feel tired, but I also feel relieved that now the worst is behind us and from here on out it will be full steam ahead to get Jack well and as soon as he is able to stand we'd like you and Lauren to standup with us, because we've decided to be married right here in the hospital chapel," said Cindy.

"Well come on girl let's get you home and get some food in you, then you can meet the twins and afterward you can go to bed early and get a really good night's sleep," I said.

Driving home Cindy dozed in the backseat while David regaled me with all the love songs to which he could remember the words. When we pulled in the drive I saw the twins come bounding out of the house running full tilt toward their daddy who was still seated in the car.

"Mike and Laura, this is Aunt Cindy, she is the wife of the man who was in the next bed to your daddy in the hospital. She'll be spending the night here and I want you both on your best behavior. Now stand back a little so Daddy can get out of the car and mind you don't knock the crutches from him while he's getting into the house," I said.

"Hi Mike, Hi Laura. It's so nice to meet you because your mommy and daddy have told us so much about you," said Cindy.

"Hi Aunt Cindy," they replied.

David by this time had gotten out of the car and was standing next to it balancing on his crutches. "Sorry Cindy, I can't be my usual chivalrous self and help you get out of the back seat," laughed David.

"No problem David, I'm quite capable of getting out myself," she laughed.

"We'll help her, Daddy," said the twins. Each of them took hold of one of her hands and pulled her up so she could get down from the car.

"Thanks you two, now take her in the house for I'm coming right behind you," chuckled their father.

Once Cindy and David were seated and they had crawled up on David's lap to hug and kiss him, the twins told Cindy that they were sorry, but they had to go finish their chores, then they'd come back in and talk to her.

"I've never in my life seen two four-year-olds as unafraid of strangers as those two seem to be," laughed Cindy.

"Neither of them know fear of any kind and believe me they'll be talking your head off at supper tonight, they take after their mom all the way," laughed David.

"Let me get both of you a drink, then I'll get supper started," I said.

"Rum and coke for me if you have it, Lauren," said Cindy.

I came back in a few minutes with Cindy's rum and coke handing it to her, then I handed David his double bourbon and I sat down for a minute to sip my own rum and coke. Then I got up to go see what I had on hand that would be quick to get ready for dinner. When I opened the icebox I saw that Carol and Beth had brought over chicken and dumplings and a cheesecake and put them in the icebox to await our return. I put the food over to heat up and went back to the living room to sit on David's lap.

"That was fast, sweetheart," said David.

"Those two sisters of mine were at it again, they left chicken and dumplings and a cheesecake in the icebox, figuring we'd be hungry and not in the mood to wait for me to cook," I laughed.

"Will I get a chance to meet them tonight?" asked Cindy.

"Actually, you'll be staying at one of their houses tonight because we only have two bedrooms here, but yes, I'll bet you they'll be running over here to see how Jack is," I said.

"It must be so nice to have sisters," said Cindy. "I've no family left in Spokane and Jack has no one."

"Do you both want to go back to Spokane?" I asked looking at David.

"Jack and I talked about it a little bit and we've about decided to stay in this part of the country," she said.

"When Jack gets his first overnight from the hospital and you two come out here, Lauren and I have a proposition to make to you," said David.

"What sort of a proposition?"

"We'll tell you both at the same time, right now you both have enough to do to get Jack back on his feet," he laughed.

"Come on you guys, go sit down at the table and I'll call the twins in, then let's eat because I'm starving," I said.

I went to the door then and called to the twins to come in for supper.

"Mommy, we already had our supper. Aunt Carol fed us, but we'll sit down and talk to you and Daddy and Aunt Cindy," they said.

"Aunt Cindy, after supper will you come out to the barn with us so we can show you our horses and dogs and cats?" asked Laura.

"I'd be happy to, Laura. I've heard quite a bit about a horse called Storm," she said.

"We have three horses, eight dogs, and two cats," said Mike.

"My gosh, and I thought I was lucky because I had a kitten when I was your age," laughed Cindy.

"Well, our cats aren't exactly pets, they're mousers," said Mike.

"Daddy," they said turning to their dad, "when are you going to be able to ride Storm with us?"

"That's my good news for you two, because Dr. Chris is taking my cast off next week and after I get used to walking without it I'll be able to walk just like new," said their father.

"Oh Daddy, that's great," they said. "We won't have to be careful of your crutches anymore and we can both sit on your lap at the same time."

"You bet you can, just give me a couple days after getting the cast off and then we three will have tons of fun," laughed David.

"Daddy!" they squealed jumping up to hug him.

"Anyone home?" we heard Carol and Beth hollering from the back porch.

"In the kitchen," I called back.

They came in then and I introduced them to Cindy. "Cindy this is David's sister Carol and this is my former boss's wife Beth," I said.

"It's so nice to meet you both. Jack has told me all about your visit to the hospital and how much fun you two were, but I thought you were actually Lauren's sisters," she said.

"Well, we're as much sisters as we can be without being blood related," they laughed.

"I'll say they are," laughed David. "They not only live here on the farm with us, but all three got pregnant at the same time, and all three went into labor at the same time."

"You're kidding, aren't you?" laughed Cindy.

"Nope we're not kidding, and we hope to do the same again one of these days before long," laughed Carol.

"What's pregnant mean, Mommy?" asked the twins.

"It means when mommies have new babies," I said to them. "Now no more questions, you two go up and get your baths because it is way past your bedtime and as soon as we get Aunt Cindy settled for the night we'll be up and tuck you in."

"But Mommy, you forget Aunt Cindy said she'd come down to the stables to meet our horses and dogs," said Mike.

"Oh, I forgot, ok you can take Aunt Cindy and show her then I want you two to double time it back here and get your baths," I laughed.

"Carol, would you mind going with them and make sure they don't forget to come back?"

"Sure sis, I want to take Lady a carrot anyway—so if you don't mind me borrowing three carrots from you I'll take one for each horse with us."

"Help yourself."

The three of them went off to the stables. Beth said she had to get back and make sure Sean was in bed, that Bill had not let him stay up any later. Carol came back with them in about 15 minutes.

"My God, Lauren, I've never seen a horse that big in all my life," laughed

Cindy. "Aren't you afraid to have the twins ride him?"

"No, both of them have been riding him since they were three and Storm watches over them when they are on him."

"Next time you come out, Aunt Cindy, we'll show you the trick we taught him," said Laura.

"I'll be looking forward to it, Laura," said Cindy.

"If you think just having these two riding Storm is scary, wait till you see the trick," I laughed.

"Come on Cindy, let's go get you bedded down at my house, because you look like you're ready to fall asleep on your feet."

"I am a little bushed," said Cindy.

"Can we kiss you goodnight, Aunt Cindy?" asked the twins.

"I'd be very honored if you did, Laura and Mike."

They flung their arms about her and kissed her. "It's been nice meeting you, Aunt Cindy. I hope you come back very soon so we can show you Storm's trick."

"Get with you two now and get your baths and no submarining, no diving, no nothing, just baths," I said. "By the time you're finished Daddy and I will be up to tuck you in, now scoot."

"Inelegant or not, I think tonight I'm going upstairs the same way I came down this morning," laughed David. He sat down on the step then and proceeding to go up them on his backside one step at a time. When he was finally seated on the upstairs floor I reached my hand to him and helped him lift himself up.

"I bet you haven't done that since you were a little boy, so welcome to your second childhood," I giggled.

"Wait till Daddy gets Mommy into bed tonight, he's going to teach her not to laugh at a wounded flier," he laughed.

"Promises, promises," I giggled.

"Believe me Mommy, that's not a promise that's a fact."

"Go sit in your chair sweetheart and I'll help you get undressed, I just want to check on the twins because I don't trust them where water is concerned I've had to clean up too many floods in the bathroom."

When I got to the bathroom Mike was just about to dive off the back of the tub. "Hey what did I tell you just two minutes ago?" I said trying not to laugh.

"Ok Mommy, but can't I do just one?"

"No not even one, get your bath and get into your pajamas right this minute."

"But Laura did it, why can't I?"

"Laura is going to hear from me as well," I said.

I turned then and almost ran back our bedroom because I didn't know how long I could keep the laughter locked up inside me.

"What's so funny?" asked David.

"I just caught Mike as he was about to dive off the back of the tub into the water," I said laughing.

"But you just told him not five minutes ago not to do it," said David.

"I know, but with the twins out of sight means do it or at least try to do it without getting caught," I giggled.

"What did he have to say for himself?"

"He said well Laura did it so why couldn't he. In the morning I'm going to have a long talk with those two and I hope Daddy will back me up," I laughed.

"I will if I can keep from laughing," said David.

We went in then and hugged and kissed the twins goodnight and tucked them into bed. David sang them their lullaby and by the time we left the room they were both sound asleep.

I helped David get undressed then I undressed myself. By the time I was finished he was sitting in his chair and I went over and sat down on his lap and curled up in his arms reaching to bring his head down so I could kiss him.

"You know baby, even after being home all these weeks, I still get a lump in my throat when we tuck those two into bed every night," said David.

"I only wish we could keep them this age forever," I sighed.

"Were you thinking the same thing as I was when you told Cindy that when Jack got leave you want to discuss something with them?"

"Of course, we'll have to ask the others, but I was thinking about maybe they'd like to build a house here on our property and be another pair of brothers and sisters for all of us," he said.

"I think it would be wonderful for Jack because none of you guys would ever let him start feeling sorry for himself, and I have the feeling that out here in the fresh air and everything that he'll probably throw his crutches away in nothing flat and he won't hardly notice he's lost a leg. I also think it would be good for Cindy because she'd have three of us to help get her adjusted to marriage and everything."

"Well since tomorrow is Friday anyway, let's ask the others at our regular

Friday get together," said David. I'll be glad when a week from Friday arrives, because by then I should be able to walk to the stable just fine and I can dance with you again," he said hugging me to him

"Come on Daddy, let's get you in bed before you fall asleep in your chair. We've both had a big day today and I think we deserve a good night's sleep."

"I am tired tonight, but it's been a really good day too," he said softly.

I helped him into bed then settled down into his arms. "Now what was Daddy saying about teaching Mommy a lesson?"

He chuckled softly, "I think Daddy's too tired tonight to teach Mommy anything, but in the morning Mommy is definitely going to get a lesson providing she still doesn't mind getting up with the rooster."

"Mommy's too tired tonight too, but she'll definitely meet you in the morning," I said kissing him.

I woke early the next morning and saw David grinning at me. "What did Daddy do, stay up all night so as to catch Mommy?"

"No, I just woke up a few minutes ago and was lying here listening to you purr, kitty cat," he laughed.

"Make Mommy purr some more Daddy, please, please," I giggled.

"You mean like this baby?" he said as his hand came down between my legs and his tongue licked at my nipple.

"Oooh just like that Daddy," I said letting my hand slide down so I could stroke his testicles, then bringing it backup to encircle his penis and stroke its head with my index finger.

"Mommy, I've got to have you right now," he moaned lifting me so I was once again astride him and he guided himself into me.

"Please, daddy, please," I moaned and my release came in shuddering waves then I felt him explode inside of me as I collapsed on top of him and felt his hands go down to cup my buttocks in them.

I started to slide off next to him but he held me where I was with his arms. "Mommy doesn't get off that lightly for giggling at Daddy last night," he said softly as he again brought me to climax and then another. "Does Mommy promise never to giggle at Daddy again?"

"I promise, I promise," I moaned as he brought me to one last climax and then I felt him once again explode within me.

When we woke it was nearly seven and we heard the twins stirring around in their room. They came running to our room and they knocked on the door. "Daddy, Mommy, are you awake yet?"

"Come in you two chatterboxes, we're awake," laughed their father.

"Daddy!" they yelled racing to him and waiting while he swung them up on the bed and hugged and kissed each one of them. Then they turned and hugged and kissed me. "We thought you two would never wake up," they laughed.

"Well, we're definitely awake now," laughed David.

"Will Aunt Cindy be having breakfast with us this morning?"

"Yes she will and you two had better get dressed PDQ so that she has time to eat before we have to take her back to the hospital to visit Uncle Jack," I said.

"Who's Uncle Jack?"

"Uncle Jack is Aunt Cindy's soon-to-be-husband and he was in the hospital with your daddy."

"Daddy, will Uncle Jack be coming to visit us too?" asked the twins.

"He sure will, but Uncle Jack had to have surgery because he was wounded flying just like Daddy was, but with him they had to take off part of his leg," said David.

"What do you mean, Daddy? We don't understand."

He showed them then, on their legs. "Uncle Jack will only have a leg down to here, just below his knee on one leg because it was so hurt the doctors couldn't fix the bottom part of it," said David.

"Will he grow another one?"

"Unfortunately, humans don't know how to grow another one, but the doctors will eventually give him an artificial one so that he'll be able to walk without crutches," said David.

"Do you mean when he comes to visit, we should be careful of him like we were of you Daddy, so we don't knock his crutches out from under him?"

"That's exactly what I mean, little ones."

"Tell Uncle Jack we'll be careful if he will just come see us," they chorused.

"Now scoot you two and get dressed, while Daddy and I get dressed," I said.

"Bet we beat you, Mommy."

"Bet you do too, love," I laughed.

They raced out of the room then and I looked up at David and kissed him. "You're such a good father, not to mention such a wonderful teacher," I laughed softly.

"Mommy enjoyed my lesson then?"

"You better believe Mommy enjoyed it, just remind me to giggle at you more often," I laughed.

"Well when Daddy gets this cast off next week, he'll see what he can do," he chuckled.

We got up and got dressed then went down stairs so I could start breakfast. Carol and Beth came over then with Cindy in tow. "Did you sleep well last night, Cindy?" I asked.

"Like a log, this farm of yours must agree with me or else it's all the good company here," she laughed.

"Did you get to meet the rest of the gang, Mark and Bill?"

"Yes briefly, but I look forward to all of you coming to our wedding," she laughed.

"Does that mean us too?" asked the twins.

"Most definitely. I want you two at our wedding."

"Daddy told us all about Uncle Jack and we can't wait to meet him, and we promise that we'll be careful and not knock his crutches out from under him," they squealed.

"Did your daddy tell you that Uncle Jack will only have one leg?"

"Yes he did, but he said soon the doctors will give him a new one then he won't need his crutches anymore."

"That's right, he won't and I'm sure Uncle Jack will be very pleased to meet the two of you," she laughed hugging both of them.

"One thing you've got to say for our brood, they don't have one bit of shyness to them," I laughed.

"Carol, Beth are you going to sit down and eat with us?" I asked.

"Sure, we'll at least have coffee with you guys and Cindy," they laughed.

"You tell Jack that the two of us intend to come visit him and that we better see him up and hobbling all over the place on his crutches when we do," said Carol.

"Yes, Cindy, tell him for us we intend to chase him down the hall, after all we can't let a good looking guy like Jack get away from us," laughed Beth.

"I think you guys are the best medicine Jack can get and I hope you do come to see him often although I'll tell you right now you're not getting that particular good looking guy, he's all mine and I'll fight for him," she laughed.

Driving back to the hospital with Cindy I said, "Cindy, you look 100% better today so I think a night at our funny farm had its desired affect."

"Lauren, thank you so much for yesterday and last night. I feel like a new person this morning and I hope the offer of having Jack and I come out once he starts getting weekend leaves still stands because I think you six people and your kids will do more for him both spiritually and physically than anything else in the world."

"Just be prepared today, because he might be in an awful lot of pain for the next two days and may get a little depressed, but tell him for me if he does I'm going to come to the hospital and box his ears," I said.

"Lauren, could I ask one more favor of you?"

"Sure, what can I do for you?"

"Would you mind coming in with me this morning? Because I'm just a little scared of what I may find and how Jack will be."

"Sure I'll come in with you, what else are sisters for."

"Lauren I do feel like you, Carol and Beth are my sisters and I hope that Jack will feel like you guys are his sisters and Bill and Mark like his brothers, because he lost his entire family when he was only ten and was raised in an orphanage," said Cindy.

"Well I'll tell him that he's no longer an orphan that he now has three brothers, three sisters and an assortment of nephews and nieces to contend with not to mention a stable full of livestock."

When we got to the room, Jack was sitting up in bed and Cindy ran to him to throw her arms around him. "Darling, how are you this morning?"

"I'm fine Cindy, a little pain, but nothing I can't tolerate now that you're here. Hi Lauren."

"Hi yourself and I get to hug you too," I laughed going to him and hugging him and kissing him on the cheek. "Carol and Beth said to tell you that they'll come see you in a couple of days and they plan on chasing you down the hall because they don't believe in letting good looking men get away from them."

"Those two would do it too," he laughed. "Cindy, you promise to protect me from them?"

"That's what wives are for, to protect their husbands from predatory females," she laughed.

"The twins said to tell you they can't wait to meet Uncle Jack since they both love Aunt Cindy," I said.

"Uncle Jack?"

"Sure, Cindy is now officially one of our sisters and you are definitely one of our brothers so get going and make jackasses out of these doctors and we'll take you to meet the rest of your family," I laughed.

"Lauren, you guys are just the best and definitely the best medicine going, maybe you ought to make the farm a half-way house for returning vets," he laughed.

"Now that isn't such a bad idea, we'll have to have a council of war on that idea when you and Cindy come out," I said.

"What's a council of war?"

"Oh it just means that we all get together for a potluck on Friday nights and a dance on our dance floor in the barn, then we bring up all the new ideas everyone has thought of during the week and discuss whether to accept or reject each idea."

"You mean you want Cindy and I to be a part of that?"

"Sure, and I'll tell you something else, when you get so you can come out weekends, we intend to offer you a chance to build a house for the two of you on our property and become a part of the Benton, Purcell, McCoy nut house. So while you're recuperating be thinking about it because we'd love to have you join us. Although you do know that by becoming a part of our little community that if one of us gets pregnant all of us get pregnant at the same time."

"How in the heck do you manage that?"

"Well we girls have a pact that way we figure the kids will always have someone their own age to play with not to mention older and younger brothers, sisters and cousins. Of course, the first time around we'll allow Cindy to catch up to us, but after that its all for one and one for all, besides it keeps you guys out of mischief."

"Before you two walked in here I was feeling kind of sorry for myself looking at the place where my leg used to be, but five minutes with you and your lunacy, I don't even care if I've a leg missing and so long as Cindy doesn't mind either, I'm one happy and one very lucky fellow."

"Glad to be of service, now take care and one or all of us will be seeing you over the next couple of weeks. I'm sure David and I will see you next week when David comes in to get his cast off, but I'm also sure the rest of your brothers and sisters will see you too. So take care and I'll leave you two alone, because poor Cindy hasn't had one minute alone since we took her to the house last night. Besides I'm sure you'd rather be holding her in your arms, than talking to me anyway," I said hugging him goodbye and waving to Cindy.

When I got home Beth, Carol and David were still sitting at the kitchen table drinking coffee and talking. "How was Jack this morning?"

"He was sitting up in bed, said he had some pain but nothing he couldn't tolerate, but said prior to our coming that he was feeling a little depressed looking at his stump, but as soon as Cindy raced in and threw herself in his arms, he was his old self again," I laughed. "Hey you guys, I promised Dr. Chris that each of us girls would visit two of the guys this next week who are facing amputation of one sort or another and try to cheer them up and let them know that we women don't give a darn whether they have one leg or two, that we still love and admire them anyway."

"Sure we're game," said Carol. "Just tell us what you told Jack and we'll pass it along to all those wonderful guys."

"That will take care of next week, but I also told Chris that we'd try and organize the women in this area to go visit the men facing deforming surgery and try to cheer them up. He said what I told Jack had practically eliminated the normal depression the guys get when they know what they are facing and that if we could get, preferably beautiful women, to visit them and tell them the same things that it would go a long way toward making the outcomes that much better and recovery quicker."

"I'll call 20 women today and Beth can call 20, then we'll get them together next week and see how many we can recruit," said Carol.

"I bet you we recruit them all," laughed Beth.

"I know I was suppose to wait until we'd put it to a vote tonight, but Jack looked like he could use some good news, so I kind of spilled the beans," I said.

"About what?"

"Well David and I talked and we'd like to offer Jack and Cindy a piece of our land on which to build their home and to become a part of our crazy farm here," I said.

"Well we vote for it and I'm sure Mark and Bill will, so that's no problem. What did he say when you told him?" asked Carol.

"He was thrilled, you should have seen the way his face lighted up, like now he really had something to offer Cindy besides his love. I told them they didn't have to give us an answer now, but to be thinking about it while he was recuperating and once he'd visited us they might want to join us but that we wouldn't be offended if they went their own way. Cindy told me that Jack had been raised in an orphanage and that she had no one either, so I think having a real family really appealed to both of them and they are such nice people."

"Did you warn them about our pact?" asked Beth.

"Yes, I told them they had one chance to let Cindy catch up with us, then it was all for one and one for all after that," I laughed.

437

"You know you guys, at the rate we are adding to this funny farm, we are soon going to have to have more land. I was thinking Lauren, why don't we sell Jack and Cindy our house and we build another one with more bedrooms?"

"I don't know, I'll have to think about that one because I love this house, but it would be nice to have more room."

"Well think about it and when the time comes either we offer them this place or to build their own house on their plot here."

"Do you know what kind of work Jack did before the war?"

"No I've never asked him, but I'll find out. Why?"

"I was just thinking," said Beth, "Bill was saying the other night that he wanted to get thinking about his new business soon because this war is finally winding down, Thank God, and he needed to decide where to locate it."

"Lauren and I've thought about that too, we thought maybe he'd want to locate it right here on the property when the time comes."

"I think that would be great and maybe you and Jack would want to think about working with Bill because I'm sure he'd rather have two men he knows and trusts than hire someone else. It would also let you be right here so if you and Lauren want to continue trying to make this a paying horse farm you'd be available to do it."

"You know, I don't even know what Bill does," said David.

"Well before he came to Washington when I worked for him he had a consulting business and also acted for various companies as a lobbyist in Washington, so I'm sure he'll probably go back into the same line of work."

"You and Jack would be great lobbyists because Congress is definitely going to listen to returning service men and if you represented companies specializing in the needs of returning service men, it would be a perfect match."

"We'll have a lot to talk about tonight at our pow-wow and as usual, you three have everything well organized," laughed David.

"It isn't that we're so good at organization, its that just unlike men we see a need and way to fill it and our women's intuition kicks in full force and we just get it done rather than discussing it to death," laughed Beth.

"Before I forget to tell you kitten, Chris called and he'll take my cast off on Tuesday at 10 A.M," said David.

"Now we've even more reason to celebrate tonight," I laughed hugging him.

"I was just thinking, if Jack is half the man I think he is, Cindy will probably be pregnant in at least a month or two, so how about we plan on 2 years from now all of us getting pregnant again?" said Carol.

"I take it sis, that you are putting us guys on notice with that statement?"

"That should be pretty good timing," I laughed, "Jack and Cindy will have their house done or else we will, whichever way we decide and our kids will be six years old and off to school, so the timing couldn't be better."

"Are you still planning on twins Lauren?" asked Carol.

"Yup, I promised my husband when he came home I'd have another set just so he'll get to experience what he missed the first time," I laughed. "Besides if we work it right that will give us another boy and another girl."

"On that note I think we'll leave," laughed Carol and Beth.

"Come on husband mine, why don't you stretch out on the couch and I'll sit with you so you can put your head in my lap, until the kids come in and want our attention," I said pulling him to his feet.

When I was seated on the sofa and David's head was in my lap he took my hand. "Kitten, do you realize how much our lives have changed in the last five years?"

"It's unbelievable isn't it? Are you ever sorry you asked me to dance that night we met?"

"God no Kitten, I just wish I had met you five years earlier."

"Me too, but then we wouldn't have been the same people and maybe the chemistry wouldn't have been there."

"Maybe, but I think the chemistry would always be there for us."

"I think you're right, we were just destined to be together," I laughed.

"Viva la Chemistry," he laughed bringing my hand to his lips.

"I'll second that sentiment," I said giggling.

"We're you really serious about having another set of twins in two years?"

"Very!"

"Well at least by then I'll have some experience under my belt," he chuckled.

"David you're going to love our babies, because when they are first born they are so cuddly and adorable and they very definitely don't ask a 1001 questions every day."

"That will be a relief, and the other two can ask them of their teachers instead of us,"

"Just remember, that until they are four or five once they get so they can walk they will be running into our room without knocking."

"I'd forgotten about that, maybe I should install a lock."

"No, no locks ever."

"Guess you're right about that sweetheart. Well if we sell Cindy and Jack this house I'll build one with a secret room where mommy and daddy can go to play," he laughed.

"Now that sounds like a wonderful idea," I giggled.

That night we met again as usual and David and I discussed having Jack and Cindy build a house or buy ours. Everyone was in agreement that by all means we should ask them to join our group. Bill told David that he'd like to have both him and Jack consider joining him in his business and thought it was a great idea to locate right on our grounds. Everyone agreed that we ought to look into purchasing the additional land bordering on our property.

"Now we girls have something to tell you, well actually forewarn you guys about, and that is that the three of us or four if Cindy decides to join us, are planning on getting pregnant in about two years because all of us want another baby and the ones we have will be in school by then," I laughed.

"Why do we even bother forewarning them, Lauren, after all we all know they can't keep their hands off us so getting pregnant should be no problem, us girls just have to coordinate our own efforts," laughed Carol.

"Do you guys ever get the feeling that they don't really need us? laughed David.

"Who cares, think of all the fun we get to have while they are trying to get pregnant," laughed Mark.

"Besides, we know from experience that they can't keep their hands off us either," said Bill.

"Hey guys, do you realize next Friday we can hold this shindig in the barn and I'll actually be able to dance with my wife again," said David.

"Way to go bro," said Mark.

"Has it been six weeks already?" asked Bill.

"No, Chris said whatever Lauren was doing, she should keep it up because my cast is coming off in five weeks and that was unheard of," said David.

"Just don't ask him what I'm doing," I laughed.

"Sis we already know what you are doing," laughed Carol.

On Tuesday we went to the hospital so Chris could take off David's cast. "While it's a relief that I can finally scratch, my leg looks deformed," said David.

"That will change in just a day or so once the air has a chance to get at it without the cast," said Chris. "Try putting your weight on it."

"My God I have no strength in it at all, and it feels just like it's going to break," said David.

"As I told you last week, use your crutches for a couple of days but put more weight on it each day and you'll soon feel normal," said Chris.

"I hope so, because it sure feels funny now," said David.

"Lauren, I want to thank you, Carol and Beth for coming to see the men who are about to have surgery this week, because the depression has lifted for all six of them, it's amazing what having a beautiful woman tell them that they don't love just whatever part is being amputated, has done for them."

"I'm glad we could help Chris, it makes us feel like we're giving back a little for what they've gone through for us. We've already got 60 women lined up to do the same thing, so whenever you need one, call one of us and we'll make sure there is someone to answer the call to arms, so to speak."

"I went before the Review Board here Monday and told them about our little experiment and the results from it and they were just amazed, so I think I'll be keeping you guys busy for the next few months. I'm wondering if it would work just as well for men who lost their sight or double amputees?"

"I know it would for double amputees, and I'm fairly certain that it might at least help those men who have lost their sight or had other deforming wounds."

"How is Jack doing?" asked David.

"He's made amazing progress and I think I'll be giving him a furlough this Friday, Saturday and Sunday," said Chris. "Do you know in addition to lifting the depression, Jack has required far less pain medication than other men undergoing the same sort of surgery without your intervention."

"Good because we're taking them to the farm and in fact, we've ask them to build a house on our property and Jack said maybe we'd want to think about making it a half-way house for returning service men, which all of us think is a good idea, so we are considering building a guest house in which to house them."

"You guys are just absolutely amazing people and I'm sure you've taken a lot of business away from the psychiatrists around this hospital. In fact, one of the psych guys was saying just the other day that he hadn't had one man who was having surgery next week come to him about anything and when he visits them on the wards, he's just amazed at their attitudes."

"When are you planning to bring your wife out to the farm, we're anxious to show you the place?" asked David.

"If you're taking Jack there this weekend, how about if we come out Friday and spend the afternoon and evening with you so I can observe Jack's reaction to the place and get a feeling for your setup?"

"Come out, the more the merrier and if you've got any other patients you'd like to bring along, just bring them with you," I said.

"We'll see you Friday about three then, if that's all right?"

"That's great because that will give the kids lots of time to play with each other and the other animals," I laughed.

"I have one man who has lost his sight and I may just bring him along to see what interaction with you guys does for him."

"Bring him along, there's plenty of room for everybody and if he wants to stay for the weekend, he'll be more than welcome, because either Carol or Beth can put him up since one of them will take Cindy and Jack," I said.

"Well I'll let you two go see Jack and I'll get back to making my rounds," laughed Chris, "I expect by Friday to see you without crutches and using only a cane."

"Actually I'm planning on dancing with my wife that night, so you're liable to see me without either cane or crutch, just this cute little bundle here on my arm," laughed David.

We went up then to Jack's room. "Hi Cindy, Jack," we called as we went in the room.

"Hi you guys," said Jack, getting up and coming to hug me.

"Hey way to go buddy," laughed David, "Isn't it amazing how fast we men can get along with only one leg when a beautiful woman is in our sights?"

"If it were anyone but Lauren, I'd knock his crutches out from under him if he had moved that fast," laughed Cindy.

"Chris tells us that he's giving you a 3 day furlough this weekend and we'll pick you up Friday morning so you can spend it with us, because the twins can't wait to meet their Uncle Jack," said David.

"I can't wait to meet them, they must be quite a pair from what Cindy has told me about them," laughed Jack.

"That's the understatement of the year, because my duo is absolutely fearless, and neither of them have a shy bone in their entire bodies. I warn you though they will talk your other leg off you," I laughed.

"Chris is coming out to the farm Friday afternoon too with his wife and kids and he may even bring another vet with him," said David.

"David, I just realized you're not wearing a cast. How does it feel?"

"Well it feels wonderful to be able to scratch at last, but it also feels like it will break or something when I put my weight on it, but I'm determined that by Friday night I'm going to dance with my wife, so I've got to keep putting more weight on it."

"Way to go buddy!"

"Have you guys given any more thought to our proposition?" I asked.

"We've talked about it and are leaning very heavily toward taking you up on it providing Jack can get a job, so we can afford to build a house," said Cindy.

"Jack what kind of work did you do before the war?" asked David.

"I was a accountant," said Jack, "Why?"

"Well Bill is starting his own consulting business right on our property and he thought maybe you and I would be interested in joining the firm with the understanding that once we learn the business we will be made partners."

"That's too generous you guys," said Jack and Cindy, "You don't even know us all that well."

"We know you well enough and believe me Bill isn't being generous because he'll expect us to learn on the job and at least you've worked in an office, whereas I just hopped all around the world reporting on news. You don't have to decide right this minute anyway, talk to Bill Friday night and see what you think."

"We've got something else for you two to think about," I said. "We were wondering if you would like to rent our house and we will build a bigger one on the property? You can rent with the option to buy eventually if you'd like, the house is big as Cindy can tell you except it has only two bedrooms."

"Aren't two bedrooms enough for your family?" asked Cindy.

"Well, that's the other thing we want to talk to you about," I laughed. "We girls have decided that if you guys decide to join us we'll give you time to get Cindy pregnant then two years after that we four girls will get pregnant again so that we all go into labor at the same time."

"Now that's what I call organization," laughed Cindy.

"Do you care if we get married first?" asked Jack.

"No, but just keep to our time table, please," I laughed.

"That reminds me, Cindy and I are getting married tomorrow in the chapel at 11:00 so we'd like all of you to come and, of course, you two are to be our attendants."

"Congratulations you two, we'll be there with bells on and twins in tow," laughed David.

"Carol, Mark and their daughter Carol Lauren will also be there as will Bill, Beth and their son Sean," I said. "Cindy do you need me to do anything toward your wedding preparations?"

"No I think we've covered it, the Chaplain here at the hospital has said he'll perform the ceremony, his name is Capt. Hollenbeck."

"Your kidding!" I laughed.

"No that's his name."

"Well he married David and I, and he also married Carol and Mark and Bill and Beth and baptized all our kids," I said.

"Now we know you two are our new brother and sister," laughed David.

"We've also voted to take you up on your idea about making our farm a half-way house for returning vets and we're planning on building a guest house on the property for them to use," said David.

"Hey Cindy, did Jack ever take you to Room 517?" asked David.

"Yes, he did," she said blushing.

"David, darling, I don't think Cindy is quite used to having their private affairs being discussed, the way the rest of us are."

"Well get used to it because where these women of ours are concerned, nothing embarrasses them," he laughed.

"Guys, we've got to get going so I can get home and practice walking, not to mention making love to Lauren without that stupid cast," said David.

"See what we mean, nothing is private in our lives," I laughed.

"You'll get used to it," laughed David.

I went to them and hugged both Jack and Cindy. "I can't wait for you to come out Friday and we'll all be here for your wedding, don't tell Capt. Hollenbeck, we want to surprise him," I said.

"See you tomorrow," they laughed.

By the time we got to where the car was parked, David was putting a good deal of weight on his leg and it appeared the crutches only gave him a little more confidence.

"Daddy, are you going to drive or do you still want me to?"

"I want to drive mommy so I can have you snuggle in my arm and feel your hand on my knee again."

"You'll be lucky if it's only your knee you feel my hand on," I laughed.

"Oh mommy I can't wait to get you home," he laughed.

"Fat lot of good that's going to do you until tonight, love, remember you've got two very inquisitive youngsters waiting for you at home. Besides I don't think they are going to let their daddy out of their sight until we finally get them bedded down tonight because I'm sure they'll be fascinated watching you learning to walk."

"Well at least I won't have to go upstairs on my backside tonight," he laughed

We got in the car and after a couple practice stops and starts David felt confident enough to drive home.

"It feels so good to be doing the driving again with you curled up in my arm kitty cat."

"It feels pretty good to me too, I've missed snuggling in your arm while we drive."

When we pulled into the drive the twins were waiting for us and they came running toward the car. When the saw that David was still on crutches they stopped and their faces showed their disappointment.

"What's the matter with you two," asked David.

"We thought you weren't going to need crutches anymore daddy, wasn't your leg any better?"

"My leg is great and I'll only need crutches for a couple of days until I get some strength back in this leg,"

Their faces brightened and they came full-tilt at him again. David put his crutches on the seat of the car and leaned against it as they came running up to him. He bent down and picked both of them up in his arms hugging them.

"Daddy, it is so nice now that you can pick both of us up and we don't have to wait our turns."

"What's more you can both sit on my lap tonight at the same time," he laughed.

"Yippee!" they shouted.

"Come on let's get this show in the house so I can fix lunch for my three favorite people," I laughed.

The twins ran ahead of us and David only used his crutches to steady him. "You know kitten, I think I could almost do without the crutches, just use a cane to help me balance."

"I'll go right after lunch and pick you up a cane at the pharmacy," I laughed. "With the progress you're making already, you'll probably be chasing me around the house by tomorrow."

"Here, take one of the crutches so I can put my arm around you right now," he laughed.

I took one of the crutches and he threw his arm around my shoulders and we walked into the house.

"Look at daddy," yelled the twins. "He's only using one crutch."

"That's right you two and this afternoon I intend to go down to the barn and watch you ride Storm and maybe I'll even ride with you."

"Honey, I think until your leg gets a little stronger maybe you should just watch because it takes an awful lot of leg strength to ride with these two."

"Maybe your right kitty cat, maybe I should give it another day before I try riding with them."

"Remember you two when daddy does ride with you there will be no rearing, no jumping, and no galloping until daddy gets more strength in his leg."

"We don't care mommy, as long as he rides with us."

"Are your chores all done?"

"Yes, we just finished them up before you came."

"Good, then go wash up for lunch and I might even be talked into hot lamb sandwiches in celebration today."

"Yippee!" came a chorus from the twins and David, and then they all started laughing.

I got the meal heated and on the table and as we sat talking my heart was filled with thankfulness that my entire family were reunited and everyone was healthy once again.

"Daddy did you and mommy see Aunt Cindy and Uncle Jack while you were at the hospital?"

"We did, and tomorrow all of us will be going to their wedding in the chapel there," he said.

"You'll have to be on your best behavior because your father and I will be part of the wedding party so you'll be on your own and we expect you both to sit still and not jabber," I said.

"We will mommy."

"David, don't let me forget to call Carol and Beth to let them know about the wedding tomorrow right after lunch."

"Ok kitten."

"We particularly want you two to be on your best behavior because the Chaplin who will be marrying Aunt Cindy and Uncle Jack is the same man who married your daddy and I as well as Aunt Carol and Uncle Mark and Aunt Beth and Uncle Bill and he also baptized all four of you kids when you were just babies."

"Do you think he'll remember us, because we don't remember him? asked the twins.

"I'm sure he'll remember baptizing you, but you were just little babies then so I'm sure he'll be surprised at how much you guys have grown."

"When will Uncle Jack and Aunt Cindy be coming to the farm?"

"That's another surprise we have for you, they'll be coming out this Friday and staying with us through Sunday," said David. "Also the doctor who took care of daddy will be coming out Friday with his family and maybe another man who lost his sight in the war, that Dr. Chris has been taking care of."

"Can we stay up later than usual that night because we want to see you dance with mommy?"

David looked at me for confirmation, "Yes we'll allow you to stay up an extra hour if you promise to go right to sleep afterwards."

"Just where do we bed all of the kids down because I wouldn't feel comfortable if they were in the house by themselves?" asked David.

"They can all bring their sleeping bags and sleep in the extra stall in the barn then in the morning they can come back to the house."

"Goody, goody, goody," shouted the twins.

"I take it that they've done this before?" asked David.

"We allow all the kids to have a camp-out in the barn at least once or twice a year, but now that you're home I suspect they'll get to do it more often."

"You kids don't mind sleeping in the barn?" asked David.

"We love it daddy, cause the hay is so comfortable and smells so good, and Storm, Lady and Sheik stand guard over us all night."

"Anyone want more to eat?" I asked.

"We're full," said the twins.

"Me too," said David.

"Then while I clean up why don't you guys go down to the barn and when I'm finished I'll come join you?"

"Hurrah!" yelled the twins. "Come on daddy, let's go see Storm."

"Right with you," said David coming over to kiss me.

"If you two decide to ride Storm, be sure that you take a chair from the dance room for daddy to sit on and watch you, because he can't handle both the chair and his crutches at the same time."

"We will mommy, we promise."

After they left, I called Carol to tell her about the wedding on the following day, and then I cleared off the table and washed the dishes. When I finished I went down to the barn. David was nowhere in sight, then I saw the twins and he riding on Storm as they cantered up to the barn area.

"Thought you weren't going to ride until your leg was stronger?"

"The kids promised to keep him at a sedate walk so I thought it would be ok and besides it's good exercise for my leg holding on to him," he laughed.

"You're as bad as the twins," I laughed, "But just how were you planning on getting down?"

"Like this," he said as the twins took Storm over to the fence where he had left his crutches. He slid down on his good leg catching the top rail with his hand, and then when he was safely on the ground he took his crutches and walked over to sit down in the chair they had placed there for his use.

"Didn't think I could do it did you, kitty cat?"

"Let's put it this way, I did have some doubts but I should have known you guys had it all worked out ahead of time."

"Hey where is everybody?" shouted Carol from the interior of the barn.

"Out here, sis."

She came out then leading Lady with young Carol following her. "We thought maybe we'd take a ride with you guys today," laughed Carol.

"Give me a few minutes to catch my breath from getting up and down on Storm and we'll take you up on it," said David.

A few minutes later he again remounted Storm, I mounted him then so that I could nestle in David's arms, then the twins mounted so that all four of us were on Storm. Carol mounted Lady and Carol Lauren mounted after her and the four of us walked the horses to the very back of the property and back. The kids all hollered and laughed and thoroughly enjoyed the fact that we were all riding together.

"Daddy nestles mommy in his arms just like she used to nestle Mike and I when we were little," said Laura.

"That's half the fun of riding, nestling in someone's arms," laughed Carol.

"It sure felt good to me," said David.

"To me too," I laughed.

"How about we give daddy a few minutes to catch his breath, then we go back to the house for lemonade?" I said.

"Us too Aunt Lauren?" asked Carol Lauren.

"Definitely you two are included," I said hugging her.

When we were all back sitting in the living room with lemonade served, Carol asked, "So what time tomorrow is the wedding?"

"Eleven and you'll never guess who is performing the ceremony," I laughed.

"Who?"

"Capt. Hollenbeck."

"Oh my God, then I know that Cindy and Jack are meant to be a part of this family," laughed Carol.

"That's what I said too sis," I said, "I made Jack and Cindy promise not to tell him who would be at their wedding so we could surprise him. We're picking up Cindy and Jack Friday morning and they'll be staying through Sunday, then Friday afternoon Dr. Chris is bringing his family out and possibly a vet who has lost his eye sight. The vet may decide to stay too for the weekend; we'll see how that goes.

"Well the more the merrier, I always say," laughed Carol.

After Carol and Carol Lauren left I called Beth. "Beth, Jack and Cindy are getting married tomorrow at the hospital chapel at eleven, I know it's kind of short notice, but Jack is doing so well they decided to move it to Wednesday."

"Short notice or not we'll definitely be there."

"You're not going to believe who is performing the ceremony."

"Who?"

"Capt. Hollenbeck. We've told them not to let him know about all of us being at their wedding, so we can surprise him.

"You're kidding, that really makes her our sister then," laughed Beth.

"That's what I told her and that's what Carol just said too."

"Oh another thing, before I forget to tell you Friday morning we're picking up Jack and Cindy for the weekend, and on Friday afternoon Dr. Chris and his family are coming out and he may be bringing a blind vet who may or may not decide to stay for the weekend."

"We'll have quite a large gathering Friday night as well as for the weekend, but Dr. Chris really is anxious to see our setup because he says the results of us talking to the vets have been very successful so far, with them showing far less depression and needing far less medication to control the pain."

"Well between Carol and I we can accommodate them all so no problem. "We'll just have to make plenty of extra food and then let Love Farms work its magic on everyone."

"Thanks for being such a good sport about all these last minute arrangements, Beth."

"No problem sis," she laughed.

Coming back into the living room I noticed that the twins were absent and David was sitting in his usual chair. "Where did the twins go?"

"They went racing back outside hollering something about going to tell Storm and the horses all the news," he laughed. "Come on mom sit on my lap."

I went over then and sat on his lap.

"Feels kind of nice to be balancing across both your knees instead of just one," I laughed. "How's your leg doing after all the exercise you've given it today?"

"Well, it aches a little, but otherwise it seems to be fine."

"Why don't you lie down on the couch for a while and rest it?"

"I will if you will, mommy."

"Come on papa," I said going to the couch and sitting down so he could lay his head in my lap.

"I thought you meant you'd lay down with me," he chuckled.

"Don't kid me daddy, you knew exactly what I meant and you were just wishful thinking," I laughed.

"Guilty as charged my love."

"Mommy, promises Friday night she'll definitely take care of all of daddy's needs while the kids are out in the barn sleeping," I laughed.

"I was thinking this afternoon while we were talking to Chris, that we might just have a goldmine here which we're just giving away."

"How so?"

"We've talked about making this a halfway house, why not work a deal with Bethesda, that every vet who comes through and who is able, spends at least two weekends here before being released. I bet Bethesda or the government would be more than happy to foot the bill since the vets would be getting additional therapy just walking around this place and riding the horses, if they can, and it would allow them to bring their wives or sweethearts which would make it additionally therapeutic to them."

"What about the kids, maybe some of them wouldn't appreciate having four small children under their feet, or maybe some of them just don't even like kids."

"There might be one or two to which that would apply, but I bet the majority would love interacting with our kids and besides, then they'd know how to approach their own kids when they get home."

"You may have something there darling, why don't you approach Chris with the idea when he's here Friday?"

"Shouldn't I talk to the others first, because it would mean a lot of work on weekends, especially for you girls because of having to serve meals?"

"They'd come with the understanding that they'd eat with one or the other of the families since we have to cook three meals a day anyway, we'd just be cooking larger portions."

"The interaction at mealtimes would be good for the guys too, make them feel more like they are a part of the family so that by the time they get released from the hospital they won't feel so funny interacting with their own families."

"Tell you what, call Chris and tell him your idea, and see what he thinks then Friday we'll put it to a vote with the others, because I'm sure they will go along with it, especially if it helps pay the bills," I laughed.

"If we do decide to do it, we're definitely going to have to get on the ball and see about purchasing the adjacent land, because we'll need room for at least two guesthouses and probably some more horses as well as an addition to the stable."

"I could give lessons in riding for those who've never ridden horses, and at least the twins will be willing to provide any assistance, not to mention entertainment, the men might need. Probably Carol Lauren will too because she's almost as outgoing as Carol, but Sean is the one that worries me, because he's so shy and reserved compared to the rest of them."

"Sean just takes a little while to warm up to strangers but he's gotten so he chatters a mile a minute with me and he's not reticent at all anymore to climb on my lap and hug me."

"Well, daddy, your such an old softie the kids all have your number, but I agree he may get over some of his shyness of strangers, especially after Friday when he sees the rest of the kids talking to everyone. That's the nice part of having all of them the same age, because their peers get the shy ones involved whether they want to or not," I laughed.

The twins came running in the door and made a beeline for their father so he could pick them up and sit them on his stomach. "Daddy, we had such fun riding with you today, can we do it tomorrow too?"

"Maybe tomorrow afternoon, but remember in the morning we're all going to Aunt Cindy and Uncle Jack's wedding."

"Oh, we forgot."

"I want to ask you two something and I want you to think about it before you give me an answer," said David.

"We promise, daddy."

"We're thinking about making the farm into what is called a halfway house for returning service men who have been wounded. A halfway house just means that before they are released from the hospital they would spend a weekend here at the farm with us to get them used to being around people again before they go home to their own families. Would it bother you two having strangers around the place, eating meals with us, riding horses with us, walking around the grounds?"

"Heck no daddy, that would be fun."

"Just remember, these men have all been wounded like I was, maybe not the exact same wounds, so they feel awfully funny about meeting strangers because they think people won't like them because they are missing arms or legs, or are blind."

They sat on their dad's chest thinking over what he had just said to them. Laura turned so she could look at Mike. "Daddy, we still think it is a good idea and we won't be scared of them and we'll try our best to make them like us," said Laura.

"Mike, what do you think, do you agree with Laura?"

"Sure daddy, Laura checked with me before she said it."

"What do you mean Laura checked with you?"

"Well when she turns around and looks at me before answering a question, she is checking with me to see if I agree."

"I'll be damned," laughed David.

"Daddy, you said a bad word," said Mike.

"Yes I did and I apologize, Mike," said David.

"If we do decide to go ahead with this project you're liable to hear swearing coming from some of the men, but I don't want you two to pick up the habit from them, what's alright for an adult to say isn't necessarily alright for a child to say."

"We understand daddy," they laughed.

The next day we all arrived at the hospital chapel about 10:30 and Jack and Cindy were already waiting in the hallway. "Jack, these are my twins, Laura and Mike."

"Hi kids, I've heard a lot about you from your Mom and Dad and from Aunt Cindy," he said.

"Can we give you a hug and a kiss, Uncle Jack, because we're very glad to meet you at last," said Mike.

"You sure can, I would like that very much."

"Be careful of Uncle Jack's leg you two," I said.

They reached up as Jack bent down from the chair in which he was sitting and put their small arms around his neck giving him a kiss and a big hug. "Does your leg hurt you very much Uncle Jack?" they asked looking at his stump.

"No not very much, it doesn't scare you does it?"

"Heck no Uncle Jack, daddy says one of these days you'll be getting a new leg from the doctor's here then you'll be able to walk without your crutches, but in the meantime we'll try to be careful so we don't hit your leg accidentally or knock your crutches out from under you—tell him daddy, we didn't knock you off your crutches did we?"

"As a matter of fact you didn't, so don't start now," laughed David.

"Hey you two, aren't you going to come give me a kiss too?" asked Cindy.

"Aunt Cindy, you look just beautiful and ever so happy," they chorused.

"I am happy, because today I'll become Uncle Jack's wife," she said hugging them.

"David, these two are wonderful, I hope we have two just like them, they didn't make me feel embarrassed at all," said Jack.

Just then Carol, Mark and Carol Lauren came up to us. "Hi Jack, Cindy, said Carol, "This is my husband Mark and my daughter Carol Lauren," she said bending down to hug and kiss Jack and then Cindy.

Carol Lauren ran to Jack hugging and kissing him as Mark shook hands with him. "Uncle Jack, mommy says you and Aunt Cindy are going to be staying with us this weekend, I can't wait for you both to come," said Carol Lauren.

"Thank you Carol Lauren, we're looking forward to it too," laughed Jack.

Bill, Beth and Sean came in then. "Jack, you've already met my husband Bill and this is our son Sean," said Beth.

"Hi Uncle Jack, said Sean going up and sticking out his hand to shake hands with Jack.

"I'm very glad to meet you Sean, I've heard a lot about you from Aunt Cindy," said Jack solemnly shaking his hand as Bill went up to shake hands with Jack.

"Well, Jack, you've met the entire farm except for the animals now and we'll introduce you to them on Friday," I laughed.

"I already feel like I'm one of your brothers you guys," he said, "Thanks for making me feel part of the group."

Just then Capt. Hollenbeck came up to where we were all gathered. "I don't believe it, didn't I marry all you guys a few years back?" he asked.

"Yes Captain you did, you married David and I first, then Mark and Carol and finally Bill and Beth and then you baptized all these kids here," I said laughing.

"Lauren, isn't it?"

"Yes, that's right."

"How do you guys know Jack and Cindy?"

"David and Jack were in the same hospital room here," I said. "We've just added Cindy and Jack to our gang out at Love Farms, so you'll be seeing us all together from now on and we expect you to baptize our next group of children."

"I remember now, you three all had your babies at the same time," he laughed.

"That's us and we're planning to do it again in about 2 years and Cindy will be included this time," I laughed.

"Wasn't Chris telling me something about you three visiting vets facing surgery?"

"That's us," said Carol.

"Chris seems to think your visit was a real boost to morale as well as physically for the men."

"We're thinking about starting a halfway house at the farm so Bethesda can send their men out to the farm for R and R a couple of times before they go back to their own families," said David. "Jack is to be our first experiment and if he survives this weekend with all of us and all our animals, then we figure it's safe to try it on the other men," said Beth.

"Guess I better get you two married right away then," laughed the Captain. "Who are your attendants?"

"David and Lauren will be our attendants," said Cindy.

"Bill, I remember now, you were David and Lauren's Maid of Honor as I recall and Mark you were David's best man."

"That's right. And before we go in for the wedding we want to officially extend you an invitation to Love Farms so you can see what's become of the place since you married Beth and I," said Bill.

"I'd like that very much, can I bring my family?"

"You sure can, how many kids do you have."

"Only one so far, and he's four so he should fit right in with your gang," he laughed. "I was a late bloomer to the marriage game."

"Come on Mike and Laura, let's get you seated, then Mommy and Daddy, will be participating in the wedding."

The ceremony was almost a duplicate of the one David and I had gone through and I looked at David as Jack and Cindy repeated their vows. He looked back and nodded and I knew he was repeating our vows at the same time, as was I.

"Congratulations Mr. and Mrs. Barber," we all chorused when the ceremony ended. "You can have a mini-honeymoon this weekend at our place and we promise none of us will disturb you until you're ready to be disturbed."

All the kids hugged and kissed them, even Sean. We women hugged and kissed them, then the men said oh what the heck and hugged them too, but stopped short of kissing Jack; they limited the kissing to Cindy.

"Come on everyone, you too Captain, we've a small reception set up in the lounge," said Carol.

"You shouldn't have bothered, Carol," said Cindy.

"Well sis it isn't much, but we had to celebrate your happy day."

We went to one of the lounges that the hospital had set aside so we could use it privately and on the table was a wedding cake which Beth had made, as well as punch for the kids and coffee for the adults. The kids watched in awe as Cindy and Jack cut their wedding cake and fed it to each other. We set their plates at one of the tables and set the kids down to eat their cake and drink their punch. The adults sat at another table.

"You guys are just the best, we weren't expecting anything like this," laughed Cindy.

"Well what are sisters for, we take care of our own," we laughed.

We laughed and talked and finally I got everyone rounded up and we took our leave of them. "David, Lauren, thank you again for everything you've done for us and please give our thanks to the others too," they said.

"You're perfectly welcome and congratulations again, you two, I just hope you'll be as happy as Lauren and I and the others have been," said David.

"We intend to make our life one long honeymoon," said Cindy.

"That's what we've always done, Cindy, and it's worked for us," I said.

"We owe you so much because if you hadn't convinced Jack that I'd love him leg or no leg and made him call me we wouldn't be standing here today," said Cindy.

"I'm just glad I was able to convince him because a blind man could see how much you two love each other and how right you are together," I said.

The rest of the week past quickly and Friday morning David and I set out for the hospital to pick up Cindy and Jack.

"Can't we come too, Daddy?" asked the twins.

"Not this time, because there won't be room for you in the car, but we'll be back before you know it then you'll have all weekend to talk to Uncle Jack and Aunt Cindy."

"Ok but hurry daddy, we can't wait to show them everything."

"We'll hurry you two chatterboxes," laughed David.

When we arrived at the hospital David remained in the car so they wouldn't ask us to move it and I went upstairs to get Cindy and Jack. "Well, you two lovebirds, you ready to go face Love Farms?"

"We're ready, I can't wait for Jack to see it," said Cindy.

An orderly wheeled Jack out in a wheelchair and helped us get him in the car, and then we were off. "It's permissible for you two to make out in the backseat, we won't peak," I laughed.

"I haven't made out in a back seat in years," laughed Jack.

"Well no time like the present to try it again, it will all come back to you," laughed David. "I know it did to me."

"This guy of mine would be willing to make out on the front lawn of the Whitehouse," I laughed, "So don't let him talk you into anything you don't feel comfortable with."

There was utter quiet from the backseat and when I turned to see if they were all right, Jack had Cindy locked in an embrace and was thoroughly kissing her. "I don't think we have to worry about them," I laughed squeezing David's knee."

When we pulled in the whole gang had come out to meet them. The twins ran to the side of the car, as did Sean and Carol Lauren. "Ok kids, stand back and give Uncle Jack some room to maneuver," said David.

"How about if we give you a hand getting out of that backseat," said Bill.

"I'd appreciate it Bill, Mark," he said handing his crutches to the twins until Bill and Mark could get him on his feet enough to take them again to hop down from the car.

"You're going to be staying with us," said Carol, "So why don't we take you over and get you settled in and then once you've had a chance to catch your breath, or anything else you might want to catch, we'll show you around a little."

"We'll take their suitcases up for them said Sean and Mike."

"Ok, but then come right back down because you're not to go into their room unless specifically invited by either Cindy or Jack," said Bill "And that goes for the girls as well."

"Jack, Cindy let me forewarn you that it might be wise to lock your bedroom door at night or when you want to be alone, because our kids usually remember to knock, but they don't always remember not to come bursting in without knocking or waiting to be invited," laughed Mark.

"We're having lunch at our house about noon, so you won't have too far to walk, but tonight we'll eat in the stable over there," said Beth.

"Give us a few minutes to get settled and let me catch my breath, then I want to see the stables and the horses I've heard so much about," said Jack.

"Uncle Jack we've got a trick we taught Storm to show you," said the twins.

"I'll show you the same trick on Lady and Sean can show you on Sheik," said Carol Lauren, not to be outdone.

"Don't you guys have ponies?" "Do you always ride the horses?" asked Jack.

"We're not babies, we've been riding the horses since we were three years old," said Laura.

"Laura, you guys must be very brave because I've never been on a horse in my life and neither has Aunt Cindy," he said laughing.

"Just wait till you see Storm, because he's as big as daddy," said Mike.

"That's what I've heard and as long as you don't expect me to ride him, I'll be more than happy to make his acquaintance," laughed Jack.

"Uncle Jack you're so funny," they laughed running to get their suitcases and carry them up to their room.

"Unfortunately Jack our bedrooms are on the second floor, so if you need help Bill and I will give you a hand just like we did David when he first came home from the hospital," said Mark.

"Thanks anyway guys, but I think I can manage, the PT has been teaching me how to get up and down steps and I've gotten pretty good at it," said Jack.

"Well if push comes to shove you can be as inelegant as I was and just do it on your backside," laughed David.

About an hour later Jack and Cindy came down and went with the kids to the stable, as did David and I. The kids and I got chairs from the dance floor so both David and Jack could sit down while they watched the kids on the horses.

When Jack saw Storm his mouth dropped open. "My God he is as big as you David," he said. "Do you mean to tell me these kids really ride him?"

"You'll see in about two minutes as soon as they get the horses bridled and hold on to your hat because what they are going to show you is going to scare the hell out of you," laughed David. "The first time I ever saw Lauren do it, we had a knock down drag out fight about it."

The kids lead the three bridled horses out to the barnyard. "You mean to tell me they don't even use a saddle?"

"Nope, never have and probably never will," I laughed.

Laura had brought out her box, which she stood on reaching up and grabbing Storm's mane she swung up then bent to give Mike an arm so he could mount as well. Sean mounted Sheik the same way and Carol Lauren mounted Lady. They maneuvered the horses a little way from us then turned them so that they were in profile to us and they made the horses rear together none of them even holding on.

"Oh my God," said Cindy and Jack together. "They aren't even holding on how do they stay on their backs?"

"It is really easy, you just hold on with your leg muscles," I laughed.

"Do you mean to tell me Lauren that you do that too?"

"Sure I've been doing that since I was about ten with various horses. David was telling you the truth we really did have a knock down drag out the first time David saw me do that, we were in the barn and a mouse skittered across the floor and I reared Storm so he wouldn't trample the mouse and David almost had apoplexy until I showed him how to do it with him seated behind me on Storm."

"I want to see you mount that horse, Lauren," chuckled Jack.

"Kids get down and let me ride Storm for a minute so I can prove to Uncle Jack that I really can mount and ride him," I said. They slid down then I grabbed Storm's mane and mounted him. "This is how you rear a horse," I laughed rearing Storm onto his hind legs just as the kids had just done. "You just lock your legs around him and move your feet forward pulling back slightly on the reins."

"Jesus, I've seen everything now, when you told Joe and I about it in the hospital I thought you were just kidding, but I see you aren't."

"Now you know why my heart was in my mouth the first time she did it when I was with her," laughed David. I've even seen her take that horse over a four foot fence like it was nothing."

"All I've got to say is if you ever do start that halfway house, you and the kids just have to show them this, because they'll thank God they are wounded and don't have to do it too," laughed Jack.

"Ok kids, get back on, daddy will give you a hand up since you left your box back by the barn." David went to them and set both of them up on Storm.

"Let's race," they yelled and all four of them gave their horses kicks and they were off galloping between the trees.

"Did you say they've been doing this since they were three?" asked Cindy.

"Well not by themselves at three, I usually rode with them and Carol and Bill with their two, but essentially, yes they were riding these horses when they were three. Of course, their legs were too short to get a really good grip on them, but somehow they managed and I've never known them to show even a second of fear."

"In some ways I'm glad I was flying in this war at the time, because I'm sure I might have blown my top again if I'd seen them riding at that age," laughed David.

"I'm beginning to think we men had it pretty good, since we didn't have the chore of telling our kids they couldn't do something," laughed Jack.

"But, Jack, I never told them they couldn't do it," I laughed, "I just assumed they could unless they proved they couldn't, then I just showed them how."

"I tried to tell you guys in the hospital, this so feminine looking female I latched onto is an out and out tomboy," laughed David.

"Well to look at you Lauren, that statement from David about you being a tomboy just didn't seem possible."

"It's very possible Jack, in truth it's a fact," I laughed.

The kids came racing up then on the horses. "You guys scared us to death," said Cindy and Jack to them.

"As soon as mommy and daddy get the fences built we're going to start jumping Storm," they said.

"David, you mean to tell me your going to allow that?"

"Sure in fact they've offered to teach me how, although now with this stiff leg I'm not sure I'm going to be able to do it, or at least not for a while," he chuckled.

"Cindy, don't you dare get any ideas from these lunatics where our kids are concerned when we have them," said Jack.

"Believe me I'm with you 100% there, darling," said Cindy.

"I hate to tell you two, but they'll do it and you'll never know it until they come running to show you what they've accomplished," I laughed.

"Laura have you ever fallen off Storm?" asked Jack.

"Sure Uncle Jack, but I always got right back on and tried it again until I got so I didn't fall off," said Laura.

"How many times did you fall off when you were teaching him to rear?" asked Jack fascinated.

"I only slid off on my bottom once," she giggled at the memory.

"Did you always just hold on when you were doing it just by the strength of your legs?"

"Of course, not, Uncle Jack, at first we held onto his mane, but then once we figured how hard we had to hold onto him with our legs we never held onto his mane again," said Mike.

"Lauren was David telling the truth that you jump four foot high fences?"

"Sure."

459

"Can you jump that pile of logs over there?"

"Sure that's just the pile that the twins have been practicing their jumping on," I laughed.

"Watch Uncle Jack we'll show you," said Laura. With that they sent Storm racing toward the logs and he leaped over it as if he'd just stepped across an anthill.

"I give up," laughed Jack.

"Jack when you get your artificial leg, why don't you come riding with me, I'll keep Storm at a walk and you'll get the feel of riding a horse and you too Cindy," I said.

"Jack you may want to consider it before telling Lauren no, because I can tell you there is nothing more romantic than riding on a horse with your wife snuggled in your arms," said David.

"Leave me out of this," laughed Cindy, "I'll keep my feet firmly planted on the ground thank you."

"I tried to get her to come flying with me once but she wanted no part of that either," said Jack.

"Oh come on Cindy, you Jack, David and I will have to go flying one of these days soon," I said.

"Aren't you scared to fly, Lauren?" asked Cindy.

"I hope not because I've got a private pilot's license," I laughed.

"Cindy, this tomboy of mine is one of the best pilot's I've ever flown with, she could fly rings around most of the guys who thought they were such hot shots," laughed David.

"Well if Cindy won't go with us, I'd sure like to go and see this wonder woman of yours fly, just to see if you're telling the truth David?"

"Maybe Saturday if you feel up to it, we can go for a couple of hours because I'm beginning to miss not flying since I returned," said David, "And I bet you are too Jack."

"I'd love to fly again, I really miss it," said Jack.

"Well then fly you shall," I said.

"How can I with only one leg?"

"That's easy enough, your bad leg is the opposite of mine, so I'll handle the rudder and break with my good leg and you handle the other with your good one," said David. "It shouldn't take us only a little practice before we have it coordinated so we'd be just as smooth as if we both had two good legs."

"If that doesn't work, I can handle the rudders and the brakes and you guys can handle the stick," I said.

"Nothing stops you guys does it," said Jack in awe.

"I've found that there's always a way around any problem if you just put your mind to it," I said. "The only time that didn't work for me was when Carol and I were both pregnant and I was out to here and Carol was just about as big. We decided we'd go flying because I missed David so much and flying made me feel closer to him. Well, we tried to fit ourselves into a Colt and quickly found out if I got the seat back far enough so I could accommodate my girth, I couldn't reach the pedals because my legs are so short," I laughed. "Carol and I started practicing on a make shift cockpit we put in our living room, but we never quite got it coordinated and we figured by the time we did, I wouldn't need her anymore because I'd already have given birth. We still decided we'd keep practicing but then we both realized that if I was pregnant again, then that would mean David was home and he could do the flying," I laughed.

"I started learning that nothing stops my tomboy, since the first night I met her, and she definitely has her own way of looking at life, love and everything else," said David.

"My dad used to tell me that if there was something he wanted me to do, as long as he told me I couldn't do it, I always did it just to prove him wrong," I laughed.

"That may be just the philosophy our vets who are facing amputation need to be taught," said Jack. First they need to know their women still want them, just as you showed me that Cindy would still want me even if I was missing a leg, then they need to be shown, that there is very little they can't do if they just make up their minds to do it, and figure a way around the obstacles."

"I know Chris has just been amazed at your progress, Jack and the fact that you required so little pain medication after your surgery," I said.

"Lauren, after you talked to me that day and I talked to Cindy and she told me the same things you had told me, I did a lot of thinking that night. I finally figured if a woman could love me even if I wasn't a whole man, then I owed it to her to do the best I could to overcome whatever handicap it left me with. The next day in physical therapy I talked the PT into letting me lift weights to build up my upper body strength so that crutches wouldn't be a problem. Then I started building muscle in my good leg so it would support me better when the time came I wouldn't have my other leg to take half the load. I made the PT show me how to get up and down stairs using only my good leg since my bad one wasn't worth much anyway. After the surgery once Cindy showed me she wasn't repulsed by my stump, I decided that I wasn't going to take a lot of the joy juice because I wanted to be alert and be able to hold her in my arms when she came to the hospital. Sometimes it got kind of tough for the first two or three days, but I just made up my mind to think about something else or to move around because I knew this brain of mine couldn't concentrate on two things at the same time. I quickly found out that when I did that I forgot about the pain for minutes at a time and now I don't think about it for hours at a time. The only time it gets really rough is when the shadow cramps start in the calf of the leg that is missing. The first time I felt them Cindy and I were in Room 517 and I was holding her in my arms when the cramps hit. She saw the misery I was in and somehow she knew to pinch the back of my arm and when she did the cramp seemed to subside a little and it went away entirely when I was making love to her, because it felt so good it was like it setoff something in my brain and that took care of the cramping. Since then I've practiced walking at least 2 or 3 times a day and going up and down stairs two or three times together and I've kept exercising my good leg and my arms so that I've kept my upper body strength and getting around on crutches doesn't bother me half as much as it did you David."

"When Chris comes today, tell him that story Jack, because somehow I think it is very important and maybe he'll know who to tell it to so that what you did becomes a regular part of pre and post surgery," said David.

"I think maybe if us vets who have been through it, could show the ones facing the same thing, they might take it better because they'll see our women love us and that we aren't letting anything stand in our way of having a normal life."

"Well you guys we've a lot to talk over with Chris this afternoon, but I think it's time we got back to the house because I'm sure Beth will have lunch ready by now," I said.

"Jack what did you think of the horses and the tricks the kids do with them?" asked Beth. "Absolutely terrifying isn't it?"

"You've got that right Beth, I think I'd rather lose my other leg than try it," laughed Jack.

"I just hope our kids aren't as fearless as your four seem to be, especially the twins," said Cindy.

"I hate to tell you, Cindy, but they will be because kids are naturally fearless until we adults teach them otherwise," laughed Beth. I know there's been many a time I've had to bite my tongue to keep from screaming at these kids not to do something because they could get hurt."

"I'm glad I'm going to have my sisters here to teach me these things," said Cindy.

"After lunch can we go see your house Lauren," asked Jack.

"Sure, anytime you're ready to see it we'll give you the grand tour."

"One thing Cindy, with three other sisters, you've always got built-in baby sitters, and if you come in late from visiting Jack at the hospital or anything else within reason you'll always find dinner fixed and in the icebox so you don't have to cook when you're too tired to crawl and your starving to death anyway," said Carol. "That goes for the men too, around here it is all for one and one for all every day of the week."

Later David and I showed them around our house. "If you still want to rent it to us with an option to purchase, we'd like to rent from you," said Jack.

"We girls will help you scour the thrift shops for furnishings for it and we'll help you redecorate anyway you want to," I said.

"Where did you guys get your furniture, it just looks so comfy and homey," asked Cindy.

"Thrift Shops, Good Will, Garage Sales, you name it and if it was marked down we picked it up," I laughed.

"Hey what's happened to all of the kids?" asked David, "I haven't heard a peep out of them since lunch and that's not like them."

"They talked Bill into going riding with them this afternoon and I think they went over to Bart's so they could do some jumping," I laughed.

"I'm sorry I asked," chuckled David.

"I don't know how you keep track of two of them the way you do, Lauren," said Cindy.

"Sometimes it can be exhausting, but most of the time my built-in mother radar just let's me know what they are up to," I laughed. "You'll find out when you have your own, it's just something built into womankind that kicks in as soon as our children are born. For instance if they are in the house and it suddenly gets terribly quiet, I know they are up to something they shouldn't be. Outside if I hear much laughing and yelling I also know they are up to no good."

Just then we heard the clatter of hooves, and the kids and Bill came trooping into the yard. "Mommy, Daddy, Bart has the cutest little puppies, can we get some?"

"Don't you think eight dogs is more than enough?" asked their dad.

"Yes, but these aren't dogs they're puppies," they said.

"Well puppies have a way of growing up and becoming dogs, so I think we will pass on the puppies," said their father.

"Oh daddy, you're getting as mean as mommy," they said.

"What you mean is you can't work both sides of the street anymore," laughed David.

"What do you mean daddy?"

"I mean that you can't play your mother and me against each other anymore, I've been around you two long enough now to know when you are trying to wheedle me into something your mother has absolutely forbidden," he chuckled.

"We're sorry we shouldn't have said you and mommy were mean, we really didn't mean it," they said sliding down off Storm and running to hug us.

"Ok you two imps all is forgiven," laughed David picking them up in his arms.

"Daddy how much bigger is Uncle Ben than you?" asked Mike.

David held his hand so that it was about a head and half taller than himself as he moved both children to one arm. "About that much taller," he said.

"I can't wait to see for myself, because I just can't imagine it," said Mike.

"David," said Jack, "Do you realize you picked the twins up and you weren't even using your cane?"

"I guess I just didn't think about it, so full steam ahead for tonight because I intend to dance with Lauren for the first time in four long years," he laughed.

Just then Dr. Chris and his family drove in the driveway. After introductions were made the kids took their kids in tow and they were off to the barn to see the animals with a whoop and a holler.

"Your kids are just like you guys, laughed Chris, not a shy bone in their bodies."

"Come on in the living room you guys and I'll give you a glass of lemonade," I said. "I see you didn't bring your other vet?"

"Dr. Ingram lives out this way and he's bringing him on his way home and will drop him off. I just hope the kids understand that he can't see."

"We've made them put on a blindfold and try to walk around the house, so they would get the idea," I laughed.

"My God," said Betty, Dr. Chris' wife, "You guys do think of everything don't you?"

"I was just saying that before you came, they have a habit of figuring out how to do whatever they want to do no matter what the obstacle," laughed Jack.

"Chris, Jack came up with some very interesting suggestions about teaching amputees how to make it easier on themselves, but I'll leave it up to Jack to tell you," said David.

We heard a car drive up in the driveway. Chris, David, and Jack went out to meet the new vet. "You guys, this is Bud, Bud on your left is David, and to his left is Jack," said Chris.

"Hi guys, I understand you are all vets too. Hope I don't get in your way too much today," said Bud.

"Hell, buddy, David here has a stiff leg from his injuries, I have only one leg, so it could well be us getting in your way," laughed Jack. "Just hold onto my shoulder and we'll get you in the house and you can meet Lauren, David's wife, and Betty, Chris' wife and later we'll introduce you to the whole menagerie."

Bud put his hand on Jack's shoulder and David got on his other side, in case Jack should have any problem walking he'd be available to help him. "Bud, just remember it's just like it was flying our bombing runs, everybody takes care of everybody else here, so don't be embarrassed if you need one of us to help you."

"Thanks you guys, I wasn't sure I really wanted to come and meet a lot of new people when Chris first invited me, but I think I'm going to enjoy it here."

"Bud, this is my wife Lauren, since you're my size she'll only come up to about your mid-chest, but watch out for her because she's a real tomboy," laughed David.

Bud held out his hand for me to shake it. Instead I went up and put my arms around him giving him a hug. "Welcome Bud, we're not formal around Love Farms everybody hugs and kisses everybody else so you might as well get used to it," I laughed.

"Hi Lauren, its nice to meet you. My gosh, you are a little girl," he laughed as he realized I had stood on tiptoe in order to hug him.

"Hi Bud," said Betty coming up and giving him a hug, I'm Chris' wife."

Just then we heard the twins running up the porch stairs. "Daddy, Mommy, Dr. Chris' kids couldn't believe how big Storm was," they hollered.

"Bud, these are my twins, Laura and Mike," said David. "Kids this is Bud, he is the vet we were telling you was coming who is blind, so if he asks for help we expect you to give it to him."

"Hi Uncle Bud," they chorused going to him and putting their arms around his legs and hugging them, "Hey, your as tall as daddy," they laughed. Bud put his hands down and hugged each of them.

"Why don't you two show Uncle Bud where the couch is then go wash your hands and we'll give you a glass of lemonade if you promise to be careful and not spill it all over.

"Come on Uncle Bud, the couch is right over here," they said one getting on each side of him and taking him by the hand. "Mommy we promise we'll be careful and please can we have our lemonade right away, because we are so thirsty.

"Where are my four kids?" asked Chris.

"Oh, they are still down at the barn with Sean and Carol Lauren, they are showing them how to ride Lady and Sheik and Storm. It took a few tries but now they can mount the horses just like we do."

"What do you mean they're riding horses?" asked Betty.

"Oh we've been riding them almost since we got to the barn, Aunt Betty, at first they didn't want to ride Storm because he's so big, but now it doesn't bother them at all," they said.

"Chris, I think you and I had better go make sure they are ok," said Betty.

"Betty, take it easy, they are fine, and the horses will take good care of them, they're used to kids riding them and they always make sure that the kids are ok," I laughed. "Besides if they've been doing it for the past hour or so, I don't think you'll get them off them now."

"Come on Betty, just to set your mind at ease we'll go check on them," said Chris laughing.

"I'm not sure seeing them is going to set your mind at ease, especially where Storm is concerned," laughed David, "But by all means go watch them."

They left then to go see about their kids.

"Is it always like this around here?" asked Bud.

"Oh Bud, you've only met half the gang, there is Carol, Mark and their daughter Carol Lauren, then there is Bill, Beth, and their son Sean, and today there is Betty, Chris and their four kids, and last but not least, Jack and Cindy. In addition to that, we have three horses, about whom you've just heard, then we have eight dogs, two cats and an assortment of chickens," I laughed.

"Mommy you forgot to tell them there was also you, daddy, and us," said the twins.

"Well since Uncle Bud has already met you I didn't think he needed to be reminded," I chuckled.

"Uncle Bud, after you have your lemonade will you let us take you to the barn so you can meet the horses," asked Laura.

"If you two promise to take my hands so you can guide me, I just might try it," laughed Bud.

"Give Uncle Bud a minute to catch his breath, you two chatterboxes, then we'll all go down and I may take along smelling salts because I have a feeling Aunt Betty might just need them when she gets a look at her kids riding Storm," I laughed.

"Who is this Storm you keep talking about?" asked Bud.

"Storm, is actually Storm King, who is our stallion and in horse circles he's about the same size as you and I," laughed David.

"If you'd like, I'll ride with you and you can ride him if you want," I said.

"When I was a kid we had horses on our farm, but I haven't ridden in years," said Bud.

"Then you know it comes back to you and while Storm is big, he's very gentle and he'll make sure you're ok and I'll be right there with you, so why don't we ride him, I bet you'll find you've actually missed riding," I said.

"Then once you get used to riding with mommy, you can ride with Laura and I too," said Mike. Laura can sit in front of you and I'll sit behind you. We promise we won't rear him or do any jumping until your ready for us to do it."

"How come you kids don't seem to mind that I'm blind?" asked Bud.

"Daddy and mommy made us put on blindfolds and try to walk around the house and at first we kept bumping into everything, then we just kind of let our other senses take over and we got around pretty good," said Laura. "Besides your nice so we don't' care whether your blind or have only one leg or anything like that."

"Thanks you two, you don't know how good that makes me feel," he said softly.

"Can we give you a real hug and kiss, now that your sitting down so we can reach you?"

"I'd love that, I'm just hoping when I get home my little boy won't be afraid of me and won't care whether or not I can see," said Bud hugging each of them.

"He won't care, we didn't care that daddy had to be on crutches, or that Uncle Jack only has one leg, he'll just be so glad his daddy is home," they said.

"Bud, they are telling you the truth, kids are very adaptable, and they see what is on the inside of person, not just the exterior," said David, "I've found that out, because my kids had never met me, because they were born when I was overseas and I was really scared that they would be afraid of me, but right from the first moment I met them they just accepted me."

"Why wouldn't we daddy, we were so glad to have you home and finally get to see you?" said Mike.

"If everyone's finished their lemonades let me get the smelling salts for Betty and we'll go down to the barn, although since Chris is a doctor I would imagine he'd know how to bring her around after she faints when she sees what her kids have been riding," I laughed.

We went to the barn then, the twins guiding Bud and David, Jack and I close behind them. When we got there, I burst into laughter, because there sat Betty looking like she might actually have just come out of a faint.

"Hi guys, how's everyone doing?"

"Well, I'm fine but I think Betty almost fainted when she got a look at Storm. I must say, he's one gigantic horse and when we saw the kids riding him I almost fainted along with her," laughed Chris.

"Hey kids, bring Storm over here so Uncle Bud can get a look at him too," I said.

"Lauren," said Betty looking at me as if I'd made the biggest goof in the history of the world.

"Betty, stop looking at me that way, Bud knows he's blind, we all know he is, but he still can see what Storm is like because he'll be able to feel him with his hands."

"Thanks, Lauren," whispered Bud, "that could have been awkward."

"Bud, around here we say it like it is, you don't need to apologize because your blind, because I know your other senses are going to pick up and do a lot of the work your eyes used to do, just like the twins senses soon adjusted when we put the blind folds on so they'd get the feeling of what it is like to be blind. And we certainly aren't going to coddle you just because your blind, we'll give you all the help you want if you ask us for it, but if we find you depending on us, we'll make sure we tell you because after a day or two here, you're not going to need us to help you as much as you think you are now."

The kids had brought Storm over to where we were standing. I took Bud's hand and placed it on Storm's shoulder so he could get a sense of his height.

"Come on Bud how about taking a ride with me?"

"I think I'd like that, because he's just about the size of my horse at home," said Bud. "Only thing is I'm not sure if I remember how to mount him and I notice he's not wearing a saddle."

"Let me mount him then I'll give you my arm, it will come back to you as soon as I do how to mount him, I'm sure."

I swung up onto Storm, then put my arm down encircling Bud's arm and gave a small tug to let him know I was ready for him to mount Storm. Taking my arm he swung up onto his back."

"Way to go buddy," laughed David, "You should have seen me try to mount him the first time I rode him with Lauren, you make it look easy."

"It's really peculiar but some of my senses did take over, and I could almost tell where I stood in relation to him, so mounting him was no problem at all," laughed Bud.

"Ok you guys, Bud and I are going for a ride, then you can have Storm back for more riding. When we get back, why don't you twins, Carol Lauren, and Sean show them your trick?"

"We will," they all chorused.

"What trick is that?" asked Bud and I could feel that he was relaxed and at ease on Storm.

"The twins ride Storm, Carol Lauren rides Lady, and Sean rides Sheik and they line them up so they are in profile to those watching, then they rear the three horses at the same time, none of them holding on with anything more than their legs. Betty is probably going to have another fainting spell when she sees that," I laughed.

"Oh I wish I could see it," he laughed.

"I'll give you a running narrative of what her face looks like, but you won't need me to describe the trick because I'm sure as a kid you did the same thing."

"You're right I did. How long have the twins been riding?"

"Since they were three and they are four now."

"Weren't their legs a little short for holding on to Storm at that age?"

"Yes, but I rode with them and being the fearless types they just took to it naturally,"

"Lauren, when I agreed to come out, I told Chris that I would stay for the afternoon but that I wanted to go back to the hospital tonight. If the offer of staying for the weekend is still valid, I'd like very much to stay for the weekend."

"The offer is still there and we'd love having you."

"Good, I understand you guys have a dance floor in the barn, can I have one dance with you?"

"You sure can, and if I see us getting too close to another couple I'll just tap your shoulder with my fingertips on which ever side that couple happens to be and no one will ever know the difference," I said.

"Thanks Lauren, I sure hope David knows what a great gal you are."

"Well if he doesn't it isn't because I haven't told him," I laughed. "Now Bud how about a fast gallop back to where everyone is and then how about if we jump Storm over a small woodpile that the twins have been practicing their jumping on?"

"I'm game if you are."

We put Storm into a gallop. When we got back by the woodpile I told Bud to hold on because I was going to jump Storm over the woodpile now, he did, and we sailed over it like nothing and came to a halt in front of the others. I dismounted and then Bud dismounted. "Thanks for a wonderful ride, I didn't realize how much I'd missed riding a horse," said Bud.

"By Sunday I expect you to be riding Lady on your own with only the twins on Storm to guide you."

"You got a deal lady," he laughed.

"Come on all of you, start back for our house so we can pick up the food then we'll all come down for potluck and a dance or two," I said. Everyone but Chris started wending their way back to our house; Chris put his hand on my arm so that I would stay behind so he could talk to me.

"Lauren, I don't know how you do it, but Bud hasn't left his room at the hospital since he was brought in and I had to actually order him to come today. Now you've got him riding horses, talking about his blindness as if it were nothing, and interacting with eight kids and with a dozen adults," said Chris.

"Chris it isn't me, he did it for himself, he just had to know that we weren't going to tiptoe around him because he was blind."

"I think we ought to fire all the psychiatrists at the hospital and hire you instead," he chuckled.

When we got back to the house, I handed out food to everyone to take over to the stable. "Bud, since you need one arm to let the kids guide you, how about you taking their sleeping bags down because you can just drape them over your other arm?" I said.

"Sure Lauren," he said smiling at me.

"Ok, wagons ho," I laughed.

When we got there the other two households were there along with Chris' kids. "Bud, there are two picnic tables at about 10 o'clock then approximately two feet beyond at 12 o'clock is the dance floor which is approximately two feet above the floor you're now standing on. Still at 10 o'clock but about two feet beyond the second table is a juke box and a cabinet with 500 records in it."

"Just sit me down where you want me," he laughed. "By the way where did you learn to give directions like that?"

"When I was learning to fly," I said.

"Don't tell me you guys have a plane too?"

"No such luck, there's a little field not too far from here where David and I go to fly. David, Jack and I are going to go flying tomorrow, want to come along?"

"I sure do, I only wish I could fly just one more time."

"No reason why you can't. David and Jack are going to fly each of them using their one good leg to operate the rudders, and brakes. You and I can fly, I'll just read the instrument panels for you—you know sort of be your navigator."

"I'd like that, it will be good to be up in the wild blue again."

"My God Lauren, don't you guys ever let anything stop you?" asked Chris.

"Nope, not when there are easy solutions or even hard ones for that matter," I laughed.

"Ok Bud, let's run the gamut and I'll introduce you to everyone. This is Carol, she's David's sister," I said.

"Welcome to the funny farm," laughed Carol hugging him. "This is Mark, or as he likes to refer to himself my better half, and this is our daughter Carol Lauren who is four."

Carol Lauren crawled up on the table bench next to him hugging him, "Hi Uncle Bud."

Bud put his arm around her and hugged her back. "Hi Carol Lauren, its nice to meet you and your mom and dad too," he said.

"This is Bill, who used to be my boss and is now my brother, his wife Beth who is now my sister—be careful because she's my size so when you reach for either of us just lower your sights a little, and last but not least this is their son Sean. Sean is a little shy with strangers at first but I'm sure he'll shake your hand."

"Hi Uncle Bud," said Sean and he too climbed up and gave Bud a hug.

"I'm not shy Aunt Lauren," he said solemnly.

"All of our kids are four years old and all about the same height as the twins," I said.

Chris introduced his four kids to him then.

"How did you all manage to have kids the same age?" asked Bud.

"Now that is a story which is about to be repeated in a couple of more years," I laughed. Beth, Carol and I all got pregnant at the same time and all of us went into labor at the same time and all of us delivered within minutes of each other."

"Did you say you intended to do it again?"

"Yes, we intend to try for us all to go into labor at the same time in about two years time, but this time we will be including Cindy as she and Jack have decided to make their home here with us," I laughed.

"Bud, don't try to figure it out, but I'm sure these four will all do exactly what they set out to do, because they have the theory that if they all have their kids at the same time then all the kids will have other kids their age to play with," laughed David.

"All I've got to say is Good Luck you guys."

"No Luck to it, its just good organization and coordination on us girl's parts," laughed Carol. "Since we all know our men can't keep their hands off us anyway, we just coordinate the timing."

"Well now I've heard everything," laughed Bud.

"Bud, we have fried chicken, potato salad, coleslaw, salad with Italian dressing for dinner tonight—just tell me what you'd like and I'll fix you a plate, then we women will get the kids plates ready for them while the rest of you help yourselves," I said.

"Lauren, I'll take a little of everything," he said.

"Which part of the chicken are you partial to sir," I asked.

"I wouldn't mind a leg and a thigh," he laughed.

When everyone had been served and were wolfing down the food, Chris said, "Lauren, David why don't you tell us how this whole Love Farms things came to be?"

So while everyone ate David and I took turns telling them how all of us met, fell in love, bought the farm, and how we were now planning on making it a halfway house for returning wounded servicemen. Jack told them about how I had talked to him when he was facing losing his leg and told them how he had prepared in physical therapy for his upcoming surgery. When we had finished Bud said, "I can only tell you from my experience what coming here has done for me. When I got stateside I stayed in my room and wouldn't even walk up and down the halls unless it was late at night so people couldn't see me stumbling around as Chris can attest. I wouldn't have come today, but he pulled rank on me and ordered me to come and I'm sure glad he did. You people have made me realize there are still lots of things I can still do that I didn't think I could ever do anymore and you made me realize I didn't have to be ashamed of my blindness."

"But Bud, why did you ever think you needed to be ashamed of your blindness," I asked. "After all it is all of us who were safe here at home that should be getting down on our knees to all you servicemen who gave so much for us."

"Maybe saying ashamed wasn't exactly the right word, but I hate having people feel sorry for me and be afraid they'll say something accidentally that will remind me I'm blind. I know I'm blind, but Lauren this afternoon when you said you wanted to show me Storm, you didn't apologize for saying you were going to show him to me when you knew I couldn't really see him, you just said it matter-of-factly and even some of the nurses at the hospital seem to get embarrassed if they accidentally say something about my seeing something."

"Bud where are you from?"

"I'm from Ohio, I have a four year old son waiting for me. My wife divorced me while I was overseas and married a plumber. She deserted our son, so some old friends took care of Bobby until I could get back home."

"What did you do before the war?"

"I had taken over my dad's farm when he died and was working it," he said.

All of us looked at one another and we all nodded our heads.

"Bud would you consider leaving Ohio and moving onto the farm with us?" asked Bill. "We've plenty of room and you could build a small house for you and your son. And before you get the idea this is charity, believe me it isn't. We need vets who have been through the experience to help us with the servicemen we expect Bethesda to send us. They'll come for two three-day weekends before they are released from the hospital which will give them time to get used to interacting with people, just like you did. We also want to make this a paying horse farm as well."

"I'm going to start my own lobbying business right here on the grounds and David and Jack are going to work for me with the idea that once they learn the business they will become my partners. You could do the same, because you could advise on what blind servicemen need and testify before Congress for those needs to be met and also help David and Lauren and Carol with the horse farm part of it. Then too you could teach blind servicemen how to ride. Of course once you learn the lobbying part of my business, then you'd be eligible for partnership as well," said Bill.

"I don't know what to say, that's a very generous offer for you to make to a guy who is a total stranger to you," he said

"No generosity involved in the offer, you'll be expected to pull your weight around here and to help with the chores the same as everyone else and as far as being a stranger, us vets weren't strangers when we were in uniform, so why should we go back to being strangers now we're home," said David.

"Please, Bud, think about it because we'd love to have you become another of our brothers," chorused Carol, Mark, Bill, Beth, Cindy, Jack and me.

"While you're thinking, remember that your son would be in familiar farm surroundings and he'd have four kids his own age to play with and when the time comes to go to school with him," I said.

"What you didn't see when Bill was making the pitch to you is that all of us who are a part of this funny farm were nodding in agreement that we wanted to make you the offer because we all think you'd fit in perfectly. Every Friday night we have this potluck and a dance, but before we start dancing we always sit and everyone tells the others any ideas they've come up with during the week and we vote either to accept or reject the ideas put forth, so it really is one for all and all for one around this place," said David.

"Yes, Bud, and all us girls promise to dance with you on Friday nights so you won't feel left out, just because at the moment you don't have a girl, which we also intend to take care of when we find just the right one for you," laughed Carol.

"Then too Bud when we go into labor in a couple of years, you can be around to watch out for our kids, while the guys are driving us to the hospital," laughed Beth.

The kids who had been gabbing with each other at their table finished their meal in time to hear us offer to include Bud in the farm. "Uncle Bud, please say yes because we want you to stay with us forever," said the twins.

"Yes Uncle Bud, so do Carol Lauren and I," said Sean.

"Thanks you guys, let me think about it for a couple of days, but I want you all to know how much the offer means to me," he said and his emotions were in his voice.

"Ok everyone, time for dancing, war council over," I said.

"Oh goody, we get to see daddy dancing with mommy," laughed the twins.

"Come on baby, it's been a long, long time since I've held you in my arms to dance with me," said David. As we got to the dance floor we heard the record *I'll Walk Alone* begin to play. "Ready darling?" asked David.

"More than ready my darling, and this time I can really enjoy it because it won't mean you're leaving," I whispered.

As the song played, Carol began to sing the words just as she had on the last night before David went overseas. David took me in his arms and we danced to our song, but this time we could listen to the music and know finally that we weren't going to be separated again. "It feels so good to dance with you again, little one," whispered David in my ear.

"Darling I love being in your arms and dancing with you again," I whispered. When the song finished, everybody clapped. "How does your leg feel?"

"It's fine, but I think for a while, at least, I'm going to have to dance one then sit one out, because it makes my leg ache a little, but its worth it," he chuckled.

"Do you mind if I dance with Bud, so he'll really feel a part of this group?"

"No sweetheart go ahead, but then I want to dance the next dance with you," he said.

I went to Bud, then, "How about it Bud ready to cut a rug with me?"

"I'm game if you are."

"Well if you men just danced the way we women do, with our eyes shut, you wouldn't have to worry," I laughed.

"That's why us guys have to keep our eyes open, because you girls shut yours," he laughed.

"I promise, this time I'll keep mine open," I said.

We went to the dance floor and we danced to *Blue Moon*. "One thing, Lauren, you're used to dancing with someone my size," laughed Bud.

"Bud, it's ok for you to hold me closer, David won't get mad and your holding me so far from you, that I can't get a sense of where your going," I laughed.

He pulled me in closer to him and we were better able to dance because now I could follow him much better. When the song concluded, we made our way off the dance floor.

"Bud you two looked pretty darn good out there," said David. "In fact, for just a moment I felt a twinge of jealousy you looked so good."

"I hope you're kidding David because I wouldn't have held Lauren so close except she told me that she couldn't follow me because I was holding her so far from me," said Bud.

"Yes buddy, I was just kidding you," laughed David.

The twins came running up then. "Mommy, Daddy, it was such fun watching you dance together."

"Glad we could entertain you two," laughed David.

"Daddy this has been so much fun tonight, because it is the first time we've had both a mommy and daddy like the rest of the kids," they said.

"Well, you have both of us from now on, and when I get a little steadier on my leg I'll dance with both of you in my arms," laughed David.

"Oh that would be so much fun, daddy, we can hardly wait."

Chris came up to us then. "David you didn't look like you were having any trouble at all dancing with Lauren, how does the leg feel?"

"Fine, it aches a little, but then it's been four long years since I've danced at all," laughed David.

"It will get stronger and after a couple of Friday night sessions of dancing with your wife, I don't think it will bother you at all."

"Well I intend to give it plenty of exercise dancing with my tomboy," said David hugging me to him.

"Bud, you looked really at home dancing with Lauren too," said Chris.

"She's a fantastic dancer and it was really fun," said Bud.

"Well, you guys, my family and I are going to take our leave of you, it's been a great day and we've really enjoyed ourselves. I was wondering if I could come out some day next week by myself and talk to all of you about this halfway house proposition because from what I've seen tonight you guys could be the best therapy our vets could get and I'd like to set it in motion as soon as possible."

"Sure Chris just give us a call whenever you want to get together and we'll be available," I said.

"Thanks again for a really wonderful day, this is the first time I've really relaxed in months. Bud, are you staying or do you want a ride back to the hospital?"

"I've decided to stay for the weekend and maybe for the rest of my life," said Bud.

"I take it you would recommend this place to other guys at the hospital?" asked Chris.

"I'd not only recommend it, but if I were in charge I'd insist on it," laughed Bud.

Carol came up then, "Bud, how about a dance, I'd like to dance with a guy taller than I am for a change because I kind of miss dancing with my brothers who are all your size or taller," laughed Carol.

"Chris, if you'll excuse us, I just promised Carol I'd dance with her. See you at the hospital on Monday," said Bud.

"See you Monday then Bud and I want to hear all your views on this Love Farms setup next week because I'm definitely going to try to promote the idea of Bethesda using it for therapy for our guys," said Chris.

"Will do Chris."

"Jack, Cindy, how are you guys doing?" I asked.

"Great, this is wonderful and I can't wait to get my new leg so I can dance with Cindy," laughed Jack.

"I think we've finally convinced you that nothing is impossible and just wait till we get you and Bud up in the plane tomorrow," I laughed.

"What's this about getting Jack in a plane?" asked Cindy.

"The four of us are going to go flying tomorrow, Cindy and all three of the guys are going to fly the plane once more with a little assistance from me."

"Jack are you sure you're up to it?" asked Cindy.

"You better believe it doll face, I can't wait to get behind the stick again," said Jack.

"Is there nothing you guys won't attempt?" laughed Cindy.

"Off hand I can't think of anything," I laughed.

"Hey kids, come on, it's time you were all in bed," I called to the children.

"Can't we stay up just a little bit more?" came the usual chorus.

"No, you've stayed up an hour past your bedtimes now, so go get your bedrolls and put them in the extra stall and I mean right now."

"Daddy," said the twins, "Please daddy tell mommy to let us stay up just a little bit longer so we can see you and mommy dance again."

"You heard your mother, next Friday you can stay up an extra hour and you can watch us dance then," he laughed.

"Go kiss everyone goodnight," I said.

They all scattered then going to each of the adults and hugging them and kissing them. I went with them to see that they got into their bedrolls. Before they all got bedded down all the adults came out to say good night to them.

"Bud, they've got all their bedrolls in the extra stall and they'll stay out here in the barn for the night tonight, it's just easier than getting them herded back to the individual houses and besides we don't like the idea of leaving them in the house alone and out here the horses will watch over them during the night," I said describing the scene to him.

"I bet they all look like little angels," he laughed.

"The only time our kids do look like angels is when they are sleeping," laughed David.

"I bet Bobby would love this," said Bud.

"Well, if you decide to stay here with us, he'll soon be one of the sleeping angels or the little devils when he's awake," I laughed.

After the kids were bedded down and admonished that they were to go right to sleep no horsing around, the adults returned to the dance floor. "Bud, how about a dance?" asked Beth.

"Sure Beth, I'm game if you are," said Bud.

"Just remember Bud, she's Lauren's size so you're going to have to take smaller steps than you did dancing with me," laughed Carol.

We danced for another hour or so then I said, "I don't know about you guys, but I think it's time we called this quits for tonight because I don't think I can stay awake much longer."

Everyone agreed. "Bud since the twins are staying in the barn for tonight, if you don't mind sleeping in a bottom bunk bed, you can stay at the house with David and I or else Beth and Bill will put you up," I said.

"Thanks for the offer you guys, but I told Beth and Bill I'd bunk in with them this weekend," said Bud.

Everyone gathered up their stuff and we all hugged and kissed and wished each other a goodnight, then we wended our separate ways back to our individual houses.

"I think everything went well today," said David, "I was really surprised how quickly Jack, Cindy, and Bud became a part of our family here thanks in large part to you my love."

I went over to sit down on his lap. "I don't think there is any big secret to it, I just think they want to be treated like normal human beings, not wounded fliers," I said putting my arms around David's neck and curling up on his lap.

"Baby, you've got a knack of making them see that a normal life is possible for them and you don't mind letting them know that you expect them to live up to their potential."

I yawned then, "Daddy, it was so nice dancing with you again tonight, especially so because I knew we had the rest of our lives to dance together."

He pulled me closer to him and bent and kissed me. "Mommy I loved having you in my arms again and dancing with you like we used to do and your right it made it even better knowing I never had to leave you again."

We went then and crawled into bed. "I can't wait until my leg is strong enough so I can pick you up and carry you to our bed again," he laughed softly. "Is mommy going to let me make love to her tonight?"

"Yes, please my darling," I said.

"Wonder if I remember how without a cast on my leg?" he chuckled.

"I'm sure it will all come back to daddy," I giggled. And it did.

EPILOG

In the months that followed our house was completed and we moved in. We continued to run our halfway house and Bethesda paid us to take returning vets who were either facing surgery or were beyond the repair of surgery. The servicemen came for two three day weekends and in most cases went away with an improved attitude and a feeling that maybe they could live more or less normal lives and that the public and their families would accept them without being repulsed by their appearance.

Jack received his artificial leg and within a month or so was walking, for the most part, without aid of either crutches or a cane except on uneven ground. He and Cindy moved into our old house.

Bud brought his son to the farm after making the decision to join us. At first Bobby was reluctant to make friends with Bud or any of the rest of us. He had been uprooted from the only home he had known and removed to this foreign environment by a father he did not know, and who was different from the other fathers because he was blind. When Bud despaired of he and Bobby ever becoming close, I told him that he would have to be patient that Bobby too was going through massive changes in his young life and he had to learn to trust again. Eventually, with Bud's patience Bobby began to accept that Bud loved him, as did the rest of us and I think our twins were instrumental in integrating him into our way of life. Within the first year Bobby settled in and became once again a normal happy little boy and he and Bud became particularly close. Bud met and married Jenny and Bobby learned to love her, as did we all and she became another sister for us.

Bill left the agency and built a small office on our grounds and Bud, David, and Jack went to work for him. Mark too decided to leave the agency for which he had worked for so many years and join Bill. By the end of two years, they had all become partners in a very successful lobbying business that catered primarily to those businesses promoting the needs of returning servicemen. The horse farm never really materialized; instead we added additional horses so that the servicemen could ride them, as could our kids. We did eventually build a small runway where we kept a Cessna and an

Apache, which we used as therapy for the servicemen who stayed with us. All of the kids learned to fly and all had their pilot's licenses by the time they were sixteen.

When the twins were six years old, I gave birth to another set of twins, Megan and Robert; Carol had a boy they named Roger; Beth had a girl they named Kate; Cindy gave birth to Jack, Jr. and Jenny gave birth to a little girl they named Rebecca. All of us went into labor at the same time, just as the three of us had done six years ago and all of us gave birth within a few minutes of each other.

David and Carol's dad and brothers visited us annually. We invited his mother to visit but she declined our invitation. We did eventually visit England and had dinner with his mother, but while David said that he had forgiven her for deserting him all those years ago, I felt that he never completely did and never trusted her.

Time was good to all of us, we were happy in our work and in each other. David and I went to Australia when our kids were all in high school or college. It was a beautiful country and I enjoyed my time there, but I think both of us were homesick for our little farm and we returned to it with joy in our hearts.

We continued our Friday night routine of potlucks and dances. David and I never did choose another song to be our song. I think we eventually knew that while *I'll Walk Alone* did have some sad memories for us, it still said all the things we had promised each other during the war years and now when we danced to it, it continued to say to us that we would always be there for each other and as the years passed our love continued to grow.

Printed in the United States
17138LVS00002B/246